# IN A WELSH VALLEY

When Ruth Greene's cousin Dora has to go into hospital, Ruth's family rallies round by going to look after the grocery shop she runs in her Welsh mining village in Carmarthenshire. This gives them a respite from the London blitz, but other dangers and excitements await them in their temporary home. Young Basil gets into mischief, while their daughter, Marina, falls in love for the first time. But can her wartime love endure?

CATRIONA McCUAIG

IN A WELSH VALLEY

*Complete and Unabridged*

LINFORD
*Leicester*

First published in Great Britain in 2007

First Linford Edition
published 2008

British Library CIP Data

McCuaig, Catriona
   In a Welsh valley.—Large print ed.—
Linford romance library
1. World War, *1939 – 1945*—Wales—
Camarthenshire—Fiction
2. Camarthenshire (Wales)—Fiction
3. Love stories 4. Large type books
I. Title
823.9′2 [F]

ISBN 978–1–84782–151–5

Published by
F. A. Thorpe (Publishing)
Anstey, Leicestershire

Set by Words & Graphics Ltd.
Anstey, Leicestershire
Printed and bound in Great Britain by
T. J. International Ltd., Padstow, Cornwall

# A Cry For Help

It was Monday morning and Ruth Greene looked with despair at the huge pile of washing. The last thing she wanted — after a restless night in the Anderson shelter — was to have to tackle the weekly wash.

As she sorted the whites from the coloureds and put them into the copper to boil, Ruth realised — with a sigh of annoyance — that she'd left her nightie upstairs.

Unfortunately she couldn't make it do for another week. Down in the shelter last night, a particularly loud explosion had made her jump and she'd splashed tea all over herself, and everyone knew that tea made an almost permanent stain if you didn't wash it out right away; she'd even heard of women trying to dye their hair with it.

'Oh, dear, somebody's getting it,'

young Basil had remarked when the noise of the explosion had faded away.

He'd sounded so like his father that Ruth had smiled. But her smile had soon faded; Bob had been out and about on his Home Guard duties, and could well have been in the thick of it somewhere in the town.

Ruth's neighbour had said to her recently, 'I think I'd rather be in London when the raids are on. I bet it would be fun, sleeping down the Tube with everyone else, having a bit of a sing-song and sharing a Thermos of tea. At least having a laugh would take your mind off what was going on outside.'

But Ruth thought that her neighbour was a very silly woman. Even though London wasn't very far away, things were much worse there than in Hertfordshire.

Ruth turned her thoughts back to the present as she trudged up the stairs to the main bedroom, which was such a mess that no amount of tidying up could do much to improve it. The window was covered with chicken wire — to prevent flying glass in case of blast — and in addition to the marital bed, two camp beds had been crammed into the room.

Under normal circumstances, Basil and his elder sister, Marina, had their own rooms, but since the raids had become heavier and more frequent, Ruth had insisted that they all stay together at night.

Marina had moaned about this arrangement, of course, complaining that Basil talked in his sleep and kept her awake. But Ruth was adamant. Whenever the sirens sounded and they needed to get down to the shelter in a hurry, then she wanted no running about in the dark wondering where everybody was.

Hearing the creak of the garden gate, she peered through the wire on the window to see a young chap in RAF uniform carefully propping his bicycle against the garden wall.

She frowned. What on earth could he

want? Surely Marina hadn't got herself involved with some boy; not after all her father's warnings about sixteen being too young for that sort of thing.

If this one was coming to ask Bob's permission to take the girl to a dance or to the pictures, then he needn't bother. He'd be sent away with a flea in his ear.

Ruth ran downstairs and opened the door, thinking that the young man standing awkwardly beside the pile of sand bags looked vaguely familiar. Perhaps she'd come across him on her volunteer days at the servicemen's canteen.

'Auntie Ruth?' The boy hesitated, his forehead creased. 'It's me, Ifor.'

Ruth's hand flew to her mouth. 'Goodness me, you've grown!' she exclaimed.

What a stupid thing to say! Of course he'd grown; she hadn't seen him since he was a small boy and now he was old enough to join the services!

'Come on in, Ifor, and I'll put the kettle on.' Ruth shepherded the boy into the house. 'You mustn't look at the mess; I'm in the middle of washday, as you can see.'

'I'm sorry to turn up on your doorstep like this, Auntie, but there wasn't time to write. I'm stationed not too far from here and I was lucky to be let out for a few hours, because it's an emergency, see?'

'Oh, dear. Nothing wrong at home, is there? It's not your dad, is it?'

'Yes, and no. That is, yes, there is something wrong, but Dad's all right, so far as we know. It's Mam. She's in the cottage hospital, with a broken leg. She was up on a stepladder, in the shop, and she fell off.'

Ruth, busy making tea and wishing she had something to go with it, made all the right noises. 'Poor thing! I'll sit down and write a cheery note to her this evening.'

Ifor shuffled his feet. 'Well . . . er . . . Auntie Ruth, Mam was wondering if you could come and sort of take over while she's in hospital, like.'

'Oh, I don't think I could do that, love! I mean, there's your Uncle Bob, and the children; I have my hands full as it is.'

'But you don't work, Auntie,' he pointed out. 'And couldn't your Marina manage here while you're away?'

A spasm of annoyance welled up in Ruth. 'You don't work,' indeed! Just like a man! What would you call cooking and cleaning, washing and ironing and mending, not to mention queuing for food, and all having to be done after broken, fear-filled nights!

'Surely there's someone else who could help your mum? Someone nearer home?' she asked.

Ifor shook his head. 'Some of the neighbours are popping in, temporary like, but they all have their own families. And Mamgu can't do for herself, and of course there's the shop. The people registered there for rations can't do without it, see?'

Ruth did see.

She felt sorry for Dora, but it really

wasn't possible for Ruth to go running off to Wales. She had her own responsibilities. It wasn't as if Dora was Ruth's sister or anything. They were only cousins.

Ruth and Dora had spent a lot of time together as girls growing up in Gloucestershire, but then Ruth had married Bob and come to Hemel Hempstead, and Dora had wed a Welshman and gone to live with him in Carmarthenshire.

Over the years, their correspondence had dwindled until it had now reached the stage of little more than cards exchanged at Christmas and on birthdays.

'How long will your mother be in hospital?' she asked now. 'Did the doctors say?'

'It's a fractured femur,' Ifor told her, stumbling over the unfamiliar words. 'They've got her leg strung up with pulleys and she's to stay like that for about fourteen weeks. After that she has to have physiotherapy. Perhaps she'll never walk again,' he finished gloomily.

'Now, now, we'll have none of that defeatist talk here!'

'I can't help it, Auntie!' He brushed away a tear. 'Mam's so worried about Mamgu and the shop. I wish Dada was here, but he's away at sea, and since Idris went and joined the Navy, I just didn't know where to turn until Mam told me to come to you.'

Poor boy, Ruth thought.

Stalling for time, she refilled his cup and asked how he liked life in the Air Force. 'Training to be a pilot, are you?'

That raised a smile.

'Oh, no. I'm ground crew. We keep the planes in working order. It's good training, mind. After the war I'll be able to get a good job as a mechanic of some sort.'

That was one less thing for Dora to worry about. Most pilots were lads not much older than Ifor himself, but for many of them their life expectancy could be counted in weeks. With any luck, Ifor would be safe on the ground while still making a vital contribution towards the war effort.

'So, tell me what to do, Auntie,' he pleaded.

'You'll have to give me time to think, love. I'll have a word with your Uncle Bob when he gets in from work. Perhaps between the two of us we'll be able to come up with something, but I can't promise.'

'But how will I know what you've decided?' asked Ifor, looking even more worried than before.

'You leave me the phone number of your camp, and I'll ring up tonight from the phone box down the road. If they can't get hold of you, I suppose someone will take a message?'

He nodded, looking a little happier.

When he had gone, Ruth went back to her washing, her thoughts in a whirl. What on earth could she and Bob do to help? Dora might just have to close the shop. It would be an inconvenience for the customers who were registered there, but things like that were happening all over Britain and people managed.

It was Mamgu who was the big problem.

Old Mair Thomas, Dora's mother-in-law, was more or less bedridden following a stroke she'd had just before the war. As Ruth knew from Dora's infrequent letters, she managed to care for the old lady with some occasional help from the district nurse, but it was obvious that Dora found looking after Mamgu a struggle. Fiercely independent, the old woman often tried to get out of bed on her own, and it was impossible to leave her unattended in case she had a fall.

'Oh, dear, but I can't go to Wales!' Ruth muttered, as she busied herself at the washboard. 'I can't be away from home for three months or more, and nobody could expect it of me.'

Dora would have to make her own arrangements, she thought, although it would have been lovely to get away for a while to a peaceful Welsh mining village. But she couldn't possibly leave the children. Who would see them safely out to the shelter on the nights when the sirens went and Bob was out fire-watching? And what if the worst happened and they were all killed while she was away looking after someone else's family? She would never forgive herself.

If only Marina was a few years older, then she could have been sent to Wales, but even if she could have coped with the old lady, there was still the shop to look after. There was a time when a capable youngster could have minded a small shop, but nowadays there was so much red tape involved, what with ration cards and quotas. Very likely the government had rules about who could be in charge. They probably had a minimum age.

No, sending Marina just wasn't possible, yet they must do something to help!

The kitchen was now full of steam, and a few damp tendrils of dark hair had escaped from under Ruth's turban.

She pushed them back, sighing. Life was full of problems.

But she would forget all about this one until Bob came home. Two heads were better than one. He might suggest that Dora should hire an assistant, some local woman who'd be glad of a few extra shillings in her purse. Why hadn't she suggested that to Ifor? Ah, well, she could bring that up when she phoned him, later.

★ ★ ★

'Oh, sorry! I was expecting to see Dr Stenson,' the man exclaimed as he stepped into the room.

The white-haired man seated behind the desk looked up with a sigh.

'Dr Stenson has joined up and I've been called out of retirement to take his place. I'm Dr Leacy. What can I do for you, Mr Greene?'

'It's this cough, doctor. I've got a tickle in my throat all the time and when I cough there's a pain in my chest. It's got me worried, I can tell you.'

'I'd better listen to your chest, then. Off with your jacket and shirt, please. Come along, man; I haven't got all day!'

Bob Greene did as he was told, reflecting that it was this older man who should have been sent to the army, not the amiable Dr Stenson. He would soon have put any malingerers in their place! But perhaps it was having to take over from Dr Stenson that had made Dr Leacy irritable; coming back into the practice when he'd been expecting to enjoy a leisurely retirement was no joke for a chap of his age.

'What is your occupation, Mr Greene?' The doctor had finished his tapping and thumpings and was now making a note on Bob's chart.

'I work at the bakery, Doctor. Making bread.'

'Hmm. Flour in the lungs, that's what's affecting you. I'm going to send you for an X-ray, just to make sure, but

I don't think there's any risk of tuberculosis. However, you'll have to give up working at the bakery.'

'But I can't stop work, Doctor! I've a wife and youngsters to support!'

'Who said anything about stopping? You'll just have to find another line of work, that's all. No chance of you going into the army, of course. It says here you had rheumatic fever as a boy and that's put the kibosh on that. Now, off you go, back to that bakery of yours, and be sure to give in your notice while you're about it. Doctor's orders, mind!'

Bob staggered out in a daze.

'And that's what the doctor told me, true as I'm standing here,' he told his employer half an hour later. 'I have to finish, no two ways about it.'

'Are you sure it's all that serious, Bob?' The baker frowned. 'I don't quite see the connection between flour getting in your lungs and this illness you had as a nipper. What does he say will happen to you if you keep on going the way you are?'

'I don't rightly know, Sid. I was so bamboozled I didn't think to ask. He just told me to give in my notice and chased me out of the surgery.'

'This is a right turn up for the books! Where am I going to get somebody reliable to replace you? All the good men have been called up! And people have to have bread, even if it is on ration and made of poor quality flour!'

'What about me?' Bob grumbled. 'I'm the only breadwinner in my family, if you'll pardon the pun! My Ruth is a good thrifty woman, but she can't manage on thin air.'

'Now, there's a thought,' Sid murmured. 'Would she like to take your place here? I could put Bessie on to bread and rolls, and your missus could do the cakes, such as they are. Not that she'd earn as much as you do, of course, being a woman.'

'No wife of mine is going out to work while I'm alive,' Bob snapped. 'I won't have it said that I can't provide for my family, and that's flat!'

'You're behind the times, man. Don't you know there's a war on? Lots of women are going out to work in factories and offices, taking the place of the poor devils who are away fighting for king and country. But it's up to you. If you say your Ruth can't come here, why, that's your business. I'll just have to look around for somebody else.'

★ ★ ★

Back at number 15 Jubilee Avenue, Ruth Greene was beginning to think about the evening meal. This being Monday, there was cold meat left over from Sunday and that, combined with home-grown salad, would make up the first course. But what could they have for pudding? Young Basil loved fried jam sandwiches but the batter would have to be made with the detested powdered egg, and his sister would turn up her nose at it, she knew.

Biting her lip, Ruth glanced out of the window, anxiously keeping an eye on the leaden sky. Her washing hung limply on the line, half dry. If it started to rain then she'd have to dash out to bring it all in and drape it over the clothes horse.

'Mum! I'm home! Is there anything to eat? I'm starving!' shouted Basil, coming in from school with his tie under one ear and his socks at half mast.

'You'll have to wait for tea, love. Your dad and Marina aren't home yet.'

Basil pulled a face that he fondly imagined characterised young love.

'Oh, her! She's standing down the end of the road ogling at a grammar school boy.' He made kissing sounds to illustrate his point.

'Now, that's enough of that, young Basil! I'm sure she's doing nothing of the sort.'

'Well, she's talking to him, anyway, and looking all goo-goo-eyed.'

'Your father will give her goo-goo eyes if he catches her.' Ruth laughed, pulling off her turban as she spoke.

'Out of my way, my lad. I must go and put my face on before your father gets home and sees me looking like this.'

Basil sauntered off, wondering if he could remove something from the bread bin without being caught in the act. What was the good of having a baker for a father if you couldn't get an extra crust now and then? The only pickings they ever got was stale bread that hadn't been sold. Good enough for toast, his mother said, and glad to get it.

It was only a few minutes later that Bob came home, but as soon as he came through the door, Ruth knew something was wrong. He looked so defeated. Was the war news bad? Was it something about the invasion?

'Bob! What on earth's the matter?'

'I had to see the doctor today,' he told her. 'Not Dr Stenson, he's been called up. It was an older chap; Leacy's his name.'

A dreadful fear gripped Ruth's heart. 'Are you all right, love? Oh, my goodness, come and sit down and I'll bring you a cup of tea.'

'No, no, just give me a minute, that's all.'

'Mum! Can I have my tea now that Dad's home?' called Basil.

'I couldn't eat a thing,' Bob groaned, putting his face in his hands. 'Give the boy my share.'

'I'll do no such thing. It's only a cold meal, being Monday. It can go back into the larder until you're ready for it. Meanwhile tell me what's bothering you.'

Moments later, Basil appeared at the sitting-room door, looking mutinous. 'Mum! I need my tea!'

'You'll get it in a minute, Basil. Now you can just go upstairs and get on with your homework.'

'But I told Frankie I'd . . . '

Suddenly Bob exploded. 'You do as your mother tells you, my lad, unless you want to feel the weight of my hand! And don't scruff along on your shoes like that. I'm not made of shoe leather!'

'But, Dad, I only . . . '

'Get out of my sight!' Bob roared, and Basil shot up the stairs without further ado.

Ruth felt her stomach clench. This wasn't like her Bob at all. He was quite strict with the children, especially with Marina — her being just a young girl — but it was rare to see him lose his temper. Something must have really upset him if he could fly off the handle like this.

'Tell me what's wrong,' she said softly.

'I've lost my job,' he told her, unable to meet her eyes.

'You've never had the sack!'

'No, of course I haven't, nothing like that; but it's worse in a way. I went to see the doctor about this cough of mine, and he says it's the flour getting in my lungs. He's made me give in my notice at the bakery because of it.'

A great sense of relief swept over Ruth. For a moment she felt quite faint. She didn't know what she'd been imagining, but nowadays you never knew what was likely to happen next, with that madman Hitler and his Nazis over in Germany.

'Oh, well, you'll soon find something else,' she soothed.

'Like what? They won't have me in the army because they say that rheumatic fever did something to my heart. I can't do heavy lifting for the same reason, so factory work is out. Now I'm told I can't follow my own trade, so what's left?'

Ruth smiled to herself as he continued to moan. Best to let him get it out of his system and then she'd spring her little surprise on him. It would kill two birds with one stone if they went to Wales. It would solve Bob's problem, and help Dora out at the same time. Really, this pronouncement of Dr Leacy's couldn't have come at a better time.

'I had a visitor today,' she said, smiling, when at last she could get a word in. 'You'll never guess who it was!

My cousin Dora's youngest, all grown up and in the RAF now, and stationed near here. It seems there's trouble at home. Dora's in hospital with a broken leg and there's nobody to look after things, not with her husband Dai and eldest lad Idris both being away at sea. That's where we come in!'

\* \* \*

Bob listened to Ruth's story, then sat looking thoughtful. 'So you're suggesting we should all go down to Wales to help Dora's family?'

'Of course,' Ruth enthused. 'And you could work in the shop!'

'So could you.'

'Oh, I could give you a hand, but you'd be much better at dealing with all the ration books and suppliers and what-not. Besides, I'll be keeping house as usual, and looking after the old lady.'

'It's hardly likely to be a permanent job for me though, is it? Three or four months at the most, and then what?'

'We'll cross that bridge when we come to it, Bob! It'll fill a gap for now.'

'Hm, yes, but will your cousin be able to pay us anything?'

Ruth looked pained. 'She's family, Bob! You don't expect to get paid for helping out. Besides, we'll have no rent to pay, and I'm sure we'll be given our food there.'

'You don't understand what I'm getting at, pet. What about this house? If we expect to have it to come back to when this little expedition is over, then we'll have to keep shelling out the rent for it while we're gone. Where's the money to come from for that if I'm not earning?'

'Oh, I see what you mean. Well, let's give it up then. The landlord won't have any trouble letting it, not with so many people getting bombed out and made homeless all over the place.'

Annoyingly Bob continued to be the voice of reason. 'And what about all our furniture? Putting it in storage costs money too, you know. And my vegetable garden! I don't want to abandon that after all my hard work.'

Like many people, Bob had dug up his cherished lawn at the outbreak of the war, and was 'digging for victory' as the government slogan went. With most food items rationed, or missing altogether from the shops, it was vital for householders to produce as much food as they could.

'We've got to make up our minds soon,' Ruth reminded him. 'I promised to get in touch with Ifor this evening. As I see it, we've got two choices: either I take the children to Wales with me, leaving you to cope alone while you look for work, or we all go. Which is it to be?'

A plaintive voice came from the doorway. 'I've finished my homework, Mum, and I'm still hungry.'

'Basil!' Ruth bawled. 'Don't you know there's a war on?'

'I was only asking,' Basil muttered. 'No harm in that, is there?'

'It's all right, son,' Bob put in. 'Your mum and I are a bit busy at the moment, that's all. Have a look in my haversack. There are a couple of buns in there. Mind you give one to your sister.'

'Cor, thanks, Dad!'

'Blast this wretched war!' Bob said. 'There isn't even a bit of dried fruit in those buns. I feel sorry for kids today, I really do. Most of them have never even seen a banana or an orange, never mind tasted ice-cream.'

'If we worked at that grocery shop we'd have first pick of anything coming in,' Ruth said, with low cunning. 'I don't mean doing anything we shouldn't, of course; but so often supplies are limited and it's first come, first served. I can't tell you how many times I've stood in a queue waiting for something tasty, only to have them run out of whatever it is before my turn comes.'

'I've said it before, and I'll say it again; I won't have us separated,' Bob insisted. 'That's why I put my foot down over the kids being evacuated. If our number's up, then we'll all go together.'

'I know, dear,' Ruth spoke softly. 'I agree with you there. But why don't we all go to Wales? I haven't heard about them bombing so far inland, and it would be a relief to do without those air raids for a bit.'

Bob seemed to have arrived at a decision. 'I tell you what, old girl. I'll pop down the road and have a word with Pete Foster, our landlord. I'll make up my mind when I've heard what he has to say.'

★ ★ ★

When Bob returned he was grinning all over his face.

'Pete has an idea, love. I asked him about this house going for a short-term let, so that we could move back in later, and he said why not leave our bits and pieces behind? He could make more money letting it furnished as temporary accommodation for someone who's been bombed out, and it would save us putting all our furniture into storage.'

Ruth was doubtful at first, but she knew that nothing was ever certain while there was a war on. If a bomb fell on their home, they'd lose everything anyway.

'But I wouldn't want strangers getting hold of my good china,' she protested. 'That was a wedding present, that was! And what about our clothes? We can't take them all with us, and if they get stolen we won't be able to replace them for love nor money!'

'Pete thought of that, too,' Bob beamed. 'I'll put a padlock on the box room and all our personal stuff can go in there. Next objection, please!'

But Ruth had nothing more to say. She was all ready for the move. She'd even made a list of things to be done.

'I'd better get off and phone the camp where Ifor is stationed. Have you any change? I want to have plenty for the call box in case they keep me waiting while they fetch him. While I'm gone you'd better discuss everything with the children. They'll have to be put in the picture.'

★   ★   ★

'You're sending us to Wales?' Marina stammered. 'I thought you said you wouldn't let us be evacuated? I want to stay here with you and Mum!'

'Me, too!' Basil piped up.

'You're not being evacuated. Well, not exactly. We'll all be going. You've heard your mother speak of her cousin in Wales, haven't you?'

'The one we call Auntie Dora?'

'Yes, that's right, Marina. Well, she's had to go into hospital, and that leaves nobody at home to look after either the shop or her mother-in-law. She's appealed to us for help. Your mother and I have talked it over, and we've agreed to give it a go. Luckily the school year is almost over, so there's no problem there.'

Basil had picked up his mother's list

and was studying it intently

'What's a mamgoo, Dad? Is it some sort of animal that we have to look after?'

'What? Let me see that.' Bob laughed. 'I think that's pronounced 'mamgee', son. It's the Welsh word for grandmother. She's Uncle Dai's mother, see?'

By the time Ruth returned, the children had accepted the idea of their temporary house move.

Marina didn't mind because her best friend was going to be spending the summer holidays with her grandparents in Torquay, leaving Marina at a loose end anyway. The idea of seeing new places and meeting new people was quite appealing. Since the war began, life had become quite boring — if you discounted the air raids!

Basil, poor boy, was entertaining greedy thoughts about all the food that would be available in a grocer's shop.

'How did it go?' Bob asked, when his wife finally returned. 'Did you get through? Did you manage to have a word with young Ifor?'

'Yes, to both questions. It seems that he was off duty and had spent the past hour hanging around the guard-house waiting for me to ring. I explained that it's going to be all of a week before we arrive, what with one thing and another. You have to work out your notice, and I must get busy with the packing.'

'I think I'll go out and take a look round the garden, love. I hope the new people, whoever they are, will take good care of my vegetables.'

Ruth laughed. 'They'll be only too glad to have the use of them.'

'Unless they're Londoners who think that everything grows on market stalls,' Bob retorted.

But Ruth knew that for Bob the fate of a few rows of brussels sprouts was the least of his worries. Only hours ago her husband had been holding down a regular job and now his world had changed in a flash.

All of a sudden she began to wonder if they were doing the right thing. Would she be able to deal with old Mrs Thomas? She hadn't any nursing experience, although surely bringing up children — with all the bathing and feeding and comforting that entailed — qualified her to look after one partially bedridden old lady. But how would Dora's mother-in-law feel about her home being invaded by a strange family? Ruth hoped she wouldn't be too querulous, especially since Basil was a normal little boy who tended to be noisy at times.

Oh, well, one thing at a time. They must look upon this as an adventure, and if things didn't work out, so what? It was only for a few weeks, after all.

# A Long Journey

After an appalling journey which had involved changing trains several times, the Greenes finally arrived at their destination.

'How do we get in?' Ruth asked, of nobody in particular. The four of them were standing in the pouring rain outside Dora and Dai's double-fronted shop in the mining village of Bedwen, but there was no sign of life in the darkened grocer's.

'It's locked,' Bob announced, rattling the door handle to no avail. 'Surely someone must be expecting us. Perhaps the old girl is all alone in the house and can't get out of bed to let us in.'

'Round here, Dad!' Marina called, from somewhere in the gloom.

At the sound of her voice, the side door flew open, illuminating them all in a beam of light.

'Here you are at last! Don't stand out there in the damp or you'll catch your deaths!'

They crowded into a cheerful kitchen, dragging their bulging suitcases behind them, and were greeted by a small, plump woman with a cheerful expression.

'I'm Mrs Parry — Bessie, that is.'

'I'm Bob Greene, this is my wife, Ruth, and these are our children, Marina and Basil.'

Bob held out his hand to Mrs Parry and, having first wiped her hands on her apron, she accepted the handshake.

'Very pleased to meet you, I'm sure. Now, just pass me your wet things and I'll hang them up in the scullery. I've a nice rabbit pie keeping warm in the oven, and I'll have it on the table in two shakes.'

Basil gave a sudden whimper. His face was the colour of putty and his hair was plastered to his skull from the rain.

Mrs Parry looked at him with pity in her dark eyes.

'Poor little chap; he's all worn out. I'll just take him up and pop him into bed, and then I'll come down and see to your meal, all right?'

Ruth made a move towards the case containing Basil's pyjamas, but was waved aside by Mrs Parry.

'I'll see to him, Mrs Greene. You go through to the scullery and wash your hands and then come and sit by the fire. You can take him something on a tray later, if he's still awake, which by the look of him I very much doubt.'

Far from being annoyed at being told what to do, Ruth suddenly felt quite safe and secure in this cosy kitchen. It was pleasant to be taken care of instead of having to worry about getting the family settled in.

She was also glad to see that the strain had left Bob's face; he, too, seemed to relish handing over the reins of command for the time being.

'She's like one of those nannies that you read about in books where the children live in a nursery at the top of the house,' Marina whispered to her mother.

Ruth smiled. That described Mrs Parry exactly.

The kitchen was a large one, one wall taken up by a huge fireplace which obviously did double duty for cooking and heating. There was a hob on each side of the fire which burned brightly in the black grate, and an iron bar which could be swung over the flames was meant to hold a pot or kettle. A small black door in the fireplace wall opened into the oven where the pie was keeping hot.

The mantelpiece itself was covered with a variety of items, candlesticks, a pair of china dogs, and some photographs framed in passe-partout.

A huge Welsh dresser on the opposite wall was filled with blue and white crockery, while the remaining space held pots and pans suspended from big old iron nails.

There were rag rugs on the stone-flagged floor.

'What a lovely kitchen,' Ruth said sincerely, her tired eyes taking everything in. The room and its furnishings seemed timeless, and the war seemed very far away.

'There, he's all tucked up in bed.' Mrs Parry beamed at Ruth as she bustled back into the kitchen. 'I thought he wouldn't be long nodding off. Now, sit up to the table and get started on your meal.'

'Aren't you going to join us, Mrs Parry?'

'Na, na, Mr Greene. I had to go home to feed the family, see? I had mine then.'

Delicious though the food was, Marina soon began to droop.

'You'd better get off to bed as well, *bach*,' she was told by Mrs Parry. 'Up you go, now. You'll soon see where things are. There are three bedrooms and I've put you in Idris's old bed. The big room is Dora's and Dai's — you'll have that, Mr and Mrs Greene. I can't think where we'll put everyone when

Dora gets out of hospital, but there, we'll cross that bridge when we come to it. No need to worry about it tonight.'

'But where is Mrs Thomas, then?' Ruth was puzzled. There had been no mention of the old lady and obviously she wasn't sleeping upstairs.

'Oh, she's just next door.' Bessie Parry jerked a thumb towards the wall. 'That used to be the parlour, but when she came to live here after her stroke they thought it best to keep her downstairs. Makes less running up and down for poor Dora, you see? I've already looked in on her and she's all right. Dead to the world, she is. I'll introduce you when I come back in the morning. She wouldn't thank me for disturbing her now.'

'But what if she wakes up in the night? What do I do?' Ruth sounded worried.

'She keeps a bell at the side of the bed, but I doubt you'll hear from her. She's been sleeping badly ever since Dora had her accident — worrying, see — and the doctor prescribed tablets for her. The district nurse will drop in tomorrow and tell you all about her, but really, Mrs Thomas is doing quite well. It's just that she shouldn't be left alone in the house, especially at night when there's nobody to call on for help.'

'What about the shop, then?' Bob wondered. 'What time do we open up in the morning?'

'No need to worry about that, Mr Greene. I'll be back first thing to show you the ropes. Mind you, we've only been able to open it for two hours a day lately, what with one thing and the other, so people will be glad to see everything back to normal. Now, I must be off home or my man will think I've eloped with Jones the milk! We'll leave these crocks to soak in the sink till morning, all right?'

In a daze, Ruth watched the kindly little woman cram a felt hat on to her frizzy dark hair and shrug her arms into a shabby coat.

'I'll say *nos da*, then,' she nodded, as

she left by the side door.

Ruth had no idea what *nos da* was; probably a Welsh form of goodbye?

'Come on, love, it's been a long day.' Bob yawned. 'You go and check on the kids while I bring the bags up.'

Ruth went first to the little room where her son was sleeping. He was curled up on the bed, still wearing his vest and underpants, and the covers had slipped to the floor. Tenderly she put them back over him and tucked them round his shoulders, casting a quick look around the darkened room as she did so.

She felt a pang as she noticed the contents of the shelves; a few children's annuals, boxes containing games of ludo and snakes and ladders, and several pieces belonging to a toy train set. They were so obviously the cherished possessions of a boy not much older than young Basil, but now. Ifor was far away from his childhood home, playing a man's part in this dreadful war. It was all wrong.

Lying beside Ruth in the strange bed, Bob was snoring softly. He had gone out like a light as soon as his head touched the pillow.

But Ruth, in that strange half-comatose state between waking and sleeping, found the events of the day flooding her mind.

She couldn't help thinking about the dreadful train journey they had endured from London to Cardiff which, she had been told, had taken twice as long as it would have done in peacetime. There had been so many lengthy and unexplained stops that she'd often felt like screaming in frustration.

The train itself had been full to bursting, with passengers packed into the smoke-filled corridors. When, eventually, an elderly man had got up and offered Ruth his seat, she'd sunk down gratefully, sure she would never be able to get up again.

Bob had commented on the various

uniforms that the other men on the train were wearing. Not only did these represent the army, navy and air force, but there were young men whose shoulder flashes proclaimed them to be from Canada or Australia.

Men and women seemed to have come from all corners of the empire to aid in the defence of the mother country and, with nothing else to do on their journey, these youngsters passed the time by singing — none too tunefully.

'Ten green bottles, hanging on the wall! If one green bottle should accidentally fall, there'd be nine green bottles, hanging on the wall!'

Basil joined in the singing with enthusiasm and, after listening with disdain for the first few verses, even Marina shook off her sulks and added her voice to the rest.

Ruth had felt a headache coming on. If only they could open a window! But she'd been afraid to get up in case somebody took her seat while she was on her feet!

But all that was behind them now. They had come to a safe haven and the adventure on which they were about to embark would provide them with a welcome break from the stress they had endured back in the Home Counties.

Turning over on to her side, Ruth slept.

# Meeting Mair Thomas

'And here is Mrs Greene, come to stay with you!' Bessie Parry spoke brightly, like a jolly dentist assuring a squirming child that this wouldn't hurt.

The senior Mrs Thomas glared back, looking for all the world like an indignant owl. She was sitting bolt upright in an old-fashioned iron bed, clutching a crocheted shawl to her ample bosom. Incongruously she wore a battered felt hat pulled low over her eyes. This headpiece was decorated with what seemed to be an entire bird, minus a few feathers.

Ruth concluded that this peculiar garment was being worn either in honour of their meeting — just as no lady would dream of going out in public without her hat and gloves — or because Dora's mother-in-law was just downright odd.

'How do you do, Mrs Thomas?' Ruth murmured.

The old lady stared back at her without blinking.

Oh, dear! Couldn't she talk? Nobody had said that the stroke had robbed her of the power of speech. This was going to make things really difficult.

'Come on, *bach*, say something,' Bessie encouraged.

Mair Thomas responded with a flood of Welsh, accompanied by a series of violent nods.

'She's being a bit awkward this morning,' Bessie muttered in an aside to Ruth. 'Come now, Mrs Thomas, let's speak English. Mrs Greene has no Welsh, see?'

Frowning, the old lady looked Ruth up and down, her gaze taking in first the polished court shoes, then travelling over the shabby tweed skirt and hand-made cotton blouse. Her eyes half closed in horror as she studied Ruth's face.

Ruth felt as if she'd been weighed in

the balance and found wanting.

It's my lipstick! she decided. The old girl probably doesn't approve of makeup. Well, I'm blowed if I'm going to take it off, like a naughty schoolgirl. She'll just have to get used to it.

She cleared her throat. 'I'm glad we were able to come and help Dora in her hour of need,' she ventured, although surely, as the sole member of the family currently in residence, Mrs Thomas should have been the one making welcoming noises.

The old lady frowned again. Then, in a creaky voice, she asked, 'Are you Church or Chapel?'

'Er, we're Church of England, I suppose.'

A grim nod greeted this information. It was obvious that the older woman's worst fears had been realised.

'There now, isn't this nice?' chirruped Bessie Parry. 'The two of you are getting on so well together. You just sit here, Mrs Greene, and you can get to know each other while I go and give Mr

Greene a hand in the shop. There was a queue forming outside last time I looked, and he won't know where anything is, never mind how to work out what's what with the ration books.'

Left alone, the two women looked at each other warily.

Mair Thomas, still wearing her hat, slid lower under the quilt, reminding Ruth of a wary tortoise retreating into its shell when confronted by a curious cat.

Ruth, perched on the edge of her chair, was unsure what to do next.

She looked around her.

The room still bore evidence of its previous existence as a parlour. The window, with its worn burgundy velvet window-seat, looked out on to a busy side street, and the view no doubt furnished Mair Thomas with some amusement as people passed by outside. She must have friends in the community; perhaps some of them tapped on the glass and waved, or even stopped to chat when the window was open.

Ruth turned her attention to the two huge pictures on the wall, reproductions of Victorian paintings, in heavy, ornate frames. She'd seen similar ones before — 'When did you last see your father?' was the title of the picture showing a small cavalier boy, hands behind his back, facing a group of stern-faced puritans. The other painting showed Sir Francis Drake finishing his game of bowls at Plymouth Hoe before sailing off to defeat the Spanish Armada.

Ruth thought that she preferred these prints to the photograph of an elderly Queen Victoria which glowered down from Dora's bedroom wall. She decided that when she went up to make the beds she would turn the old girl's face to the wall.

Her reverie was interrupted by a tap on the door.

'Safe to come in, is it?' A uniformed nurse slipped into the room, beaming. 'I'm Nurse Jenkins. How do you do?'

'How do you do? I'm Ruth Greene.'

'What on earth are you doing in bed with your hat on, Mrs Thomas?' The nurse laughed as she dropped her bag on to the sideboard.

'It's a lovely day out there, now that the rain's stopped. As soon as you've had your blanket bath, we'll open that window and let you get some fresh air. Now then, I'm just going to have a word with Mrs Greene here, and then we'll get started.'

Glad to leave the over-warm room, Ruth followed the nurse out into the passage.

'Phew, that was uphill work,' she muttered.

'Oh, you'll soon get used to each other. She's come a long way since she had her stroke, but she's a bit resentful of the fact that she can't bustle about the way she used to. You can't blame her, can you?'

'I suppose not.'

'Moving in with her daughter-in-law was a big step for her, and poor Dora having to go away and leave her must have seemed like the last straw. She can get herself in and out of bed now, so she doesn't need a lot done for her any more, that's one good thing. You'll need to take her meals in on a tray, and deal with the commode, of course, but other than that the main thing is to have someone on the premises in case of anything unforeseen happening.'

'What sort of meals should I give her?'

'She's on a regular diet. She's a bit fussy, but you'll soon get used to that. Bessie Parry can give you some pointers, I expect. Basically, if the old girl throws her plate at you, you'll know that she doesn't like your cooking.'

Ruth's jaw dropped, and Nurse Jenkins threw her head back and roared.

'If you could see your face! Only joking, I was, see?'

'Very funny, I'm sure!' Ruth grunted.

★ ★ ★

Going through into the kitchen, Ruth found her daughter staring out of the window.

'It isn't like I'd imagined Wales to be, Mum.'

'What did you expect, people running round with harps tucked under their arms?'

'Oh, Mum! No, it's all these fields. You said this was a coal-mining place, and it doesn't look like that to me. And this is the only shop within miles, by the look of it. What on earth am I going to do here? I thought there would be a cinema at least!'

'We're on the outskirts here,' Bessie Parry explained, having heard Marina's words as she came in from the shop. 'We have the colliery, right enough, and before you go very far you'll see the coal tips, but this is sheep-farming country as well. And when you go down into the town you'll see plenty of other shops; we've got Broad Street and Quay Street and the High Street as well, full of shops they are.'

'Then why have this shop out here at all?'

'Because there are plenty of people living round about it. Why should they have to trudge two miles and back to the Home and Colonial, carrying a heavy shopping basket, when they don't have to?'

Catching sight of Marina's woebegone face she relented somewhat.

'But there, I don't suppose window shopping at the fishmonger's or the haberdashery is quite what you had in mind! But don't you worry, love, we have a very nice cinema, and there's quite a good library. We even have tennis courts and a football pitch down the Rec. I'll have to introduce you to my girl, Marged. She's about your age, and she can show you around.'

'You just have the one child, Mrs Parry? I was so exhausted when we came in last night that I can't quite remember what you said.'

Ruth was hoping for small boys, for Basil's sake.

'Oh, I have a son as well. Tim, that is. He's down the pit with his da. Nineteen he is, two years older than our Marged. But we'll soon find some friends for young Basil, never you fear. Over-run with little boys we are round here.'

Although feeling a little shy at the prospect of getting to know a strange girl, Marina looked forward to having someone to squire her around.

But when Mrs Parry eventually introduced her children with an air of motherly pride, it was Tim who impressed Marina the most. It took only one look to know that she was in love. With his dark eyes and black hair, the stocky young Welshman was quite the handsomest boy she had ever met.

'No, not a boy,' she corrected herself, 'a man.'

According to his mother he had been working at the colliery since leaving school at the age of fifteen, and bringing home a wage that was almost as good as that earned by his father. Marina felt sure that she had met her destiny. If only he would invite her to the pictures or something! Perhaps she should work on Marged to get him to ask her out.

*   *   *

On visiting day, Ruth went to see Dora in the cottage hospital. 'Thank goodness you've come!' Dora greeted her. 'I've been going mad wondering what's happening at home. Have you settled in all right? How are you getting along with Mamgu? Is there any word from the boys?'

'Whoa, one thing at a time!' Ruth laughed. 'Yes, we're beginning to get settled in, and here are a couple of letters which the postman handed to me just as I was leaving. And Mamgu is . . . well, Mamgu!'

'I know what you mean.' Dora sighed. 'I could put a different name to her, but Sister's got a swear box and I've contributed too much to it already, I'm afraid! Being strung up here is no joke, I can tell you!' She indicated the ropes and pulleys which kept her leg up in the air.

'It must be a real nuisance for you. But is Mrs Thomas really that difficult?'

'Well, of course I've tried to keep the peace, for Dai's sake. No man wants trouble between his wife and his mother, but the plain fact is she's never taken to me from the very beginning. She doesn't think I'm good enough for her precious son, even though I've been a good wife to him. But I'm not Welsh, and I'm not Chapel — although I do attend services at the Wesleyan Methodist and the boys have been brought up in that religion.'

'I think she believes I'm a scarlet woman because I wear lipstick,' Ruth said, grinning. 'I caught her giving me a really old-fashioned look. Actually, it reminded me of the look on Bob's face when Marina experimented with one of my old lipsticks and some rouge. He sent her upstairs quick sharp to scrub it off!'

'One of these letters is from Dai,' Dora gloated. 'I'll keep it to read later, for a treat.'

She fingered it lovingly before tucking it under her pillow.

'I wonder why Mrs Thomas dislikes the English so much?' Ruth mused. 'The whole town can't feel the way she does. Why, your friend Bessie Parry welcomed us with open arms.'

'I often think it's because Mamgu was born back in Victorian times, when things were very different here; no wireless and so on to introduce people to the outside world. As far as I know she's never been out of her own valley, so anyone from a bit farther afield is looked upon as outlandish and threatening. Folk have had the same outlook for centuries, I expect. It dates back to the days when strangers suddenly appearing meant trouble and had to be seen off.'

'But this is 1943, and there's a war on! We're all in it together, aren't we?'

'Yes, well, there are things you ought

to know about my mother-in-law, Ruth. She's had a hard life, one way or another. When she was still quite young there was a cave-in at the mine, and her two brothers were killed. Her father was on the same shift but they managed to get him out alive. He survived, but he was never the same again, and the family lived from hand to mouth from then on. It didn't help that the mine owners were English; not that that had anything to do with it, I suppose.'

'How dreadful!'

'It marked her for life, as far as I can see. Dai often heard his grandmother say that she didn't know how she'd have stayed sane after all that, if it hadn't been for her strong religious beliefs. Anyway, I understand that's why they let Dai go to sea. Mamgu said there was no way she was letting him spend his life underground, and that was that.'

'I can see why,' Ruth murmured, resolving as she spoke to try to be more patient with Mair Thomas if she could.

She looked around the ward, which at that moment seemed a cheerful place. The walls were lined with beds, twelve on each side of the long room, and there was a long cupboard in the middle, made colourful with numerous vases of flowers.

'The flowers are from our visitors,' Dora explained. 'Sister says it's better to have them there than on our bedside lockers, and that way everyone can share the enjoyment of them. Some people never get a visit at all. Either their homes are too far away, or they're all alone in the world. Still, there are worse places to be when you're feeling poorly. There's always something going on, something to see.'

'But you must get bored at times, trussed up like a Christmas turkey!'

'Oh, I can listen to the wireless when I want to,' Dora told her, indicating a set of headphones. 'And I have to admit that I'm getting a good rest here, being waited on hand and foot. The only thing I worry about is what would happen to me in an air raid, when I can't get out of this bed. Not that we've had any raids in this part of the world up to now, but if one did come, I'd be a sitting duck, never mind a turkey!'

Ruth felt it was time to change the subject.

'What do you think of the Parry children?' she asked Dora.

'Marged and Tim? Oh, they're nice enough, I suppose. Why do you ask?'

'Because Marina has started going about with the girl, ever since Bessie introduced them.'

'She'll come to no harm with Marged, Bessie will see to that.'

'I didn't think she would. It's just that Marina has her eye on Tim and I happen to know she's been pestering Marged to set up a date with him. Now they're all going to a sing-song at the Methodist chapel and Bob is less than pleased about it, I can tell you.'

Dora tried to hide a smile. 'Hardly a den of vice, is it? What's Bob afraid of?'

'I think he's afraid that Tim will ask

to walk Marina home, although between you and me, it's more likely to be the other way around! I've managed to persuade Bob to let her go if the girls promise to stay together as a group, but he's still not at all happy about it.'

'The girl is sixteen, Ruth! Almost a young woman. You can't keep her wrapped up in cotton wool for ever. Surely it's better to let her mix with boys in a controlled setting than wait until she's eighteen and called up into the women's services or something. Then she really will be like a lamb amongst wolves if she doesn't know how to look after herself.'

'And that's another thing!' Ruth sighed. 'According to Bob, there's a yawning gulf between Marina and Tim. She's just a schoolgirl and he's a grown man, for all there's only three years' difference in their ages.'

'Just stop worrying! It'll all come out in the wash!' Dora said blithely, with all the assurance of a mother of two boys.

Irritation flooded through Ruth.

Bringing up a daughter was no joke, and she and Bob were just beginning to find that out!

★ ★ ★

Unbeknown to Ruth, Bessie Parry was at that very moment having a quiet word with her son on the subject of Miss Marina Greene.

'Sweet on you, she is, *cariad*.'

'Never!'

'There's none so blind as those who won't see, son.'

'That's silly, Mam. It's just a schoolgirl crush, if anything. Besides, I'm thinking of asking Catrin Harris to walk out with me.'

Bessie's eyes brightened. 'Well, now, that would be very suitable, I'm sure!'

'Don't go planning the wedding just yet, Mam!' Tim chuckled. 'I'm just taking the girl to the pictures, that's all.'

But Bessie went about her work with a spring in her step. One of these days, Tim would be ready to settle down, and when he was, Catrin Harris was just the sort of girl she would have chosen for him. A local girl, and a miner's daughter, Catrin would know exactly what was expected of her as a miner's wife.

Meanwhile, it looked as though Marina might be making a nuisance of herself, always hanging around, coming to the house with some excuse — such as wanting to borrow a book from Marged — but really on the off-chance of running into Tim.

Marged, of course, lost no time in teasing her brother about being a heart-throb. While his fond mother believed that Tim was by far the best looking young man for miles around, to Marged he was just the brother she'd grown up with. He was all right, she supposed, but nothing to write home about!

'That girl can make eyes at him all she likes,' Bessie told Marged, 'but it won't do her any good, see. Now, what I want you to do, Marged Parry, is to introduce her to some of the grammar school boys, some nice lads her own age. Once she gets to know some of them, she'll leave our Tim alone. Emlyn Richards, now. She could get to fancy him.'

'Yes, Mam.' Marged answered her mother meekly, but she had no intention of letting Marina get anywhere near Emlyn. She wanted him for herself! They might make up a foursome, though, if Emlyn could find someone who was halfway decent for Marina.

'And don't forget you promised to do something about young Basil,' Bessie continued. 'He can't spend all his time kicking an old tin can along the street the way he was doing yesterday. Don't some of your friends have little brothers that he can play with?'

'Yes, Mam.' Marged went upstairs to tidy her room before Bessie could get started on that subject.

★ ★ ★

Feeling bored, Basil had eventually taken himself off to the recreation ground, known locally as 'the Rec'. Other than some rundown tennis courts and some goalposts, the place didn't have much to recommend it, but it did provide somewhere for children to let off steam.

Standing on the sidelines, Basil watched enviously as a group of boys kicked a soccer ball about to the accompaniment of shouts and laughter.

When the ball suddenly came his way, he didn't hesitate for a moment. Instead of simply kicking it back into play, he sprang into action, dribbling the ball until he reached the middle of the throng.

If there was one thing he was good at, it was playing football. The boys watched him appreciatively, and when one of the largest called out, 'Want a game?' he joined in eagerly.

By the time the other boys had drifted off to their homes, he was one of their number and had agreed to join their side the next day, when they were to play against another team in a friendly match.

'What on earth have you done to your sandals?' his mother snapped when at last he reached home, hot and dishevelled.

'Nothing, Mum.'

'Nothing! I'll give you nothing, my boy! Just look at those toes, all scuffed. If they get worn out you'll have to keep wearing them, holes or no! Even if we could afford a new pair for you, I don't know where we could find them. There's nothing in the shops. Don't you know there's a war on?'

Basil let his mother's tirade flow over his head. What a fuss about nothing! Wisely he didn't mention that he'd been playing football. He knew that he wasn't supposed to kick a ball about while wearing his sandals, but what else could he have done? Did she expect him to race all the way home to get into his boots, and then turn right around to go back to the recreation ground? By that time, the other boys would have gone their separate ways and Basil would have lost his chance. As it was, he'd been accepted by them, and he'd be going back again tomorrow.

'Sorry, Mum!' he said cheerfully, before she had the chance to tell him that he had to stay in as a punishment.

'All right, but don't let it happen again!' she scolded.

★   ★   ★

The next day, Ruth caught Basil as he was slinking out of the house, hoping to be unobserved by anyone, especially his mother.

'And where do you think you're going, Basil Greene?' she called out.

'Up the Rec. Some boys have asked me to play on their team. I've got my boots on, like you wanted.'

Ruth nodded, glad to know that he was making friends. Mind you, if she'd known what this football match would lead to, she wouldn't have been so complacent, but she had too much on her mind to worry about unforeseen consequences.

Bob, too, was fitting into his new surroundings. In fact, it was a long time since she'd seen him so relaxed and cheerful.

'Len Parry's invited me to drop in at the Red Dragon on Saturday night,' he told her. 'Len says he'll introduce me to some of the local chaps. You don't mind, do you, love? I wish you could come, but women don't go into pubs around these parts.'

'That's all right, love. You go and have a nice time. Perhaps I'll invite Bessie over for a cuppa. The young people are going to a debate at the chapel, and she'll be all on her own.'

The Red Dragon was crowded, and Bob listened with interest to what the miners had to say — spoken in English, so he wouldn't feel left out.

Most of them seemed well educated, or at least well-read, and the conversation was lively. It was easy to see why

Wales had the reputation of being a nation of orators.

'It's good of you to come here to run the shop for poor Dora,' one burly man said. 'How could you get away from your job in England? On your holidays, are you?'

'Not exactly. I'm out of work at the moment.'

'What trade you in, then?'

'I'm a baker, but I've had to pack it in — doctor's orders. Lung trouble, caused by all the flour, so he says.'

'Ah! Something like the silicosis miners get.' His new friend nodded. 'Coal dust, see?'

'They won't even take me in the army,' Bob went on. 'A dicky heart caused by rheumatic fever as a lad, or so I'm told.' He always felt compelled to explain why he wasn't serving in the armed forces. People were inclined to look down their noses at you if you weren't in uniform. They didn't go so far as to bestow a white feather on you, like they used to do in the Great War, but he still didn't want people to think he was a slacker.

Next the talk turned to the rumours about German spies being parachuted into Britain. Bob had heard them all before when he was in the Home Guard. If you noticed anything suspicious at all, you were supposed to perform a citizen's arrest and ask questions later.

'I expect the same thing is happening on our side,' he offered to the discussion. 'Our lot being dropped into occupied territory, I mean. Perhaps to link up with the Resistance. How else are we supposed to know what's going on?'

The evening passed so quickly that he was quite surprised when the landlord called for last orders. Apparently closing time was eleven o'clock, and the local bobbies were strict about enforcing the law.

'Of course, the pubs don't open tomorrow,' Len reminded him. 'Sunday, see. No drinking in Wales on the Sabbath.'

Another custom that Bob found unusual was that every man got to his feet for the singing of the Welsh national anthem before leaving the building. Bob had never seen anything like that in England, not that he had been much of a pub goer as a rule.

'Here you are, then.' Bessie smiled at him when he arrived back at what he was beginning to think of as home. She stood up, rolled her knitting into a neat bundle and stowed it in a clean flour bag. 'I hope my Len took good care of you, Mr Greene.'

'Yes, thank you. Very kind. Would you like me to see you home?'

'Na, na. It's only a few steps, and I don't suppose Hitler will be hiding round the corner to make a grab for me. If he is, I'll poke him in the eye with my knitting pins!'

Laughing, she made for the door, fastening her cardigan as she left.

'Is Marina in yet?' Bob asked Ruth, looking up at the ceiling as he spoke.

'Bless you, yes! It's gone eleven!

She's been in bed this past hour, and Basil's been up there since nine o'clock, reading his *Beano*. And Mrs Thomas is all tucked up, too, so it's just you and me. Do you fancy a nice cup of Horlicks?'

'Not on top of two pints of ale, thanks. I wouldn't mind something to eat, though. Have we got anything spare?'

'I could do you some bubble and squeak,' Ruth offered. 'It's a good thing we have Dora's garden to rely on. At least we won't go short of vegetables while we're here.'

Upstairs, their son was lying on his back on top of the covers, deep in thought. His football game had gone well, and he'd managed to score two goals which had made him popular with the other boys.

When the game had been over, they'd invited him to go down to the river with them, where they'd lain on their stomachs, trailing their hands in the water in the vain hope of catching a fish. As with their elders, the boys' talk of the moment had to do with the possibility of spies in their midst, and what they would do if one was sighted. They boasted that they would bring the spy down with a rugger scrum, and sit on him while they tied him up using knots which some of the older boys had learned in the Scouts.

'But what if he's got a gun?' Basil asked. 'We might get shot.'

There was silence for a long moment as they considered this.

Then Rhodri, the oldest boy, who by common consensus was the leader of the gang, frowned at Basil. 'Where d'you get your name from, then? Funny sort of name, it seems to me.'

'It's not in the Bible,' another lad chimed in.

'How would you know?' Basil scoffed. 'I bet you haven't read the Bible. Not *all* of it, anyway.'

'Everybody knows that Basil isn't in the Bible, and it's not a Welsh name, either.'

'That's because I'm not Welsh!' Basil was no cissy and he could stick up for himself. 'Where I come from, they've never heard of some of your names either. Gwilym and Dewi and Meurig. I bet those aren't in the Bible either, so there!'

There was a low growl from the group of boys, and for a moment Basil thought he was going to have to run for it.

Rhodri stepped up and thrust his face into Basil's. 'Where you from, then, eh?'

'Hemel,' Basil replied. 'We're from Hemel.'

They left him alone then, and he was free to wander home without hindrance. So why was it that he had a sick feeling in his stomach and felt that he hadn't heard the last of this?

# A Wonderful Day For Mamgu!

Ruth was still struggling to get along with Mamgu. It had reached the point where she had to steel herself to go into the older woman's room, which irritated Ruth no end. It wasn't as if Mair Thomas was openly rude or difficult; it was the silent treatment that was hard to take.

Ruth took in tasty meals on a tray to her, only to have her good food looked at glumly.

'Anyone would think I was giving her bread and scrape,' she complained to Bob. 'It's not my fault if there isn't much variety — that's down to rationing; she gets the same as us, and plenty of it. Honestly, it bothers me to see her pushing good food around her plate as if I'm a rotten cook!'

'Ah, but she polishes her plate clean, doesn't she? I haven't noticed a crumb coming back to the kitchen, for all she's so old and feeble.'

'Still . . . ' Ruth grumbled.

Nurse Jenkins came in only once a week, so it was left to Ruth to perform what she thought of as nursing tasks, which included washing Mamgu's face and hands, combing her long white hair, and making the bed. Ruth also cleaned the room every day, unhappily aware of Mamgu's beady eyes on her as she trundled the carpet sweeper over the faded rug.

'She makes me feel like an unsatisfactory housemaid,' Ruth moaned to Marina. 'She doesn't take her eyes off me for a minute. Perhaps she thinks I'm going to run off with the family valuables, such as they are.'

'Oh, Mum! Don't exaggerate!'

'Exaggerate my foot! You try looking after her and see how she treats you!'

'No fear! It's not my job, is it? I didn't ask to come down here to the back of beyond where there's nothing to do and nowhere to go!'

Caught between the devil and the deep blue sea, Ruth decided to take a break and to go to visit Dora at the cottage hospital.

'Come for me to cheer you up, have you?' Dora grinned.

'What do you mean?'

'Well, you've got a face like a wet weekend, old girl. Mamgu playing you up, is she?'

'Not really; she's just giving me the silent treatment. I must admit, though, it's getting me down a bit.'

Ruth had decided not to say too much about Mair Thomas. True, Dora had had a private moan about life with her mother-in-law, but she might get defensive if an outsider went on in the same vein.

'No, it's Marina who's playing me up. I don't know what's come over that girl. She used to be such a sweet little thing, and now she's as grumpy as a bear. She snaps back at everything I say, and as for helping me around the house, why, wild horses couldn't drag her anywhere near the washing up.'

'Get Bob to have a word with her, why don't you?'

'Bob? A fat lot of good that would be! She's all sweetness and light when he's around, so he doesn't see the awkward side of her.'

''Sweet sixteen and never been kissed',' Dora quoted. 'I bet that's what's wrong with her, Ruth. Didn't you tell me she has her eye on that young Parry chap?'

'Oh, him! I was a bit worried for a while, but it seems to have come to nothing, and I must say, I'm glad. He's nice enough but he's too old for her. Three years' difference is nothing when you get to our age, but she's a sixteen-year-old schoolgirl and he's a working man, going on for twenty.'

'You've said all this before, and my advice was to let things run their course. You know what they say about forbidden fruit tasting the sweetest?

How do you know they're not seeing each other on the sly?'

'Because Bessie told me that he's courting a girl his own age called Catrin Harris. Very suitable, according to his mother. I think she has hopes that it'll come to something, and why not? With the wage he's bringing in he could probably afford to get married in a couple of years, and what's more, being in a reserved occupation he won't get called up. Of course, this explains why Marina's been going around with a face like a thunderclap. She knows there's no chance for her.'

'She'll have to worship from afar, then, won't she? Never mind, she'll change her tune when some other likely lad comes on the scene. What about my Ifor?'

'What about him?'

'I daresay he'll be coming home on leave one of these days. Perhaps they'll take a shine to each other?'

'But they're cousins.'

'Only second cousins.'

Ruth murmured something noncommittal. She couldn't say so to Dora, of course, but privately, she regarded Ifor as a bit wet behind the ears. She couldn't imagine how he was getting on in a barracks full of older and tougher men. She hoped that the timid lad wasn't getting bullied. Marina would make mincemeat of him, she was sure.

'How's Bob getting along in the shop?' Dora asked. 'I want to be able to tell Dai all about it when I write. There isn't much I can tell him about life in the hospital — one day here is much the same as the next, and anyway, the last thing he needs is to read about my moans, especially when there's nothing he can do about it.'

'How is Dai?'

'Safe and well, as far as I can make out. Of course, he can't say where his ship goes or what he's doing, because everything is censored, so his letters are a bit dull, too. But at least when I get one then I know he's still alive. Or, at least, he was when he sat down to write it.'

An uncomfortable few minutes passed as they contemplated this, until Ruth felt compelled to break the silence.

'Bob loves it in the shop. With his smiles and banter, he's got all the local ladies eating out of his hand. He seems to love meeting the public. There was nothing like that at the bakery, of course; it was all working behind the scenes there.'

There was a sudden clatter which drew all eyes to the end of the ward, where a hapless probationer had managed to let a tray slip through her fingers.

'Now the fat's in the fire!' Dora grinned. 'Just keep your eye on Sister and you'll see why they call her Captain Bligh!'

Sure enough, Sister had sailed down the ward and was now castigating the drooping nurse. Sister kept her voice low, but they could tell that she was bristling with indignation, and after a few minutes the girl picked up the bits and pieces and fled through a nearby door.

'That's the sluice,' Dora explained, 'the place where they wash bedpans and all that. It's also the place where they hide from Sister when they want an illicit smoke or — more often — a little weep.'

'Poor girl,' Ruth sympathised. 'Accidents happen, so why be so hard on her? I wonder what Sister said?'

'Oh, I can tell you that, I've heard it often enough — 'You'll never make a nurse, Nurse!' '

They laughed at the absurdity of it, and then Ruth consulted her watch.

'If I run I might just catch the four o'clock bus. If I miss it, I'll have an hour to wait and it looks like it's about to rain.'

They kissed the air above each other's cheeks, and Ruth hurried away, pausing at the door to wave back at Dora.

The outing had done Ruth good, and

she was full of high spirits as she went to catch her bus.

★　★　★

When Ruth reached home the shop was closed, as it usually was at that time of day. The locals knew that they could always tap on the side door if they needed something after hours, although most women preferred to shop as early as possible so as not to miss a share of some coveted item that had been delivered that morning.

Ruth hoped that Bob had kept the fire on in the kitchen, where the kettle was kept perpetually steaming on the hob.

But Bob was nowhere to be found. Was he in the garden, hoeing the vegetables?

Ruth peered out of the window, but the yard was deserted.

Then she heard the murmur of voices coming from Mamgu's room. It wasn't the day for Nurse Jenkins to call; was

Bessie in there, trying to cheer the old lady up?

Ruth tapped on the door and went in.

What she saw made her jaw drop with amazement. There was Bob, in his shirt sleeves and with his tie off, sprawled in a chair, babbling on about some funny incident that had taken place back when he'd worked in the bakery, while Mamgu was listening with rapt attention.

As Ruth watched, the story came to an end, and Mamgu responded with an open-mouthed grin, showing her false teeth.

What was going on here? Not only had Bob come into the holy of holies and sat himself down, but Mamgu was actually smiling!

'What on earth were you doing in Mamgu's room?' Ruth wanted to know once she had a moment to ask Bob about it. Not that she minded, of course, but she was surprised by it.

Bob shrugged. 'I don't know. I had

nothing better to do, and I felt sorry for the old girl, I suppose, sitting in there all alone with nobody to talk to. She must get lonely.'

Ruth had already taken Mamgu's tray in to her, and the rest of them were sitting around the kitchen fire, having their own meal.

'Vegetable pie again?' Basil grumbled. 'Where's the meat?'

'Eat what you've been given and be thankful,' his mother said automatically. 'If you don't like it, write and tell Herr Hitler.'

'I was thinking,' Bob went on, 'that there's really no reason why Mrs Thomas has to stay in that room, not now that she seems to be getting better. She should be in here with us. The only trouble is, she can't hobble more than a few steps, so how could we manage to get her in here?'

'There's a wheelbarrow out the back, Dad. Mamgu could use that,' Basil piped up, smirking.

'That will be quite enough, young

man! No, I shall make enquiries to see if anyone knows of a wheelchair we could borrow. Just think, Marina could take the old girl down town. The fresh air would do them both good.'

Marina's face showed just what she thought of that idea!

Ruth wasn't sure whether Bob was serious or not; he was good at joking with a straight face. But whatever the truth of the matter, it appeared that Bob was genuinely interested in Mamgu's well-being, because he soon came up with another idea.

★　★　★

'I've been looking at that reclining chair in Mamgu's room,' Bob announced the following morning.

'Yes, I rather fancied that myself,' his wife told him. The chair was made of highly polished wood and upholstered in a plum coloured uncut moquette. It looked fairly old, but Ruth had decided to look out for something similar once they were back home. She might find one like it in a second-hand shop.

'Next time you're in Mamgu's room, have a look at the back of it, Ruth. It goes up and down like a deckchair. A piece of the frame folds out and can be pushed into one of three slots so you can choose to sit up fairly straight, or lean back in one of two positions. Well, if you have no objection, I'm going to bring that chair in here for Mrs Thomas. It may take a while for her to shuffle across the floor to get in here, but with one of us on each side, she should be able to manage it.'

'Well, of course I don't object, love! It would be too bad if I did, when she's in her own home and we're the visitors. I don't know what she'll say to the idea, though. You know how shy she is.'

'You just leave her to me, love. I have my winning ways, you know.'

Ruth was amazed when Bob explained his plan to Mamgu and she saw the yearning look which came into the old lady's eyes. Ruth was quite sure that if she'd been the one to mention it, she'd have met with a firm refusal, or been subjected to the silent treatment again.

* ★ ★

When old Mrs Thomas was comfortably installed in the kitchen, wiping a tear from her eye at the pleasure of it all, Ruth had to admit that Bob had handled the situation very nicely.

Bessie Parry, calling in to see if all was well, clapped her hands in glee when she saw what had taken place.

'There's lovely to see you sitting out, Mair, *bach*!' She smiled. 'The kitchen today, the shop tomorrow, isn't it?'

A flood of Welsh erupted from Mamgu. Although Ruth couldn't understand a word of it, she could tell from the old lady's face that she was delighted by this turn of events. This would certainly be something for Ruth to tell Dora on her next visit to the hospital.

Yet again Ruth felt sorry for the

impatience she so often felt when dealing with Mair Thomas. No wonder the poor dear was grumpy when she had nothing to do, hour after hour, but reflect on her woes. Her only son was away at sea, facing goodness knew what dangers, and her grandsons, too, were in the thick of things, and what could Mamgu do to help? Nothing at all, being forced to sit in bed all the time like a bump on a log.

Bessie Parry turned to Marina and handed her a note. 'This is from our Marged, *bach*. Make sure she gets it, she told me, as if I could forget!'

The envelope was a brilliant mauve, and smelled of violets.

'Thanks, Mrs Parry. I'll read it later.'

The girl rushed from the room and Ruth hid a smile.

'Later, my foot! She can't wait to see what it's about, and she doesn't want us to see her face while she's reading it!'

Ruth could recall her own teenage years, and now found it rather sweet to watch the girls with their little secrets.

Marged lived just a few yards down the road and could easily have popped in with her news, whatever it was. But no, sending a dramatic little note was much more interesting. It probably ended with 'don't tell a soul' or 'eat this'!

* * *

Marina found the note entirely satisfactory. Marged had managed to persuade Tim to go with them on a picnic 'up the mountain' and Emlyn Richards would be going with them to make up the numbers.

Marged warned Marina not to say a word to anybody about the two boys going with them, in case Mr and Mrs Greene put a stop to it.

Talking Tim into going along with the plan had taken some doing.

'Picnics, is it? I'm a grown man, Marged. I've better things to do with my time than go hiking up the mountain with a sandwich in my pocket!'

'You'd go like a shot if Catrin Harris was invited!'

'That's different.'

'Please, Tim! Marina wants to see Emlyn Richards, only her father won't let her go unchaperoned. He says she's too young for boyfriends. But if we went too, then he'd think there was no harm in it.'

Tim looked at her through narrowed eyes. 'I thought *you* were sweet on Emlyn Richards?'

'That was just a passing fancy,' Marged lied. 'Marina can have him, and welcome.'

'Well, I'll see if Catrin wants to come. I might be interested then.'

That wasn't what Marged had in mind, but there was nothing she could do about it. Anyway, it might turn out to be the best thing in the long run if Marina had to watch Tim spooning with Catrin. She'd know then that there was no hope for her. It was being cruel to be kind, as Mam would say.

However, as it turned out, Catrin

turned up her nose at the idea. 'I said I'd go to the pictures with Gwyneth on Saturday, Tim.'

'Can't you do that another time?'

'No, I can't. It's 'For Me And My Gal' and I've been waiting to see that.'

'Then I'll take you myself one evening. It's going to be on all week.'

'No, I don't want to let Gwyn down, not now we've made all our arrangements. Anyway, what's so special about going up that old mountain? We've been going up there all our lives. If it's having a meal with me you're after, you can come to the house and have your tea at the table. There's silly you are, Tim Parry!'

Somehow this caught him on the raw. 'There's nothing silly about wanting to spend time with the girl you love,' he said huffily.

'Don't be such a baby! Just because I want to go out with Gwyneth for once, it's not the end of the world. We can go up the mountain any old time.'

'Well, if that's how you feel!' Tim was

red in the face now, and beginning to feel sorry for himself.

Catrin's eyes flashed. 'I won't be bossed around by the likes of you, Tim Parry! You don't own me, and if I want to go out with Gwyneth, then I will. So put that in your pipe and smoke it!'

Catrin turned away and marched down the street with as much dignity as she could muster while tottering on high-heeled sandals.

Tim stared after her, seething. Well, he'd show Miss Harris a thing or two! He'd go along on this picnic and make sure that Catrin got to hear about it. He wouldn't let on that it was being arranged so that young Emlyn could get to know the visitor from England. Let Catrin think he was interested in the girl himself.

Marged was delighted when she heard about it. 'Mind you don't tell Mam that Emlyn is coming with us,' she warned Tim.

'Why not? Mam likes him, doesn't she?'

'I know that, but she might let it slip to Mrs Greene.'

Tim shrugged. None of that was his business.

That was when his sister had raced upstairs to write a jubilant note to Marina.

All she had to do now was make Emlyn Richards fall in with their plans, and that shouldn't be difficult because he'd been dropping hints about fancying Marina. And when he saw that Marina was only interested in Tim, then he would turn to Marged!

# Spies!

Ruth leaned out of the window, frowning. Basil was at it again, aimlessly kicking a tin can down the street.

'What on earth is the matter with that boy, Bob? He looks like he's lost a shilling and found sixpence!'

Her husband frowned. 'He's not getting into mischief, is he?'

'Well, no, but at this rate it won't be long before he does. Basil! Coo-ee!'

Summoned by his mother, Basil trudged reluctantly back to the house.

'Don't you have anything better to do, child?' she questioned him.

He shook his head.

'Then why not go up to the recreation ground and see if there's a game of football going on? Won't the other boys be there at this time of day?'

'I dunno.'

Ruth lost patience with him. 'Either

you go and find out or you can put in an hour weeding the garden. Now, which is it to be? I don't want the neighbours to see you moping around like a wet weekend. They'll think I'm not bringing you up properly.'

'All right, Mum.' Basil wandered off, his head hanging low.

'And pick up your feet!' Ruth bawled after him. 'Or you'll have the soles worn through. Do you hear me?'

Basil headed for the recreation ground but, surprisingly for that time of day in the summer holidays, it was completely deserted.

He supposed he'd better go and see if his erstwhile friends were down by the river. Mum would be sure to ask if he'd met them, and he knew better than to fib.

The other boys stared at him without speaking as he approached. He was uncomfortably reminded of that picture in Mamgu's room, with the cross-looking men questioning the cavalier boy. Dad had explained to him about a civil war that had happened in the olden days, which meant that the English had been fighting each other instead of being pitched against an enemy, like now. The bad men wanted to catch the boy's father and they were trying to make him tell. The picture had impressed Basil. He would never betray his own father, no matter what anyone tried to do to him.

Rhodri Evans was the first of the boys to speak.

'Hey, you! When we asked you where you come from you said Hemel, didn't you?'

'Yes. So what?'

'So I told my da and he says that's the German word for heaven, see?'

Basil's jaw dropped. 'I never knew that. Names aren't supposed to mean anything. They're just places.'

'Da says we all come from heaven in the beginning. So now we know what you are, Basil Greene. You're a spy!'

It was a moment before Basil managed to find his voice.

'Don't talk daft! I'm nine years old! They wouldn't drop me out of an aeroplane on a parachute. I've never been up in a plane in my life.'

'Ah, but you're only camo-whatsit, that's what I think.'

'Camouflage,' another boy supplied.

'That's it. Your da is the real spy, see.'

Basil's first impulse was to leap forward and bop the older boy on the nose, but something told him that it would be better to keep quiet and hear what else was said. Being accused of spying was a serious business. You could go to prison, or worse.

'My father is not a spy. He works in a grocer's shop.'

But Rhodri kept on, confident that he knew what he was talking about.

'My father told me what he read in the paper,' he said, loudly and confidently. 'Not all spies get sent here by parachute. There are others who pretend to be ordinary people. They've been living here since before the war, and they change their names so that we think they're English, and then they try to find out things to tell the enemy. I bet that's what your da is up to!'

'My father's English!' Basil shouted. 'And he'd never do anything like that!'

'So you say. So why did he just turn up here in the middle of the war, when he should be fighting in the army or something? It looks fishy to me.'

'He wanted to be in the army, but they wouldn't let him join. I think he's too old or something. And we came here to help Auntie Dora, 'cos she's in hospital, and Uncle Dai is away at sea. Somebody has to look after the shop and the old granny.'

Blank stares greeted this explanation.

'I bet he's got one of those radios hidden away so he can send messages to Hitler,' Rhodri persisted.

It was useless to keep protesting, Basil knew. Their minds were made up and nothing he could say would make any difference.

'You're all nuts!' he shouted. 'And I'm not staying here to listen to this.

I'm going home!'

'Good riddance to bad rubbish! And you tell your da that we're on to him!'

Basil ran until his chest hurt and he had to stop. He was gripped by a dreadful fear. Of course his father wasn't a spy! Any fool would know that! But the whole country seemed to be gripped by spy fever. Even the posters at the railway station, with their frightening slogans, seemed to indicate that you had to be on your guard all the time. *'Careless talk costs lives.' 'Be like Dad, keep Mum.' 'Loose lips sink ships.'*

Should he warn Dad about what the boys had said about him? He knew from half-overheard conversations between his parents that people accused of being enemy aliens were being taken from their homes and locked up in prison camps.

Basil didn't know what an alien was, but it sounded sinister.

Could that happen to them?

The trouble was, if he went home

and said anything, his parents would simply laugh and tell him not to be so silly — that the boys were talking through their hats, as the saying went. Perhaps it was best to keep quiet for the moment. The boys might not do anything, and if they did speak out, nobody paid attention to children anyway.

★   ★   ★

'I'm worried about Basil,' Ruth told her husband some days later. 'Do you think he's sickening for something? He looks like he's seen a ghost, and yesterday tea-time he even refused pudding. That's not like him.'

'He's just bored, love. Missing his old friends, I expect. What happened to those lads he was playing football with?'

'He doesn't seem interested in them any more. I expect they've fallen out, the way kids do.'

Bob told her not to worry. It was bound to sort itself out in time. But

Ruth did worry. Wasn't that what mothers were for?

When she went up to tuck her son into bed that night, she sat down beside him to have a little chat.

'Everything all right, is it, love?'

'When are we going home, Mum? I don't like it here.'

'Missing your friends, are you? I'm afraid we can't go back just yet. You know why we're here. We have to wait until Auntie Dora is on her feet again and everything gets back to normal.'

'How long is she going to be in hospital, Mum?'

'Quite a while yet, I'm afraid. And then she has to have physiotherapy — that means exercises to strengthen her muscles. When people lie in bed for a long time, their muscles get flabby.'

'Then how am I going to get to school when September comes?'

'That's something your dad and I will have to discuss when we get a minute. I expect we'll have to see about putting you in the school here. You'll fall behind if we don't.'

Basil was horrified. If he was forced to attend school five days a week, then he'd be at the mercy of those boys and others like them.

'Can't I go to boarding-school?' he bleated.

'Boarding-school? Whatever gave you that idea? Of course you can't! We've hardly got two halfpennies to rub together, let alone hundreds of pounds to send you away. Now you roll over and go to sleep. Things will look brighter in the morning.'

He did as he was told, but sleep refused to come.

Downstairs, Ruth was speaking to Bob.

'Basil has just reminded me that we have to make a decision about school when the autumn term comes. I suppose one of us will have to go and speak to the local headmaster, to see if they have room.'

'I'm certainly not going back to school!' Marina announced.

'I want you to stay on and get a good education, my girl,' said her father. 'I've always thought you might train for something worthwhile. Teaching, say, or nursing.'

'No, Dad! As soon as I'm old enough, I'm joining the Wrens. That's if the war isn't over before then.'

'No daughter of mine . . . ' he roared, but Ruth motioned to him to calm down.

'We'll discuss this later,' she said, aware that Mamgu was watching this little family disagreement with interest. 'But if we do let you leave school — and I'm not saying that we will, mind — you needn't think you'll be sitting around here all day, filing your fingernails. You'll have to get a job to tide you over. It's about time you contributed something towards your keep.'

'Aw, Mum!' Marina pouted, dismayed by this unwelcome new idea.

★　★　★

'This won't be much of a picnic without decent food,' Marina complained to her mother. 'Remember when I was little? When we had that outing to Whipsnade Zoo and we took all that food? Pork pies, chocolate cake, egg sandwiches. And bananas!'

'And you fed your banana to one of the monkeys.' Ruth smiled. 'What I wouldn't give to taste a banana now! One day we'll have all that again, just you wait and see. Meanwhile you'll just have to make do with what we can spare.'

'But lettuce sandwiches, Mum! Really!' Marina sidled into the shop, where the remains of a large round cheese sat on the counter, waiting to be sliced up with a wire and weighed out for some lucky customer.

'Give us a bit of that cheese, Dad,' she wheedled. 'I need something to liven up these sandwiches.'

'You've had your ration for the week, my girl. It's not my fault if you've eaten it all at once.'

'Two ounces! It's hardly more than a mouthful. Isn't there anything else, then?'

She wandered around the shop, looking at the shelves, but everything she fancied took 'points'.

Bob ignored her. He was busy weighing out sugar into small blue bags so as to save time when customers came in to buy it. He was surprised that his daughter hadn't given him more of an argument but instead she rushed off, saying that she didn't want to keep Marged waiting.

He wasn't to know that two young men were hovering around the corner, watching for her arrival.

★　★　★

'So, what's so special about this famous mountain?' Marina asked Marged as they all set off.

'We're going up to the *gorsedd*,' Marged explained.

'What's that?'

'You'll see when we get there,' Tim told her.

It was a stiff climb up the hillside, and Marina fell into step beside Tim, leaving Marged and Emlyn to follow on. This, of course, suited Marged very well.

At last they reached the summit, and the whole town lay below them, looking like some toy village. Over to one side, the brooding colliery and the ugly slag heaps marred the landscape, while on the other, green fields, dotted with sheep, presented an illusion of peace. At that moment the war seemed very far away.

'And this is the *gorsedd*!' Emlyn announced proudly. 'I bet you don't have anything like this where you come from!'

Marina gazed in awe at the circle of giant stones. It reminded her of pictures she'd seen of Stonehenge, but on a smaller scale.

'I suppose this is where the druids came to worship,' she said. 'How on earth did they get these rocks up here? They must weigh a ton!'

The idea of hundreds of people — slaves, probably — pushing these great slabs up the mountainside was mind-boggling, to say the least. She said as much to Tim, who shrugged.

'The old people around here say that these aren't ancient stones at all. They were put here in the last century, when there was a revival of Welsh culture. There may have been druids in traditional robes performing their ceremonies here, but they were ordinary men, not mysterious beings from the dark ages.'

'Oh.' Marina was a little disappointed, but it still provided a topic of conversation, and she didn't want to appear tongue-tied in front of him.

'It still must have been difficult, setting all this up. Did they use horses, or what?'

But Tim was tired of the subject. 'Come on, let's put our food on the flat rock in the middle and share what we have. What did Mam give us, Marged?'

'Welsh cakes — with about one currant in each — and *tarten gennin*.' Marged smiled, and reached into her basket. 'That's leek flan to you, Marina. What did you bring, Emlyn?'

Emlyn's jaw dropped. 'I didn't know I was supposed to bring anything. You didn't say.'

'Emlyn Richards! You're stupid, you are!'

'When people ask you to tea, they don't say bring your own food. What's different about picnics?'

'In case you hadn't noticed, most people take something with them these days when they're invited out for a meal, so that other people don't have to dip into their own rations. Now we've got four people to feed on barely enough for three!'

'You didn't say!' he insisted.

Tight-lipped, Marged turned her back on him, but Marina noticed that, when it was time to divide up the *tarten*, Emlyn received a generous slice while Marged made do with a much smaller piece herself.

Marina herself was being watched with interest by Tim. Until now he had thought of her as a schoolgirl, but today she seemed much older. Dressed in a fresh gingham frock, topped with a white cardigan borrowed from her mother, she seemed to be closer to his own age. Perhaps it was because of her hair, which she was wearing loose instead of in her usual plaits.

These days, since the argument over the picnic, there was a distinct coolness between himself and Catrin Harris. Perhaps there was no harm in him getting to know Marina a little better. Nothing too serious, of course, but then, she wouldn't expect anything like that, would she? One of these days, she'd be going back to England and that would be the end of it. Ships that pass in the night.

'There's a hop in the Town Hall next Saturday night, Marina. Want to go?' he asked.

'Oh, yes, please,' she breathed. 'I'd love to.'

'Will your da let you?' Marged was doubtful.

'I'm sure I can talk him round.'

Nothing short of a miracle would make Bob Greene say yes, but Marina was not about to admit that in front of Tim. If necessary, she'd slip out of the house to go to the dance, and face the music later!

'I've got a better idea,' Marged said, understanding this without needing to be told. 'I'll get Mam to ask him, shall I?'

While Marged's mother had strong principles when it came to how girls should behave, she did at least allow her daughter to take part in such blameless pleasures that the town afforded.

'I've got nothing to wear,' Marina said, worried.

'Oh, that's all right. Nobody dresses up. Just wear an ordinary skirt and blouse. And don't bother about stockings, either. They're too precious to waste on a hop. All the girls wear ankle socks. So, do you want me to talk to Mam, or not?'

★ ★ ★

Bessie Parry picked her moment to mention the dance. She arrived at the house just as the Greenes were finishing their evening meal.

'I've brought that pattern you wanted to borrow, Mrs Greene. It should knit up lovely. Did you get that old grey jumper unpicked yet?'

'I don't know what you wanted to go and do that for,' Bob mumbled through a mouthful of scone. 'I always liked you in that.'

'Oh, Bob! I've darned the elbows so many times that there's more darn than sleeve! I'm going to knit it up again with short sleeves, from this new pattern.'

'No need for that, love! You could just re-do the sleeves. No need to change the whole thing.'

'You're missing the point, dear! I'm sick to death of the old rag. Mrs Parry's pattern has a pretty stitch in it. That'll make a change, and that's what I'm determined to have!'

Bessie saw that it was time to change the subject. She turned to speak to Marina. 'Are you going to the hop this Saturday, pet?'

'Um, I don't know, Mrs Parry. I'd really like to, but . . . '

'Marina doesn't go to dances,' Bob announced. 'It's kind of you to think of her, but she's far too young for that sort of thing.'

'This isn't exactly a dance, Mr Greene. It's just some of our young people getting together to shuffle around to gramophone records. It's well supervised, and there's certainly no drinking or anything wicked like that. I'm letting our Marged go.'

'I don't know . . . '

Bessie played her trump card. 'I'll be sending our Tim with them. He'll keep his eye on them, he will.'

'Go on, Bob, where's the harm?' Ruth smiled. 'If it makes you feel any better you can deliver the girls to the hall yourself, and fetch them home afterwards.'

'Mum!' Marina groaned.

'Well, if Tim is definitely going, I'm sure I can trust him to look after the girls. All right, then, I'll say yes, but you're to be home by nine, mind.'

'Nine? Dad! But it goes on until ten!'

'That's my last word, my girl! Take it or leave it.'

The problem was, of course, that whoever you had the last dance with was also the person who walked you home, and Marina was determined that that should be Tim Parry!

Marina was about to argue, but then her mother caught her eye.

'Leave this to me,' Ruth mouthed.

# Troubled Times

'So give me all the news! I'm so bored, sitting here. Now I know how Mamgu feels. At least I've got hope that I'll be back on my feet in a few weeks. She could be lying around for the rest of her days,' said Dora, when Ruth next went to visit her.

'Then that's where you're wrong. She's been sitting in the kitchen with us, *and* she's muttering about going into the shop to give Bob a hand.'

'I don't believe it! How did that come about?'

'Bob used his charm on her, that's what. I just don't understand it, Dora. Here's me, dancing attendance on her, all sweetness and light, and it's like water off a duck's back. All Bob has to do is get masterful and she not only does what he says, but is all smiles with it.'

'It's because he's a man, Ruth. Women of her generation were brought up to think that men always know what's best. I bet Bob laps it up.'

'He does rather,' Ruth agreed. 'Still, in this case he seems to have known what he was doing. Your mother-in-law is much happier, and I don't have to run around with trays any more.'

The ward seemed a happier place, too, today. It appeared that Sister was off duty for a couple of days and a young blonde woman, known as 'Staff', was in charge in the interim. The young nurses bustled about, singing as they went, and even the bedclothes seemed more relaxed. When Sister was present everyone was tucked in so tightly that not a wrinkle could be seen in the blue bedspreads.

'At least she can't fasten me down, not with my leg strung up like this,' Dora said when Ruth remarked on this. 'Honestly, does it really matter whether the sheets are straight or not? You should be here when Matron's round is coming up. Everything has to be really shipshape by then. Even the wheels on the beds have to face in a certain direction.'

'Speaking of ships . . . '

'Before you ask, no, I haven't heard from Dai. I don't suppose any letters have come to the house?'

'No. I'd have handed anything over at once.'

Dora wiped a tear from her eye. 'I've written, of course, giving him my address here, but I haven't heard a thing this week. Every time they bring the post round I keep my fingers crossed, and then I'm disappointed, knowing I have to get through another twenty-four hours before there's another chance.'

Ruth didn't know what to say. The life of a merchant seaman was hard enough in the normal way of things, but in wartime it was even more fraught with danger. The dreaded U-boats with their torpedoes were prowling under the sea like giant sharks, dealing out death and destruction.

And Dora's son, Idris, in the Royal Navy, was in danger, too, although neither Ruth nor his mother knew exactly what he was up to, or even where he was, because those matters were kept secret in case the enemy latched on to the information.

'What about your lot?' Dora asked, pulling herself together with an effort. 'All right, are they?'

'Oh, yes. Bob's in his element in the shop. In fact, he's talking about us getting a little shop ourselves after the war. He enjoys being his own boss and he's getting to know all the customers. Do you know, a woman came in for her cheese ration the other day, and asked for a single ounce. 'But you're entitled to two ounces, Mrs Richards,' says Bob.

' 'Oh, I know, Mr Greene', she says, 'but if I take it now, I know I'll eat it all at once. If you keep some of it here, then I'll have something to look forward to, see?' '

'Poor Mrs Richards. She's another

one with a son at sea. An ounce of cheese! Honestly, that would be funny if it wasn't so awful. What do you miss the most, Ruth?'

Ruth had to think. 'Being able to have a heaped teaspoonful of sugar in my tea. That saccharin just isn't the same. And crumpets, with lashings of butter seeping through on to the plate.'

'Oh, stop it, do! You're making my mouth water.'

'Well, you did ask! Anyway, back to what we were saying before — Marina is on cloud nine over some hop the youngsters are going to on Saturday night.'

'No! You mean Bob's going to let her go?'

'Yes, but not without a great deal of fuss. He doesn't want her jitterbugging with a lot of lads she hasn't even been introduced to.'

'Dear old Bob.' Dora laughed. 'I don't think the Methodists do much jitterbugging. This will be far more sedate — foxtrotting about, with the chaperones telling the youngsters not to dance too close together, and the minister's wife standing at the door in case couples try to go outside to smooch!'

'Speaking of chaperones,' Ruth said, giggling, 'Bob wanted young Basil to go to the dance with Marina, to keep an eye on her! Well, Marina was having none of it, as you would expect, but it was Basil who surprised me. He got really angry. He shouted something about not being a spy, and that he hated the lot of us. Then he raced upstairs and slammed his bedroom door so hard that I was surprised it didn't come off its hinges. Bob and I were amazed. That's not like Basil at all.'

'Kids! Who knows what goes on in their minds? So, what's Bob going to do now?'

'He was still harping on about delivering the poor girl to the dance himself, but I think Bessie Parry's finally talked him out of that by saying that her son will look after both Marina and Marged. I'm afraid Marina has a crush on Tim, though. I hope it won't lead to anything or the fat will really be in the fire.'

'Oh, no, it certainly won't.' Dora shook her head decisively. 'Tim's courting Catrin Harris, that I do know.'

'Catrin Harris?'

'A girl his own age. You see that woman three beds down? In the blue bed-jacket? That's Catrin's auntie. She comes for a natter with me sometimes. She thoroughly approves of Tim Parry. He's got a steady job, one he'll probably have for life, *and* he doesn't have to go away to war.'

'Mining can be a pretty dangerous occupation, though.'

'True, but you can't go through life worrying about what could happen. If you had the safest job in the world it wouldn't stop you being hit by a bus or something. You know what they say about having to go when your number's up.'

Ruth shivered. 'Ooh, this is a morbid conversation! Let's change the subject. Tell me about all these other women in the ward. What's wrong with them, do you know?'

Dora, it seemed, knew about everyone's ailments. There was little Mrs Prior, who had practically starved herself by giving most of her rations to her young children. She had lost so much weight that the doctors believed she must have some awful disease — until they found out what she'd been doing. Now they were keeping her in hospital so that she could build up her strength again.

'Although what's the betting that once they let her out she'll go on just as she did before?'

'You can understand it though, can't you?' Ruth pointed out. 'At least my kids are old enough to understand what rationing means, even if they do grumble. It must be terribly hard if you have little ones crying for second helpings when there isn't enough to go round in the first place. It would break my heart.'

On the way home, Ruth considered what she had learned about Tim Parry. It was a relief to know that he was seeing someone his own age and was unlikely to be interested in Marina. No doubt the Harris girl would be at the dance, and Marina would see them together and realise there was no chance for her. After that there would be high drama, and Ruth would be left to pick up the pieces.

# Basil Finds A Friend

Emrys Rees was a retired miner. Since the death of his wife from cancer, shortly after the outbreak of war, he had kept himself to himself, not wanting to mingle with his fellow man. He seldom went to the Red Dragon, and when former workmates greeted him on the street he responded with a curt '*Bore da*' and walked on.

It had been a great sorrow to Glynis Rees that she and Emrys hadn't been blessed with children, and there had been a time when her husband agreed with her, but not now. Any family they had had would have been caught up in the war now, at best serving in faraway places, at worst possibly being killed or maimed.

But Emrys was fond of children, although he knew few of them very well. And so, when he caught sight of a small boy hanging around the allotments, he was intrigued.

He noted that the child wore a faded grey shirt, and shorts that had been bought too large, to allow for growth. In that regard, his appearance was much the same as most local boys in these days of clothes rationing, but something marked this child out as being different. Emrys was unable to put his finger on what it was, but it was there.

Perhaps it was a lack of confidence, a feeling of being out of place somehow?

Emrys knew that feeling. He'd felt like that himself, ever since Glynis had passed on.

'*Bore da!*' Emrys called.

The boy looked up and came closer to where Emrys was adjusting his bean poles.

'Sorry, sir, I can't speak Welsh.'

'English, is it? That's what we'll use, then.'

Everybody in Bedwen spoke both languages, except for some of the very old people, who preferred to use Welsh all the time, even though — or perhaps because — they'd been forced to learn English at the school.

In the old days, when Queen Victoria was on the throne, their native tongue had even been banned in the classroom and the playground, the idea being that anyone who wished to get on in the world needed to be able to converse in the first language of the Empire.

A lot of nonsense, Emrys had always thought; it didn't matter what language a man spoke when he was down the pit.

'Would you like a carrot?' He pulled one out of the ground and dusted it clean on his moleskin trousers.

'Thanks.' Basil accepted the offering and began to crunch it between small white teeth.

'Not playing with your mates today, then?'

'No, I haven't got any.'

Emrys blinked.

'Well, that's awful! Surely there must be somebody who'd give you a game of football? Or is it cricket you play, you being English? Not much call for that round by here, see? Where are you from, then?' he asked, and was taken aback at the change that came over the boy.

'I'm not a spy! My dad's not a spy!' Basil shouted, clenching his fists.

'Nobody said you were, *bach*!'

'You would if I said where I was from, and I won't tell you, so there!'

Emrys debated with himself whether to explore this further, or to leave well alone. Children got hold of some funny ideas at times.

However, he considered himself to be a good judge of people and he sensed that the boy was almost at breaking point, so he decided to risk it.

'What's wrong, *bach*? Why don't you tell me what's up? It may be that I can help. Two heads are better than one, they say.'

As Basil burst out crying, Emrys reached over and patted him on the back.

'If things are that bad, you'd better tell your mam and dad about it, eh?'

'I can't!' the boy sobbed. 'If I say anything they'll send my father to prison, and we'll never see him again. What if they shoot him or something?'

What in the name of goodness had the man done? The last thing Emrys wanted was to get involved in something dodgy. It came to him then that these must be the people who were standing in for Dora Thomas at the shop. He'd never met the man; was it possible that he was dealing on the black market and putting the stuff through the shop? The Thomas family were stalwarts of the chapel. They would never get over the shame. Still, something urged Emrys to probe further.

'What makes you think your da could go to prison,' he asked carefully.

Basil stared back at his new friend, searching his face as if trying to decide whether he could be trusted.

'It's the boys. The ones I was playing

with. They said my father's a German spy. They said he's here to find out information to send to the enemy. It's a big fat lie, that's what it is!'

'That's just games, boyo. Having you on, they are.'

'No, sir, when I told them where we were from, they said that I was talking German, and I'm a spy. I said that was daft, and then they said it must be Dad.'

Emrys closed his eyes in exasperation. 'And where *are* you from, *bach*?'

'Hemel, sir. Hemel Hempstead really, only we always say just Hemel. It's a place in Hertfordshire, sir.'

This meant nothing to Emrys, and he couldn't see the connection with spying.

'Who was it started all this nonsense?'

'Rhodri, sir. I think his surname is Evans.'

'Oh, ay, I know the family. Well, you run along now, and let me have a bit of a think. Between the two of us, we should be able to make sense out of this.'

'You won't tell the police, will you?' Basil was still anxious.

'Na, na, you can trust me.'

Basil sped off, not altogether convinced.

Emrys sat on an upturned pail and took a pull on his pipe. He'd heard the tales about spies, and it was probably true that Britain had been infiltrated by enemy agents, just as the British were likely to be sending men and women into occupied territory abroad. All that was hush hush, of course, but it didn't take much of a brain to work out what was going on.

However, he was willing to bet that the people at the grocer's shop were in the clear. The woman — this boy's mother — was connected to Dora Thomas in some way, and they'd come to Bedwen to help out while Dora was in hospital, there being nobody else to take care of Mair Thomas in her absence. There was no way the enemy could have arranged all that!

Bessie Parry was amazed when she found Emrys standing on her doorstep. 'Emrys Rees. Fancy seeing you here! *Sut yr ydych chwi?*'

He agreed that he was well enough.

Sitting at Bessie's kitchen table, he fumbled for the right words.

'These people up at the shop. All right, are they?'

'All right? Oh, they're very healthy, so far as I know.'

'Na, na, *merch*. What I mean is, can they be trusted?'

Bessie bridled. 'I don't know what you're getting at, Emrys Rees, but they seem decent enough to me, coming all this way from London to help poor Dora.'

'Not London. The little chap said something about a place called Hemel.'

'That will be Basil. What's all this about, then?'

Emrys had known Bessie for years and decided he could trust her.

'It's those boys, Rhodri Evans in particular. They've got it into their heads that these people at the shop are enemy agents, and the boy is being made to suffer for it.'

'Stuff and nonsense! Well, there's only one thing to do. Even if the child has sworn you to secrecy, you must go and speak to Bob Greene and let him deal with it. These things have a habit of snowballing if they're not nipped in the bud.'

Despite her mixed metaphors, Bessie was talking sense, and within minutes, Emrys found himself in the little shop, facing Basil's father over the counter.

'What can I do for you, sir?'

Emrys looked around cautiously. 'Your little boy isn't within earshot, is he?'

'Basil? No, he's running an errand for my wife. Why, what's he been up to?'

Emrys plunged straight into his story, and was taken aback when Bob guffawed.

'Kids! What will they think of next?'

'I think this is a bit more serious, Mr Greene. Oh, I'm sure the constable won't be marching you off in handcuffs just yet, but your boy is extremely distressed by all this. And it can only get worse as time goes on. He can stay away from the other children now, but once school starts again they'll have him where they want him. It could come to blows.'

'Then what do you think I ought to do?'

'Call on Gareth Evans, Rhodri's father, when you get a moment. He's a reasonable man. He'll help you to sort this out.'

The two men shook hands as Emrys took his leave.

★   ★   ★

'Anyone for a game of Snap, or Happy Families?' Basil asked hopefully. Tea was over, his sister was clearing the table, and the shop was closed for the day. This was the time he liked best

131

because if he was lucky, one or both of his parents would pay attention to him.

'Not now, Basil. You and I are going for a walk.'

Basil looked up at his father in surprise. 'But it's raining, Dad, coming down cats and dogs, and my mac is leaking. Can't we go for a walk tomorrow instead?'

Marina came in from the scullery just then and her father caught her eye.

'Go upstairs for a bit, love. Would you mind? Or if you'd rather, go in and chat to Mamgu. I want to have a word with your brother in private.'

Raising her eyes to the ceiling, Marina did as she was told. She'd known for days that the kid was up to something and now, whatever it was, he'd been caught out doing it. Would he never learn?

'You'd better hear this, too,' Bob told his wife. 'Come and sit down.'

'Can't it wait? I've got a sink full of pots, and now that you've sent Marina off, I'll be stuck doing them all myself.'

'They'll still be there when we've finished.'

'That's what I'm afraid of,' she retorted.

Basil felt like screaming. Why couldn't they just get on with it, whatever it was? He twisted his features into what he hoped was an angelic expression.

'It has come to my attention,' Bob began, putting on what Ruth thought of as his pompous manner, 'that some boys have been saying some very silly things to you.'

'What sort of things, Bob?' asked Ruth.

Basil had gone white and his mother didn't like the look of him. This sounded serious.

'Well, Basil? What have you got to say to us?'

'Nothing, Dad.'

'Are you sure about that?'

'Yes, Dad.'

'Then I must tell you that I know all about it.'

'If you know all about it, then what

are you asking me for?' his son burst out.

'Don't be cheeky, lad. I wanted to hear your side of the story before taking action. Now, is this right? Rhodri Evans and some other boys think we're enemy agents because we're not Welsh, is that it?'

Ruth gasped. 'What rubbish! They can't have come to that conclusion just because we're English! We're all Britons, aren't we? All in this together? Oh, whoever started this crazy talk deserves a good clip round the ear!'

'I don't think it's because we're English, Mum, and it wasn't really Rhodri. It was his dad that said we were Germans, not him. Unless Rhodri's fibbing, of course.'

'Well, I'm going to get to the bottom of this before I'm much older. I'm going round to see this man — Gareth Evans his name is — and I'm going to have it out with him.'

'Dad, no!'

'Oh, yes, I am, and you're coming

with me, so don't give me any more of your lip. Get your mac on, leaky or not, and we'll go and get it over with.'

'You will be careful, won't you, Bob? Don't do anything you might regret.' Ruth's hands were tightly clenched inside her apron pocket as she spoke.

'I'm not about to punch him, if that's what you mean,' said Bob.

\* \* \*

Gareth Evans greeted them pleasantly enough, and ushered them into a kitchen that was very similar to their own. Despite the fact that it was midsummer, the air was chilly from the damp, and there was a fire burning in the grate.

Bob sat down on the chair that was pulled out for him, and Basil stood at his father's shoulder, ready to run if it should become necessary.

'We haven't been introduced, but I've seen you in the Red Dragon, Mr Greene. Now, what can I do for you?

My wife hasn't been asking you for tick at the shop, has she? I know Dora Thomas doesn't allow that.'

'Nothing like that, Mr Evans. The fact is, there seems to be a bit of a problem between your boy and mine. This is rather awkward, but your lad's been putting it about that I'm a spy, some sort of German agent, and the other children are giving Basil here a rough time over it.'

Rhodri's father smothered a grin, but realising the seriousness of the accusation, quickly pulled himself together.

'You're sure about this, boy? Perhaps they were talking Welsh and you got the wrong end of the stick.'

'Yes, sir. I mean, I didn't get the wrong idea; that's what they said.'

'And furthermore,' Bob put in, 'your son seems to have been acting on something you said about all this.'

'Has he indeed! Well, we'll see what he's got to say for himself now! Rhodri!'

Rhodri came clattering down from

upstairs, only to stop short when he saw Basil, accompanied by a strange man.

'What's all this I hear about you accusing Mr Greene here of being a spy?'

'Well, he could be, Da. We're always hearing about how we should watch out for spies. It said so on the wireless, and the *Meistr* told us that at school as well.'

'Listen here, boyo,' said Rhodri's father sternly, 'I know you've never set foot outside this town, but there's one thing you've got to learn. There are lots of people in the world who are on our side. Just because Mr Greene isn't a Welshman, doesn't mean he's with the enemy!'

'Oh, I know that, Da, I'm not stupid. But it was you who told me they're Germans.'

'What? I did not! What's the matter with you, boy?'

'You did, Da! I asked Basil where he's from and he said Hemel.'

'So what?'

'And you said that's what the Germans call Heaven. You did, Da, you did! And it was you that told me ages ago about everybody coming from Heaven when they're born, so if Basil came from the German part of Heaven — well, that's suspicious, see?'

Gareth Evans groaned. 'I seem to remember you asking me something like that,' he said, 'but I didn't pay much attention because I was trying to hear the nine o'clock news. I thought you said Himmel, see? Himmel!'

Rhodri's face was blank, and Basil merely looked bewildered.

'I see it all, now!' Bob laughed. 'I expect you said Hemel, didn't you, Basil? We're from Hemel Hempstead, Rhodri, a small town not far from London. It's thoroughly British, and so are we.'

Mr Evans nodded.

'So there you are, son. It doesn't pay to jump to conclusions. Next time, come to me first if you think you've found a nest of spies. Now, I expect you've something to say to Basil here, haven't you?'

Rhodri shuffled his feet before muttering an insincere, 'Sorry!'

'I must apologise for all this, Mr Greene,' said Gareth Evans. 'If only I'd realised what was going on, I'd have put a stop to it at once. My wife is a close friend of Dora Thomas, see. Visits her up at the hospital, she does. Very grateful to you for coming to stay, Dora is. I tell you what we'll do.' Gareth Evans beamed. 'To make it up to you, Basil, you can come here to tea on Sunday. How will that be?'

'That's very kind,' Bob told him, when it became clear that Basil wasn't going to respond. 'I'll see that my wife sends a bit of something to eat along with him.'

'Na, na! If there's not enough to go round, our Rhodri can go short for once. It'll save me sending him to bed without his supper as punishment for all this upset that's been caused.'

And with that the whole nasty

business came to an end. Satisfied, the two men shook hands.

The cold lump which had settled on Basil's stomach ever since this terror began was now starting to dissipate. At the same time it was with a sharp sensation of guilt that it occurred to him that, lurking in the far reaches of his mind, there had been a tiny suspicion that his father might have been in league with the enemy after all.

He knew he would never be able to forgive himself for that, and he would certainly never forgive Rhodri and his henchmen.

He wanted to cry out that he hadn't really thought such a thing, and certainly never would. The idea had just crawled unbidden into his mind.

Yet young as he was, he knew he must never tell anyone about this, or his father would be hurt beyond belief, and he couldn't bear that.

# Trapped!

Ruth felt quite sentimental as, that Saturday night, she waved her daughter off on her way to the hop.

'Just think, our little girl is going to her first dance!' she said softly. 'Oh, Bob, they grow up so fast, don't they?'

'Too fast!' he grunted.

'Remember our dancing days? How they used to spread soap flakes all over the dance floor to make it slippery and easier to glide across?'

'They won't be doing that tonight, old girl. Soap flakes are as scarce as snowballs at the equator as it is, never mind wasting them on such foolishness. Switch on the wireless while you're on your feet. I could do with a bit of music.'

The comforting voice of Vera Lynn, the Forces' Sweetheart, filled the room. Ruth sang along with her: 'There'll be bluebirds over, the white cliffs of Dover, tomorrow, just you wait and see . . . '

'Can I go out, Mum?' Basil interrupted.

'Out? Where do you want to go at this time of night?'

'It's only seven o'clock, Mum.'

'Didn't you hear me? I said, where do you want to go?'

'Down to the Town Hall, to see what they're doing. I want to watch them going in.'

'I can't imagine what for. It'll just be a few boys and girls dressed in their ordinary clothes, going to play a few records and have a dance about. Not like in my young day, when we knew how to do things properly.'

'Mum!'

'Oh, let the boy go,' Bob groaned. 'Anything for a bit of peace and quiet. What's the point of having the wireless on, if I'm not allowed to listen to it?'

'Well, go on then, Basil,' said Ruth, 'but you're to be back here no later than eight o'clock, do you hear me?'

'Yes, Mum.' Basil sped off before his parents could change their minds.

He deeply resented the fact that he had to go to bed at eight o'clock. It wasn't so bad in winter, when the evenings were dark and cold and it was a pleasure to huddle under the blankets, but summer was different. He would lie there, tossing and turning while the sun was still shining outside, and he could hear the shouts of luckier children playing in the distance. But no matter how much he pleaded to stay up later, his mother was adamant. He was a growing boy, and he needed his sleep.

★   ★   ★

But Basil wasn't on his way to the Town Hall because he was interested in the dancers. No, he was more interested in what they might have to eat.

Basil had been to tea at Rhodri's home, as arranged, and had enjoyed playing bagatelle, a game which was new to him.

When they had tired of this the two boys had sat on the stairs, talking.

'Are you going to the hop?' Rhodri had asked.

'Of course not. It's stupid. You might have to talk to girls.'

'Ah, but they're having food.'

'What sort of food?'

'Pop and biscuits, I think. Last time, they had spam sandwiches.'

'How do you know?' Basil said, his voice full of scorn.

'My cousin Catrin was here. I heard her telling Mam. She goes to the hop with Tim Parry, Catrin does. The thing is, they keep the food in the back room until half-time. And I know where there's a little window. We can get inside and help ourselves.'

Basil tried not to look shocked. 'Wouldn't that be stealing?'

'Na, na. It's for everybody who goes to the hop, see? We wouldn't take it all, just a little bit. They'd never miss it. Stands to reason — they don't know how many people to provide for.'

'Well, if you think nobody would mind . . . '

Basil's mouth watered at the thought of sinking his teeth into a spam sandwich, and how long was it since he'd tasted orange pop? It didn't occur to him to wonder why — if the food was there for everyone — it would be necessary for them to climb in through a window.

'I'll meet you there, then,' Rhodri grinned. 'Seven-fifteen, sharp. That gives the ladies time to put out the food, see?'

When Basil had gone home, Rhodri told himself that his plan was foolproof. He'd help the other boy through the window and then run off, leaving him to face the music.

Rhodri was still smouldering over the episode of the spies. So, he'd been wrong about the Greenes; what of it? It was everyone's patriotic duty to keep on the look-out for stuff like that. People should have been pleased with his efforts.

Mr Greene had been a sport. He hadn't shouted, or asked for Rhodri to be punished, and even Da had said 'boys will be boys' and said they'd let it go this once.

It was Mam who'd jumped on him like a ton of bricks.

'That poor young boy!' she'd gasped. 'Imagine what you've put him through. It's a sharp lesson you need, boyo!'

The lesson had come only that morning, when he'd had to miss the Saturday matinee at the pictures. Mam had refused to give him the empty jam jar which — if you didn't have the necessary tuppence — was the price of admission to the cinema.

Fuming, he'd decided that he had to make Basil suffer too.

\* \* \*

When Basil reached the High Street, it was to see a number of young people heading for the Town Hall, girls arm in arm, boys slouching along in small groups.

Spotting Rhodri loitering in the doorway of the draper's shop, Basil hurried to join him.

'Duck down!' Rhodri hissed. 'Don't let anybody see us!'

Basil couldn't see that it mattered, but he entered into the spirit of the game until the last of the dancers had disappeared inside the hall. Then the pair of them darted along the deserted street.

'Round the back!' Rhodri ordered, leading the way to a small window set high in the wall. It was the sort which had to be opened from the bottom, and someone had already pushed it up by about three or four inches.

'All clear!' Rhodri whispered. 'Come on, I'll give you a bunk up.'

'How will you get in, then?'

'I won't need to. You pass the stuff out to me, and then you come back out yourself.'

Boosted up by Rhodri, Basil scrambled

through the window, grazing himself painfully on the knee as he fell off the sill.

He hesitated beside the table where the food was set out. No sandwiches, but there were some stale-looking rock cakes and several bottles of pop.

At that moment, Basil heard voices from the other side of the door.

'It's good of you to bring jam tarts, Mrs Griffiths. The young people will be grateful, I'm sure.'

'It's only that awful imitation stuff with parsnips in it,' the invisible Mrs Griffiths replied. 'Still, it's better than nothing, I suppose.'

In a panic, Basil looked for an escape route. He knew he couldn't reach the window without help, and there wasn't any sort of box or chair he could use, even if he'd had time to put it in place.

Looking around wildly, he wrenched open a nearby door, slipping inside in the nick of time. It was a deep cupboard with shelves on three sides, stacked with box files and heavy ledgers. His heart pounding, he sank down on the floor.

'Just put them on the table, Mrs Griffiths. You can come and fetch your plate later. I believe you're one of the chaperones for this evening? How can you stand that horrid jazz music? Give me a nice bit of opera any day.'

'They could hardly dance to Rigoletto!' the other woman laughed, but she was rudely interrupted by a snort of outrage from her companion.

'Well, really! They've left this cupboard with the key in the lock, and all the important council papers inside! I'll hand the key over to Councillor Morgan, and give him a piece of my mind with it!'

There was a loud click, after which the footsteps receded, and Basil was left alone in the dark. He fumbled for the handle but it wouldn't turn.

He was locked in.

★  ★  ★

Inside, the hall was full of people, but nobody was dancing. The girls were standing about in small groups, talking with false animation — pretending not to notice the boys — while the young men in question leaned against the wall and eyed the girls.

'There's Emlyn,' Marina whispered. 'I wonder if he's going to ask you to dance, Marged? Shall I wave to him? He might come over.'

'Don't you dare!' Marged hissed. 'I don't want him to think I'm fast! Better to wait till everybody's dancing.'

'I wouldn't want to be first on the floor, either,' Marina told her. 'I'd be mortified to have everyone looking at me. That's if anyone asks me to dance at all,' she added.

'Oh, don't worry!' Marged hastened to reassure her. 'They always have a Paul Jones to get everybody mingling, and if that fails, Tim will dance with you.'

Before leaving home, Marged had punched her brother on the arm and warned him that if he didn't give Marina a dance or two, she'd never speak to him again.

'It's the least you can do when the poor girl is a stranger here,' she'd told Tim, and their mother, coming into the room in time to hear this, had agreed.

'I promised Mrs Greene you'd watch out for that girl of hers, our Tim, so mind you don't make a liar out of me.'

'I may, or I may not, Mam. That's the best I can say.'

It all depended on whether Catrin was at the dance, Tim told himself. Naturally, she would expect him to dance with her. That was the whole point of being part of a courting couple; you had someone to go to social events with.

Unfortunately for Catrin, she arrived at the hall in the company of her next-door neighbour, Harry Lloyd. It wasn't her fault that they both happened to be heading in the same direction. Besides, she'd always liked Harry. They'd known each other since they were toddlers and Catrin thought of him as an adopted brother.

Strolling along the street behind Marina and his sister, Tim saw Catrin and Harry arriving together. Catrin smiled at Harry as they reached the door, and he took her by the elbow to steer her inside. Neither of them noticed Tim, whose face turned red with annoyance.

'Why, isn't that your Catrin?' Marged asked him brightly.

'You know very well it is!' Tim growled. 'And don't call her *my* Catrin!'

'But I thought the two of you were going together?' Marged asked innocently, winking at Marina. 'Are you going to land one on Harry Lloyd's nose?'

'I don't care what she does. We're not married. She's free to please herself.'

Marina was delighted. Her pleasure at coming to the dance with the Parrys had been tempered by the knowledge that if Catrin were present, then Tim would gravitate to her and Marina wouldn't get a look-in. Now, if she played her cards right, he might turn his attention to herself after all.

Catrin saw the trio entering the hall. She frowned at the sight of the pretty girl at Tim's side. How dare he turn up with somebody else? It was bad enough that he hadn't offered to call for her at home.

Not for the first time, she wondered what had gone wrong between them. What had she done that was so terrible?

When her friend, Gwyneth, had invited her to go to the pictures to see 'For Me And My Gal', she'd accepted without a second thought. That sort of film wasn't Tim's cup of tea at all. Far better to go with Gwyn, even if it meant paying for themselves. Why couldn't Tim understand instead of taking the huff because she wasn't free to go on some old picnic up the mountain with him?

Catrin glared across the room at him, but he wasn't looking in her direction.

Instead, he was talking to that simpering English girl.

Now the music was playing loudly, and several couples were moving happily in time to the beat. Marina was thrilled when Tim asked her to dance. She hadn't much experience, but he steered her expertly across the floor and he didn't tread on her toes once.

There was a break while the record was changed, and then he led her on to the floor again, taking it for granted that she'd be in agreement. She was blissfully unaware that he had one eye on Catrin Harris, who, to show that she didn't care, was chattering animatedly to a girl friend.

'Can we have a ladies' choice?' Catrin whispered to Gwil Jones, the elderly man in charge of changing the records. He was the Town Hall janitor in everyday life.

'In a minute, *bach*. Wait till I get a slow one going. Is that all right?'

Catrin nodded. That would give her time to decide whether to ask some other boy to dance so as to make Tim jealous, or to go over and drag him off from under that awful Marina's nose.

Out of the corner of her eye she saw her cousin, Rhodri, edging his way into the hall. What was he doing slinking around like that? This dance was for the over sixteens, no kids allowed. Besides, what was he doing, out at night? According to Catrin's mother, the boy had been up to mischief of some sort and was being punished.

Rhodri edged his way towards the room where the snacks were laid out. It was one thing to urge Basil into mischief but quite another not to know what had happened to him. Not that his conscience was troubling him, he just needed to have his story straight if questions were asked later.

'And where do you think you're going, boy?'

Rhodri recognised Mrs Phillips, a stern lady who played a part in many of the town's organisations, such as the Red Cross and the Friends of the

Library. She was not a person to be argued with.

'Just looking, I was, Mrs Phillips.'

'Then you can go just looking outside. There's nothing to see here.'

'What's in there?' he asked desperately, looking at the inner door.

'Nothing that need interest you. Off you go now, or I'll be having a word with your mam the next time I meet her.'

There was nothing for it but to leave the hall. But where could Basil be? Hiding, perhaps? Or had he been apprehended already and taken to the police station?

Out on the street Rhodri began to laugh. He'd played a good joke on that stupid Basil. This was turning out better than he'd hoped.

★ ★ ★

Inside the cupboard, Basil knelt on the linoleum-covered floor, listening to the throbbing of the music. He gave a tentative knock on the door, expecting it to be flung open by some irate person, but nobody came. He would have to wait until the crowd came in during the interval for refreshments.

He knew he was in big trouble. When he was eventually set free, questions would be asked. They would want to know what he was doing there.

Climbing into the Town Hall through a window had been a bad thing to do. He knew that now. At the time, it had seemed like an adventure, but that was not how his parents would see it. What would the authorities do to him? Would he have to go to court? At least he hadn't stolen anything, because there hadn't been time.

The music stopped, and suddenly the room was filled with voices as the young people crowded in, handing over their money and accepting their snacks. At one point Basil thought he recognised Marina's voice, and that stopped him from banging on the door again. If it was known that she was his sister, then she might be blamed, too.

Eventually the room beyond the cupboard door fell silent once more as the dancers returned to the hall and the music started up again.

An hour passed, although for Basil it seemed like an eternity. Finally, the music stopped altogether and he could hear the faint sounds of retreating footsteps and doors banging in the distance. The dance was over. Now he would shout for help.

'We'll come back in the morning and clear up the mess in there,' Mrs Phillips announced to Gwil Jones, who held the door open for her before locking up and leaving.

There was silence, and Basil was alone in the dark.

# Where Is Basil?

'Where on earth is that boy?' Ruth looked at the clock for the fifth time in as many minutes. 'I told him he had to be back by eight o'clock. You heard me tell him that, didn't you, Bob?'

'What's that? Oh, yes. I expect he's lost track of the time. Look, it's time for the nine o'clock news; I can't miss that. Wait until it's over and then I'll go and have a look for him.'

He leaned over to switch on the wireless.

'This is the BBC Home Service,' the announcer said, in clipped tones.

Ruth got up to peer out of the kitchen window. For once she couldn't settle to listen to the news. It would be all doom and gloom as usual, with perhaps a bit of propaganda thrown in so that ordinary people wouldn't lose heart. Bob maintained that the government probably suppressed the news of some quite disastrous happenings for that very reason. This war was being waged on the home front as well as abroad.

But what was any of that, compared with a missing child? Basil should have been home an hour ago, and there was still no sign of him. Had he stayed out on purpose? It wasn't like him to be so naughty.

Ruth gave herself a mental shake. Bob was right, of course. The boy didn't possess a watch, and with these light evenings it would be easy to imagine that it was earlier than it was. Perhaps they'd left the door open at the Town Hall and he was gazing enthralled at the dancers. While that hardly seemed likely, what other explanation could there be?

The tinkling of a bell sounded from the parlour, warning her that Mamgu needed attention.

Ruth went in to see what the matter was.

'Sorry to bother you, Mrs Greene.

It's my Bible, see? Left it on top of the piano, I did, and I didn't want to fetch it myself.'

'No, indeed,' Ruth murmured. 'I don't think you're up to walking all the way across the room by yourself.'

'I like to read the Scriptures last thing at night,' Mamgu explained, accepting the leather-bound volume into her gnarled hands. 'Sort of settles me for sleep, see?'

'I could do with something to settle myself,' Ruth told her.

'Nothing wrong, is there?'

'No, no; it's just that the children aren't home yet. Marina has gone to that hop, as they call it, with the young Parrys.'

'I heard about that from Bessie. Your girl will be safe enough if her Tim has anything to do with it.'

'I expect so. It's my little boy I'm more worried about. He should have been home ages ago, but so far he hasn't turned up.'

Mamgu smiled. 'Boys will be boys!'

The two women were getting along much better these days. Mamgu seemed happier about their living arrangements since she'd been able to join the family in the kitchen, and Ruth had become used to the older woman's ways and was more tolerant of her foibles.

Now they chatted like old friends until Mamgu swallowed a yawn, and Ruth bid her goodnight.

When she returned to the kitchen the news was over and Bob was banking down the coal fire.

'It's just struck ten. They'll be coming out of the dance about now. Perhaps I'll take a stroll down the road to meet them. I could do with a stretch.'

'I'm coming with you, Bob. Just wait while I run up and fetch my cardigan.'

'No need for that, old girl. It's best you stay here, in case Basil turns up while I'm out. He'll be frightened if he comes in and finds us all missing.'

'I'll give him missing!' Ruth snapped, but she knew that what her husband said made sense. She happened to know that Basil hadn't yet recovered from all the worry of that silly spy scare. He'd had a nightmare in which his parents had been taken away by the police, and although she'd assured him it wasn't likely to happen, he hadn't been totally convinced. Children were such funny creatures. All sorts of strange ideas got into their heads.

★   ★   ★

Marina was feeling extremely pleased with herself. The dance had gone well and she'd spent a good deal of the evening with Tim. And even when she had been asked to dance by one or two other chaps, Tim hadn't gone near Catrin Harris. He'd even paid for Marina's drink, although she'd brought sixpence with her for the purpose.

Now they were strolling homeward in the balmy summer air, but Marged had linked arms with both Tim and Marina, so it was unlikely that a goodnight kiss was in the offing.

Still, it was fun to dream, and when they were standing outside her back door he might ask her to go out with him again.

These hopes were dashed when she saw her father striding towards them. How embarrassing! He'd promised faithfully that he wouldn't come to meet her like a child being collected at the school gates. She was sixteen years old! Didn't he trust her?

'Dad! What are you doing here?'

'Where's Basil? Isn't he with you?'

'Basil? Isn't he at home? Why should he be with us?'

'He went out earlier, saying he meant to walk up to the Town Hall to watch the folk going in. I couldn't see any harm in it, so we let him go. He was supposed to be back by eight, but so far there's no sign of him.'

'I'll come and help you search for him,' Tim volunteered at once. 'He'll be with some of his mates, and I know all the places where little boys like to go. I was young once!'

'You go home and tell your mother what's happening,' Bob ordered Marina, 'and before you ask, you can't come with us. Your mum's upset enough as it is, without worrying about you going missing as well.'

Marina shrugged and trotted off with Marged. What an end to her lovely evening! She could kill that young brother of hers.

Ruth was relieved to see her daughter but by this time she was near to tears.

'Dad said to tell you he's looking for Basil, and Tim Parry is going with him. You mustn't worry, Mum.'

'I mustn't worry, you say! Of course I must worry. Anything might have happened. He could have fallen into the river and drowned. He might even be at the bottom of a disused mine shaft somewhere!'

'Mum, Mum, calm down. The mine is miles away, and what would he be doing there anyhow?'

Marina wisely said nothing about the river. She happened to know that the boys spent many happy hours there, paddling or trying to fish. Basil hadn't played with them since that business with Rhodri, but what if he had wandered up there alone? He might have slipped on a wet rock and been swept away by the current.

'Shall we have a cup of tea while we're waiting, Mum?'

'Our ration's all gone,' Ruth told her.

Marina sighed. This blessed war! She couldn't even offer her mother a drop of tea to calm her nerves.

'I could go into the shop and borrow some against next week's ration. That wouldn't be wrong, would it?'

'Better not. Once we start that, we'll never catch up.'

Each person was allowed only two ounces of tea each week, which was nothing compared with pre-war consumption. Even when you reused the same tea leaves over and over again, it still wasn't enough.

Hunched over in their chairs to catch the remaining heat from the fire, the pair of them waited in silence for news.

Meanwhile, the two men marched through the town, passing the Town Hall — which was locked and deserted — on their way to the river.

'It's lucky you brought your torch, Mr Greene. It'll be almost dark when we get there. We're just going on the off-chance, mind. If anything had happened we'd have heard by now.'

'My thoughts exactly, but the river is the first place my wife will ask me about, and I'll be able to reassure her on that point at least.'

But the riverbank was deserted, and although Tim led the way to the recreation ground and the other places that Basil was most likely to be, it was as if the child had vanished off the face of the earth.

'I think we should fetch the police,' Tim said at last.

'Yes, I'm afraid we must,' Bob agreed, his face white.

Stretched out on the floor of the cupboard, Basil lay cold and alone.

* * *

'Do you mean to tell me there's no sign of him at all? Something must have happened to him. Oh, what are we going to do now?'

'Hush, you'll wake the old lady,' said Bob, putting his arm around his wife's shaking shoulders. 'Tim Parry has gone to alert the police. He'll be back at any moment with the constable.'

True to his word, Tim had gone to the constable's home and, although he was officially off duty, the man got up at once, reaching for his boots.

Llew Roberts was a stocky, dark-haired man with an air of confidence about him. He strode into the Greenes' kitchen as if he belonged there and sat himself down in front of the fire, which by now had blazed up again, having been stirred by Marina.

'No need to worry just yet,' he said easily. 'Little boys run away from home all the time, but they come back as soon as they get hungry. I did it myself when

I was this lad's age. Basil, you say his name is? Has he been worrying about anything lately? Or maybe he's been into mischief and doesn't want to come home for fear of what he'll face?'

'No,' Bob told him, just as Ruth chimed in with, 'Yes, he has.'

Llew looked from one to the other.

'So, which is it, then?'

Bob explained the trouble Basil had had with the other boys.

'But that's all behind us now. I've put a stop to it. The ringleader has been punished by his father, and I doubt he'll cause any more trouble now.'

'Basil went to tea with him only this afternoon,' Ruth put in.

'The ringleader, you say? Now who would that be?'

'A boy called Rhodri Evans.'

'Gareth Evans' boy?' asked Llew. 'I may as well have a word with him. He might just know something. Would you like to come along, Mr Greene?'

'I'm coming too!' Ruth cried, and this time there was no argument from her husband. The situation was so serious that no-one had the heart to keep her out of the picture.

'You'd better stay here, Marina, in case Mamgu rings,' she instructed.

'What'll I do if Basil shows up, then?'

'If that happens, you can see him into bed. We'll deal with him in the morning.'

'All right, Mum.' Marina noticed with a sinking feeling in her stomach that her mother had said 'if', not 'when'. It would be terrible if something dreadful had happened to her young brother. He could be an awful nuisance at times but, underneath it all, she loved him. Not that she'd ever tell him that!

★　★　★

'All right, all right! I'm coming!' Gareth Evans unlocked his front door and flung it open, amazed to see the quartet who were waiting on the doorstep. 'What's up, Llew? Not come to arrest me, have you?' He laughed uncertainly.

'Can we come in, man? This is official business, see?'

As they filed into the kitchen, Mrs Evans came down the stairs, tying the sash of her dressing-gown as she came. Her hair was done up in curlers and her face was smeared with cream.

'What's going on, Gareth?' she demanded to know.

'We need a word with your boy, Gareth,' said Llew. 'Basil Greene has gone missing. Looked everywhere, we have. Searched the whole town. We're hoping that Rhodri may be able to shed some light on it.'

'Of course he can't,' Mrs Evans bristled. 'He's in his bed. Your little boy came here to tea, Mr Greene, but he left hours ago. We haven't seen him since.'

'You may not have seen him,' Llew corrected, 'but what about Rhodri? Did he go out to play after tea?'

'Well, he did go up to the Rec for a bit. No harm in that, is there?'

'No harm at all, Mrs Evans.'

'Oh, can't we all stop beating about the bush like this?' Ruth cried. 'Can't you see we're wasting time? Basil could be lying injured somewhere. We simply must find him as soon as possible!'

'Exactly,' Llew said. 'Can we see your Rhodri now, please? Even if he has nothing to tell us, at least we'll have followed up that line of enquiry.'

Gareth went to the foot of the stairs.

'Rhodri!' he bawled. 'Can you hear me? Come down here, boyo, quick sharp! The police want a word with you!'

This was the summons that Rhodri had been dreading. He came slowly down the stairs, dressed in his shabby striped pyjamas and bunny slippers and looking far younger than his ten years.

The constable looked at Rhodri sternly. 'Now then, boyo, listen carefully. Your young friend has gone missing.'

'Has he?' Rhodri opened his eyes wide and Llew knew at once that the child was involved in Basil's disappearance.

'So, you know who I'm talking about, then!'

'Oh! Not really, but I expect it must be Basil if his parents are here?'

Cheeky young devil, thought Llew.

'What I want to know is, did you see anything of the boy when you went out to play after tea?'

'No, I didn't.'

'Are you quite sure about that?'

'He's already said he didn't!' Mrs Evans snapped, coming to the defence of her pet lamb.

'Please, Mrs Evans. Let me handle this. I want you to think very carefully, Rhodri. I believe you know more about this than you're letting on. Where was Basil when you saw him last?'

'Rhodri!' Gareth roared. 'Speak up this minute, boy, or do I have to take my belt to you?'

Rhodri burst into tears. He was no match for the two men. He knew they were going to wring it out of him sooner or later.

'He was at the Town Hall,' he

sobbed. 'That's all I know, honest!'

'That sounds right,' Ruth spoke up. 'When Basil asked if he could go out, he said he wanted to go and see the young people going into the dance. I thought at the time it seemed odd, but Basil gets funny ideas in his head sometimes. Perhaps he thought they'd all be wearing fancy dress. Anyway, there didn't seem any harm in letting him go, so long as he was home by eight o'clock. But then, when he didn't come, and he didn't come . . . ' She broke off, her poor face puckered with emotion.

Bob put his arm round her shaking shoulders and murmured something in her ear.

Llew Roberts turned back to Rhodri. 'Come now, Rhodri lad. You must know more than that. Did he go inside the hall? Was he still at the hall when you left? Was anyone else around at the time?'

Rhodri hung his head, not daring to look at Llew. But his eyes flew open when his father took him by the shoulders, shaking him none too gently.

'You're not telling the whole story, are you, lad? Better get if off your chest now, or it'll be all the worse for you later on. What were the two of you doing at the hall, eh? Up to no good, I'll be bound!'

Rubbing his eyes with his knuckles, Rhodri continued his tale.

'We heard they had pop and biscuits at the dance, Da. Basil thought we might be able to get some, see? So I bunked him in through the little window at the back. But then I heard somebody coming, and I had to run for it. I don't know what happened after that.'

'Leaving your mate to face the music!' Llew said scornfully.

'I did try to get in to see what was going on, but a lady stopped me at the door and sent me away. I didn't dare ask her if she'd seen Basil, because if he was hiding somewhere then she might find him and he'd be in trouble. That's all I know, honest!'

'Honest? You don't know the meaning of the word!' his father said in disgust. 'Get back up those stairs and we'll sort you out in the morning!'

Rhodri scuttled off, his mother following him, clucking like a hen.

'Can we get into the Town Hall at this time of night?' Bob asked. 'We've looked everywhere else we can think of. It's just possible that Basil did manage to hide somewhere inside, as the boy says.'

'We'll go and wake up Gwil Jones. He's the caretaker. He'll have a key.'

Llew Roberts led the way out of the Evans's front door, promising to come back the next day.

'Because there's more to this than meets the eye, Gareth man! That boy of yours knows more than he's letting on, and breaking into a public building is serious business, see? You should. straighten him out before he goes to the bad in a big way.'

The little party hurried silently

through the town, each with their own thoughts and with Ruth shaking inwardly, praying for Basil to be found alive.

Roused from his comfortable bed, Gwil Jones led the way to the Town Hall.

'I don't know what the world's coming to. Isn't it bad enough there's a war on, without such nonsense as this?'

As expected, the hall seemed deserted.

'Basil!' Ruth shouted. 'Basil! Are you here? Can you hear me?'

'Mummy!' A muffled voice reached them from far away, and Ruth caught her breath.

'Mummy!' There it was again.

'It's coming from the cupboard where they keep the ledgers and that!' Gwil shouted. 'Hang on, I'll get the key!'

There was an endless pause while he hurried off to the main office, and then he wrestled the door open while Ruth and Bob looked on in a fever of anticipation.

Basil looked up at them, blinking in the light. 'I thought nobody would come until Monday,' he sobbed.

Ruth reached out and gathered him into her arms. The post mortems could wait until later. For now, it was enough that her son was safe.

# Marina Gets A Job

'How are things going with you and Emlyn?' Marina asked Marged, more out of politeness than because she really cared. She had to keep in with Marged if she wanted to maintain contact with Tim Parry!

'Oh, he's lovely!' Marged boasted. 'Taking me to the pictures this week, he is.' She failed to mention that Emlyn had been pestering her about Marina, asking if she thought there was any chance for him with her.

'She likes somebody else, I think,' Marged had answered truthfully. 'How would you like to go to the pictures with me, Emlyn? There's sure to be a good film coming on when the bill changes.'

'Might as well. There's nothing else to do around here,' he'd muttered.

That response was hardly what

Marged had hoped for, but as her mother was fond of saying, 'From little acorns, great oak trees grow.'

'Our Tim and Catrin Harris had a big row the other day,' she said now, to Marina.

'Really!' Marina was delighted to hear it. 'What was it about — do you know?'

'I could hardly miss knowing, could I, the way they were shouting at each other. In the parlour they were, and me in the kitchen, see? She wanted to know why he didn't ask her to dance at the hop the other night, and he said he had to look after you, because you're a visitor and he promised your mam.'

Marina giggled. 'I bet she didn't like that.'

'Well, she told him that she didn't care what he did, she wasn't interested — and our Tim said if that was the case, why did she bother coming all the way over to the house? After a bit she stormed out, slamming the door behind her. He didn't bother going after her, which was probably what she was hoping for, so there you are.'

'They could make it up, though. I wish he'd ask me to go out with him. Do you think he might?'

'Maybe if I twist his arm.' Marged caught sight of her friend's face and knew she'd said the wrong thing. 'Oh, I didn't mean it like that, Marina! I was only thinking that he might be off women for a bit, if Catrin's thrown him over, see? How about arranging another foursome with Emlyn?'

'To do what, though? I don't want to go up the mountain again. I broke the strap on my sandals last time, scrambling over that rough ground.'

'I could ask Tim. I'm sure he'd come up with something. How would you fancy going down the pit, to see where he works?'

'Not on your life. You're not getting me going a mile underground in a tiny cage.'

'You could see the lovely pit ponies,' Marged said, grinning.

'No, thank you very much. And stop teasing. I believed you for a minute there!'

'How silly you are! Listen now, I think we should see if we can make you look a bit more grown-up than you do. Tim goes for the more sophisticated type. You're still a schoolgirl in his eyes. Very pretty, I'll grant you that, but a lot younger than Catrin Harris, in more ways than one.'

'I'm not a schoolgirl any more,' Marina insisted. 'Didn't I tell you I've finished with all that, never mind what my parents say. But Mum says that if they let me leave school then I've got to find a job, but I don't know where to start. It's not as if we're staying here for ever, is it? And who's going to employ me if they think I'll be throwing in the towel before they've got me trained?'

'Actually I'm in the same boat,' Marged sympathised. 'I left school a year ago, but Mam needed me at home for a while when she wasn't well. What I'd really like to do is to work at the telephone exchange. It's supposed to be a lot of fun. I happen to know that one of the girls is leaving to get married, so there's going to be a vacancy. Why don't we go and ask about it before they have a chance to advertise?'

'I'd have to ask Mum. She might not be very keen.'

'No. Try for the job first, and then you can go and tell her afterwards if you get it. If they turn you down, she'll be none the wiser.'

Marina hesitated. 'I don't know. We've just had a lot of trouble with my little brother and they're still on edge. There's been a lot of talk about people telling lies and keeping secrets. I don't want them thinking I can't be trusted.'

'Nonsense! It's not the same thing at all. Just say that I'm trying for a job and I want you to come with me for moral support. If you did get offered a job you could just go home and say you were in the right place at the right time.'

'What would we have to do at this telephone exchange, then?'

'You sit in front of a switchboard; people ring up to ask for a number and you put them through. Frances — that's the girl who's engaged to be married — told me they have such fun there. Sometimes they listen in to the conversations and they overhear all sorts of things.'

'Surely they're not supposed to do that?'

'Everybody knows you mustn't say anything confidential over the phone, so what difference does it make?'

Marina still wasn't sure about going for an interview. It was one thing to stop going to school, which she'd never enjoyed very much in any case, but quite another to step into the grown-up world of work.

'It would make Tim look at you differently if you worked at the telephone exchange,' Marged said slyly, 'and think what you could do with the money you earned!'

'I'd have to give it to Mum for my keep.'

'Not all of it, surely? She'd let you keep some for clothes and makeup.'

'Makeup! I can't see Dad agreeing to that!' Marina groaned, but the idea was beginning to take hold. 'All right, let's do it!'

★　★　★

Very few people in the town possessed a telephone of their own. There was one at the Town Hall and several at the colliery, and some of the bigger shops were also on the phone. Other than that, only the more important people qualified for one. They included the two doctors, the mine owner, the police and the clergy. Other people had to make do with one of the public call boxes, where they had to feed coins into a slot before the operator would put them through.

When you were successfully connected, you pressed Button A to continue the call and your money disappeared inside a locked container;

otherwise you pressed Button B to get your money returned. Children made a habit of nipping into the phone booths to see if anyone had forgotten to press Button B; it was surprising what you could buy with the proceeds.

'Yes, I suppose it's all right for you to go with Marged when she goes for her interview,' Ruth told Marina. 'It'll give you a chance to see how these things work before your own turn comes. Having an interview, I mean. Not that they'll let you into the room with her, I shouldn't think.'

'No, Mum.'

But just in case, Marina made sure she was as well turned out as possible. She polished her old school shoes and darned a hole in her ankle socks. She might look shabby, but she could at least be clean and tidy.

Nobody was more surprised than Marina when she was offered a job!

Marged had been accepted at once. The supervisor had known her for years and didn't even bother to talk about references or experience.

'I suppose you heard about Frances leaving? Well, this saves us the cost of advertising in the paper. When can you start?'

'Right away!' Marged had beamed.

'Good. We're really short-staffed. Another of my girls is engaged to an Air Force chap and she's determined to marry him as soon as possible, so she'll be off to live in England, just like Frances!'

That was when the supervisor turned to look at Marina and seemed to like what she saw.

'I don't suppose you want a job as well, do you?'

Marina was about to open her mouth to explain her circumstances, but Marged got in first.

'This is my friend, Marina Greene. She lives near us, up the Llandeilo Road.'

'Very well, Miss Greene; what do you think? Would you like to come and work here?'

Marina swallowed hard. 'Yes, please, I'd like to, very much!'

'Good! Then you're hired!'

★ ★ ★

Basil scuffed along with his eyes downcast, well aware that if his parents saw him he'd be yelled at and told to pick up his feet. But he didn't care. Nobody cared about what he wanted or what he thought! His only friend in the world was Mr Rees, the old miner. He would go and talk to him.

However, when Basil reached the allotment he was disappointed to find that his friend was nowhere to be seen. He decided to wait for a while to see if the man turned up. There was nothing else to do anyway.

He reached over to pull up a carrot.

'What's going on here, then?' Basil hadn't heard Emrys padding up behind him in his old plimsolls. He dropped the carrot as if it was burning hot.

'I didn't mean to steal, Mr Rees,

honestly!' he stammered.

'Did anyone say anything about stealing? I offered you a carrot the other day, so what's another one between friends?

'I heard about your bit of trouble the other night, boyo,' the old man went on, choosing his words with care. While he certainly didn't mind giving the child a carrot, he didn't want to give the impression that he condoned the taking of things that belonged to other people, no matter how small.

'How do you know about that, Mr Rees?'

'Oh, Gwil Jones is a pal of mine. At school together, we were, back in the dark ages. I met him in the tobacconist's just now, and he mentioned having a bit of excitement. Thought the Germans had landed, he did, when Llew Roberts come pounding at his door. Quite relieved, he was, when it was only because of a little lad locked in a cupboard where he had no business being in the first place.'

Basil's face turned the colour of his friend's beetroot.

'It was all a mistake,' he muttered.

'You can say that again! I suppose you had a thrashing when you got home? I hear Rhodri Evans won't be able to sit down for the next week or so.'

But Basil's parents hadn't lain a finger on him. When he'd reached home that night, carried on his father's shoulders, he'd been put to bed, soothed and petted by Ruth. His last thought as he'd drifted off to sleep had been that everything was going to be all right.

He had reckoned without Rhodri spilling the beans. The next morning both Bob and Ruth had read him the riot act.

'To think that any child of mine would even consider breaking into town property with the idea of stealing what was inside!' Bob thundered. 'The Greenes have always been as honest as the day is long. How has it come to this, I ask myself?'

'There wasn't anything there but a few rock cakes, Dad!'

Bob clenched his fists inside his trouser pockets. For two pins he'd let fly, but somehow he managed to control himself. The boy had to learn, but he was only a child, and had to be dealt with accordingly.

He had issued a little sermon about how it was wrong to steal, but it had been hard to tell if anything was truly sinking in.

Then it had been Ruth's turn. When Basil saw the tears rolling down his mother's face he had almost started to blubber himself. She was extremely disappointed in him, she'd said quaveringly.

'Can I go now?' he'd asked, when his mother seemed to have run out of words.

'No, you may not!' Bob had told him. 'We haven't decided on your punishment yet. For a start, I'm going to stop your pocket money for a month.'

'But, Dad! How am I going to get my *Beano*?'

'You should have thought of that before. Maybe doing without for a time will be the best thing for you.'

Basil had sloped off, feeling very hard done by.

Now he stood in Emrys Rees's allotment, his head drooping in shame.

'I didn't get a hiding but they won't let me see Rhodri any more,' he announced, aware that Mr Rees was expecting a reply to his question. 'And they've stopped my pocket money, so I won't be able to get the *Beano* or any sweets for weeks! It just isn't fair!'

'It sounds fair enough to me, *bach*. It's in the Bible, see. 'Thou shalt not steal'. If you do wrong, you have to take the punishment. That's the law, see, both God's and man's.'

Well, he'd said his piece. Maybe if the boy kept coming to see him at the allotment instead of getting in with bad companions, it might be a good thing. There wasn't much he could get up to there. Maybe he could help with the weeding and suchlike? It might make the lad feel better about himself if he had something useful to occupy him.

'Have you ever tried your hand at gardening, young Basil?' he asked him now.

'Dad won't let me touch the garden, Mr Rees. I tried weeding once, as a surprise, but he said I pulled up the young vegetable shoots by mistake. He said he didn't do all that digging and hoeing and planting to have me coming along behind him undoing all his good work.'

Emrys had to smile.

'There is a knack to gardening, true enough. I could teach you how to tell the difference, *bach*, if you'd like to try. My old back isn't what it used to be, see. I could use a helper now and then.'

In truth he was extremely fit for his age, and could have shown many a younger man a thing or two, but Basil wasn't to know that.

'All right, Mr Rees. I'll ask Mum if I

can come down each day and give you a hand.'

'That's right, *bach*. You tell your mam what you'll be getting up to and then she won't have to worry.' Then he told Basil to run along because the Town Hall clock had just struck twelve, and he'd be wanting his dinner.

Basil ran off happily. Mr Rees was his friend. Who needed Rhodri when they had Mr Rees?

# An Exciting Night Out!

Ruth was feeling a lot more cheerful. After all her worries over the children, both of them now seemed to have settled down nicely.

Marina was happy in her new job, and in the excitement of it all she seemed to have forgotten all about her infatuation with the Parry boy. It had only been puppy love, of course, but even so, it had still been a worry to her parents.

As for Basil, he was happy working with Emrys Rees on his allotment. Ruth hadn't been sure about this at first, but when she'd spoken to Bessie about it, she'd received a glowing report of Emrys, whom the Parrys had known all their lives.

'He'll come to no harm with Emrys, Mrs Greene, take it from me. He'll be a good influence on the boy.'

Ruth had winced at that, but guessed that Bessie hadn't meant anything by it. Basil had come under the influence of that dreadful Rhodri and had behaved badly as a result, but he was just as much to blame in his own way.

Although her children seemed to be happy and settled, however, Ruth herself was beginning to fret under the dull routine which she had to endure day after day.

She said as much to her husband.

'You should get out more, love,' he told her.

'I do. I go down town and do my shopping, and I've taken out membership at the library. But none of that is very inspiring. Can't we do something together occasionally?'

'We go for walks together, don't we?'

'I mean, can't we go *out* together sometimes? The pictures or somewhere?'

'Can't be done, love. You know we can't both be out in the evening, leaving the boy by himself, and then there's

Mrs Thomas. She's the main reason we came down here in the first place. I tell you what, why don't you have a word with Bessie Parry? The girls are good friends now; why can't the two of you be the same?'

When Ruth made a tentative approach, Bessie was delighted.

'You can come down the chapel with me on Wednesday nights, Mrs Greene, to our ladies' group. We have speakers and classes and that. Some of it is very interesting, all about how to manage with the rations. We learned how to make a lovely fatless sponge last month. Not that it's as good as the cakes I used to make before the war, but then, nothing is the same as it was. Seven o'clock it starts. Shall I call for you at half-past six, then? We can walk down together.'

'You go along, love,' Bob said later, when Ruth told him about the ladies' group. 'Do you good to get out for a bit.'

Ruth was less than enchanted with

the idea but at least she'd have other adults to chat to, and she might make new friends.

As it happened, the first person she met was Eileen Evans, mother of the dreadful Rhodri. Despite everything, Ruth was prepared to greet Mrs Evans politely, if coolly, and she was annoyed when the woman literally stuck her nose in the air as she sailed past.

'Ignore her,' Bessie said comfortingly. 'She always was a bit touched!'

The speaker for the evening was a hearty woman in a green overall, and the subject of her talk was Make Do And Mend, which was one of the familiar slogans of the war. She displayed several items which, she said, they might like to copy.

One was a gingham dress for a little girl, which had undergone a startling transformation after being worn out by its owner, or possibly a succession of owners. The top half of the bodice had been replaced by a yoke and sleeves knitted in obviously recycled wool.

'It isn't new yarn, of course,' the presenter explained. 'The idea is that you unravel a worn pullover and use that.'

'It seems silly to me,' Mrs Evans argued. 'I mean, why use wool at all? Why not bits of material from some other old frock?'

'Certainly you could do that, madam. This is only meant to start you thinking by demonstrating what is possible. Now I want to explain how you can turn your summer frocks to give them a new lease of life.'

'Oh, I wouldn't dream of wearing an old frock inside out!' Mrs Evans complained, causing Ruth to raise her eyes to the ceiling.

Someone in the audience tittered, but the presenter soldiered on.

'The idea here is to unpick all the seams and then sew the dress up again, so that the faded pattern is now on the inside. With a bit of rick-rack braid added, or some different buttons, it could be made very smart indeed.'

Ruth rather liked the idea. She had a favourite dress that she'd owned since she was first married, but it was sadly faded now and she'd been on the point of cutting it up for dusters.

'The trouble is,' she told Bessie in an undertone, 'I'd have to sew it by hand, and the seams might give way at some inopportune moment.'

'No need for that,' Bessie whispered back. 'You can have a loan of my old treadle. Come round to the house any time, and I'll show you how to thread it up.'

'Thanks!' Ruth whispered back.

While tea was being served, several of the other women came over to be introduced to Ruth. One wanted to sign her up for Red Cross meetings, while another wondered if she could sing soprano, as they were trying to recruit new members for the choir.

Ruth regretfully declined the offer to join the choir. She enjoyed warbling away as much as the next woman, but she knew she would let the side down if they ever got her in a choir robe. The Welsh were famous for their voices and she'd heard some magnificent singing coming from the Methodist Chapel on Sunday mornings. The beauty and the power of their music reached as far as the bedroom over the shop where the Greenes were having a lie-in.

'Enjoy the evening, did you?' Bessie asked her as they were walking home.

'I thought that idea of knitting door mats out of old stockings was quite good,' Ruth answered diplomatically. 'I might try that when we go back to Hemel. I've a good few in a bag at home, all too far gone to mend, I'm afraid.'

'You should cobble them up if you can. At least they'd give you a bit of warmth on your legs, not like colouring them with gravy browning like some women do.'

'You haven't seen these old stockings of mine, Mrs Parry. They're more ladder than leg, if you get my meaning.'

Bessie sighed. 'Ah, well, you can but try.'

'I say, what on earth was the matter with that woman, treating me like a bad smell under her nose?'

'Eileen? I told you, she isn't quite sixteen ounces to the pound. It's this business with the boys, of course. She's embarrassed, and I would be, too, if any of mine behaved the way Rhodri does. It's not just childish mischief he gets up to. It's downright devilment. If they don't take him in hand soon, he'll be in real trouble before he's much older. And a word to the wise, Mrs Greene — make sure he stays away from your Basil.'

'Oh, don't worry. We've already impressed on Basil that he's to have nothing more to do with Rhodri.'

'That isn't quite what I meant, Mrs Greene. There's a mean streak in that boy, and it showed itself when he was very small. I used to be a teacher in the Sunday School, see, looking after the little ones, and Rhodri wasn't just a handful, he was — well, I don't know how to put it. Wicked is too strong a word to use for a Christian child, but I thought that about him, even then.'

Ruth was inclined to dismiss this as a bit much. Bessie was a staunch member of the chapel, and Methodists were well known for their strict moral code.

Ruth prided herself on being honest and truthful, and she was trying to bring up her children to have similar values, but she didn't think of herself as being overly strict.

Still, both sets of beliefs were no doubt good in their own way, she thought. They could exist perfectly well side by side.

'You remember what I'm telling you, Mrs Greene,' Bessie remarked, her expression serious. 'I wouldn't trust that boy further than I could throw him, and that's a fact.'

'You surely don't mean that he'd try to hurt Basil?' Ruth was incredulous.

'I don't say he'd do your boy any physical harm,' Bessie countered, but would say no more.

# Dreadful News!

Marina loved her job and quickly learned what was expected of her. The only thing she disliked about it was the clothing she was expected to wear — a horrid black dress with a removable white collar and cuffs.

'It's what most women have to wear when they go out to work,' Ruth explained. 'In shops, offices, even in restaurants. It's very practical, really. Black doesn't show the dirt and the white bits are easy enough to wash and dry overnight. Think yourself lucky that your uniform was provided for you. Buying a dress would set you back eight clothing coupons.'

'But it's second hand!' Marina wrinkled her nose. 'And it must have been made for some bigger person. See how it hangs on me? And why do we have to dress this way when nobody ever sees us? I'd rather wear trousers like a land girl, or dungarees like women in factories have to do.'

'Perish the thought!' Bob had been passing through the kitchen and heard the tail end of this conversation. 'No daughter of mine is going to wear trousers! You don't want to get a reputation for being fast.'

'I don't see why, Dad! Girls wear tennis shorts, and jodhpurs for riding, so what's the difference?'

'Personally I think we women *should* be able to wear trousers,' Ruth announced. 'Stockings are hard to come by, and you men in your trousers have no idea what it's like to wear a skirt in winter! I'd like to make you all wear a kilt for a day or two and see what you thought about women in trousers then!'

Bob ignored her. When this beastly war was over, women would give up working on the land and in factories. They'd go back to being housewives, and never don trousers again.

As it was, his daughter was looking far too grown up these days for a girl not yet seventeen. He couldn't put his finger on what had made the difference; possibly it was the hairstyle. There was a big difference between wearing your hair in plaits and putting it up in a roll, as the girl was doing now.

He said something to that effect, but she looked him straight in the eye and said that working in the telephone exchange was like the army; your hair wasn't allowed to touch your collar.

★ ★ ★

'Have you heard any juicy conversations yet?' Marged asked Marina when she finally had a chance to catch up with her friend. They were on different shifts and rarely had a chance to speak to each other.

'No, I haven't. It's not very nice to eavesdrop on people's private chats.'

'Oh, listen to her! Telephone calls are like postcards. If you don't want people to know your business then you should write a letter and seal it. Don't be so hoity-toity, Marina!'

But Marina thought that listening in was like reading someone's diary.

However, all her good intentions were to fall by the wayside when she put through a trunk call to the doctor's wife.

'I'm putting you through now, caller,' she said, in her most professional voice, waiting until the other party came on the line; occasionally something went wrong and crossed wires resulted in a mix-up.

'Hello, Mum! Can you hear me? I'm calling to say that I've got a few days off from the hospital and I'll be home on Friday, all right?'

Marina was about to pull out the plug when her attention was attracted by what the girl said next.

'Do you know those new people at the shop?'

'I know who you mean, dear, but I never go in there. We're registered at the Home and Colonial. Why do you ask?'

It would have taken a stronger person than Marina to tune out at that moment. She felt she had to know what was being said in case it was something about her family. She almost stopped breathing in her effort not to be discovered.

'Oh, it's just that they're related to the Thomas family, aren't they?'

'I believe so. I seem to recall that the woman is Dora Thomas's sister.'

'Well, one of the nurses in my set has a brother in the Navy, and she's been terribly upset because his ship was torpedoed and she didn't know if he was all right. Anyhow, she had good news this morning when he phoned to let her know that he was safe. She was on duty with me at the time, and Sister actually let her take the call, the circumstances being what they were. Joan has mentioned me in her letters to him, so he knows where I'm from, and he told her that Idris Thomas was on his ship, but was lost when it sank. Sad, isn't it? Oh, dash it — is that the pips already? And I'm out of change. See you on Friday, Mum.'

Idris! It was all Marina could do to stop herself from breaking into the conversation to demand to be told more. In a panic she rushed to her supervisor.

'I've had bad news,' she gasped. 'I'm just going to pop home, all right?'

'You're not, you know!' The woman snorted. 'People are depending on you. Don't you know there's a war on? You'll stay at your post until your shift is up, Miss Greene. Pop home indeed! I've never heard such a thing!'

So Marina had to stay where she was, which was highly unnecessary because few other calls came in that afternoon.

★ ★ ★

It was also a quiet afternoon in the shop. Bob Greene was sitting on a high stool behind the counter, reading some government directive which had come in the post. Mamgu was seated nearby, hoping that one of her cronies would drop in for a chat.

'I could do with a cup of tea,' she remarked, just as the very same thought was going through Bob's head.

'I'll go and make one, shall I? I'll be back shortly, Mrs Thomas.'

But at that moment the doorbell jangled, and Bob turned back to the counter, ready to serve the customer. He froze when he saw that the new arrival was a fresh-faced boy, delivering one of the dreaded telegrams from the War Office.

'Telegram for Thomas,' he piped up.

Mamgu's face turned white. 'Not my Dai!' she moaned.

Bob accepted the envelope in a shaking hand. Neither of them noticed that the boy had left, letting the door swing to behind him.

'Do you want me to open this, Mrs Thomas? I mean, it's not addressed to me, but there's nobody else here.' Bob knew he was babbling but he really didn't want to break bad news to her. What if she had another stroke on the spot? Where on earth was Ruth? There should be another woman here at a time like this.

The old lady was looking at him now, with such misery in her eyes that he thought it best not to keep her in suspense any longer.

Using his penknife he slit the telegram open.

'We regret to inform you . . . enemy action . . . It's Idris, Mrs Thomas. I'm afraid his ship has been sunk.'

'Dead, then, is he?' she quavered.

'It says missing, presumed drowned. I'm so sorry, Mrs Thomas.'

She began to rock back and forth, keening softly.

Bob slipped into the kitchen. That cup of tea was needed more than ever now. He wondered if he should put a drop of something into Mrs Thomas's cup. He understood that she had signed the pledge years ago, but did that include lacing a hot drink for medicinal purposes? According to her, strong drink was the devil's tool, and he didn't want to be accused of starting her on the downward path.

What else could he do, then? Reaching for a little bottle which Ruth kept on the mantelpiece, he shook two aspirin tablets into his hand.

Ground up in the tea they should take the edge off her pain.

When he went back into the shop, she was still rocking back and forth, with her apron over her head, but she stopped when he offered her the cup and began to drink the tea quite sensibly.

The doorbell jangled again. This time it was a tall, balding man who was not one of their regular customers. He looked none too pleased and Bob wondered what was up. He wasn't left wondering for long.

'Are you Greene?'

'Yes, that's right. Can I help you?'

'I certainly hope so. It's about the

vegetables you sent round. I think you've been overcharging your customers and I want to know what you mean to do about it.'

Bob frowned. 'I don't understand. We don't sell vegetables. I just grow them for our own use, as do most people nowadays.'

'That wasn't what your boy told me when he brought them to the door.'

'My boy? Oh, I don't think so . . . '

'Well, he gave his name as Basil Greene!'

★   ★   ★

Ruth was faced with the unenviable task of breaking the news of Idris's loss to poor Dora. 'Better make sure you put the ward sister in the picture before you say anything,' Bob counselled. 'It's bound to come as a terrible shock and Dora may need a sedative or something. I only wish we had some sort of knock-out drops to give Mrs Thomas, but she's insistent that she doesn't want anything.'

'Can't you come with me?' Ruth begged. 'Surely it won't hurt to close the shop for once. You can put a notice on the door, explaining that there's been a bereavement.'

'Sorry, love; you'll have to manage on your own. I have something important to do while you're gone.'

Ruth was so distraught at the thought of what lay ahead of her that she didn't ask what could possibly be more important than the loss of poor Dora's son. Instead, she made her way to the cottage hospital feeling quite sick with dread.

Dora received the news with dangerous calm. 'I always knew something like this would happen. I begged him not to join the Navy. Isn't it enough that I have to worry about your father being at sea, I told him, but would be listen to me? I might as well have been talking to the wall.'

There was silence for a while, and then she asked, 'Do you think they'll let us bury him in Bedwen? I'd at least like to have a grave to visit. Idris wouldn't seem so far away then.'

Ruth gulped. Hadn't Dora taken in what the telegram said?

'It said, 'missing, presumed drowned',' Ruth murmured.

'Oh, yes, of course. 'Full fathom five my father lies.' Remember doing that in school, Ruth? Was that Shakespeare or Dickens?'

'Shakespeare, I think. The Tempest.'

Ruth knew very well where the quotation was from. She remembered learning the words because she'd thought them so beautiful and mysterious.

'*Full fathom five my father lies;*
*Of his bones are coral made:*
*Those are pearls that were his eyes . . .* '

She would never think them beautiful again, and she certainly wasn't going to finish the quotation for Dora.

'Of course, they wouldn't bring him home, even if he'd died on a battlefield,' Dora said, nodding. 'They don't, do they? They bury people over there.'

She sounded so reasonable that Ruth was frightened. It was shock, of course. Should she call Sister? But that good woman was already on her way, bearing a hypodermic syringe in an enamelled dish.

'Doctor wants you to have this, Mrs Thomas,' she said kindly, rolling up the sleeve of Dora's nightgown.

It was as if the prick of the needle punctured Dora's composure as well as her skin, for suddenly she began to weep, hard, wrenching sobs that shook her whole body.

'Where is Dai?' she cried. 'Is he coming? I want Dai! I want Dai!'

Aware of alarmed stares from the other patients, Sister beckoned to a hovering probationer. 'Fetch some screens and put them around this bed, Nurse. Quickly, now! Don't stand there gawping like an idiot.'

'What should I do?' Ruth asked, worried. 'Would it be best if I left now?'

'You stay with Mrs Thomas until she falls asleep,' Sister directed. 'She may not respond to you, but it will be a comfort if she knows that you're with her. We'll take over after that. Sad to say, I'm afraid this isn't the first time one of my patients has had such bad news. In a day or two, I'll ask Mrs Matthews to have a word. She lost one of her own sons who was fighting in Africa. She'll know just how your cousin is feeling.'

Waiting for the bus which would take her home, Ruth wondered whether Dai Thomas might be given compassionate leave to spend time with his wife. Probably not. Did he even know that Idris was gone? The War Office must have the lad's home address, which was why the telegram had come to the shop, but nobody would have thought of notifying Dai. Perhaps she ought to get in touch with him; but how? He was off on the ocean somewhere, doing the dangerous job of ferrying vital supplies to Britain and assisting with troop movement to other countries. At least, she supposed he was. Civilians weren't supposed to know what was going on.

'Mum!' Ruth got off the bus and looked around to see her daughter hurrying towards her. 'Have you heard the news? Isn't it dreadful? I wanted to come home to be with you all, but I wasn't allowed.'

'Poor Idris, you mean? We had a telegram. I've just come back from breaking the news to Auntie Dora.'

'How awful for you! How did she take it?'

'She was very distressed. She broke down in the end and Sister had to give her something. Even so, I doubt it's really sunk in yet. I'll have to go back in a day or two, and I'm not looking forward to it one bit.'

'You look a bit shaky yourself, Mum. Why don't we pop into that little tea-room and see if they've got anything worth eating?'

'Yes, why not? I could do with something before I face them at home.'

'Oh, you mean Mamgu! She's bound to be terribly upset too.'

'Yes, and she seems convinced that Idris's father will be next on the casualty list. It's no good telling her that it won't happen because in his line of work I'm afraid it's all too likely.'

'I hate this war!' blurted out Marina.

Ruth reflected that the same sentiment was probably being voiced all around the world at that moment. Why, oh, why did men like Hitler and Mussolini, and that Japanese emperor, have to be so hungry for power, sweeping all before them? Surely they couldn't all be as mad as hatters, but she could think of no sane explanation for their actions.

★ ★ ★

Back at home, Bob had been waiting for Basil to come in from school. He was about to have an interview with that young man, which neither of them would enjoy.

What on earth had possessed the child to do such a wicked thing,

219

especially so soon after that other episode on the night of the dance.

Bob's visitor to the shop that afternoon had been a Mr Russell, a retired schoolmaster who lived in a quiet road on the other side of the town. He had opened his door earlier that day to a boy who had an assortment of very fine vegetables in a trek cart.

'One of those two-wheeled jobs that Boy Scouts use for carrying their equipment,' he'd explained, in case Bob didn't understand what he was talking about. 'I had no quarrel with the vegetables themselves; very fine specimens they were indeed. But the prices seemed greatly inflated. I have my own garden, so I didn't want any, but I have two elderly maiden ladies living next door and they rely on me to keep an eye on anyone 'knocking around', as they say.'

'And this boy gave his name as Basil Greene?'

'Oh, yes. He spoke up quite readily

when I asked, 'And who is your father and what does he do?' and he said that you own this shop. So, as you see, here I am, and I'd like an explanation!'

'There's something not right here, Mr Russell. To start with, this isn't my shop. I'm simply running it for my wife's cousin while she's in hospital. And yes, my son is called Basil Greene, but he has no authority to sell the vegetables I grow. Furthermore, when I last looked outside, there were none missing! All I can say, Mr Russell, is that I shall look into this and report my findings to you later.'

Bob underwent a great deal of heart-searching while waiting for Basil to come home. He would have dismissed the story as nonsense had it not been for the fact that Russell had been given Basil's name. But why on earth would the child have been hawking food produce from door to door? Was it some scheme to make a bit of pocket money, to replace what was being withheld from him as punishment for the Town Hall caper? Had he somehow purchased them wholesale, as it were, and then had to charge exorbitant rates in order to make a profit?

The back door banged, and Basil came racing in. 'Dad, Dad, something awful's happened!'

Bob sighed. He'd intended to keep the news of Idris's death a secret until this other business was cleared up, but probably the news was all around the town now and the boy had heard it from one of his new classmates.

'Yes, it's very sad, Basil. You must be very kind to Mamgu now.'

'Why? Has something happened to her?'

'I'm talking about the sad news we've had, about Auntie Dora's son, Idris, being killed at the war. Isn't that what you're talking about?'

'No, Dad. I didn't know. Was his ship blown up or what?'

Bob prayed for patience. Basil had never met his cousin, and at his age he was far too young to understand the tragic consequences of war.

'Come and sit down, old chap, and I'll tell you what we think happened.'

This topic dispensed with for the time being, Bob thought it wise to get down to business before the mood was broken.

'Now, what was your news, then, Basil? Something awful, you said?'

'Yes, Dad! Poor Mr Rees! Somebody went to his allotment in the night and stole all his vegetables! I thought he was going to have a fit!'

# More Trouble For Basil

Emrys Rees felt as though all the stuffing had been knocked out of him. When he'd turned up at his allotment that morning, he hadn't intended to actually do any work. After he and young Basil had attended to the patch the evening before, there hadn't been a weed left in sight and the two of them had gloated over the rows of ripening vegetables.

But now, Emrys couldn't believe his eyes as he sat on his upturned pail, too disheartened even to light up his pipe.

He'd been counting on those vegetables to see him through the coming winter. A chap had to do something to keep body and soul together, especially now, when rationing could only be stretched to a little more than a shilling's worth of meat to do the whole week. That might amount to a single

224

pork chop and three or four sausages, and heaven only knew what they put in sausages nowadays. Mostly bread and sage, probably.

But that was only part of what was distressing Emrys. Ever since his dear wife had died, he had used his work at the allotment as a way to handle his grief. All the digging and hoeing had brought a kind of peace.

Now that had been taken away from him, too.

He got up stiffly and wandered around, looking at other people's plots.

Brinley Harris had some fine cauliflowers coming along, and little Miss Rice had some very nice heads of cabbage. Nobody else had suffered any loss. The vandals had confined their activities to his garden alone.

Who could have done this? At first glance, seeing the wreckage, he had suspected some animal, but no, that couldn't be it. Dogs might have dug holes, and he'd occasionally had rabbits going for his lettuce and carrots, but this had the hallmark of human hands. The carrots and parsnips had been pulled up systematically and his curly kale seemed to have been chopped off with a knife.

It was too late in the season to replant now. Anger surged through his body. Why should this have happened to him? He'd always done his best to treat others as he'd have wanted to be treated himself, and so far as he knew, he didn't have an enemy in the world.

As a rule, Bedwen was a law-abiding place. But Emrys read the newspapers, of course, and he knew that there were bad apples who turned the upheaval of war to their own advantage. War profiteering was illegal but not unknown; most goods could be obtained on the black market.

Should he report his loss to the police? There was probably not much point. They could hardly conduct a house-to-house search looking for surplus produce. He smiled grimly at the very idea.

He might question his fellow gardeners when they turned up later; somebody might have seen something.

So he remained sitting on his upturned pail, sunk in thought, too dispirited to make a start on clearing up the mess. Neither did he make a move to go home. There was nothing for him there.

When Basil had arrived after school, it had been evident from his reaction that the chaos was just as much a shock to the boy as it had been to him, and Emrys had chided himself for having wondered, just for a brief moment, if the child might have been responsible for the disaster.

'What happened, Mr Rees? Everything looked so lovely yesterday, and now look at it! It's all spoiled.'

'I don't know, *bach*. It was this way when I turned up this morning, see?'

'But why would anybody do this? I don't understand.'

Emrys had no answer to this.

'Whoever it was doesn't know much

about gardening,' Basil went on, reaching down to pick up the green potato foliage. 'You said the spuds weren't ready to harvest yet. Give them another week or two, you said. Shall I give you a hand clearing up, Mr Rees? Perhaps it won't look so bad if I dig it over a bit.'

'No, no, *bach*. You go on home now.'

Basil ran home feeling highly indignant on his friend's behalf. All set to blurt out the story, he was shocked when his father broke the news of his cousin's death. Unfortunately, lots of people did die in the war and Basil had never met Cousin Idris. Of course, he felt saddened in a general sort of way, but he had no sense of a personal loss.

Finally Bob stopped going on about Idris and asked his son what it was that he'd been about to say. Basil needed no second bidding.

'Oh, Dad, it's so awful I can't believe it! Somebody has gone to Mr Rees's allotment and stolen all his stuff! All his lovely carrots and onions and potatoes and . . .'

'Never mind reciting the garden catalogue to me, son. Just tell me what happened.'

'I told you, Dad! I went there on the way home from school, to see if any weeds had come up in the night, cos that's my job now — Mr Rees shows me what the weeds look like, and then I pull them up. But when I got there, Mr Rees was just sitting about, looking sad. He said somebody must have come when the place was deserted and taken all his vegetables away. Isn't that the meanest thing you ever heard, Dad?'

'Yes, yes, Basil. Now, keep quiet for a minute and let me have a think.'

Like Emrys Rees, Bob now felt ashamed of himself for having suspected Basil of any wrong-doing. He knew his son well, and could always tell when he was keeping something from him. It would have taken a better actor than Basil to play the innocent after pulling a stunt like that. He decided to take the boy into his confidence.

'Something very strange happened

today,' he began.

'Yes, Dad?'

'A gentleman came to see me. His name is Mr Russell, and he lives on the other side of the town. Apparently a boy called at his house offering to sell him vegetables. Mr Russell became suspicious when the asking price was much too high. It was as if the boy had no idea how much to charge.'

'Cor! I bet he's the one who stole from Mr Rees!'

'Possibly.'

'But, Dad! Why did the man come to see *you*?'

'Well, lad, Mr Russell came here because, when asked to give his name, the boy said it was Basil Greene.'

Basil's eyes opened wide. 'Then he's a big fat fibber. It wasn't me who stole the veggies and tried to sell them! You do believe me, don't you, Dad?'

'Yes, Basil, I believe you. The thing we have to work out now is, who was that boy?'

'Rhodri, Dad! I bet it was Rhodri!'

★ ★ ★
Their first port of call was Mr Russell's house. Fortunately he was at home when they arrived.

'Ah, Mr Greene! Good of you to report back so promptly!'

'I won't beat about the bush, Mr Russell. This is my son, Basil. Is this the boy who attempted to sell vegetables to you early this morning?'

'No, it is not.'

'Are you quite sure about that?'

'Of course I'm sure, man! I'm hardly in my dotage yet!'

'Then would you mind coming along with us? We have a good idea of what's going on here, and we'd like you to take a look at the boy who I think might be the culprit.'

Eileen Evans was furious when she opened her door to the trio.

'Not you again! I thought we'd seen the back of you, I did.'

'We'd like a word with Rhodri, please. Is he here?'

'No, he's gone out with his father, up to the Rec.'

At that moment, Gareth and Rhodri came round the side of the house; Rhodri carrying a football and looking cheerful and carefree. But his expression changed when he saw the visitors. His gaze travelled from Bob to Mr Russell, and then he bolted. His father caught him by the collar and hauled him back.

'Now what's he done?' Gareth Evans demanded, as he struggled to control his squirming son.

'Is this the boy, Mr Russell?' Bob asked.

'Yes, it is,' came the firm reply.

'Then, Mr Evans, I'd like Rhodri to explain why he has been trying to hawk stolen goods around the town, giving his name as Basil Greene!'

There was a gasp from Mrs Evans before she slid gracefully to the ground.

★　★　★

After a time, life settled back down for the Greene family. Their feelings of sadness over Idris were still raw, and they would continue to mourn, but life had to go on. Like many other families, they just had to get on with it.

Mamgu derived some comfort from the fact that at long last she'd received a letter from her son, Dai. It was impossible to tell where it had been posted, and much of its contents had been blacked out by the censor's pen, but it meant the world to her.

Dai had handled that same flimsy paper, which she folded and unfolded twenty times a day, and at night she slept with the letter under her pillow.

'Poor old girl,' Bob confided to Ruth. 'It's hard losing a grandson at her age.'

'It's hard at any age,' his wife retorted.

Ruth was still smarting from the awful blunder that she'd made when visiting Dora that day. The poor thing had been saying over and over again how much she missed Idris.

'You don't know what it's like, losing a child.'

'Oh, I'm sure I do! I was desperate when Basil went missing.'

When Dora's eyes flashed, Ruth knew she'd put her foot in it.

'Really, Ruth! There's no comparison, no comparison whatsoever. Your Basil spent the night locked in a cupboard. My Idris is dead and gone!'

'But at the time I really believed that something must have happened to Basil, that's all I meant,' Ruth stammered, but Dora was in a huff and wasn't prepared to listen.

As for Basil, he felt disillusioned and betrayed, and he said as much to his father.

'Why did Rhodri want to get me into trouble like that, Dad? It was really, really beastly.'

'According to what Rhodri told his father, he didn't set out to frame you, lad. It was only when Mr Russell demanded to know who he was, that he blurted out your name because he was afraid of getting caught.'

'If you believe that, you'll believe anything,' Basil retorted, quoting his sister whose favourite saying this was at the moment.

'Don't be cheeky!' Bob frowned, but he was inclined to agree with Basil that Rhodri had planned the whole business with malice aforethought.

'What will happen to Rhodri now, Dad?'

'Don't ask me. It'll be up to Mr Rees if he wants to press charges.'

'Poor Mr Rees, though. He needed those veggies for the winter. Can't we give him some of ours? There's enough in that garden to sink a battleship.'

Thanking his lucky stars that Mamgu wasn't in the room to hear this unfortunate remark, Bob agreed that, if Basil would lend a hand with the weeding, they might be able to help Emrys out.

★  ★  ★

Marina was perhaps more affected by her cousin's death than her parents were. Being romantically inclined, she thought of Idris as a sort of Sir Lancelot — young and pure, a knight in shining armour, who'd died for his country. She also now understood for the first time that in times of war nobody's survival was certain. That meant that you had to squeeze all the enjoyment out of life that you could, while you had the chance.

She'd been waiting patiently for Tim Parry to invite her out, but it hadn't happened. Dare she precipitate matters?

Printed in one of Ruth's women's magazines there had been a letter written to the 'agony aunt' on just this subject. The writer had explained that she liked a certain young man at her place of work and she was sure the feeling was reciprocated. However, he seemed too shy to ask her out. Would it be all right for her to do the asking?

'No,' Aunt Anne had replied. 'It does not do to appear too forward. Gentlemen prefer to be the ones to make the first move. If he really likes you then he will pluck up the courage to ask you out. Why not make up a party of your friends to go rambling or cycling, and invite him to be part of the expedition? He will not feel threatened and then, in a more relaxed atmosphere than the office provides, you can get to know each other better.'

'Good grief!' Marina thought. 'She's Victorian — even though Queen Victoria's dead!'

And anyway, they had already done the group thing. What was the worst that could happen if she asked Tim for a date? It would be mortifying if he said no, but she decided to risk it.

An old film, 'Jesse James', was coming to the cinema. Tim enjoyed action movies, and this one, about the famous American outlaw, should be just his thing. It had been released in 1939, so it wasn't new, but there was no harm in that. She would have preferred something musical and romantic, but she supposed she could sit through this so long as Tim was by her side. She wasn't sure if he liked Henry Fonda, but Tyrone Power, who portrayed Jesse, was certainly a dreamboat. She had his picture, cut from a film magazine, in her scrapbook back in Hemel.

'"Jesse James"? Might be worth seeing,' Tim mused. 'Are you offering to pay for me, Marina?'

'I thought we'd go dutch,' she said firmly. If he wasn't gentleman enough to pay for her ticket then she certainly wasn't going to waste her hard-earned cash on him. There was a limit!

She might share her sweet ration with him, though. Not chocolate, but toffees in a bag. She imagined leaning close to him to offer the bag, their hands touching as they both reached inside for a sweet.

★　★　★

Marina was delighted when, as they reached the cinema on the appointed evening, she caught sight of Catrin Harris standing in the queue with her friend, Gwyneth.

When Catrin noticed Tim she sent a furious glare in his direction.

'If looks could kill!' Marina thought, smothering a giggle. She whispered something to Tim, forcing him to incline his head towards her in order to hear what was being said. Just let Catrin conclude that they were being all lovey-dovey, thought Marina, as she simpered up at Tim.

The film wasn't bad. Marina wondered if the real Jesse James had been as handsome and daring as he was portrayed, or was he just a criminal who had preyed on the innocent? She'd always thought that the Wild West must have been a romantic place, but it might not have been so wonderful in real life.

On their way out of the cinema, they came face to face with Catrin and her friend. Marina immediately tucked her arm into Tim's and he did nothing to shake her off. Tim nodded to Catrin and didn't seem to mind when she tossed her head and deliberately turned her back on him.

Now came the exciting part! Walking home in the gloom, Marina had the perfect excuse for clinging to Tim. With no street lamps on, it was hard to see where you were going and she stumbled on purpose, giving a little squeal as she fell against him. With this encouragement he bent down and grazed her cheek with a gentle kiss.

'Oh, I did enjoy this evening,' she murmured. 'I really like a good film, don't you? I hope we can do it again sometime.'

'Might as well,' he told her.

She reached home in a daze of delight, which was heightened when he kissed her again, this time on the lips in a lingering fashion.

It took her a long time to get to sleep that night, with the result that she made mistakes at work the next day. She accidentally cut off an important trunk call which led to a demand from an irate customer to speak to her supervisor but Marina didn't care. She was in love, and she felt as if she were floating on air.

For his part, Tim had mixed feelings. He still loved Catrin, but she had to be brought to heel. No man wanted a wife who insisted on having her own way. Her place was to consider him in all things. When the time came for him to marry, Tim wanted a wife like his mother, who spent all her life catering to Len Parry's whims and was glad to do so.

It was good that Catrin was jealous. If she saw enough of him with Marina Greene, then she'd cave in and apologise for treating him in such an off-hand manner.

But Tim didn't feel that he was just using Marina. Oh, no, there was more to it than that. She had grown up a lot in the past few weeks and she was a very pretty girl. Then, too, her English ways had a novelty about them and he felt that he'd like to get to know her better.

Bessie Parry didn't suspect a thing. She believed her son was just being kind to the little visitor at the shop.

The misunderstanding between Tim and Catrin would iron itself out in time. Where there was true love, these things usually worked themselves out in the end.

Marged was the only one who saw through Tim.

'See you don't push Catrin too far or you'll lose her for good,' she warned.

'See if I care,' he countered.

'And mind you don't hurt Marina, either,' she snapped. 'She's my friend, see?'

★ ★ ★

'Good morning, Mr Thomas. I'm Lorna.' Bob looked round from the tins he was stacking on the shelves.

'Oh, good morning, er, Laura. Can I help you?'

'It's Lorna. I've come about Idris, Mr Thomas.'

Bob suddenly realised what she'd said. 'No, no, I'm not Mr Thomas. The name is Greene. I'm working here temporarily.'

'Oh, I see. Then where can I find Mr Thomas, please? Or his wife, if that's not possible.'

'Mr Thomas is away on active duty, and I'm afraid that his wife is in hospital. Would you like to tell me what this is about? Possibly I can be of assistance.'

Tears gathered in the girl's pale blue eyes. She really was a very pretty young woman, he noticed. Her light brown hair was gathered into the sort of arrangement that his own wife and daughter wore, and her clothing — although shabby now — had once been good. The coat and skirt fitted her slender figure to perfection.

'I'm Idris's fiancée,' she said quietly.

'I didn't know anything about what had happened until I read the casualty lists in the paper. I came as soon as I could, Mr Greene.'

'Oh, dear. I really don't know what to say. I'm sorry for your loss, of course, but beyond that . . . '

'Do you mind if I sit down, Mr Greene? I don't feel very well.'

'Of course. Of course. Do forgive me, Miss — er — Lorna. I was caught on the hop. I don't think we knew that Idris was engaged, you see.'

The girl sank down on to the wooden chair which was kept for customers to use while their orders were made up. She did look a bit wan. Bob hoped she wasn't going to faint.

'Look, you stay here. I think I'd better fetch my wife.'

He dashed into the kitchen, leaving the door ajar. He hoped this wasn't some ploy to shoplift. After Basil's experience with Rhodri, Bob had become cynical. If a mere child could be so Machiavellian, goodness knows what a grown woman might do.

Ruth had just placed some sour milk in a cloth and was in the act of hanging the bundle over a basin to drip. By the look of it she was making cottage cheese. Before the war she would have poured the milk down the drain, but they couldn't afford to waste it nowadays.

'Can you come?' he hissed. 'There's a girl out there who says she's Idris's financée.'

'What are you whispering for? Speak up, do. I can't make out a word you're saying.'

'Just come, all right?' he urged.

Ruth knew what to do at once. She took the girl into the kitchen, where the kettle was boiling merrily. She could at least offer her a cup of tea, the universal remedy for problems of all kinds.

What on earth would they do if the supply ships could no longer get through, and tea disappeared from the shops as so many things had already done?

'So, you're Idris's young lady, my husband tells me.'

'Yes, that's right. We were going to be married on his next leave, but now . . .' She broke down and began to sob noisily.

'I'm so sorry.'

There was little more that Ruth could say. All across Britain, and throughout the empire, similar scenes were being enacted as wives and mothers, sisters and sweethearts, had to face the fact that they would never see their loved one again.

Not that the knowledge of this did anything to soothe the individual sufferer, such as this poor girl.

'And I've come all this way to see his family, but your husband tells me that there's nobody here belonging to Idris!'

'Actually, his grandmother is here, Mrs Thomas senior, but she isn't very well.'

Lorna's face brightened at once.

'Then can I speak to her?'

'Perhaps in a little while. She's sleeping just now. As I said, she's rather frail. You mentioned having come a long way. Where are you from?'

'Portsmouth.'

'Oh, that *is* a long way.'

Ruth was thinking fast. They couldn't let this girl travel back to Portsmouth today — she would have to stay the night; but where on earth were they to put her? The house was full to bursting as it was.

And would Dora want to see the girl?

Perhaps she would, as a last link with Idris. That would mean keeping Lorna under this roof for a longer period.

And how were they to feed her? Would it be crass to demand her ration book, considering that she was almost a member of the family, and one who had been bereaved at that?

'What are your plans now, then? I suppose you have a job to go back to?'

To Ruth's dismay the girl let out a cry of anguish. 'I can't go back there! I've nowhere to go! I'm expecting

Idris's baby and my parents have thrown me out of the house. That's why I've come to Wales, you see? I thought Idris's parents might take me in because it's their grandchild, isn't it?'

'I don't know what to say,' Ruth said, shocked at this revelation. 'It's not up to me, is it? You can stay here tonight, and then we'll go to the cottage hospital tomorrow afternoon to see Dora — that's Idris's mother. It's lucky you've come today because they only have visiting hours once a week, and that's tomorrow.'

She knew that she was babbling but she'd never been in a situation like this before. One thing was certain: she couldn't turn the poor girl out on the street, as her parents had evidently done. What sort of people would do that to their own daughter anyway? Surely they'd think again after the original shock had worn off.

Lorna's meeting with Mamgu was something of an ordeal. Of course, in Mamgu's young day, the workhouse would have been the only place of refuge for a young girl in disgrace.

She looked at Lorna through narrowed eyes.

'Engaged, is it? How come Idris never mentioned you then? Wrote to his mam regular, he did, and no word of getting married.'

'It was just arranged on his last leave, Mrs Thomas. Of course, he would have broken the news in time, but he was killed first, wasn't he?'

The girl dabbed at her eyes, looking pathetic.

Another thought occurred to Mamgu. Her body might be partly crippled now but she was a shrewd old lady.

'Mr Greene said you mistook him for my son, Dai. How is it you thought that Dai might be here, then?'

'This is his home, of course. Where else would he be?'

'Where he'd be is away on his ship! Didn't Idris tell you that?'

'I expect he did, but I'd forgotten,' the girl faltered. 'This has all been such a shock to me, you see. First I found out I was expecting a baby, and then my parents told me I had to go. I've been beside myself with worry.'

Mair Thomas looked thoroughly disapproving.

'In my day you went to the chapel first to say your vows before you thought of that sort of thing! And now your parents have cast you out and you've come to us, expecting us to pick up the pieces!'

'Idris was afraid he might get killed, Mrs Thomas. I didn't think it was so very wrong to give him a bit of comfort before he went back to the war. After all, we were engaged. And as for coming here now, I thought the family might be glad to know that, even thought they've lost Idris, his child is on the way. Your great-grandchild, Mrs Thomas.'

'Hmm!' Mamgu didn't look convinced. 'Well, you'll have to wait and see what Dora has to say about this, won't you?'

Once again, poor Ruth went to the hospital as the bearer of bad news. She hoped Dora wasn't going to shoot the messenger, so to speak. Things were still a bit stiff between them as a result of Ruth's awkward handling of Dora's grief.

'You wait here,' Ruth instructed Lorna when they reached the door of the ward. 'I'd better go in first and prepare Mrs Thomas.'

Dora looked up, surprised, from the magazine she was leafing through.

'Hello, Ruth! What brings you here? I thought you weren't coming this week. You said something about a Red Cross meeting; packing comforts for the troops, wasn't it?'

'I had to give that a miss. We've got a bit of a problem at home.'

'Don't tell me Bob's got himself in a muddle with the ration books or something?'

'No, no, nothing like that. It's, well, a

251

young woman turned up yesterday, from Portsmouth. She says she's Idris's fiancée.'

Dora's jaw dropped.

'It's the first I've heard of him being engaged! Why would he want to keep a thing like that secret?'

'I can't answer that, Dora, but that's not all. Apparently she's expecting a baby, and Idris is the father.'

Dora screwed up her face so that the lines on her forehead and around her mouth deepened.

'This is all I need! I suppose I'd better see the girl, though, hadn't I? Where is she now?'

'Waiting outside the door,' Ruth told her.

# Marina Becomes A Spy!

Lorna had been staying with the Greenes for almost a month, and tempers were becoming frayed.

Marina hated sharing her room with the older girl, not least because it was so small. More than once she'd come home from work to find Lorna's things taking up space on her bed, but when she complained, Lorna said there wasn't enough room in the wardrobe.

She'd even hinted that Marina should give up her bed!

'I get so tired now that I'm expecting. You wouldn't believe how much my back aches, and that camp bed is hopeless.'

'It's a lot better than what you'd find in the workhouse!' Marina snapped.

'There's no need to take that tone with me! When it boils down to it I have more right to be here than you do, since

I'm the mother of Idris's child. You people are only visitors here.'

These spats were becoming more frequent, but the worst of it was that Lorna didn't show her true colours to the other members of the household. She was all sweetness and light in front of everyone else, especially Bob, who felt sorry for her.

'Try to show a bit of sympathy,' he suggested, when Marina had a moan to him. 'It's not easy for her, you know, being in a mess like this. Try to imagine how you'd feel in a similar situation.'

'I wouldn't *be* in a similar situation, Dad! I'd have more sense!'

'I should jolly well hope so,' he countered.

After getting nowhere with him, Marina went to talk to her mother.

'I can't take much more of this, Mum! She's driving me up the wall! She's really nasty to me and she snaps at me all the time for no reason. She reckons that we're just interlopers, living here, and it's obvious that she can't wait for us to move out so that she can have a bedroom all to herself. Well, the feeling's mutual. Honestly Mum, I don't think I can stand to share a room with her for five more minutes.'

'I don't know what you expect me to do about it, my girl. Where else could we put her? You tell me that.'

'There's plenty of room in the parlour, Mum.'

'What, put her in with Mamgu? I don't think so. You may not have noticed, but Mamgu has taken a violent dislike to Miss Lorna Pearson.'

'Then somebody round here has seen sense,' Marina mumbled. 'I wish we could go back to Hemel. I can't wait for the day!'

'Can't you, love?' Ruth spoke slyly and her daughter reddened.

Returning to England would mean saying goodbye to Tim Parry, and Ruth had a pretty good idea of the way the wind was blowing.

Poor old Bob still thought his

daughter was going out with a group of young friends, with Tim accompanying them as a sort of minder. He had no idea that Marina and Tim had become a twosome.

Ruth had been against this at first, with Tim being older and more worldly wise, but she knew she had to cut the apron strings sooner or later, so for now she was turning a blind eye.

In a way it was good that Lorna was here; her presence would serve as an awful warning to Marina in case she was ever in danger of getting carried away.

Even so, it wouldn't do any harm to have a little chat about the situation with Dora, she thought, when she next went to see her at the cottage hospital.

'Look at you!' she exclaimed, when she entered the ward and approached her cousin's bed. 'How does it feel to have both your legs down flat?'

'Wonderful! I can turn over on my side at last, and what's more, I can scratch my leg now they've taken the plaster cast off. How are things at home?'

'A bit fraught, I'm afraid.'

'The effect of having a little cuckoo in the nest, I suppose?'

'Exactly.'

'It'll be even more difficult once I come home. I'll be having physiotherapy for a bit, of course, but I can't wait to get out of here. You've all been so good, and I don't want to impose on you any longer than I have to, but I was hoping that you could stay on with us for a bit. I wouldn't mind sharing with Mamgu, and with her room being on the ground floor I wouldn't have to tackle the stairs. Still, it will be a full house, won't it?'

'Have you thought about letting Lorna stay after we've gone back to Hemel? She could help you around the house — perhaps even serve in the shop? I can't say she's proved very willing up to now, but perhaps she'd be different with you. According to Marina the girl seems to regard us as interlopers.'

'Cheeky madam!'

'What does she mean to do with the baby when it comes, I wonder? Has she discussed her plans with you?'

Dora shrugged. 'She mentioned having it adopted, but I don't know what the chances are of that. Most people are taking care of evacuees as it is.'

'Is that what you'd like to see happen?'

Dora sighed.

'Not really. I hate to think of my first grandchild going to strangers or ending up in an orphanage somewhere. I think Lorna would like me to take it myself, but I don't know if I'm up to taking on a baby at my age.'

'That's a bit of a cheek, isn't it, palming it off on to you? Surely it's her responsibility?'

'I know, but I keep coming back to the fact that this baby is my own flesh and blood. Idris may be gone, but he'll live on through this child. One idea going through my mind is that Lorna can stay with me and when the baby comes she can go out to work while I keep an eye on him or her. After all, I do work in my own shop. I can juggle both jobs, so to speak.'

'There's one thing you haven't mentioned,' Ruth murmured.

'What's that, then?'

'Well, her own parents. Pearson, isn't that their name? This is their grandchild, too. I know they've been very unkind, but I'm sure they were in shock when they gave the poor girl the 'never darken my door again' routine. They may be regretting it now, but can't do anything about it because they don't know where she is. I do think you should contact them, Dora. See what they have to say. If they are still dead against welcoming her back home, then you'll have to think again.'

'Oh, I've thought of it already. I've even suggested contacting her parents to Lorna herself, but she refuses to part with their address. Says it's no use. Their minds are quite made up.'

'Who's that staying in your house, Marina?' Tim wanted to know, having caught a glimpse of Lorna sunning herself on the wall at the side of the road. 'Not from round here, is she?'

'Her name's Lorna. She comes from Portsmouth.'

He whistled through his teeth. 'Think she'd go out with me if I ask her nicely?'

Marina was cut to the quick by this insensitive remark.

'I shouldn't think so,' she said, in as cold a voice as she could muster. 'She's Idris's widow. At least, they were engaged and planning to marry on his next leave. What I mean is, she's bereaved, and grieving.'

'Maybe I could cheer her up, then,' he leered. Marina wasn't sure he was serious, but she resolved to put a spoke in his wheel without delay.

'I doubt it. She's expecting a baby!' she snapped.

'Oh, well then, better not get involved,' he remarked. 'Don't want to get a bad reputation, do I?'

'Oh, no, that wouldn't do at all,' she said, fuming. She was beginning to wonder what she'd ever seen in Tim Parry. To think that she'd dreamed about him for so long, only to learn that her idol had feet of clay!

Then, one day, Marina overheard a conversation between her parents.

'Dora feels she ought to contact the Pearsons, to give them a chance to reconcile themselves with their daughter,' Ruth said.

'That certainly seems like the right course of action to me,' Bob agreed.

'The only trouble is, Dora hasn't been able to worm their address out of the girl. She keeps saying there's no point, that they don't want to know. And Portsmouth is such a big place, and Pearson is quite a common name. We thought perhaps you could try speaking to Lorna, Bob. After all, she seems to have taken quite a shine to you.'

'Count me out! This is women's stuff. I'm not getting involved, no fear!'.

Marina tiptoed softly up the stairs. Lorna was splashing about in the bath tub, using up all the hot water in the geyser. She surely wouldn't have taken her handbag in there with her, so it must be lying around in their room. Snooping through someone's private possessions was beastly, but in this case Marina thought it was justified.

Finding Lorna's home address was easy enough, as there were several documents in the bag, including her identity card, ration book, and birth certificate. In this time of air raids people kept their valuables with them at all times, and from studying Lorna's papers, Marina could see that, until now, Lorna had lived in the same house as her parents since the day she'd been born.

Grabbing a pencil and a slip of paper, Marina jotted down the address and, for good measure, the first names of the Pearsons as well. Then she returned the documents to Lorna's handbag, taking care to replace them in the pocket where she'd found them. As she did so, a photograph fell to the floor.

It showed a rather handsome young man, dressed in naval uniform. Idris, of course.

But when she turned it over, the writing on the back told a different story.

'*To my darling Lorna, all my love, always, Freddie.*'

★   ★   ★

Sitting up in bed, Dora glanced over some recipes in a magazine that she'd borrowed from the patient in the next bed. The one for rissoles sounded not half bad, even if the main ingredient did seem to be oatmeal. Still, you could do a lot with the addition of herbs, and she had those in her garden at home.

She looked up and saw a middle-aged couple coming into the ward. Either they were new visitors who didn't know when visiting day was, she mused, in which case it was a miracle they'd got past the ball porter, or someone in the ward was on their last legs.

The pair stopped at the desk to have a word with Sister, and they evidently passed muster because now they were headed in Dora's direction.

Dora suddenly realised who they must be and she smoothed down her hair and made sure her bed-jacket was hiding any exposed flesh which the skimpy hospital nightdress didn't cover.

'Mrs Thomas?'

'Yes, that's me.'

'I'm Edith Pearson and this is my husband, George.'

'How do you do?'

'How do *you* do? We're Lorna's parents, of course. We had your letter, Mrs Thomas, and we came as soon as we could. May we sit down?'

'Please do.' Dora indicated the upright wooden chair that waited beside her locker. 'Perhaps you'd like to borrow Mrs Franklin's chair, Mr Pearson?' she added, indicating her bed neighbour.

'Just you bring it back when you've finished with it, that's all!' that lady insisted. 'Somebody took it away last visitors' day, they did, and my Morgan had to stand up all afternoon like he was waiting for a bus.'

That settled, the Pearsons looked at each other and began to talk in turn, like a music hall team.

'We've been so worried ever since our girl disappeared, Mrs Thomas.'

'We've looked all over Portsmouth, but never a sign of her. Of course, we had no way of knowing she'd gone to Wales!'

'It was good of you to take her into your home, but there's something here we don't understand. Several things, actually. First of all, we knew that Lorna was engaged, but we'd never heard of your son until we got your letter.'

Dora felt it was time to get a word in.

'We knew nothing about Lorna either, Mr Pearson. I understand that the engagement came about during Idris's last leave and, well, we both know what happened soon after that. Idris had no time to write and tell us, of course.'

'We were so sorry to hear of your son's death,' Edith Pearson murmured. 'You must find it very hard to come to grips with it.'

'Thank you. I'm starting to come to terms with it now, but at first I didn't want to believe it.'

'Something we have to come to terms with is that Lorna is expecting a baby,' George Pearson said. 'Of course, these things do happen, especially in wartime, but I wish she could have confided in us instead of running away like this.'

'I don't understand,' said Dora, frowning. 'She said you did know — that was why you threw her out of the house. That's the main reason I agreed to have her with us. The poor girl had nowhere else to go.'

'Is that what she told you, Mrs Thomas?' Edith's Pearson's expression was deeply shocked. 'No, I'm afraid you've got the wrong end of the stick. Quite some time ago, Lorna got to know a young naval officer, called Freddie Mitchell. She brought him home to meet us and I must say, we took against him from the start. He was a real rough diamond, Mrs Thomas.

'Well, when the two of them announced they were getting engaged, we weren't pleased, I can tell you. Then George made some enquiries about the boy and discovered that he was a real bad lot. He'd been in trouble with the police. He'd also had a string of girlfriends and we felt sure he was leading our girl up the garden path.'

Edith Pearson sighed, and turned to look at her husband, who took up the story.

'I told Lorna that we wouldn't stand to have a son-in-law like him in the family, and that she'd have to break it off with him. Well, it's all water under the bridge now, because the lad went down with his ship, as it happens. But at the time of the argument, Lorna got really upset at us and stormed off, out of the house. I can only think she must have broken off with Freddie and taken up with your Idris somewhere along the way, because we've heard nothing of her since, until we got your letter.'

'So, what are you going to do?' Dora asked.

'We'll take her home with us, today, if you'll be good enough to give us directions to find your home.'

'That's good, but what I really meant was, what about the baby?'

'That's something we'll have to work out with Lorna, Mrs Thomas.'

'But please don't forget that he or she is my grandchild,' Dora pleaded.

'We'll be in touch,' Edith promised.

After they'd left, Dora fell back upon her pillows, savouring the moment.

Until now she hadn't realised just how much stress she'd been under, feeling responsible for the girl.

She began to feel really rather cross about the whole thing, too. They had all been taken in by that young minx and her tale of cruel parents. But by the sound of it, her parents were quite ready to swallow their disappointment and stand by her, so why had she come all the way to Wales with her sob story?

Could she have meant to get money out of them or something? She had already lived at their expense for quite some time!

★　★　★

Once again, Bob, on duty in the shop, was the first to know what was happening. This time he was addressed by his proper name, and George Pearson explained that he and his wife had come directly from the hospital where they had spoken to Dora.

'Is our daughter here, Mr Greene? We've come to take her home.'

'My wife told me that Dora was

going to write to you,' Bob said. 'I'm glad you had a change of heart, Mr Pearson. Lorna is your daughter, no matter what she's done.'

For the second time that day, the Pearsons had to tell their side of the story.

Not surprisingly, Lorna was none too pleased to see her parents.

The usual ritual of tea and explanations disposed of, the Pearsons prepared to leave.

'Say thank you to Mrs Greene,' Edith prompted.

'Thank you for having me, Mrs Greene,' Lorna murmured, like a child who was leaving a not particularly enjoyable birthday party.

'Goodbye and good riddance to bad rubbish,' Mamgu muttered, when the door had closed behind their unwelcome guest.

'That's a bit harsh, isn't?' Bob remonstrated.

'Not a bit of it, Mr Greene. I didn't take to her from the first. Her eyes are set too close together.'

Ruth laughed. 'We can't help our looks, Mrs Thomas. The girl does have good taste, at least; she chose your grandson, didn't she? And she is going to give you your first great-grandchild, which is something in her favour.'

'I didn't ask her to,' Mamgu grumbled. 'And now look what's happened. The *baban* growing up without a dada.'

\* \* \*

'I'm glad that's all over,' Ruth told her husband, as he took the camp bed apart and she gathered up the bedding to await wash-day Monday. 'Let's hope everything goes well from here on. Dora will be coming home soon, so that's something to look forward to.'

'I suppose that means we'll be heading home ourselves one of these days. Should I write to old Pete and see about getting the house back?'

'Perhaps not yet, dear. Dora did say something about our staying on for a bit. She won't be back to normal just yet, after all that time in hospital.'

Marina was delighted when she heard that Lorna had gone.

'Thank goodness for that! Wasn't it clever of Auntie Dora to talk her parents round?'

'From what they told us, I don't think she needed to. They were very worried when she disappeared and were immensely relieved when they had Dora's letter.'

'But they chucked her out when they found out she was expecting!'

'Apparently not. They knew nothing about that. They did have a row ages ago when a chap she'd been seeing turned out to be a bad lot and some harsh words were said.'

'Freddie somebody?' Marina cried.

'How did you know about that? Did Lorna tell you?'

'She carries a photo of him in her bag, Mum. His name is written on the back.'

'She can't have known Idris very

long, then. She probably fell for him on the rebound. Well, the poor girl's been doubly bereaved now. That other chap was lost at sea, too.'

Marina was glad now that she'd said nothing to Lorna or Ruth about that photo. What a thing to happen. She could imagine nothing worse than falling in love with a man who turned out to be a rotter.

After a moment's pause, she realised that of course she could imagine something worse, and that was falling in love with someone who went away to war and got himself killed.

# A Miracle!

Marina was alone in the house. It was her day off and she was determined to enjoy it to the full, but the trouble was that she couldn't think of anything exciting to do and had no one to do it with anyway.

Marged was at work because they were on different shifts; they hardly ever saw each other any more.

Tim was also at work. Marina tried to imagine him crawling along, far below the surface of the earth, and failed. Or could it be that she was no longer really interested in him? He was beginning to bore her. Catrin Harris could have him back and welcome.

It was early closing day and Marina's parents had gone out for a walk, Ruth saying that she wanted to pick some hips and haws to display in the house. Dora was expected home the next day and the house had been cleaned from top to bottom to welcome her.

Basil was also out, at school, and Mamgu was having her afternoon nap, worn out with the excitement of looking forward to her daughter-in-law's return. Although she was usually quiet, old Mrs Thomas had more or less talked herself to a standstill in the past few days, directing Ruth to fetch this here and to put that there.

When the back door opened and the most gorgeous young man stood framed in the doorway, Marina was about to tell him off for walking into the house without knocking, but she found it hard to get her breath. For a moment, she felt quite light-headed. Once again it was love at first sight.

'Who are *you*?' she said at last.

'I'm Idris. Who are *you*?'

'Idris? But you're dead!' Marina's hand flew to her mouth. 'I mean, that is, if you're Idris Thomas!'

'Of course I'm Idris Thomas! But you haven't answered *my* question.'

'I'm your cousin, Marina Greene,' she said faintly. 'We've been staying here while Auntie Dora — your mum — has been in hospital.'

What on earth was going on? How could this possibly be Idris?

'Honestly, we all thought you were dead,' she stammered again.

'That was a mistake, *bach*. I got a bit too close to the pearly gates, but my number wasn't up and they sent me back again. So here I am, turning up like a bad penny!'

'I can't take it in. They're planning to hold a memorial service for you at the chapel! They would have done it sooner if Auntie Dora hadn't been in the hospital. She's coming home tomorrow, as it happens.'

'Look, you must have got my telegram!' he told her. 'Sent days ago, it was. I came as soon as I could, expecting to have the fatted calf killed for me, and now this. And you say nobody knows a thing about it?'

'You may have to make do with a

couple of sausages!' Marina was slowly recovering her equilibrium. 'Meat is on the ration, in case you hadn't heard!'

He nodded. 'Put the kettle on, then, *bach*, while I bring in my kit bag.'

In a daze, she did as she was asked. Obviously there was a story to be told, but there was no point in asking about it until Mum and Dad returned as he would only have to repeat it all to them.

'Good cup of tea, that,' he said, smiling, once they were sitting at the table, looking at each other with growing interest. 'Any more in the pot? And where have you hidden Mamgu? How is she?'

'She sleeps in the parlour now. In fact, she should be waking up from her nap at any moment. Shall I go and break the news to her?'

'Oh, no, I think that's my job, don't you?'

He got up and put his head round the parlour door.

'Time to wake up, Mamgu, unless you mean to sleep the whole day!'

The old lady stared at her grandson in astonishment. Then she held out her arms and Idris went to her, kneeling down on the floor at her bedside so he could share her embrace.

Marina stood in the doorway, watching them. They were speaking Welsh now, and she couldn't understand a word of it. However, it didn't take a knowledge of the ancient Celtic language to know what was going on.

Tears of joy were rolling down Mamgu's wrinkled cheeks as she held Idris's face in her hands. She seemed to be asking question after question and not getting any answers.

Marina wasn't needed here. She tiptoed away in time to hear her parents arriving back from their walk.

'What's that thing doing here?' Bob demanded, kicking the kit bag which was lying just inside the door. 'I could have tripped over that and broken my neck!'

'Oh, is it young Ifor, home on leave?' Ruth smiled. 'Dora will be so happy to see the boy when she finds him waiting to greet her!'

'She'll be happy, all right, Mum, but it isn't Ifor who's come home. It's Idris!'

'Idris! Don't be so silly, Marina. What a thing to say! And not in very good taste, either, I'm sorry to say.'

'Hello, Auntie Ruth!' Idris appeared in the doorway, grinning.

Ruth's hands flew to her mouth.

'Well, I never did!'

She and her husband seemed to be frozen in place.

Bob recovered first. 'Idris, lad! This is wonderful! But where have you been all this time, and where have you come from now?'

'Not heaven, obviously. Look, I'm dying for a bath. Is there any hot water? We'll all sit down together after tea and I'll tell you all about it then.'

'This is the most wonderful news, of course,' Ruth muttered, when Idris had disappeared upstairs, 'but I do think he might have let us know. Him turning up like this could have given Mamgu another stroke.'

'I don't think you need worry about her, Mum. She was overjoyed, of course, but funnily enough Idris's sudden appearance didn't seem to come as a shock. And anyway, he says he did send a telegram.'

'Well, I certainly didn't see any telegram coming here,' Bob said.

'I bet I know what happened,' Marina said. 'Remember that letter from the Inland Revenue that was sent on from Hemel? I bet you . . . '

There was no letter-box in the shop door, and the elderly postman usually stepped inside to deliver the post. If the shop happened to be closed, he pushed the letters under the door. The tax envelope had gone under the mat and hadn't been discovered until Ruth had moved it to sweep up.

Marina darted into the shop and, sure enough, there was an orange envelope waiting to be discovered. Telegrams were supposed to be handed to the recipient in case there was a reply to be sent, but this one had probably come when nobody was about and the boy had wanted to get rid of it.

'He should be reported,' Bob grunted.

'Whose kit bag is that? What's it doing here?' Basil had come home from school, looking as if a whirlwind had struck him. His tie was unknotted, his shoelaces were trailing on the floor and he seemed to be covered in dust.

'Go into the scullery and wash your face and hands, Basil. Tea will be on the table shortly!' Ruth directed.

'And tuck your shirt in, too!' Bob ordered. 'You're not coming to the table looking like that, my boy.'

At that moment Idris came down the stairs, looking very smart. He had put his uniform back on after his bath, and Marina wondered if this was because he had no civilian clothes to wear, or if there was something in the rules which said he had to dress that way.

Basil was enthralled by the sight.

'Cor! Are you in the Navy, mister? Were you a friend of my cousin Idris? He was a hero, you know. He went down with his ship.'

'I don't know about being a hero, boyo, but *I'm* Idris, see? And as you can see, I didn't drown when the ship went down.'

'Cor!' Basil said again. Just wait until school tomorrow. He'd be the centre of attention all right, with this tale to tell.

When tea was over, Idris leaned back in his chair and unfolded his story. In deference to the women present he said little about the terror of that night; of the death and destruction that was all around the crew of his ship when it was torpedoed; of the plunge into the dark, icy waters, and the stress-filled hours that followed as they waited in their over-filled lifeboats for rescue.

'We were picked up by another British ship, but that was sunk too, not long afterwards. In that second attack I was knocked out cold. Presumably I was put into one of the lifeboats along with the rest, and eventually transported to hospital. I was unconscious for days and the nurses told me later that they had no idea who I was. I'd lost all my belongings, of course, and they had no means of identifying me.'

'But surely some of your shipmates knew who you were?'

'We were separated in all the confusion, Uncle Bob. I suspect that all those in the lifeboat with me were men from the other ship, the one that rescued us from the second attack. As I found out later, hundreds were lost that night, and I imagine the authorities believed I was among them. It wasn't until I came back to my senses that I was able to explain who I was.'

★　★　★

The next day, Dora came home to a flurry of excitement. The whole family was crowded into the doorway when the ambulance drew up, and Dora was helped down by the uniformed attendants. Aided by a walking stick, she made her way slowly to the house.

She and Ruth kissed the air above each other's cheeks as the rest of the family stood by, beaming.

'Someone's here to see you, Auntie Dora! Somebody really special!'

Basil had been warned to keep quiet about the surprise which awaited her, but he'd been unable to contain his excitement and blurted this out.

Dora clasped her hands together, dropping her stick in the process

'It's Ifor, isn't it? They've given him leave so he can welcome me home.'

There was no stopping Basil now.

'No, it's not Ifor! Guess who it is, Auntie, guess!'

'Don't tell me it's my Dai!'

'Oh, better than that, Auntie!'

'Nothing on earth could be better than that at this moment, Basil love.'

'Yes, it could! Yes, it could!'

'What do you say then, Mam?' Idris stepped out of the parlour.

After a moment of stunned silence, Dora began to sob, and tears ran down the faces of all those who stood watching as she ran towards her son. Ruth said later that nobody would ever have imagined that her cousin had just come out of hospital after months of suffering with a broken leg.

A bird on the wing could not have flown any faster, she insisted.

# Loose Ends

During the next few days there was a steady stream of visitors to the Thomas household as friends came to shake Idris by the hand, rejoicing in his survival.

Others came to welcome Dora home.

Mamgu kept a permanent smile on her face, and who could blame her?

'She keeps me awake half the night, telling me what a miracle it is that Idris is alive,' Dora told Ruth. 'Mind you, I'm more than happy to put up with it! I've written to tell Dai, of course, although goodness knows when he'll receive my letter.'

'What about Ifor, then? Have you written to him?'

'Of course. Oh, I do wish that both Dai and Ifor could get leave to come home and celebrate with us, but it's no good wishing for the moon! Just as well, in a way, because I don't know where we'd put them.'

Marina had volunteered to give up her room, which after all belonged to Idris by right, but he'd refused, moving in with Basil.

Needless to say, Basil was absolutely delighted to be sharing with his hero, and plagued him with questions.

Idris was very patient with the boy, answering in a kindly fashion but toning down his responses because of the child's age. In any case he preferred not to think too deeply about what he had experienced. Terrible images flooded into his mind every time he closed his eyes to go to sleep.

'I'm going to join the Navy when I grow up!' Basil enthused.

'That's nice, dear,' Ruth murmured, thinking, 'Not if I've got anything to do with it!' Still, he would probably have changed his mind by the time he reached his teens. Only last week he'd wanted to be an engine driver.

Dora was overjoyed because Idris was

to be given a shore job, at least for the time being. Despite his robust appearance the doctors had decreed that, after his terrible ordeal, he wasn't well enough to return to sea.

Something which didn't go unnoticed by their mothers was the fact that Marina and Idris were becoming increasingly drawn to each other.

'Wouldn't it be nice if they made a match of it?' Dora whispered to Ruth one evening, when the two young people were laughing over a game of Beggar My Neighbour.

'They're cousins,' Ruth countered.

'Second cousins! Anyway, cousins marry all the time, don't they?'

'Marina is much too young to think about that sort of thing.'

'She's almost seventeen!'

'Don't be so silly, Dora. When Idris goes back to wherever they send him, they'll forget all about each other.'

Dora wasn't so sure. Neither was Tim Parry.

'You don't seem to have time for me

these days,' he grumbled. 'Always hanging around that cousin of yours, you are!'

'We all thought he was dead, Tim! We're just thrilled to have him back, that's all.'

Tim glowered at her. 'Is that all?'

'Of course. Look, if you're feeling left out, why don't you come and join us? I'm sure Idris would love to see you.'

'I might ask Catrin to come to the pictures with me,' he countered.

'That sounds like a good idea, Tim. Or maybe you'd like us to make up a foursome?'

He shrugged. That didn't sound like a good idea to him. Catrin might fall all over the conquering hero as well. How could he compete with that?

★ ★ ★

'Will you write to me after I go back?' Idris asked Marina, when his leave was almost up.

'Of course I will!'

She was thrilled that he'd asked, but there was something which had to be settled first. She bit her lip, wondering how to bring up the subject.

'What's the matter, *cariad*? Something wrong?'

'I was just thinking that Lorna might not like it.'

'Lorna? Who's she?'

Marina frowned. 'Your fiancée, of course!'

Now it was Idris's turn to look blank. 'What are you talking about? I'm not engaged, never have been. I don't have a fiancée.'

'But if she's having your baby you'll have to marry her, won't you, to give the child a name?'

'Is this some kind of joke?' Idris was angry now. 'I don't know what you're accusing me of, Marina, but I don't find this amusing, see.'

They were sitting out on the back step with the kitchen door open behind them. Marina heard hesitant footsteps which told her that her aunt was nearby.

'Auntie Dora!' she called. 'Could you come out here for a moment, please?' She turned back to face Idris. 'If you won't listen to me then you'd better hear what your mother has to say.'

'What is it, dear?' Dora limped outside and stood leaning on her walking stick.

'We've just been talking about Lorna Pearson,' Marina began.

'You mean *you* have!' Idris interrupted angrily. 'Do you know what this is about, Mam?'

'Oh, dear! I knew this had to be discussed sooner or later, but I've put off saying anything about it to you because I didn't want to spoil your leave.'

'What is all this, Mam? I don't know any Lorna Pearson!'

'I have to sit down, son. Can we all go inside?'

When they were seated, Dora took up the story.

'This young woman turned up here from Portsmouth after reading your name in the casualty lists. She said that the pair of you had become engaged during your last leave, and that you planned to marry in the near future. Then, when she found that she was pregnant with your baby, her parents turned her out of the house.'

'So having nowhere else to go,' Marina continued, 'she came here, thinking that we'd look after her. That the Thomas family would, I mean. She didn't know about us staying here.'

'I can't believe this!' Idris scratched his chin, beginning to look more puzzled than angry. 'Where is she now, this Lorna Pearson?'

'Back with her parents,' his mother told him. 'We managed to trace them and they came down to Wales to take her back with them. The odd thing is that they knew nothing about the expected baby, and neither had they thrown her out of their home. There had been a falling out between the girl and her father, but that had something to do with her getting engaged to a no-good rascal. From what was said, we assumed she'd given him up and started seeing you instead. It all seemed a bit sudden to me, but people do have these whirlwind romances in war time, of course.'

'A no-good rascal, you say? I wonder who he was?'

'I think I know,' Marina told him. 'She carried a photo around with her. I wish I had it here to show you. His name was on the back; Freddie. I think his name was Freddie Mitchell, or something like that.'

'I knew him! We both hung around with the same crowd during the time we were in Portsmouth. I'm sorry to hear that he's been killed, but it's true that he was no good. There was a lot of talk about his bragging about all the girls he'd led up the garden path.'

'I see what happened!' Marina cried, her eyes sparkling. 'Freddie got engaged to Lorna — with no intention of marrying her — and when she learned she was expecting his baby, he said he wanted nothing more to do with her. She was desperate, so she looked through the casualty lists to find someone who had also been in Portsmouth at the right time. Then she turned up here to take advantage of your family!'

Idris threw back his head and laughed. 'My goodness, *cariad!* What sort of books have you been reading?'

Marina blushed, but she stuck to her story. 'I can't make you believe me, Idris, but just tell me why else would she'd come here posing as your fiancée if you've never heard of her before?'

'Marina's right so far as that goes,' Dora said, nodding. 'Oh, the first part of your idea is just supposition, dear. But we can't deny what happened after she arrived here. She was quite convincing, Idris. I even thought of letting her stay on, and helping her to bring up the baby — my grandchild, as I believed — but then the Pearsons came and took charge of her. Now, of course, I know it was all a confidence trick. Perhaps she'd have tried to get money out of me, or even gone off after the baby came, leaving it with me like a little cuckoo in the nest!'

'For all she knew I could have been married.' Idris had no choice but to accept the story now.

'Easy enough to find out your circumstances if she went to the authorities, claiming that she'd had a relationship with you,' Dora said.

'I'll have to sort all this out when I return to Portsmouth, Mam. That young woman is going to get a shock, in more ways than one!'

# Time To Go Home

'We'll be home for Christmas!' Basil carolled joyfully. 'I can't wait!'

'Do you mean you can't wait for Christmas, or you can't wait to go back to your own house?' Dora smiled.

'Both! I don't like it here.' Catching sight of his mother's frown, he hastily changed his tune. 'Sorry, Auntie Dora! I don't mean I don't like your house, or staying with you; only that some not very nice things have happened to me since I came here.'

'Rhodri, I suppose. Well, I can't say I blame you. He's been very unkind and badly behaved, by all accounts.'

'I'll miss Mr Rees, though. He's nice. If I'd stayed, I could have helped him plant his garden next spring.'

'Never mind, you can come back to visit one of these days, and you'll see him then.'

'Well, I've thoroughly enjoyed being here.' Bob beamed. 'Running a shop is right up my alley. I was saying to Ruth that I'd like to get a little place of our own after the war. A tobacconist's and sweet shop, perhaps.'

'What will you do in the meantime, though? You wouldn't think of going back to your own trade, I suppose?'

'Not if the doctor has anything to do with it. No, I'll see if I can get a job serving in a shop somewhere in Hemel. I feel I have the experience to manage one, but we'll have to see. If there aren't any vacancies for managers then I'll work as a shop assistant to tide us over.'

'Make sure it's in a sweet shop, Dad!' Basil piped up, making everyone smile.

'And Marina will have to see what's available for her, now that she's joined the ranks of the world's workers,' Bob remarked.

'Ah, well, Bob, I've been thinking about that. Marina has a good job here, and she's settled in nicely. What would you think of her staying on with me?

I'm still a bit below par, and she'd be a help to me in the house.'

'Well, I don't know; she's a bit young to be leaving home.'

'Leaving home, my foot! She'll be with her family here, and I'll keep an eye on her.'

Bob was still not convinced. 'You'd need to keep an eye on her, Dora. I'm beginning to think there's something going on between her and that young Parry chap. They're not sweethearts, are they?'

He looked round in surprise as his wife and her cousin groaned.

'You're behind the times, Bob Greene!'

'What's that, love?'

'Never mind,' Ruth sighed.

Marina was in seventh heaven. She'd had a letter from Idris, to say that he'd called on the Pearsons and had an awkward interview with Lorna and her father.

Pearson had been belligerent at first, but then Lorna had broken down and admitted what she'd done. Her poor father hadn't known where to look. He'd apologised profusely and kept saying that he didn't understand how she could have behaved the way she had. That wasn't the way she'd been brought up.

In floods of tears, Lorna had told Idris and her parents what had really happened, although Idris did wonder if they were crocodile tears. She'd already shown herself to be untruthful, so what was one more lie?

But it seemed that Marina's theory had been quite correct. Lorna had continued to see the disreputable Freddie until, to her horror, she'd discovered that she was pregnant. She'd told him about it, expecting him to stand by her, but instead he'd shrugged her off, asking her what she expected him to do about it. He'd even questioned whether the child was really his.

And next thing, he'd been killed in action.

'*That was when she thought of me,*'

wrote Idris. 'Apparently we had mutual acquaintances, and it was from them that she heard that I'd also been killed, as was thought at the time. Her nasty little scheme just grew from there.'

After writing on more general topics, Idris finished the letter by saying one or two things which brought tears of happiness to Marina's eyes.

They were too personal to share here, but it's enough to say that love will flourish, war or no war, and when Bob, Ruth and Basil went back to England, and Tim went back to Catrin, Marina stayed behind at the little shop in Bedwen, confident in the knowledge that Idris really was her knight in shining armour.

## THE END

*Other titles in the*
*Linford Romance Library:*

## TO LOVE AGAIN

### Catriona McCuaig

Jenny Doyle had always loved her brother in law, Jake Thomas-Harding, but when he chose to marry her sister instead, she knew it was a love that had no future. Now his wife is dead, and he asks Jenny to live under his roof to look after his little daughter. She wonders what the future holds for them all, especially when ghosts of the past arise to haunt them . . .

# FINDING THE SNOWDON LILY

## Heather Pardoe

Catrin Owen's father, a guide on Snowdon, shows botanists the sites of rare plants. He wants his daughter to marry Taran Davies. But then the attractive photographer Philip Meredith and his sister arrive, competing to be first to photograph the 'Snowdon Lily' in its secret location. His arrival soon has Catrin embroiled in the race, and she finds her life, as well as her heart, at stake. For the coveted prize generates treachery amongst the rivals — and Taran's jealousy . . .

# KEEP SAFE THE PAST

## Dorothy Taylor

Their bookshop in the old Edwardian Arcade meant everything to Jenny Wyatt and her father. But were the rumours that the arcade was to be sold to a development company true? Jenny decides to organise a protest group. Then, when darkly attractive Leo Cooper enters her life, his upbeat personality is like a breath of fresh air. But as their relationship develops, Jenny questions her judgement of him. Are her dreams of true love about to be dashed?

# LEGACY OF REGRET

## Jo James

When Liz Shepherd unexpectedly inherits an elderly man's considerable estate, she is persuaded it is in gratitude for her kindness to him. But doubts set in when Steve Lewis, in the guise of a reporter, challenges her good luck. Was there another reason for her legacy? And why is Steve so interested? She comes to regret her inheritance and all its uncertainties — until Steve helps her find the truth and they discover the secret of their past.

# RETURN TO HEATHERCOTE MILL

## Jean M. Long

Annis had vowed never to set foot in Heathercote Mill again. It held too many memories of her ex-fiancé, Andrew Freeman, who had died so tragically. But now her friend Sally was in trouble, and desperate for Annis' help with her wedding business. Reluctantly, Annis returned to Heathercote Mill and discovered many changes had occurred during her absence. She found herself confronted with an entirely new set of problems — not the least of them being Andrew's cousin, Ross Hadley . . .

# HARRIER 809

Britain's Legendary Jump Jet and the
Untold Story of the Falklands War

**Rowland White**

**CORGI BOOKS**

TRANSWORLD PUBLISHERS
Penguin Random House, One Embassy Gardens,
8 Viaduct Gardens, London SW11 7BW
www.penguin.co.uk

Transworld is part of the Penguin Random House group of companies
whose addresses can be found at global.penguinrandomhouse.com

Penguin
Random House
UK

First published in Great Britain in 2020 by Bantam Press
an imprint of Transworld Publishers
Corgi edition published 2021

A CIP catalogue record for this book
is available from the British Library.

ISBN
9780552176354

Typeset in ITC Stone Serif by Jouve (UK), Milton Keynes.
Printed and bound in Great Britain by Clays Ltd, Elcograf S.p.A.

The authorized representative in the EEA is Penguin Random House Ireland,
Morrison Chambers, 32 Nassau Street, Dublin D02 YH68.

Penguin Random House is committed to a sustainable
future for our business, our readers and our planet. This book
is made from Forest Stewardship Council® certified paper.

1

For Mike and Christine, for Lucy

*I asked the navy to invent a plausible scenario in which the carrier would be essential. The only one they could conceive was a prolonged naval battle in the straits of Sumatra, in which the enemy had Russian MiGs on the adjoining coast, but we had given up our bases in the area; this seemed too unlikely to be worth preparing against.*

*Oddly enough, no one suggested the only relevant situation which has actually arisen, namely the landing and supply of British forces in the Falklands against opposition from Argentina.*

Denis Healey, Secretary of State for Defence, 1964–70

# CONTENTS

*Author's Note*                                                     xi
*Acknowledgements*                                                 xiii
*Maps*                                                             xvi

Prologue: Scramble!                                                   1
Part One: Task Force                                                  7
Part Two: Into the Danger Zone                                      163
Part Three: La Muerte Negra                                         255
Part Four: STUFT                                                    355
Epilogue: Phoenix Rising                                            425

*Glossary*                                                         433
*Bibliography*                                                     445
*Appendix: British Aerospace Sea Harrier FRS.1*                    457
*Picture Acknowledgements*                                         461
*The Post-Credits Stinger*                                         465
*Index*                                                            469

# AUTHOR'S NOTE

This is a story I've wanted to write for a long time. I was eleven years old when Argentina invaded the Falkland Islands. The heroic exploits of the 'Sea Harrier fighter-bomber aircraft' so meticulously and memorably described by Ian McDonald, the bespectacled civil servant charged with sharing news of the war, made a big impression on me. As an avid reader of Second World War aircrew memoirs and the vividly drawn stories that filled the pages of *Commando* comic, *Victor* and *Warlord*, I could scarcely believe that there were daily reports of dogfights in newspapers and on TV.

The two frontline Sea Harrier squadrons that travelled south with the Task Force, 800 and 801, have been well served by books written by pilots who flew with them, and both *Sea Harrier Over the Falklands* by 801's Commanding Officer, Sharkey Ward, and *Hostile Skies* by 800's David Morgan are recommended. I've read and reread and enjoyed them many times. But I kept finding myself drawn to 809 Naval Air Squadron. Hurriedly pulled together after the invasion and sent south barely three weeks later, their story looked like the most interesting and unusual of the lot.

I wasn't disappointed. Nor did I expect my research into 809 to reveal a much bigger story hiding in the shadows. And one that, still classified to this day, had never been told before.

Those who've read any of my previous books will be familiar with the presentation of the material. While I've tried to tell a fast-paced story, I've not massaged the facts in order to do so. Everything that follows is, to the best of my knowledge, a true and accurate account of what happened. I've drawn on a wide variety of sources and this is reflected in the dialogue in the book. Where it appears in quotation marks it's either what I've been told was said, or what's been reported in previous accounts or records, published and unpublished. Where speech is in italics – sometimes the call-and-response checks that accompany any military flying – it represents genuine dialogue that's been taken from another source to add richness to a scene. I hope it can be argued with a degree of confidence that it's what would have been said. Finally, where internal thoughts are included in italics, they are accurate recordings of what participants told me they were thinking at the time.

As ever, I hope this is a book that does justice to all those whose stories I've told. And, of course, any mistakes are my own.

R.W.
Nant-y-Feinen
January 2020

# ACKNOWLEDGEMENTS

I first met Tim Gedge nearly ten years ago at a Taranto Night dinner following the publication of *Phoenix Squadron*. I told him then that I was keen to tell the story of 809 Naval Air Squadron's Falklands War. He was enthusiastic about the idea then and remained so, despite, I imagine, thinking it would never happen. I'm enormously grateful to him for his time, support and patience. Without him, the squadron Commanding Officer, on board I couldn't have written the book. I also need to thank his pilots, David Braithwaite, Bill Covington, Alastair Craig and Hugh Slade, all of whom were similarly generous. It was a pleasure and a privilege to meet and speak with them all. Likewise, on the engineering side, Bob Gellett and Colin Burton. Pilots Simon Hargreaves and Clive Morrell joined 809 when it returned to the South Atlantic aboard HMS *Illustrious* after the war, but flew with 800 NAS during the fighting. They too were kind enough to share their memories with me. As was Sharkey Ward, boss of 801 during the war. Neither Jock Gunning nor Willy McAtee went south with 809, but both talked to me about their support of the squadron's revival at Yeovilton. Former Phantom Observer Leo Gallagher also helped prepare 809 for war and provided valuable insights from within the Department of Naval Air Warfare at the MoD. These provided a perfect complement to my conversation with Admiral of the Fleet Sir Ben Bathurst, then heading the department. Sir Ben went on to become First Sea Lord in 1993 and I'm thankful to him for sparing time to talk to me. While he was 1SL, the position of Second Sea Lord was held by Admiral Sir Michael Layard. A distinguished former fighter pilot, Sir Michael was Senior Naval Officer aboard *Atlantic Conveyor* during the Falklands War. I'm hugely appreciative to him for sharing his mesmerizing account of that ship's tragic loss. Perhaps the most unexpected contribution to the Fleet Air Arm side of the story came from Graham Hodinott, who flew the De Havilland Heron that carried three 809 pilots from Yeovilton to Coningsby to train against the French. The devil's in the detail, and I'm thankful for the colour his recollections provided.

My questions didn't begin and end with the Fleet Air Arm, though, and I'm grateful to David Oddy, Mick Murden, Malcolm Smith and Laon Hulme for their willingness to help me better tell the story of their ships, HMS *Brilliant* and HMS *Exeter*.

The Air Force also played a crucial role. I had always intended to include something of the story of 1(Fighter) Squadron RAF, whose Harriers travelled south alongside 809 aboard *Atlantic Conveyor*, and so it was a real pleasure to meet Bob Iveson and talk to him. Once I got started, though, a previously little known aspect of the RAF's involvement in the war assumed greater and greater importance. In pursuit of this I spoke to a wide range of former RAF personnel. Some of them, like Sir Mike Knight, Simon Baldwin and Bob Tuxford, have become friends since our paths first crossed on *Vulcan 607*. That doesn't diminish my gratitude to them for their help with this book. It was also a great pleasure to talk to former Air Attaché to Brazil Jerry Brown again and be able to tap into his expertise on the wider impact of the Falklands War throughout Latin America. Dave Watson, Colin Adams, Mike Beer, Iain Hunter and Air Vice-Marshal John Price also shared their recollections of the time. All provided valuable insights and all have my thanks.

The least direct RAF contribution was also one of the most welcome. Squadron Leader Kev O'Brien somehow manages to squeeze in two other lives as an adventurer and historian alongside a day job in the RAF Regiment. Kev championed my cause inside the Air Force as well as unearthing and sharing some fantastic documentary material.

Throughout, I've been lucky enough to be able to lean on people far more expert than me for information. At the Fleet Air Arm Museum, Catherine Cooper and Barbara Gilbert have, as ever, done a wonderful job of finding piles of top-drawer information. Graham Rood at the Farnborough Air Sciences Trust also dug up a little gold. Sir Donald Spiers, John Roulston and Paul Stone shared deep understanding and fascinating first-hand experience of the world I was exploring. Nick Cook, Douglas Barrie, Jon Lake, Paul Beaver and Nick Stroud all know much more than me about this sort of stuff. Fortunately, they've all gone out of their way to help me, allowing me to benefit from their insights and vast specialist knowledge. In Argentina, aviation writer Santiago Rivas has done the same. Late in the proofreading stage, I was also fortunate to be able to draw on aviation writer Denis J. Calvert's keen eye for detail and encyclopaedic knowledge of the Harrier. And even later in the proofreading, Nick Greenall and the great Jon Lake were kind enough to share their expertise to help iron out a few more wrinkles.

Once again, Lalla Hitchings's contribution has been immense. Without Lalla there would be no book. The hours of interviews you've transcribed for me over the years rather beggars belief. Thank you! A shout-out too for the extraordinarily talented Keith Burns, whose painting of John Leeming's guns kill is included in the plate section. If that's whetted your appetite – and I'd be astonished if it hasn't – go to keithburns.co.uk to see more.

By contrast, Jo Whitaker had nothing to do with the book whatsoever, but she did ask, and I said yes, so she gets a mention.

Mark Lucas and Bill Scott-Kerr are thoroughly deserving of inclusion, however. My agent and publisher, Mark and Bill have been with me every step of the way and that makes me feel like the luckiest author around. At this book's inception, we all agreed that it would be a shorter effort. They were both powerless to stop it growing and growing, but their support, enthusiasm and encouragement never wavered. Huge thanks.

Working alongside Bill at the mighty Transworld Publishers is a large, dedicated and talented team across editorial, design, production, sales, marketing and publicity. Eloisa Clegg, Viv Thompson, Josh Benn, Phil Lord, Richard Shailer, Anthony Maddock, Gary Harley, Tom Chicken and Tom Hill have all helped bring *Harrier 809* to life. And, once again, my eagle-eyed copy-editor Dan Balado has made me look a good deal less careless than I am.

At work, Louise Moore continues to manage the occasionally reluctant-to-be-managed with understanding, intelligence and compassion. It's a finely judged effort and I'm enormously appreciative of it.

As ever, though, I must finish with a heartfelt thank you to my amazing wife and kids Lucy, Rory, Jemima and Lexi. It's with you that I really lucked out. I'm never happier than I am when I'm with you. I'm in awe of you all. And, Lucy, I said once that 'I scorn to change my state with kings.' Still true.

# The Falkland Islands

- ○ Place of interest
- ✈ Military airport
- ◄■► Combat Air Patrol station
- ▲ Mountain peak

60°00'W
59°30'
60°30'W
51°00'S
61°00'W

W7

Pebble Island

Many Branch Harbour

**Port Howard**
Mount Maria ▲ ○

51°30'S
W6

King George Bay

Mount Adam ▲

WEST FALKLAND

Hornby Mountains

Shag Cove

Swan Island

Mount Sullivan ▲

W10

**Fox Bay** ○

52°00'S

W4

Cape Belgrano

W5

*South Atlantic Ocean*

52°30'S
61°00'W
60°30'W
60°00'W
59°30'W

**English – *Argentinian* place names**

East Falkland – *Isla Soledad*

Falkland Islands – *Islas Malvinas*

Goose Green airfield – *BAM Condor*

Pebble Island – *Isla Borbón*

Pebble Island airfield – *EAB Calderón*

Port Howard – *Puerto Mitre*

Port San Carlos – *Puerto San Carlos*

Stanley – *Puerto Argentino*

Stanley Airport – *BAM Malvinas*

West Falkland – *Isla Gran Malvina*

**South Georgia**

Bird Island

Prince Olaf Harbour

Fortuna Glacier

Leith Harbour

King Edward Point

Grytviken

Ocean Harbour

N

South Atlantic Ocean

0 — 25 — miles

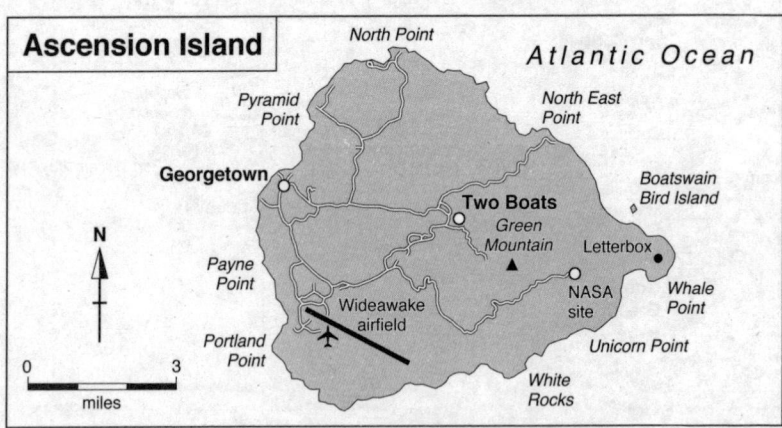

**Ascension Island**

North Point

Atlantic Ocean

Pyramid Point

North East Point

Georgetown

Two Boats

Boatswain Bird Island

Green Mountain

Letterbox

Payne Point

Wideawake airfield

NASA site

Whale Point

N

Portland Point

Unicorn Point

White Rocks

0 — 3 — miles

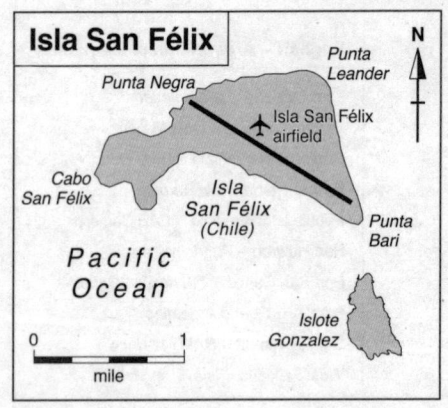

**Isla San Félix**

Punta Negra

Punta Leander

N

Isla San Félix airfield

Cabo San Félix

Isla San Félix (Chile)

Punta Bari

Pacific Ocean

Islote Gonzalez

0 — 1 — mile

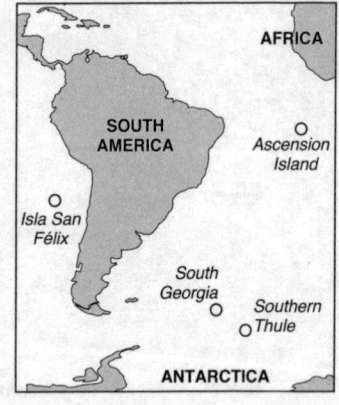

AFRICA

SOUTH AMERICA

Ascension Island

Isla San Félix

South Georgia

Southern Thule

ANTARCTICA

Latin America

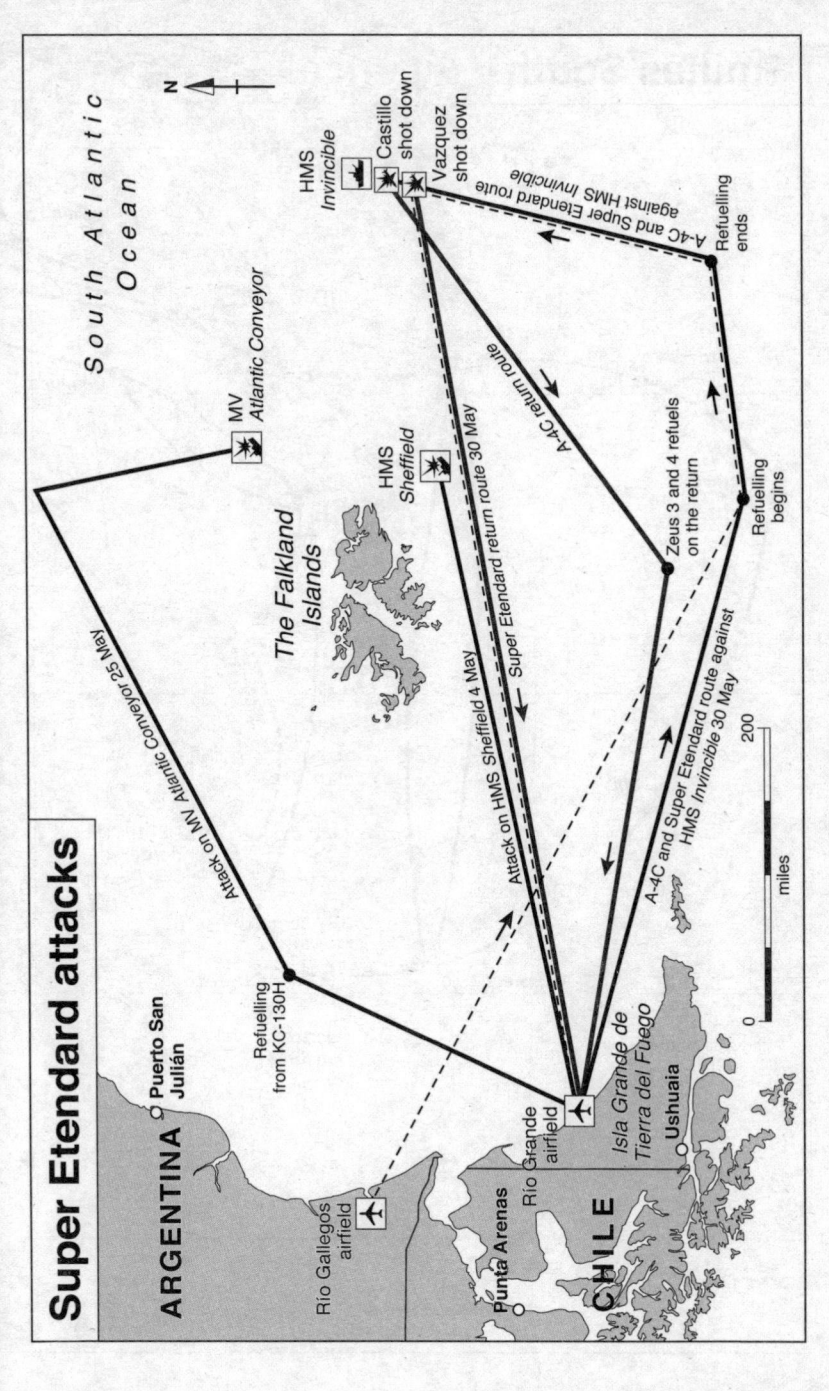

# Super Etendard attacks

ARGENTINA

Puerto San Julián

Rio Gallegos airfield

Attack on MV Atlantic Conveyor 25 May

Refuelling from KC-130H

MV Atlantic Conveyor

South Atlantic Ocean

N

HMS Invincible

Castillo shot down

Vazquez shot down

A-4C and Super Etendard route against HMS Invincible

Refuelling ends

A-4C return route

The Falkland Islands

HMS Sheffield

Super Etendard return route 30 May

Attack on HMS Sheffield 4 May

Zeus 3 and 4 refuels on the return

Refuelling begins

A-4C and Super Etendard route against HMS Invincible 30 May

Rio Grande airfield

Isla Grande de Tierra del Fuego

CHILE

Punta Arenas

Ushuaia

miles

0    200

# Routes South

N

Gander

Washington

March
Airforce Base

Bermuda

Hawaii

BELIZE

PERU/CHILE
border

Tahiti

Easter Island

San Félix

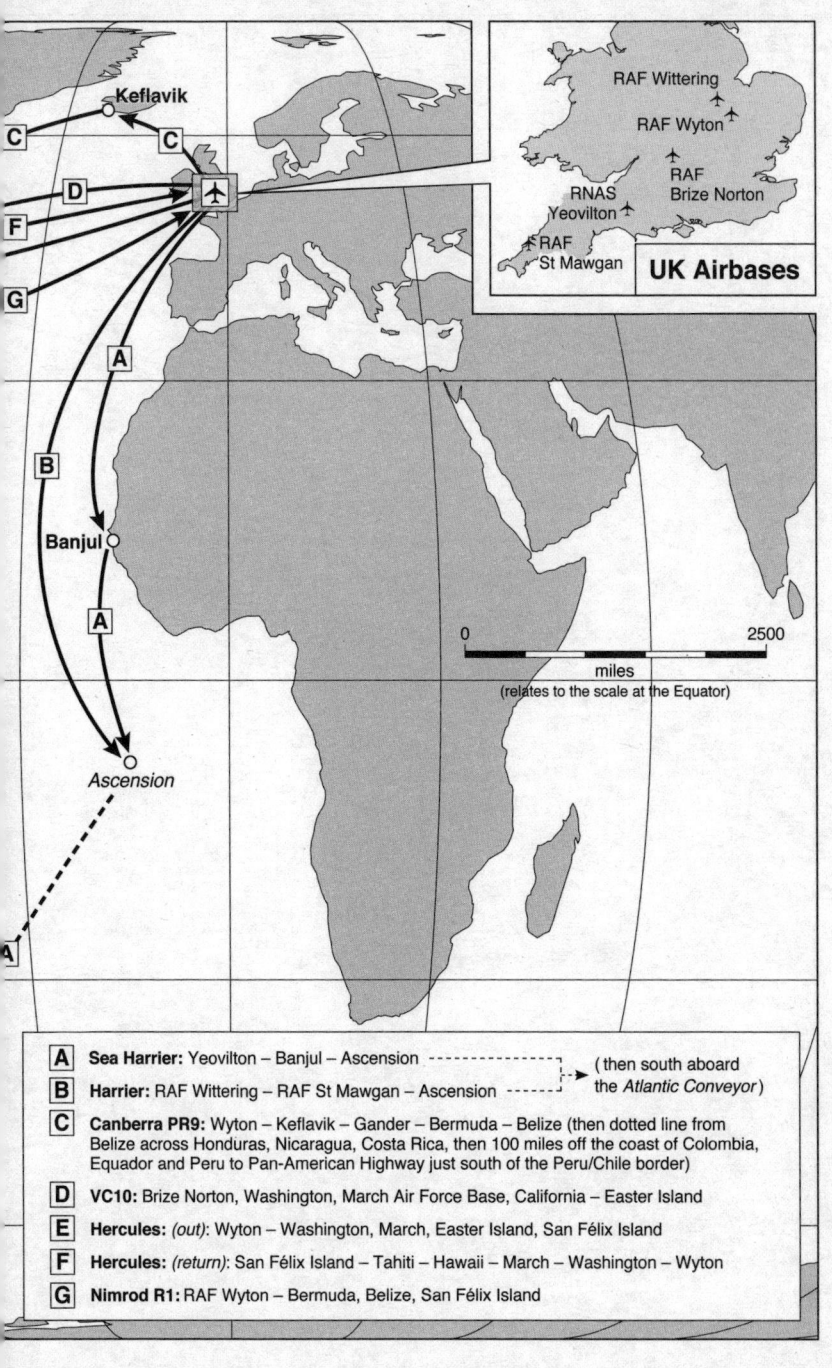

**UK Airbases**
- RAF Wittering
- RAF Wyton
- RNAS Yeovilton
- RAF Brize Norton
- RAF St Mawgan

Keflavik

Banjul

Ascension

0 — 2500
miles
(relates to the scale at the Equator)

| A | **Sea Harrier:** Yeovilton – Banjul – Ascension ------------ ┐ ( then south aboard |
| B | **Harrier:** RAF Wittering – RAF St Mawgan – Ascension ------ ┘→ the *Atlantic Conveyor* ) |
| C | **Canberra PR9:** Wyton – Keflavik – Gander – Bermuda – Belize (then dotted line from Belize across Honduras, Nicaragua, Costa Rica, then 100 miles off the coast of Colombia, Equador and Peru to Pan-American Highway just south of the Peru/Chile border) |
| D | **VC10:** Brize Norton, Washington, March Air Force Base, California – Easter Island |
| E | **Hercules:** *(out)*: Wyton – Washington, March, Easter Island, San Félix Island |
| F | **Hercules:** *(return)*: San Félix Island – Tahiti – Hawaii – March – Washington – Wyton |
| G | **Nimrod R1:** RAF Wyton – Bermuda, Belize, San Félix Island |

# PROLOGUE

Scramble!

*If I were you I'd buy the Sea Harrier.*

Admiral Sergey Gorshkov,
Admiral of the Fleet of the Soviet Union, 1967–85

*HMS* Hermes, *South Atlantic, 21 April 1982*

Lieutenant Simon Hargreaves checked his canopy was closed and locked. Beneath him, the flight deck pitched as the carrier turned into wind. By holding up five fingers against the cockpit perspex he confirmed to the aircraft handlers that his Martin-Baker Mk.10 ejection seat was armed and the safety pins stowed. He continued running through the pre-start checks.

*LP cock – on. Battery masters – both on. Check voltage. Jetpipe temperature.*

All good.

He turned on the booster pumps, selected START, pressed his stopwatch and punched the starter button. Immediately behind him he heard, and felt, the whine of the Rolls-Royce Pegasus engine spooling up. He set the throttle to idle and carried on working through the checklist, making sure his fighter's navigation system was aligned – vital if he was ever going to find his way back to 'Mother' out here over the South Atlantic, midway between Brazil and Namibia, over 1,000 miles from land in any direction.

Outside, the last ground locks were removed.

*Flying controls – full and free movement. Flaps . . . check.*

He could hardly believe his luck. The youngest and least experienced member of 800 Naval Air Squadron, he'd only been out of training for a couple of months. It was just weeks since he'd landed on board HMS *Hermes* for the very first time. And now he was being scrambled to intercept an unidentified radar contact approaching the Task Force from the southwest at 20,000 feet.

At 1130Z he'd been preparing to fly a training sortie. Fifteen minutes later, after the order to launch, the armourers had removed the training rounds from beneath the wings and sharpened his fighter's dark grey lines with a pair of ghost-grey AIM-9L Sidewinder heatseeking missiles. Live rounds. Beneath the fuselage was a pair of 30mm ADEN cannon. There hadn't been time to load them.

The shadower had been picked up at a range of 160 miles. But now it was almost on top of them.

*Trim at 5° nose up, check fuel, flaps – full.*

Hargreaves checked his canopy and ejection seat again. To his right, the Flight Deck Officer directing the launch signalled him to wind up the engine. Eyes on his instruments, Hargreaves advanced the throttle lever to 55% to make sure his engine rpm was within limits. After checking the engine nozzles, he placed the flat of his hand against the glass of his canopy to accept the launch.

Standing to his right, the FDO whipped down a green flag and crouched to the side of the take-off run that stretched ahead towards the ski-jump over the ship's bow.

The young fighter pilot slammed the throttle lever to the stops with his left hand. Engine gauges flicked round their dials in harness with the big Rolls-Royce turbofan winding up behind him. A second later, 10 tons of thrust began to overwhelm the brakes, scrubbing stationary rubber across the rough metal flight deck. Then Hargreaves released the brakes and the jet leapt forward, accelerating fiercely to 90 knots in just three seconds before pressing its pilot further down into his seat as it nosed up the ramp and over the bow. As soon as the cockpit cleared the deck he pulled the nozzle lever back to the short take-off stop then left the controls alone, allowing the Sea Harrier to arc through a ballistic trajectory as she accelerated to wingborne flight.

Capitán Luis Dupeyron saw it all from 20,000 feet as the Fuerza Aérea Argentina Boeing 707 banked to get a better view. After first locating the British fleet using weather radar, the crew of the big jet freighter, serial TC-91, made visual contact with the Royal Navy ships at 1138Z. But after a six-hour flight to find the Task Force, when Dupeyron, the Argentine Naval Observer on board, saw *Hermes* turning into wind below them he knew it was time to go. The curving white wake meant the British carrier was preparing to launch fighters. On Dupeyron's instruction, the 707 was soon climbing away through 35,000 feet, her pilots eking as much speed out of the old airliner as they could.

On paper, the SHAR could reach 40,000 feet two minutes after brakes off. In practice, with the target already turned tail and gaining altitude, Hargreaves didn't have a great deal of performance to spare. If he let impatience get the better of him and pulled the nose up, his speed would drop off, and rather than finding himself on the wing of the target he'd have to dive to build up speed again. He kept the speed high, resisted the temptation to try to climb too quickly, and was rewarded for it. Ahead, the distinctive shape of a Boeing 707 airliner began to resolve. As he approached more closely, so too did the pale blue roundels that adorned it. And the words FUERZA AÉREA ARGENTINA in black capitals painted behind the flight deck.

*Holy Schmoly*, he thought, *this isn't just an airliner off course, it's Argentine military.*

Hargreaves struggled to keep the surprise out of his voice as he reported what he'd found back to *Hermes*. 'TC-91,' he confirmed, reading the jet's serial number to them, partly to reassure himself he wasn't seeing things.

'A plane is coming!' shouted a crewman, his face glued to one of the small windows that ran up and down the Argentine freighter's cabin.

'Where?'

There was no time for an answer. Looming just off the 707's port wing was a Sea Harrier, blue and red roundels clearly visible against the dark sea grey. Armed, intentions unknown. Adrenalin coursed through the veins of everyone on board the big FAA transport. They knew they were defenceless in the face of the interceptor flying alongside them. The Sea Harrier manoeuvred lazily from one wing to the other like a cat toying with a mouse. But when the British fighter dropped back, out of sight from TC-91's cabin windows, the hearts of those on board beat a little faster still. It was from behind that the infrared seeker heads of the fighter's Sidewinder missiles would most easily lock on to the hot exhaust from the four turbojet engines. On the flight deck, the crew braced themselves for the impact of the missiles.

Hargreaves was gentle on the controls though. Hard manoeuvring would have cost him energy and seen him lose ground to his quarry. And as the 707 continued to climb towards 40,000 feet the Sea Harrier's performance advantage became even more marginal. Instead he watched them, the crew's faces peering out from portholes stitched along the pale blue cheatline that ran the length of the fuselage.

*Zero chance of escape*, he thought.

Twelve minutes after first formating on the Argentine jet, Hargreaves peeled away for the last time. At no point did he ever make any attempt to communicate with them, but there was never any doubt that they were at his mercy. *Next time*, he thought, *I might have to shoot this thing down.*

Five hours later, TC-91 touched down at Ezeiza Airport in northern Argentina, the eight passengers and crew relieved to have succeeded in locating the British fleet and to have survived their first encounter with the Fleet Air Arm. It had been an unsettling experience, though. *The coming confrontation*, realized one of the pilots on board, *will not be easy.* But, he thought, perhaps the British were also beginning to appreciate that recovering the Falkland Islands would be no walk in the park.

As the Royal Navy Task Force continued south, a message was passed from the British government to the Argentine Junta via a Swiss diplomatic back channel. It made clear that, should the Grupo 1 reconnaissance missions continue, their aircraft would be fired on.

Without warning.

# PART ONE

Task Force

*Upon my arrival in Berkeley Sound East Falkland, – I investigated the matters in question and finding them to be of the most inquisitous and illegal character, – I determined to break up and disperse this band of pirates, many of whom had been sent from the prisons of Buenos Ayres and Monte Video, and were thus let lose to prey upon a peacable and industrious part of our community.*

Captain Silas Duncan,
USS *Lexington*, 3 February 1832

# ONE

## On immediate notice to embark

*RNAS Yeovilton, 31 March 1982*

THE FIRST SIGN of trouble at Royal Naval Air Station Yeovilton, the Somerset headquarters of the Royal Navy's Fleet Air Arm, came late on a Wednesday night with a phone call from Scotland. The Operations Officer aboard HMS *Splendid* called wanting to know if FONAC (Flag Officer Naval Air Command) could arrange for a hydraulic pump to be transported from Devonport dockyard to Faslane, the Scottish home of the Navy's nuclear submarine force, by nine a.m. the following morning. *Splendid*, the Navy's newest nuclear attack boat, had been hauled off the trail of a Soviet Victor class hunter-killer and told to return to base with all despatch where she was now being stored for war. Yeovilton's duty Sea Heron, one of three old piston-engined De Havilland airliners used by the air station for hack work and VIP transport, was already committed, having battled her way through foul weather to deliver stores to Portsmouth. By 11.15 FONAC had made arrangements for a 750 Squadron Jetstream T2 from RNAS Culdrose in Cornwall to make the delivery to Faslane instead.

Half an hour later the phone rang again. The Department of Naval Air Warfare (DNAW) were calling from Ministry of Defence Main Building in London. Could a stripped-down Westland Wessex V helicopter, complete with crew and maintainers, be ready to load aboard a Royal Air Force Hercules bound for Ascension Island in the morning? There was no hint of what was to come. This remote mid-Atlantic outpost, one of the UK's last colonial possessions, was about to displace Chicago O'Hare as the world's busiest airfield. FONAC's telephone didn't stop ringing for the next three months.

And another British overseas territory was the cause of it all.

In Moody Brook Barracks, Port Stanley, the Commanding Officer of Naval Party 8901, the small detachment of Royal Marines charged with the defence of the Falkland Islands, told his men 'tomorrow you're all going to earn your pay'.

The next day, the first day of April, Lieutenant Commander Tim Gedge was sitting in a lecture hall in Gosport, listening to his new boss, Rear Admiral Derek Reffell, explain the intricacies of the naval redundancy programme. The Senior Service was to be savaged by swingeing cuts to its frontline imposed by the new Conservative Party Defence Secretary, John Nott. HMS *Invincible*, the Navy's brand-new aircraft carrier, was all but on her way to join the Royal Australian Navy, the number of destroyers and frigates was to be reduced by around a third, and HMS *Endurance*, the Antarctic Patrol Ship, was to be disposed of. It was only through the direct intervention of the First Sea Lord, Admiral Sir Henry Leach, that Nott had been persuaded of the need to retain the two assault ships HMS *Fearless* and HMS *Intrepid*. To have lost them alongside *Invincible* would have made Reffell's position as Flag Officer Third Flotilla, or FOF3, responsible for the Navy's carriers and assault ships, practically redundant too. But even with their stay of execution, another fact remained: with fewer ships, fewer people were needed to sail them.

As the Admiral continued, Gedge was pulled out of the presentation to take a phone call from the Commander in Chief Fleet's office. He must, he was told, report to CINCFLEET at Northwood HQ in northwest London in half an hour.

'I may be the aviator on the staff,' Gedge told them, 'but I don't have a helicopter. It'll probably take me two hours.'

'That's far too long,' came the reply.

Tim Gedge's soft-spoken manner and apparently gentle demeanour gave little indication that he was one of the Royal Navy's most experienced and accomplished fighter pilots. After discovering that the Glasgow University Air Squadron would pay for him to learn to fly while he studied for an engineering degree he was bitten hard by the flying bug. A year later aviation had so displaced engineering in his affections that he left academia altogether to follow in the footsteps of an uncle who'd flown seaplanes in the Navy in the 1930s.

After flying training he was posted to all-weather fighters, flying De Havilland Sea Vixens off HMS *Victorious* in the Far East. Recognizing his ability, the Navy sent him to the RAF's Central Flying School before posting him to RNAS Lossiemouth as the Qualified Flying Instructor on 764 Naval Air Squadron, the Fleet Air Arm's elite Air Warfare School. Returning to the frontline as QFI on 892 NAS, HMS *Ark Royal*'s F-4 Phantom squadron, he'd begun to plan for a career with BOAC when his eight-year short service naval commission came to an end. Faced with losing him to the airlines, the Navy offered him £1,500 to persuade him to extend his commission to twelve years. But it was poor compensation for the prospect of losing four years' worth of seniority with BOAC. Instead, he told them what it would take to keep him. The next morning he was called in to see 892's Commanding Officer.

'Tim,' the boss began, 'I've just had a very surprising call from London; as of eight a.m. you are on the General List and you're off to do the Air Warfare Instructor's course.'

There was no argument. *My bluff*, Gedge thought, *has been totally called*. And he wasn't unhappy about that at all. Now enjoying the security of a permanent commission, he completed the AWI course as 764's Senior Pilot before earning his watchkeeping tickets aboard the frigate HMS *Jupiter* in Singapore, and completing another tour with *Ark*'s Phantom squadron as Senior Pilot. Postings to Dartmouth as Aviation Officer at Britannia Royal Naval College and as Brigade Aviation Officer to the Royal Marines followed, but in 1979 he was sent to RAF Wittering to learn to fly the Harrier. The same year had seen the Royal Navy take delivery of its first British Aerospace Sea Harrier FRS.1. And Gedge had been flying the SHAR, as the Navy pilots quickly christened their new jump jet, until just two months earlier, when he'd joined FOF3 as fixed-wing adviser to the Admiral. As much as there was to do, he couldn't help feeling that his new office job paled a little in comparison to being a fighter pilot.

As he drove north in a black naval saloon borrowed from the Gosport motor transport pool, Gedge tuned in to BBC Radio 4. News bulletins included the latest reports on the simmering crisis in the South Atlantic, now nearly a fortnight old.

After an illegal landing by Argentine scrap merchant Constantino Davidoff on the British territory of South Georgia on 19 March, Margaret Thatcher's government despatched the ice patrol ship HMS *Endurance* to intervene, prompting a chorus of jingoistic headlines in the British press. A bit of provocative graffiti and the hoisting of the Argentine flag? A gunboat would teach them some respect. But signals intelligence soon reached London that perhaps Davidoff's salvage operation, already dependent on the support of the Argentine Navy who referred to the enterprise as Operation ALPHA, heralded an altogether more significant military interest in South Georgia and the neighbouring Falkland Islands. And Britain's response, or at least how it was perceived in Argentina, actually accelerated the process.

A week after the ALPHA landings, the Swiftsure class nuclear-powered hunter-killer submarine HMS *Superb* sailed from Gibraltar on Operation SARDIUS, prompting press reports of her departure. While SARDIUS would actually see *Superb* sail north towards the Shetland-Faroes gap to find and track a Soviet Victor II submarine, in Argentina, naval commanders assumed, not unreasonably, that *Superb* was on her way to the South Atlantic. Believing they'd triggered the despatch of the one thing capable of preventing Operation BLUE, a long-standing plan to occupy the Malvinas, the Admirals knew the seaborne invasion of the Falkland Islands was now a race against time. They had ten days before they expected *Superb* to arrive. The British did nothing to disabuse them of that because, as the First Sea Lord put it, 'it did not profit us to do so'. In fact, the first boat ordered south was *Superb*'s sister ship, HMS *Spartan*, on 1 April. The confusion was immaterial. All that mattered was that for the Argentine Navy's Commander in Chief Admiral Jorge Anaya, the price he'd extracted for supporting General Leopoldo Galtieri's accession to power in December 1981 – the new leader's blessing for Operation BLUE – must now be paid without delay. Or the opportunity would be lost.

Arriving at Northwood by lunchtime, Gedge parked and was taken straight through to the Commander in Chief's office. CINCFLEET himself, Admiral Sir John Fieldhouse, was absent, but the combined presence of so many senior naval commanders waiting for him was scarcely less imposing. After a cursory welcome, the questions began.

'If we are to go operational, what assets would FOF3 wish to send?'

'Where are we going?' Gedge asked with deliberate ingenuousness. 'What's the operation?'

'We can't tell you that. It's too highly classified and you don't have the security clearance.'

'Assuming we're going to the Falklands,' Gedge volunteered, pausing only to clock some slightly nervous blinking among his audience, 'we need to send all the carriers and all our fighter aircraft' – knowing full well that meant just two carriers, HMS *Invincible* and HMS *Hermes*, and twenty Sea Harriers – 'and we need to look at whether we take anti-submarine aircraft based on intelligence.' Gedge was queried about the numbers of Sea Harriers. Over the previous two years he'd embarked his squadron aboard both ships and knew their capabilities well. 'Twelve in *Hermes*' – the larger of the two carriers – 'and eight in *Invincible*.'

Gedge was instructed to return to Fort Southwick, the old Napoleonic-era fort overlooking the Solent from which FOF3 conducted its business, and to ensure that the Sea Harrier squadrons were ready for possible action.

'What should I tell the COs?'

'You can't tell them anything. Just make sure that they're on immediate notice to embark.'

As Gedge drove back to Portsmouth with as much speed as possible, the BBC was reporting that an invasion of the Falkland Islands was supposedly imminent.

It wasn't the first time the Royal Navy had been asked to forestall the possibility of Argentine action against British South Atlantic territories. In 1976, HMS *Endurance* discovered a small detachment of Argentine soldiers on Southern Thule. In direct response, nothing beyond a protest from the Foreign & Commonwealth Office was done. But, as talks between Britain and Argentina over the future of the Falkland Islands got underway the following year, Operation JOURNEYMAN saw the despatch of HMS *Phoebe* and HMS *Alacrity* towards the South Atlantic. And while the two frigates and their Royal Fleet Auxiliary support ships loitered at a considerable distance from the Falklands, Britain's first nuclear submarine, HMS *Dreadnought*, patrolled within 4 or 5 miles of the islands, prompting a conversation within the Argentine Admiralty about whether their own submarine force could do anything about it. The answer, despite the recent introduction of new diesel-electric submarines bought from Germany, was no.

The frustrating truth for Argentina was that it was no more able to contest British naval power in 1977 than it had been in 1833 when two Royal Navy warships, HMS *Clio* and HMS *Tyne*, re-established British sovereignty over the islands.

In 1774, after less than a century of frankly half-hearted exchanges of sovereignty with France and Spain, the British left their settlement at Port Egmont on West Falkland, naively hoping that a plaque asserting that 'Falkland's Ysland, with this fort, the storehouses, wharf, harbour, bays, and creeks thereunto belonging, are the sole right and property of His Most Sacred Majesty George III' would be sufficient to retain possession.

In Britain's absence, control of the former Spanish settlement of Puerto Soledad in East Falkland passed to the United Provinces of the Río de la Plata, newly independent from Spain in 1816. In reality, it wasn't much of a bauble; little more than a port in a storm for a lawless American sealing fleet. But when Captain Silas Duncan of the US Navy's twenty-four-gun sloop-of-war USS *Lexington* intervened in an attempt by Buenos Aires to impose a little order on the behaviour of his countrymen, his response was to destroy Puerto Soledad and declare the islands 'Free of all Government'. The vacuum left in *Lexington*'s wake was promptly filled by *Clio* and *Tyne* and the islands had remained in British hands ever since.

The United Provinces of the Río de la Plata formally became the Argentine Republic in 1860. And, unlike in 1833 and 1977, in 1982 Admiral Anaya knew he had a brief window in which to reverse the historic injustice and humiliation suffered by his country before the arrival of any meaningful British naval force that might stop him.

Back at Fort Southwick, Tim Gedge phoned the two Sea Harrier squadron bosses. He caught Lieutenant Commander Andy Auld, the taciturn Scot who'd recently taken the reins of 800 Naval Air Squadron, at Yeovilton. 800 were supposed to be going on Easter leave the following day. Their counterparts on 801 had already dispersed, so their piratical CO, Lieutenant Commander Nigel 'Sharkey' Ward required a little more tracking down. Gedge told them both that leave was cancelled. Both squadrons needed to be ready to embark aboard the carriers. Auld and Ward had put two and two together and knew what was brewing, but when they asked Gedge for confirmation, his hands were tied by his instructions from Northwood.

'Listen to the BBC,' he told them.

With the Argentine invasion force still at sea, President Reagan, after hours of trying, was able to speak to General Galtieri. The President had no desire to see war between two allies but told Galtieri that Argentina would unavoidably be seen as the aggressor. In an hour-long conversation with the General, Reagan left him in no doubt about Britain's determination to fight. Following the call, Galtieri spoke to Admiral Anaya, the driving force behind an invasion now codenamed Operation ROSARIO. It's too late for second thoughts, Anaya is reported to have told him, because his ships were already in formation off the Falklands.

At 2.55 a.m. on 2 April, FONAC took a call from Northwood HQ telling them that *Invincible* and *Hermes* had been brought to immediate notice to sail. Each required an expanded Sea Harrier squadron and a full complement of Westland Sea King HAS.5 anti-submarine helicopters. Whether or not to embark the 'Junglies', the troop-carrying Sea King HC.4s, was yet to be decided.

# TWO

## A ferocious display

CAPTAIN JEREMY 'JJ' Black and his wife were sound asleep at home in their picturesque Hampshire farmhouse when the phone rang. Black cursed as he reached over to silence it. It was four a.m. He picked up.

'Is that Captain Black?'

'Yes,' he replied, his voice betraying his irritation at the early morning disturbance.

'I have just received a signal from the Commander in Chief ordering *Invincible* to be brought to four hours' notice for sea by twelve hundred hours tomorrow.'

'What for?' he asked, recognizing the voice of the ship's Duty Officer.

'Oh, there's some trouble brewing in the Falkland Islands, a landing by the Argentinians or something.'

JJ Black had been Captain of HMS *Invincible*, the Navy's newest aircraft carrier, for just three months. And on the face of it, his qualifications for the job were unusual. After joining the Navy aged thirteen in the immediate aftermath of the Second World War, he had, by the time of his nineteenth birthday, been to war in Korea aboard HMS *Belfast* and patrolled the jungles of Borneo with the Royal Marines in search of Communist insurgents. In the years that followed he'd fired the 15-inch guns of HMS *Vanguard*, Britain's last battleship, and served aboard destroyers, cruisers and aircraft carriers before being given command of a coastal minesweeper, HMS *Fiskerton*, in the Far East, during which time he came under heavy fire while taking part in the dramatic rescue of Western hostages from terrorists in Brunei. Command of destroyers and staff jobs in the MoD followed. But Black, a Gunnery Officer, had never been an aviator. In the Royal Navy, unlike their US counterparts, it was not a prerequisite for the Captain of an aircraft carrier. That Black had achieved the rank despite its absence from his CV, though, was a mark of the high regard in which he was held by the Senior Service.

'Make the General Recall,' Black instructed, and told the Duty Officer to inform *Invincible*'s Heads of Department to get to work. Now wide awake, his mind cycled through all that needed to be done to bring the 20,000-ton ship back to life, not least the formidable task of reassembling the ship's company, currently scattered far and wide on leave following a successful series of exercises in challenging weather off Scotland and Norway.

Black couldn't help but wonder whether, after the early morning excitement, it wouldn't all just blow over. A phone call to his friend Admiral David Halifax, Chief of Staff to CINCFLEET at Northwood, put paid to that notion. 'This is for real,' Halifax told him. 'Jump to it.'

Before heading into Portsmouth, another concern nagged at the Captain. His daughter and her friend were supposed to be celebrating their eighteenth birthdays with 120 of their closest friends on *Invincible*'s quarterdeck that evening. If Wellington could attend a ball the evening before the Battle of Waterloo, then he had every intention of holding a party for his daughter before his ship sailed, but he thought it might be prudent to make contingency plans. Eating a bowl of cereal, he walked round to his next-door neighbour who, conveniently, worked as Supply Commander to the Royal Naval Barracks in Portsmouth. Black explained that there was a chance he'd have to relocate his daughter's party to the barracks wardroom. 'I'd be so grateful if you could make the arrangements.' Black thanked him and, still eating his breakfast, returned home, leaving a surprised but seemingly unfazed neighbour in his wake.

That Friday morning, the atmosphere in the Sea Harrier squadron crewrooms was charged. Following the heads-up from Gedge the previous day, the two frontline Sea Harrier squadron bosses, Andy

Auld and Sharkey Ward, had each received a wake-up phone call around the same time as JJ Black.

When the Duty Officer of 899 NAS, the Sea Harrier's headquarters and training squadron, called his CO, Lieutenant Commander Neill Thomas, to tell him the balloon had gone up, the boss was unconvinced. 'Yeah?' he responded. 'Pull the other one.' Then he put the phone down and went back to bed. He needed to: along with most of his squadron, he'd only enjoyed about three hours' sleep. The squadron's run ashore the previous evening had got a little out of hand when a group of football fans took exception to the sight of 899's squadron boss sporting a grass skirt and singing on stage in Bristol's Beer Cellar. After the police intervened and A&E had patched up those requiring it, two coaches finally delivered them back to Yeovilton at around half past midnight.

It took another phone call from the Duty Officer to persuade Thomas he really had to get up. The 899 boss dressed quickly and headed in to work.

800's Air Engineering Officer, or AEO, had already called his counterpart on 899 to inform him that the two frontline squadrons needed three of his jets. The effort to fill their cockpits was also in full swing. After less than twenty-four hours' leave in the States, Lieutenant Al Curtis was already on his way back to the UK aboard an RAF VC10. 845 Squadron would have a Wessex helicopter waiting at Brize Norton to bring him back to his unit. At Yeovilton, Sharkey Ward and Andy Auld were like two playground football captains picking teams. Even with Curtis en route, Ward was still down a couple of players. His Senior Pilot (aka SPLOT) had discovered he was allergic to *Invincible*'s air conditioning system. While he received treatment he wouldn't be deploying. In his place, Ward bagged Robin Kent, one of Neill Thomas's instructors from 899. Grateful for the experience they added, he was also given John 'EJ' Eyton-Jones, Paul Barton and Mike Broadwater from 899. Then there was Major Willard T. McAtee of the United States Marine Corps, 899's AWI.

A veteran of dangerous close air support missions over Vietnam in the propellor-driven Rockwell OV-10 Bronco, McAtee had arrived at Yeovilton for an exchange tour with 899 NAS less than a week after EJ. The two became firm friends on the basis that, when McAtee risked being disciplined for querying the wisdom of his instructors by using phrases like 'Are you shitting me?', EJ could dig him out by explaining 'What he *meant* to say was . . .' EJ was also quickly on hand to sort things out when McAtee arrived unannounced in a Sea Harrier at the MoD's Farnborough test centre offering, by way of explanation, 'Well, I screwed up. I'm lost.' But the Navy quickly realized that Willy McAtee was a rough diamond, not only a vastly experienced Harrier pilot but also a Weapons Instructor who'd arrived in the UK armed with a copy of the Marine Corps TACMAN, the tactical manual detailing sight settings, bomb clearances and weapons release parameters for the AV-8A. They gave him a week's training in the peculiarities of low-level navigation in the UK and made him the squadron AWI.

And Ward told him to come with 801.

'OK, cool,' replied McAtee, who was of the view that you couldn't have a war without inviting the Marines.

As an American exchange officer, McAtee, alongside the Fleet Air Arm chain of command, also had an obligation to the Marine Corps. He called the US Embassy in London to speak to the Assistant Naval Attaché, a Marine grunt full Colonel.

'Colonel,' he said, 'I'm packing my stuff and going to war, so you won't be hearing from me for a while.'

'You're doing what?'

'I'm going to war.'

'What are you talking about?'

'You know, the Falklands.'

'Don't move.'

'I'm going with the boys,' McAtee told him.

While McAtee was trying to force the issue with his superiors, Neill Thomas hit a brick wall with his own. Despite long experience as a naval fighter pilot and, with 899 divvied up between 800 and 801, no longer having any kind of meaningful squadron to run, the Navy told him he was staying put. They regarded the idea of sending an extra Commanding Officer to either 800 or 801, each of which already had a perfectly good one, as an embarrassment. 'I'll be a good boy,' he told them, 'won't tread on any toes . . .' But as desperate as he was to go, he was getting nowhere. Instead he turned his attention to trying to rustle up more jets.

At Fort Southwick, Tim Gedge was already doing just that and going about things in a characteristically meticulous fashion. In flawlessly neat handwriting, he produced a thorough audit of the status of the Sea Harrier force. He'd recommended to CINCFLEET sending twenty jets. As well as the necessary airframes and pilots, he also had to make sure the squadrons had sufficient weaponry, radars and avionics. He tallied up the contents of the two carriers' magazines. With seventy-five 1,000lb bombs on board, *Hermes* had room for another twenty-four. With thirty-six, *Invincible* could manage just another twelve. Both ships could take another 3,000 rounds of 30mm ammunition. Between them, they had sixty-seven AIM-9G Sidewinder heatseeking missiles. One hundred more were to be delivered to Portsmouth dockyard by Monday morning.

For now, he discovered, he was short of two of the twenty Blue Fox radar sets he needed for the SHARs to be able to employ their weapons effectively.

With 899 split between 800 and 801, each frontline squadron was now eight jets strong. That was all that Sharkey's expanded squadron needed for *Invincible*. To provide 800 with twelve airframes, Gedge could scrape one more aeroplane out of 899, and bring a couple out of long-term storage at RAF St Athan, where a number of brand-new jets were kept as attrition reserves. Then, potentially, there were SHARs being used for trials work by the Aeroplane & Armament Experimental Establishment (A&AEE) at Boscombe Down.

At lunchtime, the BBC's *World at One* reported that the Falkland Islands were now in the hands of the Argentine Junta.

Three hours later, in a ferocious display of jet noise and sea spray, eight of the Sea Harriers allocated to 800 Squadron embarked on HMS *Hermes* as she was tied alongside at Portsmouth.

The 28,000-ton carrier was hardly in the first flush of youth. She'd begun life in 1944 as HMS *Elephant*, when her keel was laid down at the Vickers Armstrong shipyard in Barrow-in-Furness. Early on in what was to be a protracted build, she was renamed *Hermes* to perpetuate the name of the world's first purpose-built 'airplane carrier'. The new *Hermes* didn't then join the fleet until 1959. Since then she'd served as a strike carrier armed with De Havilland Sea Vixens and Blackburn Buccaneers throughout the sixties, then a helicopter assault ship through the early seventies, before emerging in 1976 after a refit as an anti-submarine specialist. By the summer of 1981 she'd acquired the distinctive-looking ski-jump over the bow that signalled the addition of the Sea Harrier to her air group. It only added further character to the lines of a ship that seemed composed more of protrusions, overhangs, appendages and afterthoughts than smooth steel.

Beside her on the dock was a shanty town of cranes, conveyor belts, Portakabins, containers and a relay race of trucks delivering stores and weaponry. Two lorries carried nothing but timber that would be used to repair battle damage. A skip stencilled 'SCRAP' sat next to the starboard forward gangway; someone had painted out the 'S'. But for all the air of the reclamation yard she had about her, the overall effect was striking. She looked purposeful and intimidating. Now, after nearly eight months of testing exercises on both sides of the Atlantic under her hard-charging Captain, Lyn Middleton, a South African former Buccaneer pilot, *Hermes* was due a lick of paint and a little TLC. After returning to Portsmouth less than two weeks earlier her island – the superstructure located on the starboard side of her flight deck that was home to the ship's bridge, Flyco (Flying Control), and her radar and communications masts – was clad in scaffolding. Her grey hull was still streaked with rust. The larger of the two carriers sailing south, *Hermes*, for all that she already looked like she'd been through a war, would be the flagship.

In the end, Neill Thomas was told he'd be joining her. A combined effort by him, his AEO and Tim Gedge at FOF3 had produced four more aeroplanes for *Hermes*. But now Andy Auld's twelve-strong Sea

Harrier squadron only had eleven pilots. As well as a pair of instructors, Thomas had already provided 800 with two of his students, but in an ideal world you wanted about three pilots for every two jets. 'What's the point,' he argued, 'of having the aeroplanes on board if you can't fly them?' And he volunteered immediately.

His persistence rewarded, the men chosen to join him were a naval test pilot drafted in from Boscombe Down, Sharkey Ward's designated replacement as CO 801, and another 899 student, Flight Lieutenant Dave Morgan, an RAF exchange pilot who over the course of the day had been told he wasn't going, then that he was going but not flying, before, like Thomas, finally being given the nod. Morgan had covered about a third of the Sea Harrier operational flying training course.

Reluctantly, JJ Black decided that he should move his daughter's party to the wardroom of the naval barracks. He had no concerns about *Invincible*'s ability to host a party as the ship's company stored for war, but he imagined what the press might make of it and realized it probably wasn't quite the image the Navy wanted to project. But it didn't stop him getting changed into full mess undress tailcoat and enjoying the occasion.

Black's determination to project an air of calm, confidence and normality would serve him and his crew well over the months ahead.

Sharkey Ward's Sea Harriers were scheduled to embark in the morning. Each was carried towards a vertical landing on a broiling pillar of 21,500lb of jet thrust that churned up the surface of the sea below. Their dramatic arrival would only add to the consternation of the archaeologists raising the wreck of Henry VIII's flagship *Mary Rose* from the bottom of the Solent that had already been caused by 800's SHARs.

Nothing could have been further from Ward's mind as he clambered out of the cockpit and bounded down to the deck. The squadron boss relished the prospect of what he'd decided would be a 'limited war'.

After successive tours flying the F-4 Phantom from *Ark Royal*, Ward, as boss of 700A NAS, the Sea Harrier Intensive Flying Trials

Unit, had played a central role in the introduction of its replacement. A short, sharp dust-up, he thought, might offer a chance to prove to doubters what the Navy's new vertical take-off fighter, in the hands of the Fleet Air Arm's finest, might be capable of. And remind both the public and politicians of how much they were needed.

For all the unshakeable confidence he had in the SHAR, Ward also knew that, still relatively new into service, there was room for improvement. He put in a phone call to Tim Gedge at FOF3 with a list of requirements. It was one of the more straightforward requests Gedge had to deal with.

# THREE

## Famous the world over

ON SATURDAY MORNING, Tim Gedge took a call from a payphone in Southampton. At the other end of the line, standing on the jetty shoving ten-pence pieces into the slot, was an AEO Gedge had known a few years earlier during his tour as SPLOT on 764 Squadron. The AEO needed to speak to a helicopter expert. But with much of the FOF3 aviation staff already on its way to join the lead elements of the Task Force in Gibraltar, Gedge was on his own. He listened as his former colleague explained that he'd been tasked with constructing two flight decks for P&O's flagship, the SS *Canberra*.

Looking around the empty office, Gedge told him, 'I'm the helicopter expert,' before the engineer began to run out of change. After they'd tried and failed to organize a reverse charge call, Gedge called him back in his phone box. An hour later, Gedge had chinagraph drawings of *Canberra*'s layout spread over his desk. But there was a problem.

Less than twenty-four hours after the invasion, the government had in place the legal instruments it needed to requisition merchant ships in support of the Task Force. In a process labelled STUFT – ships taken up from trade – ferries, container ships, tugs, oil-rig support ships, trawlers, refrigerated cargo ships, tankers and cruiseliners were pressed into action as troopships, hospital ships, minesweepers, repair ships and helicopter carriers. In total, fifty-two ships from thirty-three different companies joined the STUFT programme. The most spectacular of these, and the first on the MoD's shopping list, was the *Canberra*. On 1 April, before the Argentinians had even set foot on the Falklands, representatives from P&O had been asked to attend a meeting 'within the hour'. They were questioned in detail about the ship, already earmarked to transport 3 Commando Brigade south. And about whether or not she might be converted to operate helicopters. Now the man given the job of ensuring she could was struggling.

'I can't make the flight deck forward,' his old colleague told him.

Building a flight deck amidships on top of *Canberra*'s swimming pool was going to be easy enough, but because the deck immediately forward of the ship's bridge wasn't flat, it would have to be built up with scaffolding. The half-moon-shaped landing pad *could* be made level, but only using greater lengths of scaffolding, which would mean they were insufficiently strong. He was going round in circles. Flat or level, but not both.

'What angle can you make it?' Gedge asked him.

'I can make it flat, but it's going to have a slope of about five degrees.'

Gedge approved it without hesitation. During his tour with the Royal Marines, he'd learned to fly a Wessex V helicopter. As part of the conversion course he'd practised landings in sloping fields. 'If I can land a helicopter on a five-degree slope, then any frontline pilot can do it.'

Gedge wasn't the only one winging it. The Navy was improvising too. There was much more at stake for the Senior Service than just the fate of the Falkland Islands.

*Invincible* and *Hermes* were all that was left of the Royal Navy's once mighty fleet of aircraft carriers. After announcing Britain's withdrawal from East of Suez, in 1966 Defence Secretary Denis Healey also cancelled the Navy's plans for the first of a new generation of carriers called CVA-01. At the same time, recognizing that even a reduced fleet needed more substantial command and control and helicopter capability than that which was on offer from mere frigates and destroyers, Healey supported plans for a new class of ship. These quickly evolved into a design for an 18,000-ton through-deck cruiser. Although not, at the time, labelled an aircraft carrier, the proposed new cruiser looked very like one. A flight deck ran the full length of the ship. From the outset, provision was made to operate 'Kestrel' vertical take-off jets. Three of the new ships were ordered, but by 1982 only *Invincible* had been delivered. And her sale to the Royal Australian Navy at a knockdown price had already been agreed.

A crimson flag striped with white flew above Semaphore Tower. 'Clear the Channel', it warned mariners, 'big ship in movement'. At 1010Z on Monday, 5 April, Captain JJ Black reached the bridge of HMS *Invincible* and was told that all his ship's departments had reported 'Ready for Sea'. Five minutes later the 20,000-ton carrier slipped her moorings and turned to leave the harbour. Ahead of him, perched on the ramp like the figurehead of a square-rigged man-o'-war, was one of 801's Sea Harriers. For such a large warship, *Invincible* looked svelte, clean and modern; less bruising than *Hermes*, which half an hour later followed *Invincible* out to sea.

The Southsea front was packed with wellwishers cheering and waving banners. Rod Stewart's 'Sailing', a song forever connected to the Royal Navy after being used to introduce a landmark BBC documentary series about HMS *Ark Royal*, played over the ship's broadcast. Black swallowed hard, deeply moved by the public's support and the faith that they placed in him, his ship and her crew. But he had little inkling of the task that lay ahead or even of the Navy's ability to succeed. The burden of responsibility weighed heavy on him.

After the shock and outrage caused by the invasion, the government's forceful reaction and the almost impossibly rapid despatch of a Carrier Battle Group seemed to have galvanized the country. The occupation of the islands was a setback for sure, but it was now time to teach the Argentinians a lesson. And, intoxicated by the spectacle of the Navy's departure, the public seemed to feel that the job was as good as done. If, just a week earlier, few people had heard of the Falkland Islands, there was even less understanding of the scale of the military challenge now facing British forces. The MoD's own planning, however, spelled it out.

In the mid-seventies, when fears of Argentine aggression prompted the despatch of HMS *Dreadnought* as part of Operation JOURNEY-MAN, other options and potential threats were examined, from the possibility of Argentina organizing a 'Green March' and overtaking the islands, as Morocco had done in Spanish Sahara, through an unarmed civilian invasion to the deployment of an SAS team. But, as the Defence Operational Planning Staff pointed out in 1976, if diplomacy and deterrence failed, distance, the probable denial of South American airfields, a lack of diversion airfields, the quality of the Port Stanley airstrip and lack of in-flight weather updates ruled out rapid reinforcement by air and made it impossible to mount long-range maritime reconnaissance. Even if a C-130 Hercules *were* to attempt the journey from Ascension, the closest British airfield nearly 4,000 miles away, the distance was such that it could only do so carrying just thirty troops. There would be no fuel for a return journey. 'The only way,' the planners reported, 'of providing combat aircraft capability in the Falkland Islands would be either deploying HMS *Ark Royal* or by using Harrier aircraft transported by sea.' Faced with an invasion, the task of recapturing the islands would 'require a major amphibious operation involving all our amphibious forces, a task force escort including HMS *Ark Royal* and substantial logistic support'.

By the summer of 1981, with *Ark Royal* and her powerful air group of Phantoms and Buccaneers no longer at the Navy's disposal, the MoD's options were more limited. If Argentina mounted a full-scale military occupation of the Falklands and a large naval task force led by an Invincible class carrier was sent in response, 'there could be no certainty that such a force could retake the Dependency'. Retaking the islands after an Argentine invasion, the paper concluded, 'is barely militarily viable and would present formidable problems'.

Following the invasion, British planners once again considered the possibilities. These ranged from the prospect of blockading Argentine ports by scuttling ships in the approaches to launching Vulcan raids against mainland targets. Perhaps most radical of all was the notion of an operation to seize and occupy land in Tierra del Fuego. It would undoubtedly, the Defence Policy Staff document argued, be a 'severe blow for Junta' but at the same time would also 'greatly reduce capacity for subsequent operations against Argentine Forces on Falkland Islands'. Every option other than sending a naval task force to blockade the islands, then evict the occupying force, looked likely either to be ineffective or to pose greater problems than it solved.

Like Sharkey Ward, the Admiralty realized that the Argentine invasion of the Falklands might present an opportunity to prove a point. From the onset of the crisis, the Navy had been the driving force behind the bullish British response. Still reeling from John Nott's 1981 Defence Review, feeling misunderstood and undervalued, this was a situation almost uniquely constructed to ensure that only the Navy could offer a solution. And in the days before the Argentine landing, with the Cabinet still at odds over how to respond, when the Prime Minister asked the First Sea Lord 'Could we really recapture the islands if they were invaded?', Admiral Sir Henry Leach had left her in no doubt at all and departed the meeting with the authority needed to assemble the Task Force.

The Argentine invasion of the Falklands couldn't have offered a better opportunity for the Navy to demonstrate its value. Eight thousand miles away from the UK, and just 300 miles from southern Argentina, they were beyond the range of the Royal Air Force to intervene and, without the Air Force as a means of delivery, the Army too.

Many still thought that, after witnessing a sufficiently impressive show of strength, the Argentinians would back down. But not all. During a brief trip home on Sunday, the day before they sailed, JJ Black had told his wife Pam that the positions of the leaders of both countries were already too entrenched. He was certain his ship would fight.

Tim Gedge, too, was sure it was war. Watching from Portsdown Hill, standing in front of Fort Southwick, he saw both carriers sail, but from his high vantage point it was a distant spectacle. Away from the cheering crowds and thronging intensity of Old Portsmouth, he was alone with his thoughts. His boss, Rear Admiral Derek Reffell, had been the last to leave *Invincible* before she sailed. Both the carriers and the amphibious assault ships upon which the success of Operation

CORPORATE was dependent were Reffell's responsibility as FOF3. It made little sense to Gedge, or indeed many others inside Fort Southwick, that he hadn't been given command of the Task Force itself.

But Gedge's mixed feelings about the departure of the carriers were more personal and immediate. As he watched the ships pass the Hard, South Parade Pier and the Round Tower and disappear out to sea, it was impossible not to linger on the thought that he was the only member of his squadron who'd been left behind.

At a recommissioning ceremony in 1980, attended by the First Sea Lord, senior Admirals, the Captains of both *Invincible* and *Hermes* and sixteen former Commanding Officers of 800 NAS, Tim Gedge had become the first Commanding Officer of a frontline Sea Harrier FRS.1 unit. He'd conducted their first embarkation on HMS *Invincible* when his embryonic unit was just two jets strong. The following year, 800 was the first squadron to operate from *Hermes* after she emerged from a refit with the striking new ski-jump used to help launch the new jump jets. Under his leadership 800 NAS had displayed the SHAR at Farnborough, strafed and bombed the ranges, kept tabs on the Soviet Navy, and been tested in mock dogfights against the best the USAF had to offer. And Gedge had come to understand just what a remarkable aeroplane the Harrier had become.

The Hawker Harrier was unique. And by the time Gedge first climbed into the cockpit of a Harrier T.4 at 233 Operational Conversion Unit at RAF Wittering, it was already famous the world over. Of scores of efforts around the world to build a practical fixed-wing vertical take-off and landing aeroplane, only the Harrier had been successful. There were aeroplanes with banks of lift jets buried in the fuselage, powerful turboprop tailsitters that required their pilots to descend to earth backwards like a rocket returning to the launch pad, swivelling wings and tilting engine pods, but nothing that matched the essential simplicity of the Harrier.

It was the last machine to emerge from under the watchful eye of Hawker boss Sir Sydney Camm, who had previously been responsible for an illustrious line of fighter aircraft that included the Hurricane, Typhoon, Tempest, Sea Fury, Sea Hawk and Hunter. Evidence of a family resemblance between the Harrier and the Hunter could be seen in the profile of the two aeroplanes' vertical tails. Camm wasn't inclined to change anything unless he had to. It's ironic, therefore, that Hawker's last great design before it became subsumed within British Aerospace was a machine as revolutionary as the Harrier. It wasn't at all how the legendary designer had planned it.

Instead he had had his hopes pinned on a large supersonic fighter design labelled the P.1121 – a successor to the Hunter, then in full production and being sold to air forces around the world. But when, in 1957, 'Statement on Defence', a White Paper produced by Defence Secretary Duncan Sandys, announced that the RAF would require no new manned fighters and that Britain's air defence would instead be provided by missiles, it was clear that the P.1121 was dead in the water. Without a domestic order from the RAF, there was no hope of export success. Work on the prototype, funded privately by the company, was abandoned.

Without the P.1121, Ralph Hooper, one of Hawker's young engineers, was at something of a loose end until a brochure for a new jet engine crossed his desk and fired his imagination.

A sort of Frankenstein-like cobbling together of the front of the big Olympus engine with the rear of a smaller Orpheus, the Bristol Engine Company's BE53 was inspired by the work of a Frenchman, Michel Wibault, on a vertical take-off fighter concept he called Le Gyroptère. Wibault's design was complicated, but another giant of the British aviation industry, Sir Stanley Hooker, whose career had taken him from the Rolls-Royce Merlin engine that powered the Spitfire, Hurricane and Lancaster to the mighty Bristol Olympus engine that powered the Avro Vulcan, saw its potential. By using a pair of swivelling nozzles to direct compressed air from the fan of the Olympus engine, Hooker's BE53 could produce lift to supplement that produced by the wing. He labelled the principle vectored thrust.

To Ralph Hooper's eyes, that looked as if it could create a short-take-off aircraft. But in discussions with his colleague John Fozard, they realized that if they also directed the thrust from the rear of the engine through another pair of nozzles, they then had an engine that, by producing four columns of jet thrust, might power a *vertical* take-off and landing aircraft.

Hooper designed an aircraft around the modified engine and

labelled it the P.1127. It was already identifiably the same machine as the Harrier that followed. Camm invited Hooker to see the drawings and told him he'd persuaded the Hawker board to finance a flying prototype. A year later, as they planned the first flight, Hooker had to confess to Camm that his engine, now christened the Pegasus, was producing less thrust than required for a vertical take-off. Camm flew into a rage, while Hooker tried to placate him with the possibility that, for the first flight at least, the P.1127 might simply use the runway like any other aeroplane.

'Why should we want to do that?' Camm barked.

'To prove that the P.1127 has good handling qualities as a conventional aircraft?'

'All Hawker aircraft handle perfectly,' Camm insisted. 'There's no need to waste time on that. The first flight will be vertical take-off!'

Of the machine that evolved over the next twenty years into the Sea Harrier, Gedge could vouch for Sir Sydney's appraisal of its handling. But at a farewell ceremony at the end of January he'd been towed around Yeovilton sitting astride a 1,000lb bomb and been saluted with a six-strong flypast by the squadron's Sea Harriers, then handed over the reins of 800 NAS to Andy Auld. Gedge's landing aboard *Hermes* on 30 December 1981, following two months of exercises with the US Navy, would be his last – 'subject', noted the Squadron Record Book, 'to the intervention of fate'.

With *Invincible* and *Hermes* gone, Gedge swallowed his disappointment and returned to his desk in Fort Southwick. At the insistence of the First Sea Lord, the fleet, come hell or high water, had been ready to sail on Monday morning. But with the Carrier Battle Group on its way, the job of making sure it was also capable of winning a war against an enemy who was not well understood began in earnest.

# FOUR

## A revolution in naval doctrine

ON PAPER, THE Fuerza Aérea Argentina was a potent force. With a frontline over 200 combat aircraft strong, they were acknowledged by the MoD to be a professional, well-equipped fighting force. Supersonic Dassault Mirage III fighters, Israeli-built IAI Daggers and American Douglas A-4 Skyhawks might no longer have been at the cutting edge of fighter design, but all were battle-proven machines, having earned their spurs in convincing fashion in the Middle East and Vietnam. Supplementing the fast jets were long-ranged but long-in-the-tooth British-built Canberra bombers and Argentina's own FMA IA-58 Pucará, a rugged twin-turboprop ground attack aircraft.

Ranged against them were the twenty SHARs aboard *Hermes* and *Invincible*. It looked like a very thin line. Eight thousand miles from home, the safety of the carriers was paramount. The most immediate threat to them came not from the Air Force but from the Comando de Aviación Naval Argentina (COAN), the Argentine naval air arm. They were the trained shipkillers. Compounding the threat, they were also capable of operating from an aircraft carrier.

In 1967, the Armada Argentina (ARA) – the Argentine Navy – had even asked the British about the possibility of acquiring HMS *Hermes*. As London tied itself in knots over whether, if they sold an aircraft carrier to Argentina, they should also sell one to Chile, the ARA bought HMNLS *Karel Doorman* from the Dutch. A former British light fleet carrier, HMS *Venerable*, that had seen service in the Pacific during the Second World War, she was refitted and renamed ARA *25 de Mayo*, after one of the country's national days. As the

16,000-ton ship steamed through the Channel on her journey to her new home, Hawker test pilot John Farley took advantage of the opportunity to land a Harrier on her flight deck. It was very much hoped in other departments that the Argentine Navy might like to buy jump jets to fly from their new ship. At the same time, British officials thought they could persuade the Fuerza Aérea Argentina to buy BAC Lightning jet fighters. British industry was to be disappointed on both fronts.

While it was believed in London that Argentine naval aviators wanted the Harrier, the Armada's Admirals opted for second-hand McDonnell Douglas A-4 Skyhawks from the United States. That the American jets cost about 10% of the price of the Harrier 'could well', noted a British Minister with admirable understatement, 'have been decisive'.

During their conversations over ships and aircraft, the Argentine Navy's Chief of Staff asked his British counterpart whether he could think of any way in which the two navies could solve the Falklands problem. That now looked as if it was on the cards – but not, of course, in quite the way that Admiral Benigno Varela had imagined.

When, in the 1950s, the possibility that Argentina might acquire an aircraft carrier had first been explored, there were concerns in Whitehall that it might be detrimental to British interests in the region. 'We cannot pretend,' acknowledged one exchange between the Admiralty and the Colonial Office, 'that the addition of a light fleet carrier to the Argentine Navy is particularly welcome.' That view remained unchanged thirty years later, not least because the COAN had recently added to its arsenal the French Dassault Super Etendard. The SuE itself, a warmed-over version of a design originally rejected by the Armée de l'Air in the mid-fifties, was a relatively unspectacular machine. But it didn't need searing flight performance to be a danger. Fitted with modern avionics and armed with the sea-skimming AM.39 Exocet missile, the SuE posed a potentially lethal threat to British ships. The first five jets were accepted into front-line service with 2 Escuadrilla Aeronaval de Caza y Ataque (Fighter and Attack Squadron) in November 1981. Whether they were yet capable of operating from *25 de Mayo* or carrying the Exocet anti-ship missile remained uncertain. A report by British Defence Intelligence classified TOP SECRET UMBRA believed both were possibilities.

During the First World War, Germany became the first country to pursue the development of guided missiles. In the end, hopes of launching biplane gliding bombs from the Imperial German Navy's Zeppelins were curtailed by the Armistice, but in the late 1930s the Reichsluftfahrtministerium (the German Air Ministry) sponsored a number of new projects. The most successful of these was the Fritz X. Within ten days of becoming operational at the end of August 1943 two direct hits from the new missile sank the 45,000-ton Italian flagship, *Roma*, preventing the battleship from joining the Allied fleet. A few months later Fritz X attacks put the British battleship HMS *Warspite* out of action for a year. But it was the sinking of another British-built warship over twenty years later that alerted navies around the world to the deadly threat from a new generation of guided missiles.

HMS *Zealous* served with the Royal Navy during the Second World War before being sold to the Israeli Navy in 1955 and being renamed INS *Eilat*. She was sunk in 1967 after being hit by three Soviet-made SS-N-2 Styx missiles fired from Egyptian fast attack boats. This triggered a revolution in naval doctrine and a scramble for similar weapons.

In France, Nord Aviation combined elements of two existing air-to-surface missiles to quickly develop a new sea-skimming anti-ship missile, the MM.38 Exocet ('flying fish'). Although initially developed as a ship-launched weapon, an air-launched version, the AM.39, soon followed.

The Royal Navy had to assume the worst about the new Argentine capability. In London, it was up to the Director of Naval Air Warfare, Captain Ben Bathurst, and his small team based at MoD Main Building to ensure that the Fleet Air Arm was best equipped to face it. Years earlier, during a previous stint in DNAW, Bathurst had been in the department when the Navy won its fight to acquire the Sea Harrier in the first place. There'd been celebration, but mainly relief.

Faced with the retirement of *Ark Royal* and her air group, the Navy began to make the case for a 'Maritime Harrier' that, operating from their new Invincible class helicopter carriers, might provide a measure of organic air defence for the fleet. In doing so they were walking on eggshells. With *Ark* gone, responsibility for providing air cover for the fleet was vested in the RAF, while the Fleet Air Arm concentrated on flying helicopters. With that decision taken, the Navy couldn't be seen to be trying to undo it. They made their case by stressing the Harrier's insignificance. 'The project is a modest one,' they argued. The cost of just twenty-five aircraft would amount to under 1% of the naval budget over ten years. 'It is,' they purred, 'an admittedly limited aircraft, but it has only a limited – though vital – job to do.' They meant only to complement the efforts of the RAF and help them husband their precious resources. The Maritime Harrier was merely a way of keeping Soviet reconnaissance aircraft at bay; the job of actually shooting down the bombers and missile carriers would remain that of the Royal Air Force. In 1975, the Admiralty's determinedly self-deprecating pitch for the Harrier was successful. An order for twenty-four Sea Harriers was placed with Hawker Siddeley.

So unimpressed were the Fleet Air Arm's frontline pilots by the prospect of seeing their Phantoms and Buccaneers replaced by the little jump jet that John Farley, Hawker Siddeley's Chief Test Pilot, was asked to try to placate them. Heckled and barracked from the outset, he quickly lost his temper. 'I am sorry,' he told them. 'I'm sure you'd like a big boat; I am sure you'd like more modern aeroplanes, but you can't have them. Nobody's going to let you have them, so shut up and listen to me telling you what you *will* have and you may be quite surprised at how useful it will be.'

Now, as the fleet sailed south towards a potential conflict that was nothing like any scenario envisioned at the time the jet was acquired, the Sea Harrier was all the Navy had.

And one thing was abundantly clear: Bathurst had to send south as many SHARs as he could lay his hands on. And find pilots to fly them. With the two frontline squadrons deployed and 899 HQ Squadron reduced to a rump, he thought the most effective vehicle for doing so would be to form a brand-new squadron. He told Yeovilton to make it so.

\*

Rear Admiral Ted Anson was known as Mr Buccaneer. A veteran of the Korean War and Suez campaign, he more than any other pilot in the Fleet Air Arm had ushered Blackburn's world-beating low-level strike jet into frontline service. As the last Captain of HMS *Ark Royal*, he'd flagged the Buccaneers off the flight deck for the last time. Now Flag Officer Naval Air Command headquartered at RNAS Yeovilton, responsibility for commissioning new squadrons was vested in him. And while there may have been much spirited debate back in DNAW about the number plate of the new Sea Harrier squadron, the final decision was Anson's. There was only ever really one possibility: 809.

The squadron's motto, 'Immortal', seemed auspicious.

More so, perhaps, than the unit's combat debut in 1941. It arrived less than two years after formal control of the Fleet Air Arm had, after twenty years of wrangling following the formation of the RAF in 1918, returned to the Royal Navy, in May 1939. And it simply hadn't been enough time to repair two decades of neglect and under-investment in naval aviation. At the outbreak of the Second World War, the Fleet Air Arm had just four frontline fighter squadrons equipped with woefully inadequate machines like the Blackburn Skua and biplane Gloster Sea Gladiator.

809 NAS was formed in January 1941 as part of the Fleet Air Arm's rapid expansion and sent to war in the Arctic aboard HMS *Victorious* in July. But flying the Fairey Fulmar II, a slow, underarmed two-seat fleet interceptor, 809 found itself worryingly outclassed by the Luftwaffe's Messerschmitt Bf-109s and Bf-110s. It was 1943 before the squadron finally re-equipped with the Supermarine Seafires it flew successfully from the deck of HMS *Stalker* until the end of the war. The squadron once again distinguished itself during the ill-fated 1956 Suez campaign flying the De Havilland Sea Venom, but in 1966 it re-formed as a Buccaneer squadron. Three years later, 809 was flying Buccs from the deck of HMS *Hermes* under the command of Lieutenant Commander Lyn Middleton, the carrier's future Captain, but it was the Immortals' next incarnation that cemented its future.

809 had flown Ted Anson's beloved Buccaneers from the deck of *Ark Royal* from 1970 until the carrier's retirement under his command in 1978, their tails emblazoned with the squadron's emblem: a phoenix rising from the flames. It was time for their resurrection.

The Admiral's staff put him through to Fort Southwick, Extension 277.

'Tim,' began the Admiral, 'how would you like to come back to Yeovilton to form another squadron?'

A broad grin broke out across Gedge's face as he processed what, in his characteristically charming way, Ted Anson had just asked him. He was so busy thanking him – practically saluting down the phoneline – that he nearly forgot to ask when he was required.

'Tomorrow at eight a.m. would be fine,' Anson told him.

In less than twenty minutes, after signing back in all the various documents he'd been working on, Gedge was out of Fort Southwick and speeding away from his desk job as fast as his Mini would carry him. Fate had intervened big time. His wife, Monika, couldn't understand what he was so excited about.

'Gentlemen,' Capitán de Corbeta Rodolfo Castro Fox told his pilots, 'the time has come to start working.' The mood on board ARA *25 de Mayo* was euphoric, but the Commanding Officer of 3 Escuadrilla Aeronaval de Caza y Ataque was under no illusions about what lay ahead.

Castro Fox had stayed up through the night during the operation to seize the islands. Up in Flyco high on the carrier's island, they had tuned in to Port Stanley's local radio station. Islanders phoned in to update their countrymen on the latest developments. Then, after Argentine forces took over the studio, the broadcasts came in English and Spanish.

The Skyhawk squadron boss had one question of his Commander: 'How do you think the English will react?'

'It'll be fixed through negotiations,' he was told. The English wouldn't be able to deal with it any other way.

They both now knew that assumption to be wrong.

The three 3 Escuadrilla A-4Q Skyhawks on board hadn't been required to intervene during the invasion. But with the British fleet now steaming south there was an urgent need to return to their home base at Comandante Espora near Bahía Blanca and begin intensive training for a war they were hardly prepared for. Not least among causes for concern was the squadron boss's own fitness. Castro Fox hadn't been in the cockpit of a Skyhawk for eight months.

Not since the accident that had nearly killed him.

3 Escuadrilla had been ashore for four months, but on 9 August 1981 six jets took off from Comandante Espora to embark aboard *25 de Mayo* for the Armada's participation in Exercise OCEAN VENTURE alongside the US Navy.

As he joined the landing circuit after a routine flight out to the ship, Castro Fox was thinking about the time away from his wife and four children. A short while later, the mainwheels slammed on to the carrier's flight deck and he felt the familiar, violent deceleration as the hook lowered from the back of his Skyhawk caught one of the six arrestor wires stretched across the deck. As it slowed, the jet bowed forward, compressing the long nosewheel oleo. He could see the edge of angled deck ahead of him. Then it all suddenly let go. Whiplashing viciously around the deck, the arrestor wire failed. As the Skyhawk reared to port, Castro Fox knew instantly that he had too much speed to stop and too little to have any chance of taking to the air again.

'Eject! Eject! Eject!' screamed the Landing Officer, watching the disaster from Flyco.

Castro Fox reached between his legs and pulled hard at the yellow handle of his ESCAPAC ejection seat.

Nothing.

With its pilot trapped in the cockpit, the jet careened over the edge of the ship and fell 50 feet, nose first, into the South Atlantic. The impact with the sea was the last thing Castro Fox remembered.

The seat eventually activated underwater, firing the pilot through the sea like a torpedo, before releasing him and sinking to the ocean floor along with the aircraft. Unconscious, Castro Fox floated to the surface, made buoyant by air trapped in his thick rubber immersion suit.

Lungs full of water, he suffered his first cardiac arrest before they managed to get him to the ship's infirmary. His heart stopped again as they tried to medevac him ashore to Puerto Belgrano naval base near Buenos Aires.

On top of that there was concussion, a dislocated shoulder, a smashed left arm and broken ribs, but after several days in intensive care Castro Fox began to recover from his injuries. When the cast first came off his left arm, though, the shattered bones carefully re-assembled with metal pins, he could barely move it.

After the accident, Castro Fox took command of 3 Escuadrilla in December 1981. By April he was still yet to fly. The material state of the squadron's jets was hardly more encouraging than his own. When he took over, just three of the unit's A-4Q Skyhawks were air-worthy; the other seven were grounded after cracks had been discovered in the wings. Nor had the failure of his ejection seat been a one-off, but an indication of a problem that was fleetwide. By the end of 1981, all but three of the rocket cartridges that fired the seats were time-expired. With the country under the control of the military Junta, the United States had refused to supply replacements. 3 Escuadrilla had had no choice but to arbitrarily extend the life of the cartridges. It no more made them safe than changing the sell-by date of a banana stopped it from turning black. *It is like*, thought Castro Fox, *flying without a parachute*. Of the seven Skyhawks with cracks in the wings, the squadron's engineers selected the five least damaged to return to flight, bringing the frontline strength to eight aeroplanes.

3 Escuadrilla really would be going into battle on a wing and a prayer.

At the same airfield, their fellow naval aviators, the Super Etendard pilots of 2 Escuadrilla, faced challenges born not of old age, but youth. The SuE was so fresh into COAN service that it was not yet fully operational. Under the leadership of Capitán de Fragata Jorge Colombo, the squadron's engineers began tuning the SuE's radar, and testing the inertial navigation system and its ability to talk to the weapons computer. Colombo divided his ten-strong squadron into pairs. None of the pilots had any detailed training in how to mount an Exocet attack. *The principle of it*, Colombo understood, *is more or less known*, but there was a gulf between having a broad appreciation of the technique and launching an operational mission against one of the world's most powerful navies. Between them they studied tactics, flight profiles and radii of action, and performed take-off and landing tests on marked runways to determine whether or not they might be able to launch attacks against the British fleet from Puerto Argentino, the newly rechristened airfield at Port Stanley.

A team of twenty-five technicians from Aérospatiale, the French manufacturer of the five Exocet missiles already delivered to the squadron, was expected to fly into Argentina in a week's time. With their assistance, the complicated job of integrating the big 1,500lb anti-ship missile with its launch aircraft would become a lot easier. Colombo and his engineers looked forward to their arrival.

With difficult decisions made regarding the jets' serviceability, Rodolfo Castro Fox turned his mind to the pilots he required to fly them. He needed experienced operators in the cockpits, not young nuggets fresh out of flight school. Former Skyhawk pilots were brought back to Comandante Espora from staff jobs and from conversion training in France for the SuE.

*To master the weapons system and tactics of a high performance combat aircraft like the A-4Q,* he believed, *requires at least a year of practice.*

# FIVE

## Limited by geography

WHEN TIM GEDGE arrived at Ted Anson's office at FONAC HQ the following morning, 6 April, the Admiral's brief was straightforward and expansive. 'Go into Yeovilton,' he told Gedge, 'and find yourself an office and some aeroplanes, form another squadron, work it up for air defence and attack, and be ready to go in twenty-one days.' Anson explained that the purpose of the newly revived 809 Naval Air Squadron was to provide attrition replacements to cover losses sustained by the squadrons already aboard the carriers. 'I'll ensure,' he added, 'that you'll have all the support you need.'

The commissioning order, signed by Anson the following day, directed the new 809 Squadron boss to proceed with 'the utmost despatch'. To be ready in three weeks, that was a given.

As Gedge got to work, the RAF was examining its options in the South Atlantic. They were limited by geography. From flying home Rex Hunt, the Falklands Governor, and the Royal Marines of Naval Party 8901 from Montevideo to flying the Special Boat Squadron (SBS) to Ascension Island, four squadrons of Lockheed C-130 Hercules transports and 10 Squadron's Vickers VC10s had already been hard at work ferrying men and materiel. Unable, for the time being at least, to play any practical role beyond that point, the RAF, through the establishment of what it called the Alert Measures Committee, applied a little creativity. Intelligence about the enemy's plans, intentions and movements would be at a premium if the fleet, operating so far from home, was to be protected. The RAF was already considering the ways in which it might provide that.

Among the first green shoots of this was an order to RAF Wattisham in Suffolk to mobilize a Marconi S259, a fully mobile air defence radar capable of providing a three-dimensional picture of aerial movements out to a distance of 120 miles.

There were hopes that the Buccaneer force based in Suffolk at RAF Honington might have a role to play, but, for now, the Alert Measures Committee was clear that RAF support for the Fleet Air Arm must be prioritized above all else.

At first, Tim Gedge thought he might simply return to his old office in 800 Squadron. On reflection, he decided to take up residence in 899's newer building. It hardly mattered. Yeovilton's Sea Harrier community was gone. The hangars were empty. He had just one jet, albeit a machine fitted with neither radar nor a navigation system.

He sat down at Neill Thomas's desk and took stock for a moment. Then, without really thinking there'd be anyone on the other side, he slid back a hatch in the wall next to his seat. Sabrina, 899's red-haired WRNS Air Staff Officer, was as surprised as he was to be staring at someone neither of them had been expecting. Initially, she seemed put out that anyone but Thomas should be sitting there, but Gedge calmly explained that she was now working for him.

'We need aeroplanes, pilots and maintainers,' he told her, 'we're forming a new squadron.'

Gedge had been lucky. Since his last Sea Harrier flight in January, and for no reason other than that he'd wanted to, he'd kept up his fast jet currency by flying Hunters out of Yeovilton whenever he got the opportunity. Now he needed anyone else who might be similarly well prepared to be put back into the cockpit of a Sea Harrier and, in three weeks' time, be sufficiently up to speed to go to war.

First on the list was Lieutenant Dave Austin, who ran the Sea Harrier Simulator at Yeovilton. Austin was trained to fly a Harrier by the RAF, but his career in a light blue uniform was not destined to be long and happy. After a premature parting of the ways with the Air Force, he'd arrived at Yeovilton as a contract pilot for Airwork, the company that operated a fleet of Royal Navy Hunters and Canberras used to sharpen the fleet's air defences. Once the Navy had cottoned on to the fact that they had a fully trained Harrier pilot on their doorstep, they welcomed him with open arms. His somewhat unusual career path was of no concern or interest to Gedge. After all, the Air Force and the Navy could view things in a very different light. Austin was a trained and capable pilot, and Gedge was pleased to have him.

Two pilots, one jet. There was still a mountain to climb.

In an ideal world he'd have taken Willy McAtee. But the State Department had put its foot down. After being told to stay put by the Embassy, he might have been unable to join Sharkey Ward, but he didn't think a trip to St Athan to bring a SHAR back to Yeovilton could hurt. When the Colonel called while he was away and was told 'the Major's gone; he's flying aeroplanes and they're going to war', he went ballistic. McAtee was ordered to call in the next day, and the next, to make sure he was behaving himself. Much to his frustration, the war was going to have to carry on without the United States Marine Corps.

Things looked briefly more promising for Lieutenant Commander David Ramsay, Gedge's old Senior Pilot and Air Warfare Instructor from 800. On exchange from the Royal Australian Navy, Ramsay was a hugely experienced operator who'd flown the McDonnell Douglas A-4 Skyhawk off the deck of HMAS *Melbourne* with VF-805. He'd been on holiday in Brussels when he was recalled to Yeovilton. And while he didn't sail with *Hermes*, that Monday evening FONAC was under the impression that Australian exchange personnel were cleared to take part in CORPORATE. Confirmation on the Wednesday that RAN exchange officers were not to go south dashed any lingering hopes he had, though.

There was Lieutenant Commander Jock Gunning, the boss of the Naval Flying Standards Flight. A hugely experienced former Sea Vixen and Phantom pilot and Qualified Flying Instructor, the Scot was now responsible for examining each fixed-wing squadron annually. But with Neill Thomas on board *Hermes*, Gunning was off to RAF Wittering to revalidate his Harrier qualifications before taking over 899 as acting CO. Gedge knew he'd be invaluable helping whip his new squadron into shape, but was told he'd have to leave him behind too. The Navy needed someone to make sure that the training pipeline didn't dry up completely. In any case, Jock was no real fan of landing an aeroplane vertically. Best avoided unless you really had to. He reckoned he was too old to be learning fancy new tricks like that. And given that the Harrier's unusual bicycle undercarriage meant that the alternative, a conventional landing, had been likened to trying to steer a wheelbarrow at 165 knots, it was clear that his aversion to vertical take-off and landing was deeply held.

And then there was Taylor Scott.

Hawker Siddeley had now been absorbed into British Aerospace, but Dunsfold remained the home of the Harrier. After returning to the Surrey airfield following a test flight exploring the Sea Harrier's stall characteristics, Chief Test Pilot John Farley was debriefing the team when the door burst open. Taylor Scott flew in announcing, 'I'm off! Back to the Navy. There's a war on!'

'I don't think it'll be settled in the next couple of hours,' Farley told him, as unruffled by his colleague's sudden arrival as he had been by earlier efforts to provoke a heavily laden SHAR to fall from the sky, 'so let me finish this debrief and then you and I can go and have a chat about it.' Before heading home for the evening, Farley and Scott briefed the Dunsfold nightshift to try to make sure as many jets as possible were prepped, and left the factory for home.

Farley was about to settle down for his dinner when the phone rang. One of the gate guards told him the Navy were on their way in and wanted all the airfield lights put back on.

'Turn all the lights back off,' Farley told him, 'and shut down air traffic because the Navy is not coming in here tonight!'

They came anyway, landing at Dunsfold in a helicopter carrying a handful of Harrier pilots who were hoping to fly away every Sea Harrier they could get their hands on. The Fleet Air Arm hopefuls were sent packing, but it was clear that they were as eager as Taylor Scott to get into the face of the Argentine Air Force.

And if anyone deserved to go it was Scott. There was nobody more intimately involved with the Sea Harrier programme. He'd been drafted in to BAe as Liaison Officer in 1978, after a tour flying Phantoms on *Ark*, to bring an operational eye to the design and function of the cockpit, radar and navigation systems. Within twenty minutes of flying with him, John Farley had realized that Scott should be running the programme.

Scott knew the Sea Harrier and its systems like the back of his hand. And, while he was now a civilian test pilot working for BAe, as a member of the Royal Navy Reserve he looked to Gedge like the perfect candidate. There was just one problem. Britain and Argentina were not technically at war. Without Queen's Order No. 2 being signed, the Navy couldn't call up the reserves. To Gedge's mind it was just crackers.

*Wasn't that the whole reason for having a reserve?*

For a bitterly disappointed Scott, there was a further kick in the teeth when he received the news that, even if he did get to go, his life insurance policy wouldn't cover him.

The Phoenix Squadron's new Commanding Officer was going to have to cast the net a little wider.

# SIX

## Death ray

'ARE YOU LIEUTENANT Bill Covington?'

'Yes,' he replied, wondering who could be phoning at such an early hour.

'I'm calling from the British Embassy in Washington. I have a signal from the MoD, Navy. You are to proceed with all despatch to Royal Naval Air Station Yeovilton for operational duties.'

'What?'

'You've got twenty-four hours.'

'Do you know where I *am*?'

Lieutenant Bill Covington was born on an RAF station in Egypt, where his father was working as a surveyor following wartime service with the Army. From their home at the entrance of the Suez Canal, the family could see aircraft carriers towering over the surrounding landscape as they made their slow progress from the Mediterranean to the Red Sea. Covington, who combined a seriousness of purpose with an easy affability, now went by the callsign 'Limey'. It had been hard won.

Now midway through an exchange tour with the US Marine Corps, he'd come a long, long way since arriving in the States. It was traditional to send your best, most experienced people on exchange, but when Covington arrived at MCAS Yuma in Arizona, the desert home of VMA-513, the Marine Corps' West Coast AV-8A Harrier squadron, he had barely fifty hours on the Harrier under his belt and hadn't yet completed his operational flying training on the Sea Harrier, let alone a tour with a frontline fast jet squadron. VMA-513 was a close air support squadron and Covington had only ever once visited a weapons range in a Harrier before leaving for the US.

But he'd been identified early by the Royal Navy as a high-flyer, earmarked for the new Sea Harrier and fast-tracked through flight training so that he could experience operating from the deck of *Ark Royal* before she was paid off. There hadn't been time to complete the fast jet training that would have seen him join the 'heavies', the Buccaneers and Phantoms, but if they kept the learning curve steep there was time to get him deck-qualified on the Fairey Gannet AEW.3, the ungainly-looking propellor-driven turboprop that provided the ship with airborne early warning of attack. He served two short tours embarked with 849 'B' Flight and hoovered up the experience, taking in everything he could about all aspects of naval aviation.

There was no getting around it, though, the Marine Corps had got themselves a Gannet driver who could fly a Harrier. But, posted to Yuma, he worked hard to become an operational gun squadron pilot. It was massively challenging, but after two years training with guns, rockets, Zuni rocket pods, napalm, 250lb bombs, 500lb bombs, 10° dive bombing, 30° dive bombing and 60° dive bombing, air-to-air and air-to-ground, by day and by night, on or off the ship – all the time having to bone up on it himself from the NATOPS manual – he'd come through. He'd *earned* that callsign, and the Marine Corps had rewarded him with a coveted slot on their WTI (Weapons Tactics Instructors) course. The Marines' equivalent of TOPGUN.

It all culminated with Covington programming a big-wing expeditionary operation involving seventy aircraft, from helicopters to fast jets. On the penultimate day of the exercise a fellow Marine Corps aviator, callsign 'Skull', turned to him and asked, 'What do you think about the Falklands?'

Lieutenant Commander Dave Braithwaite was having the time of his life. He'd spent the last couple of months dogfighting in the clear blue skies above California. Since 1981 he'd been on exchange with VX-4, the US Navy's operational test and evaluation squadron based at NAS Point Mugu. Barely a day went by without him strapping himself into the cockpit of a Grumman F-14A Tomcat or F-4S Phantom and pitting himself against the best pilots and jets the US Navy had to offer. And while he had to acknowledge that the big swing-wing Tomcat really was the all-singing, all-dancing superfighter of legend, it was the Phantom that had stolen his heart. As superb as the Tomcat was, he could make the F-4 *dance*.

Growing up in Sussex, Braithwaite had been single-minded in his ambition to fly heavies like the Phantom from the deck of a carrier. As a teenager he'd rejected an offer to train as a pilot with the RAF in favour of the Fleet Air Arm. Then, after being accepted by the Navy to train as a helicopter pilot, he had persuaded his father, who as Chief Education Officer for East Sussex also served on the Admiralty Interview Board, to explain to their lordships that his son didn't want to fly helicopters. A letter arrived in Lewes the next day telling him he'd be training as a fixed-wing naval aviator. Three years later, in 1967, he was flying the De Havilland Sea Vixen FAW.2 from HMS *Hermes*. But in 1973 he joined *Ark Royal*'s Phantom squadron where, for the next five years, his affection for the big interceptor grew stronger.

Braithwaite's posting to VX-4 was his second exchange tour in the States. His first, as an instructor flying F-4s with VF-121 at NAS Miramar, had seen him go through TOPGUN school. On top of that, he was a graduate of the Fleet Air Arm's own fiendishly demanding Air Warfare Instructor's course, a qualification he'd put to good use as AWI on 700A Naval Air Squadron, the Sea Harrier trials unit, developing tactics and procedures for the Navy's new jet.

Now he was looking forward to getting his hands on the new F/A-18 Hornet, the US Navy's latest fighter. But when the British-accented voice on the other end of the line asked 'Is that Lieutenant Commander Braithwaite?' he knew something was up. People usually just called him 'Brave'. He'd been 'Dave the Brave' ever since choosing to land a stricken Sea Vixen aboard the carrier rather than eject in order to save the life of the Observer flying with him.

Bill Covington raced into the squadron to tell them he was on his way and wasn't sure when he'd be back. Don Swaby, the second-in-command, handed the young British pilot his leather flying jacket.

'This has been to Vietnam,' he told him. 'It worked for me. Take it with you and good luck.'

At the Marine Air Warfare Training School, they realized that Covington would be the first graduate of the WTI course to go to war. 'We'd better get you passed out!' He was handed his badge, and told he was now a Marine Corps Weapons Tactics Instructor. 'Wear it with pride.' Before Limey left, his instructor injected a note of caution: 'Be careful, Bill. You still have a lot to learn. You're not the full enchilada yet . . .'

Braithwaite greeted Covington at LA airport with a knowing smirk. Bluff, provocative and mischievous, Brave was one of the Fleet Air Arm's big characters. The pair caught a British Airways flight back to Heathrow from LA. Somehow word reached the 747's crew that they were ferrying two Royal Navy fighter pilots back to the UK to go to war. After being invited to the flight deck to meet the Captain, they returned to their seats on the jumbo's top deck. But the VIP treatment had barely started.

'Drinks,' they were told, 'are on British Airways.' And so, in the space next to the first-class lounge cinema screen, they invited their fellow passengers to join them for an impromptu drinks party. These had a habit of breaking out whenever Brave was around.

With the effort to find qualified pilots in full swing, at Yeovilton Tim Gedge was trying to stand back and consider the questions that needed asking. This time around, the most difficult thing about forming a squadron was not just putting in place the administrative structure and assembling the mountain of paperwork and reference material required. He'd done the practical and procedural once before with 800 and knew how to go about it. Instead he had to identify what 809 might require or benefit from in addition before going to war – training, trials, intelligence, equipment. Given a more or less blank cheque by the Admiral, he asked himself not how do I get, but *what do I need*?

Top of the list were AIM-9L Sidewinder air-to-air missiles. On the day of the invasion, Gedge had noted that, while the carriers were reasonably well stocked with the earlier AIM-9G model, they carried none of the more advanced AIM-9L. There were just nineteen to be found aboard the Royal Fleet Auxiliary stores ship *Resource*. On the same day, Lyn Middleton, the Captain of *Hermes*, had told his superiors that getting hold of the new model was critical. So too had Sharkey Ward, 801's CO.

Everyone wanted the Nine Lima. And for good reason.

In the summer of 1958, as tension mounted over the Communist bombardment of Taiwanese islands, American and Chinese warships stared each other down in the Formosa Straits. High above them, Taiwanese F-86 Sabres tried and failed to get within gun range of the Communist Chinese MiG-17 Frescos flying overhead with impunity. Capable of flying faster and higher than the Taiwanese jets, the Soviet-built MiGs were untouchable. A month later, on 22 September, the Taiwanese pilots rejoined the battle with a new trick up their sleeves. By the end of the day they'd destroyed at least ten of the high-flying Chinese MiGs. The occasion marked the combat debut of the AIM-9 Sidewinder missile and it showed that, armed with the right weapon, a fighter didn't necessarily need to outperform its opponent.

The new missile's development flew in the face of the then state-of-the-art in missile design. While large American aerospace companies like Hughes and Raytheon poured Air Force and Navy money into ever more complex, sophisticated and apparently fallible radar-guided systems, a small team at the US Naval Ordnance Test Station at China Lake in the Mojave desert tacked the other way. 'It's easy,' argued the team's leader, Dr William B. McLean, 'to build something complicated; it's hard to build it so it's simple.' The key to success, thought McLean in 1946, was to *put the fire control in the missile instead of the aircraft.* A year after the end of the Second World War, he set his mind to building what amounted to an autonomous robot that, once fired by the pilot, would guide itself to the target with no further outside input or direction.

McLean first sketched the 'heat-homing' seeker head that would make that possible on an envelope in 1947. Developed as an R&D exercise, without official support, the project advanced under McLean's exacting leadership, and by 1953 China Lake test pilots were able to amuse themselves by swooping in behind trucks, trains and Greyhound buses to see if they could get their missiles to lock on. But it was footage of an old B-17 Flying Fortress spiralling to the ground after a direct hit that finally helped persuade Washington to take an interest.

The new heatseeking missile was christened Sidewinder, named after the local horned rattlesnake that hunted at night in the desert by detecting the infrared radiation given off by its prey.

Such was the confidence in the new generation of air-to-air missiles that, after breaking every sort of speed and altitude world record under the sun, the US Navy's hot new interceptor, the McDonnell Douglas F-4 Phantom II, entered service in 1960 without a gun. And yet in combat in Vietnam the Sidewinder proved to be far from infallible. By the end of the war just one in five Sidewinders had hit its target. The Sidewinder was extremely short-ranged; it needed a clear, unbroken view of the target's jet exhaust and so had to be fired from behind. That required a degree of cooperation from a target who was likely to be more inclined to try hard manoeuvring, flying into cloud or pointing towards the sun. All worked in confounding the missile. It didn't like wet weather either, and at low altitude over water it found it hard to acquire the target at all.

All in all, the AIM-9G looked like a weapon that, used at low level in the grim late-autumn conditions faced by the British Task Force in the South Atlantic, was going to be well out of its comfort zone.

But the Nine Lima was another matter altogether. Its design had been shaped by the experience in Vietnam to address every one of its predecessor's shortcomings. A brand-new seeker head gave it an all-aspect capability – it was the first Sidewinder that could be fired at the target from any direction, even head-on. New double-delta canards endowed it with the ability to generate 35g loads as it raced towards its prey. No aircraft, let alone its pilot, could cope with that. It was, in the words of one of the team at China Lake, 'a death ray'.

Tim Gedge spoke to DNAW in London, who assured him that the missiles were on their way. Further AIM-9Gs had been appropriated from an order destined for Singapore, while a quantity of the much-coveted AIM-9Ls had been raided from the RAF's NATO stocks at Leuchars in Scotland. More importantly, a hundred more had been requested from the Americans. The plan was to have them airfreighted direct to Ascension's Wideawake airfield to await the arrival of *Hermes* and *Invincible*. If, that is, *Invincible* ever arrived.

Three days earlier, and just hours out of Portsmouth, *Invincible*'s engineering department heard a sound they recognized and didn't like at all. The Engineer Officer took JJ Black aside and told him, 'Sir, we have a suspicious knocking from the starboard coupling in the gearbox.' Black's heart sank. This wasn't the first time it had happened, but previously, the ship had spent a fortnight alongside with full dockyard assistance to put it right. The gearbox itself was the size of a small house, the offending coupling a 3-ton lump of metal. While the problem was investigated, thoughts of humiliation and failure churned through Black's mind. *Invincible* was irreplaceable, and to have to abandon the mission was unthinkable. Powered by four Olympus gas turbines derived from the jet engines used by Concorde, the only replacement coupling for the carrier's gearbox – and there had been no guarantee they would have one – would be at the Rolls-Royce plant in Derby, and with the Task Force already 80 miles southwest of Land's End, delivering such a massive piece of machinery was going to be a challenge. But after the coupling was despatched to RNAS Culdrose in Cornwall by road, a big twin-rotor RAF Chinook helicopter delivered it to the flight deck. Led through thick fog to the ship by a radar-equipped Navy Sea King, it was an impressive piece of airmanship from an RAF crew completely unused to operating at sea. Within twenty-four hours of discovering the problem the means to fix it was safely aboard. It remained a huge ask of the ship's engineering department, but *Invincible* was back in control of her own destiny. The Captain, wearing his trademark baseball cap with 'JJ Black' emblazoned across the back and drinking tea out of a mug that just read 'Boss', hoped he'd not let his concern show.

As the weather cleared, Black watched from the bridge as Sharkey Ward's Sea Harrier squadron launched a handful of sorties. One of them would end with one of Ward's pilots, fresh out of training, performing a deck landing at sea for the first time in his life. Another would see 801 carrying live AIM-9G Sidewinder rounds beneath their wings for the first time.

The Nine Limas were yet to arrive in the ship's magazines.

# SEVEN

## Gonadal noises

WHEN NEWS OF the invasion broke, three members of B Squadron SAS were at Quantico, the FBI headquarters in America, training the FBI in counter-terrorist techniques. The successful assault on the Iranian Embassy two years earlier had made the Regiment's expertise a valuable commodity.

With the Task Force on its way they no longer thought teaching G-men was the best use of their time. After contacting Hereford to say so, they were told to make their way to Andrews Air Force Base in Washington, from where they'd be picked up and flown to Pope Air Force Base, a short drive from Fort Bragg, home to the US Army's Delta Force Special Operations unit. The bond between the two units was a close one, not least because Delta Force owed its existence to the Regiment. 1 Special Forces Operational Detachment-Delta, as Delta was more properly known, was set up in the mid-seventies by Colonel Charlie Beckwith, following an exchange tour with 22 SAS in the sixties. It was unashamedly modelled on the elite British unit. There was now an opportunity to return the favour.

The trio from Stirling Lines were in North Carolina to try out Delta's new man-portable anti-aircraft missile, the Stinger, and, more importantly, to try to persuade them to let the Brits have a few. Dressed in civilian clothes, they were surprised to be quizzed en route to Pope by an eager crewman about their views of the American political system. It struck the Regiment men as oddly off key. On arrival, things took an even stranger turn when a red carpet and salutes from a welcoming party of senior USAF officers suggested that they were being afforded altogether more respect than they merited. As they finally made it to a waiting car, the two Delta Force operators who'd watched the whole charade on the tarmac unfold started laughing hard. They'd told the Air Force that their guests from the SAS were British MPs on an official visit.

Just two members of Delta Force were subsequently involved in the discussion following the SAS's arrival at Fort Bragg: one of the men who'd greeted them at the airport – an old friend – and the Colonel of the unit who, years earlier, had himself successfully completed SAS selection. Stinger was at the time a deeply classified programme, but over the next days the three SAS men were briefed in and given the opportunity to train with it. Impressed, one commented that 'some of these would definitely come in handy in the Falklands'. The missile was immediately made available. Then Hereford said they also wanted portable satellite equipment. Just six hours later, around thirty AN/PSC-3 TACSAT terminals were supplied without demur – approved, without the knowledge of the SAS team at Fort Bragg, by the Pentagon. Not even during the Second World War had assistance been provided with such alacrity.

Hereford's new toys were loaded on to a rented Hertz truck and, hidden in plain sight, were driven to Dulles International Airport in Washington. The SAS troopers followed behind as passengers in the Delta Force Colonel's car. On the ground at Dulles was a waiting 10 Squadron Vickers VC10 C.1, ready to spirit them and their haul back to Brize Norton without delay. The crew of the RAF transport jet could only speculate about the nature of their mysterious, top-secret cargo. But they were in no doubt at all about the importance that had been attached to it. A C-130 Hercules would be on the ground at Brize, ready, with the VC10's load transferred, for an immediate departure for Ascension Island.

Providing 24/7 access to a network of relay satellites enabling reliable, real-time encrypted conversation across vast distances, the TACSAT kit had the potential to play a critical role in the defence of the fleet. Two people on different sides of the globe could talk as if they were in adjoining rooms. But for that to really count, a way still needed to be found of gathering timely intelligence in the first place. For now, though, the Task Force could rely only on its own resources: the radars, missiles and Sea Harriers they had with them.

Sending them into battle with Nine Limas could make a critical difference.

While the British were talking tough, US officials, alarmed at the prospect of their closest ally boxing itself into a disastrous repeat of the 1956 Suez crisis, were not entirely convinced by their confidence.

Listening to British Defence Secretary John Nott 'making gonadal noises about the ability of the British fleet to sustain operations indefinitely in the South Atlantic', US diplomat James Rentschler was doubtful. *Despite the onset of formidable winter conditions – the ice, the snow, the 60-foot seas, the constant Antarctic gales, and the vulnerabilities of an 8,000-mile supply line?* He kept his thoughts to himself, but it was not a view confined to the State Department. 'UK action could not succeed,' Secretary of Defense Caspar Weinberger was told. Such were the logistic and military challenges faced, compounded by the limited resources of the British Task Force, that senior US military leaders concluded that the British mission was both 'futile and impossible'.

But while senior figures in the Pentagon watched the unfolding crisis with a mixture of astonishment and fascination, they were willing, despite Secretary of State Al Haig's ongoing efforts to act as an honest broker, to provide immediate and significant assistance. To the anglophile Cap Weinberger – a man who in 1940 had tried to enlist in the Royal Air Force – and the Secretary for the Navy, Cambridge University graduate John Lehman, the idea that the Pentagon would do anything else seemed inconceivable. Their sympathies were clear. Initially it was less a political decision than a simple manifestation of the inescapably close relationship between the two militaries. There were already established channels for sharing intelligence, and an effective formal and informal network on both sides of the Atlantic that already dealt with the sale, loan and transfer of equipment on a daily basis. Nothing needed to change; no decisions needed to be made. Providing it remained a concern between the Pentagon and the MoD, military to military, Weinberger told the DoD that all British requests for equipment and support short of US participation should be granted immediately. The first requirements were for aircraft fuel to be delivered to Ascension Island. And AIM-9L Sidewinders.

To John Lehman, that represented a bare-bones minimum. As far as he was concerned, the Royal Navy, without adequate radar, and without supersonic interceptors, was deploying its Task Force to the South Atlantic *without effective protection against air attack.*

In his last weeks as squadron boss of 800 Squadron, Gedge knew that clearance trials for the AIM 9L had been scheduled for later in the year. They were now brought forward to the end of the week. Time on the ranges at RAE Aberporth, off the Welsh coast was booked. FONAC tried to rustle up a chase plane to observe the test firings while Taylor Scott and Dave Ramsay took up one of 899 Squadron's two-seat Harrier T.4s to work out the various flight profiles they'd use during the trials. Navy weapons engineers attached to A&AEE at Boscombe Down had already laid the groundwork. Denied the necessary integration information from the US, they'd been forced to dismantle a Nine Lima seeker head, then design and test their own modification to the SHAR's weapon system. Their efforts had been sufficiently successful for Dave Ramsay to be despatched to RAF Valley in Anglesey with instructions from Gedge to stay there until the trials were complete. If the Australian Air Warfare Instructor wasn't going to get to go south, at least he'd get to fire more Sidewinders than anyone else.

That evening, after a refamiliarization flight in a T.4 the previous day, Tim Gedge finally strapped himself back into the cockpit of 809's only Sea Harrier and went flying. His only other pilot, Dave Austin, had already been up in her three times since breakfast, spending three hours practising air combat manoeuvring against Yeovilton's Hunters. This was going to be the pace of things.

On Good Friday, 9 April, Tim Gedge barely had time to welcome 809's newest recruit before he had to fly up to RAF Valley to see how Dave Ramsay was getting on. Al Craig was a welcome addition to the ranks, though.

A week earlier, as the Task Force prepared to sail, Craig had been playing golf at North Luffenham in Rutland with his squadron boss, Wing Commander Peter Squire, when the CO had turned to him and said, 'Alastair, shouldn't we be playing bowls?'

An experienced former Buccaneer pilot with 809 Squadron

aboard *Ark Royal*, Ulster-born Craig was on exchange with 1(Fighter) Squadron RAF flying Harrier GR.3s at Wittering in Cambridgeshire when he got the call from Yeovilton. He was told there'd be a car waiting to bring him back to Somerset the next morning. There was barely time to tell his wife he was off and pack.

As he was driven across the country he couldn't help but notice the ever greater concentrations of army lorries clogging the roads as they approached the southwest.

*This is getting serious*, he thought.

He'd no sooner arrived than an old mate from his Buccaneer days came barrelling up. 'We got the name!' he enthused. 809 had been a popular choice for the new squadron number plate.

Gedge welcomed him back. A ground attack pilot his entire career, Craig was going to have to concentrate on learning the rudiments of fighter combat. For now, he just needed to get a feel for the new jet after two years flying the RAF's GR.3. Equipped for entirely different roles, there were a few obvious differences to contend with, like the raised cockpit that contained a substantially different suite of instruments and displays. Under the skin, more powerful puffer jets around the aeroplane's extremities made for slightly unfamiliar handling in the hover. But he was airborne by nine that morning. As a flying machine the SHAR was similar enough to a GR.3 for Craig to be signed off on his first familiarization flight with what felt to him like little more than 'Can you spell Sea Harrier? Right! Great! Strap in!'

At RAF Valley, Gedge was presented with a new problem. The navigation system on the Sidewinder trials aircraft had failed. In order to keep Ramsay's jet serviceable, he was going to have to remove parts from his own then take a calculated risk on flying it back to Yeovilton. Needs must. A separate issue arising from the missile launch rails was unexpected, though. The reprofiled canard fins at the front of the Nine Lima meant it no longer fitted on to the SHAR's launch rails. That would normally need an expensive manufacturer's redesign and recertification to be sorted out. He asked the Chief Petty Officer responsible for arming the aircraft if there was anything that could be done.

'Well, we *could* just file down the rails we've already got to make them fit . . .'

Gedge told him to crack on.

*Must be one of the cheapest modifications ever,* he smiled to himself, before climbing back into the cockpit of a now half-serviceable ZA190 and returning to Yeovilton. He squeezed in a handful of practice vertical landings before taxiing back to the hardstanding.

Dave Braithwaite and Bill Covington arrived at Yeovilton main gate that evening after being offered a lift from Heathrow by a man they'd met on their flight from LA.

On arrival at the Yeovilton main gate Brave explained who they were, but beyond that, he confessed, 'I've no idea what we're doing.'

'Well, you're Senior Pilot on 809.'

That sounded good. 'Thank you very much!' he replied, before asking who else was in the squadron.

'Tim Gedge is your CO.'

And that was it. They were ushered into the base and headed straight for the bar. It was Happy Hour. Work would begin in earnest in the morning.

# EIGHT

## Over the horizon

JUST AFTER DAWN on 5 June 1967, the Israeli Air Force launched an audacious surprise attack against Egypt. In barely half an hour, the IAF French-built fleet of Mirage IIIs, Super Mystères, Mystères and Ouragans had destroyed nearly 200 Egyptian aircraft on the ground. More were shot down in the air as they tried desperately to respond. Half of Egypt's Air Force was removed at a stroke; the other half were confined to the ground by the destruction of their runways. As well as bombs and rockets, the Israeli jets carried a French-designed weapon called Durandal. Slowed down by retro-rockets, the bomb then fell vertically beneath a parachute towards the ground before, in the last moments, being driven deep beneath the surface by another set of rockets, resulting in a large, difficult-to-repair crater. By sundown on 10 June the Six-Day War had been won decisively by Israel.

It was the second time in just over a decade that the Egyptian Air Force had been largely wiped out on the ground. First time around, during the Suez crisis in 1956, much of the destruction had been meted out by the RAF, flying from Malta and Cyprus, and the Sea Hawks, Sea Venoms and Wyverns of the Fleet Air Arm operating from three aircraft carriers: HMS *Albion*, *Bulwark* and *Eagle*.

Air superiority could be established in two ways: Air Defence – intercepting and shooting down enemy aircraft (and Tim Gedge's efforts to hasten the AIM-9L into service were in pursuit of that); and Offensive Counter Air – attacking the enemy on the ground to cut off the air threat at source.

The trouble with the latter was that it was a role that had never been envisaged for the Sea Harrier. From the outset it was expected to operate only at sea, beyond the reach of land-based fast jets. That was its very *raison d'être*; its strike capability was intended for use against naval targets. And even that, so early in the jet's service life, remained a relatively austere proposition, dependent solely on 30mm cannon shells, unguided 2-inch rockets (both of which were likely to be of little more than nuisance value) and 1,000lb iron bombs.

Just after two o'clock in the morning on Easter Saturday, 10 April, CINCFLEET Northwood signalled FONAC and DNAW asking for advice on airfield denial weapons for the SHAR. As the squadrons aboard *Hermes* and *Invincible* began dropping 1,000lb bombs against wooden splash targets towed at a safe distance behind the ships, a study into whether or not Durandal might be added to the Sea Harrier's bag of tricks was quickly put in hand.

The threat posed by the runway at Port Stanley was now a major preoccupation at Northwood. Attacks against the Task Force could arrive from the mainland, from the ARA carrier *25 de Mayo*, or from Port Stanley. From mainland bases in southern Argentina, Air Force Mirages and Skyhawks would, without air-to-air refuelling, be operating at the limits of their range. There was mixed intelligence on whether the Fuerza Aérea Argentina had maintained an ability to extend the range of the Skyhawks and SuEs using in-flight refuelling. Nor was it, ultimately, something over which the British had any control, but the prospect of attacks being launched from 300 miles closer to the Carrier Battle Group, from either *25 de Mayo* or Port Stanley, had to be stopped. 'The fleet's position in the war area demands air superiority,' wrote Sharkey Ward, and he urged his squadron to be bold. *He Who Dares*.

Over the Easter weekend, the SHAR squadrons on *Invincible* and *Hermes* planned missions against both the Argentine carrier and the runway. Without stand-off weapons, both tasks relied on the element of surprise. On the basis that most of the Argentine air defences around Stanley were visually aimed, 801 planned to attack in the middle of the night. Eight jets loaded with airburst and retarded 1,000lb bombs and 2-inch rockets would come screaming in from the IP (initial point) at Volunteer Point on the east coast of East Falkland. If possible, it was hoped that the SBS might help by destroying the Argentinians' air defence radar.

'Secrecy,' the plan underlined, 'was paramount as the success of an airfield attack at Port Stanley is directly proportional to that secrecy.' That was less easy to come by with any assault on the Argentine carrier, which would need to be attacked in daylight, and was expected to be protected by a pair of British-built Type 42 destroyers, *Hercules* and *Santísima Trinidad*. The latter ship had, rather inconveniently, had her state-of-the-art Sea Dart surface-to-air missile system tuned during a visit to Portsmouth barely six months earlier.

801's planning cell, led by Ward's AWI, Flight Lieutenant Ian Mortimer, concluded that against the Type 42 the British jets were extremely vulnerable. To have any hope of success they'd require fourteen SHARs, two of which were to act as decoys with the sole aim of tying up the air defence radars of the destroyers. The twelve remaining jets, split into two groups of six, would then attack at the lowest height possible armed with 1,000lb bombs. Mortimer was icily realistic about the Sea Harriers' chances of success:

```
Carrier on its own - easy.
Plus 1 x Type 42 - possible but some attrition.
Whole force - forget it.
```

At least the latest intelligence from DNAW suggested that the COAN's new Super Etendards were not yet capable of operating from *25 de Mayo*. That meant that they, like the Fuerza Aérea Argentina Mirages, Daggers and Skyhawks, would have to operate at range from mainland airfields like Río Gallegos or Río Grande in Tierra del Fuego. The British fleet could plan its self-preservation on that basis. They'd know where the Argentine attacks were coming from. They just wouldn't know when. Because missing from the Task Force air defences was a vital piece of the jigsaw.

It was an omission well understood by Lieutenant Commander Hugh Slade. The affable young fighter pilot was just five years old when he decided he wanted to be in the Navy. He signed up twelve years later.

During four years at Dartmouth he was given a taste of all the various different specializations available to him. A few days aboard a submarine proved to be more than enough, but a flight in a De Havilland Chipmunk during which a fire-breathing former Spitfire pilot threw the little trainer around the sky as if he had a Messerschmitt on his tail turned out to be one of the defining moments of his life. He made his decision to fly at the same point as the Fleet Air Arm realized it needed to train a new generation of pilots to fly the Sea Harrier.

Like his friend Bill Covington, he was boosted through flight training and sent to fly the Fairey Gannet AEW.3 from the deck of *Ark Royal*. And it was here, while serving with 849 'B' Flight, that he learned about the principles and practice of airborne early warning.

The Admiralty had sponsored trials of airborne radar to locate surface ships as early as 1937, but it was research in America, using a British invention shipped across the Atlantic in 1940 after the fall of France, that led to success. The cavity magnetron, which produced the powerful microwaves required for radar development, was described by its grateful recipients as 'the most valuable cargo ever brought to our shores'.

In early 1944, as American ships and aircraft battled Japanese forces across the vast expanses of the Pacific, the US Navy initiated Project CADILLAC. Named after the mountain in Maine whose peak is the first point in the continental United States to see the rising sun, it was an ambitious effort to produce a flying radar station that might look over the horizon to provide the fleet with early warning of attack. It was too late to see service before the end of the war, but the vulnerability of radar picket ships sent upthreat to alert the main body of the fleet to impending raids underlined the need for it. The distant, solitary sentry duties performed by the picket ships had made them live bait for the Kamikazes.

In 1949, the Douglas AD-3W Skyraider, equipped with a Hughes AN/APS-20 radar that could pick up ships and formations of aircraft at ranges of 100 miles or so, finally entered service with the US Navy. Following the outbreak of the Korean War in 1950, the Royal Navy ordered fifty Skyraiders of their own.

By 1978, 849 Squadron's handful of Gannet AEW.3s were all

the Navy had left. After inheriting the Skyraiders' AN/APS-20 radars and bolting them beneath the forward fuselage like a great upside-down mushroom, most of the Gannets' radars were now in the hands of the crabs – the nickname used by the Fleet Air Arm for their light blue counterparts. With the RAF assuming responsibility for the organic air defence of the fleet, the AN/APS-20s had been relocated once again, finding a new home attached to the noses of 8 Squadron's Avro Shackleton AEW.2s. As the British Task Force sailed south in April 1982, 8 Squadron remained firmly ensconced at their home base of RAF Lossiemouth near Elgin in Scotland. From there, even with a maximum endurance of nearly fifteen hours, these ancient descendants of the old Lancaster bomber were not going to be much help.

As it had been in March 1945, when fighting alongside the US Navy at the Battle of Okinawa, the Royal Navy would be dependent on radar picket ships for warning of impending attack. In the Pacific, with little time to react, Fleet Air Arm fighters had been unable to stop the Kamikazes getting through to the carriers. *Indefatigable*, *Formidable* and *Victorious* all took hits.

Hugh Slade was the last of its SHAR pilots that the Navy was able to scrape up for 809, and he also had the furthest to travel. After the demise of the Gannet, he'd flown Sea Harriers with Sharkey Ward on 700A, the Intensive Flying Trials Unit, and 801 before being sent to Nowra Naval Air Station in New South Wales. Here, the Royal Australian Navy was going to train him to become an Air Warfare Instructor. But he'd only been flying VC-724's A-4 Skyhawks and Macchi MB-326s for a couple of months when the High Commission in Canberra told him he was booked on to a flight home the following night. After watching the television news, he'd been expecting the call.

Slade's baby daughter Hannah was just two months old when she travelled out to Australia with him and his wife Josephine. Having now to leave them both behind in Australia as he rushed back to the UK was deeply upsetting. 'Don't worry,' he tried to reassure Josephine before boarding the Qantas flight back to Heathrow, 'it'll blow over.' *Surely*, he thought, *someone is going to see sense.*

It wasn't a view shared by his counterparts in Argentina.

*

At Base Aeronaval Comandante Espora, the Super Etendard pilots of 2 Escuadrilla Aeronaval de Caza y Ataque had been organized into two-man sections. The plan was to operate in well-practised pairs, providing for more robust communication and navigation during long, challenging over-water attack profiles and redundancy in the event of technical failure. On 10 April, the squadron practised air-to-air refuelling from the Fuerza Aérea Argentina's two Lockheed KC-130H Hercules tankers. If they managed to perfect the technique, the extra range would give the SuEs the ability to come at the British from any direction. And that greatly complicated the nature of the threat posed by Jorge Colombo's men.

The Royal Navy had no choice but to focus their limited resources on defending against where they *assumed* any attack might come from. But without airborne early warning, and without sufficient numbers of Type 42 radar pickets to provide 360° protection, the British were forced to accept that there were blind spots. There remained a desperate need to try to weigh the odds more heavily in favour of the Task Force and its small force of Sea Harriers and missile-armed air defence ships.

The Royal Air Force faced an entirely different problem. It was difficult to see how it might actually place itself in harm's way. And while initial studies focused on the Buccaneer, it was soon overtaken by the prospect of using the Avro Vulcan B.2.

Approaching the end of its long career as a nuclear bomber, it was due to be retired in just three months' time. But the big, charismatic delta-winged jet had potential. If it could be converted back to the role of conventional bomber it might, supported by a fleet of Handley Page Victor K.2 tankers, help address Northwood's reluctance to hazard the Sea Harriers in counter air missions. Armed with twenty-one 1,000lb bombs, the Vulcan provided an alternative means of putting the Port Stanley runway out of action.

While the Alert Measures Committee explored that and other options, including the possibility of forward basing in New Zealand and even Antarctica, ACAS (Ops) – Assistant Chief of the Air Staff, Operations – Air Vice-Marshal Ken Hayr, to whom the AMC reported, had his eyes on another prize, one that might just prove crucial to improving the fleet's chances of survival.

It was time to phone an old friend.

Wing Commander Sidney Edwards was mowing the lawn at his home near Marlow in Buckinghamshire when Ken Hayr called. Nearly thirty years earlier, the two men had been through officer training at the RAF College, Cranwell before going through the Hawker Hunter conversion course together.

'How long will it take you to get to Northwood?' Hayr asked.

'About an hour, sir.'

'Make it forty-five minutes and I'll see you at the main gate.'

Edwards was there in forty-three.

In a briefing room attended by senior personnel from all three armed services, Hayr explained that, in a few days' time, Edwards would be deploying to Chile on a covert mission. A fluent Spanish speaker following a tour as Air Attaché at the British Embassy in Madrid, Edwards had both diplomatic and intelligence experience, and the required high levels of security clearance. Reporting directly to Hayr, his role would be to act as liaison with the Chilean authorities, facilitating whatever assistance for Operation CORPORATE that he could. He would be the man on the spot, authorized to make decisions and recommendations and to take action as required – whatever could be done to help tip the balance in favour of British forces fighting to retake the Falklands.

'You should tell nobody where you are going or what you are going to do,' Hayr stressed, 'not even your wife.' He could tell her only that he was deploying on special duties until further notice. Hayr told Edwards he would call her periodically to reassure her that her husband was safe and well.

Over the next forty-eight hours, Edwards was briefed by the Chief of the Air Staff, Air Chief Marshal Sir Michael Beetham, and Intelligence and Operations staff at the MoD, before crossing White-hall to talk to the South American desk at the Foreign & Commonwealth Office on King Charles Street. He was driven to see Brigadier Peter de la Billière, Director Special Forces, at his office in

Chelsea. Unlike those he'd met in the MoD, de la Billière was wearing uniform and a holstered sidearm on both hips. And at the Chilean Embassy on Devonshire Street in Marylebone he met the Chilean Ambassador and Air Attaché, who were encouraging about his prospects. He was told he should expect a warm welcome in Santiago and excellent cooperation from the country's armed forces, in particular General Fernando Matthei, head of the Air Force.

'Like you, he's a Hunter pilot,' added the Air Attaché. 'You'll have a lot to talk about.'

Sidney Edwards would soon be coordinating some of the most closely guarded secret operations of the war.

# NINE

## Powder blue and salmon pink

TIM GEDGE SAT down in his office with his new Senior Pilot and Air Warfare Instructor the morning after their arrival from the States. He asked Dave Braithwaite to try to tailor a programme for 809's pilots that somehow condensed a nine-month operational training course into three weeks. Again, Gedge asked, What do we need? What should we be asking for?

Freshly minted as a Marine Corps WTI, Bill Covington was eager to bring to bear all he'd learned. But before he even got into more careful consideration of weapons and tactics, it was immediately obvious to him that the squadron's aircraft could do with looking a little more suited to the theatre they were deploying to. Four jets had now arrived from St Athan in various states of repair, but all shared the gloss dark sea grey and gleaming white undersides that was the standard livery for the Navy's Sea Harriers. Camouflage it was not. Gedge talked to DNAW to see what could be done.

They were already on the case.

Lieutenant Commander Leo Gallagher, a former F-4 Phantom Observer, had already visited the Royal Aircraft Establishment at Farnborough and been promised a report by their resident expert, Mr Philip J. Barley of the RAE's Defensive Weapons Department. That had yet to materialize, though. And so it was time to drag Mr Barley back from his Easter holidays.

Before he'd stepped into the cockpit of a Sea Harrier Bill Covington was on his way to Farnborough, the home of British aeronautical research and development.

Housed in an unprepossessing prefab, Mr Barley's workshop was pure Caractacus Potts. A collision of specialist scientific apparatus, optical equipment, tripods, mounts and model aeroplanes in all shapes, sizes and colours. Barley had been a student of the history of aircraft camouflage since the seventies, when the MoD ran trials using a pair of Hawker Hunters. Finances no longer allowed for that. Instead, Barley had Bert, the model-maker from the RAE's 40 Department, to build lots of Airfix kits. As the only contemporary RAF jet available in 1:24 scale, Bert's models were all, conveniently enough, of Hawker Harriers. And so Barley dug out his 1980 technical report evaluating the effect of different paint schemes on detection of the Harrier from the ground. Without access to real, airborne Hunters he'd set up his equipment on the flat roof of the Portakabin belonging to the RAE's Institute of Aviation Medicine to ensure that he could take his photometric measurements against an unbroken background of sky.

Covington listened carefully as Barley explained the principles of his work. Two things were key: reducing the contrast against the sky, and creating an element of uncertainty about which way an aeroplane was facing. Beyond a distance of a couple of miles it made no difference at all, but if in a dogfight an opponent thought up was down, and back was front, even momentarily, it was a valuable marginal advantage.

Fighter pilot and scientist discussed the priorities. What were the prevailing conditions like? The expected operational tactics? Based on what he imagined 809 would face, Covington explained that two main scenarios needed to be addressed: high-altitude interception and reducing the visibility of the jet as seen from below.

Drawing on lessons learned in the 1980 trial Barley began to consider the possibilities, thinking a five-colour scheme might work, with different shades of grey applied to either convex or concave parts of the airframe. The lightest shade would be used to reduce the distance from which dark shadows beneath the wings or the Harrier's big black elephant's-ear engine air intakes would give it away. Matt paint would be a must to reduce the possibility of sunlight glinting off the aircraft. The national markings would be toned down into pastel shades of powder blue and salmon pink. Perhaps even a false cockpit painted on the underside.

'How many aircraft do you have to paint?' Barley asked.

'Eight,' Covington replied.

'When?'

'Soon as you can.'

The Royal Navy was not alone in choosing to paint their peacetime jets in a handsome gloss grey and white scheme. The French thought it suited the Super Etendard too. And that was the colour, with the addition of the pale blue and white of the national flag to the rudder, that adorned the five jets belonging to the Armada Argentina. But while useless open-source information like that was relatively easy to come by, hard intelligence about the combat readiness and capability of the Argentine SuEs and Mirages was tougher to unearth. Tim Gedge wanted to know about the nature and quality of the threat, not orders of battle and notional top speeds. Judging by the content of the briefing documents he was being sent by the MoD, Jane's, the publisher of great breezeblock reference books on defence, was having a bumper month. Everyone seemed to have been stocking up with the latest edition. But if he was going into combat with aircraft designed and built on the other side of the Channel, it didn't seem unreasonable to want to know more than that. Even better, he wanted 809 to train against them in the air.

As boss of 800, Gedge had enjoyed warm relations with the Commanding Officer of one of the Aéronavale's two Super Etendard squadrons based at Landivisiau in Brittany. It was barely a fortnight since his successor, Andy Auld, had played host to a flight of four SuEs during which the SHARs appeared to have come out on top. But the SuE was never intended to be a dogfighter. It was an attack jet, and now Gedge needed to interrogate that capability a little more thoroughly. It was time to extend another invitation to his French counterpart. Gedge phoned him, but, it turned out, the situation was now very different. The CO of the Aéronavale squadron was very sorry but his hands were tied. He'd have been only too willing to come over to Yeovilton, but he'd been told no. From above.

Instead of insights into the SuE, DNAW produced a report on the birdstrike hazard to fast jets in the South Atlantic drafted by the Aviation Bird Unit at Worplesdon in Surrey. Gedge learned that 'unlike the birds encountered around the British Isles many of those in the South

Atlantic are very large'. The report included a map of albatross distribution in South Georgia, and while it acknowledged that the Falkland Islands' largest bird, the gentoo penguin, 'was incapable of flight' it warned that they could jump a bit, albeit not 'very far off the ground'.

Also from Surrey came a Senior Scientist from the Defence Operational Analysis Establishment at West Byfleet. Gedge's formal request for a comprehensive brief on the Argentine capability appeared to have borne fruit. Before the squadron briefing, Gedge invited his visitor into his office for coffee to hear a little more about what he planned to say. The DOAE were proud of having been able to tweak an existing computer program to model and predict the course of the Operation CORPORATE air war. Prior to getting into the detail of that, the civil servant once more ran through the kind of numbers-of-aircraft information anyone could glean from Jane's. So far it hardly seemed worth gathering his pilots. Then the analyst told the 809 Squadron boss that their modelling predicted that most of the Sea Harriers were going to be shot down by the end of day two.

'Thank you very much for the briefing,' Gedge managed equably. 'I'll see you out.'

'But,' began the shocked scientist, 'I want to brief your people.'

'No,' Gedge told him politely, but unequivocally, 'you're not going to if that's what you're going to say.'

The scientist wasn't having it. He'd come all the way to deliver his pearls of wisdom and wasn't going back until he'd done so. Eventually Gedge called up the Master at Arms to have him escorted out. As the insults hurled at him by the apoplectic civil servant receded into the distance, Gedge called Captain Peter Williams, Yeovilton's Commanding Officer, to explain what had happened; that he wasn't prepared to have his pilots exposed to such ill-informed and entirely counter-productive guff.

'You might well have some sort of complaint about it in due course,' Gedge told him, then heard a commotion down the line from the Captain's office.

'Tim, I think it's just arrived . . .'

There was better news from Dave Ramsay at Valley. When Gedge phoned to find out how the trials were going, he was told the trials team had packed up and gone home. His initial reaction was irritation. He'd given Ramsay clear instructions not to return to Yeovilton until they were complete. But when he finally caught up with the Australian pilot, Ramsay explained that he'd been trying to reach Gedge on the phone. They were done. Six shots, six hits. One hundred per cent.

It was cause for encouragement, but the analysts at DOAE weren't the only ones who had concerns about the levels of Sea Harrier attrition that Task Force commanders should prepare for. And one of them was Gedge's boss at Fort Southwick, Rear Admiral Derek Reffell, who, prior to the launch of Operation CORPORATE, had enjoyed responsibility for the Navy's carriers and amphibious ships. Reffell had produced a graph suggesting that, through a combination of combat losses and unserviceability, just ten Sea Harriers would be operational by the end of the first week of the war. He predicted that on each day that the Sea Harriers faced determined resistance from the enemy it was likely one or two would be lost. 'And this,' he concluded, 'may well be an optimistic estimate.'

Director of Naval Air Warfare Ben Bathurst was asked to sense-check the Admiral's assumptions and deductions. Without actually contradicting him, Bathurst presented an interpretation that sounded a good deal less categorical than the dismal picture painted by Reffell. All the same, he acknowledged the need to bolster the small Sea Harrier force – but, he pointed out, he was trying to do just that. 'It is intended,' he reassured them, 'to give this the highest priority with 809 NAS.'

Yet while the Navy's Sea Harriers may have been a desperately finite resource, they were not the only fast jets in the British arsenal that were capable of operating from the deck of an aircraft carrier.

# TEN

## A transatlantic affair

As a young Wing Commander in 1969, after tours on Hunters and Lightnings, Ken Hayr had taken charge of the RAF's first Harrier GR.1 squadron, 1(F) Squadron at RAF Wittering. He was the third Commanding Officer in less than six months. The first had been killed in a flying accident; the second didn't take to vertical take-off and landing. But Hayr quickly fell in love with the Harrier, shepherding its revolutionary new capability into RAF service. There were deployments to Cyprus, Sardinia and Norway, and operations from rough fields and forest. And in May 1971 he led a detachment to HMS *Ark Royal* to explore the feasibility of operating from a ship. Hayr was in Flyco when, after the 'heavies' had launched, the weather clamped down. Following a succession of failed attempts by the Phantoms and Buccaneers to land on deck, Wings (the ship's Commander Air) ordered them all to divert to the mainland. The fog was so thick that, as the heavies overshot, it was barely possible to see them as they accelerated away past the island. But Hayr's two jets were also airborne.

'Couldn't the Harriers just have a go at landing? They've stacks of fuel.'

Before Hayr got an answer, one of the GR.1s emerged from the mist, with his nozzles down, slowly descending along the glidepath. Its pilot had spotted *Ark*'s wake, slammed the nozzles forward to the brake-stop and been able to decelerate fast enough to be able to stick an immediate vertical landing on board.

It was the first evidence that the Harrier could take off and land at sea in conditions that would keep conventional carrier aircraft lashed firmly to the deck. And Hayr had no reason to believe that the current generation of Harrier pilots would have any more difficulty doing so than he and his pilots had.

A decade on, in the days after the Task Force sailed, Air Vice-Marshal Hayr contacted 1(F)'s current boss, and former Red Arrow, Wing Commander Peter Squire, just to sow the seed. If, he asked, the squadron's Harriers were used to reinforce the Fleet Air Arm Sea Harriers, what modifications and training might be required? He'd even signalled the Navy suggesting that, based on his own experience, RAF Harrier GR.3s could, if required, fly direct to the carriers as they steamed south.

At DNAW, an initially reluctant Ben Bathurst was persuaded by CINCFLEET that whatever reinforcement the RAF could provide was welcome. And, since Hayr had first helped usher the Harrier into frontline service in the late sixties, over 150 had been delivered to the RAF.

In truth, Hayr knew that the Task Force would be better served if his GR.3s took more time to prepare. Expected to carry out ground attack missions in a land war against Warsaw Pact forces fought across the plains of central Europe, if they were going to become an attrition reserve for the Sea Harriers, the jets would need modifications and new weapons clearances. Their crews would need air combat training. Realistically, they wouldn't be ready to join the fleet en route.

Fortunately, there were other plans afoot.

Squadron Leader Bob Iveson picked up his flying jacket and walked out of the briefing room. A large man with a thick walrus moustache, Big Bob had the appearance of a military officer from a bygone era. But while he might have looked at home in the open cockpit of a Sopwith Camel, a Hawker Harrier awaited him. Ahead was the prospect of leading a four-ship of GR.3s across the Atlantic to Goose Bay for Exercise MAPLE FLAG 9, where 1(F) would get to enjoy the spectacularly good low flying that Canada's NATO training ranges had to offer. If he was honest, given the crisis brewing in the South Atlantic, it seemed a little strange they were still going, but 13 April had been fixed as the departure date and the powers that be were sticking to it. But just as Iveson got to Ops Desk to sign out the jet, the squadron boss came running in.

'Hang on,' Peter Squire said, 'the squadron are still going, but someone's got to go and have a look at a ship.'

That was definitely not what Iveson was expecting. He was pointed in the direction of the phone, picked up the receiver and found himself talking directly to the Assistant Chief of the Air Staff. Ken Hayr explained that he wanted an expert opinion view of a container ship that was currently alongside in Liverpool Docks.

'I need you to tell me if you think we can put Harriers on it, vertical only; we don't need to fight from it, just get them down there as reserves. The only snag is that there's a meeting at two p.m. today and I need to know by then.'

Iveson looked at his watch. It was already 8.30 in the morning. Peterborough to Liverpool wasn't looking too clever.

'How am I going to get there?' he asked.

'My jet's landing as we speak.'

Outside, a Hawker Siddeley Dominie T.1, the RAF's version of the HS125 business jet, descended across the A1 towards the threshold of Runway 26, landed and taxied up to the hardstanding.

Bob Iveson was chosen for good reason. It wasn't that as a boy he'd contemplated joining the Fleet Air Arm in defiance of his father, Hank, a decorated Second World War RAF bomber pilot and Squadron Commander. Instead, ACAS (Ops) wanted to draw on Iveson's experience flying Harriers on exchange with the US Marine Corps.

After winning a flying scholarship and finishing top of the class during flying training, Iveson was chosen as one of the first pilots to join an RAF Harrier squadron straight after earning his wings. So when he joined VMA-542 at Marine Corps Air Station Cherry Point, North Carolina, in 1976 with 850 hours under his belt, he immediately became the most experienced Harrier pilot in the squadron. The only other pilot who even came close was his friend Terry Matkey USMC. And Matkey had clocked up much of his flight time on exchange with an RAF Harrier squadron. The two pilots couldn't have provided better evidence of the way the Harrier, from its inception, had always been a transatlantic affair.

\*

Without American support, it's entirely possible there'd never even have been a Harrier; at least not one that existed beyond the confines of Ralph Hooper's sketchbook. As early as 1959, NASA saw enough potential in the embryonic British jump jet design to provide encouraging technical reports. And while the Hawker board might have sanctioned building two P.1127 prototypes without any official backing, it was American money from an organization called the Mutual Weapons Development Program based in Paris – a sort of military start-up incubator – that largely financed the construction of the expensive BE53 Pegasus engines on which flying prototypes were dependent. Indeed it was the same agency that had introduced Sir Stanley Hooker to Michel Wibault's Gyroptère in the first place. Such was the lack of British government interest or support that one senior USAF General was sure that without intervention 'an all British P.1127 would die a natural death – it would just wither away'. And so the Pentagon proposed the creation of a multinational evaluation squadron to conduct a series of trials using a development of the P.1127 known as the Kestrel. For nearly a year British, American and German pilots flew the Kestrel from fields around Norfolk, losing one and badly damaging another in a hard vertical landing which allowed its Luftwaffe pilot, Lieutenant Colonel Gerhard Barkhorn, a Second World War ace with 301 Allied kills to his credit, to claim 'Drei hundert und zwei' as he walked away from the broken jet.

With the conclusion of the trials in 1966, six Kestrels were shipped back to the US where, designated the XV-6A, they flew for NASA and the USAF for another three years. When the Kestrels were flown from the decks of the assault ships USS *Raleigh* and *La Salle* and the supercarrier *Independence*, the US Marine Corps followed it all with mounting interest. Then in 1968, a young Marine Corps officer told his boss, the General responsible for determining the Marine Corps' aviation needs, 'Sir, I've just seen a film I've gotten from the British Embassy . . .'

The footage of the Harrier GR.1, now in production for the RAF, stunned the General. With nearly one and a half times the thrust of the Kestrel and armed with twin 30mm cannon and five weapons hardpoints beneath the wings and fuselage, the Harrier was a machine of a different order altogether. Unlike the Kestrel it was a real *warplane*. And one which, through its unique ability to use rough-field sites ashore, had the potential to unshackle the Marines from their dependence on the US Navy to get their fast air close enough to the forward edge of battle to give the grunts on the ground air support when they needed it.

Within months, a pair of USMC test pilots had flown the Harrier at Dunsfold and reported back enthusiastically. The Marines' conviction that the Harrier was the airplane for them hardened throughout the seventies. After a fierce battle for funding, over a hundred Harriers, known in the US as the AV-8A, were eventually delivered to the Marine Corps. All were built in the UK.

But if the Harrier owed its existence to support from America, the Pentagon was now suggesting that the jump jet's future development depended on the UK returning the favour.

In Washington, the Department of Defense held London's decision not to participate largely to blame for the collapse of an ambitious plan to build a second-generation Harrier labelled the AV-16. In its place came the AV-8B, a more modest upgrade that it was expected would deliver most of the cancelled jet's capability at a fraction of the cost. But by the end of the decade the new programme too looked fragile. And the RAF was unsure whether or not the AV-8B offered the speed and manoeuvrability it required of a new Harrier. The US Secretary of Defense told his British counterpart if the UK didn't buy the jet in preference to BAe's alternative design for a 'Big Wing' Harrier GR.5, 'the United States was unlikely to buy any'.

In 1979, with the programme in the balance, Bob Iveson was one of two British pilots sent out to the US Navy Test and Evaluation Center at Patuxent River to fly the new YAV-8B prototype and report back.

A few years on and it looked like Iveson's evaluation of a ship's potential as a Harrier carrier might see him pulled into a war that could make or break the jump jet's reputation. There was just one problem with that, though.

By the end of his exchange tour with the Marine Corps, Bob Iveson had qualified as an Attack Training Officer and on leaving was commended by the US Secretary for the Navy for his contribution to 'updating and rewriting the AV8 Tactical Manual that is now employed throughout the Marine Corps'. But, ironically, despite Hayr's confidence in him, the one thing his time with VMA-542 had not provided him with was much experience of ships. British foreign policy over Japan had prevented him from deploying to the Pacific with the rest of the squadron. Instead he'd been limited to a handful of take-offs and landings aboard passing amphibious carriers as they sailed up and down the eastern seaboard. He'd barely even left the cockpit.

Nonetheless Iveson and Bruce Sobey, 1(F)'s Senior Engineering Officer, climbed aboard the little 32 Squadron liaison jet and took their seats for the short flight to Liverpool's Speke Airport. They were told a helicopter would be waiting for them on arrival.

# ELEVEN

## Vast experience and a big heart

OVER LUNCH, ELSPETH and the boys discussed what they thought he should take with him now he was joining the 'Armada'. That morning, her husband, Captain Michael Layard, had been on gardening leave, looking forward to taking up a new post as Captain of HMS *Seahawk*, the Royal Naval Air Station at Culdrose. Then came the call from the Navy Department at the MoD explaining that they were going to convert a container ship into an aircraft carrier to take Sea Harriers and helicopters down to the South Atlantic. They wanted him to sail with her.

Layard, a distinguished former fighter pilot with experience commanding a frigate, had the perfect CV to become Senior Naval Officer aboard the MV *Atlantic Conveyor*, a twelve-year-old container ship requisitioned from Cunard as part of the government's STUFT programme. She was currently laid up in Liverpool awaiting a thorough survey before conversion.

As much as Layard might have wanted to take a reminder of home with him to war, his son suggested leaving the framed collage of family photos behind, 'just in case it doesn't come back!'

The idea of converting a merchant ship into an aircraft carrier was not a new one. In 1940, the *Hannover*, a captured German banana boat, had her masts, upper bridge and much of her superstructure removed to make room for an unbroken 368-foot-long flight deck from which a small squadron of tubby little Grumman Martlet fighters could operate. She was commissioned as HMS *Audacity* and sailed in defence of Convoy HG76 as it steamed between Britain and Gibraltar in 1941.

For four months the pilots of 802 Naval Air Squadron lived in very unmilitary splendour in the old freighter's twelve staterooms, while putting up fierce resistance against long-range German Focke-Wulf Fw 200 Condor bombers and U-boats. But in the end *Audacity* was unable to protect herself and, on 21 December, was hit by torpedoes; with her bow blown off, she sank ten minutes later. But the concept was proven and other merchant carriers followed.

The introduction of the now familiar intermodal shipping container in the 1950s had revolutionized the freight industry. Its subsequent ubiquity prompted a dramatic re-evaluation of the notion of the merchant carrier. In the US the ARAPAHO programme and in the UK SCADS – the Shipborne Containerized Air Defence System – promised standardized, pre-fabricated aviation facilities able to transform an average fast container ship into a vessel capable of operating helicopters and V/STOL aircraft within forty-eight hours – a new generation of plug-and-play merchant carriers capable of defending the sea-lanes in times of emergency.

And while, in April 1982, neither ARAPAHO nor SCADS was any more than a paper project, the studies were dusted off inside the MoD in time for Layard's arrival for a day of meetings about how best to configure and operate *Atlantic Conveyor*. The following morning he caught a train from Euston to Liverpool Lime Street to go and see her for himself.

On boarding the 15,000-ton ship, Layard was greeted warmly by her Master, Captain Ian North. A veteran of the Second World War's Battle of the Atlantic, the rotund, white-bearded mariner was a man with vast experience and a big heart. Born in Doncaster, the avuncular old seadog had been just fourteen years old when he first went to sea in 1939. Now fifty-seven, North was a highly respected and popular ship's Captain, regarded by his crews as firm, fearless and fair, and by Cunard as the man to turn to whenever a new class of vessel, route or procedure required breaking in. He seemed to be tailor-made for the challenge ahead.

Layard liked him immediately. Despite North's twelve-year-old ship having been laid up for nine months, a walk around the cargo areas and weatherdecks revealed little of concern other than his tendency to stop and chat as he negotiated the ship's companion-ways. Layard got the impression that the regular pauses in their progress around the ship were largely so that the Captain could catch his breath. But while he may not quite have been at fighting weight, the Master seemed unfazed by the prospect of going to war. Instead he radiated pride in his ship and her crew.

From the bridge, *Conveyor*'s potential as a makeshift aviation ship was obvious. There was no time for the kind of work imagined by the SCADS programme to turn her into a genuine Harrier carrier, but fitted with landing pads fore and aft, as a means of getting reinforcements to the Task Force, she fitted the bill.

Before leaving the docks to catch his train back to London, Layard looked back at the ship's 40-foot-high black slab-sided freeboards and white superstructure that towered above him and he thought about how she might defend herself from air attack.

Similar considerations continued to occupy 809 Squadron. On his return to Yeovilton, Hugh Slade was surprised to get a phone call from DNAW asking him about the capability of the A-4 Skyhawk flown by both Argentina and the Australian Navy. He tried to explain that he'd barely finished the this-is-how-you-fly-it part of the course.

'Surely we've got all this info somewhere?' he asked.

'Not really,' they told him. There were plenty of intelligence assessments of Soviet MiGs, Sukhois, Yaks and Tupolevs, but the American-built jet was never supposed to be the enemy. That also meant, however, that dotted around both Yeovilton and the wider defence establishment the knowledge was there; it's just that it was to be found in pockets of personal expertise and experience. Brave's time at TOPGUN and Point Mugu meant he was well acquainted with the A-4. After frontline tours on VF-805 flying the Skyhawk for the Royal Australian Navy, Dave Ramsay knew it inside out. He'd even written a report for the RAN a year earlier comparing it in detail to the Sea Harrier. That, clearly, had not been made available to the MoD. Instead they'd found an experienced US Marine Corps aviator who told them that in a low-speed dogfight the early-model A-4 operated by the Argentinians was 'extremely good', adding that it could claim kills against the Harrier 'if flown by reasonably experienced Argentinians'.

He should have known that his assessment of the Skyhawk's chances against the Harrier was not shared by all of his fellow leathernecks. Far from it. Because it had been the Marine Corps that had first explored the Harrier's unique attributes in air combat.

From day one, the Marines planned to equip their AV-8A Harriers with Sidewinder missiles. Because of its ability to deploy forward, using rough-field sites, the Harrier would likely have to fend for itself against whatever opposition the enemy put up. And so when the first Marine Corps Harrier squadron, VMA-513 'The Flying Nightmares', formed in 1971, developing an air-to-air capability was a priority. By the mid-seventies the Harriers had taken on pretty much every other machine in the US arsenal. They'd even deployed to Area 51, the top-secret facility at Groom Lake, Nevada, where they encountered real, live MiGs operated by the USAF as part of a highly classified deep black programme. And they beat them all.

The secret was the Marines' exploitation of a technique called VIFFing – vectoring in forward flight. By rotating the nozzles of the Pegasus engine in wingborne flight, Marine Corps pilots were achieving turn ratios that computer modelling – or *physics* – suggested weren't possible. At least not without losing so much speed and energy that you became a sitting duck. The trick was to use the technique sparingly; to tweak the nozzles briefly to nudge the nose more tightly into the turn before rotating them backwards again before too much forward speed was lost. An additional benefit, it seemed – and one which neither the computers nor Harrier Chief Designer John Fozard's calculations had predicted – was that by artificially lowering the load on the wings using the vectored thrust from the engine, the Harrier was turning more tightly than its small wing should theoretically have been capable of. When he first received a phone call from an excited Marine Corps test pilot saying it was so, Fozard refused to believe it. But in the end it was undeniable.

'There is no aircraft in the world which can stay behind a Harrier,' claimed another VMA-513 pilot. 'You can decelerate faster than any aircraft in the world, unless it hits a brick wall.'

*

If fleet air defence had been all about dogfighting, 809 would have been in great shape, but the ability, as Hugh Slade put it, to knife-fight in a phone box was just one element of the fleet interceptor's toolkit. And in the opinion of the MoD's scientific advisers, the Defence Scientific Staff, 'the SHAR lacked the range, speed, sufficient missiles and high speed dash and acceleration capability of a true Fleet Air Defence fighter'.

Dave Braithwaite tended to agree. To a point, at least. Admittedly, as he'd strapped himself back into the cockpit of the little Sea Harrier FRS.1 after returning from Point Mugu, his first thought was *Oh dear, here we go again*. A couple of weeks earlier he'd been burning holes in the sky in the cockpit of a Grumman F-14 Tomcat. *A meaningful aeroplane. All the same*, he thought, *any fighter pilot can tell when there's bullshit around*. Too much of what he was reading about Argentine capabilities, not to mention what was being said about the SHAR, seemed overstated. Top Trumps stuff not informed by operational experience or understanding.

And if there was a decent enough appreciation of the A-4 Skyhawk, useful intelligence on the Argentine fighter threat in the form of the Mirage III remained sketchy. A decades-old A&AEE evaluation praised its good performance and imagined it 'should be one of the leading supersonic fighters' but was less than enlightening.

Once again, Dave Ramsay was able to provide some insight as he'd trained with Royal Australian Air Force Mirages back home. Supersonic, and armed with radar-guided missiles that outranged the SHAR's Sidewinder, in the right hands they certainly had the potential to cause problems.

Brave too had some knowledge to share. While in the US he'd had access to combat reports written by Israeli Mirage pilots, but they made for cold comfort. Between 1966 and 1974 they'd chalked up nearly 300 kills against a well-equipped enemy. In less than a decade, thirty-five IAF pilots had, with at least five kills to their names, become aces. Nearly forty former IAF Neshers, a pirated Israeli copy of the more manoeuvrable Mirage 5, had since entered service with the Fuerza Aérea Argentina, where they were known as Daggers.

In the end, though, there was really only one way to establish the nature of the threat they posed: in the air.

Tim Gedge continued to push hard for a chance to pitch 809's Sea Harriers against the Mirage and Super Etendard in 1 v 1 air combat training. Eventually the French Defence Attaché in London complained to the RAF about the 809 CO's efforts. It was vital, stressed the Marine Nationale Admiral, that any French support for the British in relation to the Falklands was kept secret. And he summarily dismissed any possibility of the Sea Harrier jousting with the SuE as 'not convenient'.

Part of the problem for France was simply that the Sea Harrier was the competition. In 1979 the Armada Argentina had once again been on the lookout for new jets to fly from their carrier. The ARA had believed they'd come close to acquiring the highly rated Vought A-7 Corsair II light attack jet from the US, but a US arms embargo put paid to that. Instead, they turned their attention to Britain and France. British Aerospace was hopeful they had convinced the Argentinians that to operate Dassault's Super Etendard from the deck would require expensive new catapult equipment to be installed on *25 de Mayo*. In support of BAe's sales pitch for the SHAR, the MoD pointed out to the FCO that it was 'extremely unlikely that the Argentinians would ever use it against the Falklands'. Ironically, the danger turned out not to be from how the ARA might use its new jets in any attack *against* the Falkland Islands, but how they would employ them in their defence.

In the end the Argentine Admirals once again opted not to pursue the Harrier, but at various points in the SHAR's life BAe had entertained the prospect of selling the Sea Jet to a long list of countries including China, India, Iran, Chile, Brazil, Australia and even France itself. The Super Etendard was in some cases the only plausible alternative. With millions of dollars of business at stake it was perhaps understandable that the French were a little coy about sharing.

At the time of the negotiations with Argentina, one argument made by the MoD in favour of selling them the Sea Harrier was that 'If the Argentinians opted for the Super Etendard then the aircraft would be available sooner and we would have no control whatsoever over the logistic support.'

With five SuEs already in the hangars at Comandante Espora, the former had certainly turned out to be true enough, but Britain had been able to exert a degree of influence over the latter. Following the imposition of a French arms embargo, President François Mitterrand was able to reassure Margaret Thatcher that Argentina would receive no further help integrating the jets and their missiles. His brother, Jacques, was CEO of the company that built them.

The technical team from Aérospatiale that 2 Escuadrilla had expected in mid-April never arrived. It meant that the complex job of coupling the big AM.39 Exocet missiles to the squadron's Super Etendards had to be figured out in country using only the manuals that had been supplied with the kit. The 2 Escuadrilla engineers and technicians greeted the news that they were on their own with understandable gloom, angry that France had broken its contract. Not only would they have to master the technical detail of setting up and fine-tuning the weapons system, they'd also have to do so without the deeper experience and understanding of the intricacies of the AM.39 that would inevitably have come with representatives from the manufacturer. The squadron would have to discover the Exocet's quirks, foibles, short cuts and work-arounds for themselves. Or nearly.

Their efforts were helped when an Argentine airline pilot on a scheduled flight from Paris to Buenos Aires brought with him valuable information on the Exocet's inertial guidance system, installation and circuitry. A disaffected technician at Dassault, the Super Etendard's manufacturer, had shared the documents with Argentine naval personnel still working in France who'd passed them to Capitán de Navío Julio Lavezzo, a former SuE pilot now working at the Argentine Embassy in Paris. Recognizing their potentially critical value to 2 Escuadrilla's technicians, he pressed them into the hands of an Aerolíneas Argentinas Captain for immediate return to Buenos Aires.

The lights in the hangar at Comandante Espora never went out. Inside, work continued around the clock beneath the wings of the

SuEs, each of which sat primed, tail low and nose high on slender undercarriage, like a mantis poised to strike.

France may have cut off the flow of any further technical assistance to Argentina, but there was nothing they could do about either the aircraft and weapons already delivered, or the knowledge already imparted. It had been eighteen months since around fifty personnel from 2 Escuadrilla had travelled to France for an introduction to the AM.39 Exocet with the Marine Nationale at Landivisiau. After completing an intensive language course at Rochefort, they had proved to be conscientious students.

As the warship sliced through the heavy South Atlantic swell, the Type 909 air defence radar scanned the horizon. Inside, Teniente de Fragata Armando Mayora sat in the darkened Operations Room of the ARA *Hercules* watching the concentric circles of the radar screen glowing orange. The Super Etendard pilot had been flown out to the Type 42 destroyer by helicopter to see for himself how well 2 Escuadrilla's preparations were coming along.

For days now, Mayora and the rest of the squadron's ten pilots had been training intensively, developing mission profiles that saw them cover long distances over the sea at ultra-low level in radio and electronic silence. In support, piston-engined Aeronaval Lockheed SP-2H Neptunes and Grumman S-2E Trackers patrolled the open water, scanning ahead with long-range radar and radar-detectors to find and report the position of potential targets. In barely a fortnight, each of the SuE pilots had logged some twenty hours of flight time. And now, thanks to the extraordinary efforts of the squadron's engineers and technicians, it was coming together.

On 17 April, a pair of SuEs launched on a training flight from Comandante Espora. After taking on fuel from an Air Force KC-130H nearly 300 miles from base, they descended towards the sea and accelerated to 500 knots to carry out a successful dummy attack against the *Hercules'* sister ship, *Santísima Trinidad*. Unlike the British Sea Harriers, armed only with iron bombs, the Exocet-armed SuEs didn't have to run the gauntlet of the British-built destroyers' Sea Dart missile defences. With his aircraft's return to base, the squadron's Commanding Officer, Jorge Colombo, felt confident that the Exocet could be launched accurately. More importantly, he knew his pilots were capable of breaching the British defences.

Ironically, rather than providing a measure of control, the export of a state-of-the-art weapons system by Britain to Argentina had simply ensured that the enemy faced by the Royal Navy was now more confident of success.

Colombo signalled the Armada Argentina Command to tell them that the Super Etendard/Exocet combination was operational.

*We asked for thirty days*, noted the 2 Escuadrilla boss with satisfaction, *it took only fifteen. The squadron is ready.*

In the months immediately before the British Task Force sailed, the Royal Navy had been refining a policy paper examining its future operational requirements. In its conclusions it admitted that the Navy's air defences suffered from some major shortcomings. It pointed out that the use of ships as radar pickets was in decline as they were both vulnerable and ineffective. The ability of the Sea Harrier to shoot down missile-carrying aircraft, it reported, 'was likely to be small'. Against the missiles themselves, it had 'none'.

In Paris, another former Argentine naval aviator, Capitán de Navío Carlos Corti, joined Julio Lavezzo at the Argentine Military Commission on Avenue Marceau near the Arc de Triomphe. Their task was to try to acquire more Exocets.

# TWELVE

## A target-rich environment

'THE ARGENTINES HAVEN'T fought a war for over a hundred and fifty years. They may have relatively modern hardware, but I believe that the last bit of up-to-date training they received was from Adolf Galland, the German fighter ace from World War Two.' On board HMS *Invincible*, Sharkey Ward had the room. As the Task Force sailed south, he and his senior team were conducting a threat reduction exercise.

Ward was a self-styled maverick. But for all his energy, skill and leadership, his inability to mince his words could also rub people up the wrong way. Cut from the same cloth as legendary Second World War characters such as Douglas Bader, David Stirling and Orde Wingate, you were either with him or out in the cold. And while, like them, he may not have had the temperament to reach high command, he inspired great loyalty and confidence from his men and from the ship's Captain, JJ Black. And now, after 801's relentless weapons training programme as the Task Force had sailed south, he'd enjoyed an intoxicating whiff of cordite. War would provide him with the opportunity to prove himself, his squadron and his aircraft. In his view, the numerical odds stacked against the small force of SHARs were to be welcomed as a target-rich environment.

Ward's planning team found it relatively straightforward to agree on tactics for countering the threat from the Fuerza Aérea Argentina's Mirages, Daggers and Skyhawks. There was more debate about how to deal with the Aeronaval's Exocet-armed Super Etendards, however. Their conclusions relied on a series of assumptions about how the SuEs would be employed, on the early detection of large-scale raids, and on throwing successive CAP (combat air patrol) pairs down the throat of the threat axis to disrupt and destroy the attackers. If, though, the SuEs came in low and fast from any direction other than that of the main attack Sharkey could offer no more than the promise that he'd have jets available to respond. Even the irrepressible 801 Squadron CO couldn't guarantee that that response would be effective. Individual ships themselves, he concluded, *could take early and appropriate Exocet counter-measures.* In effect, without sufficient time to position his fighters upthreat, they were on their own. Ward was loath to admit it, but without airborne early warning he couldn't guarantee full air superiority. And he cursed the RAF's inability to provide the global air defence the fleet had been promised.

But while in the Falklands the Navy would be operating beyond the range of the RAF AEW and fighter cover, it didn't mean that the Air Force was sitting on its hands.

The same MoD policy paper that had been so clear about the difficulties faced by the Navy in defending itself against missile attack stressed the need for adequate warning of impending attack to coordinate the reaction. Included on the list of ways in which that warning could be provided were satellites, communications intelligence, electronic surveillance, radar and the rapid exchange of information.

For satellite coverage of the region, the British would be dependent on what the United States was willing to provide. For the rest, the country – and the RAF – would have to rely on its own resources.

RAF Wyton was the home of RAF ISTAR (Intelligence, Surveillance, Target Acquisition and Reconnaissance). From model-makers building scale reproductions of Warsaw Pact targets to liaison with 'E' Division at GCHQ, the air station near Huntingdon in Cambridgeshire was the distillation of a Royal Air Force intelligence-gathering capability that had once been much more extensive. However, it continued to enjoy an impressively full spectrum of capabilities. And when it came to taking photographs, responsibility rested with the English Electric Canberra PR.9s of 39(PR) Squadron.

After two decades flying photo-reconnaissance missions around the world, the unit's boss, Wing Commander Colin Adams, was now anticipating 39's demise at the end of May. With just five aircraft to its name, 39(PR) was to lose its status as a full squadron. And what would become 1 PRU (Photographic Reconnaissance Unit) wasn't going to need a Wing Commander to run it, so his time in the cockpit of the PR.9 would also soon be coming to an end. He'd had a remarkable run though.

After entering Cranwell in 1958, Adams had spent over twenty years flying photo-reconnaissance in the Canberra, sneaking around the edges of places of interest like Syria, British Guiana, Guatemala, Yemen, Indonesia and China. In January 1982 there'd even been the prospect of deploying to North Africa after the Prime Minister's son Mark Thatcher got lost in the Sahara during the Paris–Dakar rally. Leaving at short notice for destinations he couldn't share with his wife and disappointing fighter pilots who struggled to interfere with his squadron's high-flying activities counted for normal. For that excitement, he had the remarkable PR.9 to thank.

While the Canberra, Britain's first jet bomber, first took to the air in the late forties, the PR.9, the most advanced British development of the jet, was regarded by some of its crews as an almost new aeroplane. With uprated Rolls-Royce Avon 206 engines delivering nearly twice the power of earlier marks, powered flight controls and larger wings, it was a strategic reconnaissance platform of exceptional flexibility and performance. The Canberra had always been a spritely performer, but the PR.9 was something of a hotrod.

While Adams had been a Flight Commander with 13 Squadron at RAF Luqa in Malta, new pilots weren't considered to be operational until they'd managed to capture a picture of the whole of Malta in a single frame. To do that required precision flying at an altitude of 66,000 feet. Adams himself had flown the PR.9 as high as 68,000 feet. By 1982, the System III camera capsule it had inherited from the American U-2 spyplane meant it could tell the time on Big Ben while flying at over 40,000 feet above the Isle of Wight.

Just twenty-three PR.9s were built by Short Brothers in Belfast. Those that remained, carefully nurtured to preserve the dwindling fatigue life of their old airframes, were now under the care of Colin Adams at Wyton. But, when the 39 Squadron boss had first been asked to make a contribution to the crisis in the South Atlantic, the plan was to leave them all at home.

The invitation to Northwood HQ from Air Marshal Sir John Curtiss had sounded almost informal – a discussion of photo-reconnaissance followed 'by lunch at my house'. But Curtiss, the Air Commander of Operation CORPORATE, who knew Adams of old, left him in no doubt about the urgency of the request.

At Northwood the following day, 16 April, he was introduced to Major-General Jeremy Moore, who would soon deploy south as Land Force Commander. Adams outlined his thoughts on capturing the required imagery of both the Falkland Islands and the location of Argentine ships. Operating out of Punta Arenas in southern Chile, the Canberras could depart south towards Antarctica, climbing to height through Chilean airspace over Cape Horn and into international airspace before doglegging east then north towards the islands at extreme altitude. There was much detailed planning to be done, but Adams was confident that by flying at over 60,000 feet or, alternatively, descending to 15,000 to 20,000 feet and using the oblique, sideways-facing cameras while standing off at a distance from the islands, the jets would be reasonably safe from Argentine attention.

There would need to be, Adams realized, some means for the detachment to be able to pass on the intelligence gleaned to the fleet in a timely fashion, but for now Curtiss simply wanted to know whether, in principle, Adams and his men could do the job.

Reassured by Northwood, the Chief of the Defence Staff recommended to his political masters that a pair of Canberra PR.9s be despatched to RAF Belize in Central America, ready to continue their journey south as soon as arrangements could be made to receive them.

Frustrated at the paucity and tardiness of intelligence from the South Atlantic, the British Chiefs of the Defence Staff had first discussed the possibility of deploying RAF Canberras to Chile within days of the invasion. Initial discussions, though, had focused on the notion of using the older, less operationally capable but longer-ranged PR.7

version of the jet. While a design for quickly adding an air-to-air refuelling capability to the PR.9 had been completed in 1966 it had never been pursued. Until now the PR.9's 2,000-mile unrefuelled range had been sufficient, but the distances and logistic challenges involved in getting recce aircraft over the Falklands were staggering.

Without diplomatic clearance to overfly Central or South American countries, the Canberras would be forced to fly east, leapfrogging from Italy to Cyprus, then Bahrain, Oman, Sri Lanka, Malaysia, Australia, Fiji, Tahiti and Easter Island to mainland Chile – forty-eight hours' flying time without counting rest periods and overnight stops. The easterly route would take over a week.

At Wyton, Colin Adams had selected those he considered to be his three most capable crews, taking the unwelcome decision to leave behind his own young navigator in favour of taking with him 39(PR)'s Nav Leader, the vastly more experienced Squadron Leader Brian Cole. All three crews underwent a rapid conversion back on to the Canberra PR.7 using jets borrowed from 100 Squadron. 'For possible deployment to Chile as part of a potential sales demonstration,' recorded the 100 Squadron Operation Record Book. But those embryonic thoughts of using the older jet were soon discarded in favour of the more capable PR.9 when the prospect of fitting a hastily designed additional internal fuel tank saw it over the line.

So Adams returned to Wyton from Northwood HQ with instructions to prepare a pair of Canberra PR.9s, their crews, and all the necessary ground support for what would be labelled Operation FOLKLORE. The requirement, he was told by Curtiss, was 'immediate'. And knowledge of the true nature of the mission was held extremely close. The engineers and ground crews were told only that they were deploying overseas. There was good reason for such secrecy.

In being able to settle on the more capable aircraft, the British had enjoyed a stroke of good fortune. It had been a conversation in Chile itself, a country that was ostensibly neutral, that had helped crystallize the RAF's plans to use the Canberra PR.9 to gather intelligence on the threat faced by the Task Force.

# THIRTEEN

## All practical assistance

SIDNEY EDWARDS WAS carrying his sword in his hand luggage. Uncertain of just what might be expected of him once he arrived in Santiago, Ken Hayr's Spanish-speaking envoy had prepared for his covert mission by packing for all eventualities. If for any reason the Chileans needed him to look the part of a Royal Air Force Air Attaché, he had the uniform, the braid and the ceremonial sword. For nearly twenty-four hours, as his scheduled flight to Chile routed across the United States before flying south to Santiago, he'd kept it in the airliner's overhead locker.

It would certainly be one of Britain's less controversial weapons exports to Chile. In 1973, footage of Hawker Hunters attacking the Presidential Palace had been beamed around the world.

At 11.52 a.m. on 11 September that year four Grupo 7 jets launched the first of twenty-four Sura rockets at the Palacio de la Moneda in central Santiago. It was the last bastion of President Salvador Allende's resistance to a coup launched by the military to curb mounting political unrest and economic chaos in the country. By the time Allende made his farewell radio address vowing never to resign, the country was already under the control of the generals. Debate raged over whether Allende, who died in the palace from a single gunshot to the head, committed suicide or was executed. What is certain is that in the years that followed thousands of Chileans died, disappeared, fled or were imprisoned under General Augusto Pinochet's hardline military government.

By 1975, Britain had imposed a ban on arms exports to the country and withdrawn its Ambassador. But a normalization of diplomatic relations with Chile in 1980 and a lifting of the embargo under the new Conservative government had already seen the sale of two warships to the Chilean Navy. There was hope of much more business to come. For now, though, the thaw in the UK's relations with Chile, and the opportunity that came with it in 1982 to cloak any British military activity on the South American mainland with the appearance of business-as-usual, was proving to be spectacularly well timed.

Within hours of landing, Sidney Edwards was taken to the headquarters of the Fuerza Aérea de Chile (FACh), where General Fernando Matthei, the Air Force Commander in Chief, greeted him warmly. Now a senior member of the country's ruling Junta, Matthei was an anglophile who'd served as Chile's Air Attaché in London in the seventies. Before they spoke, the RAF fixer handed Matthei a letter of introduction from Marshal of the Royal Air Force Sir Michael Beetham, the British Chief of the Air Staff. It was hardly necessary. The head of Chilean Air Force Operations, General Mario López, was an old friend who'd served as Air Attaché in Madrid at the same time as Edwards had been in the Spanish capital. López embraced him, slapping his back heartily. The other assembled Chilean top brass could be in no doubt about Edwards' credentials and it was soon agreed that, while it must remain secret, the British would receive all practical assistance. But it would come at a cost.

The next day, Edwards met General Vicente Rodriguez, the head of Chilean Air Force Intelligence and the man General Matthei had decided should be the British Wing Commander's main point of contact. Rodriguez showed Edwards around his own headquarters, sharing up-to-date intelligence on Argentine dispositions, encouraging him to ask whatever he wanted of his staff, and explaining that, as chairman of the country's Joint Intelligence Committee, he could guarantee the assistance of all Chile's armed forces.

With the carrot dangled, General Matthei had Edwards brought back to his office for another meeting. This time, it was just the two of them.

'Nothing specific to discuss,' Matthei told him, 'I just want to make sure you're getting all the help you needed.'

Edwards assured him that General Rodriguez had been most helpful. He also had good news for Matthei. He'd just received a signal confirming that preparations were being made to airfreight six surplus RAF Hunters to Chile to bolster the existing FACh squadrons within the week; another seven had been identified and would follow as soon as they were ready. Also now being given priority treatment were Chilean requests for Blowpipe anti-aircraft missiles. If the General was delighted by the sudden absence of red tape and procrastination over what had been ongoing export negotiations, Edwards then presented him with a fresh opportunity.

With the balance of the conversation working so far largely in Chile's favour, Edwards made a request of his own. 'Would you,' he asked, 'allow us to base some RAF photo-reconnaissance Canberras in Chile?' He outlined the need for up-to-date intelligence and the exceptional imagery the PR.9s would bring back while flying, he explained, 'at very high altitude in Chilean and international airspace'.

'I'm familiar with the Canberra's qualities,' Matthei told him. And he really was. Chile had wanted to add the PR.9 to its Air Force inventory to help with 'land survey tasks' for some time. Previously denied the opportunity to do so for either financial or political reasons, the General saw his opening. He let Edwards finish making his case and then turned him down. 'The Canberra is such a distinctive aircraft,' he said, 'that we would not be able to keep its presence in Chile a secret.'

Before Edwards had had a chance to absorb the bad news, Matthei proposed an alternative arrangement. 'If you were prepared to sell some to Chile at an acceptable price, the sale could be portrayed as part of Chile's defence procurement. Obviously, some RAF air and ground crews would be needed initially to train their Chilean Air Force counterparts.'

Edwards listened, hope rising.

'There could be no better way of carrying out this training than to mount the sort of reconnaissance sorties you've described,' Matthei concluded.

London eagerly embraced the General's suggestion, asking only that, at least until the take from the first few missions was in, the acquisition of the FACh's newest asset was not made public. But the

RAF air and ground crews who'd be flying to Chile were already hard at work.

The main threat, it was thought, would come from the Mirage IIIs of the Fuerza Aérea Argentina. At RAF Wyton, Colin Adams and his crews considered their vulnerability to interception by the Argentine fighters. It had long been considered sport within the PR.9 community to fish for attention from fighter squadrons. In the early seventies, Canberra crews only had to include the word 'Embellish' when they filed their flight plan to invite them to try their luck.

But while the Lightning jockeys were capable of *reaching* the altitudes flown by the Canberra it was not the same thing as making a successful interception. And although flying above 60,000 feet the spyplane had to be handled pretty gingerly, it was better able to manoeuvre at that height than the fighter.

If threatened in the skies over the South Atlantic by FAA Mirage IIIs, a machine that was known to be capable of zoom climbing to a height of over 70,000 feet, Adams was hopeful that they would fare no better in a stratospheric turning match than their British counterparts. But it would at least help to know they were coming. And the recently installed Marconi AN/ARI18228/6 Sky Guardian radar warning receiver could warn the Canberra crews of the frequency and bearing of enemy radars at a distance of up to 120 miles.

In the week of his meeting at Northwood, Colin Adams flew a trial using the Sky Guardian. To help the crews familiarize themselves with the nature of anything the RWR might detect, Wyton's Electronic Warfare Operational Support Establishment prepared cassette tapes of the various different radars operated by the Argentinians. And with support from Boscombe Down and the jet's manufacturer, 39(PR) Squadron's engineers were working on modifications that would further enhance the Canberra's range and survivability. Such was the pace of things that, as they looked to reinstate underwing pylons that had gone unused for as long as anyone could remember, they were using lengths of metal pipe they'd found stored behind the Wyton NAAFI. Adams could only applaud and admire his men's initiative.

\*

Photo-reconnaissance was only part of the story, however. While high-resolution photography from the Canberras could, once analysed, provide vital intelligence on Argentine positions, it was only one element of the overall picture. It was, literally, a snapshot, offering comprehensive detail of a moment in time. That knowledge was invaluable in any assessment of the enemy's strength, capability and disposition, not least when it came to targeting for any offensive air campaign. But it could not alert the British fleet to when an attack might be imminent, nor buy the time the Task Force needed to organize its defences. And it was to addressing this shortcoming that Sidney Edwards attached the very highest priority.

Tierra del Fuego is the southernmost point of the South American continent. Shared between Argentina and Chile, a territorial dispute between them had, in 1978, nearly erupted into war. Terrible weather delayed a planned Argentinian invasion, and subsequent Papal mediation saw them pull back from the brink, but the region had remained the main source of tension between the two countries. And since the Argentine Junta's rash decision to invade the Falklands, their Chilean counterparts feared Tierra del Fuego could be next. Anti-aircraft missiles and guns defended Punta Arenas, Chile's main airfield in the region, while a detachment of Northrop F-5E fighters from Grupo 7 maintained QRA (Quick Reaction Alert). The region's largest landmass, the Grande Isla de Tierra del Fuego, was split down the middle by the border. The Argentine side was home to an airfield at Río Grande and a naval base at Ushuaia. The Chilean side, though, was home to the high ground. And the southernmost range of the Andes provided the Fuerza Aérea de Chile with the ideal location for powerful long-range search radar capable of detecting any Argentine air activity in or out of Río Grande, Ushuaia and the Air Force Base at Río Gallegos, a couple of hundred miles to the north.

Inside the Chilean Air Force Intelligence HQ, Sidney Edwards asked General Rodriguez whether he could have access to FACh radar plots: 24/7 radar coverage enabled Chilean operators to track the time, height, direction, speed and numbers of every Argentine aircraft operating out of the country's southern airfields. Rodriguez agreed without demur.

From Tierra del Fuego, FACh radar intelligence would be passed back to Santiago via a secure communications link. Within a few days of his arrival in Santiago, Edwards knew he had access to information that had the potential to improve the fleet's ability to defend itself substantially: real-time intelligence on incoming raids. Furthermore, he and Rodriguez realized that, if it was possible to position another radar set near the Argentine border, coverage could be enhanced. And neither Rodriguez nor General Matthei had any objection to the possibility of the British providing one.

This was excellent news, but for a brief moment Edwards thought he might never get the chance to share it with London. Before he left the FACh Intelligence HQ for the day, he watched Rodriguez misjudge an effort to retrieve some documents from his briefcase. The case fell to the floor with a crash, spilling papers, a pistol, two spare clips of ammunition and three hand grenades across the carpet. The General cursed and apologized as he and his surprised British guest bent down to gather it all up.

'No harm done,' Edwards said as he helped scoop up the General's belongings, 'the pins are still in the grenades.'

But armed only with a sword, the RAF man could be forgiven for thinking that, in General Pinochet's Chile, he was a little outgunned.

Back at the Embassy, Edwards signalled Ken Hayr to bring him up-to-date with developments. The supply of a mobile radar was already in hand. A week earlier, HQ Strike Command had told RAF Wattisham in Suffolk that it needed a Marconi S259 radar with all associated equipment and personnel brought to forty-eight hours' readiness to move. There was a possible requirement, said the signal, 'to provide a radar control and reporting facility from a remote location'.

But there was one potentially serious problem. Edwards was concerned about how he was going to pass on the radar information from Tierra del Fuego to where it was needed, when it was needed. It was all very well knowing that a pair of strike fighters had launched from Río Grande, but unless there was a way to relay that information from the Chilean Air Force Intelligence HQ in Santiago to a Task

Force sailing 600 miles off the coast of Argentina without delay, his possession of it became next to useless.

Fortunately, as he'd soon discover, Ken Hayr had that covered too.

While, behind the scenes in London and South America, the RAF prepared in secret for a possible deployment to the South Atlantic, their activity down in Somerset was attracting a good deal more publicity. CINCFLEET had gratefully accepted the RAF's offer of a handful of Harriers to augment the Sea Harrier attrition reserve being worked up by Tim Gedge. And so, after spending just a single night in Canada, the Harrier GR.3 pilots of 1(F) Squadron were brought straight home again aboard an RAF Nimrod.

After landing back at Wittering at ten p.m. on 14 April, they were at Yeovilton by nine the next morning being briefed on how to launch from the practice ski-jump the Navy had installed at the airfield. Each of the 1(F) pilots was going to get five launches. And it was hoped that newspaper reporting of the event would be noticed in Argentina, sending a very clear message to the Junta about the resources Britain was able to bring to bear in support of the Task Force.

The ski-jump was a dazzlingly simple British innovation that enabled the Sea Harriers to launch from the carriers at greater weight and with greater safety. Steaming through Far Eastern waters in 1964, HMS *Victorious* had seen her aircraft confined to the deck when the blistering tropical heat jammed the steam catapult required to launch them. The experience got Lieutenant Commander Doug Taylor, the young Engineering Officer responsible for their smooth operation, thinking that there must be a better way. The result, over a decade later, was the ski-jump. By finishing their short take-off with a ramp, the SHARs' own brutal acceleration was lent ballistic assistance, ensuring the jet was always climbing as it left the deck, however much the ship's bow might be pitching up and down through the swell. In doing so the ramp provided five or six seconds of grace in which the SHAR could accelerate to wingborne flying speed. The ski-jump had no moving parts, required no maintenance, needed no power and cost nothing to operate – the naval aviation equivalent of discovering perpetual motion.

*Nothing to it*, realized Bob Iveson as he powered into the sky from the end of the ramp. The short take-offs he'd practised from the flat decks of US Navy assault ships were more demanding, an awkward combination of thrust, deck, space and control inputs throwing the jet out of trim at exactly the moment the nosewheel left the bow. This, by contrast, thought Iveson after his first attempt, was *in trim; over the top; fantastic.*

It would have taken weeks to construct a ski-jump over the bow of *Atlantic Conveyor*. The naval dockyard at Devonport had days. Tim Gedge met Michael Layard on board. The two men knew each other from way back, when they'd both flown Hunters on 764 NAS, the Fleet Air Arm's TOPGUN squadron, at Lossiemouth. Today offered a rather less high-speed challenge. The two fighter pilots walked around the deck along with the members of the dockyard team who'd be carrying out the work. They moved around the ship identifying which deck fittings to remove and keep, marking up the deck with chalk as they went.

'What's the ship's beam at this point?' Gedge asked as they approached the bow of the ship.

'Ninety-two feet.'

Gedge had found his landing pad. 'We'll make it ninety-two feet square.' The larger of the two Harrier pads at Yeovilton was ninety.

He and Layard decided to keep two walls of containers down each side of the ship to act as weather breaks for the precious cargo of aircraft and, potentially, to serve as engineering spaces and further storage. With the Harrier's landing pad near the bow it was assumed they'd need to lose the ship's tall forward mast as a potential obstacle.

'Leave it,' Gedge told them. Unable actually to see the pad beneath them from the cockpit, it would be the only visual reference point his pilots had when they came in to land.

With the fundamental decisions made, Layard and Gedge returned to the ship's living quarters to continue the discussion. With accommodation and facilities for a crew of around thirty, numbers were a major concern for Layard, but 809, Gedge assured him, would occupy a very small footprint.

Self-protection remained a worry too. Discussions at the MoD about the possibility of installing a containerized Seawolf missile system went nowhere. The necessary kit had actually been acquired and test-fired at the Aberporth range in the seventies. It was now in storage with BAe, but the best estimate for installing it and getting it operational was eight weeks. Layard asked about the possibility of fitting chaff cannons, able to fire clouds of foil strips that spoofed an incoming missile into thinking there was a juicier target. For a ship that could effectively serve as a third aircraft carrier, it seemed like a bare minimum. But apart from a 7.62mm general-purpose machine gun, or GPMG, on each bridge wing, *Conveyor* would be defenceless.

'Don't worry,' they told him, 'you'll be escorted wherever you go. You won't need self-defence armament.'

Layard also resolved to do something about the ship's bone-white superstructure. The least he could do was get it painted grey.

As Gedge left the ship to return to Yeovilton, the deck was already alive with activity. Pad eyes and container stools were being noisily cut away, throwing up showers of orange sparks, while great steel sheets for the landing pad were being craned on and welded over forward hatches. For now she resembled a construction site, but *Atlantic Conveyor* was being transformed into a unique new naval asset. In a week's time, 809 would have their ship. But the squadron's boss was still short on pilots.

# FOURTEEN

## Purposeful *and* elegant

HAPPY HOUR IN the Officers' Mess bar at RAF Gütersloh was looking like a good one. The Harrier base in West Germany was playing host to aircrew from various different NATO air forces who'd been taking part in an air defence exercise. But it was now the weekend. By 7.30 most of the assembled had already got a few pints in when, unexpectedly, two of 3(F)'s GR.3 pilots, John Leeming and Steve Brown, were summoned to meet the Station Commander in the mess reception. Leeming tried to think of anything he'd done wrong, but figured his conscience was clear.

'What do you two think you're doing on Monday morning?'

'Flying to Wildenrath for some air combat training with F-4s in the Ardennes,' came the reply.

That, it quickly turned out, was the wrong answer.

The well was dry. The Navy was all out of Sea Harrier pilots. Students, like Dave Morgan and Andy George, who could be sent south, had been. With Dave Ramsay, Willy McAtee, Taylor Scott and Jock Gunning out of the picture, 809 had clawed their way to a sum total of seven pilots. But with the promise of one more SHAR delivered a month early by BAe after an accelerated build it looked as if Gedge would have eight or even nine jets to load aboard *Atlantic Conveyor*. Ted Anson had promised him all the support he needed. It was time to take him up on it. And to look to the RAF.

'We need experienced current GR.3 pilots, at least on their second tour in a Harrier,' Gedge explained to the Admiral, 'but they need to have done a tour on single-seat, radar-equipped fighters.' He knew full well he was looking for former Lightning pilots.

In Flight Lieutenant Murdo McLeod, 3(F) Squadron at RAF Gütersloh had the perfect candidate. Not only was the Scot a Lightning pilot, he'd also done a tour flying Phantoms with 892 Naval Air Squadron aboard *Ark Royal*. McLeod and his Observer were the last crew ever to be catapulted from the old carrier's flight deck. But while he'd have been ideal, McLeod was in Canada taking part in MAPLE FLAG. And so it was John Leeming and Steve Brown who found themselves rumbling back towards Somerset in the rear-facing passenger seats of a fat-bellied 60 Squadron Hunting Pembroke C.1. They were to report for duty at RNAS Yeovilton at eight a.m. on Monday, 19 April.

Brown and Leeming were enjoying breakfast in the Yeovilton wardroom on that Monday morning when they first encountered their new CO. The Sea Harrier Operational Conversion Course comprised over one hundred separate sorties taking in navigation, weaponry, air combat manoeuvring, air interception and reconnaissance. Over fifty hours of instruction in the air were usually devoted to the radar alone. After Dave Braithwaite had pared the syllabus down to its bare bones, Brown and Leeming would get just four. In total, the two 3(F) 'mercenaries', as they'd taken to describing themselves, would be getting about ten hours in the cockpit of a Sea Harrier before they went to war. It was a fraction of what, during the Battle of Britain, the RAF had given new Spitfire pilots.

Tim Gedge told them breakfast was over. Their first day of intensive ground school lay ahead. Experience in the cockpit of the GR.3 was going to help them get to grips with the Sea Harrier as a flying machine. But it was the most obvious external difference between the two aircraft – and the feature that enabled the SHAR to function as a fighter – that was virgin territory: the Blue Fox radar in the nose.

'Purposeful *and* elegant!' extolled the Sea Harrier's Chief Designer John Fozard. He was thrilled about the good looks he'd bestowed on his new creation. Minimum change was the mantra that underpinned the SHAR's evolution from the RAF's land-based ground attack jet. To ensure the lowest financial and technical risk, anything that *could* remain unchanged was left alone. Minor tweaks like the addition of tie-down lugs, drainage holes and the replacement of magnesium components with less corrosive aluminium ones were all essential. But, to accommodate a radar set, the shape of the Harrier's nose had required more radical attention. The SHAR's pipe-smoking Chief Designer went as far as to build a full-scale mock-up of his proposed new nose and cockpit layout to help win approval for this obviously major change to the airframe. But for all that more space was needed, the real reason it looked the way it did was simply that it was to Fozard's liking. Inside the radome it was a different story.

There wasn't a lot about the little Blue Fox radar to impress a former Phantom backseater like Leo Gallagher. With the F-4's retirement from the Navy went the jobs of a cadre of Fleet Air Arm Observers who, as part of the Phantom's two-man crew, had become expert in using the big interceptor's powerful AWG-11 pulse-Doppler radar to pick up low-flying aircraft over land or sea at distances of 60 miles or more. The introduction of the single-seat Sea Harrier saw the backseaters grounded, but not discarded.

After climbing out of an 892 Phantom for the last time, Gallagher had been seconded to British Aerospace at Dunsfold, where he'd helped develop and fine-tune the new fighter's radar.

A low-risk development of the Lynx helicopter's Seaspray radar, the Blue Fox was perfectly adequate as a means of finding a high-flying Soviet Tupolev Tu-95 Bear sent to shadow the fleet, but it struggled to look down and pick up low-flying fighters against the background clutter from land or sea. Without the pulse-Doppler technology required to distinguish movement against a stationary background, it all just looked the same.

But after Dunsfold, as one of two Chief Tactics Instructors on 700A NAS (Sharkey Ward's Sea Harrier trials unit), Gallagher continued to try to wring the best possible performance from the Blue Fox. Up to the summer of 1981 he'd lectured every single new SHAR pilot on how to use it. From the squadron COs to the most junior Joes, they all owed, to a greater or lesser extent, their ability to get the most out of Blue Fox to Leo Gallagher.

And now he'd been drafted in from a new posting at DNAW in London to try to help get Tim Gedge's motley crew of newbies, retreads, veterans and crabs over the line. Back at the MoD, with admiration, affection and perhaps a little envy, 809 were sometimes labelled 'Fred Karno's Circus' after the music-hall-era slapstick comedian. They were the Fleet Air Arm's own Dirty Dozen. *The only thing we don't have*, thought Gallagher with a smile, *is a guy out of clink.* And he wished he was going south with them.

Having helped write the book on the Blue Fox radar he was realistic about its strengths and weaknesses. Some of the more extravagant claims made on its behalf by enthusiasts like Sharkey Ward were, he thought, *bollocks*. But while conscious of its limitations he was happy to concede that, used properly, it was a great help. It was reliable, had a decent enough look-up capability, and, by being slaved to the nav system, it could help get you round into a target's six o'clock. Most of all, it was easy to get the hang of, and he thought that it was probably that simple fact that lay at the heart of Sharkey's fondness for it: as a pilot, Sharkey didn't have to sit in the Observer's coal hole on a Sea Vixen trying to interpret raw radar imagery. And, right now, given that some of Tim Gedge's pilots had zero experience of operating a radar, user-friendly was pretty much top of his list of priorities.

But there was so little time. It was going to be bare essentials. Gallagher was equipping them to survive. And he realized that part of the challenge was actually trying to make sure they didn't get too sidetracked by the radar display. They needed to keep their eyes outside the cockpit.

'Here are the rudiments,' he told them, 'but for God's sake fly the aeroplane!'

Unless the MoD managed to persuade the Indian Navy to part with two of the Blue Fox radars that they'd bought for *their* Sea Harriers, then getting distracted by a radar wasn't, for a couple of 809 pilots at least, going to be a problem in any case. Negotiations with officials at the Indian Embassy in London were ongoing.

Of all the things on Tim Gedge's to-do list, having a chat with an anxious crane driver wasn't one of them.

After visiting *Atlantic Conveyor* and saving her forward mast, he'd wondered how he was going to familiarize his pilots with using it as a landing aid. A phone call to Yeovil Crane Hire had provided the answer. As he prepared to go flying, Gedge looked out of the window of his office to see the yellow Coles Crane parked at the end of the runway with the jib extended to 100 feet and angled at 10° to imitate the *Conveyor*'s mast, only to spot the driver still sitting in the cab. Gedge, eager to get airborne and see whether or not his improvisation did the trick, sent someone out to go and get him only to get a message back saying he couldn't leave the cab with the engine running.

Gedge invited him in for a cup of coffee and pointed across the airfield at the formidable sound and fury pouring off a hovering Sea Harrier. 'If you stay in your cab, that Harrier is going to be eight to ten feet from your nose and you really don't want to be there.'

Point made, Gedge saddled up and flew a circuit of the airfield, before slowing to a hover about 10 feet from the top of the crane. Edging gently backwards to follow the slope of the jib, he brought the jet down on to its wheels next to the mobile crane's squat, wheeled base unit. Worked like a dream, he thought, realizing his success meant a formal trial could be avoided. He asked Brave to programme a few vertical landings in front of the crane for the rest of the squadron. And that was that. No other naval fast jet in existence could qualify for deck landing with so little fuss. Let alone do so with pilots who had never flown from a ship before.

From the cockpit of his A-4Q Skyhawk, Capitán de Corbeta Alberto Philippi picked out *25 de Mayo* steaming below – a small grey shape scoring a white line across the ocean. After a staff job ashore, it was good to be back in the cockpit and returning to the ship. Especially now. It would have been painful not to be part of this; to have had to watch from the sidelines as his brothers in arms prepared to defend the Malvinas as part of the Armada's Task Force 79. He focused on the job in hand. He'd been lucky enough to survive when, in 1961, a landing accident aboard *25 de Mayo*'s predecessor, *Independencia*, had led to the loss of the North American SNJ-5C Texan he'd been flying. When things went wrong on the deck of an aircraft carrier you didn't often get a second chance. God, he always felt certain, was looking out for him.

After a fast run and break down the port side of the flight deck, the eight A-4Q Skyhawks of 3 Escuadrilla Aeronaval de Caza y Ataque joined the landing pattern. One by one the rugged little attack jets resolved in the distance, high above the ship's churning white wake, their Pratt & Whitney J-65 engines trailing oily smoke behind them.

Listening to terse, calm instructions over the RT and responding almost subconsciously to the lights of the mirror-landing sight that reported the accuracy of his descent to the carrier's angled flight deck, Philippi guided his jet in on finals, his control inputs on the throttle stick gentle and unhurried. For too long the Colossus class carrier looked to be an impossibly small target, then in a rush, as the Skyhawk raced over the round-down, she was suddenly 20,000 tons of unyielding steel. Philippi drove the Skyhawk hard into the deck, slamming the throttle to full power as the jet bounced heavily on its tall undercarriage. Then he was thrown forward against his straps. But with the fierce deceleration came reassurance: the arrestor hook that hung beneath the A-4's jetpipe had caught one of the six wires of the MacTaggart Scott Mk.12 arrestor stretching across the deck. Safely down, Philippi chopped the power. The Skyhawk rolled back a touch, dropping the arrestor wire to the deck. Then, as his pale grey jet was marshalled to its parking spot, the wire retracted back into its housing like the flex of a vacuum cleaner, until it once more stretched across the deck, ready to trap the next jet in the pattern.

For nearly two weeks, after disembarking following the occupation of the Falklands, the squadron had trained intensively from BAN Comandante Espora, the naval air station they shared with 2 Escuadrilla's Super Etendards. Like their sister squadron, the Skyhawk pilots had been training against the Type 42 destroyers *Hercules* and *Santísima Trinidad*, the two most capable air defence ships in all of South America, directed by the Grumman S-2E Tracker squadron with which they shared *25 de Mayo*. To give themselves a chance of getting in under the 909 radar and avoiding detection they stepped their descent to low level, from 500 feet at 100 miles out to less than 100 feet from 50 miles until a final run-in to the target over the last 30 miles below 50 feet. Once they had the target in their sights, they'd manoeuvre to avoid the defences before streaking across at twenty-second intervals in order not to get fragged by the bombs dropped by the previous jet. Training with the ARA's sophisticated Type 42s allowed 3 Escuadrilla to study radar recordings of their attacks. The flying required to penetrate the ship's defences was not for the faint-hearted *but*, confirmed one of the pilots after their work-up, *we knew how to do it*.

With tactics rehearsed and honed ashore, it was now vital to get back on board the ship. Carrier flying skills eroded fast. And so, after two weeks ashore, they were coming back to where they needed to be to keep them sharp – where they belonged. As the remaining jets landed on, ARA *25 de Mayo* steamed into wind off the coast of Argentina, making 23 knots, to reduce the effective landing speed of the jets by the same amount. Without wind over the deck, the margins became slimmer. Worse, insufficient wind limited the war load an A-4 could carry when launching from the ship's steam catapult. But wind, fortunately, was not something that, in the South Atlantic, was usually in short supply.

# FIFTEEN

## Flint-eyed and inscrutable

INSIDE THE CONTROL cabin of the Westinghouse AN/TPS-43 radar, the men of the FAA's Grupo 2 de Vigilancia y Control Aéreo tracked the approach of the Navy's Super Etendards. Since deploying four jets to Río Grande in Tierra del Fuego, the pilots of 2 Escuadrilla had been mounting training flights out over the South Atlantic, staging mock attacks against the ARA *Alferez Sobral*, an 800-ton ocean-going tug. But it was important for them to see the airfield at Puerto Argentino, the former Port Stanley. Their trials earlier in the month had shown that, in an emergency at least, using the runway at BAM Malvinas – the occupiers' name for Stanley airfield – was an option. After familiarizing themselves with the lie of the land, the SuE Flight Leader thanked air traffic, advanced the throttle and climbed away to the west, leading his men back to the mainland.

The islands had been home to the command and control team from VYCA Grupo 2 since 1 April, when they'd flown in late in the evening aboard an Air Force C-130. Five days later they were providing round-the-clock coverage, but, concerned about how exposed and vulnerable they were at their initial location near BAM Malvinas, they moved, during the night of 13 April, to a site tucked in closer to the town. Working in conjunction with four other AN/TPS-43 radar stations dotted along the crescent-shaped coast of Patagonia, the operators of the Fuerza Aérea Argentina were in possession of a more capable radar than the British. With over 200 miles' range, the US-built radars provided three-dimensional coverage. Not only could they track speed, direction and distance, but at the same time, unlike any single air defence radar possessed by the Task Force, height. And since acquiring the system in 1980, the Argentine operators had become expert in its use. The air picture they could generate and their ability to manage it had the potential to be one of the most important assets in the Argentine arsenal. Throughout April they used the constant stream of air traffic to and from the mainland to tune their equipment and refine their skills, identifying fixed echoes and possible British flight paths. But they were not alone in trying to build a more comprehensive picture of the skies over the South Atlantic.

On Wednesday, 21 April, a pair of heavily laden Vickers VC10s from 10 Squadron RAF climbed away from Brize Norton and set a course for Dulles International Airport in Washington. But that was not their final destination. After a night's rest on the East Coast they would continue their journey west to March Air Force Base in southern California. From there they'd head out over the Pacific, flying almost due south towards a small volcanic island in the South Pacific. Barely 15 miles across and located over 2,000 miles west of the Latin American mainland, Easter Island was one of the most remote inhabited islands in the world. It was home to nearly 1,000 carved stone heads known as *moai* and one single runway. And since 1888 it had belonged to Chile.

For public consumption, the journey undertaken by Ascot 2830 and Ascot 2831 was coyly described as a 'route training flight', but it was nothing of the sort. And as they descended towards their Polynesian destination, a passenger on board one of the two RAF transports, Squadron Leader Peter Robbie, thought about what might lie ahead. One of the three Canberra pilots selected by Colin Adams for Operation FOLKLORE, he was leading the advance party. And travelling with him, loaded aboard the two VC10s, was all the support equipment required to sustain what was to be an open-ended mission.

Expected to be operating without local support, they were not travelling light. A fully supported aerial survey detachment required a minimum of twenty personnel to fly and maintain the aircraft and at least the same again to man a mobile Reconnaissance Intelligence Centre, or RIC, housed within a pair of prefabricated ATREL cabins.

Film processors and printers were needed. A camera bay for servicing the photographic equipment required a 50 by 30-foot inflatable shelter. To keep the PR.9s serviceable, the detachment needed to be self-sufficient in everything from spare engines and tyres to lightbulbs. All would have to be kept undercover along with generators, tools, jacks, trolleys and hydraulic rigs. Consumables such as fuel, oil, hydraulic fluid and oxygen had to be readily available. There were tents to accommodate personnel. And tents in which to store and service the extensive array of survival kit each pilot and navigator needed to fly high-altitude, long-range missions over near-freezing water.

Once they were on the ground at Easter Island, it was Robbie's job to get it all crossloaded on to a pair of waiting RAF C-130s already in country without attracting too much attention from a Soviet spy satellite thought to be passing overhead every hour and a half. The two RAF turboprops had had their British roundels and fin flashes painted out and replaced with Chilean markings. One of them was identified with the words FUERZA AÉRA DE CHILE painted on the fuselage. In the haste to disguise their true identities, 'Aérea' had been misspelt.

Given that the VC10s were ferrying as much as 40 tons of men and materiel required for Operation FOLKLORE out from the UK, it would have been a shame not to have also found room for a pair of signallers from 264 (SAS) Signal Squadron. Part of the Royal Corps of Signals, the unit had been established to provide dedicated communications support to the SAS. Although not badged members of the Regiment itself, 264 enjoyed respect for being exceptionally good at what they did. And now they had an opportunity to demonstrate that once again, using the AN/PSC-3 satellite radios on loan to Hereford from their friends at Fort Bragg.

After Sidney Edwards had expressed concern about how he might share radar intelligence on Argentine air movements without delay, Ken Hayr had ensured that part of the haul from Delta Force was diverted straight to Santiago. Consisting of a backpack, a handset and a small LP-sized satellite dish mounted on a tripod, it attracted little attention. And General Rodriguez had readily agreed to let Edwards install the aerial on the roof of his building – an inconspicuous addition to the antenna farm already there. With the signallers installed in the FACh Intelligence HQ, Operation SHUTTER, a further element of the RAF-led effort in Chile to provide the Task Force with greater warning of air attack, got underway.

On the same day that the VC10s left the UK bound for Easter Island, a C-130 Hercules C.1 from 70 Squadron RAF took off from Ascension Island on a seven-and-a-half-hour round trip. In the hold, packed in buoyant waterproof boxes, were more of the Delta Force SATCOM sets, destined for D Squadron 22 SAS. Four hours after leaving Ascension's Wideawake airfield they'd been rolled out of the back of the C-130 in the company of one of the SAS troopers who'd originally escorted them back from Fort Bragg. Both were picked up by seaboats from HMS *Invincible*.

'The passenger,' noted the ship's war diary, 'believed to be a member of the SAS, seems to possess a limited vocabulary and even the politest question from the Commander as to his state of health receives only a grunt of *"Hermes"*, which we eventually assume to be his desired destination and send him there, complete with a range of weapons that accompanied him.'

By the end of the day, the SAS man and his luggage were safely aboard the flagship.

It was proving to be a busy day for the Task Force flagship. One of her young Sea Harrier pilots had just become the first of them to make contact with the enemy.

Simon Hargreaves had been scrambled to intercept the Argentine Boeing 707 shadowing the British fleet. Carrying hastily fitted live Sidewinders beneath his wings, he'd spent twelve minutes in close formation with the enemy jet, leaving its crew in no doubt that he held their lives in his hands. With the reconnaissance jet safely on its way back to Argentina, he returned to the carrier to recover on board.

His hands gently working the throttle and stick, he held station to port of the flight deck before crabbing sideways across the ship. The SHAR hovered briefly then descended vertically towards the flight deck. As the dark grey jet bounced heavily on its stocky bicycle undercarriage, Hargreaves cut the power. The belligerent whine of the big Pegasus turbofan behind him fell sharply as he ran through his post-landing checks.

*Water injection – off. Tailplane trimmed to +4°. Flaps – up.*

He checked his brake and rotated the nozzles aft, ready to taxi to a parking spot under the direction of the deck handlers.

After Hargreaves's successful interception of the Fuerza Aérea Argentina Boeing 707, the mood throughout the Task Force changed.

They were no longer out of reach.

This was real.

'Well done,' congratulated one of the young SHAR pilot's squadron mates, before adding, 'You managed not to do anything rash like shoot him down!' As the first of them to encounter the enemy, Hargreaves's return to the crewroom was greeted with excitement and curiosity, but not without a predictable amount of pisstaking. The truth was, though, that every one of his squadron mates would have given their eye teeth to be in his position.

Since leaving Ascension Island on 18 April, the atmosphere aboard *Hermes* had become more freighted with anticipation. Not least because the Task Force Commander, Admiral John 'Sandy' Woodward, had now made the carrier his flagship. It was from aboard the veteran carrier that he would direct the war. And Tim Gedge wasn't alone in raising an eyebrow at the former submariner's appointment.

Woodward himself thought he'd got the job simply by virtue of being the closest Flag Officer to the frontline at the time of the invasion. Not by much. As one of just three sea-going Admirals in the Navy he'd been leading the ships of the First Flotilla during Exercise SPRINGTRAIN off Gibraltar.

*My good fortune*, he wrote in his diary after receiving a signal from CINCFLEET telling him that Argentina had invaded the Falklands.

As flint-eyed and inscrutable as Clint Eastwood in the midday sun, Woodward was an intimidating figure; appraising, brusque, intolerant of fools and highly regarded. But given that his priority was to establish air superiority and enforce the exclusion zone prior to landing ground forces, his experience of naval aviation seemed limited. The Admiral, though, possessed one of the sharpest minds in the Navy.

Prior to taking command of the twenty-two frigates and destroyers of the First Flotilla, he'd served as 'Teacher' – a revered position within the Submarine Service. With that came responsibility for running the legendarily tough Perisher course used to select all Royal Navy submarine captains. It was a role that required deep tactical knowledge, quick thinking, an understanding of human nature, and the ability to soak up stress and make tough decisions without giving a damn what anyone else thought of you.

However, in a thirty-six-year naval career, Woodward had spent just one week at sea aboard a carrier. He was only too aware that he needed to get up to speed fast. While he may not have enjoyed a close association with the Fleet Air Arm he was in no doubt about the nature of the war that lay ahead, or how critical the two carriers would be to his prospects of success.

*Lose* Invincible, he thought, *and the operation is severely jeopardized. Lose* Hermes *and the operation is over.*

The anti-air warfare posture of the Battle Group was raised immediately. The interception of the Argentine Boeing brought forward by a day plans to keep a Sea Harrier on alert 24/7. From here on, though, both *Hermes* and *Invincible* would keep a fully armed aircraft on deck at Alert 5 – ready to be scrambled within five minutes – with two further SHARs at Alert 20.

Unlike the more progressive preparations aboard *Invincible*, *Hermes*, at the insistence of her Captain, Lyn Middleton, had been practically on a war footing since leaving Portsmouth harbour. Anything that could burn or cut had been removed. Mirrors and glass had all been stowed. Cushions, pillows and mattresses were simply thrown overboard. Anyone unfortunate enough to be allocated a cabin below the waterline had been forced to abandon it in case of torpedo attack. Some of the 800 Squadron pilots were sleeping in the crewroom.

*Invincible*'s Captain, JJ Black, had decided that, on balance, the benefits of his fighter pilots getting a decent night's kip outweighed the risk of them being killed in their sleep by toxic smoke from a burning mattress. Alert and well rested, he figured they might just be the difference between his carrier getting hit by an air attack or not.

That afternoon *Hermes* scrambled another SHAR in pursuit of an unidentified contact travelling east at 38,000 feet around 100 miles south of the ship. After picking up the bogey on the jet's Blue Fox radar at a distance of nearly 40 miles, the pilot, Flight Lieutenant Dave Morgan, armed his weapons and climbed towards the target, soon catching sight of four white contrails tracing a line across the clear blue sky. But as he closed to a distance of 2 miles and 5,000 feet below it was soon clear that this time it was no Fuerza Aérea Argentina intelligence-gathering mission. Instead, Morgan found himself flying in very loose formation with a civilian jumbo on a routine trans-atlantic flight. After the excitement of the squadron's encounter with the Escuadrón II 707 earlier he couldn't help but feel a twinge of disappointment, albeit tempered by relief.

Morgan might have returned empty-handed, but the military intruder was to return that night when, at 0230Z, an 801 Squadron Sea Harrier from HMS *Invincible* was scrambled to intercept a high-level bogey approaching from the northeast. Again the pilot manoeuvred himself into a firing position and tracked the Argentine Boeing for over half an hour before it finally turned away to the southwest. As the Rules of Engagement stood, the SHARs could do no more than 'visibly escort the aircraft and dissuade it from overflying the force'. But without permission to fire a shot across the bow, dissuasion was more dependent on the nerve of the 707 crew than on anything the Fleet Air Arm pilots could do.

Acquired by the Navy to 'Hack the Shad', the SHAR was doing exactly what it was designed for – except, that is, for one very important detail. Instead of getting 'hacked', the shadower was allowed to return to base at BAM El Palomar unscathed with valuable intelligence on the position, progress and capability of the British fleet.

Aboard *Hermes*, Admiral Woodward asked himself the question *Am I going to let this 'Burglar' go on reporting our position back to Argentinian headquarters? Or am I going to splash him?* An act, he knew, that would show blatant disregard for the Rules of Engagement. But as his Battle Group ploughed south he was acutely conscious that, in the absence of any airborne early warning, his only surface search capability lay with the SHAR's Blue Fox radars. Woodward signalled Northwood, urging them not just to give him permission to shoot the burglars down, but to make sure the Argentinians knew it. Two days and one interception later, during which the crew of the 707 TC-91 heard the pilot of the Sea Harrier flying alongside them asking for permission to shoot, the reconnaissance flights came to an end.

For the time being at least.

And not before news had been passed on to the Fuerza Aérea Argentina's elite fighter squadron, Grupo 8 de Caza, that the British Sea Harriers sent up to intercept the 707s were armed with the latest Nine Lima version of the Sidewinder missile. There was no doubt at all in the mind of the unit's boss, Comodoro Carlos Corino, that this made his squadron's job considerably more difficult. Since providing a pair of Mirage IIIs to cover the invasion, he and his pilots had been analysing the capabilities of the Sea Harrier and planning their tactics. Flying at the limits of their range, they were going to have to try to make sure they got the basics right and play to the Mirage's strengths. If they nailed that, though, the Mirage III would be a dangerous opponent.

Back at Yeovilton, Tim Gedge continued his pursuit of better information about the French fighter. Dave Ramsay's appreciation of the type's Australian record was a useful insight into what 809 might expect.

The RAAF still used the Mirage as its primary frontline fighter and understood its strengths and weaknesses well. To its credit it was fast, small and hard to see, particularly from head-on, and it enjoyed well-sorted, harmonious flight controls and few vices. It had an extremely fast rate of roll that very few other jets could match. And in exercises like COPE THUNDER, Australian Mirage jocks had achieved 'kills' against the USAF's highly regarded new F-16 Fighting Falcons. Provided that they enjoyed good radar control from the ground and kept their speed high, mounting hit-and-run, slashing attacks, the Australian Mirages were able to cause a few surprises. Flying at supersonic speed and working together as coordinated pairs against subsonic jets like A-4 Skyhawks and Hawker Hunters, the Mirage could cause havoc.

There was a lot riding on the SHARs' new AIM-9L Sidewinder. And while there was justifiable confidence in the missile, the French-made Matra R.550 Magic used by the Argentine Mirages was believed by the Royal Navy's own Directorate of Air Warfare to be superior to the AIM-9G that was still carried in large numbers by the Task Force. The Magic was assessed by the Defence Science Staff to pose a 'very significant' threat.

A shipment of brand-new R.550 Magic missiles, despatched by sea before the invasion, had just arrived in Argentina. They may not have been Nine Limas, but they were probably the next best thing.

Further east, the fighting had already started.

# SIXTEEN

## A remarkable piece of flying

THE LOSS OF two Wessex helicopters caused near despair in Downing Street. As the fate of seventeen men hung in the balance on a storm-swept glacier high on a South Atlantic island, the Prime Minister asked herself, *Is the task we have set ourselves impossible?* Operation PARAQUET, the campaign to retake South Georgia, was supposed to be a welcome hors d'oeuvre to the main event. Although not militarily important, ejecting the Argentine occupiers from the island was an important political statement of intent, designed both to demonstrate British resolve and establish a successful momentum in the days leading up to battle being joined in the Falklands themselves. A small flotilla of ships, led by the County class destroyer HMS *Antrim*, carrying a company from 42 Commando Royal Marines and D Squadron 22 SAS, was despatched by Sandy Woodward to achieve the task.

Inspired by the heroics of Ernest Shackleton, who at the end of his epic boat journey across the Southern Ocean from Elephant Island had crossed South Georgia's Fortuna glacier to reach the settlement, and salvation, at Grytviken, the SAS decided that an approach from the same, unlikely direction offered them an element of surprise. But, after being flown on to the glacier aboard a Westland Wessex helicopter, fierce Force 12 winds violently relieved the first team of their equipment and any possibility of shelter. After surviving the night, dawn saw some of the troop showing signs of frostbite and hypothermia. Their mission was hopeless, and their Commander requested an extraction.

Three helicopters were sent: a pair of Wessex HU.5 troop carriers and *Antrim*'s radar-equipped Wessex HAS.3 to lead them through the dreadful conditions. But whiteout conditions atop the glacier saw the two HU.5s lost in quick succession, leaving the soldiers stranded and exposed. As *Antrim*'s Wessex HAS.3, the sole surviving cab, felt its way down the mountainside towards Possession Bay, her co-pilot radioed the ship.

'Feet wet. ETA one five. Regret we have lost our two chicks.'

'Roger, out,' came the reply. Then silence, until a couple of minutes later, as those in *Antrim* tried to digest the news, the RT crackled to life again: 'Confirm what you have lost.'

'Our two chicks.'

'Oh . . .'

With the potential loss of life still unknown, Margaret Thatcher wept when first given news of the disaster. It was the worst possible start to PARAQUET, an operation ordered to boost morale and stiffen resolve. *Is the weather,* she asked herself, *going to beat our courage and bravery?*

It was not.

In a remarkable piece of flying, the crew of *Antrim*'s Wessex, Humphrey, ascended once more to the crash site where, after dumping their kit, all seventeen D Squadron men were crammed into the anti-submarine helicopter's small, cluttered cabin. With a four-man crew on board, Humphrey was dangerously overloaded to the tune of nearly a ton. But somehow the pilot, Lieutenant Commander Ian Stanley, managed to bring his leaden machine safely back to the deck. As his men tumbled out of Humphrey's cabin door, Major Cedric Delves, D Squadron's CO, counted them out.

*It doesn't seem possible,* he thought, as he realized that every last one of his men had been returned alive.

Three days later, as Mrs Thatcher's War Cabinet met at Chequers, a signal was received from HMS *Antrim* reading: 'Be pleased to inform Her Majesty that the White Ensign flies alongside the Union Flag in Grytviken South Georgia. God Save the Queen.'

After an attempt to land reinforcements by submarine ended with the crippled boat limping back into Grytviken harbour, Argentine forces surrendered fifteen minutes after the British launched their assault. With the surrender of the garrison at Leith harbour the following day, Operation PARAQUET concluded successfully without loss of life on either side. And, with victory in South Georgia, the whole British adventure in the South Atlantic was back on track.

But, of the six helicopters first deployed to South Georgia aboard the *Antrim* group, a third had been lost within twenty-four hours of the operation commencing. And Fuerza Aérea Argentina C-130 Hercules, Canberra B.62 bombers and the 'Burglar', the Boeing 707 whose attentions had been so exercising Sandy Woodward, had all flown over South Georgia with impunity. The need to get more Sea Harriers down south was well illustrated.

At RNAS Yeovilton, the 809 Squadron boss was examining his options for doing just that.

In May 1919, in support of the world's first transatlantic flight, the US Navy positioned a fleet of seventy-three warships along the route between Newfoundland and Lisbon via the Azores. Should the crews of the three Curtiss NC flying boats get into trouble, they could be confident that at any point along their journey, help was reasonably close at hand. Now Tim Gedge was wondering about the possibility of something similar for 809, although his demand for ships would be rather less burdensome. The numbers just about worked, Gedge realized. A speed, time and distance study suggested his squadron would be able to self-ferry to Ascension. If he could get diplomatic clearance to fly over Morocco, 809 could island-hop from airfield to airfield under their own steam, leapfrogging from the Canaries to the Azores, to Cape Verde and on to Wideawake. Diversion airfields were an issue, but that was also true of flying the SHAR off the deck of a carrier. And, if a safety net was required, they could position a frigate.

*We've never trialled it*, he thought, *but we can land. Even if we can't take off again we won't lose the aircraft.*

In the end he never had to worry about whether or not the Moroccans' painfully slow diplomatic clearance process could be accelerated: the MoD had decided they'd be using RAF Victor K.2 tankers to refuel them en route. And Gedge was told to report to RAF North Luffenham for a week's ground school on the principles and procedures of in-flight refuelling. With barely a week left to prepare his squadron for combat it beggared belief. *Why do I need to learn the theory of how a refuelling pod works?* He didn't, was his angry conclusion, and neither did his pilots. He despatched a signal announcing that all of them were already in-flight refuelling qualified in the SHAR, although in reality the Fleet Air Arm had yet even to try air-to-air refuelling in the Sea Harrier. All his pilots, though, had at least tried it in other aircraft. 809, he said, would only require a single sortie's worth of refresher training. *The Sea Harrier's a pretty responsive aeroplane*, he told himself, *it can't be that difficult*. And it wasn't, except for one thing.

Hanging heavy off the wings of the little Sea Harrier, the two big 330-gallon ferry tanks looked almost as if they were the floats of an old seaplane. Carrying over three times the fuel of the SHAR's standard 100-gallon combat tanks, they offered a dramatic increase in range. As far as the 809 Squadron boss was aware, the longest flight the Navy had ever undertaken in the SHAR was something in the region of an hour and a half. The ferry tanks could double that. But, since being delivered to Yeovilton along with the jets themselves, they'd never been used.

Flying alongside Gedge as he completed his own AAR refresher, Taylor Scott's SHAR carried a pair of the big tanks. He knew his boss at BAe, John Farley, had managed the more delicate challenge of landing vertically aboard the wooden-decked Spanish Navy carrier SNS *Dedalo* while burdened with them. But after his own training sortie Scott reported that they did significantly affect the Sea Harrier's manoeuvrability and responsiveness.

Rather than risk something so unfamiliar, Gedge opted to stick with the tried-and-tested 100-gallon combat tanks. With his squadron of pilots having enjoyed so few hours on the SHAR, with so much to try to get on top of, and with so little time in which to do it, it didn't make sense to add a further wrinkle to the programme. Especially when, Gedge learned, the squadron's departure date had just been pulled forward a week without explanation.

809 were heading to war on 30 April.

The two 39(PR) Squadron Canberra PR.9s were already on their way, skirting around the northern rim of the Atlantic. Colin Adams and

**Above**: Jump jet. On 21 October 1960, three years after initial design work started, test pilot Bill Bedford flew the Hawker P.1127 prototype for the first time at Dunsfold Aerodrome in Surrey. The revolutionary little vertical take-off and landing jet remained tethered to the ground throughout.

**Left**: Born in 1893 during the reign of Queen Victoria, Hawker Chief Designer Sir Sydney Camm had been responsible for the design of a long line of iconic aircraft including the Hurricane, Sea Fury and Hunter before overseeing the team that designed the P.1127 – the machine that would evolve into the Harrier.

The Harrier GR.1 entered service with 1(F) Squadron RAF in 1969. In 1971, a detachment led by the pioneering V/STOL unit's first CO, Ken Hayr, conducted successful trials aboard HMS *Ark Royal*, the Royal Navy's last conventional aircraft carrier. Four years later the Navy ordered twenty-four Sea Harriers to operate from three new Invincible class carriers.

Two years earlier, Hawker Siddeley Chief Test Pilot John Farley flew the Harrier from the deck of Argentina's freshly acquired aircraft carrier *25 de Mayo* as she sailed home from Rotterdam for the first time. A US offer of cheap second-hand A-4 Skyhawks headed off the Argentine Navy interest in buying the Harrier.

**Left**: A month after the first flight of the Sea Harrier FRS.1 in August 1978, John Farley and Sea Harrier Chief Designer John Fozard celebrate the first launch from a ski-jump. The ski-jump, designed to assist short take-offs at sea, was demonstrated in public at that year's Farnborough Air Show.

**Below**: Lieutenant Commander Tim Gedge, CO of 800 NAS, the first frontline Sea Harrier unit, flies over HMS *Hermes*, a former conventional carrier refitted with a 12° ski-jump for Sea Harrier operations.

Tim Gedge and Captain Linley Middleton celebrate 800's first embarkation aboard HMS *Hermes* with a glass of champagne. Note the thick rubber immersion suit worn by Gedge to protect him in the event of an ejection over water. Standing behind them is John Locke, Middleton's Executive Officer and second-in-command.

In September 1981, during a deployment to the United States aboard *Hermes*, 800 NAS Sea Harriers performed for the crowds at the Pratt & Whitney factory in West Palm Beach, Florida. The perception that the jet was more of an airshow novelty than a serious warplane was not uncommon at the time.

**Above**: TOPGUN. Often underrated, the Sea Harrier proved to be an unexpectedly lethal opponent when 800 Squadron flew air combat training sorties against the USAF's highly regarded new F-16 fighter. Photographs of the F-16 caught in the SHAR's gunsights made the papers.

**Right**: After two years as CO, on 20 January 1982 Tim Gedge handed over command of 800 Squadron to Lieutenant Commander Andy Auld. To mark the occasion, the squadron towed Gedge around the Yeovilton flightline on an inert 1,000lb bomb.

In a further gesture to their departing CO, the squadron staged a six-aircraft flypast. At the time, the frontline SHAR squadrons were only five-strong, barely enough to maintain a round-the-clock air defence for any substantial length of time.

On 1 April 1982, Argentine forces seized the Falkland Islands. An Argentine Air Force A-4 Skyhawk rounds the national flag at Base Aérea Militar Malvinas, formerly Stanley Airport. Note the Pucará turboprop attack aircraft on the ground, just two of a more substantial force deployed to reinforce the occupation.

*Hermes* stores for war. Despite having only recently returned to Portsmouth after being at sea for the previous two months, Lin Middleton's ship was brought to four hours' notice for steam. 800 Squadron was ordered to re-embark on the afternoon of 2 April.

**Left**: Admiral Sandy Woodward was given command of the Task Force despatched to recapture the Falkland Islands. A career submariner, Woodward was known for his exceptionally sharp mind and no less brusque manner. The larger of the two carriers, HMS *Hermes*, was made his flagship.

**Right**: Captain JJ Black. A highly regarded former gunnery officer, Black had assumed command of HMS *Invincible*, the first of the Navy's new class of anti-submarine carriers, in early 1982.

**Right**: Phoenix Squadron. Less than a week after the invasion, in anticipation of the twenty Sea Harriers embarked on the carriers suffering unsustainable losses, 809 NAS was recommissioned to provide attrition replacements. Tim Gedge was given command and told he had to be ready to deploy in three weeks.

Cunard's SS *Atlantic Conveyor* approaching New York before the war. A 15,000-ton fast roll-on, roll-off container ship working routes between Europe and North America, she was quickly identified by the Ministry of Defence as a means of carrying 809 Squadron south.

**Right**: After sailing from Liverpool, *Atlantic Conveyor* was modified in the naval dockyards in Devonport to equip her with helicopter pads fore and aft, workspaces and military communications equipment. The conversion was completed in less than ten days.

**Left**: *Atlantic Conveyor's* Master, Ian North, with Captain Michael Layard, appointed Senior Naval Officer aboard the ship. One of Cunard's most experienced captains, North was a veteran of the Second World War Atlantic convoys. It was Layard's job to prepare the Merchant Navy's crew for hostile waters.

**Left**: 1(F) Squadron, based at RAF Wittering, was tasked with sending six Harrier GR.3s south aboard *Atlantic Conveyor*.

**Above right**: Expected to operate as fighters, 1(F)'s jets were quickly cleared to carry AIM-9 Sidewinder heatseeking missiles and modified to operate at sea with additional tie-down lugs, and holes drilled in the airframe to allow sea water to drain away.

First contact. On 21 April, a Sea Harrier was scrambled from HMS *Hermes* to intercept an Argentine Air Force Boeing 707 shadowing the progress of the Task Force. The picture was taken using the F95 camera in the fighter's nose.

The Sea Harrier taken from inside the Argentine 707. The British pilot, Lieutenant Simon Hargreaves, said later, 'I had live Sidewinders locked on him – if I had fired he would have been dead.'

Simon Hargreaves after landing back aboard *Hermes* following his interception of the Argentine Boeing.

**Above**: Warpaint. Photometric apparatus set up on a flat roof at Farnborough's Royal Aircraft Establishment to test the effectiveness of experimental camouflage. A new low-visibility paint scheme for 809's Sea Harriers drew on this research.

**Right**: RAE model-maker Bert Edwards building Airfix kits for the Defensive Weapons Department's camouflage research. It was simply chance and good luck that Airfix produced a big 1:24 scale model of the Harrier.

**Left**: One of 809's freshly painted Sea Harriers in the company of a jet wearing the Fleet Air Arm's smart pre-war livery. The new scheme, known as Barley Grey after the RAE scientist who devised it, was designed to be effective at medium altitude against grey South Atlantic skies.

**Right**: In preparation for their deployment, 809 Squadron also trialled large 330-gallon ferry tanks but decided against using them, opting instead for the tried and tested 100-gallon combat tanks and multiple in-flight refuellings.

Esprit de corps. Shortly before flying south, 809 Squadron flew a photo sortie over southern England designed to signal strength in depth to an enemy that would soon meet the Sea Harrier in battle.

Brian Cole, flying XH166, led the pair. In the cockpit of the other Canberra was Flight Lieutenant David Lord. His crewmate, sealed inside the nose of the jet, was navigator Flight Lieutenant Ted Boyle. After leaving Wyton on 20 April, they flew northwest to Keflavik in Iceland and on to Gander in Canada. On the 21st they spent the night at the US Navy air station at Kindley Field, Bermuda before continuing on to RAF Belize in Central America the following day.

Much work had gone into preparing the two spyplanes for Op FOLKLORE before their departure. A new chaff dispenser fitted in the flare bay had been trialled against a Lightning F.6 from RAF Binbrook in Lincolnshire, and had successfully broken the lock from the fighter's Airpass radar. But a more front-footed approach to self-defence was also in train.

The pipework snaffled by 39(PR) Squadron engineers from round the back of the Wyton NAAFI had been put to good use plumbing AN/ALQ-101 jamming pods, borrowed from the Buccaneer force at RAF Honington, to the jet's freshly restored wing pylons. Proving flights over the electronic warfare range at RAF Spadeadam in Cumbria were arranged. If successful, the new kit would spoof Argentine radars into believing the Canberra was somewhere other than where it was – a useful trick when people are trying to shoot you down.

But perhaps the most unusual element of deception that had gone on behind closed hangar doors was the simplest. Although still wearing their standard RAF khaki green and dark grey camouflage, the PR.9s had seen their British roundels and fin flashes painted over and replaced by the blue and red shield of the Fuerza Aérea de Chile. Then removable British national markings had been papered back on to the wings, fuselage and tail prior to undertaking the ferry flight across the Atlantic to Belize.

Before they left, the 1 Group AOC, Air Vice-Marshal Mike Knight, had visited the Op FOLKLORE crews at Wyton. Their difficult and demanding mission may be top secret, he'd told them, but they had the potential to make a critical difference to the coming war. The public wouldn't know the extent of their contribution but they should have good reason to be grateful.

\*

Just a few miles up the A1 at RAF Wittering, a single two-seat Harrier T.4 thundered into the air, tucked up its undercarriage and climbed away from the airfield. In the front seat, Bob Iveson completed his checks and turned towards the southwest. In the back was Peter Squire, the squadron boss. The two 1(F) pilots were on their way back to Yeovilton to meet Tim Gedge and Captain Mike Layard, the Senior Naval Officer of *Atlantic Conveyor*, the ship that would carry both 809 and 1(F) south from Ascension. As well as discussing the logistics of the embarkation and journey south, there was an opportunity to brief Gedge on 1(F)'s progress at Wittering. If the two squadrons were going to be sharing the burden of reinforcing the SHARs already deployed to the South Atlantic, the flow of information between 809 and 1(F) needed to be comprehensive.

Modifications to the RAF jets to allow their operation from the carriers had been made. Tie-down shackles had been added and holes drilled into the airframe to let excess water drain away. For short take-offs from the deck, the jet's nosewheel steering had been enabled. Tweaks had been made to the avionics to prevent interference from the ship's radar. And, critically, Ferranti had produced a piece of kit called FINRAE, a trolley-mounted unit that it was hoped would mean the Harriers could align their own on-board navigation and weapons computers. Without it, they'd be relying on what amounted to dead reckoning and pre-Second World War fixed gunsights.

As well as lining up live firings of Sidewinder missiles and trials with the Royal Navy's 2-inch rocket pods, the GR.3s had even, after much procrastination, been cleared to train at ultra-low level. Flying through a valley at 600 knots just 100 feet from the ground was, one of the 1(F) pilots thought, *like flying through a tunnel*. It was possible to focus a few degrees either side of the nose, but the world in your peripheral vision was nothing more than an alarming blur.

The RAF mud-movers had also been mixing it with Binbrook's Lightnings and Hawker Hunters flown by 79 Squadron instructors from the Tactical Weapons Unit at RAF Brawdy in Pembrokeshire, Wales, grateful for the opportunity to play the role of an A-4 Skyhawk for the day. But there were more interesting developments to report on the air combat training front. Squire and Iveson brought

Gedge up to speed and, for reasons the 809 Squadron boss now properly appreciated, were gone by mid-morning. In the rush to get back to Wittering, Iveson even forsook the opportunity to garner any more practice launching off Yeovilton's ski-jump.

Quite right too, as far as Dave Braithwaite was concerned. He couldn't see the need. In fact, 809's Senior Pilot had never been off the end of a ski-jump in his life and, until he launched from the deck of *Invincible* or *Hermes* in anger, he had no plans to. *If the crabs can do it* . . . he reasoned. *And after all*, he told himself, thinking of the USAAF's retaliation against Tokyo after Pearl Harbor, launched from the deck of the USS *Hornet, Jimmy Doolittle got away with it, didn't he?* As far as he was concerned, taking off was the easy bit. It was what happened once you were airborne that mattered.

As he learned from Tim Gedge after Squire and Iveson's departure, he was going to be spending the next day as a guest of the RAF trying to get to grips with exactly that. Along with Bill Covington and Hugh Slade he was, as he liked to put it, going to have something *meaningful* to focus on. Just not quite in the way they'd all been hoping for.

# SEVENTEEN

## Not in the slightest reassuring

'THE BRITISH,' ANNOUNCED the old man during a radio interview, 'have asked for the loan of Super Etendards and Mirages to study their strengths and weaknesses.'

Marcel Dassault, the driving force behind the French planemaker that bore his name, wasn't averse to a little mythmaking. He was not, after all, actually even called Dassault, but Bloch. But in 1946, after barely surviving the Second World War in Buchenwald concentration camp, he adopted the *nom de guerre* given to his brother, General Paul Bloch, by the Resistance: d'Assault.

A decade later, the prototype Mirage III flew for the first time. Massive global export sales followed, all of which only fuelled Dassault's very high opinion of himself and his company. The success of the Mirage allowed him to promote the notion that Dassault was different, a company underpinned by brilliance, inspiration and passion. Presented with a good story that reflected well on Dassault, well, why not?

While both the French and British Defence Ministries were eager to deny the reports that spiralled out of Dassault's mischievous claim, he was not completely wide of the mark. Although Tim Gedge's efforts to arrange an informal encounter between 809's Sea Harriers and his French counterparts had met with an emphatic *non*, negotiations higher up the food chain had been more fruitful.

Major Jean-Yves Testard began his descent towards RAF Coningsby. His journey to Lincolnshire had started at Base Aérienne 'Guynemer' at Dijon-Longvic in Burgundy. Named after one of the leading French aces of the Great War, it was now home cornerstone of the Armée de l'Air's Mirage III air defence fleet. Testard was flying a two-seat Mirage IIIBE belonging to the 2ème Escadre de Chasse. The rear seat was empty. But it wouldn't remain so for long after he'd landed at the British fighter station. Testard was anticipating a busy, exhilarating couple of days.

While Coningsby was the headquarters of the RAF's Phantom force, Testard's business today was not with them. Instead, using Coningsby provided a measure of cover for activity his government and that of the British were very much hoping would remain under wraps. As chance would have it, just three months earlier the two countries had formalized a programme of DACT (Dissimilar Air Combat Training) known as Exercise TYPHOON. It was now hoped – largely to soothe what the British regarded as the nearly neurotic concerns of the French arms industry – to use TYPHOON to explain away France's willingness to help train British pilots to combat the Mirage III. A young Testard had yet to join the Armée de l'Air when, in 1971, the 2ème Escadre had trained the Fuerza Aérea Argentina pilots who flew them. If anyone in France was enjoying the irony of the situation, they weren't admitting to it.

As Testard flew in from Burgundy in Mirage 261/2-ZF, at the Marine Nationale air station in Landivisiau, Brittany, the Aéronavale Super Etendard pilots taking part in TYPHOON looked forward to joining him. Meanwhile, a ground support party slowly rumbled its way to Lincolnshire aboard a twin-tailed, piston-engined Nord Noratlas 2501 freighter. 'You're not there yet' went the transport squadron's unofficial motto.

After his arrival at Coningsby, Testard taxied immediately to the safety of a thick concrete hardened aircraft shelter. Capable of protecting aircraft and crews from bomb blast, fallout and poison gas, the HAS would also keep evidence of French cooperation with the British safe from prying eyes. Should questions be asked about what was going on, the line politicians were to take was simple: 'Our forces naturally maintain close contacts with their French opposite numbers, and joint training takes place regularly.'

They set off early. Given the relatively sedate pace of the old piston-engined De Havilland Heron C.1, you needed to allow time. But at least they were travelling in the Admiral's Barge with its distinctive green cheatline. Now used to ferry Ted Anson between the naval air stations under his command, XM296 had previously served with the Queen's Flight. Dave Braithwaite, Bill Covington and Hugh Slade settled into deep leather seats and looked out of the big square cabin windows as the four-engined aeroplane throbbed into the air. Might as well get comfortable. The flight to Lincolnshire was going to take the best part of an hour and a half. The weather didn't look too promising.

Brave, Covington and Slade had mixed feelings about what was on offer. The first and most significant issue was that they were arriving as passengers in the Heron rather than in the cockpits of a formation of SHARs. In order to preserve the illusion that this was business as usual under the terms of Exercise TYPHOON, it had been decided that the Sea Harriers couldn't be seen anywhere near Coningsby.

There hadn't been much less paranoia about the prospect of the RAF Harriers being spotted either. Two days earlier, the Station Commander at Coningsby had briefed Peter Squire and his men about the need for secrecy. The next day, after returning from Yeovilton, Squire, Iveson and the five other pilots chosen to sail south on *Conveyor* were flying in and out of Wittering, meeting the French jets for a series of 1 v 1 and 2 v 2 combats out over the Wash, before trundling up to Coningsby in the backseat of a little De Havilland Chipmunk, borrowed from one of the RAF's Air Experience Flights, for the debrief. Now it was the turn of the Sea Harrier pilots. Sort of.

Jean-Yves Testard lit the SNECMA Atar 09C engine of his Mirage inside the HAS. Only then did the thick armoured doors roll open. Marshalled forward, the Frenchman nudged the throttle with his left hand and the jet began to roll. He dipped the brakes before taxiing out of the shelter. Camouflaged in grey and green, the needle-nosed delta emerged beneath overcast skies. In the backseat, Dave Braithwaite scanned the instruments as they taxied towards the runway threshold.

At Point Mugu, on exchange with the US Navy, Brave had gained experience in evaluating any new and unfamiliar aircraft. But he was going to have to try to do it at one remove today. Nor were he and the other 809 pilots going to get the chance to duel with the

French aircraft as an opponent themselves. Instead, they'd been offered a slightly unsatisfactory kind of halfway house: a backseat ride with Major Testard in the Mirage while *he* flew against the Harrier GR.3s of 1(F) Squadron. What they'd learn from watching the performance of the RAF ground attack pilots was uncertain. He'd have preferred to be in the front seat, but, resting his hands and feet on the stick and rudder, he'd at least be able to follow Testard's movements as he flew the jet.

Cleared for take-off by the Coningsby tower, Testard advanced the throttle through full military power and into reheat. The Atar engine's jetpipe flared as raw fuel was sprayed into the exhaust – nearly 2 tons of extra thrust. As he released the brakes it was immediately obvious to his passenger that the Mirage lacked the savage low-speed acceleration of the Harrier. In fact, Braithwaite soon discovered, the French jet's sleek shape didn't allow it to out-drag the Harrier until both jets were already flying at speeds of over 400 knots.

Acceleration was just one of the items on Brave's list. There were eight other categories he and his 809 colleagues wanted to try to explore, including low-speed handling, high-speed handling, high angles of attack, visibility and ergonomics. He wanted a better appreciation of how the Mirage might be flown against the Harrier to best advantage. But to his great frustration, Testard, by accident or design, seemed keen on trying to meet the GR.3s on their terms, engaging in slow-speed combat at high angles of attack. It required a heavy hand on the throttle and plenty of reheat to keep the Mirage in the game. But if allowed to get slow, trying to recover flying speed meant, once committed to combat, the Mirage would always call 'Joker' – low fuel requiring it to disengage from the fight – before the more frugal Harriers. And yet, despite apparently giving himself every disadvantage, Brave was concerned that Testard still seemed able to claim kills on the Harriers with more frequency than he should have been able to. Depressingly, Bill Covington and Hugh Slade reported a similar experience.

There was no possibility of repeating the exercise with the single-seat Super Etendards they met over the Channel, but the GR.3 pilots reckoned they were, if not sharper performers than the supersonic Mirages, then more aggressively and effectively flown. They would also concede that, above 15,000 feet, the advantage lay with the

Mirage. *At height*, reckoned Bob Iveson, *it's a lot better. A lot of times, they'd have got a missile away.*

As ever, much would depend on the quality of the opposition, but following a conversation with the French pilots involved in Exercise TYPHOON training at Coningsby, the French Defence Attaché reported that 'the Argentine pilots were considered to be good'. 'The Harriers,' he added, 'had proved to be vulnerable to the Matra R.550 Magic missiles in a steep climb.'

And for Bill Covington, fresh out of his US Marine Corps WTI course, this last point was key. Just as much as they needed to get to grips with the aeroplanes, they needed to return to Yeovilton with an appreciation of the weapons systems they carried. At the end of the day's flying, he, along with Brave, Hugh Slade and the handful of GR.3 pilots brought up from Wittering in the Chipmunks, talked at length with the Mirage and SuE pilots. The French flyers were extremely forthcoming about the weapons envelopes, radar ranges, weapons system capabilities and fuzing. It was clear that, below 5,000 feet at least, the Mirage III's radar was so affected by ground clutter that it couldn't be used either to range the guns or achieve a lock-on with the radar-guided R.530 missile. The heatseeking R.550 Magic was a different proposition though. In successful trials, targets flying as low as 50 feet had been taken out.

The next morning, Peter Squire signalled his AOC with details of what had been learned.

'Harrier tactics,' he wrote, 'must be to remain at low level to minimize effectiveness of Mirage systems. Even at ultra-low level, turning will increase chances of a kill by R.550 or guns.'

The Sea Harrier pilots, Squire assumed, would be drawing their own conclusions and considering their tactics in response. They had done just that.

During the slow, bumpy return to Yeovilton aboard the Heron, the three of them talked as Brave produced a handwritten report on the day's activity. The results weren't pretty. All three had been disappointed by the performance of the 1(F) GR.3s against the Mirage and frustrated not to be able to employ their own specialist training and tactics as air defenders. For all their unquestioned skill as pilots, the

RAF Harriers were mud-movers, low-level specialists lacking both the expertise and the aeroplane required for air combat. It was like asking a boxer to play tennis. Innate coordination and athleticism would count, but it took time and practice to develop real proficiency.

And winning any encounter with an Argentine Mirage was only half the battle. The SHARs had to try to protect the fleet from Exocet attack by the Super Etendards of the Argentine Navy's 2 Escuadrilla Aeronaval de Caza y Ataque.

Covington had quizzed the Marine Nationale SuE pilots about the jet's Agave radar and the capabilities of the Exocet missile. What he heard in reply was not in the slightest reassuring. Based on what the SuE pilots felt they could say about the Exocet, it had been made clear that the threat was significant. He left with a better appreciation of the missile's kinetic performance, and of its electronic systems, its search patterns, its kill criteria and its resistance to decoys. The Royal Navy, Covington realized, was going to have to find some way *to fuck with it*.

Tim Gedge met them on the apron at Yeovilton. As the three 809 pilots clambered down the Heron's rear steps in their flying suits it was immediately obvious to Gedge that all was not well. With the Admiral's car waiting to whisk them off to brief Ted Anson, the squadron boss pulled them to one side and asked them what was wrong. They described the less than stellar performance of the GR.3s and Testard's apparent control of fight in the Mirage.

'Would you have lost if you were flying a Sea Harrier?' Gedge asked.

'No,' was the resounding answer.

'Then as far as I'm concerned the exercise hasn't happened and we won't talk about it.'

Brave didn't even record it in his logbook; Covington noted only that he'd flown forty minutes on 23 April in an aircraft he described as 'TYPE 1'.

It was Gedge's job to make sure his fighter pilots were confident of success. This was now the second time he'd had to bury bad news in an effort to preserve the morale of his new squadron. But he hadn't reckoned on the Admiral being rather less circumspect.

Inside Ted Anson's office, Dave Braithwaite led the conversation, and once again had to go over the disappointing performance of the

GR.3s against the Mirage. The Admiral listened before responding by sharing the conclusions of the DOAE attrition analysis.

'The modelling,' he said, 'says we're going to lose fifty per cent of the Sea Harriers.'

*Shit*, thought Hugh Slade, *there aren't that many of us to start with*.

It smelt like bullshit to Brave. Like so many others, the boffins at West Byfleet had fallen into the trap of taking everything at face value – weapons systems, speeds, ranges – and he knew it didn't stand up to real-world experience.

'What's your view, Bill?' asked the Admiral.

'Without airborne early warning I can't see how we can guarantee the carriers a hundred per cent against Exocet,' Covington replied, 'and if the Argentinian pilots are as good as we are we could end up trading kill ratios of one to one.' Even as he said it he realized how chilling that prospect sounded. 'But they're not as good,' he concluded firmly. 'We're better.'

'That's what I think,' Anson agreed, and picked up the phone to CINCFLEET at Northwood.

'Green light for Aviation,' he told them.

Forced to consider the possibility of losing ships and aircraft, Covington's first thought was of his wife Penny, just returned from Arizona to the UK. Slade, given pause by the DOAE report, became acutely aware of the distance separating him from his own wife, Josephine, and their baby daughter. *We're off in a few days*, he realized, and their absence suddenly cut deep. He couldn't countenance the thought of his wife and daughter being so far from any kind of familiar support network. He phoned Josephine in Australia and told her that she and Hannah needed to come home as soon as they could. They could worry about paying for it another time. Right now, he wanted to see them and, more importantly, he needed them home amongst friends and family.

At RAF Wittering too there were sleepless nights and anxiety dreams. All the 1(F) pilots were given will forms to fill in before they departed for Ascension.

Brave didn't see any need at all to put his affairs in order. He was just going to bull through. *I'm not going to die*, he told himself, and lit a cigarette.

# EIGHTEEN

## Consistently underrated

'There is a nervousness on board,' reported JJ Black's secretary. Like a party whip, the Lieutenant's job was to keep his ear to the deck and ensure the Captain was in tune with the mood of his ship. But since sailing from Ascension, the atmosphere aboard *Invincible* had shifted. 'The ship's company,' continued the secretary, 'now believe that we will fight.' With the carrier already sailing in the southern latitudes and no apparent hope of a diplomatic settlement, what had seemed unlikely now felt imminent. And the Captain was the only man on board the carrier with any firsthand experience of combat. Black decided he should talk to his ship's company over the CCTV network.

As *Invincible* journeyed south, reminders of what she might face accumulated. While Black was prepared to let his crew keep their foam mattresses, paintings and curtains stowed, cushions, after a flammability test showed they went up like a torch releasing an angry storm of acrid, choking smoke, had been removed and piled up on the quarterdeck. Of the ship's silver and commemorative valuables, all that remained aboard was a twisted silver toast rack from the carrier's First World War namesake that had survived the first Battle of the Falklands after being blown inside the wardroom piano by the blast from a German shell.

Fire drills used thunderflashes and smoke to add realism. If that weren't enough, 1lb charges dropped into the water just outside the hull would ring through the ship's compartments. And at the call of 'Action Stations, Action Stations, assume NBCD state one, Condition Zulu' the ship's company would race to pre-arranged positions pulling on white cotton anti-flash gloves and masks to protect them from burns as they bundled through the ship's narrow passages. Their progress was barely slowed by the lifejackets and one-time immersion suits they now had with them at all times. Hatches were locked closed behind them, sealing the warship into separate airtight, watertight compartments.

Everyone now carried an identity card listing name, rank, number and blood type as required by the Geneva Convention. And after morphine monojets were issued to the crew the ship's surgeon demonstrated how to jab them into your leg during a short broadcast from the on-board TV studio. 'Have a good war,' he signed off with a smile. It was JJ Black's turn next.

'After refuelling,' he explained, 'we are going to push on south for a rendezvous with the Type 42 destroyers *Sheffield*, *Glasgow* and *Coventry*.' With them and the Seawolf-armed frigates *Broadsword* and *Brilliant* in close as goalkeepers, the Carrier Battle Group's air defence screen would be in place. And this, supported by Royal Fleet Auxiliaries, would be the formation in which the two carriers would close on the Falklands. For nearly half an hour Black detailed the balance of British and Argentine forces and tactics, ships, and weapons available to both sides. As ever, the Captain exuded calm and confidence. He tried to be systematic in addressing all possible threats and how the Task Force planned to meet them. He warned against the dangers of stress. 'Get as much rest as possible,' he advised. 'Our task is to establish air superiority over the Falkland Islands exclusion zone and maintain it for about a month.'

As Black approached the end of his allotted time, he realized that, having prepared the rest of his address, he'd not given any thought to how he was going to sign off. Unable to craft anything particularly erudite at the same time as he spoke, he concluded, more by accident than design, with something rather more memorable: 'I have described the various threats and our planned responses, and as far as I'm concerned, we'll piss it!'

The effect was electrifying. As he climbed seven or eight decks back up to his cabin from the studio, a dozen sailors stopped him to agree: 'You're right, sir – we'll piss it!' There were soon signs on the doors confirming 'We'll piss it with JJ'. Printed T-shirts followed. It had been, thought Black, *like setting fire to the gorse on Dartmoor at the end of summer.*

Then, just as morale had turned a corner, *Invincible*'s Captain read the report on Exercise TYPHOON produced by Dave Braithwaite, Bill Covington and Hugh Slade. The details of the combat training with the French at RAF Coningsby didn't make for reassuring reading. At the end of the evening Command briefing, Black took Sharkey Ward to one side and asked him to read the signal from Yeovilton.

As Ward took it, he saw the look of concern in the Captain's eyes. He could see why. Although the report didn't mention the three 809 pilots by name, the 801 Squadron boss thought he'd got it figured out from the details in the signal. Then he set out to rubbish the report and its authors.

'Don't worry about what this says, sir. I know exactly who these three SHAR boys were.' He explained that none of the three pilots were what he would describe as 'Aces of the Base'. Their tactics were inadvisable – but predictable for the pilots concerned. They didn't measure up to the 801 team, nor had they, unlike his pilots, proven themselves against the F-15, F-5E and F-16, all of which, he said, would 'knock spots off a Mirage III'. 'In my view,' he concluded, 'the report isn't worth the paper it's written on.' It was a convincing demolition and, with respect to allaying the worst of his Captain's fears, a useful exercise in threat reduction. The trouble was that, on this occasion, the charismatic 801 Squadron boss had got completely the wrong end of the stick, misunderstanding the signal's content and its provenance.

The 809 pilots hadn't, as Ward supposed, been flying the Sea Harrier. Nor even the Harrier, of course. They hadn't actually been flying at all, but, rather, were flown as passengers in the Mirage. Any questionable tactics used against the Mirage could hardly be laid at their door. Nor were they quite as green as Ward claimed. Brave, after all, had been Sharkey's own AWI when 899 Squadron had trained against the USAF's F-5s and F-15s.

The report was never supposed to be an exercise in oneupmanship, though. It was simply an objective assessment of the Mirage's capability. But in defence of the Sea Harrier and his squadron, Ward was like a proud parent, unable to see, or at least acknowledge, his child's shortcomings.

'Are you blowing smoke up my arse again, Sharkey?' Black asked. As they steamed towards the Total Exclusion Zone, the carrier's Captain needed a squadron boss like Ward, exuding confidence and an unshakeable belief in the SHAR's superiority. But if the task was to establish air superiority over the islands, he couldn't afford to have any doubts about the ability of the small Sea Harrier force to do the job. And, despite Ward's vigorous dismissal of the report from Yeovilton, they continued to nag away at him. Unlike the Mirage, the jump jet was untested in battle. *Surely*, Black worried, *if the Israelis have chosen to buy the French-designed aircraft, it must be a capable machine?*

The Navy had spent so long underselling the SHAR's potential in order to acquire the jet in the first place that a Gunnery Officer like Black could perhaps be forgiven for having reservations. The Harrier, after all, had once been famously derided by critics as a machine incapable of carrying a matchbox across a playing field. And on paper they seemed to have a point. The SHAR was subsonic, lightly armed and relatively short-ranged. But it had also been consistently underrated.

# NINETEEN

## A disadvantage well known and understood

SINCE THE END of the Second World War, fighter aircraft designs had become inexorably bigger, heavier, more complicated and much more expensive. Inside the Pentagon, though, a maverick USAF Colonel called John Boyd had led a rearguard action against this trend to excess. Boyd's Energy-Maneuverability theory revolutionized fighter design and could be distilled into a single, elegant equation:

$$P_s\left[\frac{T-D}{W}\right]V$$

Specific energy ($P_s$ equals Thrust minus Drag over Weight multiplied by Velocity. It really boiled down to a simple calculation of how much excess power a fighter aircraft had in reserve in any given situation. And how quickly, as a result, it could regain energy lost through hard manoeuvring in a dogfight.

Instead of *Guinness Book of Records* baubles such as absolute maximum speed or altitude, Boyd's theory valued excess power. And the Sea Harrier had that in spades. It was an essential requirement of vertical take-off and landing. You needed a thrust-to-weight ratio of greater than 1 or you couldn't hover any more than a man wearing lead shoes could swim.

As a SHAR left the ski-jump from the bow of *Hermes* or *Invincible* carrying a pair of Sidewinders, twin ADEN gun pods loaded with 30mm ammunition, two 100-gallon combat tanks and a full internal fuel load, it enjoyed a thrust-to-weight ratio of around 1:1. By the time it had burned off fuel reaching its CAP station, it was more like 1:2. This was the kind of surplus power not seen in Western fighters until the introduction of the McDonnell Douglas F-15 Eagle and General Dynamics F-16 Fighting Falcon in the late seventies, both of which were directly influenced by John Boyd's work.

Up to about 400 knots there wasn't much that could out-drag the Sea Harrier at low altitude. US Marine Corps trials in 1976 had seen a Harrier climb to 30,000 feet thirteen seconds faster than an F-4 Phantom. And, because of its ability to VIFF, when it came to losing speed in a hurry, nothing else came close.

Alongside excess power and low weight, Boyd valued simplicity and small size. And curiosity about the clear superiority of the American F-86 Sabre over the MiG-15 in Korea also led him to further conclusions. According to his theory the MiG should have held the advantage, but in poring over the data Boyd realized that all-round visibility from the cockpit of the F-86 was better and that powered-flight controls conferred an agility advantage on the American jet. It could flick from one manoeuvre to another more quickly than the MiG.

These were all qualities shared by the SHAR.

And it all meant that against the latest, most advanced American fighter designs, the little Sea Harrier, so obviously a direct descendant of Ralph Hooper's original 1950s design for the Hawker P.1127, was perfectly capable of holding its own.

Tim Gedge had the pictures to prove it.

In May 1981 he'd taken 800 Squadron up to RAF Lossiemouth on the shores of the Moray Firth for a series of bombing trials on the Garvie Island range. On arrival they discovered that the base was also playing host to the F-16As of the 4th Tactical Fighter Squadron based at Hill AFB in Utah, who were participating in the RAF's annual Tactical Bombing competition. It was the Fighting Falcon's first overseas deployment, but, just four months after declaring themselves operational with the new jet, the 'Fightin' Fuujins' won the contest convincingly with a score of 7,831 out of a possible 8,000 points.

Having forcefully demonstrated the superiority of the F-16 as an attack jet, the six 4th TFS pilots seemed to Gedge rather scornful of the Sea Harrier. Until, that is, gunsight film of the F-16 filling the frame began to appear around the base. Now they had the F-16 drivers' attention, further encounters were arranged and produced similar results. Gedge didn't recall having lost a single combat. The

800 boss wasn't sure how the photograph of an F-16 made its way into the hands of the *Daily Telegraph*, but he had been delighted to see it in print.

The F-16 was the ultimate expression of Boyd's Fighter Mafia: a small, lightweight fighter with a thrust-to-weight ratio of greater than 1. But it had been brought down a peg or two by Tim Gedge's SHARs in the skies over Lossie. The Mirage III flown by the Fuerza Aérea Argentina, for all its needle-nosed, paper-dart slipperiness through the air, had a thrust-to-weight ratio of less than 0.6.

John Boyd wouldn't have fancied its chances.

Before that could be put to the test, though, the SHARs had to get past the Mirage's medium-range radar-guided R.530 missiles. And on that front there had been an unwelcome development at Yeovilton.

Leo Gallagher watched the four blips converge on the centre of the radar screen. Two pairs of fighters heading towards each other from opposite directions – a classic 2 v 2 intercept. It was a picture the former F-4 Observer and Tactics Instructor couldn't have been more familiar with.

The two sections accelerated towards the merge before one of the defending jets peeled off to port, gaining altitude and separation, ready to carve back round to starboard on to the tail of one of the attackers. Meanwhile, his wingman made a minor correction on to a collision course with the incoming jets. He was going to fly straight through the middle and, at a closing speed of over 1,000 knots, take advantage of the AIM-9L Sidewinder's ability to acquire a target from head-on. The tactic was called 'the Hook'. And if the SHARs could get inside the enemy's longer-ranged R.530 missiles it had the potential to be a tactic that would be hard to beat. But as much as the success of the Hook was dependent on the all-aspect capability of the Sidewinder, it also required you to see your opponent before they saw you. But it was abundantly clear, in Gallagher's expert opinion of the radar picture, that *some of the SHARs stood out like dog's bollocks*.

As well as practising air combat manoeuvring in different combinations against each other and the station's Hunters, 809's cadre of pilots had spent as much time as possible training for ground-controlled intercepts – flying under the direction of Fighter Controllers using ground-based long-range radars.

Once deployed on CAP in the South Atlantic, 809 would spend much of their time under the control of destroyers and frigates responsible for ensuring that the SHARs were positioned exactly where they needed to be, when they needed to be there, to meet any incoming raid, and that the layers of the fleet's air defence remained separate and deconflicted. If a SHAR chased a target into the arcs covered by a Type 42's Sea Dart missile or even the shorter-ranged Seawolf missiles aboard the Type 22 frigates it was liable to become as much a target as any Mirage or Skyhawk. And so learning to operate under the direction of skilled Fighter Controllers was critical to 809's success. But it was while conducting these interceptions that their counterparts at Yeovilton, which was home to the Royal Navy's Fighter Control School, first noticed a radar picture they couldn't explain.

Some of 809's SHARs simply appeared to be a lot bigger than others. And, as a result, the 'D's – as the Navy likes to call its Fighter Direction Officers – were picking them up on their screens a lot further out. It was a concern and a puzzle.

Every aircraft has its own particular radar signature. Very broadly, the bigger the aircraft, the bigger the radar return. But shape is also a factor, and features like the cavernous air intakes and exposed fan of the Sea Harrier's Pegasus engine had a magnifying effect on the jet's radar cross-section, or RCS. From head-on that was a disadvantage well known and understood by the Navy, but it didn't account for the huge discrepancy between different airframes.

But 809's fleet of SHARs, drawn at short notice from various different sources, was still anything but uniform. Some were relatively well used; some were box fresh. Through a process of elimination, Gallagher and the rest of 809's radar specialists realized that the problem lay within the squadron itself.

The windblown, salt-sprayed deck of an aircraft carrier at sea is a particularly unforgiving environment in which to keep a finely tuned, multi-million-pound piece of electrical and mechanical engineering. In an effort to protect their jets from the elements, the Fleet Air Arm had long had a voracious appetite for WD-40.

Originally formulated in the fifties and used to protect the skins of Atlas nuclear missiles from corroding in their silos, the water-displacing oil quickly became ubiquitous in the aviation industry. And in preparation for sending their new SHARs to war lashed to the exposed deck of *Atlantic Conveyor*, 809's engineers had not held back in reaching for their blue and yellow aerosol cans. And it was the slathering of WD-40 that was making all the difference.

The choice facing 809 appeared to be less than ideal: corrode or be shot down.

Test pilot Dave Poole would have taken either option over staying at home, but with barely a week before 809 deployed, he was given crushing news.

In the seventies, after completing a course at the Empire Test Pilots School he'd returned to the Phantom frontline where he'd been able to outfly 892's Senior Pilot using the pole-handling skills he'd acquired at Boscombe Down. To the enthusiasm for high-speed, high-g manoeuvring that had earned him the nickname 'Hooligan', he'd added a soft touch: an ability to eke out the best of the jet's performance around the fringes of the performance envelope. He was top of the list of pilots Tim Gedge wanted to take south. But he was also the Navy's only qualified Sea Harrier test pilot. Ted Anson told Gedge that he was going to have to leave him behind.

Gedge protested as strongly as he could. 'We need him,' he told the Admiral. 'His personal kit's already in *Atlantic Conveyor*.' But that was never going to make a difference. Hooligan was required in the UK for what would be an extensive test-flying programme in support of new systems and fits being developed for the war. Anson was unmoveable. Poole was to remain, and it was up to Gedge, as his Commanding Officer, to break the news to him.

If Gedge was frustrated, Poole was bitterly disappointed. At the mercy of a decision that had been out of his hands, he could only vent his deep unhappiness about it to Gedge. The die was cast, though. Hooligan's trunk was unloaded from *Conveyor* and brought back from Devonport. Two weeks later, Poole received a further kick in the teeth when he was forced to eject from a heavily loaded, out-of-control Sea Harrier that ended its own journey off the end of the

Yeovilton ski-jump by writing off a number of cars in the control tower car park.

As far as Mike Layard was concerned, Hooligan's kit was one of the few things actually being *un*loaded from *Conveyor*. As the ship's Senior Naval Officer he had been struggling to get Northwood and the MoD to agree on what was needed and, as a result, what was to be carried. Plans seemed to change every half hour. And as work on the ship's conversion neared completion, the nature of her cargo had continued to chop and change.

*I'll never be rude about the dockyards again*, Layard promised himself. Their efforts had been heroic. The ship had been transformed. Inside, the hold had been strengthened with steel plating and modifications had been made to the communications and firefighting equipment. A system for conducting RAS – replenishment at sea – had been installed, allowing her to be refuelled en route by Royal Fleet Auxiliary tankers. From the superstructure to a large flight deck just aft of the bow, the deck was lined with shipping containers stacked three high providing storage, maintenance space and protection for the aircraft she would soon host. The second landing pad aft would facilitate helicopter operations at sea.

Instead of her normal crew of thirty-four she would be carrying around 120. A pair of Portakabins had been installed on the upper deck to accommodate twenty-four of them. The upper deck was also home to a series of troughs built along one side that drained straight into the sea. Fresh water from the ship's two evaporation plants was going to be at a premium, and if members of what was now labelled Naval Party 1840 used these newly installed urinals, it would save on fresh water being wasted by flushing the heads. Once she was joined by the soldiers, sailors and airmen she was carrying south, the nickname *Atlantic Convenience* was almost inevitable.

All week convoys of trucks had ferried men and materiel to *Atlantic Conveyor* from Yeovilton. On board one of the 3-tonners, Petty Officer Bob Gellett sat surrounded by some of the ground equipment and spares required by 809. Of the twelve maintainers the squadron was taking south, just he and Noel Irish, wedged inside another truck alongside a load of 2-inch rocket pods, were sailing from Devonport, tasked with unloading and organizing 809's stores aboard *Conveyor* prior to the rest of the squadron joining at Ascension.

*Atlantic Conveyor* had already embarked five Boeing Vertol Chinook HC.1s from 18 Squadron RAF and another six Wessex HU.5s of the newly re-formed 848 Naval Air Squadron. Inside she carried nearly the entire UK stock of aluminium matting with which a 1,000 by 38-foot forward airstrip, taxiways and hardstandings for the Harriers were to be built; a tented city; twelve rigid-hulled combat support boats; fork-lift trucks; and storage and pumping facilities for 40,000lb of aviation fuel. But when she had first been pressed into service to ferry attrition replacement aircraft it had not been thought necessary to make arrangements for a magazine. Only much later did the need to get further explosive stores down south see the 18,000-ton ship loaded with:

- 240 600lb RAF cluster bombs
- AS12 air-to-surface missiles (rocket motors and warheads crated separately)
- SS11 air-to-surface missiles (boxed)
- 7.62mm ball rounds in cases
- conventional grenades
- phosphor grenades

The rush to convert her, and the late decision to carry explosive stores, meant that the Navy's Magazine Safety Committee was not involved in the process. Instead, the cargo was simply stowed according to UN hazard categories marked on the boxes and a desire to place them as deep inside the ship and as far from the accommodation areas as possible. No Sea Transport Officer from the Department of Trade was available to come and inspect the results. Which was just as well as they'd have had a fit. *Conveyor* was clearly in breach of *all* DoT regulations.

Mike Layard was eager to get to sea, though. He and his ship had a job to do. He phoned his wife Elspeth to say farewell only to have to call her back later in the day to say that there was a twenty-four-hour delay. 'Up, down, up, down,' she wrote in her diary. 'I feel like a yoyo on a string.'

# TWENTY

## A third flat-top

'TIME,' BEGAN THE TV ad to a backdrop of ticking clocks and dramatic chords. 'When you fly air cargo, time really is money.' As an image of a striking bare-metal 747 swept across the screen bearing the legend 'FLYING TIGERS' behind the cockpit and sporting two distinctive diagonal red and blue stripes across the rear fuselage, the voiceover promised, 'It's on time or it's on us.' Across the bottom of the screen, the small print warned that 'some restrictions apply. Call Flying Tigers for details.'

And that's exactly what the MoD did.

Formed in the wake of the Second World War and named after the American volunteer fighter unit with which the company's founders had served in China during the war, the Flying Tiger Line had grown into the world's biggest cargo airline. 'If the Tigers can't move it,' went the industry mantra, 'then nobody can.' And compared to the time they'd flown Shamu the killer whale, the six surplus RAF Hunters the MoD needed delivered overnight to Santiago were a breeze.

Chartering the Tigers, though – an outfit so eager to do what it did with style that it had even set up its own record label, Happy Tiger Records – was hardly going inconspicuous. But while the timing of the Hunters' despatch to Chile may have raised a few eyebrows, when the big silver Boeing 747-200 freighter took off from RAF Brize Norton with its cargo of Hawker thoroughbreds on Sunday, 25 April, there was nothing else to suggest that it was anything other than a straightforward, if rather swiftly processed, arms deal.

\*

On the same day, a little over 20 miles to the other side of Cirencester, the departure of another transport aircraft, a 30 Squadron Lockheed Hercules C.1, was recorded in the unit's Operations Record Book. XV292 was also bound for Chile. But the C-130 crew that climbed away from RAF Lyneham to the west were very definitely not broadcasting details of their final destination. All that was known about the mission being flown by Flight Lieutenant Morris and his four-man crew was that they were taking part in Operation FOLKLORE. That this was an effort to deploy the 39(PR) Squadron Canberra PR.9s to the South Atlantic was not shared. The less said the better.

Looking down from the bridge across the lashed-down Wessex helicopters and bladeless Chinooks, Mike Layard watched as the pale grey jet slowed to a hover alongside the ship, her nose pointing aft. *Atlantic Conveyor* had slipped out of Devonport dockyard the previous day. Now anchored in Plymouth Sound, she had only to complete First of Class trials with the SHAR before she could begin the long journey south.

Carefully balanced on a raging haze of 10 tons of thrust pouring from the Pegasus turbofan through the engine's four nozzles, the SHAR edged forward and sideways, yawing slowly until the nose was perpendicular to the length of the ship. A hypnotic balance of power and delicacy. The water seethed white beneath her as she inched over the gunwales and came to a halt over the pad. She descended vertically, dropping hard over the last few feet on to her undercarriage, then settled on the ship's forward flight deck. The noise fell away as the pilot pulled the throttle back to idle.

Inside the cockpit, Tim Gedge looked around him, taking stock of his new surroundings. Absorbing the picture. He advanced the throttle again to 55% and rotated the nozzles to 40%.

Duct pressure 55 psi. *Good*. Brakes on.

With his left hand he pulled the nozzle lever back to the hover-stop. A second later he slammed the throttle forward to full power and immediately felt the jet become light on its feet as the powerful Rolls-Royce engine took the strain.

He checked his instruments again as he rose vertically from the pad, noting with satisfaction that the tall mast to his left was serving as just the kind of visual reference he had intended.

Layard watched the SHAR describe a wide, low circle around the Sound before approaching from the other side of the ship. One Red 90 landing and take-off, one Green 90; port and starboard. And with that, the First of Class trial was complete. He wouldn't see 809's SHARs again, nor the RAF's GR.3s from 1(F) Squadron, until Ascension.

As XZ438 climbed away to the north there was no more to do; nothing to further delay their immediate departure.

Over the last ten days expectations of *Conveyor* had grown. She had become more than simply a vessel for transferring stores and aircraft south; she was now a potentially valuable addition to the fleet – a third flat-top. There was new communications equipment and the machinery necessary for RAS, but despite Layard's best efforts she was to all intents and purposes unarmed. She had sprinklers and fire extinguishers, but not the sealed compartments required of a warship to contain battle damage. Members of Naval Party 1840 had already christened the huge, open lower deck that ran the length of the ship the 'Cathedral'. And then there was the Merchant Navy crew. Layard would have his work cut out preparing them to go to war, even getting them to acknowledge that that was what was happening. *They are not in the right frame of mind*, Layard felt as he got to know the small ship's company.

Only Ian North, the ship's fifty-seven-year-old Master, had any experience of what was to come. North gave the order to weigh anchor, ready to sail into hostile waters again for the first time since 1945.

Tim Gedge hadn't been back to Plymouth City Airport since running Britannia Flight, the small squadron of De Havilland Chipmunk T.10s the Navy used to provide officer cadets with air experience. As well as a handful of piston-engined Royal Navy trainers, the former RAF airfield was now home to Handley Page Heralds and De Havilland Dash-8 commuter airliners plying routes to and from the Channel Islands and the Scillies. And so Gedge's arrival in a front-line jet fighter caused a few raised eyebrows. But after completing the sequence of proving flights from *Atlantic Conveyor*'s newly installed landing pad he needed to top up the tanks before returning to Yeovilton.

As he climbed away from the little airport he turned and looked out towards the Sound.

*Conveyor* was already gone.

That evening, Elspeth Layard noted the ship's departure in her diary: 'Well, he has really gone now and the yoyo will be at the end of its string until he returns – soon, I hope. It's all very well being self-sufficient, but it would be good to know that he'll be back sometime.'

# TWENTY-ONE

## A whole load of misfits

From the cockpit of the two-seat Hunter T.8M camera ship, Jock Gunning thought they looked magnificent. While the station photographer snapped away next to him, Gunning felt almost euphoric at the sight of the eight 809 Squadron SHARs flying in formation beside him. It hardly seemed possible. Not one of the eight pilots in the Sea Harrier cockpits, appropriated from other jobs and other corners of the world, had been part of 809 for more than three weeks. And they were putting on a hell of a show. Despite the varied provenance of the Sea Harriers in the formation, the jets, all now sporting Philip Barley's carefully calculated shade of grey, looked like a homogeneous, cohesive unit.

They looked like a squadron.

After painting a single jet in the five different shades of grey designed to disguise its attitude, it had been felt it was just too complicated and time-consuming. In the end, a slightly lighter shade was applied to the underside of the wings and tailplane, but otherwise it was Mr Barley's light grey scheme all over. Against pale grey skies at altitude, only the SHAR's black radome stood out, contrasting against the background like a polar bear's nose against the snow. But they'd all been custom-sprayed in the Yeovilton paintshop over the last week or so. They looked factory fresh, unlike the SHARs of Gedge's old squadron aboard *Hermes*, which had been crudely painted over in dark sea grey by hand using broad brushes. In the process, all of them had lost the bright red, white and gold 800 Squadron flash on the tail, designed by Gedge's wife Monika, that had so distinguished them in peacetime.

But trying to create a sense of esprit de corps was still important to Gedge with his new squadron. Especially, perhaps, because it was being forced to grow up so quickly. And so alongside the pale pink and powder-blue low-visibility national roundels, Gedge also had the 809 emblem, the phoenix rising from the flames that had adorned the tails of the squadron's Buccaneers in the seventies, painted on the tails in the same pastel colours. It was a nice touch. So too were the lo-vis 809 Naval Air Squadron velcro patches displaying each pilot's name and wings on the chests of their flightsuits.

As the eight SHARs joined, broke, wheeled and swooped around the southwest skies they used the callsign 'Phoenix'. And Gedge, Phoenix Leader, wanted them noticed. This wasn't just about looking good. It was a statement. In just three weeks the Fleet Air Arm had built a brand-new fast jet fighter squadron from nothing. And they were on their way south. Gedge and the whole of the Royal Navy establishment wanted the enemy to see it and to know what was coming. This spoke of strength in depth from an opponent who was playing for keeps. Looking out over the wings of XZ438 at the formation, the CO couldn't help but feel proud of what they'd achieved.

With good reason, felt his Senior Pilot. *It can't have been easy,* thought Brave, *to put a whole load of misfits together and make a squadron.*

But 809 were not the only ones doing that. Nor were they the only Phoenix squadron preparing for war.

Jimmy Harvey thought his fighting days were over. After surviving the Second World War as an RAF pilot, the Anglo-Argentinian returned to South America, wanting to put the death and destruction he'd endured behind him. After joining Argentina's fledgling national airline following the war, he retired in the seventies to work as the pilot of a Gates Learjet 24D executive jet. But when, in April 1982, Captain Jorge Luis Paez, a former Fuerza Aérea Argentina pilot, came knocking, Harvey didn't hesitate.

During the 1978 crisis over the Beagle Channel, Argentina had formed a paramilitary unit of civilian aircraft to fly in support of the

Air Force in any potential conflict. It was christened Escuadrón Fénix. The invasion of the Falklands saw the squadron's reincarnation. Offered the opportunity to opt out because of his British heritage, Harvey said, 'I am Argentine, Jorge, and the islands are Argentine. I want to participate.' The Learjet he flew joined eight others – a pair of Douglas C-47s, a clutch of twin-prop aircraft and helicopters and a single Hawker Siddeley HS125 business jet belonging to the state-owned oil company Yacimientos Petrolíferos Fiscales.

Tito Withington, another Anglo-Argentine RAF veteran, was commissioned to fly for Escuadrón Fénix alongside Harvey. The prospect of war with Britain filled both men with real sadness. But while the coming conflict may have been brought on by a reckless, unstable military dictatorship, neither felt they could leave their young compatriots to fight and die in a war they had little hope of winning without lending their own skill, insight and experience.

Much of the flying undertaken by Escuadrón Fénix would be simple transport and communications work around the mainland, but the high-performance jets like the HS125 and Learjets had a more hazardous contribution to make.

During the Second World War, Withington had flown daring missions for Bomber Command, dropping chaff over the Berghof, Hitler's vacation home in the Bavarian Alps, to distract the German radars. Now he and Harvey were hoping to dupe British radars. Fast enough to mimic incoming Mirages and Skyhawks, the Learjets were to fly diversion missions, saturating and confusing the British radar picture to provoke an unnecessary response from the Sea Harriers, spreading the small force thin and pulling them away from incoming raids flown by the Fuerza Aérea Argentina's fighter-bombers.

And, equipped with relatively sophisticated navigation and communication suites compared to the more primitive avionics carried by the attack jets, they would fly out over the South Atlantic on reconnaissance missions in search of British ships. Unarmed and flying without ejection seats, Argentina's Phoenix Squadron pilots were issued with standard military flightsuits and Mae West lifejackets. There was a lot riding on the accuracy and reliability of the jets' Omega radio navigation system.

*

Leo Gallagher tried to instil a healthy measure of mistrust among 809's new pilots in the Sea Harrier's navigation system. From experience he knew it was a mistake to rely on the Sea Harrier's Ferranti navigation heading and attitude reference system too completely. When NAVHARS worked, it worked well, but it also had a tendency to go awry. And because it was linked directly to the head-up display in front of the pilot's line of sight it was easy to get seduced by any error. Nor was it especially easy to use. Gallagher had heard one test pilot liken it to 'trying to work out your tax return on a calculator strapped to your ankle while driving around central Guildford at rush hour'. And that was when it was working. It could fail as often as one in twenty sorties. The NAVHARS was just one of a long list of unfamiliar items of avionics that those new to the SHAR had to try to get to grips with. There was also the HUDWAC (head-up display weapon-aiming computer) and the Marconi Blue Fox radar. All of it was complex, multi-mode digital kit operated by a dense array of cathode ray tube screens, buttons, switches and lights.

While the flight controls and primary instruments were familiar enough, the rest of it was completely new to those like Al Craig, Bill Covington, John Leeming and Steve Brown, who'd all come to the Sea Harrier from earlier generations of Harrier optimized for ground attack not fleet air defence. It was too much to be able to stay ahead of it all.

Since arriving at Yeovilton with his 3(F) Squadron, Leeming had crammed in air combat, night flying, his first air-to-air refuelling since his Lightning days eleven years earlier and hovering trials next to the crane, but after two or three attempts to work the radar he had had to admit defeat. With respect to the Blue Fox, he noted wrily, it was very much a case of 'DNCO' – Duty Not Carried Out. And now, after twelve dizzying days in Somerset, he was wrestling with the next step into the unknown. *Where the fuck*, he wondered to himself, *is Banjul?*

Tim Gedge was surprised to see Brave back in his office quite so quickly. After discarding the idea of using the big 330-gallon ferry tanks and uncertain of the ability of the SHAR's new liquid oxygen system to cope with a longer flight direct to Ascension, 809 had settled on a route that included an overnight stop in the capital of The Gambia, the little former British colony in West Africa. Gedge asked his Senior Pilot to check the flight plan for snags. After just three-quarters of an hour Brave returned and told the boss it all looked good. It was supposed to be a six-hour flight, but the only important thing, he reckoned, was getting in and out of the airfields. *Everything else in between is just flying along doing nothing.* And there wasn't time to waste on that.

For reasons that still weren't clear, Gedge was going to have to lead his squadron to Ascension Island before the end of the week then sit there, kicking his heels, until *Atlantic Conveyor* arrived five days later. After their arrival on the mid-Atlantic outpost, pressure on Wideawake's single runway and a lack of space on the hardstanding would keep them grounded. Hurry up and wait. Given the inexperience of pilots like Brown and Leeming it was a huge frustration. Leaving early was effectively cutting the training available to his two self-styled 3(F) Squadron 'mercenaries' by a third. On top of that, the RAF were telling him that a lack of tankers meant he was going to have to deploy the squadron in two waves: the first six on Friday and the two pilots left behind the following day.

At dusk on Wednesday, 28 April, Gedge took delivery of his last SHAR when Willy McAtee flew into Yeovilton aboard ZA194. After an accelerated build at the BAe factory at Dunsfold, 809's newest recruit had taken to the air for the first time ever just five days earlier.

Steaming 200 miles to the northwest of the Falklands, the Armada Argentina's Task Force 79 braced itself for the arrival of the British fleet. Escorted by the ARA's two Type 42 destroyers the Argentine carrier, *25 de Mayo*, launched A-4Q Skyhawks of 3 Escuadrilla on reconnaissance missions to the north of the Total Exclusion Zone in anticipation of the appearance of the British from the northeast. To aid their pilots' ability to navigate over the large expanses of open water and to accurately record and report any contacts, two of the squadron's jets had been fitted with additional very low frequency radio equipment. On the 28th, four Grumman S-2E Trackers of the Escuadrilla Aeronaval Antisubmarina joined the ship. All had been equipped with a homegrown radar warning receiver assembled from commercially available components. But it gave them the chance of picking up British radar emissions at a greater range than their own AN/APS-38 radars could detect enemy ships. With the embarkation of the Trackers, the Skyhawk squadron concentrated on its preparations for a strike against the British ships.

Task Force 79 received orders to 'remain as a potential threat' and to 'operate when there is an opportunity'.

*25 de Mayo*'s Trackers stepped up their patrols.

Leo Gallagher was working at DNAW inside MoD Main Building when he took the phone call from Yeovilton. Ted Anson's office had important intelligence to pass on. During a visit to the French Embassy in London, a French Navy pilot flying Wessex HU.5s with the Fleet Air Arm Junglie squadrons had learned that not only did the Argentine Super Etendards have an air-to-air refuelling capability using a pair of KC-130 Hercules tankers, but Argentine Navy engineers had successfully coupled the SuE with the AM.39 Exocet missile.

In the same week, a pilot contracted to the Falkland Islands Government Air Service, flown out of Stanley by the occupiers on a Boeing 737, claimed that the runway there had been extended. He was thought by the MoD to be a reliable witness. If true, it had the potential to dramatically increase the threat to British ships.

Hard intelligence was still thin on the ground.

# TWENTY-TWO

## A deserted stretch of
## the Pan-American Highway

COLIN ADAMS WAS furious. Prior to their arrival in Central America, a signal had been sent requiring that his Canberras' presence and purpose must be kept secret. But, after it had been decided locally that perhaps the British Forces Belize Orders Group should also be briefed in, as a courtesy, it felt as if *everyone* was now in on Operation FOLKLORE.

It wasn't the 39(PR) Squadron boss's only concern. He and his crews had been put up in a hotel in Belize City and were being ferried in and out of the airfield by an Army driver. It complicated the process of planning what was already a flight fraught with risk and difficulty. And it was proving exceptionally difficult to get information to and from Peter Robbie, already in Chile with the advance party and trying to prepare the ground for the PR.9s' deployment. But the frustration felt by Adams and his crews as they waited in the sticky Caribbean heat of Belize for a green light to deploy south paled in comparison to the difficulties endured by his colleague in Santiago.

Robbie flattened himself down against the backseat of the car and pulled the blankets over to cover himself up. Each visit to the British Embassy in Santiago first required permission from his Fuerza Aérea de Chile minder, then this clandestine approach, the RAF Flight Lieutenant hidden from view like a criminal being driven from a courthouse. Without access to a secure phoneline, the only way of getting information to his CO, sweating it out in Belize, was through Northwood, via the SAS SATCOM link to Hereford.

There was a little less need for subterfuge as he scouted around the country, assessing FACh air stations for their suitability as forward bases for the PR.9 deployment. But from the moment he reached the mainland he could tell his hosts were nervous about the prospect of the Canberras' arrival. And he knew nothing of the cover story hatched by Sidney Edwards and General Matthei that Operation FOLKLORE was nothing more than the despatch of a British Military Training Team to Chile to work temporarily with the FACh and their newly acquired high-altitude spyplanes. It all made for an uncomfortable mission.

The distances didn't help. The country's northern border with Peru was further from Cape Horn in the south than London was from Timbuktu. But in the days since his arrival from Easter Island Robbie had visited five different air bases, often ferried from one to the other inside one of the RAF C-130s that had been hastily repainted in FACh livery. The Herc's crew all wore the US-issue flightsuits used by their Chilean counterparts. Each had been given a patch carrying a Spanish-sounding name to velcro to their chests.

From the arid brown hills and deserts of the north he flew to the Base Aérea de Bahía Catalina in Punta Arenas. The wild forests, glaciers and fjords of Tierra del Fuego, all bathed in perpetual rain, couldn't have offered a greater contrast. And it was here, on the Argentinians' doorstep, that it so clearly made sense to launch the Operation FOLKLORE missions from. But it felt like the frontline. Already anxious about the intentions of the Argentine Junta in the region, the FACh maintained a detachment of armed F-5s on Quick Reaction Alert, ready to respond to any incursion from their hotheaded neighbours to the east. The civilian terminal that shared the airfield with the military had its windows papered over, while flight attendants insisted their passengers lower the blinds both in and out of the airfield.

In Punta Arenas, Robbie discussed the prospective PR.9 operation with the FACh personnel at the base. They pointed out the poor, changeable weather, strong winds, Argentine spies and a need to operate under cover of darkness. There was a radar-equipped Argentine picket ship steaming off the coast, they said. They seemed paranoid that instead of routing south out over the Southern Ocean, the British Canberra crews would somehow drop the ball and fly directly east after take-off. Straight into Argentine airspace.

*They'd like to be helpful*, Robbie thought, but he got the impression *they're clearly trying to scupper the whole thing*. It wasn't up to them, though. If the plan had General Matthei's backing, his subordinates had no choice but to try to make it work.

The Chileans insisted on being represented at the planning and briefing of the first FOLKLORE mission. But with that caveat agreed, Robbie made his recommendation to Sir Mike Knight back at 1 Group headquarters in Bawtry, South Yorkshire: the Canberras should mount their reconnaissance missions over the Falklands from Punta Arenas. But to get them into Chile in the first place required a little ingenuity. Unable to fly direct from Belize over Colombia, Ecuador and Peru, even Los Cóndores air base in Iquique was going to be too far south for the PR.9s to reach, while the closer civilian airfield in Arica would be too conspicuous. Instead, Robbie recommended that his squadron's jets land on a deserted stretch of the Pan-American Highway about 30 miles south of the Peruvian border, refuel from a waiting RAF C-130, then take off again from the blacktop to continue south to Tierra del Fuego.

Even this would see Colin Adams and his wingman flying into Chile on fumes. And the MoD wanted them to do it at night.

As the helicopter rose above the roof of the hangar the full force of the gale assaulted it, forcing it backwards over the ground. The pilot pulled on the collective with his left hand and, with his right, wrestled with the cyclic to dip the nose of the little SA315 Lama into the storm. The Chileans had been right about the wind at Punta Arenas.

Strapped into the back, Sidney Edwards could only admire the skill of the FACh pilot fighting the controls ahead of him. Gradually, the helo gained the upper hand, but it seemed to take an age even to reach the far side of the airfield. As they crossed the perimeter, buffeted and battling, they picked up speed towards the southwest, but their progress over the ground was painfully slow. And after twenty minutes the pilot received word that the gusting winds at their intended destination would make any landing unsafe. He rolled the

Lama into a steep left-hand turn to swing the tail of the Lama round and they raced back to the airfield, chased by the wind.

After they'd landed safely, Edwards shook the pilot's hand and congratulated him on his skill, but his inspection of the Chilean radar site was going to have to wait for another day.

Next time, armed with a pair of binoculars, Edwards was flown around the region aboard one of the Grupo 6 DHC-6 Twin Otters based at Punta Arenas. The rugged little utility stayed low while her passenger scouted for potential locations to site the S259 radar being prepared back at RAF Wattisham. Flying close to the border he was able to observe the Argentine port of Ushuaia with ease. And as much as they might not like it, Argentina could do nothing about it. No more than they could prevent the deployment of a British radar convoy, now codenamed Operation FINGENT, from doing the same.

A Flying Tigers 747-200 was booked to leave Brize Norton bound for Santiago on 5 May with a stopover in San Juan, Puerto Rico. Estimated time of departure was 1600Z. Like Operation FOLKLORE, the deployment of a Royal Air Force radar convoy was characterized as an opportunity to 'demonstrate and train local personnel on the operation and maintenance' of the new equipment. That the Chileans would get to keep it all after the war had no bearing on the direct contribution it would make to the fighting, while manned by the eleven-strong RAF detachment accompanying it. But the FINGENT deployment was still deemed so highly sensitive that, throughout their time in Chile, the airmen would only wear civilian clothes. They were provided with purchase orders and told to buy their own cold-weather gear. Each needed a valid passport. They were to pick up their travellers cheques at Brize before departure.

Helpfully, the Operation Order provided detail about whose side everyone was on. In the friendly forces column were:

```
1.  RAF BRIZE NORTON SUPPORT SERVICES
2.  BRITISH AIR ATTACHE STAFF SANTIAGO (WG CDR EDWARDS)
3.  OTHER UK FORCES PERSONNEL IN CHILE
4.  CHILEAN FORCES
```

In the enemy column there was just one entry:

ARGENTINE FORCES ASSOCIATED WITH THE ILLEGAL
OCCUPATION OF THE FALKLAND ISLANDS

On the Yeovilton flightline, 809's eight Sea Harrier FRS.1s stood chocked and waiting on the concrete. An immaculate rank of spotless, identical machines. A red ladder hung from the starboard side of each cockpit, inviting the arrival of its pilot. On the other side of the jet, the in-flight refuelling probe, bolted to the port engine intake, extended out and forward like the proboscis of some giant insect.

Inside the squadron briefing room, Tim Gedge hadn't seen scenes quite like it. It was normally just the CO, Ops Officer, Met Officer and the crews themselves, but today the room was crowded, the eight SHAR drivers in their baggy khaki flying suits engulfed by a tide of navy blue, gold-striped epaulettes and stiff white shirt collars. Peter Williams, Yeovilton's CO, was there. And, very unusually, a number of the 809 pilots' wives had joined them too. Gedge was glad they'd covered the nuts and bolts – the minutiae of the route, heights, speeds and the refuelling plan – the previous evening before repairing to the wardroom to raise a glass or two to what lay ahead. A few Horse's Necks for the road. The mood had been expectant.

There was little more to do today than to run through weather and the timings with the list of aircraft and pilots chalked up on the blackboard behind. Then enjoy a few words from Williams acknowledging their impressive achievement in getting to this point and wishing them luck with whatever lay ahead.

The pilots said their farewells, then squeezed into and pulled on thick rubber immersion suits over their flightsuits to protect them in the event they were forced to eject over the sea. They fastened their Mae Wests and picked up their flying helmets, then walked out to the waiting Sea Harriers.

Ronald Reagan was eager to get away on vacation in the Caribbean. The National Security Meeting on Friday morning, 30 April, was the last piece of business before he and Nancy left Washington. But after lamenting the UN's inability to keep the peace, the President sanctioned the release of a statement to be delivered by his Secretary of State, Al Haig, following the close of the meeting. After Argentina's rejection of the Secretary of State's final proposal for a negotiated settlement, it stated that the United States would 'respond positively to requests for materiel support for British forces'. James Rentschler, the State Department official who'd been travelling with Haig, left Buenos Aires for the last time with a rather more pointed view of the Junta's intransigence.

'Fuck you, Argentina,' he wrote in his diary.

Opening the meeting, CIA Deputy Director Admiral Bobby Ray Inman outlined the gathering military situation around the islands. 'The major problem the British now face,' he said, 'is making the airfield at Port Stanley inoperable,' and he explained how he expected they were going to try to do that.

As they finished up, Haig, who'd spent the last month pursuing a punishing schedule of shuttle diplomacy between London, Buenos Aires and Washington, told those around him in the White House Cabinet Room that, with his own effort now out of road, 'the British are going to go ahead and do some damage'.

Within hours, an armada of British aircraft waiting in the dark at Wideawake airfield, their anti-collision beacons flashing, started their engines. The noise from fifty-two Rolls-Royce turbojets seemed to make the ground quake. Operation BLACK BUCK, the longest bomber raid in history, was about to get underway. Success or failure would hinge on one of the most fiendishly complex aerial refuelling plans ever devised. And on the reliability of the thirteen old V-bombers that had to make it work.

Just four minutes after take-off, Squadron Leader John Reeve, the Captain of the single Vulcan tasked with carrying out the attack, pressed the RT button on his control column.

'Blue Two unserviceable,' he announced with a heavy heart. 'Returning to base. Blue Four, you're on.'

One down. The Vulcan mission to cut the runway at Port Stanley was in the hands of the airborne reserve. And experience earlier in the day suggested that, when it came to air-to-air refuelling, there was a lot more that might still go wrong.

# TWENTY-THREE

## Any self-respecting fighter pilot

THE FIRST WAVE of SHARs took off from Yeovilton at 0930Z on 30 April. The three jets only got as far as Penzance before John Leeming's oxygen system failed. He was just ten minutes into a six-hour flight that he knew from experience was now going to feel a whole lot longer. He'd been short of oxygen before, on a non-stop from Bahrain to Binbrook in a 5 Squadron Lightning F.6. Told he couldn't divert in to Akrotiri in Cyprus he'd pressed on, but by the time he was back on the ground in Lincolnshire he was shattered.

Leeming pressed the RT button to tell Dave Braithwaite, the Flight Leader, what was going on, but he knew that, ultimately, the decision on whether or not he'd have to scrub was his own. Without oxygen, he'd have to cruise a whole lot lower than Brave and Bill Covington, but he thought he'd manage. While Brave and Covington settled at 30,000 feet, Leeming dropped down to 20,000 to 22,000 feet. That would give him a cabin altitude of 10,000 to 12,000 feet. The rulebook said that without oxygen he shouldn't climb beyond 10,000 feet, but he knew the limit used by the Americans was 14,000. There was room to push it a little. And if he could remember the basics of how the radar worked, he'd be able to keep track of Brave and Covington flying above and ahead.

The SHAR flight rendezvoused with the two RAF Marham Victor K.2s over the sea south of Land's End and the loose formation of jets trailed south, their planned route skirting around the edge of France, Spain and Portugal before threading their way through those countries' Atlantic islands. The Sea Harriers refuelled little and often. Keeping the tanks as full as possible lent you options.

Before passing the Brittany peninsula, one of the two Victors transferred fuel to its wingman and turned for home. The long-slot tanker continued south with the three Fleet Air Arm jets in tow until announcing that both the wing-mounted Mk.20B refuelling pods used to refuel the SHARs had failed. There was still the central hose drum unit, but the Sea Harriers hadn't been cleared by Boscombe Down to use it. Designed for use by larger aircraft and capable of delivering at a greater rate, it was believed to be too heavy. There was every chance it would overstress the probe and cause it to shear off like a lizard's tail to protect the aircraft itself from damage. But without fuel, Brave, Covington and Leeming were going to have to find a diversion field. Or, failing that, bang out and lose the fighters. Both options looked like a pretty ignominious opening of 809's account. With Leeming already bending the rules, the SHAR pilots decided to conduct their own trial with the centreline hose. If the probe broke they'd be no worse off than they already were.

Brave was first to prod for fuel, approaching from below and behind the Victor towards the trailing hose. At the end a large spoked basket, pulled through the air like a shuttlecock, bobbled gently in the slipstream, waiting to catch the SHAR's probe and funnel it towards the valve at its centre. An inescapably male/female coupling. Brave tried to ignore it all, focusing instead on the fluorescent orange lines marked on the Victor's pale belly. They offered a more reliable guide to success than chasing the basket. Nudging the throttle lever, Brave set up a gentle overtake, grateful for the little SHAR's nimble handling. Given the way things had developed, it was just as well his section weren't wallowing around the sky with the big 330-gallon ferry tanks slung under the wings. Leaving them on the ground at Yeovilton had been the right decision.

Covington and Leeming followed their Flight Leader's example to complete another of the fourteen separate refuellings the two-leg flight plan to Ascension required. The four British jets continued on what was becoming, thought Covington, *an interesting sortie*. As they passed abeam Galicia in northwest Spain they tracked further out into the Atlantic, losing sight of land.

'Position' came the request from the Victor. Then, from his seat in the rear of the cabin, the tanker's Air Electronics Officer broke the news that the big jet's navigation suite had failed. They assumed the SHARs had inertial navigation kit of their own. And they did. In theory.

Despite their immaculate appearance, 809's jets were hiding a few snags under the skin. Bill Covington didn't have a radar. And Dave Braithwaite's NAVHARS had packed up. Without it, he'd been navigating using a pencil line on a chart and a stopwatch, calculating the effects of altitude, windspeed and direction on their progress. He looked at the map sitting on his lap and marked off where his own dead reckoning told him they were. He thumbed the RT button and, without qualification or demur, confidently confirmed the formation's position.

Reassured, the Victor, with her two navigators on board, continued to lead the formation on their way south to The Gambia.

Covington, whose *working* NAVHARS had suggested a different position to Brave's, was relieved when he saw Senegal's distinctive Cap-Vert peninsula emerge from the hazy blue skies ahead. With the country's capital Dakar on the nose, there were just 100 miles to run. The three high-flying jets began their descent into Banjul's Yundum International Airport, meeting John Leeming on their way down.

*Went like clockwork*, thought Leeming with a wry smile as he taxied to the apron. And he cracked open the canopy a few inches to get a little welcome air flowing through the glasshouse cockpit.

In winter dawn breaks late so far south. But as the sun finally rose over the horizon at 0846 local time, a single S-2E Tracker from the Escuadrilla Aeronaval Antisubmarina was already on her way home to ARA *25 de Mayo*. Using the new Tectronix electronic surveillance kit, the crew of the twin-engined patrol aircraft had picked up a contact 113 miles north of the Falklands. Two further Tracker missions launched from the Argentine carrier later in the day. Both returned with strong contacts and UHF and VHF radio intercepts. *25 de Mayo* had found the British Carrier Battle Group.

When the 3 Escuadrilla attack jets launched, each armed with four 250kg Mk.82 Snake Eye retarded bombs, the raid against the British was to be led by Alberto Philippi. Forty-three years old and married with four children, Philippi hadn't needed asking twice to return to the squadron from a posting ashore. At the time of the operation to seize the Malvinas, one in three of the pilots in his old unit had been little more than a rookie. A former Commanding Officer of the Skyhawk squadron, Philippi knew his long experience in the cockpit of the A-4Q could count.

As he anticipated leading the squadron into action against a hornets' nest of British defences, Philippi took comfort from his faith. 'Not one leaf falls from a tree if it is not the will of God,' he told himself.

In West Africa, Bible verse appeared to be a long way from the thoughts of a handful of Philippi's British counterparts. Drinking, smoking and laughing, six 809 pilots admired the view across the mouth of the River Gambia. The first few beers had barely touched the sides. Beyond a kidney-shaped swimming pool fringed with palm trees, the sea lapped at a butter-coloured beach. Sundowners in Banjul's Caledonian Atlantic Hotel and Resort really weren't a bad way to go to war.

Led by Tim Gedge, the second section of SHARs had touched down on Yundum's long runway half an hour after the first. The squadron boss had taxied in to the hardstanding, completing his post-landing checks as he rolled along the concrete towards the whitewashed control tower and the distinctive-looking terminal building. He'd shut down the jet and undone his harness, eager to climb out of the cockpit and peel out of his immersion suit. The Gambia in May was no place to be sealed in thick watertight rubber.

The Man from Del Monte-style white suit worn by the British consular official who'd greeted them looked like a much better bet.

'Don't worry about the Senegalese troops guarding the airport,' he'd reassured them after welcoming them to the country, 'there was a coup last year.'

Still in their flightsuits, the pilots had clambered into the back of a minibus. As they left for their hotel, the squadron's maintainers, who'd flown into Banjul aboard a Hercules, were already swarming all over the aeroplanes.

Inside the minibus, a walkie-talkie had crackled into life. It was the airport manager.

'Tim,' he'd said, 'we'd like to supply some in-flight rations for you to take with you. What would you like?'

For a moment, Gedge had been stumped.

'I'll leave it up to you,' he'd suggested. 'Whatever you think any self-respecting fighter pilot would like to eat.' And Gedge had thought no more of it. Thirst, not hunger, was 809's priority.

After checking into the hotel the six 809 pilots had made their way outside, grabbed a table beneath a thatched parasol, and got stuck in. By the end of the evening, a fully dressed Dave Braithwaite was in the pool. But high spirits were understandable. When the group of exuberant fighter pilots finally called time and returned to their rooms it would be the last any of them would see of a proper bed for many weeks.

'Tomorrow will be one of the most demanding days of our lives,' JJ Black had told his ship's company as HMS *Invincible* steamed towards the 200-mile Total Exclusion Zone that had been declared around the islands. Now, as he stood shaving in his cabin, he knew his crew's fate, that of the Task Force and of the success of the whole adventure lay in the hands of the Sea Harriers. He wished he could be more certain of the superiority claimed by Sharkey Ward, but he was by no means sure. He thought about the Argentine aircraft ranged against them. Good aeroplanes against a handful of unproven Harriers. He drew the razor across his face before rinsing the blade in the sink. *I wonder*, he mused, *if we'll have any aircraft left by tonight.*

At 0530Z on Saturday, 1 May, *Invincible* crossed into the TEZ and sailed on to a position about 100 miles east-northeast of East Falkland.

# PART TWO

## Into the Danger Zone

*Reacher said nothing.* We can't fight thirty people. *To which Reacher's natural response was:* Why the hell not?

Lee Child

# TWENTY-FOUR

## All the meat on the grill

THE ARGENTINE PLAN was to take on the Sea Harriers. Successive waves of Mirages and Daggers launched from Río Gallegos and Río Grande mounting slashing, diving attacks from high altitude would carve into the small British fighter force. Two kills, even if they came at a higher price to the Fuerza Aérea Argentina, would be a literal decimation of the SHARs.

It was 0940Z on 1 May. Local time on Argentina's east coast trailed three hours behind and darkness still clung to the airfield when word reached Río Gallegos that a British Vulcan bomber had attacked the airfield at BAM Malvinas, the former Stanley Airport. Riding hot white spears of fire from their jetpipes, a pair of Grupo 8 Mirage IIIEAs was scrambled. Tucking up their undercarriage, they climbed away in the chill air and into sunlight, their cruising altitude towards the islands exposing them to the first glow of the rising sun. Each of the supersonic fighters was armed with a pair of the most capable missiles in the FAA arsenal, the Matra R.550 Magics. Their pilots were confident in the Mirage. If they stayed high and fast, they believed, they'd hold an advantage.

But unable to establish contact with the controllers operating the AN/TPS-43 radar on the islands, they were flying blind. The short-range Cyrano radar in the nose of each jet was never going to be able to pick up trade without first being vectored towards it by ground control. The pilots returned to Río Gallegos empty-handed. It was a frustrating opening shot for the Argentine fighter pilots.

*

Just as the first Argentine Mirage flight returned to base, twelve Sea Harriers launched from HMS *Hermes*. Armed variously with 1,000lb iron bombs fuzed to airburst, retarded thousand-pounders and cluster bombs, each of which contained a further 147 smaller bomblets, the SHARs formed up and tracked towards the islands for the first time.

Split into three sections, the 800 Squadron jets attacked the airfields at Stanley and Goose Green. Before the main attack, the four jets from Red Section had lobbed twelve thousand-pounders at the airfield defences from the east.

'Bombs gone,' called Red Leader as Black Section sliced in over the coast from Berkeley Sound, hugging the ground between Mount Low and Beagle Ridge. While the defenders' heads were turned in the direction of the initial attack, squadron boss Andy Auld led the five Black Section jets in from the northwest. The retarded bombs, it was hoped, would add to the damage caused by the Vulcan, which had left a single deep crater at the runway's midpoint. The cluster bombs were to take out aircraft, fuel, equipment and personnel. Anything above ground and unprotected was vulnerable. But to carry out the attack, the SHARs had to safely negotiate the batteries of radar-guided Roland missiles and 20mm Oerlikon cannon shielding the airfield.

Further west, Tartan Section streaked in low towards the grass strip at Goose Green to attack the detachment of FMA IA-58 Pucarás based there. Operating from makeshift airfields, the indigenously built turboprop had the potential to harass the British operation. Designed for counter-insurgency, the Pucará may not have posed the same level of threat as the fast jets flying from the mainland, but it was rugged and heavily armed.

*Only madmen*, thought one of the defending Argentine soldiers, *would fly so low*. Later examination of the gun camera footage suggested that most of the Sea Harrier pilots were approaching their targets between 5 and 15 feet from the ground. With so little warning of attack, Argentine defences were hard-pressed to respond effectively.

All twelve British jets returned safely to the carrier. Only the last of them to flash across the airfield had suffered any damage at all – a hit from a single 20mm cannon shell in the tail. Concerned that it might have affected the reaction controls that enabled the precision flying required of hovering, its pilot, Flight Lieutenant Dave Morgan, opted to bring his jet in over *Hermes'* stern with 50 knots of forward speed in what was called a rolling vertical landing. A manoeuvre not cleared for the SHAR by Boscombe Down or the Navy, it was to be the first time it had been performed at sea, but it posed no problems. It was an early indication of what the little Sea Jet might bring to the fight.

Within an hour and a half of going to war, the Sea Harrier had already demonstrated a flexibility and robustness that, as the campaign developed, would prove vital.

After he'd taxied forward to the base of the ski-jump, Morgan completed his post-landing checks and shut down the jet. As the SHAR, a jagged fist-sized hole in its tail visible from the bridge, was chained to the deck, his legs began to shake.

'I'm not allowed to say how many planes joined the raid,' reported the BBC's Brian Hanrahan from on board the British flagship, 'but I counted them all out and I counted them all back.'

And in the 800 Squadron crewroom relief gave way to exuberance. The anxious, tight-lipped focus that had preceded the mission was long gone. As a young Winston Churchill, reporting on skirmishes on India's northwest frontier in the late nineteenth century, had observed: 'Nothing in life is so exhilarating as to be shot at without result.'

Sharkey Ward was feeling rather differently about the progress of his war so far. His proposal to lead a night-time raid against Port Stanley had gone by the wayside with the decision to launch the long-range Vulcan attack from Ascension. And to learn that, once the V-bomber's twenty-one 1,000lb bombs had stirred up the hornets' nest around the Port Stanley airfield, 800 Squadron would then be staging their own dawn raid just beggared belief. So much for any element of surprise, he thought, boiling at the stupidity of it all.

So far, at least, the air battle against the Argentinians hadn't done much to improve his mood. Successive pairs of 801 Sea Harriers had been vectored from their CAP stations by the 'D' aboard HMS *Glamorgan* towards trade, but on each occasion there'd been little more than shadow-boxing. Mirages and Daggers, controlled from Port Stanley, approached at heights of 25,000 feet or more, hoping to tempt the SHARs up from 15,000 feet to meet them. On one occasion, the CAP pair was told by the 'D' that the enemy jets were just 2 miles away, but there was no sign of them.

Dry-mouthed with tension, the 801 pilots had scoured the skies around them, but could see no sign of bogeys that, with visibility of over 10 miles, they should have been able to eyeball. Only when one of them pulled his SHAR up into a vertical climb to scan the sky above with his Blue Fox radar did he detect the Argentine jets flying beyond a veil of high cloud up near 35,000 feet. With no possibility of reaching them, the SHARs returned to their CAP station.

Trident Section, another pair of SHARs led by Ward's Senior Pilot, was vectored on to a pair of Daggers but had no more luck. The two Grupo 6 pilots of TORO Flight punched off their drop tanks in anticipation of combat with the Sea Harriers, but saw no sign of the British jets. But they were more or less on top of each other. In the uncertainty, the British pilots mistook the Argentine tanks, streaming a white mist of unburnt fuel as they fell past, for an incoming radar-guided R.530 missile. By the time their report of a suspected missile launch against them reached *Invincible*'s Ops Room, it had been misinterpreted as an Exocet attack against the carrier, causing the ship to go to Action Stations. Nerves were stretched thin.

Sharkey Ward tried to take what positives he could from the morning's frustrations. His pilots had gained valuable experience. *The Mirages*, he'd had to conclude, *are obviously not too keen on mixing it*. He wanted to see a result, though. And for that to happen the enemy had to join the battle.

Capitán Gustavo 'Paco' Garcia Cuerva was sure that they'd had a shot at a pair of Sea Harriers. After mistakenly directing a flight of four Skyhawks *towards* the approaching British fighters, the Vigilancia y Control Aéreo Grupo 2 controllers realized their error. They hauled them off and instead vectored Garcia Cuerva and his wingman, Primer Teniente Carlos 'Daga' Perona, in pursuit of the SHARs as they returned to their CAP station. But, after hitting 'bingo' fuel, the two Grupo 8 Mirages had no choice but to abandon the hunt and turn back to the mainland or risk ditching before reaching home.

During the debriefing at Río Gallegos, as they planned for another sortie to the Malvinas in the afternoon, Garcia Cuerva made no secret of his eagerness to engage the British fighters. Frustrated that a lack of fuel had forced them to abandon what had seemed to be a promising position, he was determined not to let it happen again.

'If we get low on fuel,' he told Perona, 'we'll try to land at Puerto Argentino, refuel and return to the continent in Alfa configuration.' If they recovered into Stanley after a fuel-draining dogfight, he thought they could, if they removed the tanks and missiles, just about get airborne from the short runway and make it back to the mainland. There was no doubting his determination, but following the damage caused by Operation BLACK BUCK, it was a plan that already seemed unlikely to succeed. And it also depended on the outcome of their next encounter with the Sea Harriers.

'Helicopter!' reported Teniente de Corbeta Daniel Manzella. 'Helicopter to the left!' Three hundred yards away, the British Westland Sea King spotted them and took immediate evasive action.

After taking off from the grass strip on Pebble Island at 1525Z, the three Comando de Aviación Naval Beechcraft T-34C-1 Turbo Mentors had flown east to Cow Bay, where there'd been reports of British helicopters. They'd been hunting for half an hour. Now they had their reward.

Each was armed with two 70mm rocket pods and a pair of 7.62mm machine guns. They weren't really warplanes at all, but little propellor-driven trainers from the Escuela de Aviación Naval, the Argentine Navy's flight school. But unable to safely fly the Super Etendards or Skyhawks from the only paved strip on the Malvinas at Puerto Argentino, the Armada had been forced to improvise. After their high-visibility orange markings were overpainted in drab green and brown camouflage, the Turbo Mentors went to war. And now, with the British air attacks against BAM Malvinas thought to herald a full-scale amphibious landing, they'd been sent in to try to slow it down.

The three turboprops swarmed towards the target. In the cockpits, Manzella and his two wingmen armed their weapons.

*

Low cloud hung over East Falkland and out to sea. Five oktas (5/8) coverage according to the morning met briefing, but from 12,000 feet it looked thicker. Flying in a loose defensive battle formation, line abreast a couple of thousand yards apart, Sharkey Ward and his wingman, Ian 'Soapy' Watson, cleared each other's sixes as they patrolled their CAP station. From 10 miles off the northeast coast, glimpses of Wickham Heights peeked through the cotton-wool mantle beneath, the occasional break in the cloud providing a window on the valleys below. A high-pressure system had pitched camp above the islands and looked in no hurry to move on. At this time of year the South Atlantic weather here seemed almost binary, switching from calm and cloudy to something altogether fiercer. On warmer days, thick fog would clamp down over the cold seas reducing visibility to a couple of hundred yards. Today was what counted for good weather.

In the cockpits of the two 801 Squadron SHARs the radio crackled into life.

'I have two, no, three contacts, slow moving,' began the 'D' aboard *Glamorgan*. The three blips on his radar screen were turning north along the coast, away from Stanley. They might be Pucarás, he suggested, 'ten miles south of you now'.

Ward and Watson hauled their jets round and began their descent, eyes glued to their radar screens as they searched for the three bogeys.

Watson painted them first. 'I have them, boss,' he confirmed, 'three contacts on radar, well below at six miles. Twenty degrees right.'

As their altimeters wound down, the two fighters accelerated towards an opening in the thick cloud carpet below them.

Manzella's wingman saw them first. The dark outlines of two Sea Harriers scorching into view beneath the clouds a little more than a mile behind. A 300mph overtake. He jabbed at the RT button.

'Wolves at six o'clock!' he screamed.

All three T-34s broke for the clouds.

'Tally ho!' Ward called as he made visual contact with one of the Armada T-34s as it climbed towards the safety of the clouds. He had to take the shot. The 801 Squadron boss checked the safety catch was flipped open and pulled back hard on the stick. As the SHAR's nose whipped up, the anti-g trousers around his legs and waist inflated, squeezing the lower half of his body to help keep the blood from draining from his head. He squeezed the trigger. Lethal streams of high-explosive shells erupted from the twin 30mm ADEN cannon pods beneath the fuselage at a rate of 1,200 rounds per minute. A shower of spent shell cases trailed in the SHAR's wake.

Manzella broke right as he found the sanctuary of the cloud cover. He could hear the judder of the British fighter's guns. Then a percussive thump immediately behind him. Faster than he could react, the dark grey shape of the Sea Harrier resolved out of the enveloping white, flashed over his cockpit like a banshee and disappeared back into the cloaking mist. The little Turbo Mentor quivered in its wake. Heart thumping, the pilot hauled the nose of his aircraft down. With the Sea Harrier screaming up through the thick cloud layer, there would be some shelter beneath. Descending into the clear air below, he made visual contact with the rest of the flight, jettisoned his weapons and redlined the throttle. He darted in and out of the cloud to evade the preying British fighter as he escaped to the south. Behind him, a single 30mm shell from his attacker had passed through the plexiglass canopy. *If I'd turned to the left*, he realized, *I'd have run right into its fire.*

After diving back down beneath the murk, Ward caught another glimpse of the three Armada T-34s before they once again shrouded themselves in the cloud layer at the first sight of him. It was hopeless. Berating himself for missing with his first snap shot with the guns the 801 boss returned to his CAP station to rejoin Watson, only for *Glamorgan*'s 'D' to report another three contacts inbound. This time they were coming in high and fast: 38,000 feet, Mach 0.95.

*Mirages*, thought Ward.

Determined to try to pull them on to the punch, he told Soapy to hold his course to give the Argentine fighter pilots the impression they'd caught the SHARs unawares.

'We'll spoof them into attacking us,' he told Watson.

'Thirty miles ... twenty-five miles,' reported the 'D', 'they are now supersonic. Coming down the hill.' Accelerating, the Argentine fighters dived towards the Sea Harriers. 'Fifteen miles.'

'Counter port!' called Ward over the radio, initiating a hard turn through 180° to face the enemy. Tight white vortices streamed off the SHARs' wingtips as they bit into the moist air. As the 801 pair levelled off to face the incoming threat, just a few seconds separated them from the merge. Adrenalin surged as the two pilots searched the skies above them.

Then, just as they had in their first encounter with the SHARs earlier in the day, the Fuerza Aérea Argentina deltas punched off their fuel tanks and turned tail.

Ward and Watson, now low on fuel themselves, made their weapons safe and rolled away to the east. Ward couldn't quell a mounting sense of frustration. Limited by the SHAR's modest performance and the short range of the Sidewinders, if the enemy chose not to fight, there wasn't really much he could do about it.

As Trident Section cruised back to *Invincible*, Ward's young wingman mulled over a less than satisfying day's work so far. A missed opportunity, Watson concluded. *I could have become an ace on day one.*

At Río Gallegos, Gustavo Garcia Cuerva and Carlos Perona prepared for their second flight of the day. Their Grupo 8 Mirage IIIs were tasked with providing top cover for a massive wave of ship attacks launched from four air bases – Daggers, Skyhawks and, for the first time, the Canberra B.62 bombers of Grupo 2 de Bombardeo flying in at longer range from the naval air station at Trelew. Forty or more sorties were planned.

*The Air Force*, thought Perona, *is going to put all the meat on the grill.*

# TWENTY-FIVE

## The Hook

EACH OF THEM armed with a pair of R.550 Magic heatseekers, DARDO ('Dart') Flight patrolled at 30,000 feet above the islands. From the cockpit of his Mirage IIIEA, Gustavo Garcia Cuerva called up the radar controllers on the ground at Puerto Argentino to ask about the condition of the runway at BAM Malvinas. The answer never came. Instead, he and his wingman, Carlos Perona, were told they had trade. Two bogeys 30 miles ahead. The northern Sea Harrier CAP.

'Jettison the tanks,' ordered Garcia Cuerva, as the two big 1,700-litre tanks tumbled away from beneath the wings of his Mirage. Twelve hundred yards to his left, Perona's starboard drop tank stuck stubbornly beneath the wing. A hang-up. It would affect his jet's performance but there was nothing he could do.

The bogeys, reported the controller, were coming straight at them, 15,000 feet below. As DARDO Flight dived towards the intercept, Perona kept his eyes fixed on the radar screen.

'Looks as though they mean business this time,' reported *Glamorgan*'s 'D' as he watched the two contacts accelerate towards the CAP pair under his control.

In the cockpits of the two 801 Squadron SHARs, the pilots stared intently at their radar screens. Steve Thomas, on his second mission of the day, picked them up first. He hit transmit. 'I've got them,' he told his wingman, Flight Lieutenant Paul Barton, flying in battle formation a mile off his starboard wing, 'ten degrees high at seventeen miles, ten degrees right.' As he watched the two glowing green contacts track down his radar screen towards them he called 'Judy!' to assume control of the intercept from *Glamorgan*. 'Fifteen miles. I'm going head-on. You take it round the back.'

The two formations of fighters closed on each other at near 1,000mph.

Barton advanced the throttle to the stops and felt the Sea Harrier surge forward. As he carved into a turn to starboard, he lowered the nose a touch to help boost his acceleration to combat speed. As they executed the Hook, both pilots armed their weapons.

'Ten miles,' reported the Puerto Argentino controller.

Failing to pick them up with his radar, Carlos Perona looked up and out of the Mirage's cockpit to make a visual search. He was immediately rewarded. The dark grey of the Sea Harrier's warpaint stood out like a sore thumb against the white cotton-wool cloud, 6 or 7 miles ahead and below. But he could only make out one of them. He knew that, like his own squadron, the British CAPs hunted in pairs. He strained to catch sight of the Sea Harrier's wingman without success. Unable to establish visual contact with a second jet, Perona had no choice but to focus on the machine he could see. He kept it in his sights as he pushed the throttle lever all the way forward with his gloved left hand. The rpm needle began to arc around the dial as the Atar engine spooled up. He needed to gain speed and height to try to take advantage of his jet's superior performance. But as soon as he pulled the Mirage into a steep climb it was clear that the big fuel tank still hanging off his wing was holding him back.

The British jet shouldn't have been able to stay with him, but Perona was surprised and alarmed to discover it was keeping pace. Even outclimbing him.

While Barton racked round from the right to try to tuck himself in behind the Mirage flight, Thomas hoped for a head-on shot at the Mirage pair. But, as he ran in from the east, the closing Argentine jets had the afternoon sun behind them. Against that background, the Nine Lima's sensitive seeker head was unable to pick up the heat from the Atar engine. And without the distinctive electronic growl of the Sidewinder's acquisition tone buzzing in his ears, he knew his missiles hadn't locked on to their target. He pulled back on the stick and rolled into a climbing turn towards the soaring Mirage. The anti-g suit inflated around his legs and waist as he was pressed deep into his seat. Tightening the turn, Thomas hauled the nose round as his jet swept upwards on a collision course.

Then they flashed across each other, SHAR over Mirage, dissecting the sky. Barely 100 feet separated them.

Thomas craned his neck over his shoulder to keep visual on the Argentine delta. Running on adrenalin, it was as if he could make out every rivet and curve of the enemy jet's camouflage. He'd seen the white helmet of his opponent in the cockpit as the Mirage streaked past beneath him. And then, as he held the turn to starboard, Thomas swept over the path of his own wingman as he dropped unseen into the Mirage's six o'clock.

Barton's ADEN guns spat 30mm cannon shells.

He'd loosed off a few rounds as the Mirage streaked across his gunsight, but he knew he'd never had a proper lead on him. But now, as the two Mirages continued their climbing turn to port, Barton rolled on to the Flight Leader's tail. The pilot seemed preoccupied with the hunt for Thomas, oblivious to the Sea Harrier 500 yards behind him.

*If he'd seen me*, Barton thought, *any red-blooded fighter pilot would have broken hard*. But there was nothing to complicate the British pilot's attack. He had to act fast, though.

Bleeding off speed as the SHAR juddered through a fierce 6g turn, he was already starting to fall behind the faster Argentine jet as it soared skyward. Now out of gun range, he switched to missiles, keeping visual on the Mirage through the top of his canopy. From behind and beneath, the distinctive delta shape was framed against the cold winter sky, its jetpipe presenting itself like a flare. The Sidewinder's acquisition tone growled in his ears. Through the head-up display in front of him, a hollow X was projected over the turning Mirage. He pressed the 'ACCEPT' button on the control column to lock the missile to the target. The growl changed to an insistent chirping at the same time as a hollow diamond boxed his view of the Mirage through the HUD. The Nine Lima was locked and tracking. Barton flipped up the safety catch with his right thumb and pickled the fire button.

'Fox Two,' he reported as the Sidewinder raced off the rail trailing an angry white rocket plume in its wake.

'Break!' called his wingman, but Garcia Cuerva's warning came too late. A moment later Perona felt a thump as the Mirage bunted forward from the impact, shedding debris behind. Perona lost control immediately as the jet, clean aerodynamics shredded, began to shake. At the right of the instrument panel, the engine gauges kicked as a bank of warning lights lit up to a devastating soundtrack of fire, hydraulic and system alarms. He shut down the engine. There was no hope of saving the aircraft, but as damaged as she was, she was still flying. He might save himself, but only if his ruined aeroplane made landfall. Because he'd opted not to wear a cumbersome immersion suit, he'd be unlikely to survive more than three or four minutes in the chill South Atlantic. Thirty miles ahead he could see salvation. He hit the RT button.

'Paco,' he called, 'I'm looking at a coast. I'm going to try to get there to eject.'

'Be lucky, asshole,' came the encouraging reply from Garcia Cuerva, 'eject safely.'

The stricken Mirage, unbalanced by the single drop tank still hanging off its starboard wing, began to roll uncontrollably. At 15,000 feet as he coasted over Pebble Island, Perona pulled the ejection handle.

Out to his right, Steve Thomas had seen Barton's missile hit home, the rear of the Mirage disintegrating from inside a violent yellow fireball.

'Splash One, Mirage,' confirmed Barton.

But Thomas was already on the trail of the Argentine Flight Leader. After witnessing the destruction of his wingman, the surviving enemy jet pulled into a steep, spiralling turn towards the cloud cover 8,000 feet below. Thomas rolled the SHAR on to its back and hauled down the nose into a vertical dive behind it. When the acquisition tone growled, he pressed 'ACCEPT' to lock on to the target. As the system began to chirrup, he fired, watching the Sidewinder streak after the evading Mirage. As the Argentine jet disappeared into the 4,000-foot cloud layer, the missile streaked in close behind it.

Thomas never saw either again. Now low on fuel, he and Barton climbed to medium altitude to return to *Invincible*. Uncertain of whether or not his Nine Lima had hit its target, Thomas would only claim the second Mirage as a 'possible'.

If Garcia Cuerva had hoped luck was on Perona's side, it had definitely deserted him. For while Garcia Cuerva's Mirage had survived the initial attack by the Sea Harrier, its encounter with Steve Thomas had no less caused its destruction than if it had been shot from the sky. Initially there was confusion about what had happened, but after Perona, who survived his ejection and was picked up by an Argentine Army helicopter, had been medevacked back to Buenos Aires for treatment of injuries sustained during the ejection, Grupo 8's Commanding Officer, Carlos Corino, revealed the truth. Or something like it.

Both Perona *and* his Flight Leader had been shot down, Corino told him. 'Garcia Cuerva's aircraft was badly damaged during the dogfight – fuel was streaming out so he couldn't get back to the mainland. He diverted to land in the Malvinas, where his Mirage exploded on landing and killed him.'

What Corino couldn't bring himself to admit was that, attempting an emergency landing on the damaged runway at BAM Malvinas, his pilot's crippled jet had been finally brought down by Argentine anti-aircraft guns. Despite being warned about the incoming Mirage, an Army Oerlikon 35mm battery got spooked when Garcia Cuerva jettisoned his weapons in anticipation of a difficult landing, and opened fire. Garcia Cuerva had cried 'They're firing at me!' over the radio before rolling away to the south and crashing in shallow water just off the coast.

DARDO Flight had been wiped out. The first air combat of the war had resulted in the loss of two of Grupo 8's most capable Mirage IIIs. And there was worse news to come for the Fuerza Aérea Argentina.

A section of three Daggers from San Julián had got through at low level to inflict relatively minor damage on the destroyer HMS *Glamorgan* and frigates *Alacrity* and *Arrow* as they steamed close to Stanley shelling Argentine positions ashore. They just managed to escape the attention of a pair of Sea Harriers as they turned for home. Out of ammunition and low on fuel, the Daggers climbed to height as the SHARs slowly gained on them from the east. Once they'd reached cruising altitude and Mach 0.9, they knew the British fighters didn't have the performance to close to within range of their Sidewinders.

But as they accelerated away to the west, another Grupo 6 Dagger, operating alone after his wingman suffered a technical failure, was vectored towards what was reported to be a single contact. But when the single glow on the screen of the Grupo 2 controller resolved into two bogeys, the Dagger's pilot, Teniente José Ardiles, knew he was outnumbered and outgunned. He jettisoned his tanks and advanced the throttle to full power as he pulled into a hard climbing turn. But he was too late. The 800 Squadron CAP from HMS *Hermes* had him, the spear of flame from his engine's reheat presenting an irresistible target to the Nine Lima. Caught near the limit of the Sidewinder's range as he tried to escape to high altitude, Ardiles was killed in the fireball. He was the cousin of the Tottenham Hotspur star Ossie.

At dusk, a pair of 801 Squadron SHARs intercepted a flight of three Canberra bombers skimming in 50 feet above the waves 150 miles northwest of Stanley. Low on fuel, the Sea Harrier pilots had to break off their attack more quickly than they'd have liked, but not before they'd taken down one of the bombers with a Sidewinder. Neither of the remaining Canberras, nor those of another section of three bombers that followed them into the air at Trelew, got anywhere near their targets.

In the 'Duty' column of 801 Squadron's Fair Flying Log, Thomas and Barton's successful sortie was marked as a 'Mirage Killer'. But while there had been kills for the Sea Harrier squadrons aboard both carriers, it had also been a frustrating and relentless day during which every pilot had flown at least twice. Their opponents' apparently poor grasp of tactics was a surprise and a comfort, but there was concern in the 801 crewroom about the level of intensity so far. During the afternoon's raids, three or four pairs of SHARs had all been separately engaged against *scores* of raiders. *If it carries on like this*, thought one of Sharkey Ward's two Air Warfare Instructors, *hardly any of us will get home*. It was simply that the maths counted against them. *If the Argentinians throw enough missiles at us*, he thought, *sooner or later some are going to hit.*

The prospect of a bloody war of attrition may have hung over the crewroom but it was the price you paid, thought 801's Senior Pilot, *for getting to strut around in a tailored flying suit and wear a big watch.*

After dark, a relieved JJ Black addressed his ship's company. 'The first day,' he told them, 'has been a success. The Sea Harriers have given an exemplary display and the scoreboard is in our favour.' *Invincible*'s Captain allowed himself to enjoy a little more of the confidence he was projecting to his crew. But the damage sustained by *Glamorgan*, *Alacrity* and *Arrow* had shown that British ships were far from invulnerable to attack from the air.

Nor, so far, had there been any sign of Argentina's own aircraft carrier, *25 de Mayo*, and her potentially lethal complement of A-4 Skyhawks.

# TWENTY-SIX

## The Midway of the South Atlantic

Capitán de Corbeta Alberto Philippi stood at the front of the 3 Escuadrilla crewroom outlining the plan for an attack on the British Carrier Battle Group. It was an hour before midnight. ARA *25 de Mayo*'s Skyhawk squadron had been organized into two divisions and rostered into watches and, at dawn, it would be Philippi's team, not that of the squadron boss, Rodolfo Castro Fox, who would be opening the Aeronaval's account. All day the A-4 crews had been tense with anticipation of an order to launch that never came. Only Philippi and his wingman, scrambled during the afternoon to intercept a radar contact that turned out to be a flight of Air Force Canberras returning to the mainland, had enjoyed an opportunity to relieve it.

3 Escuadrilla's pale grey Skyhawks were ranged on deck, lashed down with chains. Each proudly displayed the anchors on the wings and pale blue and white rudders, and the legend 'ARMADA' writ large on the fuselage that distinguished them from their Air Force counterparts. The squadron's maintainers had worked tirelessly to prepare the jets for the mission. Low-drag 500lb Mk.82 Snake Eye retarded bombs lay cradled in trolleys waiting to be bolted beneath each aircraft's fuselage. Chalked on one of them was the name of its intended recipient: HMS INVINCIBLE. How many each A-4 could carry would depend on the weather and the distance from the target. Unable to close the distance before nightfall, *25 de Mayo* and her escorts began to zigzag south as the sun dropped below the horizon.

Based on position reports from a series of recce flights flown by the Tracker squadron, Philippi explained, the British Task Force was steaming around 200 miles to the southeast. A further Tracker sortie was ongoing. They'd have an update on its return. Armed with that information the six Skyhawks, each carrying four Snake Eyes, would launch at first light to press home the attack. Carrier against carrier. The battle in prospect had an epic quality about it that was impossible to ignore.

*The Midway of the South Atlantic*, thought one of the pilots, recalling the epic WWII carrier battle between the US and Imperial Japanese navies.

In the end, the prospect of missing out on such a famous encounter was too much for the squadron's CO to bear. As he listened in on the briefing, Castro Fox stood up and approached Philippi.

'Please,' he said, resting a hand on his shoulder, 'this is my squadron's first combat mission. Will you please let me have the honour of leading it?'

Philippi had every sympathy for Castro Fox, so recently returned to the cockpit after his terrible accident, but he wasn't prepared to give it up.

'I'm sorry, no,' he replied. 'I'm on the roster and I'll take the mission.'

Only when he later spoke in private to the ship's Intelligence Officer did Philippi have pause for thought about the wisdom of his decision. Faced with the layered missile defences of the British Carrier Battle Group – Sea Dart, Seawolf and Seacat missiles – the analysis suggested that only four of the six-strong strike force would make it through to the target, and that only two would safely return to the ship. The stark reality of what it would cost him and his men to try to deliver sixteen bombs on target hit home. The thought sent a chill through him.

Two hundred miles northwest of *Invincible*, Flight Lieutenant Ian Mortimer descended from altitude. It was just after midnight local time and like flying inside an inkbottle. The only light came from the dim glow of his own instruments. He covered the next 40 miles flying at 200 feet above the grim South Atlantic swell. Alone and in radio silence, the 801 Squadron AWI had launched on a probe mission to locate the Argentine carrier group.

An hour earlier, *Invincible* had detected emissions that matched the signature of the AN/APS-38 search radar fitted to S-2 Trackers operating from *25 de Mayo*. Did that mean the Argentine carrier was close? Task Force Commander Sandy Woodward knew that the Argentine fleet was at sea with task groups north and south of the islands, but was some kind of pincer attack imminent? The southern force, led by the cruiser ARA *General Belgrano*, was being trailed by one of his nuclear-powered hunter-killer submarines, HMS *Conqueror*, but the Argentine carrier had slipped her tail. He had to find her.

*We've got it wrong*, thought Mortimer. Enveloped by the night, he'd seen not a glimmer of light beyond the cockpit since leaving the ski-jump, nor had there been any alarm from the radar warning receiver mounted in the SHAR's tail. Then that all changed.

*All hell's broken loose*, he thought as he was lit up by the fire control radar of a Type 42 destroyer armed with long-range Sea Dart missiles. The RWR display next to his right knee highlighted the range and direction of the powerful 909 radar. He withdrew, before once more turning towards the threat and, at a safer distance, turning on the SHAR's Blue Fox radar. On the radar display screen he counted five contacts glowing green less than 25 miles ahead of him. He noted the position of the threat on the NAVHARS, switched off his radar, then tipped his lonely SHAR into a steep turn back in the opposite direction.

*Time*, he reckoned, *I fucked off.*

At dawn on 2 May, *Invincible* went to Action Stations in anticipation of an attack by the Argentine Navy Skyhawks. By lunchtime 801 had launched six pairs of SHARs on CAP, those upthreat toward the northwest braced to repel the inbound strike. But none came. There had simply not been enough wind. Heavily loaded with bombs and fuel, the 3 Escuadrilla A-4Qs needed at least 40 knots of wind over the deck to launch from *25 de Mayo*'s elderly catapult. By steaming into wind at 20 knots the ship could generate half of that. But an additional 10 knots of assistance offered by a light southwesterly breeze just wasn't going to cut it. There was bitter disappointment among the 3 Escuadrilla crews and anger from some that the order to strike hadn't come a day earlier when the winds were more favourable.

'We were ready to die in order to stop the Task Force,' said one of the pilots, reflecting the mood within the whole squadron. Luck had not been on their side. 'The South Atlantic,' he continued, 'is wild this time of year with gale-force winds, but because of the unbelievable weather we can't do a thing.'

*For this war*, noted another, *we need something like an American Essex class carrier, with two catapults and capable of 30 knots.*

Or, just as British Aerospace had pointed out in 1979, they needed Sea Harriers.

After a three-hour flight from Banjul, Tim Gedge jumped down from the cockpit of ZA190 on the Wideawake dispersal.

*Like a scene from* M\*A\*S\*H, he thought as he looked around the airfield. Beyond a showcase for the variety to be found in the RAF's multi-engine fleet there were stores dumps and human activity in all directions. Captain Bob McQueen, the Senior Naval Officer on Ascension, greeted him but, as the feeling returned to the SHAR pilot's legs following hours strapped into an ejection seat, the tone of the welcome was a little unexpected.

Halfway between the UK and the Falklands, the sleepy British territory, so critical to the logistics of fighting a war 4,000 miles further south, was creaking under the strain. And responsibility for keeping the show on the road rested firmly with McQueen, a former naval aviator. Such was the pressure on the island's meagre facilities that McQueen had taken to checking the names of personnel disembarking from the streams of RAF transports flying in and out of the airfield. One RAF padre, told by McQueen that, while his spiritual guidance was surplus to requirements, he was welcome to stay and hump stores around, decided to climb back aboard his VC10 and return to the UK without delay. If your name's not on the list you're not coming in. Greeting new arrivals with mirth was unusual, though. And, as Gedge saluted and shook hands with the island's potentate, McQueen seemed to be laughing at him.

Admittedly, he and his pilots needed to scrub up a bit. The airport manager in Banjul had decided that the most suitable in-flight meal for any 'self-respecting fighter pilot' was a large tray of unpeeled prawns and fizzy drinks. Some of his pilots rejected them as a flight hazard, but Gedge managed to move it around the cockpit as he completed his pre-flight checks before wedging it along the port console for take-off. Actually eating them presented its own challenge. Gloves had to come off. Then the oxygen mask. And that meant bolting as many *gambas* as possible before hypoxia began to blur your vision. The drinks weren't a whole lot more suitable. By the time Brave landed, the can of Coca-Cola that had geysered all over the canopy when he opened it at altitude, then frozen, had thawed during his descent and dripped all over him.

But none of it quite seemed to justify McQueen's apparent amusement at Gedge's efforts to introduce himself and his squadron. Then the 809 boss looked over his shoulder and caught sight of one of the squadron's maintainers gleefully removing bottles from ZA190's cockpit as if he was unloading a distillery delivery van. Most of their personal kit had travelled ahead of them in trunks aboard *Atlantic Conveyor*. But, unsure of what deprivations they might have to endure on Ascension before joining the ship, Tim Gedge was taking no chances. Secreted around the cockpit of ZA190 in whatever space he could find were four or five bottles of whisky from the Yundum Airport duty free.

Preparation was all in the detail.

The next morning, Al Craig and Hugh Slade announced their arrival by smoking in low over Wideawake for a fast run and break before landing. Arriving in Banjul a day after their comrades, they'd been encouraged to beat up the airfield by the tower to impress the High Commissioner's wife as she waited to greet them with her husband. She'd nearly been witness to a dramatically more spectacular show when the roar of the Sea Harriers panicked a flock of storks into the air in their path as they speared through the airfield overhead. *They look as big as donkeys*, Craig had thought as he contemplated the court martial that would surely follow if he hit one.

Air Traffic Control on Ascension was rather less enthusiastic about the SHARs' flamboyant performance.

'Why haven't you read your NOTAMs?' demanded the RAF controller after running over to the Sea Harrier pilots as they clambered out of their cockpits. Had the two fighter pilots read the Notices to Airmen relating to Wideawake, they'd have known that only straight-in approaches to the runway were permitted. And for good reason: 809's two new arrivals had just flown straight over a live firing range.

'I don't read NOTAMs when I'm going to war!' Craig told him.

'Good for morale,' laughed the Army Range Safety Officer when he met Craig in the bar of the Exiles Club later that evening. He'd called ceasefire as he saw the two SHARs screaming through low over the heads of his soldiers. The roar of the Pegasus engines rolling across the range had prompted wide grins in their wakes. 'Wonderful for the troops!' he concluded.

There wasn't much to dampen anyone's spirits. The news from down south was all positive and this contributed to an almost surreal atmosphere on Ascension, at once both at the heart of things and 4,000 miles distant. Every day at sunset a different military band beat the retreat. It acted as a starting gun on the evening's drinking. And booze felt like it was probably the best way for 809 to bond with their new neighbours at Two Boats. The ramshackle little village at the foot of Green Mountain was also home to the Vulcan crews who'd just mounted the epic BLACK BUCK raid against Stanley airfield.

On arrival at Wideawake, it was immediately obvious to Tim Gedge and his crews why their departure for Ascension had been so dictated by the availability of the Victor tankers. Most of the fleet had evidently been committed to the long-range Vulcan attack. 809's transit to the island had been supported by instructors and students from the Victor Operational Conversion Unit flying whatever aircraft they could scrape together.

Flight Lieutenant Martin Withers and his crew landed safely back at Wideawake just a few hours after the first wave of Sea Harriers touched down. The scale of the operation was impossible to ignore. So too was the impressive feat of airmanship that had seen the crew of Vulcan XM607 make a successful precision attack at night against a well-defended target several thousand miles away.

*The one thing,* thought Gedge, *they're going to need when they arrive back up here is a few beers.* He made sure they had a couple of cases. The bomber crews and their Fleet Air Arm housemates drank into the night, toasting a job well done and the success of the campaign so far. Their noisy celebrations were not universally welcome.

'Be quiet!' shouted one of the C-130 Hercules crews trying to sleep nearby.

'You've only flown two hours today!' taunted the jet pilots. 'You must be out of crew time!'

The to-and-fro continued unabated.

*Pathetic*, reflected Dave Braithwaite as he lit another cigarette. It was childish stuff. And he was enjoying every second of it.

The Vulcan boys deserved their beer. Not only had Withers and his crew managed to crater the runway at its midpoint, ending any hope of Argentina safely using the Port Stanley airfield as a diversion for their fast jets, but the impact of 607's stick of bombs had reverberated in Buenos Aires. The Vulcan was designed and built to be a strategic bomber. And the effect of its combat debut, twenty-six years after it had first entered service with the RAF in 1956, had been eminently strategic.

# TWENTY-SEVEN

## The Swiss army knife of aeroplanes

THE THIRTEENTH OF August 1940. Reichsmarschall Hermann Goering called it *Adlertag* – Eagle Day. And it was the first day of the greatest aerial battle the world had ever seen. Enjoying a numerical superiority of nearly three-to-one over Fighter Command's squadrons of Spitfires and Hurricanes, Goering predicted that his Luftwaffe would defeat the RAF in just three days. And with the destruction of Britain's air defence, it was expected that a seaborne invasion of Britain could follow. A few weeks later, though, the Battle of Britain had become a brutal, gruelling war of attrition in which both sides were suffering unsustainable losses and damage to men and materiel.

By early September, a number of British airfields had been seriously degraded and frontline squadrons were operating at just 75% of their allocated strength. More worrying for Fighter Command was the depletion in the number of experienced, combat-ready pilots. The Luftwaffe was hardly in better shape. But at a point when the pressure on the RAF's defences might have really begun to bite, Fighter Command was let off the hook.

Incensed by a handful of Bomber Command raids against Berlin, Hitler ordered a change in tactics. And on 7 September, instead of continuing with their debilitating campaign against the RAF in the air and on the ground, the Luftwaffe were ordered to target British cities instead in an effort to bomb the country into submission. It was a disastrous intervention by the Führer that gave Fighter Command the opportunity it needed to regroup, rebuild and reorganize against an enemy who, in focusing on large raids, had become more predictable and straightforward to counter.

And on 2 May 1982, following the first day's encounters over the Falkland Islands, the Fuerza Aérea Argentina made the same mistake.

Mauled by the Sea Harriers on the few occasions any meaningful combat had developed and concerned that mainland targets were now vulnerable following the BLACK BUCK raid, the FAA's Mirage III interceptors were withdrawn from the fight. Never again would they go on fighter sweeps out to the Falklands hunting for the SHARs. Nor would the Daggers, armed with air-to-air missiles, continue to be tasked as fighter escorts to bomb-laden attack jets. After the disappointing return from 1 May, Grupo 8's boss, Comodoro Carlos Corino, had to accept that *our primary mission for the Mirage III is to intercept the Vulcan*. Any sustained effort to deplete the small British fighter force in the air was abandoned.

Instead they would have to tackle it at source by going after the carriers. That job fell to the Super Etendards of 2 Escuadrilla Aeronaval de Caza y Ataque, but the first day's fighting had proved no more fruitful for them than for the Mirages and Daggers.

After taking off from Río Grande at 1938Z a pair of Exocet-carrying SuEs was forced to abort their mission after their KC-130 tanker suffered a fuel leak. As they'd attempted to refuel, both of the 2 Escuadrilla strike jets knew they'd been picked up by British radar. Further proof, as far as the unit's Commander, Jorge Colombo, was concerned, of his conviction that *the Super Etendards must be always solitary hunters. Surprise and discretion our most precious operational characteristics*.

During the Battle of Britain, the Chain Home and Chain Home Low network of radar stations had proved to be a critical advantage to Fighter Command's ability to defend the country against the Luftwaffe. As it was in 1940, so too in 1982. After a confusing start to the day, the radar operators of the Vigilancia y Control Aéreo Grupo 2 had found their feet, providing incoming Argentine jets with accurate reports on the position and movements of the Sea Harrier CAPs awaiting their arrival. From inside their air-conditioned mobile control room secreted on the outskirts of Puerto Argentino they'd guided the Mirages towards the enemy and warned the bombers when they became the focus of the SHARs' attentions. They had reported the positions of the British warships as they approached the islands.

Some of their countrymen already owed their lives to VYCA 2's appreciation of the battlespace.

If their value to their own side was clear, however, they were also acutely aware of how valuable a target that made them to the enemy. The unit had gone to great lengths to conceal the big AN/TPS-43 antenna close to farm buildings and ensure it was invisible from the sea. The operators' cabin, protected by over 200 soil-filled oil drums, was located 75 yards away near residential accommodation. The generators had been hidden halfway between, beneath one of the island's few trees. There was no other single Argentine unit ashore on the Malvinas with greater potential to influence the outcome of the war. But if the British wanted to remove them from the game, they would have to find them first.

*Hermes'* Captain, Lyn Middleton, liked to describe the Sea Harrier as the Swiss army knife of aeroplanes. The clue was in the SHAR's designation, FRS.1: Fighter, Reconnaissance, Strike, Mark One. After successfully performing both the first and last of its given roles, a single jet was flown high across Stanley airfield by Neill Thomas to complete the set by sundown on day one.

Mounted beneath the cockpit on the starboard side of the Sea Harrier's front fuselage was a single Vinten F.95 camera. Optimized for low-level photography, the F.95 wasn't the ideal piece of kit with which to take post-strike photographs from 20,000 feet, but it was more than enough to see the line of 1,000lb bomb craters that had been stitched across the airfield by the Vulcan. And what was clear was that the BLACK BUCK mission had succeeded by the slenderest of margins. Of twenty-one bombs dropped, only the very first of them had torn up the runway surface. Released a split second later and all would have missed. But it proved the validity of the plan. Cutting across the runway as they had meant that Martin Withers' crew had a 90% chance of success. It also illustrated the inescapable fact that, despite the enormous challenge of hitting it, the runway was a large, immovable target that was impossible to disguise or hide. Just as a twenty-year-old Vulcan bomber on the cusp of retirement could hit it with unguided iron bombs so a Sea Harrier with a single F.95 camera could capture its picture. But that was it. The SHAR was the only means available of providing Task Force commanders with any real-time photographic reconnaissance. And other enemy assets would be a good deal harder to spot.

Back at Northwood headquarters, Air Marshal John Curtiss, the Op CORPORATE Air Commander, was frustrated by the inadequacy of the intelligence coming back from the Task Force. If there was to be any hope of conducting a serious offensive air campaign against the islands' occupiers, the first requirement was for more systematic photo-reconnaissance. From that it would be possible to assemble a jigsaw puzzle of overlapping high-resolution photographs. Analysis by skilled photographic interpreters could pinpoint Argentine command and control facilities, anti-aircraft defences, fuel dumps, stores, troop dispositions, and the AN/TPS-43 radar that had already been able to limit the damage meted out by the Sea Harriers. But to produce such a comprehensive appreciation of the situation at ground level required a dedicated reconnaissance asset. A spyplane.

It was close to being the longest operational sortie ever flown by the Canberra PR.9. Fuel would be critical. Colin Adams had once stayed airborne in a PR.7 for over eight hours, but in the shorter-ranged PR.9, carrying the heavy camera fit installed in the two jets deployed to RAF Belize for Op FOLKLORE, the flight was going to be a stretch.

*Every drop will count*, realized the 39(PR) Squadron boss as he and his crews planned and refined their route to northern Chile. Since arriving in Central America communications with Peter Robbie's advance party had been frustratingly patchy, but concern about fuel and the diplomatic complications prompted by any direct route between Belize and Chile had been constant. To have any chance of reaching their destination they were going to have to cruise-climb on a southeasterly track across Honduras, Nicaragua and Costa Rica. Clearance to do so would be neither requested nor given. But intelligence suggested that it was unlikely any of them could do anything about it. While Nicaragua waited for delivery of a squadron of MiG-21s from the Soviet Union via Cuba, Honduras was the only country equipped with a fighter that had any chance of reaching the PR.9s. But the challenges of scrambling an armed jet to make an unexpected high-altitude interception were substantial. Adams felt confident that the two 39(PR) Squadron jets would be long gone before the Fuerza Aérea Hondureña's old Dassault Super Mystère B2s were even out of the hangar.

Beyond Central America lay Colombia, Ecuador and Peru. Such a cavalier attitude to entering *their* airspace was likely to end badly. All three possessed modern, well-equipped air forces operating squadrons of supersonic Mirage jets. And Peru, more than any other country in Latin America, was vocal in its support of Argentina. Adams suggested skirting around Peru's 1,500-mile coastline at a distance of 100 miles. His navigator, Brian Cole, argued that tucking in closer, at 50 miles, would shave the overall distance to Chile and usefully increase their fuel margin. Crucially, at 50 miles offshore the RAF jets would still be flying way beyond the limits of Peru's sovereign airspace. While Argentina's ally might not welcome the puzzling presence nearby of a pair of Canberra PR.9s dressed in Fuerza Aérea de Chile markings, they could not legitimately hinder their progress.

It would buy the RAF flyers a little more leeway, but they still took the decision either to tow the jets out to the end of the runway before starting the engines, or taxi out then hot-refuel on the runway threshold to top up the tanks before an immediate departure.

Adams and his crews were no less concerned about the fine detail of their arrival in Chile. The squadron boss had already signalled 1 Group HQ back in the UK to tell them that the MoD demand that they land in the dark was a non-starter. *Plainly unacceptable*, Cole had thought. *We'd not only be very low on fuel, but would have to make a visual approach to land on a totally unfamiliar stretch of road.* And landing anywhere except a runway wasn't a procedure that was in any way part of 39(PR) Squadron's normal repertoire. On top of that there'd be no up-to-date met information, nor any radar control. A compromise was reached. After descending to low level at first light, the PR.9 crews would radio ahead with 15 miles to run from their Pan-American Highway landing strip. At that point a series of Verey cartridges would be fired to light a flare path to the makeshift runway threshold. Unlikely to have the fuel to go around again, they'd get one shot at it.

If during this last critical phase of the flight anything went wrong – and running out of fuel was a real possibility – they were,

Adams briefed his men, 'to point the aircraft out to sea and eject while still over land'.

In Chile, Peter Robbie boarded a disguised RAF C-130 and flew north to the Arica Province. Arriving just after dawn, the big four-engined transport settled on to the highway on soft tyres. On board was another RAF Hercules crew and, as ever, their Chilean minders. The C-130 crew was impressed with the slickness of the Fuerza Aérea de Chile operation to close the road to traffic and prepare it for the arrival of the Canberras – clearly it was something practised regularly. And the dress rehearsal proved the validity of the 39(PR) Squadron plan. When the PR.9s arrived through the soft glow of the new day, they would cross-refuel from the C-130's own tanks before immediately taking to the air again from the road for the final leg of the journey south to Punta Arenas.

And from there it was Robbie and his navigator, rather than the two crews who'd just staged south over 7,000 miles from Belize, who were tasked to fly the first FOLKLORE photo-reconnaissance mission out over the South Atlantic.

39(PR) Squadron was not the only RAF unit wrestling with the challenges of getting their aircraft into theatre. Landing a Harrier GR.3 with 330-gallon ferry tanks bolted beneath the wings wasn't easy at the best of times. The disproportionately large drop tanks played havoc with the jump jet's centre of gravity. The strong wind whipping across the runway at RAF St Mawgan in north Cornwall should have made it impossible. It was way outside cleared limits for the awkwardly configured jets. 'On no account,' they were told by their Station Commander, 'is anyone to exceed crosswind limits.' But faced with the prospect of either diverting to another airfield or jettisoning the tanks, the 1(F) Squadron pilots gritted their teeth and landed anyway. Shaving 20 knots off the normal approach speed and applying reverse thrust after touchdown seemed to do the trick. Anything else would have put at risk their planned HAWK TRAIL deployment to Ascension early the next morning. And that, flying direct for over nine hours, was set to be the longest-duration Harrier flight ever attempted.

With the jets safely on the ground, the 1(F) pilots repaired to the Officers' Mess bar, where they had unexpected company.

Back home in his Cornish constituency for the weekend, Defence Secretary John Nott had driven up from his seventeenth-century farmhouse, Trewinnard Manor in St Erth, to meet the Harrier pilots before their departure. He seemed buoyant about the progress of the campaign so far. And although he wouldn't be drawn on the details, he was eager to share news that further dramatic developments were imminent.

'In the next twenty-four hours,' he told them, 'a major event will have occurred.'

# TWENTY-EIGHT

## Like wind blowing through a chandelier

It took fifty-seven seconds for the first torpedo to find its target. One of a fan of three Mk.8 torpedoes fired from the Churchill class nuclear hunter-killer submarine HMS *Conqueror* at 1901Z on Sunday, 2 May, it struck ARA *General Belgrano* amidships, just forward of the cruiser's two rear 6-inch gun turrets.

Eight hundred pounds of Torpex, a high-explosive mixture of RDX, TNT and powdered aluminium accelerant, ripped through the middle engine room, two mess decks and the dining hall.

The initial blast killed over 270 crewmen as well as two civilian brothers working as barmen in the 'Soda Fountain'. The explosion tore a 60-foot-wide hole in the 12,000-ton cruiser's main deck. The ship shuddered and groaned, her forward progress stopped as surely as if she'd hit a harbour wall. Sailors were thrown from their feet and from bunks as the lights blinked out. Moments later, before they'd had time to process what was happening, a second torpedo speared into them, removing everything forward of the No. 1 gun turret. A vicious plume of black smoke, water, steam and shrapnel erupted 80 feet into the air as *Belgrano*'s bow began its descent to the ocean floor. Within an hour, the rest of the ship would follow.

With orders to attack any British ships that came within range, *Belgrano*'s crew, thought her Captain, had been *eager to pull the trigger*. Armed with fifteen 6-inch-calibre guns and escorted by the two Exocet-armed destroyers ARA *Hipolito Bouchard* and *Piedra Buena* that, along with the tanker *Puerto Rosales*, completed the Armada's Task Force 79.3, she was, if unchecked, capable of inflicting real damage. But now, as darkness fell and the weather worsened, nearly 800 survivors from her crew huddled in high-visibility orange liferafts awaiting rescue. A power failure caused by the first torpedo strike meant they had been unable even to send a distress call.

Fifty miles to the southwest, after running deep to escape any counter-attack launched by the two Argentine destroyers, *Conqueror's* sonar operators listened to the chilling sound of the great ship's death throes. At first they were confused by an unfamiliar tinkling noise, like wind blowing through a chandelier, as *Belgrano's* ruined hulk sank to the bottom. Only later did they realize that it was the sound of fire and hot metal being doused by cold water. A thousand little sparkles of steam.

News of *General Belgrano's* destruction reached HMS *Hermes* from Northwood HQ at 2245Z. Sandy Woodward greeted it with relief. He had feared his own Carrier Battle Group being trapped in a classic pincer movement between Task Force 79.3 to the south and the *25 de Mayo* group, TF 79.2, to the north. *Unless we are extremely lucky,* he'd thought, *we could find ourselves in major trouble,* fighting off a low-level attack from *25 de Mayo's* Skyhawks from the north while Exocets and 6-inch shells streamed in from the south. Frustrated by the inability of the three British hunter-killer submarines in theatre to find and track the Argentine carrier, he had instead tried all day to force a change in the Rules of Engagement from Northwood that would allow *Conqueror* to remove the southern claw. The sinking of the *Belgrano* was shared with *Hermes'* crew via the ship's broadcast.

In the 800 Squadron briefing room, Dave Morgan was on his feet before the cheering had subsided. Mounted on the bulkheads of the SHAR pilots' lair were recognition boards collaged with photographs and silhouettes of Argentine aircraft and ships – Mirages, Skyhawks, Super Etendards and the carrier *25 de Mayo*. Attracting a little less interest from the fast jet squadron were the traditional lines of the *Belgrano*. Launched in 1938, the former US Navy warship had (as the USS *Phoenix*) survived the Japanese attack on Pearl Harbor in 1941 and fought with distinction throughout the remainder of the war, and had served with the Argentine fleet for over thirty years. But her storied career was over. Morgan scored a cross through the old cruiser's photograph with a chinagraph pencil.

During one of the many late-night conversations that followed the invasion, as Margaret Thatcher grappled with the challenges and realities of mounting a military operation to recapture the Falklands, she had asked Sir Henry Leach, the First Sea Lord, 'Admiral, what would you do if you were Commander in Chief of the Argentine Navy?'

On this hypothetical, Leach was in no doubt. 'I should return to harbour, Prime Minister,' he replied, 'and stay there.'

'Why?'

'Because I should appreciate that although I could take out some of the British ships, they would sink my entire navy. It would take years to recover, if indeed it were practicable to do so.'

Had there been any doubts about that prior to *Conqueror*'s icily efficient despatch of their second largest combatant, they were now gone.

At 1630Z the following day, ARA *25 de Mayo*, her escorts and the rest of the Armada's surface fleet were ordered to withdraw from the combat zone. Confined to Argentine coastal waters, the carrier would play no further part in the conflict. The A-4Q Skyhawks from 3 Escuadrilla disembarked and returned to their home base at Comandante Espora without reward.

On the day *25 de Mayo* began her retreat, Alberto Philippi was once more scrambled from the carrier's deck in pursuit of unidentified bogies. Again, though, they turned out to be returning Air Force jets. The Skyhawk pilot's war still lay ahead.

As disappointed as he and his fellow naval aviators had been not to launch an attack from the carrier, it's doubtful they would all have survived a raid against the British Carrier Battle Group steaming in open water. When their time came, the odds would not be stacked quite so heavily against them.

Every morning on Ascension, Tim Gedge attended Bob McQueen's commanders' briefing. Prior to getting started, McQueen questioned each of those present about their mission and the number of personnel they'd brought to his island in order to carry it out. At eight pilots, eight jet fighters and just twelve maintenance personnel,

Gedge knew 809's footprint was deemed to be acceptably small. Nor was the squadron, grounded until *Atlantic Conveyor*'s arrival, adding to the relentless demands on Wideawake's overworked air traffic controllers. But so far news from the South Atlantic was good.

And then it wasn't.

Harrier Chief Test Pilot John Farley returned to his hotel room in St Louis, Missouri and switched on the television. Since flying out to the US in early April he'd been working with McDonnell Douglas, the American company leading development of the next-generation Harrier, the AV-8B. He was enjoying flying the new jet, but was desperate to return to Dunsfold to help with the programme of modifications being made to the Sea Harrier to enhance its combat capability. While away, he'd had to rely on US TV news bulletins to keep abreast of events in the South Atlantic. As frustrating as he found the situation, though, he was at least, he thought, getting a more comprehensive impression of the war than British viewers. All the American networks drew heavily on video shot by the Argentinians. Tonight's footage shocked him, though.

As the camera panned across the wreckage of the Sea Harrier he recognized the serial number: XZ450. She'd been the first SHAR to fly. He'd been at the controls for her maiden flight in August 1978. And she was the last Sea Harrier he'd flown before leaving for the States. Now she'd been reduced to wreckage strewn across the rocks of East Falkland. The camera zoomed in and he recognized part of the reaction control system hanging forlornly out of the wingtip.

Unaware of the fate of the pilot, he couldn't help but feel sentimental about the loss of the aeroplane. Perhaps though, he thought, there was a silver lining. The downed jet was the very same machine he'd been flying on the day of the invasion. Slung beneath the wings, while he conducted stall trials, were Sidewinders and a pair of Sea Eagle anti-ship missiles. Of the twenty SHARs that had deployed aboard *Hermes* and *Invincible*, only XZ450 had the Sea Eagle control panel in the cockpit. But the Argentine investigators combing through the wreckage wouldn't know that. If the threat of British hunter-killer submarines hadn't been enough to confine the Argentine Navy to port, the possibility of air attack by low-flying Sea

Harriers armed with long-range sea-skimming Sea Eagle missiles was more than enough to seal the deal.

But XZ450's unique weapons fit had rather more direct and tragic consequences for her pilot, Lieutenant Nick Taylor. While taking part in a three-ship low-level attack against the airfield at Goose Green, Taylor's Sea Harrier was hit just behind the cockpit by high-explosive shells fired from a heavy-calibre 35mm Oerlikon cannon.

After the alarm of his radar warning receiver alerted Taylor's Section Leader, Gordy Batt, that he'd been locked up by the anti-aircraft battery's Skyguard guidance radar, he broke hard right, dumped chaff from beneath the airbrake, then jinked left again to release the weapon's grip. But Taylor never enjoyed the same shot at survival. Dunsfold's ad hoc installation of the Sea Eagle trials equipment had required the removal of the jet's RWR. Without it, he didn't realize the immediate, deadly danger he was in from the Argentine Army's radar-laid guns and made no effort to evade them. Flying straight and level across the target on his bomb run he didn't stand a chance. XZ450 was breaking up before it even hit the ground.

Tim Gedge was the first of the SHAR fraternity on Ascension to learn about the loss of one of their own. With that came the grim job of telling his squadron. They were waiting outside on the bus used to ferry them to and from Two Boats. Gedge climbed on board and broke the awful news. Taylor was a friend to many of them. Inherent in their suitability to join the new squadron, 809's pilots shared long experience of military fast jet flying. All had lost friends before. And while, throughout the seventies, *Ark Royal*'s squadrons had bucked the trend, Gedge, Dave Braithwaite and Al Craig had first joined the Fleet Air Arm frontline when life was cheaper for a naval aviator. For Bill Covington, still raw from the death of a friend in a flying accident in Yuma, it was a double blow. Two close friends in the space of a few months. *A shock to the system.* Anger at Taylor's loss now fuelled his determination.

809 had expected war. It had never, from the moment of its hastened inception, merely been about a show of force. With Nick Taylor's death, though, that expectation materialized into something sharper-edged and more personal.

There was worse to come.

# TWENTY-NINE

## Routine radar and communications research

GENERALLY SPEAKING THE *Daily Star*'s diet of pin-ups, prurience, celebrity news and outrage was of little interest to readers in Chile. But as the red top covered the events in the South Atlantic with screaming 100-point headlines, there was one report that prompted deep concern in Santiago.

'Last week,' reported the tabloid, 'Phantom fighters secretly flew to southern Chile, via Ascension Island, from an RAF base in Suffolk. With them went six giant RAF Victor tankers to refuel them in the air . . . Defence sources say the Phantoms will be more than a match for the Argentinians' 50 French Mirage fighters.'

Unfortunately for British military planners, while the RAF's F-4 Phantoms may well have been more than a match for the Argentine Air Force, the rest of the report was completely untrue. But as he struggled to reassure his Chilean hosts, Sidney Edwards couldn't help but wonder about the source of the story. *Misinformation planted by Argentina?* He thought it might be. And such was the difficulty it caused his mission in Santiago, it may as well have been. Reporters approached the British Embassy for comments. And while both Chile and the UK dismissed the story about the deployment of Phantoms as baseless, their denials required careful wording. A report from Reuters that followed a few days later suggesting that Britain had secured an agreement to use airfields in southern Chile only added to the unease in both London and Santiago about the imminent deployment of the 39(PR) Squadron Canberra PR.9s from Belize.

\*

As a young pilot, Colin Adams had celebrated Christmas at RAF Wyton by dropping a hundred loo rolls from the flare bay of his Canberra. All had streamed beautifully except for the one that hit the station's overly officious Ops Officer. That stunt had earned him an immediate bollocking from the Station Commander. And it had now provided the 39(PR) Squadron boss with the germ of an idea about how the take from Op FOLKLORE might quickly be placed into the hands of the Task Force. If real-time intelligence was required then a circuitous journey from Chile via the UK in a diplomatic pouch was hardly going to cut it. But if, after being processed by the RIC in Chile, photographs could be airdropped from the PR.9s on subsequent recce missions the intelligence might be more timely and useful. In anticipation, the 39(PR) Squadron detachment had flown out with a supply of polythene bags, masking tape, flotation material and spare red 'Remove Before Flight' tags that they hoped would make any parcels easier to find and pick up. It was evidence of the attention to detail the RAF recce crews had tried to bring to the task.

In the mess at RAF Belize, Adams and his crews listened to the BBC World Service as they planned the mission ahead. The weather, gleaned from normal commercial airline met reports, was favourable. But the dangers and difficulties were hard to ignore: an illegal climb through Nicaraguan and Costa Rican airspace in radio silence with their IFF (identification friend or foe) transponders turned off before a long, anxious high-altitude cruise around Argentina's west coast allies, before a gasping arrival on an unfamiliar road in Chile in the grey light of dawn.

*Hell or bust*, thought the squadron boss.

Then, at lunchtime on the day when, after nightfall, they were expecting to deploy, they were told it was scrubbed. Operation FOLKLORE was off. No explanation was given. They were bitterly disappointed. So much effort had been put in and, for all the risks, they had been confident of being able to do what was required of them and make a valuable contribution to the British campaign to retake the islands.

Sadly, the possibility that the operation might be exposed, and the political and diplomatic fallout that would follow, had clearly been deemed too great.

Peter Robbie's advance party was ordered by Sidney Edwards to clear Chilean territory without delay. Such was the indecent haste of Robbie's Raiders' departure that when the two RAF C-130s carrying them and their ground support equipment arrived in Tahiti from Easter Island, none of the required diplomatic clearances had been completed. After being questioned by a French Admiral about the reasons for their unannounced arrival, the crews were told their aircraft would be impounded until the necessary approvals were agreed. For the next five days they were stuck in paradise. Hawaii, their next stop, was going to have to wait.

They weren't the only ones having trouble with their paperwork, either. Leaving Brian Cole, David Lord and Ted Boyle behind in Belize, Adams claimed a seat on the first RAF VC10 flight back to the UK to see if he might be able to keep alive any hope of his squadron deploying. Staging through Washington before flying east across the Atlantic, Adams fell foul of US customs and immigration.

'You haven't got a visa,' the official told him.

'Oh for fuck's sake,' replied Adams.

Without the Canberras, the British would continue to rely heavily on intelligence from the United States. And while the Border Patrol may not have got the memo, Cap Weinberger's Department of Defense was bending over backwards to help. Since declaring its hand on 30 April, America's support for the British campaign had become far more wide-ranging and substantial.

After quantities of AN/ALE-40 chaff and flare dispensers were made available for the Sea Harriers and Harriers, Yeovilton's US Marine Corps exchange officer, Willy McAtee, flew up to RAF Upper Heyford, the Oxfordshire home of USAFE's 20th Tactical Fighter Wing. The unit's big swing-wing General Dynamics F-111E strike jets already used the self-protection system. McAtee was met from the cockpit of his Hawker Hunter by an Air Force Colonel and ushered into a briefing room filled with files and folders piled on a large table.

'All the stuff you requested to read is here,' the Colonel told him, 'so, go read.'

Unable to take any of it away with him, McAtee memorized what he could, scribbled notes on his forearms to remind him of the rest, and took what he'd learned back to Yeovilton to disseminate.

Other offers of help had the potential to be a good deal more conspicuous.

In conversation with Nico Henderson, the British Ambassador to the United States, at a garden party in Washington on 2 May, Weinberger confided that he was waiting to hear whether or not he might be able to provide additional support by sending a US Navy aircraft carrier. Steaming just off Gibraltar, the 100,000-ton nuclear-powered USS *Dwight D. Eisenhower* had already been earmarked to provide top cover should the Falklands Crisis precipitate a situation requiring the evacuation of US citizens from Argentina.

'I'm thinking,' Weinberger told him, worried about the thin grey line of Sea Harriers defending the fleet, 'that she might serve as a mobile runway for you.' The US Secretary of Defense clarified that this didn't mean that US forces would be directly engaged against the Argentinians on Britain's behalf.

'I suppose,' Henderson wondered aloud, 'US reconnaissance planes could fly off the carrier and provide information for us?' And he was enthusiastic about the prospect of using 'Ike' as an additional deck from which to operate British jets. To a fault.

Not entirely grasping the formidable practical and operational obstacles involved, the Ambassador warmed to his theme. 'How would you view the idea of Buccaneers using the carrier?' he asked, before clarifying that they would be 'manned, of course, by the RAF'. To make a supercarrier available would be far more effective, Henderson thought, than anything the US could do to impose trade sanctions on Argentina, while failing to appreciate that it would take months if not years to regenerate the ability to fly the Buccaneers from an aircraft carrier, irrespective of who was flying them. In London, First Sea Lord Sir Henry Leach was quick to dismiss the idea, as generous as he acknowledged it to be, as completely unworkable.

Instead, Sir Henry and the other Defence Chiefs considered asking the Americans to provide in-flight refuelling support. Might it somehow, they wondered, fall outside the definition of 'combat assistance' that had been explicitly excluded from the declaration of US support?

There were no such concerns about satellites. And with any possibility of 'Ike' making her presence felt in the South Atlantic at least fifteen days' steaming away, it was the NRO – the National Reconnaissance Office, the top-secret agency responsible for the operation of American spy satellites – that was best placed to help build an intelligence picture of Argentine dispositions and intentions.

The NRO's VORTEX satellite had only been launched aboard a Titan IIIC rocket from Cape Canaveral the previous October, but it was pressed into action in support of the British, collecting signals intelligence, or SIGINT, from communication intercepts and the detection of radar activity. It was VORTEX that had first helped pinpoint the Argentine Navy carrier group after picking up the radar sweep from one of the two Type 42 destroyers escorting *25 de Mayo* as she steamed to the northwest of the British Task Force.

SIGINT – both communication and electronic intelligence – from US satellites was both welcome and valuable to the British campaign. But while Defence Chiefs were happy to draw on whatever their ally was prepared to share, they remained eager to bring their own intelligence-gathering resources to bear. And although the MoD may not have had a constellation of British spy satellites at its disposal, the demise of Operation FOLKLORE had not brought to an end the RAF's ambitions in Chile. Once again, the focus fell on RAF Wyton, where three aircraft dedicated to the collection of SIGINT were stationed.

51 Squadron was perhaps the most secretive unit in the RAF. Since the early 1960s they'd flown a small fleet of specially equipped Canberra B.6s and Comet 2Rs on Cold War intelligence-gathering missions coyly described as radar proving flights, or RPFs. 51 Squadron deployed around the world, from Iran to Hong Kong, and from the Baltic to Indonesia, while their role was seldom discussed publicly nor even acknowledged. Back at Wyton, a ground support unit of over forty linguists and radar technicians conducted first-line analyses, before passing the take to GCHQ's T Division and J Division to pore over. All just 'routine radar and communications research', said the unit's Operational Record Book. In 1974 the squadron had re-equipped with an extensively modified version of the

RAF's Hawker Siddeley Nimrod maritime patrol aircraft. A development of the De Havilland Comet, the world's first jet airliner, the Nimrod was a design with real pedigree, but, other than its basic outline, 51 Squadron's R.1 version had little in common with its sub-hunting sibling. Inside and out the new airframe was peppered with aerials, antennae and receivers designed for the interception of enemy communications and the pinpointing and identification of air defence radars. In the big jet's cabin a crew of up to twenty-five Special Operators – scanners, searchers and loggers – processed the take, sustained by a never-ending flow of food and drink from a small galley.

51 Squadron had been on standby since early April. But with Op FOLKLORE faltering, it was decided to bring them into play. Ken Hayr signalled Sidney Edwards in Santiago.

'Please nip out to San Félix Island as soon as possible,' he said, 'and report on its suitability for Nimrod operations.'

Operation ACME was on.

San Félix rose low out of the southern Pacific Ocean like the head of an alligator from a mangrove swamp. Barely 2 square miles of barren volcanic rock located 500 miles west of the Chilean mainland, it was home to a 6,000-foot runway bisecting it from cliff to cliff, an underground naval base hidden in a large cavern and a small military garrison. A real-life Tracy Island. But it wasn't *Thunderbirds* that first occurred to Sidney Edwards as the Chilean Navy Embraer EMB 110 Bandeirante made its approach.

'It looks like an excellent location for a James Bond film,' he remarked to Vicente Rodriguez as they circled to land.

The Air Force General laughed, knowing Edwards hadn't even seen the subterranean deep-water harbour yet.

At the controls of the little twin-turboprop was Commander Pedro Anguita, Chief of Staff of the Servicio de Aviación de la Armada de Chile – the Chilean Naval Air Service. Such was the sensitivity of the mission that rather than assign a squadron pilot to ferry the head of Chilean Air Force Intelligence and his British companion to the Navy's island outpost, Anguita took the job himself.

As they came in low over the threshold, Edwards took a look at the jagged rocks and steep ground falling away to sea. *There's no room for error*, he thought.

For the rest of the day Edwards inspected the remote island air base, checking the surfaces of the runways, taxiways and hardstandings for anything that might damage a large, relatively low-slung aircraft like the Nimrod R.1. He asked questions about the load-bearing, gradient and construction of the runway, about airfield lighting, and about the logistics. San Félix was hardly set up for sustained operations of a 50-ton, four-engined spyplane. The island's available jet fuel would be swallowed up *at one gulp*, even if, as seemed likely to Edwards, the R.1's Captain would have to take off and land from what was a relatively short runway carrying a minimum fuel load. But if they airlifted in the necessary AVTUR fuel in 50-gallon drums aboard C-130s and found a discreet airfield on the mainland where, under the cover of darkness, the Nimrod's crew could fill the jet's tanks before the mission, then San Félix Island could offer the perfect secret operating base. Remote, secure and safe. No one would ever know.

While Edwards discussed the logistic and administrative requirements that 'a large RAF aircraft' might need with the Base Commander and his staff, Rodriguez confirmed that an airport at Concepción, 300 miles south of Santiago, could be made available for the Nimrod to refuel. During its time on the ground, paramilitary police would restrict public access to the airfield.

As the Bandeirante droned through the night on its long return to the capital, Edwards wrote up a detailed signal on the facilities at San Félix and the proposal to use Concepción as a refuelling stop. When he finally arrived back at the Embassy in the early hours of the morning, he handed it to the Duty Clerk for immediate encryption and transmission to Ken Hayr back in London. They had a plan.

The Nimrod's arrival in theatre was still days away, though. So too was the delivery of the additional S259 air defence radar and its crew from RAF Wattisham. Sidney Edwards' tapestry of interlocking operations in Chile, SHUTTER, ACME and FINGENT, was in train, and, once ready, it would provide the British Task Force with greater intelligence and early warning of air attack. But it was not yet ready.

# THIRTY

## A new era of naval warfare

THE WEATHER ON 4 May was foul. Typical for the time of year. Jorge Colombo still wished that he was in the cockpit of one of the two Super Etendards as they taxied out. But the 2 Escuadrilla boss had set the rules: each pair of his pilots would get their turn. After his aborted mission on the first day of the fighting he would have to wait until his name came up again. So, braced against the squalling winds and showers in a leather flying jacket adorned with unit patches, he watched the jets, each weighed down with fuel and a single 1,500lb AM.39 Exocet missile beneath the starboard wing, accelerate away from the runway, tuck up their undercarriage and climb away into the mist. Their anti-collision beacons blushed the cloud until they were gone. He had his doubts about the Junta's wisdom in provoking a war with the world's third largest navy. But, after the shock of being ordered to prepare the SuE for war, he'd been immensely proud of what his squadron had achieved. He offered a silent prayer for his pilots. The weather, he thought, would lend them a measure of protection against the British Sea Harriers.

It was 0945 in Río Grande.

Three-quarters of an hour later, the crew of a Lockheed SP-2H Neptune from the Armada's Escuadrilla Aeronaval de Exploración detected three surface contacts 60 miles to the northwest on radar. They'd tried to mask the true purpose of their mission by flying a search pattern, suggesting that they were looking for survivors of the *Belgrano*, but they were acutely vulnerable to the British air defences. After plotting the position of the potential targets, the old piston-engined maritime patrol aircraft descended to low level and turned away to the west. As they made their escape, the Neptune's pilot, Capitán de Corbeta Proni Leston, pressed the RT button on his control yoke.

'Gaucho?' he enquired.

'Vasco,' confirmed the reply.

And Leston transmitted the targeting coordinates to the pilots of the incoming Super Etendards.

52°48S/57°31W. Flight Leader Capitán de Corbeta Augusto Bedacarratz punched the numbers into the SuE's Sagem UAT-40 attack computer. Flying through volleys of rain, he and his wingman, Teniente de Fragata Armando Mayora, continued in radio silence, descending to a height of less than 100 feet. Sandwiched between the dark sea surface and a moving ceiling of low grey cloud, they pushed their throttle levers forward and accelerated to a speed of 500 knots.

At 1104 local time, after a small course correction to starboard, Bedacarratz flew into another squall of rain and pushed the button to launch the missile.

As his Flight Leader's jet emerged from the shower, Mayora saw the fire of the Exocet's exhaust burn bright through the gloom, trailing a fierce white rope of smoke as it raced away.

'You launched?'

'Sí.'

Mayora immediately punched the launch button in the cockpit of his own jet. A second and a half later the big missile dropped from the Super Etendard's wing and accelerated ahead, disappearing into the fog.

The missile struck HMS *Sheffield* amidships two minutes later with the kinetic energy of a 75-ton railway locomotive travelling at 60mph. The impact alone ripped a 15-foot-long gash into the destroyer's starboard side 8 feet above the waterline. Then the Exocet's 370lb high-explosive fragmentation warhead detonated.

The blast tore through the ship's galley, severely damaging nearby compartments including the machinery spaces below. The ship's main generators, internal communications and water supply were lost immediately. With unspent solid rocket fuel from the missile acting as an accelerant, the spread of fire quickly outstripped the ship's company's ability to fight it.

As darkness began to fall after a valiant four-hour battle to save his ship, at 1751Z Captain Sam Salt reluctantly gave the order to abandon her. Less than three-quarters of an hour later, the 266 survivors of the attack were off the ship. Of them, twenty-four were injured, four seriously.

Twenty men had lost their lives.

Bedacarratz and Mayora were back in the crewroom at Río Grande when, at 1716 local time, the BBC World Service reported that HMS *Sheffield* had been hit and abandoned. Until that point all they'd been able to tell the squadron was that the missiles had launched successfully. Now they had confirmation that at least one had struck home. With that came pride and satisfaction that in mounting a successful Exocet attack against a modern warship 2 Escuadrilla Aeronaval de Caza y Ataque had ushered in a new era of naval warfare.

Amid the congratulations, the pilots admitted to a brief moment of alarm when, early in the hour-long flight back to the mainland, Bedacarratz thought he'd been painted by the Blue Fox radar of a Sea Harrier and shouted a warning to Mayora. But the SHARs, vectored in from their CAP station to a dead reckoning position based on brief radar contact by HMS *Glasgow*, found nothing. *Glasgow*'s single-sweep glimpse of the SuE was assessed as spurious.

Bedacarratz's scare turned out to be no more than his embarrassed wingman, who, after his Flight Leader's rattled RT call, remembered that he'd forgotten to shut down the Agave radar in the nose of his own jet.

*If you English had early-warning aircraft*, thought Mayora, *then you might have caught us*.

But they did not. And, with the loss of the *Sheffield*, their absence had been tragically hammered home.

*Atlantic Conveyor* was now less than a day out of Ascension. Two days earlier, anchored off Freetown's Deep Water Quay to refuel in the fetid heat of a Sierra Leone summer, they'd conducted a fire and life-boat drill. The lucky ones had been lowered to the water inside the boats by davits. The rest, a pick and mix of merchant sailors, stewards, cooks, Chinese laundrymen and military personnel from Layard's own Naval Party 1840, had to scramble down nets and ropes to the lifeboats. At the same time, local traders, approaching in canoes filled with goods and trinkets from fruit to local arts and crafts, tried to climb *up* the ropes to sell their wares to the visitors.

After exchanging a couple of plastic water containers for a striking pair of antelope horns mounted on a plinth, Bob Gellett, one of the advance party of 809 Squadron engineers, emerged from it all with a smile on his face. He was already wondering how his new trophy might colour his eventual arrival aboard HMS *Hermes*.

By contrast, after his lifeboat's shambolic efforts at any kind of useful rowing, *Conveyor*'s Third Officer, Martin Stenzel, just prayed they weren't going to have to take to the boats again any time soon.

There were some concessions to the freighter's new role as an ersatz aircraft carrier. The ship's expansive bridge had become a rudimentary operations centre, equipped with a VHF, HF and SATCOM communications suite. A new ship's broadcast system was installed for the benefit of the aviation department – 809's engineers, flight deck handlers and the twelve-strong battle damage repair team from MARTSU, the Navy's Mobile Aircraft Repair, Transport and Salvage Unit. A naval watch system had been set up and three damage control teams established, manned jointly by the Navy and Merchant Marine. And there were regular emergency and Action Stations drills. With the help of the ship's Master, Ian North, Layard trained *Conveyor*'s officers of the watch in how to manoeuvre the ship in response to torpedo, bomb or missile attack. The heavy steel of the rear-loading ramp was thought to offer the greatest protection. Unarmoured and unarmed, *Conveyor*'s best defence was simply to present her backside to any threat.

A day after leaving Sierra Leone, *Atlantic Conveyor* had sailed into southern waters. On crossing the equator her Merchant Navy crew all qualified for a war bonus: a 150% pay increase for every week they spent in what their paymasters at Cunard deemed to be the war zone. But Layard knew that for all the changes to their routine, and even following the campaign's opening shots, they were struggling to get to grips with the prospect of violence that lay ahead.

That innocence came to an end on 4 May when, during his nightly broadcast to the ship's company, Layard cleared the lower decks with the news that HMS *Sheffield* had been 'mortally damaged' by an Exocet missile.

In the ship's bar, Third Engineer Charles Drought was enjoying a Happy Hour beer with friends before dinner. The three men listened in stunned silence as Layard described the fires and loss of life.

'What in God's name is an Exocet missile?' Drought asked his colleagues.

None of them could answer him. But they were agreed that *Sheffield* was supposedly a state-of-the-art warship with every defensive aid. What chance did they have?

'We're bloody sitting ducks,' concluded the Chief Engineer.

No longer thirsty, they left their half-finished drinks and walked through to the dining saloon. But they'd lost their appetites too.

*The shock*, Layard recognized, *was palpable. Sheffield*'s destruction came as a terrible wake-up call to *Conveyor*'s civilian crew. But he now had their attention, and that was a good thing. From here on, their reaction to the Action Stations siren was electric.

Loosing off a ten-round clip of 9mm ammunition from a Browning Hi-Power semi-automatic offered a welcome distraction to the 809 pilots still smarting from news of Nick Taylor's death. Under the watchful eye of a Royal Marine Colour Sergeant and the squadron AWI, Bill Covington, the eight flyers had taken to the ranges. An hour and fifteen minutes' worth of training on the Hi-Power was just one of the items on the 809 ground training programme drawn up by Tim Gedge and his Senior Pilot, Dave Braithwaite. The game of baseball the squadron subsequently lost against Wideawake airfield's American contingent after throwing down the gauntlet over lunch in the American mess was not.

Neither activity was on the list of the twelve things one was supposed to do to pass the time while on Ascension. From sitting on the beach watching green turtle hatchlings make their way to the sea for the first time, to climbing Green Mountain to see the cloud forest that resulted from former Kew Gardens director Joseph Hooker's planting of the island in the nineteenth century, Gedge figured they could squeeze in two a day before embarking on *Atlantic Conveyor* to go to war. But it was pretty slim pickings. And after ticking off the museum in Georgetown with its collection of communications ephemera, medical equipment and ship's bells, the lure of the Exiles Club got stronger. When the news that HMS *Sheffield* had been lost reached the Ascension squadron, the place became irresistible.

On a good day, the sight of the Royal Marines band Beating Retreat at sundown was enough to stir the soul. But, a few pints down, watching from the Exiles Club balcony against the strange, alien backdrop of Ascension on a day of such emotional intensity it was almost unbearably moving. Along with the rest of the Royal Navy contingent in the bar, 809 leaned into the drinking in commiseration and defiance over the first loss of a British warship in combat since the Second World War.

By the time the RAF Harrier pilots of 1(F) Squadron arrived for a drink, finally reunited after what had been an eventful, uncomfortable flight to Ascension, the Exiles Club was in the throes of what one of them could only describe as a 'monster piss-up'. The evening didn't stop at that. After opening their wallets in Georgetown, 809 Squadron hosted an RPC back at Two Boats, an invitation that was taken up by a substantial number of revellers.

Tim Gedge's evening ended with a visit to the island's hospital to retrieve Al Craig. 809's QFI had been booked into the small medical centre by his Senior Pilot with some desperately serious but entirely fictitious illness.

Meanwhile, Brave himself was last seen lying fully clothed in a bath, enthusiastically tucking into a late-night egg banjo.

Back in London, inside MoD Main Building, Ben Bathurst's response to the sinking of the *Sheffield* was rather more practical. And it was immediate.

# THIRTY-ONE

## A million-to-one chance

*SHEFFIELD* HAD BEEN one of three Type 42 destroyers on picket duty, 10 miles upthreat of the next screen of air defence ships. She'd been positioned there solely because the Fleet Air Arm was no longer capable of providing early warning of air attack. As the Director of Naval Air Warfare, Ben Bathurst was in a position to try to do something about that. It was not his fault that a replacement for *Ark Royal*'s Gannet AEW.3s had been deemed unnecessary. Nor could any blame be placed at the feet of his predecessors. Lyn Middleton, running DNAW before taking command of *Hermes*, had, as with all things, been forceful in his view that the fleet needed AEW. But it had been decided years earlier that there was insufficient hangar space aboard the Invincible class ships to accommodate it, and now Middleton found himself at war without that critical piece of the air defence jigsaw. Within hours of the attack on *Sheffield*, though, Bathurst had commissioned an urgent report exploring the options for addressing that absence.

Once again, the RAF's old Avro Shackleton AEW.2s were considered and quickly dismissed. The old warhorse, a derivative of Avro's famous Lancaster bomber, was the last piston-engined aeroplane in frontline service with the Air Force. But it didn't have the range to operate from Ascension and had no in-flight refuelling capability. Even if a bridgehead on the Falkland Islands had been established and the necessary facilities were in place in theatre – not least a runway – 8 Squadron's Shacks would need to stage through South America to get there. And four of them too, if twenty-four-hour coverage was to be guaranteed. Furthermore, the vintage Rolls-Royce

Griffon engines they shared only with a Spitfire PR.XIX from the RAF's Battle of Britain Memorial Flight required high-octane AVGAS fuel, not used by any other frontline aircraft. Even the Fuerza Aérea Argentina had seen fit to retire its own Lancaster derivative, the Avro Lincoln B.2, fifteen years earlier. It was a non-starter.

The RAF looked at developing an ad hoc AEW aircraft by fitting the Shackleton's AN/APS-20 radar to BAe's Coastguarder, a military development of their HS748 twin-turboprop airliner, and to the C-130 Hercules. The challenges inherent in each proposal seemed to outweigh its potential usefulness, and in the end the RAF concluded that, once the Falklands were retaken, ground-based radars and F-4 Phantoms operating from the islands themselves were the best they could do.

At DNAW, Bathurst quickly realized that there was no feasible fixed-wing solution. He had asked FONAC to look into the possibility of reviving the Gannet. With the ski-jump-equipped carriers now limited to operating V/STOL aircraft, they too would have to have been shore-based, but given their small size it would at least have been possible to transport them south by ship. While the Fleet Air Arm managed to ferret out sufficient airframes, engines and radars, though, the difficulties of refurbishing the aircraft and equipment and assembling a cadre of experienced personnel in any reasonable timeframe put the idea out of reach.

Leaving no stone unturned, Bathurst considered airships and balloons as potential AEW platforms. Airship Industries had flown its new Skyship 500 from Cardington in Bedfordshire for the first time the previous year. Again, though, Bathurst ruled them out because of the time it would take to generate such a radically new capability. The Skyship 500 would have to wait another few years before it carried a Royal Navy officer into the air – in the shape of Commander James Bond in *A View to a Kill*.

Bathurst then focused his attention on the prospect of using a helicopter. And with that decision made, Project LAST was born.

The first Sea King built by Westland flew in 1969. Two years before that, the West Country helicopter manufacturer had proposed fitting an AEW radar to its new naval helicopter, an American design built in Yeovil under licence from Sikorsky, but despite repeatedly submitting studies to the MoD throughout the seventies, it had remained a paper project. The Sea King quickly became Bathurst's preferred option, though.

Initially, with the big twin-engined anti-submarine helicopter in such demand in the South Atlantic, the Navy was reluctant to release the airframes and asked him to consider RAF machines like the tandem-rotor Chinook HC.1 and the smaller Anglo-French Puma HC.1 utility helicopter. None, though, made as much sense to use as the foundation for a new naval AEW system as the machine already operated by the Fleet Air Arm in large numbers.

Before he approached Westland he enlisted the help of the Royal Signals and Radar Establishment in Malvern, Worcestershire, to identify the best radar set to employ, options ranging from the Gannet's old 1940s-tech AN/APS-20 to the Foxhunter radar under painful and protracted development by Marconi for the RAF's new Tornado ADV interceptor. A private venture, outlined by Thorn EMI, to modify the Searchwater radar they produced for the RAF's Nimrod MR.2s, to provide air surveillance as well as the surface search capability used by the RAF, looked to be the solution. Fitted with Searchwater, a Sea King patrolling at a height of around 10,000 feet would, calculated the radar's manufacturer, be able to see over the horizon to detect a Super Etendard at a distance of over 50 miles.

Which might have prevented the next tragedy to befall the small, close-knit Sea Harrier fraternity.

809 heard it first from Bob McQueen. As they prepared to embark on *Atlantic Conveyor*, now anchored off the island, the Senior Naval Officer told them, 'We've got bad news on the Sea Harrier.'

Gedge's pilots leaned in. 'What?'

'I'm not allowed to tell you,' McQueen told them, knowing his effort to give them only what information he had been authorized to share had already misfired.

The SHAR pilots started throwing names at him. Friends, former squadron mates. It was a grim guessing game that chipped away at McQueen's resolve.

'It's actually EJ and Al Curtis.'

It seemed impossible to credit. John Eyton-Jones was one of the Fleet Air Arm's big characters. Curtis, less extrovert, was also a popular, generous-spirited figure. They were missing, presumed dead. It seemed inconceivable that two such experienced, well-liked aviators could have simply collided in fog. A million-to-one chance, but it was still the most likely of all the various explanations put forward.

The two 801 Squadron pilots had been part of a three-ship flight launched from *Invincible* soon after dawn on 6 May to provide CAP for Sea Kings hunting for submarines near the still-burning hulk of HMS *Sheffield*. The Observer aboard one of the anti-submarine helicopters reported a brief radar contact. But the Sea King HAS.5 Sea Searcher radar lacked the moving target indicator needed to give it any useful air-to-air capability. Sea Searcher was not an AEW radar. *Invincible's* powerful Type 1022 search radar could see nothing and so the target was assessed to be flying at low level, below the carrier's radar horizon. Less than forty-eight hours after a contact dismissed as spurious had launched an Exocet missile at HMS *Sheffield*, though, no one was taking any chances.

Al Curtis was sent to investigate, and descended into the low cloud. He was soon below *Invincible's* radar and VHF radio horizon. EJ requested his own vector towards the contact under investigation by his wingman. Then he too dropped away from the clear skies at medium altitude into the clag. And out of radar and radio contact with the carrier.

Twenty miles had separated them at the point when they were both still visible as bright orange blips on radar screens in *Invincible's* Operations Room.

With the low-level pair unreachable from the ship, the pilot of the third SHAR, Lieutenant Commander Mike Broadwater, tried to raise them over the RT without success. A search-and-rescue operation continued throughout the day without finding any trace, and at sunset it was called off. EJ and Al were gone. It was, recorded 801's war diary, 'a very sad day for the squadron'. That barely covered it. They were devastated.

On Ascension, Al Craig tried to console himself with the thought that EJ and Al had just been welcomed into the long bar upstairs with all the other aircrew he'd known who'd lost their lives over the years. *It's like Valhalla for naval pilots*, he thought, *it's not a bad place*.

Bill Covington's thoughts turned immediately to the desperation of the families back home. The Navy car driving up through all the married quarters and stopping; the padre getting out and walking to the front door to deliver the hopeless news to the next of kin. While he had been close to Nick Taylor, he and Penny were good friends with Al Curtis and his wife Pam who, in a ghastly twist of fate, was heavily pregnant with a baby daughter. Al's death was a terrible blow, and back home inside the Yeovilton pressure cooker Penny, he knew, would be feeling it acutely.

The community of pilots' wives in Somerset provided mutual support. They visited each other, talked, played bridge together and comforted one another. It was at once distraction and empathy. But Jacqui Auld and Alison Ward, married to the two squadron bosses, found the uncertainty punctuated by heartbreak desperately hard. Elspeth Layard hoped the imminent arrival of Pam Curtis's baby would provide her friend with a ray of hope to cling to. And she wondered how poor Sally E-J was bearing up. *It's like a nightmare*, she thought. To make matters worse, they and their husbands had become the object of fevered interest from the press.

Bill Covington knew that he had the easier time of it. Wrapped up in the camaraderie of the new squadron, making the last preparations to fly out to *Conveyor*, he had the luxury of focus and shared purpose. 809 at least had a job to do. And now, more than ever, they were required to do it. With the loss of EJ and Al, *Invincible*, the ship leading the air defence of the Task Force, was down to just six Sea Harriers.

Less than a week in and the Task Force had lost 15% of the Sea Harrier force on which the outcome of Operation CORPORATE depended. Task Force Commander Sandy Woodward railed in his diary that night about losing two SHARs chasing what seemed obvious to him was not trade for the CAP. 'All so bloody unnecessary,' he wrote. But the low-level air picture was a confusing one. And the fleet's air

**Above**: Operation FOLKLORE. RAF Canberra PR.9 spyplanes deployed to Belize in anticipation of flying reconnaissance missions over the South Atlantic. The plan called for them to fly on to northern Chile, land on a stretch of the Pan-American Highway at dawn, refuel from a waiting C-130, then continue on to Punta Arenas.

**Above**: Taken in late April from the window of a departing 10 Squadron VC10, this previously unseen photograph shows a 30 Squadron C-130 Hercules, its RAF markings painted out, on Easter Island alongside a Chilean Air Force C-130. The British aircraft was deployed in support of Operation FOLKLORE.

**Above**: Operation ACME. A single Nimrod R.1 of 51 Squadron RAF deployed to San Félix Island and carried out a number of SIGINT missions in support of the Task Force.

**Above**: A map of the route flown during ACME 4 produced to brief Britain's Chief of the Air Staff, Air Chief Marshal Sir Michael Beetham, on the RAF's remote South Pacific spy mission.

**Above**: From the ashes. The eight 809 Squadron pilots pose in front of their aeroplanes on the RNAS Yeovilton flightline. From left to right: Dave Braithwaite, Hugh Slade, Bill Covington, Tim Gedge, David Austin, John Leeming, Steve Brown and Alastair Craig.

**Left**: Harrier carrier. Prior to *Atlantic Conveyor*'s departure for the South Atlantic, Tim Gedge flew a number of vertical take-offs and landings in Plymouth Sound to complete First of Class trials and prove the ship's suitability for fixed-wing operations.

**Above**: En route. One of the 809 Sea Harriers takes on fuel from a 57 Squadron Victor K.2 tanker during the ferry flight to Banjul's Yundum International Airport in The Gambia.

**Above**: Argentine Navy A-4Q Skyhawks of 3 Escuadrilla Aeronaval de Caza y Ataque embarked on ARA *25 de Mayo* in anticipation of the arrival of the British task force. Unlike the Sea Harriers, they relied on catapults and arrestor wires to launch and recover to the flight deck.

**Right**: ARA *25 de Mayo*. Named after Argentina's national day, the Argentine carrier had served, as HMS *Venerable*, with the British Pacific Fleet during the Second World War before enjoying a twenty-year career with the Royal Netherlands Navy. She was refitted and commissioned into the Argentine Navy in 1969.

**Below**: 3 Escuadrilla planned to welcome the enemy with an attack on the two British carriers, an encounter that one of the pilots said would be akin to the 'Midway of the South Atlantic'. But launching heavy, bombed-up Skyhawks would require the assistance of strong winds over the flight deck . . .

**Above left**: Lieutenant Commander Nigel 'Sharkey' Ward, Commanding Officer of 801 NAS, embarked on HMS *Invincible*. There was no greater advocate for the Sea Harrier than Ward and he relished the opportunity war provided for the SHAR to prove the doubters wrong.

**Above right**: On day one of the air war, Ward's first encounter with the enemy ended in frustration when an Argentine Navy Turbo Mentor escaped into cloud after receiving a single direct hit from Ward's 30mm ADEN cannon.

**Below**: The first engagement between Argentine Air Force Mirage IIIs and their opponents ended decisively in the Sea Harriers' favour. To Sharkey Ward's disappointment, the Grupo 8 fighters never again went looking for combat with the SHARs.

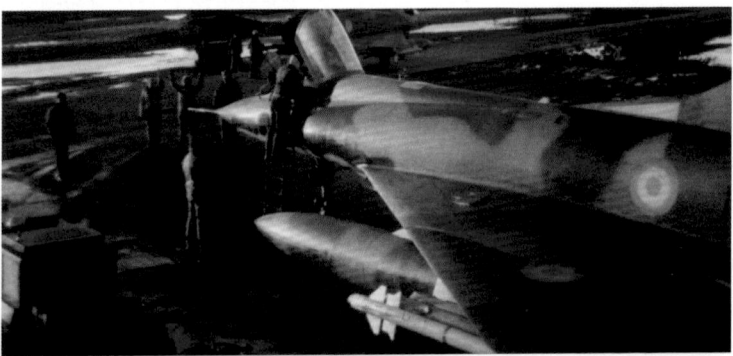

**Right**: Revenge. After the sinking of the cruiser ARA *General Belgrano* by the nuclear submarine HMS *Conqueror*, Argentine Navy Lockheed Neptune patrol aircraft scanned the seas for British targets while they appeared to be searching for survivors of the *Belgrano*.

**Left**: 2 Escuadrilla Aeronaval de Caza y Ataque operated the new French-built Super Etendard strike fighter.

**Below**: Exocet. When technical help from France was cancelled after the invasion, Argentine Navy engineers were able to successfully marry the sea-skimming Exocet missile to the Super Etendard attack jet without assistance.

**Above left**: A Super Etendard of 2 Escuadrilla Aeronaval de Caza y Ataque launches an Exocet missile.

**Above right**: After being hit by two Exocet missiles, HMS *Sheffield* was abandoned, burnt out and eventually lost, the first British warship sunk by the enemy since the Second World War. The attack sent shockwaves through the British Task Force.

**Left**: 1(F) Squadron pose for the camera aboard *Atlantic Conveyor*. From left to right: Peter Harris, Jeff Glover, Mark Hare, John Rochfort, Jerry Pook, Peter Squire and Bob Iveson, with Tony Harper sitting.

**Right**: Alert 5. A single armed Sea Harrier was ranged on *Atlantic Conveyor*'s forward pad in the hope of intercepting the Argentine Air Force 707 that was tracking their progress south. Despite support from Victors launched from Ascension there was a strong possibility that, if scrambled, it would be a one-way mission.

**Above left**: Drivin' south. A previously unseen picture of *Atlantic Conveyor* on her way from Ascension Island to the Total Exclusion Zone around the Falklands. Offered some protection from the elements by the containers stacked on either side, the Sea Harriers, Harriers and helicopters are ranged on deck between them.

**Above right**: 809 Squadron enjoy the hospitality aboard *Atlantic Conveyor*. From left to right: Alastair Craig, Dave Braithwaite, Hugh Slade, John Leeming, Bill Covington and Steve Brown.

**Right**: After arriving in theatre, 809's Sea Harriers were split between *Hermes* and *Invincible*. All 1(F)'s Harriers went to the former. One of the GR.3s is visible on deck in this previously unpublished photograph of *Hermes* on operations in the South Atlantic.

**Above**: Sea King HC.4. The Commando variant of the Westland Sea King was used both for the SAS raid against Pebble Island and the covert insertion of an SAS reconnaissance team into Tierra del Fuego. When the mission was compromised, 'Victor Charlie', the aircraft pictured here before the war, was abandoned and destroyed by its crew in Chile.

**Above left**: Birds of a feather. All three Harrier varieties aboard *Hermes* are pictured here. In the foreground one of 1(F) Squadron's Harrier GR.3s; behind it is one of 809's paler Barley Grey Sea Harriers, with a pair of the dark sea-grey 800 NAS jets ranged beyond it.

**Above right**: 1(F) Squadron enjoyed a destructive first few days in theatre. An Argentine Army Chinook burns after being hit by cannon fire from Mark Hare's GR.3 during a dawn attack with Jerry Pook on 21 May.

**Left**: Previously unseen picture of a Sea Harrier over the Falklands taken by Al Craig using the F95 camera mounted in the nose of his jet. Craig's first sortie over the islands on 21 May was an eventful one, resulting in the shooting down of a Pucará by Sharkey Ward.

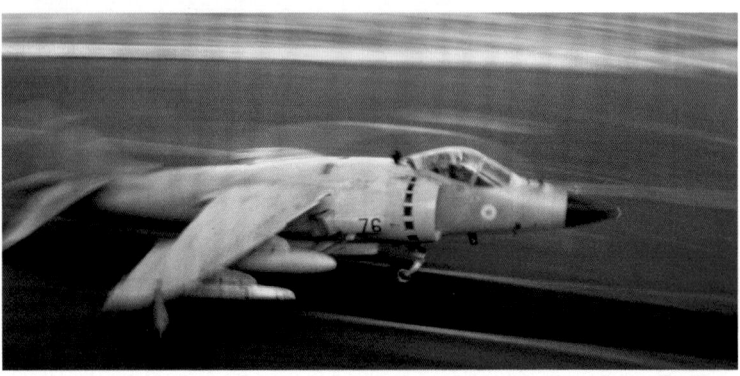

**Above**: An 809 Squadron Sea Harrier launches from HMS *Hermes*. A former CO of the squadron, the carrier's Captain, Lin Middleton, had his doubts about the pale grey camouflage and pastel roundels.

**Above left**: Hovering Sea Harriers recover aboard *Hermes*. The absence of Sidewinders suggests they've seen action. Before nightfall on 21 May, the day of the British amphibious landings, SHARs from both carriers would account for nine enemy fast jets for no loss of their own.

**Above right**: Al Craig and Dave Braithwaite in the 801 Squadron crewroom aboard HMS *Invincible*. Sitting behind them is Steve Thomas, whose pairing with squadron boss Sharkey Ward proved fruitful. Note the white anti-flash hoods they're wearing, ready to pull up over their faces if the ship is attacked.

defences had proved to be incapable of adequately responding to, let alone stopping, an attack by the Super Etendards.

*What*, Sandy Woodward asked himself, *can we do about that? Without airborne early warning*, he concluded, *not a lot.* He had little choice but to continue to position the Type 42s upthreat and, if they proved unable to defend themselves, regard them, however reluctantly, as expendable. Without the few extra minutes' warning of air attack they could provide, the carriers were too exposed. And they were very definitely *not* expendable.

However vigorously Ben Bathurst might be pursuing the prospect of a new helicopter-borne AEW radar for the carriers, Woodward needed greater warning of attack *now*. But while the RAF's ability to provide AEW cover for the fleet had been defeated by geography, their more lateral, clandestine efforts to provide Woodward with some kind of real-time intelligence were about to bear fruit. As the Admiral sat at the desk in his cabin recording his fears and frustrations in his diary, two very different aeroplanes were en route to Chile from the UK.

At 1425Z the previous day, a single Nimrod R.1 took off from RAF Wyton. In the pilots' seats, Squadron Leaders Lambert and Brice trimmed the aircraft and turned to the west as they climbed to cruising altitude. Behind them, the aircraft was unusually full. XW664, a jet that had been hurriedly updated to TRIM 5/82 standard for the Operation ACME deployment, carried another twenty-eight personnel from 51 Squadron. So that flight crews could be rested over the three-day journey, the R.1 flew with three pilots and three navigators on board as well as the usual complement of Special Operators and signallers. Sitting out the first nine-hour stage, the squadron boss, Wing Commander Brian Speed, would take over as navigator for the second leg. Their destination, after routing via Bermuda and Belize.

51 Squadron's ground support equipment had travelled from Wyton to Brize Norton by road where, once again, the RAF's transport hub was playing host to one of the Flying Tiger Line's eye-catching silver Boeing 747-200 freighters. After arriving in Puerto Rico late at night on 5 May, the jumbo took off again at lunchtime the following day

and routed south across Venezuela, Brazil and Bolivia. Unlike the RAF's Canberras, Nimrods, VC10s and C-130s, the civilian charter had no problems flying across countries hostile to Britain's cause, but it was performing a mission no less vital to the UK's campaign in the South Atlantic than any of them.

On board, under the command of Squadron Leader Kendall, was a ten-man RAF 'sales team' flying to Chile with the S259 radar requested by Sidney Edwards. Composed of operators from RAF radar stations around the UK from Cornwall to Aberdeenshire, and the military air traffic control centre at RAF West Drayton, Kendall's team was deep on experience. Beneath them down in the jumbo jet's hold were the radar, generator and operators' cabin along with stores for the anticipated thirty-day deployment. The Marconi D-Band radar was employed by the RAF to provide 'extension of early warning cover by forward deployment'. While Opération FINGENT might have been dressed up as a straightforward export sale, the S259 radar, in tandem with the Army signallers already in country with their SATCOM radio in the Chilean Air Force Intelligence HQ, was going to do exactly what it had been acquired by the RAF to do.

Still looking immaculate against the rust-brown volcanic backdrop of Ascension, 809's eight Barley Grey Sea Harriers had been grounded for nearly a week, shunted off to the far side of the airfield out of the way of the relentless procession of logistics flights coming in and out of Wideawake. From RAF VC10s and C-130s to chartered civilian freighters, British Airways 707s and HeavyLift's big Shorts Belfast turboprops it was a comprehensive parade of the UK's military and commercial air transport capability. There was further variety on offer from America. The world's largest aircraft, the vast Lockheed C-5A Galaxy, was an occasional companion to the larger number of Lockheed C-141 Starlifters from the USAF's Military Airlift Command, now openly supplying weapons and materiel to British forces. And it was one of 809's maintainers who first noticed the bounty that had just been unloaded from one of the latter.

As Petty Officer Colin 'Ollie' Burton helped prepare the SHARs for the short hop to *Atlantic Conveyor*, he spotted an A-frame loaded with AIM-9L Sidewinders. As a 'Bombhead' – one of the squadron's armourers – he recognized the Nine Limas immediately. It was too good an opportunity to resist.

'We could do with some of those on board,' he told the pilots.

Without further complication or permission, he directed the crew of an 18 Squadron Chinook HC.1 that the missiles needed to be loaded on to *Conveyor*. And for good measure, he thought, they might as well throw in the 30mm ADEN cannon ammunition he'd found too. He and his fellow Bombheads could worry about the laborious job of breaking it down and reassembling it for the right-hand feed guns of the SHARs once they were on the ship.

At 1430Z the next day, the last of three 809 SHARs dropped loudly on to *Conveyor*'s forward landing pad at twenty-minute intervals – Steve Brown following Dave Austin and Hugh Slade, for his first ever deck landing. The initial five 809 jets had landed on in the morning after conducting a radar sweep around the island. The squadron was now embarked for the first time since 1978, when its Buccaneers had last catapulted off *Ark Royal* prior to her decommissioning. Already on board were 1(F) Squadron's six Harrier GR.3s.

Of the six RAF pilots who completed the same hop the previous day, only Bob Iveson, during his exchange tour with the US Marine Corps, had ever flown from the deck before. The soft pitch and roll of the ship in the calm tropical swell off Ascension was as gentle an introduction as they could have hoped for. Once aboard, the fourteen jets were rolled into a tight herringbone pattern between the walls of shipping containers on either side of the deck. Iveson and Peter Squire remained on board. The remaining four 1(F) GR.3 pilots were lightered to the MV *Norland*, a cross-Channel car ferry requisitioned to carry 2 PARA (the 2nd Battalion, Parachute Regiment) to the fight.

At 2200Z, with her lights turned off, *Atlantic Conveyor* weighed anchor and, in the company of the other ships of the Amphibious Task Group, began her journey south, now part of a formation known to the Navy as TG 317.0.

# THIRTY-TWO

## Three irreducible concerns

LED BY THE assault ship HMS *Fearless*, the flotilla gathered strength as it steamed south; her sister ship, HMS *Intrepid*, sailed from Ascension a day later. The Royal Marines' 3 Commando Brigade and 3 PARA travelled aboard P&O's 45,000-ton flagship SS *Canberra*. With 2 PARA, these were the troops who would spearhead Britain's mission to recapture the Falklands. Another North Atlantic ferry, the MV *Europic Ferry*, was taken up from trade just to carry their heavy equipment and ammunition. Five landing ships named after King Arthur's Knights of the Round Table – *Sir Galahad*, *Geraint*, *Lancelot*, *Percivale* and *Tristram* – were joined en route. And there were Royal Fleet Auxiliary oilers and stores ships in company too. Three frigates, *Antelope*, *Ardent* and *Argonaut*, escorted them.

And while Sandy Woodward's Carrier Battle Group blockading the Total Exclusion Zone could, if they succumbed to the Argentine air threat, certainly lose the war before their arrival, only the 5,000-strong force of troops sailing south with the Amphibious Task Group could actually win it.

The battle lines were drawn. To have any chance of victory, Argentina now had to do two things: remove or destroy one or both of the British aircraft carriers; and prevent the British from landing ground forces on the Malvinas. Once the Royal Marines and Paras were ashore in strength, the game was up for the Junta as surely as it had been for Nazi Germany after it turned on the Soviet Union and declared war on the United States after Pearl Harbor.

The British, by contrast, had to protect *Invincible* and *Hermes* at any cost, and then, once TG 317.0 was in theatre, successfully mount a difficult, high-risk opposed amphibious landing, codenamed Operation SUTTON, under the command of Commodore Mike Clapp, sailing south in *Fearless*.

Both sides, though, had already had their wings clipped by their opponent. Following the sinking of the *Belgrano*, and the retreat of the Armada Argentina to coastal waters, the Royal Navy had largely won the war at sea. Outclassed by the Sea Harriers on day one, and anxious about the threat posed by RAF Vulcans to the mainland, the Fuerza Aérea Argentina abandoned any hopes of further depleting the small British fast jet force in aerial combat.

But after Nick Taylor was shot down over Goose Green, the Royal Navy decided it could no longer hazard its precious, shrinking force of Sea Harriers on low-level ground attack and reconnaissance missions which put them within reach of demonstrably lethal Argentine air defences. And with that, any hope of mounting an effective, systematic counter air campaign to degrade the capabilities of the occupying forces was lost. The SHARs could do no more than harass them with the occasional thousand-pounder lobbed from a distance or dropped from altitude.

More importantly, the Exocet attack on the *Sheffield* had sent shockwaves throughout the fleet.

For JJ Black, *Invincible*'s apparently unflappable Captain, existence was distilled into three irreducible concerns: *Will I be alive tonight? Have I provided for my family? Am I prosecuting this war as best I can?* His heart froze at the prospect of losing men or aeroplanes to enemy action, but he had to project confidence. *Any sign of weakness, the slightest hint of concern*, he thought, *could be infectious*. Black auditioned for an officer to broadcast details of incoming raids before settling on one who seemed able to convey news of an air attack with no more excitement than an airline pilot warning of a little turbulence ahead. And he made sure that whenever he was visited in his cabin, he always appeared to be sufficiently underwhelmed by it all to be relaxing in the company of a good paperback. His people drew strength from it.

Aboard *Hermes*, Task Force Commander Sandy Woodward was content to be a good deal more abrasive. But he could do little more than urge his Captains to up their game, while he tried to balance the need to position his carriers out of harm's way, while still sufficiently close to the islands for the SHARs to mount meaningful combat air patrols. That was assuming they could get airborne at all. The fog had barely lifted since it had claimed the lives of two of his pilots three days earlier.

Rather unexpectedly, it looked as if 809 Squadron might be the next SHAR unit to make contact with the enemy.

To the dismay of those within it, TG 317.0's departure was announced by Defence Secretary John Nott and subsequently reported by the BBC World Service. It therefore came as no surprise when, a day out of Ascension, HMS *Argonaut* picked up a high-flying contact on her Type 965 radar. The bogey's behaviour suggested that, after being warned off the Carrier Battle Group two weeks earlier, the Burglar was back. Now the shooting had started, that had the potential to be a good deal more significant than its earlier incursions.

'The whole war depends on the survival of [the Amphibious Task Group] main body,' signalled *Argonaut*'s Captain to the TG 317.0 Commander. 'The enemy,' he continued, could be expected to 'make extraordinary efforts to attack the undefended Task Group.' Their ability to do anything about it, he pointed out, was limited by what he described as 'a complete lack of air defence assets'. But that wasn't quite true. While the short-range Seacat missiles carried by the frigates may have been no use in the circumstances, they had *Conveyor*. And she had 809 Squadron. Mike Layard was asked Mike Clapp whether there might be a way of putting one of the SHARs to work.

In the summer of 1940, as Fighter Command's Spitfires and Hurricanes diced with Messerschmitts in the skies over eastern England, Britain was engaged in another campaign upon which her survival was equally dependent. Unlike the Battle of Britain, the Battle of the Atlantic was fought far from view. And while Winston Churchill was lavish in his well-earned praise of the Few, it was the war at sea that concerned him even more greatly. 'If we fail in this,' he told the First Sea Lord and Chief of the Air Staff in November, 'then we lose the war.'

His concern was well founded. It was barely four months since the Luftwaffe first introduced the Focke-Wulf Fw 200 Condor into service and this long-range four-engined maritime bomber had dramatically exposed the vulnerability of the convoys when out of range of land-based fighter cover.

Flying from their base in Bordeaux-Mérignac, KG40, the first squadron flying the new aircraft, could reach as far as the Azores in the southwest or Iceland to the north. In their first two and a half months of operations they'd sunk nearly 90,000 tons of Allied shipping. Operating in conjunction with the U-boats, the Condors quickly earned a reputation as the 'Scourge of the Atlantic'.

In response, Britain improvised. And by the end of the year, a plan to fire knackered, battle-scarred Hawker Hurricanes and Fairey Fulmars from merchant ships using catapults or batteries of 3-inch rockets was approved. But for the pilots of the RAF's Merchant Ship Fighter Unit and 804 Naval Air Squadron it was often a one-way mission. If out of range of land when they launched, the pilots had no choice but to bail out or ditch and hope to be fished out of the water.

On 3 August 1941, a former Grand National-winning jockey, turned Royal Navy Reserve pilot, Bob Everett scored the Hurricats' first kill, when he shot down a Condor in defence of a convoy returning from Sierra Leone before ditching. The 804 Squadron pilot was awarded the DSO for his achievement.

The Fw 200 Condor had been designed in the late 1930s as an airliner for Deutsche Lufthansa before its military potential was realized after the outbreak of the Second World War. Now, a little over forty years since Everett splashed his Condor over the Bay of Biscay, the Fleet Air Arm was hoping to repeat the trick. 809 wanted to launch a single-seat interceptor from a merchant ship to shoot down other airliners that had been pressed into military service: the three Boeing 707s being used by the Fuerza Aérea Argentina to track British ships. It was a prospect that the squadron boss and his Senior Pilot both relished. Each of them had a number of Sea Harrier firsts to their credit, but Tim Gedge and Dave Braithwaite both wanted this one on their CVs.

*This*, thought Gedge, *is a real opportunity.*

After leaving Ascension, all the jets had been washed down with fresh water and liberally covered in WD-40 then cocooned in tailor-made green polybags to protect them from the elements. It was of particular importance to sheathe the RAF Harriers. In developing the Sea Harrier for the Navy, BAe had marinized the airframe. Not so the GR.3. Salt water corroded the Air Force jet's magnesium components. Maintainers noticed that if you listened carefully you could hear it fizzing. While the 1(F) Squadron jets were left lashed down on the starboard side of the deck, a single Sea Harrier was debagged and prepared for action. The Sidewinders and 30mm ammunition liberated from Wideawake were going to come in handy.

The Victor tankers had been in the thick of it from the beginning. Until the revival of the Vulcan's in-flight refuelling capability they had been the only aircraft in the RAF's inventory capable of reaching the theatre of war from Ascension. After mounting long-range maritime reconnaissance missions, facilitating the BLACK BUCK raids and supporting the Harrier and Sea Harrier deployments, they'd now added the newly AAR-capable Nimrods and C-130s to their growing clientele list. Back home, an American agreement to provide USAF KC-135 tankers for Op TANSOR, the refuelling support required by the RAF Phantoms and Lightnings defending UK airspace, freed another two Victors to leave Marham in Norfolk for the mid-Atlantic. By mid-May, thirteen of the big former V-bombers were squeezed on to the hardstanding at Wideawake. That at any given time a number of them were likely to be airborne made the job of finding space to park them all a little easier. A request from the Amphibious Task Group for tankers to support their plans to scramble a Sea Harrier in pursuit of the Burglar would make it easier still.

Borrowing the language used by the Fleet Air Arm for the mission, the Victor crews labelled their plan 'Hack the Shad'. It was soon given the official codename Operation GRAMMERIAN. And, of everything they'd so far been required to do in support of the South Atlantic war, this was the task that had most in common with their most frequent Cold War tasking of keeping the fighters flying.

*Conveyor's* port bridge wing quickly assumed the mantle of Flyco on a ship that seemed to be evolving, with each further mile south, into a third aircraft carrier. In the makeshift military spaces made available to NP 1840, the effort to establish a SHAR on Quick Reaction Alert took shape. Along with Mike Layard, Gedge and Braithwaite established the tactical approach to making the interception. Using fuel and performance tables, the two SHAR pilots worked out a flight plan, testing different weapons configurations against the need to carry as much fuel as possible.

Without a full-length flight deck, the need for a vertical take-off was a given. But relying solely on the 21,500lb of thrust provided by the Pegasus engine to get airborne would limit the weight of fuel and stores that could be carried. At least now, though, as the ship steamed away from the equator, the air and sea temperature was cooling down. They could extract more performance from the engine as a result. The whole mission, Gedge thought, was another chance to challenge a few misconceptions about the Harrier. And they died hard.

Gedge remembered the occasion in 1980 when, as boss of 800 Squadron, he'd taken five SHARs down to the French Aéronavale air station at Hyères as guests of the Etendard squadron there. After rolling out charts of the south of France during a briefing, the French CO had asked him, 'How far can your aeroplane go?'

'We can go as far as you can,' Gedge told him.

And, after the 17 Flottille boss had drawn a derisory-looking radius on to the map, Gedge sketched a low-level route that took them north towards Grenoble and returning across the Alps before flying out to sea and switching back to Hyères. Five or six hundred miles. Gedge's counterpart muttered, frowned and shook his head, but agreed to lead the way. After a couple of the Aéronavale jets had returned to base en route, Gedge rubbed it in by squeezing in a quick 2 v 2 practice air combat before landing.

A vertical take-off wouldn't require excessive amounts of fuel. The issue was simply weight. With clean wings and a full internal fuel load of 4,400lb, Gedge and Braithwaite calculated that the greatest distance they could reach and return to the ship was 183 miles. Add a pair of Sidewinders and loaded ADEN gun pods then a reduced fuel load of 2,500lb, and that radius of action came down to 100 miles. That was still, though, equivalent to launching from London and making an intercept in Salisbury. More than enough, given that new Rules of Engagement from Northwood decreed that any Argentine shadower had to close within 30 to 40 miles of the British ships before 809 were authorized to shoot it down.

On the forward pad, 809's maintainers prepared the jet for action, testing the systems and reattaching the refuelling probe that had been removed prior to bagging her up for the journey. They removed the 100-gallon drop tank from each of the two inboard pylons. No point in carrying the empty, dead weight.

Colin Burton and the rest of the squadron's armourers loaded the gun pods with chain-linked 30mm ammunition. Then they unlocked the white shipping container on the starboard deck behind the pad and removed a pair of Sidewinders. After bolting them on to the outboard pylons they tested the seeker heads using infrared torches. And, just as it had done at China Lake during the missile's development, the AIM-9's heatseeking electronic eye tracked them as unerringly as a predator choosing its prey.

As the Fleet Air Arm prepared to counter the enemy's intelligence-gathering effort, the RAF were already engaged in a little aerial espionage of their own.

# THIRTY-THREE

## If you can't take a joke

THERE WAS NEVER a good time to lose an engine. But for the twenty-eight souls aboard Nimrod XW664 flying Operation ACME 4, the first of 51 Squadron's top-secret SIGINT-gathering missions, it seemed particularly lousy. There was no option, though. After the Flight Engineer reported the total loss of oil pressure to the No. 1 engine, they had to shut it down. Leave it running without oil and you risked catastrophic failure. And in a jet like the Nimrod, with its four Rolls-Royce Spey engines buried in close-coupled pairs inside the wingroots, engine trouble had a habit of being contagious.

'Shutting down number one engine,' reported the Nimrod's Captain, Squadron Leader Lambert. 'HP cock off . . . LP cock shut.'

Behind him, the Flight Engineer confirmed, 'One HP air supply lever is off.'

The preparation for the sortie had been meticulous, although hardly helped by trouble with the SATCOM link to the UK. But Northwood HQ had insisted on changes to the flight plan to minimize the risk of the mission being compromised. Only then was the Detachment Commander, Brian Speed, given clearance to fly. After launching from San Félix Island on 9 May, the 51 Squadron jet had landed at Concepción two hours later to refuel, before taking off again at 0445 local time. The Nimrod tracked south, parallel to the Argentine border, as far as Patagonia before reversing course overhead Bernardo O'Higgins National Park and retracing her steps. As dawn broke over Concepción a little before nine, Lambert rolled into a gentle turn on to a heading of 330°, out to sea and into jeopardy.

Flying on three engines wasn't in itself a problem for the

Nimrod, but landing was another matter. Ahead lay a short, sloping runway on a remote, unfamiliar island of barely 2 square miles in area. It was already less than ideal, but the loss of the No. 1 engine meant he'd lost half the reverse thrust from the two outer engines that he'd normally have used to slow the jet down. They were going to be asking a lot of the brakes.

And, inevitably enough, ACME 4 came with a cherry on top.

On today's flight, not only was he responsible for the safety of his aircraft and the lives of his crew, but also that of Commander Pedro Anguita. The Chilean naval air arm's Chief of Staff, who'd first introduced Sidney Edwards to San Félix, had joined them for the sortie. The British spyplane was flying a deniable operational mission from inside a neutral country carrying a senior member of that country's military on board as an observer: if it all went pear-shaped it was going to take some explaining. But if you can't take a joke, so the saying went, you shouldn't have joined.

Lambert thumbed the RT button on the Nimrod's control yoke to prepare San Félix for their arrival. 'Pan, Pan, Pan,' he began before identifying himself, his position and the nature of the problem. It stopped short of Mayday, but the Pan signal would leave them in no doubt about the seriousness of the situation aboard XW664.

In the Captain's terse transmission, concerned only with the safety of the aircraft, there was no mention of the fact that the team of Special Operators behind him had enjoyed a fruitful night hoovering up a particularly abundant flurry of signals and communication activity in Argentina. And that had not happened without some provocation.

A couple of hours before XW664 took off from Concepción, a single Sea Harrier, '004', had been launched into the dark from the deck of HMS *Invincible*. In the cockpit, his instruments dimmed almost to the point of invisibility, Sharkey Ward had relished the tranquillity of a high-level transit to East Falkland. From 35,000 feet, beneath a canopy of bright stars, he could pick out the lights of Stanley. After sweeping the skies for enemy aircraft with his radar, he switched the Blue Fox to air-to-surface mode, reduced the power and descended towards Choiseul Sound. A low-level run-in towards the target, Goose Green airfield, followed. Beneath his port wing was neither a missile nor bomb, though, but a Lepus flare carried on the outer pylon. Burning with a six-million-candlepower intensity, it had the power to turn night into day. With that came the potential to goad the islands' defenders into believing that the British were launching a full-scale amphibious assault.

Guided by the jet's NAVHARS weapons and navigation computer, Ward ran in over the water. Following the instructions projected on to the head-up display, he pickled the flare, feeling a bump through the airframe as it was ejected from the pylon. Then he poured on the power and pulled back on the stick to climb to height, counting down the seconds until the flare, descending towards the airfield beneath a small parachute, brought an earlier-than-expected dawn to the Argentine garrison.

From Goose Green the 801 Squadron boss flew west across Falkland Sound to Fox Bay to repeat the trick before returning for a tricky recovery to the carrier in poor visibility and buffeting 40- to 50-knot winds.

By morning in Buenos Aires, radio stations were reporting that the British had landed troops on the Malvinas. And throughout the night, before the country's civilian population woke up to the news, the 51 Squadron Nimrod had been hoovering up the Argentine military's surprised reaction to it. The flap caused by Sharkey Ward's solo sortie ensured it was SIGINT gold.

From where Lambert and his co-pilot were sitting in the R.1's cockpit, it looked almost as if they were approaching the flight deck of an aircraft carrier. There was a low approach over water before XW664 flashed over the edge of the island towards the threshold of runway Two Nine. Behind them, in the cabin of the big jet, the Nimrod's crew and their Chilean guest had tightened their straps and were braced, prepared for the worst. With one engine shut down, Lambert was coming in hot. The crosswind coming in from the northeast didn't help. And with only 6,000 feet of runway sloping gently away ahead of him he needed to try to bring her down on the numbers. Not many things as useless to a pilot as runway behind you.

The mainwheels thumped down on the tarmacadam, the big jet bouncing heavily on the hydraulic oleos. While Lambert kept her rolling straight, bringing the nose down on to the undercarriage, his co-pilot chopped the power, pulling back the throttle levers of the three remaining R-R Speys to idle.

Then, with the sea visible beyond the western limit of the runway, Lambert stood on the brakes. And it was a whole lot more forceful than the four-wheel bogies of the main undercarriage were entirely happy with. But, unable to use reverse thrust from the failed engine, he had no option. He could overstress the brakes or go off the end of the runway into the sea. In the end it was more than the jet could take. First one of the mainwheel tyres burst, shedding rubber behind the decelerating aircraft in a puff of white smoke. Then another tyre disintegrated in protest at its treatment by Lambert.

But it was enough.

By adding wrecked undercarriage to his jet's list of complaints alongside the No. 1 engine's ruptured main bearing seal, XW664's Captain had brought her in to San Félix in one piece and saved a valuable intelligence take for dissemination and analysis. A SATCOM link to the UK would be open until 1500Z. It was expected that Northwood would use the comms window to share further tasking with the Detachment Commander, Brian Speed. Instead, they received news that XW664 was going nowhere until a replacement engine and new mainwheel assembly were flown out from the UK.

# THIRTY-FOUR

## A topsy-turvy world

KEEPING AN ARMED Sea Harrier on deck alert didn't do much to make Tim Gedge or his Senior Pilot's journey more comfortable. Working in shifts, Gedge and Brave shared the responsibility. One day on, one day off. It meant the pilot on alert had to hang around the bridge in his immersion suit, ready to scramble down the ladders to deck level to get strapped into the cockpit. But there was good food at least, and games of bridge and the ever-present Rubik's cubes to keep them occupied. There was also Captain Birdseye – *Conveyor*'s Master, Ian North – to talk to. It was impossible not to warm to him.

Just as NP 1840's Senior Naval Officer, Mike Layard, had been charmed by the old merchant mariner's sea stories, so too were the Harrier pilots now on board. Gedge had particularly good reason to be grateful. Captain Birdseye had given up his day cabin for the 809 boss to share with David Baston, the CO of 848 NAS, the new Wessex helicopter squadron travelling south alongside the SHARs and GR.3s. Situated high up in the ship's superstructure, the views through the big windows were excellent. Even better, it housed a large fridge full of beer that, however hard Gedge and Baston tried to empty it, was restocked whenever they left the room. Eventually, Gedge learned that convention on merchant ships dictated that all the booze belongs to the Master and that he sells it to whomever he wants to sell it at whatever price he deems suitable. But any attempt by Gedge or Baston to pay was rebuffed by North. And so, inevitably, his day cabin became the preferred venue for squadron gatherings. North himself would often join them, while mix tapes Gedge recorded before leaving home played on the little cassette player he'd bought to take south.

Mounted on the bulkhead was a gold-headed cane in a glass cabinet. North was the first Cunard Master to have been awarded it by winning the race to be first to reach Montreal Harbour along the St Lawrence seaway after the thawing of the winter ice.

'How did you win?' Gedge asked, fascinated by the very notion that anyone could race a container ship that didn't give much away to HMS *Invincible* in size.

'I overtook the other ship through a large bend by sailing over the shallow bit.' An extraordinary bit of seamanship, and a measure of North's skill as a ship handler.

Bob Iveson, one of the two 1(F) pilots who were billeted on *Conveyor*, encouraged him to share tales of the Second World War convoys. North had been a boy sailor, just fourteen, when, after war broke out, he'd first gone to sea. The Navy, he told Iveson, could learn a thing or two from the way they did it in the war. It would certainly be a whole lot easier to keep the Task Group together if, instead of using radios to find each other every morning, they simply tied a fender on to half a mile of rope and trailed it behind them for the next ship to follow.

'It's so easy!' North laughed. 'But I can't convince the Navy to do it!'

The Argentine invasion had thrown the Royal Navy, the Merchant Navy and the Royal Air Force together into a situation none of them had anticipated or trained for. All had been forced into an unfamiliar and, for all the determination to get the job done, sometimes uneasy cooperation. The trouble was, everyone tended to think that their way was the right way.

That the four GR.3 pilots on board *Norland* had to be ferried across to *Conveyor* by helicopter probably didn't add to their enthusiasm for the programme of briefings scheduled during the transit south. For the Navy, the aircraft were just one of a range of weapons systems available to the fleet. By contrast, the RAF revolved around the aircraft that were the service's *raison d'être*. Perhaps that alone accounted for 1(F) Flight Commander Jerry Pook's assessment of some of the briefings from the 809 pilots. He'd been willing enough to listen to what they had to say about the particular requirements of flying from a carrier deck, but he dismissed what was said about air combat as *bullshit and duff gen*.

Drawing on experience honed in the US at TOPGUN and the Marine Corps' WTI course, Brave and Bill Covington delivered the air combat briefings. A last-ditch escape manoeuvre briefed by Covington that combined a split 'S', VIFFing, and deploying full flap above the specified limit of 300 knots might overstress the jet, but it wasn't going to kill it. And it might just shake off any Mirage locked on to your six o'clock, and mean you and your aircraft got to live to fight another day.

'It doesn't apply to us,' Pook told the GR.3 crews. 'We'll not overstress our aircraft.'

Covington was shocked. *We're going to war*, he thought, *and all of us need as much knowledge as possible*. You never knew when it might save your life.

Pook later gave his own briefing to the GR.3 pilots on VIFFing and how to use the Sidewinder, Brave's thoughts on missile combat having not, as far as Pook was concerned at least, passed muster. And yet, for all that the 1(F) Flight Commander, as much as he liked the 809 pilots as individuals, appeared to have circled the wagons against the Navy, his prickliness wouldn't turn out to be entirely misplaced. Covington, Braithwaite and Co. may have been doing their best to help prepare the RAF squadron for life and war aboard an aircraft carrier, but not everyone, they would soon discover, was quite as well disposed towards them.

For now, though, it wasn't Pook or the RAF who were going to be launching from the deck in pursuit of the Fuerza Aérea Argentina. Instead, Tim Gedge was trussed up in the thick rubber immersion suit when the order to bring the alert SHAR to five minutes' readiness came through from HMS *Fearless*. One of the frigates escorting the TG 317.0 had picked up an unidentified radar contact that it suspected was the Argentine Burglar.

A few hundred miles to the north, Op GRAMMERIAN got underway.

The primary Victor K.2 was already on its way from Ascension, launched alongside a second tanker in anticipation of a SHAR mission. Rules of Engagement had been changed, allowing the Task

Group to shoot down any aircraft that could be positively identified as hostile, and, on the day that the Junta had announced that the Amphibious Task Group represented a legitimate target, that meant any Argentine military aircraft coming within 40 miles of the convoy. After taking on fuel from the second Victor, the primary tanker continued south before descending to an altitude of 25,000 feet overhead the Amphibious Task Group. The crew then settled into a lazy racetrack pattern, ready to pick up the 809 Squadron Sea Harrier as required.

On board *Conveyor*, Jerry Pook watched the maintainers prepare the SHAR for launch. He reckoned that if Gedge made the intercept he was going to be *critically short of gravy*.

Should the situation demand it, though, the Victor was cleared to descend to a height of 2,000 feet in support of a low-level Sea Harrier CAP. No one was in any doubt about the challenges that an attempt to intercept the big Boeing might throw up.

Carrying his helmet, Gedge weaved his way forward along *Conveyor*'s deck through the maze of polybagged Harriers and helicopters towards the single SHAR squatting ready on the forward pad. He climbed up the ladder and lowered himself into the cockpit. And there he sat for an hour before the sortie was cancelled after the Burglar turned for home.

Escuadrón II's Boeing 707, serial TC-92, would be back the following day. But this time it would be Dave Braithwaite's turn.

The long-slot Victor patrolling overhead was a reassuring presence, the last of a four-strong Victor formation that had launched from Wideawake to position a single tanker over the Task Group. They had her for five hours, between 1200Z and 1700Z. After *Argonaut*'s radar operator once again picked up what he suspected was the Argentine reconnaissance flight, Brave was brought to five minutes' readiness to launch.

Like the CO the previous day, the Senior Pilot strapped in and cycled through his pre-flight checks. Scribbled on his thigh were the serial numbers of the three Fuerza Aérea Argentina 707s. Outside, the squadron's maintainers removed the protective caps from the seeker heads of the two Sidewinder missiles.

Then the order came through to scramble.

Braithwaite ran through the pre-start checks before he was told to stand down. There seemed to be some uncertainty about the air picture. The suspected Argentine shadower appeared to have been joined by a pair of Soviet Naval Aviation Tupolev Tu-142s, known to NATO as the 'Bear F', long-range maritime reconnaissance aircraft staging out of Conakry in Guinea, West Africa. With that confusion, the order to launch was cancelled. The Soviet Navy machine had every right to operate unmolested over international waters this far out in the South Atlantic. And so the Cold War threat for which the SHAR had been largely designed and built to counter was, on this occasion, off limits, while its presence prevented the interception of an unarmed airliner, operated by an Air Force to which the British had been eager to sell aeroplanes, which had been confirmed as hostile.

It was a topsy-turvy world.

Brave shut down the jet and cracked open the canopy. For all his eagerness to get airborne, he couldn't help but feel the mission was marginal, the chances of safely returning the SHAR to *Conveyor* slim. *If we have to go*, he thought, *the aircraft will probably be lost*. As a result there could be no uncertainty. If you went after the Burglar, *you really had to shoot the bloody thing down*.

As if gloating over the frustration they'd caused, the two red-starred Bear Fs descended to low level and stooged around above the Task Group for half an hour, the sun glinting off their bare metal skins. Satisfied that they'd been nuisance enough, their pilots poured on the power from the big Kuznetsov turboprops, and the two swept-wing silver beasts climbed away with a buzzsaw howl, their sixteen contra-rotating propellors shredding the air as they clawed their way to altitude.

Behind them, the alert SHAR was lashed to *Conveyor*'s deck and made safe. The Victor, orbiting above it all, rolled out on to a northerly heading to begin the three-hour transit back to Wideawake. And Brave rejoined the rest of the squadron inside for a beer and a cigarette. Next time, perhaps.

And when the time came, London would be ready for it. Patience finally having worn thin, Downing Street approved a draft press release in anticipation of the successful destruction of the Burglar:

DRAFT PRESS RELEASE FOR ARGENTINE 707/C130 ENGAGEMENT

At [time] an Argentine military aircraft engaged on surveillance duties against our own forces was shot down by a [missile/aircraft]. We have no reports of any survivors.

We warned the Argentine authorities on 23rd April and again on 7th May that all Argentine aircraft engaging in surveillance of British forces would be regarded as hostile and were liable to be dealt with accordingly.

The aircraft which is a type we know the Argentines use for military purposes [Boeing 707/C130] was [outside/inside] the TEZ and it was clear from its observed behaviour that it [intended to obtain/was engaged in acquiring] intelligence about our forces.

The intelligence gained from this type of surveillance operation can be used to direct air, surface ship and submarine attacks against our forces, with consequent risk to British lives.

The need for such action in our self-defence can easily be avoided if Argentina heeds our public warnings in future.

For now, though, 809's jet remained clamped to the deck. Nor were Gedge and Braithwaite the only Sea Harrier pilots who were frustrated at being deprived of an opportunity to show their mettle.

Apart from his own Lepus flare attack on Goose Green and Fox Bay, Sharkey Ward's squadron had barely left the flight deck since the day EJ and Al Curtis had been lost to the gloom. 801 hadn't had any contact with enemy aircraft for nearly a week. Day after day the met report recorded variations on a theme: 'sky obscured'; '8/8 cloud cover'; 'visibility 200m in fog'. The 'suitability for offensive air operations', it concluded, was 'poor in fog and low cloud'.

The squadron had no option but to stand down, although filthy weather, CIA analysis suggested, handed an advantage to the all-weather Sea Harriers over their Argentine opponents. And indeed, when *Invincible* was next to launch 801's SHARs on 14 May, the squadron war diary made mention of an improvement in the weather. It wasn't really much to write home about. There was still a 5-mile-deep smothering of solid cloud between 1,000 feet and 28,000 feet to contend with.

But there was one aircraft in the Argentine arsenal that was every bit as capable of operating at night, at low level and in all weathers: the Super Etendard flown by the Argentine Navy's 2 Escuadrilla Aeronaval de Caza y Ataque.

On 10 May, while the Sea Harriers aboard *Hermes* and *Invincible* were still grounded by the weather, a pair of SuEs launched an attack against Royal Navy warships as they sailed within unrefuelled range of the strike jets' home base. On this occasion, though, their run-in was welcome. And by prior arrangement. The two Aéronavale jets had taken off from the French naval air station at Landivisiau in Brittany to stage a simulated Exocet attack against a small flotilla led by the Type 82 destroyer HMS *Bristol*. As the British ships began their journey south to reinforce the Task Force, the French, more willing to assist if it was out of sight, had offered to help sharpen their reflexes. And the *Bristol* group would have cause to be grateful for that before reaching the TEZ.

The Marine Nationale SuE pilots, meanwhile, couldn't help but watch the performance of their Argentine counterparts with fascination. Would they do any better against the British? *Probably not*, thought the Aéronavale pilot who'd acted as liaison during their time training in France.

For the Argentine pilots, though, there had been frustration.

After introducing themselves so spectacularly with the destruction of the *Sheffield*, 2 Escuadrilla had been unable to launch another mission against the British Task Force. Their first had been reliant on the targeting information shared by one of the old piston-engined SP-2H Neptunes of 1 Escuadrilla Aeronaval de Exploración. But the two veteran maritime patrollers were now simply worn out.

In its heyday in the sixties, the Neptune unit had twelve aircraft on strength. By January 1982 they'd managed to get just two airborne to meet the Whitbread Round the World race as it approached Argentina from New Zealand. And as war dawned three months later the squadron's engineers were struggling even to do that.

One of the two Neptunes, 2-P-111, had been made airworthy using what amounted to a home-made engine, its Wright R-3350 Cyclone a Frankenstein's monster of parts cobbled together from five other engines. By any peacetime standard the aeroplane would have been grounded. But it flew on until the middle of May, by which time both Neptunes were springing problems like patients being lost to intensive care. Throughout the campaign they'd been shuttling back and forth between Río Grande and their home base at Comandante Espora near Bahía Blanca for running repairs, but on 15 May the squadron had to concede defeat. Having distinguished themselves by finding the survivors of the *Belgrano* and targeting the *Sheffield*, the engineering challenges had finally overwhelmed them.

Just when, on San Félix Island, 51 Squadron RAF had got the better of theirs.

The civil register suggested the Boeing 707 belonged to Gambia Airways, but the jet was unmarked and owned by an Irish leasing company called Omega Air. The crew was American and refused to tell any of the RAF engineers and aircrew on board who they worked for.

Since leaving the Irish Army the previous year, former Intelligence Officer Ulick McEvaddy had, with his brother, acquired an ex-Pan Am Boeing 707 stranded at Dublin Airport, reduced it to scrap and used the money made to acquire more 707s. They'd soon stopped pulling them apart and instead leased and chartered airworthy jets to Gambia Airways – in which they had a 49% stake – and customers around the world including the Pentagon and Ministry of Defence. Omega was the perfect operation to deliver the replacement Rolls-Royce Spey and mainwheel assembly required to return XW664 to flight.

Landing in Santiago on 12 May after leaving RAF Brize Norton at 0945Z the previous morning, the Nimrod spares were transferred from the 707 to a C-130 and flown out to San Félix Island, where 51 Squadron's engineers swapped out the damaged engine and repaired the undercarriage.

With Squadron Leader Brice taking over in the Captain's seat, the British spyplane took to the air again at just after midnight to embark on a near eleven-hour SIGINT mission, ACME 5. This time, after the dramatic conclusion to the previous ACME mission, Pedro Anguita chose not to join them.

On Latin America's Atlantic coast, 2 Escuadrilla remained grounded. Without the old Neptunes leading the way, Jorge Colombo's Super Etendards had no way of safely finding their targets without exposing themselves to British air defences. The squadron was going to have to find another way of pinpointing the British ships.

# THIRTY-FIVE

## A zebra's backside

'IF YOU LAUNCH,' Bill Covington told Mike Layard, 'you're going to lose the aeroplane.' From *Conveyor*'s bridge they looked ahead towards the Alert 5 SHAR, and the 809 Air Warfare Instructor didn't like the look of it at all.

Neither, it had to be said, did Brave. While he sat in the Sea Jet's cockpit preparing for a Red 90 vertical take-off, the ship was moving alarmingly beneath him. As she rolled to port, the nose of the little fighter pointed over the guardrails towards the heavy swell. Grey seas filled his field of view as he pitched forward against his straps. The ship held him there for a moment, before she began her roll back to starboard, whipping him through vertical until he was couched in his ejector seat on his back looking at the sky like a patient in a dentist's chair. The attitude indicator projected on to his head-up display told him they were rolling through 30°.

It had been two days since Victors had been able to offer tanker support. With fresh demands on the Victor fleet from modified Nimrods and C-130s, now also capable of taking on fuel in-flight, the maths no longer worked.

If scrambled, the 809 SHAR was on its own.

'The conditions you're asking that aircraft to launch and recover in,' Covington continued, 'are making this highly problematic.'

Fleet Air Arm pilots didn't make a habit of being overly impressed by a bit of weather. In the characteristically understated language of a naval aviator, Covington's statement suggested that the conditions were more than a little sporty. Launching was one thing, but trying to hover and land on such a treacherous deck without rolling back into the guardrails or one of the shipping containers, not least the one nearest the pad loaded with Sidewinders, was quite another. The decision, ultimately, was simple. 'Is this for real?' Covington asked. And in acknowledging that on this occasion the order from *Fearless* to launch was merely an exercise, Layard agreed they should scrub. If the radar operators aboard the frigates had been confident that they had the Argentine Boeing in their sights it would have been a different matter, but it was senseless to risk flying the SHAR just to prove it could be done.

A relieved Dave Braithwaite returned to the bridge, happier to devote himself instead to thinking about how best to allocate the 809 pilots, now that word had come through that the squadron was to be shared equally between the two carriers.

It had been decided that the CO was going to *Invincible*. With two squadron bosses, 800's Andy Auld and 899's Neill Thomas, already aboard *Hermes*, the flagship didn't need another. So Gedge was going to be joining Sharkey Ward's team. The rest was back-of-an-envelope stuff. With *Invincible* leading the air defence effort, it made sense to send them the pilots with fighter experience. *Hermes* would get the mud-movers.

After a career spent trying to escape the attention of fighters, while flying ground attack in Buccaneers, Etendards and Harrier GR.3s, Al Craig wasn't quite sure why that meant he was off to JJ Black's ship with Gedge, Brave and Dave Austin, but the laid-back Ulsterman took it in his stride. Tim Gedge, he'd thought, had proved to be a superb CO – understanding, in control, and on top of things. And he knew Sharkey would be leading from the front. It looked like a good combination.

Bill Covington, Hugh Slade, John Leeming and Steve Brown were going to *Hermes*. Also going to the bigger ship were the six 1(F) Squadron Harriers. With a mixed complement of over twenty SHARs, GR.3s and Sea King helicopters aboard, she was going to look and feel more like a big-deck strike carrier than at any time since 1970, when she had last embarked her squadrons of Sea Vixens, Buccaneers and Gannets.

But first of all, *Atlantic Conveyor* had to deliver her precious cargo to the Task Force. And as the big container ship plunged south the greater danger now was not from Argentine ships and submarines, but from the elements.

Heated by the sun, warm air rises from the equator and circulates towards the poles, descending at around 30° north and south. In the age of sail, ships becalmed here by a lack of wind were often forced to throw livestock overboard to eke out their dwindling reserves of fresh water. As a result they became known as the Horse Latitudes, and beyond them, as the air cooled and was deflected towards the poles by the Earth's rotation, the strength of the wind increased. In the southern hemisphere, unobstructed by the continental land masses of Asia, Europe and North America, the winds became fiercer still. Mariners called them the Roaring Forties. And they brought with them heavy seas and treacherous conditions.

Ian North took the helm himself, drawing on forty years' experience at sea to stop his ship turning turtle. Fifty-knot winds drove steep rolling waves of 20 to 30 feet. Snakes of angry white foam skittered across the surface of the dark water. *Conveyor* thumped and juddered as she pitched through the sea, ascending peaks then surfing down the other side before slamming her bow into the bottom of the trough, seemingly stopping dead. Slowly she'd recover forward momentum as the fo'c's'le swung up in anticipation of the cycle starting again. Sheets of spray slapped at the thick glass of the bridge as she pounded up and down through the storm. But of most concern to her Master was his ship's ability to cope with the severe rolling.

*Conveyor* had left the UK without working stabilizers. The retractable horizontal fins that swung out amidships below the waterline usually helped counter any rolling motion. The lack of stabilization would have been more of a discomfort than a danger, except that it was combined with a very atypical cargo distribution that was helping amplify the effects of the heavy seas.

Without a full load of laden containers layered three deep and six wide forward and aft of the superstructure, *Atlantic Conveyor* was dramatically underweight. It meant that the distance between her centre of gravity and the axis around which she rolled was too small. She should have been loaded to sail with a metacentric height, or GM, of a couple of centimetres. Instead it was over 2 metres, and as a result she was more or less bobbing around on the surface of the sea.

Time and again the SHAR pilots on the bridge watched as North grabbed the wheel to break the rolling motion by turning the ship. But it needed to be judged carefully as the very act of turning the ship at high speed was in itself a cause of roll.

An effort to return to the *Norland* the GR.3 pilots who'd flown over to *Conveyor* for briefings by helicopter had to be abandoned as unsafe and so, facing the discomfort of a sleepless night without a bunk aboard the tossing and turning ship, the 1(F) pilots turned to alcohol. They were joined, just as they had been two days earlier to celebrate the squadron's seventieth birthday, by their 809 NAS counterparts.

John Leeming, seconded to 809 from the RAF with Steve Brown, was rather taken by the way his Senior Service comrades-in-arms described their ship's unsettling situation. A zebra's backside's got us, they told him. You only had to look at the closely packed isobars on the met map illustrating the large, bad-tempered depression that had them in its clutches to see what they meant. Now happily describing himself as 'a naval type', Leeming took it all in his stride. But for all his easy-going confidence at sea, the reality of their situation was never far from the surface. 'I was not in a dream,' he wrote in his diary, 'and would very soon be in a combat zone.'

Major Cedric Delves looked out with satisfaction at the destruction he and his men had wreaked on Pebble Island, the enemy's Isla Borbón. Through the cockpit windows of the Westland Sea King HC.4, over the shoulder of the 846 NAS pilot, the horizon burned fiercely, illuminating the pre-dawn. Over the intercom, the Navy Aircrewman behind in the cabin reported that they were good to go. It was a relief to be back aboard the big twin-engined helo, cocooned once more from the freezing wind outside and enveloped in the reassuringly familiar scent of oil, metal and burning AVTUR jet fuel.

Job done.

A little over three and a half hours earlier Delves had led a helicopter-borne raiding party of forty-five troopers from D Squadron SAS in an operation that bore all the hallmarks of the legendary

North African missions that had built the Regiment's reputation during the Second World War. Then, legendary SAS Originals such as David Stirling and Paddy Mayne had set about the Luftwaffe with gleeful abandon. Today – Friday, 14 May – the destruction of Argentine aircraft had been their objective.

Supported by naval gunfire from the twin 4.5-inch guns of the destroyer HMS *Glamorgan*, steaming up and down the gunline 6 miles north of the coast, D Squadron's target was Estación Aeronaval *Calderón*. The grass airfield was home to the little T-34 turboprops that had so narrowly escaped the attention of Sharkey Ward and Soapy Watson's SHARs on the first day of the war. And after 800 Squadron's attacks on Goose Green its complement had grown when it took in six of the Fuerza Aérea Argentina's heavily armed IA-58 Pucará COIN aircraft.

Sandy Woodward had wanted them gone.

As the Admiral began to focus on the amphibious landings that would follow the arrival of HMS *Fearless*, *Atlantic Conveyor* and the rest of TG 317.0, he calculated that the Argentine light attack force at EAN *Calderón* were just four minutes' flying time from San Carlos, where it had been decided by Mike Clapp and Brigadier Julian Thompson, Commander of 3 Commando Brigade, that British forces were to be put ashore. And, as he'd pored over his charts in his day cabin, looking across the 19 miles that separated Pebble Island from San Carlos Water, a snake's tongue of water licking into the East Falkland from the northern entrance of the Sound, he'd known that was no notice at all.

Carrying M16 assault rifles with three spare magazines taped to the stock, 200 to 400 rounds of belted GPMG ammunition, a couple of mortar rounds, claymore mines and, in some cases, M-72 LAW anti-tank weapons, the D Squadron assault force had destroyed or put out of action all eleven Argentine aircraft, leaving chaos, confusion and an ammunition dump cooking off in their wake.

The SAS Sabre Squadron had climbed back aboard the four Sea Kings with no more than a concussion and a relatively minor shrapnel wound between them. But, as the big helicopter thrummed back towards the carrier, dawn breaking to the east, one thing kept nagging at their CO: he and his men hadn't destroyed the radar. Hadn't even seen it. This, though, had been the target that, when the decision to launch the raid was made, Woodward had stressed was to be given the very highest priority. Only when Delves had acknowledged this did the Admiral tell him: 'Make it so.'

The Argentine radars near Stanley and at Goose Green were a known concern, but rumours of a third search radar at Pebble Island had taken hold quickly. One of the SHAR pilots had been painted by a radar that his RWR suggested was transmitting from a mobile set operating from the little auxiliary airfield. When a signal from the CO of 22 SAS, travelling south aboard HMS *Fearless*, floated the same supposition, it reinforced Woodward's fear that the landings at San Carlos might be fatally compromised. An eight-man SAS recce patrol that had gone in days ahead of the main assault saw no evidence of a radar, but the Admiral just couldn't afford to take the risk.

For all D Squadron's success at Pebble Island, the status of the radar was uncertain.

Woodward was acutely aware of the advantage to the Argentine air effort provided by the AN/TPS-43 radar at Stanley, warning Northwood that 'attainment of air superiority is not possible while these radars are in operation'. And he was forced to admit that, with the resources at his disposal, he had 'no real prospect' of doing anything about them.

At Northwood HQ, the Op CORPORATE Air Commander, John Curtiss, shared the Admiral's frustration.

# THIRTY-SIX

## Dangerous again

As STATION COMMANDER at RAF Brüggen in Germany in 1971, John Curtiss had overseen the formation of the RAF's first dedicated F-4 Phantom FGR.2 tactical reconnaissance squadron. Slung beneath the centreline of each jet was a massive sensor pod designed and built by EMI. Contained within were four F.95 cameras, two F.135 cameras, an infrared scanner, sideways-looking radar and even an in-flight film-processing capability. The fan of the cameras meant a single low-level pass could bring home a 5-mile-wide take. It was information like this upon which RAF Germany built its plans for taking on the Warsaw Pact forces ranged against it. Now, deprived of any possibility of using the RAF's own Canberra PR.9s from Chile to acquire similar intelligence, Curtiss was concerned that the Task Force had simply afforded too little priority to both reconnaissance and the planning and execution of any effective Offensive Counter Air campaign that might follow.

The fog lifted on 14 May. When SHAR operations from *Invincible* and *Hermes* resumed, each of the jets heading out on CAP was loaded with a single 1,000lb bomb on the centreline pylon. Confined to higher altitudes following the loss of Nick Taylor's SHAR to Argentine triple-A, the Sea Harriers had been reduced to dropping handfuls of thousand-pounders from 18,000 feet. While the pilots used to enjoy the sport of pickling the bomb then standing the jet on its starboard wing to try to record its impact with the SHAR's single F.95 camera, they rarely captured pictures of the explosion. It was largely hit and hope. And, unless the enemy was unfortunate enough to be directly underneath, of little more than nuisance value.

As the SHARs struggled to degrade the Argentine air defences, Curtiss wrote a paper outlining his thoughts on how best to tackle the problem. Whether it was through air attack, naval gunfire or Special Forces direct action, Woodward's forces, he argued, were not focusing enough on key targets like the search radars, surface-to-air missiles and radar-laid anti-aircraft guns.

Alongside the Air Commander's efforts to try to bring some long-distance influence to bear on the prosecution of the counter air campaign, the RAF was also trying to apply a little creativity to how it might be able to achieve the same results more directly.

Two years earlier, the Royal Aircraft Establishment at Farnborough had trialled a forward-looking infrared sensor aboard an old piston-engined Vickers Varsity T.1. Now, within a fortnight of a decision, it was thought that a two-seat Harrier T.4 equipped with a similar system could be in theatre by early June. With a FLIR operator sitting behind the pilot, the T.4 would be able to accurately acquire and attack well-defended targets in total darkness, or act as a pathfinder and target-marker for larger numbers of single-seat Harriers flown by pilots wearing Night Vision Goggles. In the end, though, while a crash development programme was thought to be technically feasible, it was felt that the risks probably outweighed the potential rewards.

So, limited to operations by day in good visibility, the 1(F) Squadron's Harrier GR.3s aboard *Atlantic Conveyor* would have to enter the fray with little more than speed and whatever cover they could claim from the terrain to protect them. That had already cost Nick Taylor his life.

The RAF pilots would pay for it too.

The Nimrod's Captain redlined the four Rolls-Royce Spey engines and tipped the big reconnaissance jet into a dive. The whole intention was to detect and record the widest possible range of electronic emissions, but that was not expected to include a fighter jet's X-band fire control radar scanning the skies for targets. But, sitting at Rack ten in the Nimrod's main cabin, operator Tony Stokes was in no doubt. They'd been painted. There was no mistaking the French-made Agave radar's distinctive transmissions. As the 51 Squadron R.1 returned from another Op ACME intelligence-gathering mission out over the South Atlantic, they had attracted the very unwelcome attention of the local air defences. While one of the COMINT – communications intelligence – specialists monitored the RT exchanges between the interceptor pilot and his controller on the ground, the Nimrod's Mission Supervisor, Squadron Leader Ian Sampson, seated at Rack seven, warned the pilots to take evasive action.

An experienced and much respected operator, Sampson knew this was febrile airspace. War with the British had hardly reduced Argentina's nervousness about her neighbour. Worried that Chile might take advantage of the fight over the Falklands to revisit their simmering border dispute at the end of the world, Argentina was forced to keep looking over her shoulder. Just to make sure they did, the Fuerza Aérea de Chile had employed its small fleet of Mirage 50s, recently acquired from France, to tease and probe along the border.

With tensions so high, it was a dangerous game. That Sampson's team could identify the Mirage as Chilean was cold comfort. As the big RAF jet plunged down through the dark, the crew remained calm, hoping not to hear Stokes's report that the fighter's radar had locked on.

On the ground, the radar operators directing the interception watched their screens as the unidentified intruder manoeuvred to try to evade their fighter. That in itself was suspicious. Only a military aircraft would even be aware it was being pursued. They'd been right to order the intercept.

After a short break, the Senior Duty Officer returned to the Operations Room to find his controllers discussing whether or not to seek authorization for the interceptor to engage the intruder once the pilot was in range. And he immediately took control of the situation.

On board the British jet, the pilots pushed the Nimrod uncomfortably close to its limits as they dashed for the relative safety of low altitude. Skimming low across the islands and inlets of the Beagle Channel would offer some protection. By dropping below the radar horizon of the Chilean fighter controllers, they would complicate the task of their pursuer by relieving him of assistance and direction. Their mood was determined. After departing Wyton the day after the *Sheffield* was hit, the ACME crews had always been up for the fight. Then, without warning, the fighter just abandoned his pursuit, peeling away from any possible intercept vector. But as tension eased among the twenty-nine-strong RAF crew, there was puzzlement about just what had transpired.

After assuming command of the intercept, the Senior Duty Officer had taken the heat out of a dangerous situation. When the unidentified aircraft had entered their airspace, the controllers at the Base Aérea Carlos Ibáñez, the Chilean Air Force base at Punta Arenas, had wasted no time in directing an armed Mirage 50 to intercept it. Such was the secrecy surrounding the British ACME missions that only the Station Commander and two Duty Officers working in shifts had been briefed into the operation. With immaculately bad timing, the only person who knew about the provenance of the 'intruder' was out of the room at the moment the Nimrod re-entered Chilean airspace. He returned in the nick of time, hauling off the Grupo 4 interceptor before it had closed on the British aircraft.

But it was all too close for comfort. Through a combination of error and eagerness the 51 Squadron Nimrod and its crew had been at risk of being shot down. And, once again, in the shape of a future head of his country's naval intelligence, Primer Teniente Enrique O'Reilly, there had been a Chilean naval aviator on board the British spyplane.

Using SATCOM equipment installed on the Nimrod, Detachment Commander Brian Speed reported to Northwood. The senior Chilean officer on San Félix was invited onboard to listen to the voice recordings of the encounter.

At the British Embassy in Santiago, Sidney Edwards was roused from his bed by the Duty Clerk to take an urgent telephone call. It was Ken Hayr in London. Confirming his identity over the open line using a pre-arranged codename, the Assistant Chief of the Air Staff sounded agitated. He normally only communicated with his man in Chile via encrypted signal, but the threat to the Nimrod required immediate investigation. Hayr used a codeword to identify the nature of the incident. What the hell had gone wrong?

A hastily convened meeting with General Rodriguez at the FACh Intelligence HQ soon provided Edwards with the answer.

There had now been three SIGINT missions flown under the umbrella of Operation ACME. But the eleven-hour sortie on the night of 17 May would be the last. While valuable intelligence was harvested by 51 Squadron, it was now felt that the political risk of the operation being discovered was too great. Despite requests from Sandy Woodward for further missions in the days prior to Operation SUTTON, the planned amphibious landing at San Carlos, by the 19th XW664 and her crew were on their way home. Operation ACME 7a, 7b, 8 and 9 simply covered the jet's return to RAF Wyton on the 22nd, where the two Canberra PR.9s earmarked for Operation FOLK-LORE had arrived back from Belize five days earlier.

With 51 Squadron's departure, the RAF's airborne effort in Chile was reduced to a pair of C-130s disguised in FACh markings. It was something. The Hercules was at least able to carry roll-on/roll-off pal-letized SIGINT equipment, but the take wasn't a patch on what a machine dedicated to the job like the Nimrod R.1 could produce. Sidney Edwards' focus now fell on Operations FINGENT and SHUT-TER, the radar surveillance and SATCOM early warning system he had set up to monitor activity at Argentina's southern air bases. And life in Santiago would become a little less fraught. For a few days at least.

At DNAW in London, Ben Bathurst had been equally devoted to the task of trying to protect the fleet from the threat of air attack. Project LAST, his response to the sinking of HMS *Sheffield*, was moving forward apace. Following a meeting with Bathurst at the MoD on a Thursday, Westland Helicopters had produced a full project report by Monday morning, promising that they could design, build and put into squadron service an AEW Sea King within three months. They proposed to hang a modified version of the Nimrod's Thorn EMI Searchwater radar from the side of the helicopter's fuselage. The antenna would be protected inside an inflatable kevlar bag that could be raised and lowered as required for take-off and landing – an ingeni-ous piece of engineering that was conspicuously a triumph of function over form. At a subsequent meeting at the Westland factory in Yeovil, Bathurst sat on one side of a table writing the operational requirement while, on the other, Westland Project Manager Jim Schofield went over the results of wind tunnel tests on the strange-looking configuration.

Bathurst calculated that two Searchwater-equipped Sea Kings could work in shifts to provide twenty-four-hour cover, seven days a week. Operating 50 miles upthreat from the carriers, they had the potential to detect and track an incoming Super Etendard skimming in low over the sea nine minutes *before* it was close enough to launch an Exocet. Ample time to vector in the Sea Harrier CAP to greet them.

Project LAST was enthusiastically endorsed by the Admiralty as a matter of 'considerable urgency'. A project like this, DNAW pointed out, would normally take at least two years to complete, but providing they could beg, borrow or steal a pair of Searchwater radars, Westland now expected the two modified Sea Kings to be flying in less than two months. It was an extraordinary effort, but still not fast enough. The AEW helos would be ready to deploy aboard *Invincible*'s sister ship, HMS *Illustrious*, when she sailed south in the summer, but *Invincible* and *Hermes* needed protection now.

Bathurst's department, though, had recognized the Exocet threat long before it materialized. The programme they had instigated to try to counter it was assigned the codenames HAMPTON and DETHRONE. And it had been helped along when, in April, the Royal Navy managed to drop and smash one of its own, sea-launched MM.38 Exocet missiles. Before sending the pieces back to Aérospatiale for repair, they took the opportunity to rummage around a bit. 'Know the enemy,' Sun Tzu had suggested.

On 17 May, the first of Bathurst's anti-Exocet initiatives arrived in theatre. A single Westland Lynx HAS.1 helicopter landed aboard each of the carriers after travelling south from Ascension aboard the stores ship RFA *Fort Austin*. Each had been modified to carry a radar reflector and an I-Band radar jammer appropriated from the Canberra T.17s of 360 Squadron, a joint RAF/RN electronic warfare training unit. The Lynx were to be kept on deck alert and scrambled in response to an incoming Exocet raid, then to hover 600 yards away from the carrier to seduce any missile away from the ship.

Trials in the UK suggested the decoy would work, but the arrival of *Invincible*'s Lynx hadn't inspired much confidence. After suffering an engine failure she'd come screaming down to the deck on one engine, only for maintainers to discover that the 'good' engine wasn't so good either. XZ725 would require a double engine change before being in a position to seduce anything.

Bathurst and his team hadn't confined themselves to exploring how the Fleet Air Arm's helicopters could better protect the fleet from air attack. There was a long list of modifications and studies designed to improve the capability of the Sea Harrier too, from the AN/ALE-40 chaff and flare pods acquired from the Americans and larger 190-gallon combat tanks that would increase time on CAP, to twin-rail Sidewinder launchers that doubled the jet's missile load out. But none were ready to deploy, while most of a plethora of exotic new weaponry being considered was concerned with developing the jet's ground attack capability.

In the fight for Falklands' skies, the SHAR continued the fight as it had started it, carrying two small 100-gallon drop tanks, cannon, a pair of short-range air-to-air missiles and the Blue Fox radar.

With the imminent arrival of 809 Squadron, Bathurst could at least claim to have substantially bolstered the depleted fighter force aboard the carriers, but it was an exercise in quantitative improvement, not a qualitative one. Yet any reinforcement of the outer protective ring was welcome, because the fleet's much-vaunted layered air defences had been exposed as worryingly patchy.

On 12 May, with 801's Sea Harriers grounded by fog, two waves of Argentine A-4 Skyhawks had attacked HMS *Glasgow* and HMS *Brilliant* as the former shelled Stanley airfield with her 4.5-inch gun. After detecting the first flight of four jets with their 909 fire control radar, *Glasgow*'s Sea Dart system failed to engage them. After they'd closed towards their targets untroubled by the two outer layers of the British air defences, Seawolf missiles fired by *Brilliant* finally shot down two of the Skyhawks. A third crashed into the sea trying to evade another missile. But when the second flight of A-4s arrived ten minutes later *Brilliant*'s missile system glitched too, allowing the Argentine fighter-bombers to attack unhindered by anything but small-arms fire.

While the bombs aimed at *Brilliant* skipped overhead like skimming stones, *Glasgow* was hit by one that crashed all the way through the ship's hull and out the other side before exploding at a distance. The destroyer was lucky, but the kinetic damage alone caused by a 500lb bomb hitting the ship at around 500mph was enough to see *Glasgow* withdrawn from the fight to be patched up.

A prerequisite for Operation SUTTON, the British amphibious landings, it had been stressed, was air superiority. The Sea Harriers and their pilots may have proved themselves superior to their Argentine opponents, but, as continuing Argentine air raids and resupply missions illustrated, they had not established what was generally acknowledged to be air superiority. As the Director of Naval Air Warfare, Bathurst felt he had a duty to point this out.

'As your Air Adviser, sir,' he told the First Sea Lord, 'I have to say that we haven't got air superiority.'

'Bugger off,' replied Sir Henry Leach.

In the shadow-boxing that had followed the opening days' aerial combat, the AN/TPS-43 radar operators of Vigilancia y Control Aéreo Grupo 2 could do little more than track the Harriers coming in at altitude, patrolling their CAP stations then returning to the carriers. Always out of range of the air defences around BAM Malvinas.

Keeping a close eye on the Harriers at least meant they could help the near daily C-130 resupply flights from the mainland thread their way in and out of the airfield without unwelcome attention. Similarly, if their fast jet counterparts faced the possibility of interception from the Sea Harrier CAP, they could be warned and turned back rather than press on and risk attracting a Nine Lima for their trouble.

But following the retirement of the SP-2H Neptunes the Armada Argentina had been looking for another way to guide 2 Escuadrilla's Super Etendards and their Exocets towards their targets. After unsuccessful trials with the S-2 Trackers, attention had turned to the possibility of using the AN/TPS-43 radar at Puerto Argentino to pinpoint the position of the British carriers.

Naval radar controllers on the islands were ordered to begin analysing the movements of the Harriers. Helped along by the Fleet Air Arm's liberal application of WD-40, they plotted the positions of the British jets at the moment they were detected on radar and at the point they disappeared. With enough data it was possible to make an educated guess as to where the British carriers might be. And while the British pilots, aware of the danger, were directed to ingress and egress from the carrier at low level for 50 miles before climbing to height over the islands, the SHAR's endurance meant that the potential for deception was limited. As long as the Fleet Air Arm continued to launch and recover CAP pairs at half-hour intervals it was possible to triangulate a reasonably accurate position for at least one of the carriers.

At Río Grande, the Super Etendard crews received the frequent updates with growing confidence. After an enforced hiatus, Jorge Colombo's men appeared to be back in business. With the radar plots from Puerto Argentino they could pinpoint the British carriers with sufficient accuracy to get close enough to launch their missiles without detection.

They were dangerous again.

As the ships of the Amphibious Task Group converged on Woodward's Battle Group, on *Atlantic Conveyor* the covers came off the Sea Harriers and GR.3s. In the small hours of 18 May, as jets sat on deck ready to fly off to the carriers later in the day, Mike Layard ordered the ship to Action Stations to rehearse the ship's response to an air attack. Zipped up in his immersion suit, Al Craig couldn't shake the wretched sight of the ship's Chinese laundrymen mustered in the anti-flash hoods and gloves issued to every warship's crew to protect any exposed flesh from burns, and yet otherwise dressed only in shorts and T-shirts.

At the CIA headquarters in Langley, Virginia, a top-secret briefing paper produced for the organization's Director, William J. Casey, reported that 'The British appear to be positioning their forces to mount significant ground operations against the Falklands some time this week.' Outnumbered more than two to one, with up to sixty Argentine fast jets mounting aggressive attacks to try to stop them, any British assault against East Falkland, it concluded, 'would be a high-risk venture'.

'The two British carriers,' it went on to note, 'would be particularly attractive targets.'

There was no mention of the ship now considered to be a third carrier.

# PART THREE

La Muerte Negra

# PART THREE

*Engage the enemy more closely.*

Signal hoisted by Admiral Lord Nelson
at the Battle of Trafalgar, 1805

# THIRTY-SEVEN

## This heaving monster

THE AIR WAS gin clear. Visibility good for 10 miles or more across a weak blue sky streaked with a few wisps of low, thin cloud. The northwesterly wind was scarcely breathing. The sea that had battered them a few days earlier now barely lapped at *Conveyor*'s dark hull as she slipped through the cold swell. A battle-worn HMS *Hermes* steamed three or four cables to starboard, her grey hull streaked with rust. The carrier's lines were broken by aircraft and stores on deck, aerials, masts, radar and the vast steel ski-jump rising from the bow like some industrial revolution feat of engineering.

Perhaps it was the sight of his new home that Steve Brown, in the cockpit of a Sea Harrier for the first time since landing at Ascension Island nearly three weeks earlier, found distracting, daunting even, as he carried out his engine checks in preparation for a Green 90 vertical take-off and a short hop to *Hermes*. He glanced at the rpm dial tucked in at the left of the instrument panel: 27%. With the nozzles set at 40° he advanced the throttle and, eyes glued on the rpm, timed the needle's progress to 55%. Just over four seconds later, and satisfied that the engine was accelerating as required, he throttled back.

Then he slammed the throttle wide open.

From *Conveyor*'s bridge, Tim Gedge looked on in horror. He had a microphone in his hand with which to pass instructions to each departing pilot, but the 809 pilot's launch was going south faster than he could possibly intervene. The SHAR lurched forward and upwards across the deck, the dorsal fin beneath the tail on a collision course with the guardrail running along the side of the pad.

After completing his engine acceleration checks, Brown had

failed to then set the engine nozzles at 90° ready for a vertical take-off. Realizing his mistake, his first instinct was to pull back on the stick, but this only exacerbated the situation. As the nose rotated skywards, the tail looked certain to clip the guardrails. He pushed forward on the stick to try to correct the jet's attitude. The nose flopped down over the side of the ship without hitting it.

*That's the end of the aeroplane*, thought Gedge as he watched Brown's SHAR drop towards the sea. But then Brown, thinking quickly, managed to arrest his descent by rotating the nozzles and riding the full 21,500lb of thrust from the Pegasus engine. In his lightly fuelled jet it was enough. Through a cloud of steam and spray the SHAR slowly hover-taxied away from the ship, carving a deep furrow of white water and swarming mist in its wake. Half a mile on Brown managed to haul his way into the air, gaining height and speed before disappearing out of sight.

But after the relief of watching his pilot save himself and his aircraft the 809 boss now faced a fresh anxiety: Brown's fuel state. None of the jets had been loaded with more fuel than they needed for the short flight to *Hermes*. And as Gedge watched the SHAR disappear over the horizon he considered his next move.

*What on earth do I say?* he wondered. *'Come back, all is forgiven!' perhaps?*

Standing alongside him on the bridge, Mike Layard and Ian North had watched Brown's narrow escape with bated breath. As the 809 SHAR finally climbed away to safety a wry smile played out across the bearded face of *Conveyor*'s Master.

'That's a novel way of doing it . . .' he said.

After making a safe landing aboard *Hermes*, a still-shaken Steve Brown shut down his engine just after 1300Z and climbed out of the cockpit. Two hours later, the three other 809 SHARs destined for the flagship had followed without incident. Apart from the fact that the ship's Captain seemed to take an instant dislike to the appearance of the ghostly grey Phoenix Squadron jets. As welcome as their arrival was, ranged next to the darker 800 Squadron machines against the dull expanse of the flight deck, 809's immaculate-looking new jump jets seemed altogether too pale and conspicuous for Lyn

Middleton's liking. And instead of red, their low-visibility insignia appeared to be painted in a shade of *pink*. The lo-vis markings stayed, but the phoenix logo on the tail wouldn't last long as the four new fighters were assimilated into the *Hermes* air group.

Bill Covington and Hugh Slade jumped down on to the crowded carrier deck and were greeted warmly by Des Hughes, 800's Ops Officer. A hive of activity, piled high with ordnance and stores wherever space could be found among the aircraft, it reminded Slade of Wide-awake airfield on Ascension, but even more cramped and overrun.

They made their way into the ship's island and through narrow passages beneath a vascular system of pipes and bundled cables that ran along the ceiling to the SHAR crewroom. The welcome was warm, but both were shocked by the strained appearance of the 800 and 899 pilots already on board. Unshaven and red-eyed, many of them looked exhausted. It wasn't hard to understand why.

For three weeks now, they and their counterparts aboard *Invincible* had maintained a continuous alert, ready to be scrambled at any time of day or night. It wasn't unusual to plan, fly and debrief three sorties a day. And *Hermes* had carried the lion's share of the ground attack burden alongside providing air defence. Denied cabin space below the waterline, a good night's sleep was hard to come by, and pilots, dressed in flightsuits and immersion suits, were asleep in chairs in the crewroom. Covington had never been in an environment that so seemed to bleed tension. And he was struck by the reality of his situation: it was the responsibility of this small band of SHAR pilots he had now joined to protect the Battle Group *whatever the cost*.

For weeks the 800 Squadron crews had been flying long hours, at great personal risk, driven by adrenalin and shared purpose. They'd lost friends, though. And there was every possibility that they would lose more. No longer was their first priority, as it was in peacetime, the safety of the aircraft, but to provide the first line of defence against a determined enemy. For all the evident stress and fatigue, though, the can-do attitude on display was unmissable. No less was expected of 809, nor was that unwelcome.

*We're being thrown into battle*, thought Covington, for the first time properly appreciating what that meant. And then, after a series of intelligence briefings, the four of them were told to saddle up. The best way to shake off the ring rust was to go flying. While John Leeming looked forward to launching himself off the deck of a ship he'd admiringly described as *this heaving monster* with Hugh Slade, Steve Brown was paired with Covington.

Peter Squire was the first of the GR.3 pilots to land on, bouncing down on to *Hermes'* deck at 1630Z. Three more RAF jets followed, flown by Jerry Pook, John Rochfort and Pete Harris, the squatter-looking, camouflaged RAF jets immediately distinctive alongside the Sea Harriers. Bob Iveson and Jeff Glover were ferried across to the carrier by helicopter along with nine of the squadron's engineering team and flyaway packs of spares. After suffering last-minute technical glitches, the remaining two 1(F) jets stayed aboard *Conveyor* and would join the carrier over the next couple of days once engineers had rectified a couple of minor unserviceabilities.

Before being taken to the 800 Squadron crewroom his men were expected to share with the SHAR pilots, Squire was introduced to Lyn Middleton.

'Right,' began the ship's Captain, after despatching an efficient greeting, 'we've got to get you briefed up so that we can get you flying.'

On the face of it, the welcome afforded the RAF reinforcements to the Harrier force was similar to what had greeted the 809 pilots: a swift induction followed by an immediate effort to launch them on an in-theatre training flight. The logic was perhaps sound enough. The sooner they were comfortable flying on and off the deck, the sooner they'd become a useful component of the air campaign.

The trouble was that when the briefing for the 1(F) pilots began as scheduled, only Squire was aboard the ship and able to attend. Jerry Pook joined them half an hour later. It was, supposedly, a good briefing, clear and to the point. But, with the launch of the GR.3s already scheduled, no one other than Squire and Pook caught more than five minutes of it.

Led by Bill Covington, Tartan Flight's two Sea Harriers launched from the deck that afternoon. For his number two, Steve Brown, a familiarization flight, a little air interception training and radio drill followed by a carrier-controlled landing was a chance to settle his nerves after his near disaster taking off from *Conveyor*.

Brown and John Leeming had been thrown in at the deep end when they'd arrived at Yeovilton from RAF Gütersloh a month earlier and had been operating at capacity ever since. Any fast jet pilot learning to fly a new aeroplane in a new role was used to a steep learning curve. It was how it was done. But ten days just wasn't close to being enough for either of them to feel they were really on top of it.

Covington felt it too. Flying from a carrier deck was familiar enough to him but, fresh out of the cockpit of a US Marine Corps AV-8A, he couldn't help but wish he was going to war with a tour on a frontline SHAR squadron under his belt so that he really knew the jet and its systems inside out.

Covington kept a close eye on his RAF colleague. Brown was still desperately unfamiliar with the SHAR's radar and NAVHARS system, and the last thing he needed was to find himself alone over the South Atlantic and unable to find his way home to Mother.

As Tartan Leader shepherded his wingman back to *Hermes*, the other more recent RAF arrivals on board were being treated with rather less care.

With the briefing over, irrespective of how much anyone had actually heard, Squire and his two Flight Commanders, Iveson and Pook, were ordered into the air, their scheduled take-off time just before sunset. Squire resisted, explaining to Wings (the ship's Commander Air) that FINRAE, the kit they needed to align the GR.3's inertial navigation at sea, was still aboard *Conveyor*. If they took off, they'd be flying without the head-up display using nothing but standby instruments. None of them had ever carried out a ski-jump launch at sea. And none had ever landed aboard a carrier at night with or without a working HUD. Wings agreed. Relieved, the three Harrier pilots had pulled themselves out of their immersion suits when word arrived that the Captain had insisted they get airborne.

Like condemned men they strapped into the cockpits of the jets and waited for the order to launch. As darkness fell, Squire asked Flyco if the launch was still on.

'Standby,' came the reply, without further elaboration.

Now seriously worried about the prospect of launching, Squire rebriefed the sortie over the RT. He kept it short: 'We'll get airborne, dump fuel, and come round for a carrier-controlled approach.'

It was pitch black when, half an hour later, Wings finally persuaded the Captain to let him stand them down.

Squire was in no doubt at all that Middleton was just imposing himself – showing them who was boss. And that evening, John Locke, the ship's Commander and Middleton's second-in-command, invited the 1(F) Squadron boss to his cabin for a more informal introduction to the ship. After pouring him a whisky, Locke told him that *Hermes* was not an especially happy ship.

'The Captain has three battles,' he said. 'He fights the Admiral's staff, he fights the ship's staff and he fights the Argentinians; and he does it in that order.' And he made it clear that Middleton was not overly enamoured with the arrival of the RAF aboard his carrier. While 1(F) offered welcome additional firepower, their unfamiliarity with shipboard operations added weight to the considerable burden the Captain already shouldered. He was keenly aware of the critical importance of *Hermes* to the successful outcome of the campaign. Responsibility for keeping her safe from both air and submarine attack lay with him. And unlike JJ Black, his counterpart aboard *Invincible*, he had to do it with Sandy Woodward – *also* unfamiliar with carrier operations – breathing down his neck. As if that weren't enough, his twenty-year-old son Ray was also in harm's way, serving as a Lynx pilot aboard *Broadsword*. 'You should expect,' Locke warned Squire, 'a very difficult time.'

But if there were understandable reasons for Middleton's abrasive manner, this wasn't of much comfort to the newly arrived RAF squadron boss. While Squire might still enjoy administrative control over his squadron, he realized that with his arrival on board all operational control now lay with the ship's Captain.

It was a sobering thought.

After settling his bar bill in the *Atlantic Conveyor* Officers' Lounge, Tim Gedge had said his farewells to Mike Layard and Ian North, thanking them and the Navy and Merchant Marine crews who'd looked after him and his squadron so well, before strapping into the cockpit of ZA190.

Squire, Iveson and Pook were all on deck when Gedge dropped on to *Hermes'* deck at dusk, expecting to stay for the night, refuel, then fly on to *Invincible* the next day. But as he pulled back the canopy, one of the ship's company attached a ladder, climbed up and handed him a note telling him to stay in the aeroplane. They were sending him on to *Invincible* right away.

With darkness imminent, he felt a stab of apprehension. While he might have been a little rusty, night flying in and of itself held no fear. What concerned him was the prospect of approaching a heavily defended aircraft carrier at war, in the dark, while observing proper RT discipline, without any prior briefing on the procedures he was expected to follow. What height should he fly? Too high and the Argentine radar would pick him up. Too low and *Invincible* might gun him down. Should he turn on his navigation lights?

He was handed a piece of paper with a callsign and some lat/long coordinates which he fed into the NAVHARS. At 2042Z he launched into the night for the twenty-minute flight to JJ Black's ship.

A reasonably leisurely approach at 5,000 feet felt as if it was pretty unthreatening. He turned on all the lights and thumbed the RT button on the stick. After addressing the ship by its callsign he announced himself: 'This is Phoenix Leader.'

His call appeared to cause undue consternation. Unknown to Gedge, Phoenix seemed to be a codeword that signalled disaster of some sort. Or triumph. Something significant at least. But after a brief RT interrogation he was recognized as the CO of the reinforcement squadron and was welcomed aboard by JJ Black.

After the Exocet attack on the *Sheffield*, the Captain had taken to wearing a flightsuit, acquired from the carrier's air group. Unlike the official-issue action working dress, it wouldn't burn and stick to the flesh in the event of fire. His ship was also playing a more front-footed role in the effort to try to meet the missile threat from Argentina.

Unknown to Gedge, *Invincible* had just returned to the Battle Group following a twenty-four-hour high-speed dash south of the islands to a position around 150 miles west to launch a covert mission against the Argentine mainland.

# THIRTY-EIGHT

## The untamed wilds of Borneo

BRAVE, AL CRAIG and Dave Austin cross-decked from *Conveyor* to *Invincible* soon after dawn the following morning, bringing the total complement of SHARs on board to ten. Sharing the deck and hangar space of the smaller of the two Task Force carriers were nine Sea Kings and the new Exocet decoy Lynx. But there was one aircraft unaccounted for.

While 809's new arrivals were welcomed aboard, three of their Fleet Air Arm comrades were looking forward to another day bivouacked under ponchos in Patagonia. After ten hours of slow progress across difficult, rising terrain strewn with fallen trees they'd barely managed to put a couple of miles between them and the burned-out wreck of their aircraft – all that was left of the Westland Sea King HC.4 helicopter in which they'd made a difficult rolling take-off from the deck of *Invincible* a little over twenty-four hours earlier.

Royal Marine Major Richard Hutchings, his co-pilot and navigator Lieutenant Commander 'Wiggy' Bennett and their aircrewman Pete Imrie were 'Junglies'. The badge of honour worn by the Navy's Commando squadrons – 845, 846 and, aboard *Atlantic Conveyor*, the newly re-formed 848 – was hard won.

During Operation MUSKETEER, the politically disastrous British and French intervention at Suez in 1956, the Navy had pioneered the use of helicopters to mount a large-scale amphibious assault from carriers at sea, but it was in the untamed wilds of Borneo where the Junglies had earned their spurs. Between 1962 and 1966 they deployed to the Far East, operating from remote jungle clearings in support of British and Commonwealth troops defending Malaysia against Indonesian aggression. The most challenging flying was often required by the SAS who from 1964 began mounting covert cross-border operations behind enemy lines.

As the relationship between the Junglies and the SAS was forged, so it continued in 1982 with Operation PLUM DUFF, a one-way mission to insert an eight-man reconnaissance team from B Squadron SAS into Argentina.

846's Sea King HC.4s had been the only machines for the job. A simpler, more rugged variant of Westland's big anti-submarine helicopter, it had the capacity to carry nearly thirty troops over 300 miles. Stripped of all non-essential items, from the winch and flotation gear to seats and even soundproofing, Hutchings's HC.4, Victor Charlie, was capable of carrying the eight SAS troopers considerably further. Any possibility of a return to the carrier was quickly discounted, but the margins for the PLUM DUFF mission remained fine. And when things started to go wrong, the problems seemed to accumulate with alarming rapidity.

After a three-and-a-half-hour flight into fierce headwinds and an unplanned diversion around an uncharted offshore gasfield, followed by thick fog as they coasted in 15 miles north of their expected landfall, the mood aboard Victor Charlie was uneasy. Unable to see in any direction, Hutchings was forced to climb out to sea before trying again to find a path through the fog. But 14 miles from the planned drop-off he and Bennett had to accept that they could feel their way no further through skies their night vision goggles couldn't penetrate. Flaring gently, Hutchings put the Sea King down on the pampas.

During the loop out to sea they'd seen lights flicker through the cloud. Now on the ground, their machine still loudly turning and burning, there were other unidentifiable lights shimmering through the darkness. In the co-pilot's seat, Bennett couldn't shake the feeling: *we're not alone*.

Unable to confirm their position, ill served by maps and fearing compromise, the SAS Troop Commander, Andy Legg, took the difficult decision to abandon the drop-off and make for the emergency drop-off. 'I'm not aborting the mission,' he told them. 'If you can just drop us fifteen miles inside Chile it'll be fine.'

'I'll do my best,' replied Hutchings before pulling on the collective to initiate a full power climb.

If Legg could lead Six Troop back into Argentina to the target on foot, PLUM DUFF might yet deliver the intelligence required for an SAS spectacular inspired by a remarkable Special Forces mission six years earlier.

On 27 June 1976, Air France Flight 139 was en route from Tel Aviv to Paris via Greece when, during the final leg of its journey, it was hijacked by terrorists. After refuelling in Libya, the Airbus A300 was flown on to Entebbe International Airport in Uganda. Five days later a flight of four Israeli C-130s landed at Entebbe just after midnight. On board was an assault force of commandos tasked with rescuing the hostages from the terminal building where they were being held. By the time the last of the 131 Squadron C-130s took off again after a ruthlessly efficient hour and a half on the ground, 102 freed hostages were already on their way to Nairobi aboard the other three aircraft. Codenamed THUNDERBOLT, the audacious operation was a stunning success for Israel's elite Sayeret Matkal special forces unit. Set up in the late 1950s, they had looked to the SAS when choosing their motto: Who Dares Wins.

Now SAS commanders in Hereford and London saw their Israeli counterparts' raid on Entebbe as a touchstone for their own ambitious plans to remove the Exocet threat to the Task Force at source.

To prevent any possible interception of the escaping Israeli C-130s by the Ugandan Air Force, the Sayeret Matkal had destroyed four MiG-17s and seven MiG-21s on the ground at Entebbe. The Armada's Super Etendards forward-deployed to Río Grande seemed ripe for the same treatment. Just as a small recce team had been put ashore ahead of the D Squadron raid on Pebble Island, PLUM DUFF was designed to pave the way for a full squadron-strength assault on the Argentine naval air station in Tierra del Fuego, codenamed Operation MIKADO.

The plan was for B Squadron to fly in to Río Grande beneath the radar to deliver a devastating *coup de main* against Jorge Colombo's SuE squadron.

They were known simply as 'The Flight'. Throughout April, the 47 Squadron aircrew who made up the RAF's Special Forces Flight had flown a series of exercises dubbed PURPLE DRAGON to test their ability to fly undetected into an unlit, well-defended airfield. They staged air-land sorties against RAF Marham in Norfolk, St Mawgan in Cornwall, Kinloss in Morayshire and Binbrook in Lincolnshire. But the results were always the same. At Kinloss they were picked up on radar 25 miles out as they crested the Great Glen. Approaching Binbrook at a height that was, thought one of the aircrew, *stupidly and ridiculously low*, they'd got closer, but not close enough to land and deplane an SAS Sabre Squadron before being shot out of the sky. And, because Binbrook sat on rising ground, they'd been able to come in *below* the level of the runway. The airfield at Río Grande was just 60 feet above sea level. Were it even possible to entertain it, a long approach at an altitude of just 20 feet would still have been too high.

Unlike Entebbe International Airport, Río Grande was home to one of Argentina's powerful Westinghouse AN/TPS-43 three-dimensional search radar and batteries of radar-laid 20mm Rheinmetall anti-aircraft cannon, six 40mm zero-elevation Bofors gun emplacements and four 30mm Hispano-Suiza cannon.

Capitán de Navío Miguel Pita, the Argentine Marine officer responsible for the air station's defence, was dismissive of any possibility that the British might attack. The notion that they could succeed in staging an Entebbe-style attack against Río Grande was, he thought, *mad*.

Prior even to making landfall, Victor Charlie had been detected on radar by ARA *Hipolito Bouchard*, an Argentine destroyer which, since the sinking of the *Belgrano*, had been patrolling north of Río Grande inside the 12-mile limit of Argentina's territorial waters. After trying and failing to make radio contact she reported the detection to controllers at Río Grande. Half an hour later, as the British helicopter climbed away to the west towards the emergency drop-off point in Chile, she was picked up and tracked by the AN/TPS-43 radar at Río Grande.

The crew of Victor Charlie knew it too. For the next five minutes they flew west with their hearts in their mouths, waiting for their hand-held Omega radar warning receiver to announce, with a change in tone from the rhythmic pulse of the search radar to a harsh electronic howl, their illumination by a fire control radar.

*A noise you do not want to hear when over enemy territory*, thought Bennett. As a precaution, Pete Imrie threw buckets of chaff out of the cabin door of the cab.

With no improvement in the weather, it was impossible to put down through cloud at the emergency drop-off. Six Troop had no option but to stay on board while Hutchings and Bennett beat west-northwest at 3,000 feet until, once clear of mountains that straddled the border, they could descend in safety over the open water of Bahía Inútil – Useless Bay – on the eastern side of the Magellan Straits.

Legg's men finally jumped down from the cabin door of the Sea King on to the saturated ground beneath. Before leaving them to continue their mission alone, Bennett conferred with their CO, pointing out their position to Legg on an old 1940s map, before pushing the map, which extended no further west, into his hand.

In return, Legg gave Hutchings's crew two high-explosive demolition charges. When the time came to abandon the helicopter, they would help in her destruction.

Weighed down with ammunition and at least 140 miles from Río Grande, Six Troop's prospects looked bleak. It was five o'clock in the morning local time. Tabbing east through the darkness with horizontal sleet and rain driving at their backs they calculated it would take them two and a half days even to get to the border with Argentina. They had food for four.

They heard the whine and thump from Victor Charlie disappear into the darkness behind them.

Three-quarters of an hour later, Hutchings landed on a secluded beach 11 miles south of Punta Arenas. While Victor Charlie's Captain remained at the controls, Bennett and Imrie set about punching holes in the aircraft's hull using survival knives and hand axes. The Sea King's boat-shaped hull was designed to allow water landings, but if they could add enough perforation, and if Hutchings could, after taking her out to deeper water, by rocking her from side to side get her to take on sea water, they expected her to sink while her pilot made his escape, pulled to safety by his crewmates on a 200-foot line. But it wasn't to be. After his crew had done their worst,

Hutchings hover-taxied out a short distance to sea, but try as he might he couldn't provoke her to start shipping water.

He returned to the beach, but dazzled by the amplified flash of the low-fuel warning light through his NVGs he came in blind, smashing the port undercarriage and pitching to the side. With the main rotor blades chewing up the sand dunes he shut down the engines and applied the rotor brake. Victor Charlie's mission was over.

After smashing the NVGs with rocks and throwing the pieces out to sea, they drained the remaining fuel from the tanks, poured petrol throughout the cabin and placed the two charges gifted by Six Troop. Hutchings lit a distress flare and threw it into the aircraft. He threw a second into the AVTAG fuel pooled beneath her. And with the blameless helicopter burning fiercely in their wake, Victor Charlie's crew headed for the hills with orders to try to avoid capture for a minimum of eight days.

They would not find out until 25 May – when, after sleeping rough for a week, they walked into Punta Arenas and were picked up by Chile's paramilitary police, the Carabineros – that Operation MIKADO had not taken place.

The following night, Andy Legg's exhausted patrol was finally picked up after making contact with another covert SAS team sent to Tierra del Fuego to find them. Three days later they were exfiltrated to a safe house in Santiago and told to await further orders.

Photos of Río Grande snatched by an ad-hoc SAS operation out of Punta Arenas using a borrowed FACh Huey helo and a standard SLR camera did little to dampen Hereford's enthusiasm for the planned air-land assault. In reality, though, it was in turnaround, postponed indefinitely. No one was more relieved than the pilots of 47 Squadron's Special Forces Flight who, as they continued to train for the mission through May, were so concerned about the lack of intelligence about what awaited them in South America that they signalled CINCFLEET at Northwood directly.

With the failure of the proposed SAS assault against the mainland, the Exocet remained as much of a threat as ever, while protection of the Task Force remained firmly in its own hands, aided by any early warning that could be provided by the radar surveillance operation in southern Chile set up by Sidney Edwards.

Since 17 May, the RAF-led effort had been augmented by flash signals from HMS *Valiant*, a nuclear-powered hunter-killer submarine now patrolling off the coast of Tierra del Fuego and observing the launch of strike packages from Río Grande through her periscope. The job of actually stopping them still fell to the Sea Harriers, and the Sea Dart and Seawolf missiles.

Yet on 19 May, when the reinforcements from *Atlantic Conveyor* were finally drawn in to the fleet's defence, it turned out not to be Tim Gedge's 809 Squadron SHARs but the Harrier GR.3s of 1(F) Squadron RAF that got the call.

At 1145Z, Peter Squire and Jeff Glover launched in quick succession from the deck of *Hermes*. Green Leader and Green Two – the boss and the least experienced of the pilots Squire had elected to take with him to the South Atlantic. Ahead of them, following their first ski-jump launch at sea, a routine air combat training mission. Although not expected to encounter the enemy, both jets carried live AIM-9G Sidewinders beneath the wings. Arming the jets proved to have been a sensible decision when, after one of the Escuadrón II Boeing 707s was picked up flying south from Buenos Aires towards the Task Force, Squire and Glover were vectored to meet it.

Green Formation climbed through a dusting of cirrus cloud to 30,000 feet towards the northeast with instructions to do no more than shadow and deter. That was optimistic given the challenges faced by the two RAF pilots.

At a distance of 150 miles Squire and Glover lost radio contact with the ship. And with neither direction from a Fighter Controller nor the Blue Fox radar carried by the SHARs, they didn't have a hope of finding the Burglar. Nor, without FINRAE, did they have any navigational aids other than a stopwatch and a compass.

After they'd recovered to *Hermes* a decision was made to place the air defence task in the sole hands of the now twenty-five-strong Sea Harrier force. The GR.3s, meanwhile, were to be dedicated to the ground attack role they were designed for and for which their pilots had trained.

Once again, though, the 707 had escaped close attention from the British air defences. At the same time, with the Fuerza Aérea Argentina considering the feasibility of arming both the long-range 707 and C-130 with Exocets, and in the case of the latter fitting multiple ejector racks beneath the wings capable of carrying up to twelve 250kg bombs, the need to do more than simply 'shadow and deter' was becoming more pressing.

As the day closed, there was no news aboard *Invincible* from the crew of Victor Charlie. Signals were sent home to Northwood. At Yeovilton, visits to the Sea King crew's next of kin would have to be arranged. Missing, presumed alive, at least.

JJ Black had been concerned about Operation PLUM DUFF from the outset. He'd enquired of Andy Legg about the targeting information, only to be shown a 1:100,000 scale map of Argentina that had once been part of the Cambridge University Library's collection. It had been printed in 1943 and was based on surveys conducted in 1931.

But uncertainty about the fate of the crew of Victor Charlie and their cargo was soon overtaken by the news from *Hermes* that another 846 Squadron Sea King loaded with men from G and D Squadron SAS had ditched in appalling weather. Of the thirty men on board there were only nine survivors. The Regiment had been cross-decking from the flagship to HMS *Intrepid* in anticipation of the move ashore. The tragedy cast a pall over the arrival of the Amphibious Task Group but could not be allowed to interfere with the final preparations for Operation SUTTON.

That evening, JJ Black spoke to his ship's company over the broadcast. 'The landing we've all been building up for,' he told them, 'will take place before dawn on the twenty-first of May.' Before urging them to continue to stay sharp and give of their best, he outlined details of the plan to land at Port San Carlos.

D-Day was fixed for the day after tomorrow.

A few hours earlier, Alberto Philippi had landed on Runway 26 at Base Contraalmirante Quijada, the naval air station at Río Grande, taxied in to the hardstanding where he parked the A-4Q alongside his wingman, Teniente de Navío Félix Medici, and shut down the J65 engine. There was much to discuss at the debriefing. Since 15 May, the 3 Escuadrilla Skyhawks had maintained a round-the-clock alert, each armed with four Mk.82 Snake Eye bombs. Today, Philippi and Medici had flown a training mission in the company of one of the 2 Escuadrilla Super Etendards, flown by their friend Roberto Curilovic, himself a former A-4Q pilot. The mixed formation of heavily armed Skyhawks led by the SuE with its state-of-the-art navigation and attack computer had the potential to offer a powerful new dimension to COAN anti-ship operations.

Philippi, Medici and Curilovic continued their conversation over dinner in the mess.

# THIRTY-NINE

## Diligence and rebellion

AL CRAIG COULDN'T help but feel a little sorry for Tim Gedge. The former Buccaneer pilot thought the 809 CO had proved to be a superb boss over the short time he'd had to prepare the new squadron. By the time they'd flown out from Yeovilton, three weeks after being conjured from nothing, they'd felt like a unit. That camaraderie had only deepened aboard *Atlantic Conveyor*. But with the splitting up of the squadron between *Hermes* and *Invincible* the esprit de corps that Gedge had tried so hard to foster was hard to hold on to.

And Sharkey Ward's insistence that there could be only one SHAR squadron aboard *Invincible*, and only one SHAR squadron CO, didn't make it any easier. On board *Hermes*, after an appeal from Neill Thomas, Lyn Middleton had agreed to recognize 899 Squadron as a separate entity. On board *Invincible*, Sharkey explained to Gedge, while he would be afforded the status and courtesy due the boss of a naval air squadron while off duty, and would attend the Command briefings, 809 would be subsumed within 801. Aboard the smaller carrier, with just ten Sea Harriers embarked instead of the twenty-one jump jets now sprawled around *Hermes*, it made more sense. But there were limits.

'Your aircraft are the wrong colour,' Ward told him, 'they'll have to be repainted.'

'I think ours are the right colour,' Gedge needled gently, explaining the provenance of the paler camouflage, 'and that *yours* are wrong.'

In the end, the carefully calculated shade of Barley Grey developed by Farnborough would stay, but, as aboard *Hermes*, the phoenix badges on the SHAR's fins were soon covered up.

Gedge had expected as much. He and Ward were chalk and cheese. Beyond the piercing blue eyes both men possessed there seemed to be little more in common. Ward, the self-styled maverick, thrived on strong opinions and a hard-charging, damn-the-torpedoes approach to leadership. Gedge may have been a more self-contained, less obvious character, but it was he whom the Navy had entrusted with the first frontline Sea Harrier squadron and who'd earned newspaper headlines for humbling the USAF's new dogfighter extraordinaire, the F-16. And it was Gedge who, in less than a month, had raised a second SHAR squadron from scratch. Whether Sharkey liked it or not he was determined to keep the 809 flame burning.

While he took a phlegmatic approach to 809's sublimation within 801 in public, privately Gedge continued to record his squadron's activity as a discrete operation as best he could – a place where diligence and rebellion intersected. 'From this week,' he noted on 20 May, 'the diary covers the 801 (*Invincible*) detachment of the squadron.' Though unable to detail the movements of Covington, Slade, Leeming and Brown aboard *Hermes*, he was meticulous in keeping up to date the Fair Flying Log for the Phoenix Squadron pilots embarked on *Invincible*, all of whom continued to wear the 809 Squadron wings on their flying suits with pride.

Thick cloud settled like smoke just 200 feet above the sea. As *Invincible* steamed south of the islands in a feint to divert attention from the amphibious forces gathering around the northeast coast, the new SHAR pilots were briefed by 801's QFI, Mike Broadwater, on every aspect of the squadron's operation, from domestic arrangements and safety equipment to flying procedures. In the end, despite Broadwater's best-laid plans, the weather curtailed his hope of getting all the 809 pilots airborne in the morning.

When, at 1230Z, the ship went to Action Stations, only Gedge and Brave began briefing to fly. 809's two most experienced pilots were launched into the clag as part of Trident Section, a four-ship familiarization and CAP sortie led by 801's Air Warfare Instructor. For most of the sortie they were flying on instruments and couldn't see either each other or anything else. Unable to launch on their own fam flight, Al Craig and Dave Austin were going to have to pick it up on the job.

The weather to the north of the Falklands, where *Hermes* was operating in support of the Amphibious Task Group, was proving a little kinder. But only a little. Tasked with an attack against a fuel dump on West Falkland, the GR.3 pilots wondered whether their first operational mission might get scrubbed as a result.

'Oh, they'll launch you in this,' came the less-than-reassuring reply, 'no problem.'

FINRAE didn't work. Despite the best efforts of the squadron's small, eighteen-man cadre of engineers on the journey south, the trolley developed by Ferranti to align their inertial navigation and attack system wasn't functioning as advertised. Without it, the head-up display and weapons system wouldn't be much help. Instead the 1(F) pilots were going to have to operate using nothing more than standby instruments, the small collection of dials to the bottom left of the instrument panel, and a fixed sight on coaming. Wind, throw, drift and anything else that might have a bearing on the accuracy of their weapons delivery would simply have to be estimated based on instinct and experience.

*We're back to pre-war technology*, thought Bob Iveson. *Even Battle of Britain pilots had moving gunsights.*

To ensure they could at least find their way through the cloud to their let-down point, *Hermes* tasked one of the 800 Squadron SHARs to follow behind, tracking their progress towards the Dolphin Point headland on the eastern side of Falkland Sound.

After briefing, they signed the Form 700s to accept the aircraft and strapped into the cockpits of the jets, their green and grey RAF camouflage an unfamiliar, almost colourful sight on a carrier deck presenting nothing other than shades of grey. Each was armed with 600lb BL755 cluster bombs – one beneath each wing and a third bolted beneath the fuselage between the ADEN gun pods.

Squire launched at 1430Z. Iveson, performing his first short take-off from a carrier deck since his exchange tour with the US Marine Corps, was next. Pook was the last to leave the ski-jump, using his left index finger to punch the undercarriage 'UP' button as he eased the nozzle lever forward. He flicked the flap lever to clean up the wings before, settled into wingborne flight, he followed Green Leader and Green Two into the gloom. They were careful to keep their speed below 250 knots to avoid provoking any unwelcome attention from HMS *Brilliant*'s Seawolf missile operators.

Neill Thomas got airborne in a Sea Harrier a few minutes after the 1(F) Squadron section. A terse RT transmission on the ATC frequency let them know he was on his way. And after staying low and slow for fifteen minutes he pushed the throttle forward, pulled the nose up and accelerated into the smothering cloud. Cruising west at 30,000 feet, he swept the skies ahead with his Blue Fox radar until the three Harriers appeared glowing brilliant orange on the little CRT screen on his instrument panel. He locked on to them and, when the time came, confident that the three radar contacts were where they should be, he thumbed the RT to tell Green Leader his formation's track looked good. He wished them luck and turned back for Mother.

As he led 1(F) Squadron into action for the first time since the Second World War, Peter Squire was struck by the peacefulness of their high-level transit towards the target. With confirmation from the escorting SHAR that all was well, he cut the power and began his descent towards the less-inviting prospect of the low-level ingress towards the target. Flying in a loose arrowhead formation, the three GR.3s dropped through the thick cloud towards the sea. At 1,200 feet they emerged into the clear air beneath it. As they closed up and accelerated over the coast of West Falkland, the distinctive drone of the engine was replaced by the percussive beat and buffeting of the airframe as it bludgeoned its way through the thick, moist air. A mile or so separated them. As well as checking the boss's six, Iveson and Pook covered each other's tails. It was second nature. As they carved into turns, condensation whipped over the top of the jets' little anhedral wings; pale vortices streamed off the tips. The boulder-strewn landscape beneath barely registered as it blurred past. Their focus was on the path ahead. At this speed and altitude it had to be.

From their IP (initial point) at the foot of Mount Sullivan, 5 miles north-northwest of the target, they slipped into escort formation. To complicate the job of the defences, Iveson was going to fly across the target at 30° off Squire's track, before Pook then streaked across on the same heading as the Flight Leader. They ran in at 500 knots, just 50 feet above the gently undulating ground beneath them before climbing to a height of 150 feet for weapons release. Ahead, through the flat armoured glass of the front of the cockpit, Iveson spotted the houses of Fox Bay settlement. And, nearby, he saw the target: 40-gallon oil drums and stacks of jerrycans, dispersed widely to protect them from destruction by any single well-aimed bomb.

*A perfect shape for a cluster bomb pattern*, thought Iveson as he watched Squire make his attack. The 147 bomblets ejected in all directions from each of the formation's nine BL755s would cause a hailstorm of submunitions. Instead of sniper rifles, the GR.3s were hunting with shotguns.

Iveson watched the first of Squire's cluster bombs pepper the target, triggering a chain reaction of secondary explosions before a massive fireball erupted, belching filthy black smoke into the sky. Seconds later he speared across the target, pickling the weapons as he went.

*A good hit*, thought Pook as he watched Green Two streak across his nose from right to left before diving back down to the height of the long grass and out over the water. Pook concentrated on making sure his own attack counted. Bombs gone, he cornered the throttle lever and made for the safety of East Head at the entrance of the bay.

It had been a clinically effective demonstration in offensive air power; well planned, professionally executed, successful. Coming in without warning from the hills, Green Section were in and out, leaving destruction in their wake, before a single shot appeared to have been fired in their target's defence.

Protected by the headland, they turned northeast and climbed back up to high altitude over Falkland Sound, their RWRs beginning to pulse to the sound of a search radar transmitting from Pebble Island.

Squire reported it in the debrief that followed their safe return to *Hermes*.

D Minus One, and it seemed that there was confirmation that the radar that had so preoccupied Sandy Woodward prior to the SAS raid against the island airfield was still operating.

Nothing was going to rub the adrenalin-fuelled smiles off the faces of Squire, Iveson and Pook though. Not yet anyway.

'Sir, not the photo again . . .' complained one of the 3 Escuadrilla pilots. None of them wanted to leave the warmth of the crewroom and head out into the cold and wet. But to a chorus of groans and eye-rolling, Alberto Philippi stuck to his guns.

'Everybody outside,' he insisted, 'the photo is an order!'

It was rare to get the whole squadron together in one place. He felt it was important to capture the moment.

Each wearing a leather flight jacket decorated with an accumulation of unit patches, including the hawk and lightning bolt of the squadron's own badge, the twelve pilots traipsed outside into the drizzle. They lined up in two ranks, some in beanie hats pulled down against the chill. Behind them, the Skyhawks were chocked up along Río Grande flightline. Then, using the little camera Philippi always carried with him, one of the ground crew snapped them smiling.

'Always in the action' went the squadron motto.

And so it would prove.


In Santiago, the British Ambassador, John Heath, was summoned to the Chilean Ministry of Foreign Affairs for an urgent meeting with Foreign Minister René Rojas Galdames. Behind the building's imposing portico and classical facade, Rojas Galdames explained that the burned-out remains of a Royal Navy Sea King helicopter had been found on a beach 18 kilometres south of Punta Arenas. It appeared not to have crashed but to have been deliberately set on fire. Despite an ongoing search there was no sign of the crew. Rojas Galdames said that he would be issuing a statement about the incident later in the day and that he had already informed Argentina.

He handed Heath a formal note of protest about the helicopter. The wreckage clearly indicated 'that British units had entered Chilean territory and violated Chilean sovereignty'.

The words were reproachful, but his eyes told a different story.

And with the diplomatic formalities complete, a broad smile broke out across the face of the Chilean Foreign Minister, leaving

Heath in no doubt at all about how Chile really felt about the intrusion.

'When are you going to invade?' asked Rojas Galdames, laughing.

Nearly 1,500 miles to the southeast, Operation SUTTON was already underway.

# FORTY

## A very odd bunch of individuals

AT 1415Z, THREE-QUARTERS of an hour before midday local time, Mike Clapp's Amphibious Task Group broke away from the carriers to begin their run in to Falkland Sound. Cloaked beneath leaden skies, the convoy steamed in at a steady 12½ knots.

Shared between the assault ships HMS *Fearless* and HMS *Intrepid*, RFA *Stromness* and the cross-Channel ferry MV *Norland* were the spearhead troops of 40 Commando Royal Marines, 2 PARA, 3 PARA and 45 Commando RM. 42 Commando were aboard P&O's flagship SS *Canberra*, while the Royal Fleet Auxiliary *Fort Austin*, MV *Europic Ferry* and the smaller RFA Landing Ships Logistics (LSL) *Galahad, Geraint, Lancelot, Tristram* and *Percivale* brought in the support elements: battlefield helicopters, engineers, artillery and medical facilities. And there were the Rapier missile Fire Units of 12 Air Defence Regiment, Royal Artillery which, once ashore, could augment the protection from air attack provided by the escorting frigates and destroyers, chief among them the two Seawolf-armed Type 22s *Brilliant* and *Broadsword*. Fighter Controllers aboard the guided missile destroyer HMS *Antrim* would be responsible for coordinating the air battle.

With the Argentine Navy confined to territorial waters and the weight of the occupiers' ground defences deployed in and around Port Stanley, it was, as ever, defence against attack from the air that preoccupied the Task Force Commander.

Sandy Woodward's day cabin was located in *Hermes'* island behind the Admiral's Bridge, a short walk from the Flag Operations Room.

Shorn of pictures, comfortable chairs and other creature comforts before he'd joined the ship at Ascension, the cream-painted 9 by 9-foot steel box provided him with a 3-foot-wide desk, a bunk, a wardrobe, a chest of drawers and an upright chair. To the side there was a small shower and head. Exposed pipes and electrical cables were the only other visual distraction. The Admiral was sanguine about the sparseness of his surroundings, though. *Concentrates the mind*, he reckoned, and there were few in the Navy that were sharper. Alone in the confines of his quarters, Woodward put it to work, thinking, processing, calculating, reflecting and making notes, sometimes privately unburdening himself of views that even he regarded as too caustic for wider consumption.

There had been different opinions on how best to protect the ships in Falkland Sound during the landings and the securing of the beachhead. JJ Black had wanted to take the fight to the enemy. Charged with responsibility for leading the air defence of the fleet, *Invincible*'s captain argued that by moving the carriers upthreat he could take out the Argentine raids before they got near the islands. With the two remaining Type 42s, HMS *Sheffield*'s sister ships *Coventry* and *Glasgow*, positioned among the islets west of West Falkland, the Sidewinder-armed Sea Harrier CAP could provide an outer ring of protection, supported by the Sea Dart screen supplied by the destroyers.

To conserve fuel, the Argentine raids cruised in at high level before dropping down low over the islands to make their attacks. Without ingressing at altitude, the Fuerza Aérea Argentina's Daggers simply didn't have the range to be a threat, but scanning for raiders silhouetted against the sky, away from the clutter generated by land and sea, the SHAR's Blue Fox radar started to become a genuinely effective piece of kit. For the same reason Sea Dart became a lethal, dependable proposition.

Furthermore, by reducing the distance between the British carriers and the Amphibious Operations Area – the AOA – Black would be able to guarantee real strength in depth in defence of the landings. Without a long transit from *Hermes* or *Invincible*, SHARs would be able to spend more useful time on CAP before bingo fuel forced them to return to Mother. They'd have combat persistence. And in any engagement with a fuel-starved enemy jet, that offered a clear advantage.

Woodward was tempted. *I can't help feeling I ought to do it*, he thought. But he'd be putting all his eggs in one basket. The plan to push the air defence screen west, he felt, *smacks of all or nothing.*

It wasn't that the Admiral was unwilling to hazard his ships to achieve his objectives.

After arriving at Britannia Royal Naval College in Dartmouth on a scholarship at the age of thirteen, Woodward was marinated in the names and achievements of legendary figures such as Nelson, Hawke, Codrington, Hood, Fisher and Jellicoe. And there was ABC, too.

Operating without air cover during the 1941 evacuation of Crete, Admiral Andrew Browne Cunningham's Mediterranean Fleet suffered terribly at the hands of the Luftwaffe's Junkers Ju 87 Stuka dive-bombers. In response to Army concerns that the loss of ships would force him to abandon the operation, Cunningham replied: 'It takes the Navy three years to build a ship. It will take three hundred years to build a new tradition. The evacuation will continue.'

The Royal Navy had always been prepared to lose ships in pursuit of victory, and Woodward was bloodless about the likelihood that he would sustain losses. But not all ships were equal. Things could go wrong at any time and it was his job to respond; but contained within all the ifs and buts there seemed one irreducible and overriding consideration: the safety of the two carriers.

If he moved them west within unrefuelled range of the land-based Daggers and Skyhawks he was taking a huge risk. *What if they make a really determined effort of, say, fifty aircraft in a major strike?* he asked himself. *What if they are prepared to lose twenty or thirty aircraft in an all-out attempt to sink one of our carriers?* The answer was inescapable. The Argentinians had already shown themselves to be capable of breaching the defences. He had to position the carriers far enough east to protect them. The weather forecast clinched it. A low-pressure centre southeast of Tierra del Fuego brought with it a frontal system extending north as far as Buenos Aires. Behind this, thick cloud would smother the islands, covering the landings until morning. Beyond that, two days of clear skies would have precluded them. But with the forecast improvement in the weather he knew to expect a furious Argentine response.

In the melee that would follow, he knew there was a terrible danger of the SHARs falling prey to his own air defences. To try to avoid the possibility of a tragic blue-on-blue, the solution was straightforward: an imaginary box in the sky above Mike Clapp's AOA, roughly 10 miles across and 10,000 feet high. The Sea Harriers were forbidden to enter under any circumstances. That guaranteed that *any* fast jet inside the box was fair game for the missiles and guns of the warships.

*A bit primitive*, thought Woodward, *but simplicity is the only sensible policy*. When one of his officers suggested that this was not how the Navy normally set up its air defence, the Admiral, after a brief attempt to explain, made his position clear.

'I don't give a damn about your bloody rules,' he said, 'this is how it's going to be done.'

After sunset, a few decks below Woodward's day cabin, the Sea Harrier pilots congregated in the wardroom bar. Two days earlier, the new arrivals from 809 and 1(F) had been excited to be reunited with old friends. Bill Covington and Hugh Slade were back among many of the pilots who'd flown the heavies aboard *Ark* during their own days on the Gannet squadron – experienced operators like Andy Auld, Neill Thomas, Clive Morrell, Fred Frederiksen and Tony Ogilvy. John Leeming and Steve Brown caught up with Dave Morgan, a former squadron mate from Gütersloh, now on exchange with 800 Naval Air Squadron. Although fresh from Sea Harrier training, Morgan still had more hours on the clock than Leeming and Brown. Many knew the 1(F) crews too. The Harrier community was tight-knit. Every single one of the jump jet pilots on board, Fleet Air Arm or RAF, had first been introduced to the aeroplane's unique capabilities on the conversion course at RAF Wittering.

Tonight, though, the Courage CSB ale was flowing a little more slowly. The mood was more subdued as the pilots considered the responsibility heaped on their shoulders. Instead of leaving whirls of smoke from expansive hand gestures, short drags punctuating animated conversation, smokers inhaled a little harder. When, like a church bell ringing in a minute's silence, the BBC's 'Lilliburlero' played over the ship's broadcast to announce the latest World Service report, the words of the MoD's spokesman, Ian McDonald, provoked a little more thoughtfulness and reflection.

In the midst of their earlier happy reunion, Morgan had been struck by what a motley collection they really were. *A very odd bunch of individuals*, he thought, *each with his own particular skills and background but very few with any meaningful experience of fighting the aircraft.* Now, as he contemplated what tomorrow would bring, his deliberations were more pointed. *Which of us*, he wondered, *will survive and who will not be going home?*

Just after 2300Z, HMS *Ardent* sailed past Dolphin Point and on into Falkland Sound. An hour and a half later she was joined by HMS *Antrim*. Forty miles to the northeast, HMS *Glamorgan* steamed close to MacBride Head. All three were to support diversionary operations designed to deceive Argentine commanders into believing the landings were underway somewhere other than San Carlos. Operation TORNADO, the *son et lumière* show of starshells, chaff delta, radio traffic and a series of feints from *Glamorgan*'s Wessex helicopter, suggested Berkeley Sound. *Ardent*'s gunfire, in support of a similarly loud and attention-seeking SAS raid, said Darwin. But *Glamorgan* had been moving up and down the east coast night after night shelling different targets ashore. When the first reports of British activity in San Carlos reached Stanley early on Friday morning, 21 May, it was impossible to be certain that they carried any more significance than any of the other attacks.

*Ardent* and *Antrim* were followed into the Sound by the assault ships, troop carriers and their escort of frigates and destroyers. Sandy Woodward could do little more than wait, and hope that the Amphibious Task Group would succeed in their task. *Fingers crossed*, he thought, aware of the inadequacy of the sentiment.

On board *Hermes*, it seemed people had lowered their voices, as if speaking in whispers might somehow conceal the night's intent from the enemy. But the time for stealth was over.

At 0350Z, as landing craft loaded with Royal Marines and Paras motored into San Carlos Water from the two assault ships, HMS *Antrim*'s twin 4.5-inch guns opened fire, delivering a barrage of 250 high-explosive rounds over the next half hour. Employed constantly since the recapture of South Georgia in April, the grey paint had long ago flaked and peeled off their barrels.

At 0730Z, as Woodward finally retired to his cabin, astonished and grateful that as yet there had been no Argentine response to the landings, 2 PARA hit the beaches. Ten minutes later, as 40 Commando waded ashore at San Carlos settlement, a little to the north of the Paras, the Admiral recorded his surprise in his diary: '0740 – still a deathly hush – extraordinary.'

While elements of 40 Commando pushed out from the settlement to set up a defensive perimeter around their position, others knocked on doors to reassure the residents. As one of the Royal Marines of Naval Party 8901, the small garrison that had tried in vain to forestall the Argentine invasion, was shepherded aboard a C-130 to be flown off the islands, he'd offered a little friendly advice. 'Don't get too comfy, mate,' he'd told the Argentine occupier, 'we'll be back.' Making good on that promise, the Bootnecks ran up the Union Flag on the Falkland Islands for the first time since 1 April.

And on *Hermes*, as the flight deck came alive in preparation to launch the dawn's first Harrier sorties, Sandy Woodward braced himself for D-Day. Win or lose.

*On this day*, he thought, *the Argentinians are going to have to fight.* And, he felt sure, *the Royal Navy will be required to fight its first major action since the end of the Second World War.*

Around the hinterland of San Carlos Water the Royals and Paras consolidated their positions ashore. Above them, instead of a ceiling of low cloud, there was a roof of sparkling stars. Aboard *Brilliant*, darkened since her approach to the Sound, it seemed as if they could see every star in the sky. The weather that had covered their approach had deserted them.

And with *Broadsword* and *Brilliant* defending the AOA in Falkland Sound, the carriers were operating without the goalkeepers that had been such a reassuring presence since the arrival of the Task Force in theatre.

# FORTY-ONE

## Big enough and good enough

IT WAS STILL dark outside when Sharkey Ward stood up in the No. 2 briefing room aboard HMS *Invincible*. In front of him his audience sat, slumped but attentive, in high-backed dark-green leatherette chairs.

It was a year to the day since he'd led 801 aboard the ship for the first time. In the spring of 1981, just five aircraft and seven pilots had embarked south of the Isle of Wight. On that occasion, in the eight days of intensive flying that followed the embarkation the squadron racked up ninety-six sorties. In doing so, an obvious problem, Ward noted in the squadron record book, was aircrew fatigue.

Twelve months on, his expanded squadron, now boosted by the addition of the four pilots from 809 Squadron, would fly twenty-eight sorties before the end of the *day* as well as enduring long periods in the cockpit on deck alert before dawn and after nightfall.

Ward's audience this morning was more grizzled than the fresh-faced squadron of a year earlier. Two of the new arrivals, Dave Braithwaite and Al Craig, had been quick to adopt the shoulder holsters worn by their more battle-worn comrades-in-arms. Neither wore the 801 Squadron patch on the shoulder of his flightsuit, but Craig had at least managed to rustle up a generic Sea Harrier patch. Just in case anyone should be in any doubt.

'Gentlemen,' Ward began, 'as you know, the Amphibious Force is right at this minute setting up the beachhead.' The 801 boss explained that, so far, there had been no reports of any significant opposition. 'But,' he added, 'pretty soon the shit's going to hit the fan and the only things standing between our disembarking troops and disaster are seven of Her Majesty's ships and the Sea Harrier.'

After the Met Officer had briefed the weather, Ward went through the coordinates of the CAP stations, fuel minima, and their use of the radar. By keeping them switched on they'd alert incoming raids to the presence of the waiting SHARs. He wanted to deter the Argentine pilots from even trying to breach the CAP. He reminded them that the 'box' over the AOA was sacrosanct.

'No mistakes, please.'

He acknowledged that, over land, their Blue Fox radars would be incapable of picking up low-flying bogeys. Instead they'd be reliant on Fighter Controllers aboard HMS *Antrim* who would be responsible for directing them towards their targets before they then had to pick them up visually. And Ward wanted his squadron right down on the deck. 'Your patrol height,' he told them, 'is no higher than two hundred and fifty feet above the sea or ground.' Only by staying low, figured Ward, would his pilots give themselves a half-decent chance of catching sight of the Argentine fast jets as they ran in. To maximize their time on station in the thick, cold air he wanted them patrolling at endurance speed. That handed the raiders an advantage, but the SHAR's low-level acceleration was good – at least up to 400 knots or so – and, he reassured them, 'you're big enough and good enough to allow for that'.

Trident Section would launch first at 1030Z, an hour before sunrise. Gold Section would follow an hour later; an hour after that, Silver Section. With a greater complement of aircraft and aircrew, *Hermes* would launch two CAP pairs for every one from *Invincible*. Between them, from dawn till dusk, the two ships would fire a pair of armed SHARs off the deck every twenty minutes. The coordinates of the CAP stations were written on the board, one to the northwest over Pebble Island, another over Swan Island in the middle of the Sound, covering the southern approaches to San Carlos. Ward asked the pilots to note them down.

The Commander of TG 317.0, the Amphibious Force, had wanted six SHARs on three CAP stations framing the AOA. Because of the 130-mile transit between the Carrier Battle Group and San Carlos, that would require another six on deck alert and a further six in transit to and from the carriers. Woodward told him he thought he could keep two Sea Harriers permanently on CAP and surge to four if raids were expected.

By mid-morning on the 21st there would be fourteen SHARs airborne. First blood, though, would be drawn by a pair of 1(F) Squadron GR.3s from *Hermes*, the first of *Atlantic Conveyor*'s brood to make their presence felt.

Dawn broke clear and cold, the front that had smothered the approach of the Amphibious Task Group trailing still blue skies in its wake. On board the ships arrayed in Falkland Sound, the Captains knew they faced a hard day ahead.

It was the anniversary, noted Commander Alan West, Captain of HMS *Ardent*, the first British ship to enter Falkland Sound the previous night, of the Battle of Crete, the Second World War engagement that had seen ABC's Mediterranean Fleet so ravaged by air attack. Forty-one years later, that remained the greatest threat to his own ship's survival.

When he took command of the Type 21 class frigate in 1980, he'd become the youngest frigate captain in the Royal Navy, but he'd already led her into harm's way. As part of the Navy's Armilla Patrol he had escorted oil tankers through the hazardous waters of the Persian Gulf. But his time with his beloved ship was nearly at an end. After commemorating the sacrifice of his ship's predecessor, sunk in Norwegian waters during the Second World War, West had been due to leave *Ardent* on 17 April. When asked by the Navy if he wanted to hand over command before she sailed south, he told them, 'You must be joking.'

West had good reason to expect a torrid time though. His ship's meagre air defences – her Mark 8 4.5-inch gun, an elderly Seacat missile system and a pair of 20mm Oerlikon cannon – were going to struggle to contain the threat from Argentine fast jets. He posted lookouts on the upper deck in the hope of providing a little more warning of imminent attack.

Ten miles to the northwest, *Brilliant* was positioned a quarter of a mile offshore outside the entrance to Many Branch Harbour, the most westerly of the seven destroyers and frigates defending Operation SUTTON. Commissioned in May 1981, she was the most modern frigate in the Navy, and, of all the ships in the British Task Force, only she and her sister ship HMS *Broadsword* were armed with the new and effective short-range Seawolf anti-aircraft missile. Under the pugnacious leadership of her Captain, Commander John Coward, *Brilliant* had been in the thick of the action since the operation to retake South Georgia. He seemed to have approached the war as an opportunity to give the lie to his surname.

Despite the responsibility bestowed on them by their possession of Seawolf, the two Type 22s weren't really air defence assets at all, but sub-hunters. They'd been frustrated in their search for ARA *San Luis* though. Sei whales, southern right whales, sperm whales, humpbacks, even blue whales – it was impossible to tell – had been erroneously identified as a submarine threat. Some of the luckless cetaceans had been torpedoed. Ultimately, Coward was sure that, like a Second World War U-boat, the Argentine diesel-electric submarine was sitting on the sea floor biding her time; but the bottom was also littered with the wrecks of old whaling ships whose metal hulks were indistinguishable from the hull of the submarine. And there weren't enough depth charges to attack them all.

Despite Seawolf's value as a last-ditch weapon, *Brilliant*'s Executive Officer, Lieutenant Commander Laon Hulme, was keenly aware of his ship's limited value in an air war. Although now second-in-command of an anti-submarine frigate, Hulme had trained as a Fighter Controller, specializing in anti-air warfare. He was going to have to follow the progress of the air battle over the Anti-Air Warfare Coordinator radio net, and stew impotently at the foolishness, to his mind, of some of the decisions being made by those responsible for managing the air defence. Despite being harnessed to the carriers in their close-protection, goalkeeping role, *Brilliant*'s 967 radar and missiles were, he bemoaned, *so short-range that we are not really involved in the action.*

With the expected Argentine response to the landings, that was certain to change. After the Seawolf system had glitched during the attack on *Glasgow*, tweaks to the software had been made to help it prioritize targets. Now, with battle looming, the forward missile launcher was on the blink. Following a day spent trying to bring it back on line, it was now deemed to be only 85% effective. Today of all days.

*That's another ten grey hairs*, thought Hulme. Wearing a white roll-neck submariner's sweater, he positioned himself in the ship's

Ops Room alongside the Command and Helicopter displays to better monitor the AAWC.

Jerry Pook was smiling as he tipped the GR.3 into its descent towards the IP at MacBride Head, the most northeasterly point on East Falkland. After checking in with *Fearless*, he'd been told Green Section's services were not required in defence of the beachhead at San Carlos. A last-minute change in tasking before launching from *Hermes* had forced him and his wingman, Mark Hare, to abandon their pre-planned mission in favour of providing close air support to the landings. But with the all-clear from the Amphibious Operations Room the attack on their original target was back on.

From the hidden observation post they would end up occupying for an unbroken twenty-six-day stretch, a four-man team from G Squadron SAS had reported an Argentine Army helicopter dispersal site northwest of Mount Kent, 10 miles west of Stanley. After two of their small fleet of helicopters had been damaged by British naval gunfire, the Comando de Aviación de Ejército (Argentine Army Aviation) had begun moving them out of harm's way at dusk before returning them to the defence of the capital at first light. But while the site might have been out of range of the ships' 4.5-inch guns it was wide open to attack from the fast jets.

As the two Harriers dived towards low level, they dropped beneath the low, rising sun behind them and back into the twilight of pre-dawn. Pook switched frequencies and thumbed the RT button.

'Green, check in.'

'Green Two.'

'Loud and clear.'

Each armed with a pair of the BL755 cluster bombs that had proved so effective at Fox Bay the previous day, the two Harriers ran in from the northeast towards the saddle between two low peaks. The barren landscape of grass and scattered boulders blurred past in shades of grey, detail barely discernible. Judging altitude was tricky. And Pook expected the helicopters to be well dispersed making them less vulnerable to attack from the air.

*Might need more than one attacking pass*, he'd thought.

Straining to pick up the dull outlines of the helicopters in the low light, he throttled back a touch to give himself a better chance of spotting them. Then, too late, he caught sight of the distinctive shapes of a big twin-rotor Chinook and a smaller medium-lift Puma as they flashed past beneath him. Both were machines the RAF had in its own inventory. Further west he saw the familiar lines of a Bell UH-1, the ubiquitous Huey that had made its name in Vietnam. Its thick two-bladed main rotor was already spinning.

Pook confirmed that his wingman had clocked them, then reefed his jet into a fast, low turn to port, using the high ground of Mount Kent to mask his path and intentions. The Harrier complained a little as the Gs mounted. Pook's g-suit inflated around his legs and torso before, as he rolled out of the turn on to a second attack run, it released him from its grasp.

His track was good. Ahead of him, the Chinook was framed through the glass of his head-up display. And then, as he pickled the bombs, he knew he'd misjudged it. In the flattening, diffusing grey of the early morning he'd not allowed enough height for the cluster bomb pattern to spread.

*You fool*, he berated himself as he flicked the Harrier into another hard turn to port. Pushed back into his ejection seat as he arced around Mount Kent to set himself up for a third pass, he looked back over his shoulder in frustration at the tightly spaced pattern of bomblets exploding ahead of the big helicopter like a fistful of gravel hitting the surface of a millpond.

Green Two fared no better. Hare had suffered a hang-up, an electrical fault ensuring that his bombs resolutely refused to leave their pylons.

The two Harrier pilots switched to guns.

Pook's third pass saw the Chinook once again emerge unscathed in his wake. Then Hare streaked towards the target behind him.

To compensate for the slight upwards elevation of the jet's twin ADEN cannon, Hare applied a touch of backwards pressure to the stick as he ran in towards the Chinook, just checking the climb at 200 feet before bunting the nose down to point the guns. He pulled the trigger on the control column with his right hand and held it there. Beneath him, 30mm shells spat from the rifled barrels at a rate of forty rounds per second. Ahead, the high-explosive ammunition chewed up the rock-strewn heath as they walked along the ground towards the Chinook. With the big helicopter in the crosshairs he held it there for a moment. In the semi-darkness the rounds flashed white as they punctured the target. With a sudden gush of flame it exploded as Hare pulled away, banking into another tight left-hand turn to follow Pook back around the mountain to set up another pass.

This time, Pook made good. On his fourth pass across the dispersal site he held the trigger down, loosing off a long burst of cannon fire. His shells ripped into the Puma, causing it too to burn.

*Spectacular*, thought Pook as the flames lit up the semi-darkness, relieved to have finally got the better of the testing conditions.

He was determined now to go for the Huey, but of the three helicopters they'd seen, it was this one, despite its spinning main rotor, that was hardest to pick out against the muted colours of the landscape. Its drab olive camouflage, despite the addition of a thick yellow identification stripe on the tail boom, barely registered until they were almost on top of it.

Unable to make out the shape of the Huey as they rolled out into the attack, Pook and Hare were forced to run in blind. On successive passes, Pook fired his guns at the position where he expected to see the helicopter resolve out of the gloom only to spot it too late to make the correction required to bring his guns to bear.

With every circuit his radar warning receiver chirruped threateningly, but while detected by the Superfledermaus radar defending the airfield at Stanley, they were out of reach of the 35mm Oerlikon cannon that were under Argentine control. That didn't mean the dispersal site was entirely undefended, though. And at low level it only took one lucky shot from small-arms fire to spoil a mud-mover's day.

Determined to line up on the Huey, Pook and Hare continued to slingshot around Mount Kent until Hare felt a thump ruffle his aeroplane's smooth progress.

'Green Two's taken a hit,' he reported.

Pook ordered him to run out to the north, then followed him. After coasting out and turning east, they climbed to height, while

Pook tucked himself up close to his wingman to check for damage. Despite picking out a hole in the bottom of the fuselage near the intake and gun mounting, he was satisfied that Hare would make it back to the carrier. Hit with a fuel transfer problem and leaching AVCAT during the twenty-minute transit back to *Hermes*, Hare landed aboard with just 400lb of useable fuel left in his tanks. Less than two minutes in the hover.

Green Flight was safe though and had removed two of the occupiers' small, vital fleet of helicopters, including the total destruction of a Chinook, and with it a third of their serviceable heavy-lift capacity. And, despite Pook's frustration, he had managed to put a few rounds through the Huey's main rotor, which at least put the machine temporarily out of commission.

So far, 1(F)'s account was substantially in credit, but the mission had given the Captain cause for concern. Following Pook's debriefing, Lyn Middleton ticked him off for his foolhardiness in making so many passes over the target. Then praised him for the tenacity he'd shown in taking out the helos – a classic shit sandwich. Pook was furious that, as the man on the spot, his decision-making had been called into question. Middleton's concern, however, would prove to be well founded.

It had taken an encounter with the Captain to spoil Jerry Pook's mood. That hadn't been required by Rod 'Fred' Frederiksen and Martin Hale. The first pair of SHAR pilots to return to *Hermes* after contact with the enemy were spitting chips before they even climbed out of the cockpits.

After a few ranging jabs throughout the morning from the force of light attack aircraft based on the islands themselves, the Fuerza Aérea Argentina big guns had arrived just before 1330Z.

Approaching low over the islands and inlets across the top of West Falkland, the two jets of LEON Flight arrived without fair warning to rake *Antrim* with cannon fire. Four retarded bombs torpedoed into the water around the ship, one catching a whip aerial and being dragged closer to the destroyer's hull. Plumes of water exploded over the superstructure as the ship's stern was bulldozed sideways. Inside it felt as if the ship was being clubbed with lump hammers.

TANDU Flight, the first wave of three Daggers from Río Grande, streaked in ten minutes later, attacking *Argonaut* and *Broadsword*. Targeting the latter, one of the brace of Type 22s, proved to be a fatal decision when a Seawolf missile brought down one of the three Escuadrón III fighter-bombers.

But PERRO Flight was hot on their heels. The second wave of Daggers went after *Antrim* again, so low that those on deck manning the machine guns felt the pressure wave as they roared overhead. This time one of the Mk.17 1,000lb bombs found its mark, crashing in across the flight deck before drilling through a magazine and coming to rest in the seamen's heads.

Unburdened of ordnance, the three Daggers rolled out over Falkland Sound and accelerated to near supersonic speed as they made their escape towards the southwest.

Vectored towards these Grupo 6 Daggers, Frederiksen and Hale pushed their throttles forward to give chase. But they never really had a chance of catching them. With clean wings, at high altitude and in a shallow dive the SHAR was cleared to a maximum speed of Mach 1.2. But in the thicker air at low level, sound travelled faster. The powerful but less than svelte little fighter was always going to hit its 600-knot maximum long before threatening the sound barrier.

As they dropped in behind the Dagger flight, Hale loosed off a Nine Lima at range. But despite the growl in his ears telling him the Sidewinder had acquired and locked on to its target, the Daggers pulled away from the pursuing heatseeker. Hale and Frederiksen could only look on impotently as the missile homed straight and true before falling away.

The two 800 Squadron pilots persisted with their fruitless, frustrating tailchase for a few miles until low fuel forced them to knock it off. They'd been powerless to do any more than try to wring a few more knots out of their aeroplanes and curse their misfortune as the Daggers quickly outpaced them and outranged their missiles.

It was hard to escape the conclusion that, on this occasion, the Defence Science Staff's assessment of the SHAR as a fleet interceptor had some merit. The Sea Jet had come up short on three counts: speed, endurance and weaponry. None of which was lost on Frederiksen who, in the early seventies, had flown the supersonic, long-range F-4 Phantom, armed with four medium-range, semi-active, radar-guided AIM-7 Sparrow missiles, from the deck of the old *Ark Royal*. Frederiksen and Hale returned to the *Hermes* crewroom with faces like thunder.

In the first action of the day, all eight Daggers that launched from the mainland would return safely to their bases to fight another day.

The British, though, were now going to have to continue the battle for San Carlos without *Antrim*. While the bomb dropped by PERRO Flight had failed to explode, the fire damage caused by the Daggers saw her forced to withdraw from the fight, her 992 search and targeting radar no longer serviceable.

Without her there was no dedicated air defence ship in Falkland Sound.

# FORTY-TWO

## Lower than a snake's belly

LAON HULME WAS listening in on the AAWC when *Antrim* told the CAP that she could no longer provide them with control or support. Standing in the low light of *Brilliant*'s Ops Room, crowded with sailors seated at glowing orange tactical displays, their heads balaclava'd in white anti-flash hoods, Hulme realized the SHARs were on their own. He reported this perilous development to the Captain.

With *Antrim* out of the picture, John Coward had taken *Brilliant* closer to *Fearless* and *Intrepid*, the two assault ships leading the operation. But in driving the ship into the confines of San Carlos Water he'd discovered that the Seawolf's computer was unable to recognize radar clutter from the surrounding hills for what it was. Unable to filter it out, the system's processing capacity was quickly overwhelmed.

*If we could just get the missiles away,* Coward fumed, *they're going to knock the Mirages down.* Without them, *Brilliant* was virtually defenceless. A brand-new warship forced to rely on a pair of Bofors guns that had rolled off a Canadian production line in 1942. *Absolutely useless.* But with news of *Antrim*'s misfortune it occurred to him that there might just be an opportunity for *Brilliant* to make herself useful again.

Looking at his XO, he asked: 'Can you provide aircraft control to the Sea Harriers?'

It would take a little improvisation, but Hulme told him he thought he could. He knew more or less where the CAP stations were. If he reconfigured the ship's helicopter control display for the longer ranges demanded by the fighters, and if the Helicopter Control Petty Officer could feed him visual reports from the bridge and the gun direction platforms, then he should be able to cobble it all together to provide a workable picture of what was going on. He'd be working like a one-armed paper-hanger to combine the sightings with the radar contacts and D-Band moving images, but needs must. High-speed three-dimensional chess was supposed to be meat and drink to a former instructor at the Navy's School of Fighter Control. That didn't stop his counterparts aboard *Hermes* chipping in when they heard Hulme assume control of the AAWC.

'Now you be very careful with our aircraft.'

'Of course we'll be very careful,' came the reply, 'we know what we're bloody doing.'

Breaking out of cloud as he descended across Darwin to his CAP station, Al Craig saw the intricate khaki and rust contours of the Falkland Islands beneath him for the first time. Lapping at the shores, the startlingly clear coastal water sparkled blue and bottle green in the low midday sun. He was struck by how familiar it looked.

*Beautiful and wild like the Shetland Islands and Scottish coast*, he thought, reminded of his time flying Buccaneers out of RNAS Lossie-mouth across the Moray Firth.

Unable to get airborne for a gentle refam sortie the previous day, Craig's first launch from *Invincible* saw him sitting on Steve Thomas's wing in a loose battle formation alongside Sharkey Ward. For Craig's benefit, the 801 boss had taken the time to brief the sortie at greater length. After the drama of the earlier Argentine raids, the AAWC net was quiet as they approached the islands. Levelling off at low level and throttling back to endurance speed, Gold Flight settled into a lazy racetrack pattern. His senses keen on his first operational mission, Craig kept a watchful eye on his wingman's six.

Despite instructions from Northwood not to use their radars while patrolling over Falkland Sound, Ward had told his squadron to keep their Blue Fox sets scanning the skies for trade. The 801 boss didn't share the pervading dim view of the radar's capability and, at the very least, he'd told his pilots, it might act as a deterrent to any incoming raid. Maintaining such close scrutiny of the little radar display was painstaking work, though, and most contacts were quickly confirmed as friendly.

When Thomas picked up a group of three ships approaching the islands from the south it seemed likely to play out the same way. He called it in to the 'D'. The formation of the ships appeared to be military.

From his station inside HMS *Brilliant*'s Ops Room, Laon Hulme acknowledged Thomas's report, but had no information about the three ships. Unable to positively identify them, he instructed the CAP to investigate.

Ward acknowledged. And as Gold Flight ran in towards the ships they armed their Sidewinders. The Nine Lima may have been an infrared air-to-air missile, but as the squadron armourers tested the missiles' seeker heads on deck while pre-flighting the jets they'd already noticed the way they would sometimes lock on to the frigates and destroyers steaming alongside the carrier. Against the freezing South Atlantic, even the cold steel of a ship offered a measure of contrasting warmth.

*Bloody hell*, thought Craig as he accelerated to combat speed, *this is getting a bit serious for a fam flight*.

Moments later, Thomas identified the target as a small flotilla of British hospital ships. Gold Flight hauled off, rolling into a turn back towards their CAP station. As the adrenalin washed away, Craig made safe his missiles.

After nearly three-quarters of an hour on station, fuel was beginning to run low. It was time to return to Mother. Ahead, Ward pulled back on the stick and began to climb back to medium altitude for the transit east. Craig and Thomas followed in his wake. As they soared past 10,000 feet, the AAWC crackled into life. It was *Brilliant*.

'I have two slow-moving contacts over land to the south of you, possibly helicopters or ground attack aircraft,' Hulme reported. 'Do you wish to investigate?'

Ward had rolled his jet into a hard descending turn to starboard before Hulme had even finished the question. 'Affirmative. Now in descending heading one six zero degrees. Do you still hold the contacts?'

'Affirmative. Ten miles. Very low.'

In the absence of any other enemy air activity, Hulme cleared Gold Flight to slice through the AOA box in pursuit of the bogeys.

Their orders were to go after British helicopters around San Carlos Water. All Mayor Juan Tomba and Primer Teniente Juan Luis Micheloud had got for their trouble was a barrage of small-arms fire and close attention from a pair of surface-to-air missiles. Their twin-turboprop IA-58 Pucarás had already proved themselves capable of soaking up battle damage. But there were limits. And Tomba and Micheloud knew they were close to where, earlier the same morning, their squadron boss had been brought down by a Stinger missile fired by an SAS patrol. After turning for the relative safety of BAM Malvinas, the two Grupo 3 pilots had then been tasked with destroying a settlement 10 miles southeast of Darwin which it was believed was being used to direct British naval gunfire against BAM Condor, their own operating base at Goose Green. After calling in a successful attack using 70mm LAU-68 rockets they had been ordered southwest in search of another suspected observation post. And into view of HMS *Brilliant*'s Type 967 radar.

'Got him, Sharkey. Looks like a Pucará on the deck, about fifteen degrees.' Steve Thomas saw it first, catching sight of one of the Fuerza Aérea Argentina machines as it emerged, tracking south, from beneath a thin layer of cloud.

The Pucarás had been hastily camouflaged in light green and sand before deploying to the islands, but it wasn't helping much. Over the muted East Falkland grassland the pale paint scheme, thought Thomas, *stuck out like a sore thumb*.

'Not visual,' Ward responded, 'you attack first.'

Thomas had already tipped in towards the target. Al Craig followed him down.

*This is getting real*, he thought as adrenalin surged through him – *this is good!*

'Watch out – Harriers!' reported Micheloud after spotting the three British fighters a few thousand feet above them.

Tomba craned his neck to see two of the Sea Harriers swooping down from behind his right shoulder. Two predatory dark grey shapes silhouetted against the pale sky.

Flying barely 50 feet above the rolling ground below, Tomba and Micheloud broke left and right. Ahead, Micheloud saw the relative safety of a low saddle joined by rising ground to each side. He turned through 90° towards it, forced the nose even lower and, hugging the earth, ran for cover. Instead of juicing the aeroplane for all of the 270-knot top speed he could wring out of it, he chopped the throttle, gently raising the nose as the speed washed off. If he kept her low and slow, it was only going to complicate the job of the interceptors. But his wingman hadn't been able to make the turn towards protection afforded by the terrain.

Micheloud watched with alarm as the Harriers went in for the kill.

It was deemed to be wasteful to expend a Sidewinder missile on one of the slow-moving Pucarás. Instead, as Steve Thomas carved down towards the target, he switched to guns and made sure his head-up display was in air-to-air mode. It was still going to be a difficult shot. With the Pucará skimming the weeds there was no way of getting underneath the Argentine machine to try to bring the two ADEN cannon to bear.

Thomas pulled back on the control column, hauling the SHAR's nose round in a descending angled-off track from the Pucará's four o'clock, trying to walk his gunsight over the target. But the picture through the HUD was tricky. The angles were all wrong. The Pucará was flying barely 10 feet above the ground, its wings level, and as Thomas dived in from 45° to starboard he was unable to frame the whole plan form of the Argentine turboprop in his sights, only a foreshortened sliver of it.

He opened fire.

A split second later heavy 30mm rounds chunked into the moorland all around the Pucará. As he rapidly overshot, the slower machine disappearing beneath the nose of his SHAR, Thomas hauled back on the stick to arrest his descent and pulled into a hard turn to port, unsure whether he'd hit it or not.

But Al Craig was just behind him. Coming on strong.

The former Buccaneer pilot tried to line himself up behind the Pucará. Like Thomas, he was diving in from height. And still unfamiliar with the SHAR's weapons system after two years in the cockpit of a GR.3, Craig was stuck using the reversion sight rather than the HUDWAC's air-to-air mode. Instead of the weapons aiming computer calculating the lead he required to hit the low-flying target, his guns were simply going to fire wherever he was pointing at the time he pulled the trigger. To actually hit the Pucará he'd have to aim ahead of it, but how far? The only way to correct his aim was by watching the fall of his shot and adjusting.

He pulled the trigger. The recoil of the two gas-powered 30mm cannon juddered through the airframe. Further back, heavy brass shell cases the size of school milk bottles clinked and clattered against the rear of the fuselage after being ejected from the side of the gun pods.

There was no tracer. No indication of the trajectory of his shells as they speared through the air ahead of him from the belly of the SHAR.

*Too expensive*, rued Craig as he kept his index finger squeezed on the trigger. A split second later he saw the high-explosive shells divot the ground behind the fleeing Pucará, throwing up spurts of earth as they exploded near a flock of sheep. The startled animals scattered, not looking too happy. *Surprise!* He released the trigger, adjusted his aim and fired again, closing fast on the target while hosing high-explosive shells at it with as much accuracy as he could muster.

*He's not blowing up like they do in the movies*, Craig thought as he barrelled over the Pucará with a 200-knot-plus overtake. He didn't know whether he'd hit it or not as he pulled out of the diving attack. Probably couldn't claim any strikes against the sheep either.

Sharkey Ward watched it all.

Instead of the screaming dives and slashing attacks from Gold Two and Three that failed to bring down the Pucará, the 801 boss had decided on a more measured approach. He dropped down low behind the target. Because of the angle of his guns he was going to have to make any stern attack from down in the weeds. But the

Pucará pilot wasn't making it easy for him. The only silver lining was that, with those long, straight wings, it was impossible for the Argentine pilot to manoeuvre hard. Any attempt to throw his machine into a steep evasive turn would see him catch a crab with fatal results.

Despite rapidly overhauling the slower turboprop, Ward had given himself time to set up his attack. With his HUDWAC in air-to-air mode, the SHAR's Hotline historical tracer sight computed the relative trajectory of his shot and projected it on to his head-up display. If he placed the reticle over the target he should hit it. No guesswork. He framed the Pucará in the sight and pulled the trigger on the control column. The jet vibrated as the big 30mm shells ripped out of the ADENs with a hammer-drill persistence, each cannon despatching twenty-five rounds a second in his target's direction.

Ward saw the Pucará's port aileron shred and fray as his shells stitched into the wing. He saw the first flashes of flame lick from the Argentine's starboard engine cowling. But there was no sign of him going down. Moments later, as the target loomed large in Ward's view, he threw his jet into a hard, flat turn away from it. His attack on the Pucará had been too fleeting. The rugged turboprop, built for counter-insurgency work, was designed to absorb punishment. It was time to try another approach.

Straining against the Gs as he held the SHAR in the steep turn, he pulled back on the throttle lever with a gloved left hand. Then, as the speed washed off, he reached forward to the flap selector on the port-side control panel and selected mid-flap.

But there was a danger inherent in sloughing off his jet's energy. In air combat, it was deemed to be axiomatic that speed was life. Sharkey Ward had weighed the odds, though. The Pucará was isolated, his wingman gone, and flying too low to manoeuvre hard. Thomas and Craig would cover his own tail. And he'd spent a good deal of his career as a Senior Pilot and Air Warfare Instructor on an F-4 Phantom squadron obsessing about how best to squeeze the last drops of performance out of the big interceptor in low-speed air combat. If ever there was an occasion to break such a cardinal rule, it was now.

He rolled out behind the Pucará, still closing on the Argentine turboprop but at a less urgent rate. More importantly, extending his flaps along the trailing edge of the wings had made a critical difference to the way he was able to frame his target. By increasing his wing area, the flaps also increased the lift provided. This had the effect of pitching the nose down by reducing the angle of attack required to fly straight and level at any given speed. By lowering the nose to counter the upwards inclination of his guns, he wasn't going to have to try to get below his target to bring them to bear. With the Pucará flying lower than a snake's belly there was little chance of that without ploughing into the ground.

Ward settled into a position a couple of hundred yards behind his target and opened up. 30mm rounds punched into the stricken Argentine aircraft, smashing into the cockpit and setting fire to the port engine. But as Ward released the trigger and pulled the SHAR into a tight turn to set himself up for a third pass, the Pucará was still airborne.

*Brave bloke*, thought the 801 boss as he considered the man in the cockpit. It didn't matter. With a first kill within his grasp, Ward's respect for a courageous adversary wasn't going to deter him.

*This time you're going down.*

It was painful to watch. From the vantage point of his own cockpit, Al Craig looked down at Ward's SHAR tailgating the doomed Pucará. As the CO's cannon spat high-explosive shells into the target, Craig could see it coming apart. The fuselage caught fire. The canopy was ripped free. Chunks of metal and jagged patches of the aircraft's aluminium skin were blown away, thrown into a filthy trail of dark smoke.

'Eject, *eject*!' Craig urged under his breath.

And, finally, he did.

No longer able to control his ruined aircraft, Tomba pulled the ejection handle. A split second later, the British-built Martin-Baker Mk.6 zero/zero ejection seat fired him clear. The Pucará had already pancaked into the spongy moorland by the time Tomba, after barely a single swing beneath his parachute, landed in a heap. From 100 yards away he watched his aeroplane burn. It seemed to him that the Sea Harrier's guns had riddled every inch of it and yet somehow he'd emerged unhurt.

*God didn't want it*, he concluded as he reflected on how close he'd come to death. He shouldn't even have been flying. He was in his second year at Staff College when, a week before the arrival of the British Task Force, he was sent to the Malvinas to help remedy a problem with the Pucará's weapons system caused by the damp air.

As the British jets climbed away to the northeast, he began the long walk towards Argentine lines at Goose Green to the northeast.

The cold began to bite.

*Right*, thought Al Craig, *now we can go home.* He'd been relieved to see the Argentine pilot finally abandon his aircraft and his parachute open, but his reaction wasn't entirely selfless. He was now worryingly short on fuel. *And*, he thought, *it's going to be a bit daft to run out of petrol on a refam flight.*

*Invincible*, made alert to the situation by Ward, steamed towards them, making use of Gold Flight's twenty-minute transit time to close to within 100 miles of Falkland Sound. Even 10 miles could make a difference to the returning fighters. Ward shepherded Craig home to Mother, making sure that his new pilot was the first of the three SHARs to recover aboard the ship, descending to the deck with his undercarriage lowered like a bee, legs trailing, returning to the hive.

Unfazed by what had been an unexpectedly eventful introduction to theatre, Craig recorded the detail in his logbook without embellishment. In the column marked 'MISSION (including Results and Remarks)' he simply entered 'CAP'. No need to make a meal of it.

Craig's refusal to be overly impressed by it all didn't stop the rest of the combined ranks of 801 and 809 pilots wanting to pick through the bones of the sortie. While they'd both seen their rounds tear up the ground, neither Craig nor Thomas knew whether or not they'd registered any hits on the Pucará. And Ward was happy to disabuse them of any lingering hopes that their shooting might have given them a share in the kill.

'You boys didn't get anywhere near it!' Sharkey ribbed them.

And they didn't disagree.

Craig was almost relieved not to have to argue. If he'd seen any of his own rounds hitting home then had the temerity to mention it, he thought, *Sharkey would've killed me!* After missing out during the fighting on the opening day of the war, the combative 801 Squadron boss had been eager to break his duck.

But if Al Craig had come home empty-handed from his first operational sortie, it had at least earned him Sharkey Ward's respect, and that was always hard won. *Crazy, but above average* was Ward's warm assessment of the man from 809. And that, in the formal language used to rate military pilots, was a rare accolade. Where Craig really scored, in Ward's view, was in his attitude. *A most aggressive pilot*, the CO reflected approvingly. And 801's Ops Officer, a former F-4 Phantom Observer, weighed in, in agreement. 'Your AI's crap,' he told Craig, who as a lifelong ground attack pilot was the first to admit his air interception skills could do with a little brushing up, 'but your aggression's quite good, though.'

# FORTY-THREE

## The valley of the shadow of death

Río Grande was still wreathed in drizzle when the six Armada jets returned to base. The dreary weather seemed to sum up what had been a disappointing morning's work for the men of 3 Escuadrilla. After disembarking from the carrier, the Comando de Aviación Naval's A-4 Skyhawk squadron had been eager to join the fight. With the confirmation that the British landings had begun, the unit's CO, Rodolfo Castro Fox, had begun briefing his men early. He'd split them into two divisions of two flights, each made up of three jets. He would lead 1 Division against a transport ship located in Fox Bay. Alberto Philippi was given command of 2 Division, scheduled to fly the same aircraft following a quick turnaround later in the day. Flying alongside him were Teniente de Navío José Arca and Teniente de Fragata Marcelo Marquez.

But soon after launching at 1315Z Castro Fox's mission had started to come unglued. The failure of the VLF Omega navigation equipment carried by each Flight Leader left them dependent on dead reckoning using a compass and stopwatch. Their target was then changed before, after they'd turned northwest on to the new heading, they were recalled to Río Grande without having cleared their wings.

Back on the ground, while their six bombed-up Skyhawks were refuelled and pre-flighted again, the returning pilots helped Philippi's 2 Division plan the next mission. The target was a frigate that was detached from the main concentration of British ships and thought to be operating as a radar picket ship.

Following the morning's raids by Air Force Daggers and Skyhawks,

3 Escuadrilla's mission planning was on a much firmer footing. Armed with hard intelligence about the disposition of the British ships based on reports from the returning pilots, Castro Fox hoped Philippi's 2 Division wouldn't suffer the same disappointment as his own. But frustration hadn't been confined to the Argentine pilots.

Hugh Slade came on frequency as he climbed from low level on his first CAP sortie. Unlike Al Craig and Dave Austin aboard *Invincible*, the 809 Squadron contingent aboard *Hermes* had at least managed a couple of in-theatre training sorties before being pitched into the fight. As he listened in, he recognized Mike Blissett's voice over the AAWC.

'I shot down an A-4,' reported the 800 Squadron pilot.

There was no disguising the adrenalin coursing through Blissett's veins. And his excitement was infectious. Slade was elated. This was it – what he'd trained for.

*It's on*, he thought as he descended towards his CAP station, anticipating trade. But he was out of luck. The two A-4s splashed by Blissett and his wingman, 899 boss Neill Thomas, proved to be the last encounter between the Sea Harriers and the raiders from the Argentine mainland for nearly an hour and a half.

After launching from *Invincible* at 1620Z with Gold Flight, Dave Austin came close. Like Al Craig, he was tagging along with an established pair on his first operational mission. After forty minutes on patrol at low level, the three SHARs were climbing away from their CAP station when Gold Two spotted a Skyhawk through a gap in the clouds. The lead pair broke out of the climb and accelerated to fighting speed in pursuit of the A-4. But they lost contact with their target in the descent. Low on fuel, and with no hope of detecting the Skyhawk over land using the Blue Fox radar, they had no option but to knock it off and return to Mother.

809 Squadron's next contact was to be rather more decisive. And yet none of Tim Gedge's pilots were involved at all.

Delivered from RAF St Athan the day after the Task Force sailed, ZA190 was 809's first aircraft. She was the jet in which Tim Gedge,

Dave Austin and Hugh Slade all made their return to the cockpit of the Sea Harrier. What little experience of the Blue Fox radar Steve Brown possessed had been honed aboard ZA190. While trialling new toss bombing techniques, Bill Covington had flown her. Dave Braithwaite had been at the controls during the formation flypast before the squadron's departure. Al Craig had delivered her to *Atlantic Conveyor* from Ascension, and with Gedge at the helm she had been the first of the 809 jets to arrive aboard *Invincible*. She belonged to them all.

At 1510Z she'd launched as one half of the first CAP pair composed solely of the men and machines that had come south aboard *Atlantic Conveyor*. Both jets sported 809's ghostly Barley Grey camouflage. 809 boss Tim Gedge was the Flight Leader in XZ491. His wingman, the squadron's Senior Pilot Dave Braithwaite, was flying ZA190.

After the 809 pair recovered aboard the carrier at 1635Z, Brave's jet was refuelled.

Three-quarters of an hour later, she was on her way back to the CAP stations as part of Trident Section. In the cockpit, Steve Thomas maintained a loose battle formation 1,000 yards or so off his wingman, Trident Leader, Sharkey Ward.

One hundred miles out from the target, Alberto Philippi throttled back and began a gentle descent from 27,000 feet towards the sea. Without breaking radio silence the two other A-4Q Skyhawks followed him down. Between the two heavy 300-gallon fuel tanks that hung under the wings, each of Philippi's jets carried four 500lb Mk.82 Snake Eye retarded bombs on a centreline pylon.

One hundred feet above a leaden sea the weather was filthy. Low cloud hung like smoke down to 500 feet issuing curtains of rain down to the water. A gusting southwesterly wind whipped the tops off the waves below. In the deteriorating visibility Philippi closed the formation. Continue on in a loose escort formation and there was a danger they'd lose visual with each other. And without any kind of useful navigational aid you really didn't want to be out in this on your own. After its failure during the squadron's first mission, the engineers had still been unable to fix the VLF Omega navigation system. Using a magnetic compass, stopwatch and an ADF bearing from a mainland navigational beacon, Philippi calculated that they had 50 miles to run until reaching the coast of Gran Malvina (West Falkland). At 7½ miles per minute, time on target was twenty minutes away.

It was time to check in with the S-2E Tracker that had been sent to patrol southwest of the islands to provide them with targeting information. After two RT calls went without reply, Philippi abandoned his attempt to make contact.

2 Division pressed on, eyes straining ahead for the first sight of land. As he led Arca and Marquez into harm's way, Philippi held on to the words of the 23rd Psalm, turning them over in his mind like a mantra: *The Lord is my shepherd, I shall not want. Yea, though I walk through the valley of the shadow of death, I will fear no evil, for thou art with me; thy rod and thy staff, they comfort me; and I will dwell in the house of the Lord forever.*

As Trident Section began their descent towards CAP station 14 over West Falkland, they could only listen in to the AAWC with mounting frustration. There were raids coming in. They could hear Laon Hulme aboard HMS *Brilliant* directing the fight. The picture was confused, but it sounded as if Tartan Section, an 800 Squadron CAP from *Hermes*, had splashed an A-4. Ward was eager to bring his height and speed advantage to bear on the situation. If *Brilliant* could point them in the right direction, he and Thomas could swoop down on the tails of the outbound jets as they made their escape.

Ward called the 'D' to get a position on the enemy aircraft.

'There's a raid coming in,' replied Hulme. 'Wait out!'

Before the end of the transmission from *Brilliant*, Ward and Thomas heard a series of clonks thump across the AAWC.

Hulme's focus was destroyed in an instant. A fusillade of 30mm cannon shells from a Grupo 6 Dagger exploded through the side of *Brilliant*'s starboard hull, spraying a lethal hail of shrapnel around the tight confines of the densely manned Ops Room. Once again the hills surrounding San Carlos had rendered the ship blind to the low-flying jets' approach.

The shred of hot, sharp metal was indiscriminate. Some just saw it fly across their field of view. Others were fortunate it only snagged their clothing. One man was bleeding from a slash across his nose. Another had been hit in the legs. The Petty Officer sitting next to Hulme was concussed by a larger piece of metal that glanced off his head, punched a hole in a cabinet the size of a two-pence piece, and left him with a suspected fractured skull. There was smoke. A beat later, the shouting started. And Laon Hulme clutched at his left shoulder in pain. He'd been hit too.

As sunlight streamed in through a hole in the bulkhead the smoke cleared and first-aiders were piped into the Ops Room to treat the casualties. Another sailor had been injured on the bridge wing.

Hulme got back on the AAWC to explain to Trident Section what was going on. 'We've just been hit,' he told the SHAR pilots, 'hang on a minute. The guy next to me has been hit in the head and I've been hit in the arm.'

Over twenty high-explosive 30mm cannon shells from the twin DEFA cannon of the Argentine Dagger had punched into *Brilliant* amidships, below the bridge. They'd torn jagged holes inside the Ops Room and Seawolf Surveillance Office and shredded the forward Seawolf launcher and wiring looms feeding the fire control computer.

At first, as the frigate began to settle down again after the shock of the strafing attack, it appeared she was out of the fight. Then Hulme realized that his 967 radar was still on line.

John Coward spoke to his ship's company to give them details of what had happened. As an afterthought he added, 'Anyone wishing to shoot at the Argentinians, draw a weapon from the small-arms store.'

Unable to intervene in the raid that had targeted *Brilliant*, Ward and Thomas continued their descent towards the patrol line. Nestled in the valley north of Mount Maria, they stooged up and down in battle formation at 300 knots between 500 and 1,000 feet above ground level. They made for a contrasting pair: Ward in the dark sea grey of 801 Squadron's original jets; Thomas, in ZA190, in 809's pale custom camouflage. At the southern end of the racetrack they rolled towards each other into a shackle turn, each clearing the other's six as they scissored back towards the north.

Ninety degrees through the turn, with his nose pointing west, Ward caught sight of a pair of Daggers barrelling in down the throat, low and fast beneath the ridgeline. He barely had time to hit the transmit button before they flashed past each other at a closing speed of over 800 knots. Ward slammed the throttle forward and hauled the nose round into a climbing turn to starboard, straining against his harness as the Gs bit to try to keep eyes on the delta-winged fighter-bombers. The time elapsed from the moment he'd first seen them to the point they streaked past each other was barely five seconds.

Steve Thomas saw them before the boss had even finished calling it in. After reading a book about the air war in Vietnam, the young Fleet Air Arm pilot had got into the habit of periodically reversing his turns in order to clear the sky beneath him. As he did so, the Daggers, their wings painted with thick yellow identification stripes, shot past west of him in echelon, 500 yards apart, barely 100 feet off the deck.

After catching sight of Ward's dark grey jet silhouetted against the pale overcast, the Daggers jettisoned their bombs and broke hard to right, streaming white vortices from their wingtips. But they hadn't seen Thomas. And when they rolled out on to a westerly heading, Trident Two dropped easily into their six o'clock. ZA190's small height advantage and the energy bled away by the Daggers' barn-door wing through the 90° turn to starboard meant that this time there was no escape.

With the Nine Lima in boresight mode, Thomas manoeuvred to position the trailing Dagger in his sights. At an altitude of 200 feet, slipstreaming him from 1,000 yards back, he framed the Dagger firmly inside the HUD symbology. The angry invertebrate growl of the Sidewinder acquisition tone buzzed through his headset. He pressed 'ACCEPT' to uncage the seeker and, checking the heatseeker was locked on and tracking, flipped up the safety catch on the control column and pickled the missile.

The Sidewinder fizzed away from the starboard rail, streaming a trail of boiling white exhaust. It climbed slightly before it seemed to catch itself, then guided unerringly into the spine of the Argentine jet between the cockpit and vertical tail. The Dagger bunted forward as the back half of the aeroplane disintegrated in a ball of flame.

*Took it apart*, noted Thomas as the pilot ejected from the spinning wreckage. But the SHAR pilot was already in pursuit of the second Dagger, now climbing in full reheat towards the sanctuary of cloud. He pulled back on the stick, raising the nose towards the target as it accelerated away. It was getting rangey. But presented with the Dagger's flaming jetpipe, the Nine Lima locked on.

Thomas pressed the fire button with his thumb.

From 500 feet, the missile speared away towards the target, now nearly 2,000 yards distant. The Sidewinder's rocket motor burned out, its fuel spent. But still travelling at over two and a half times the speed of sound, its momentum saw it get close enough to the fleeing Dagger to trigger the missile's laser proximity fuze close to the port wing.

The 20lb annular blast fragmentation warhead threw out a lethal, expanding buzzsaw of metal rods. It proved as damaging to a Dagger's health as had Thomas's earlier direct hit. Moments later the pilot ejected.

But neither Thomas nor Ward had seen the third member of RATON Flight. There had always been three Daggers.

After his Flight Leader first glimpsed the Sea Harriers and called 'Break!', Gustavo Piuma had racked his jet into a hard right-hand turn and advanced the throttle through the detente into full afterburner. Raw fuel sprayed into the Atar engine's jetpipe delivering nearly 14,000lb of thrust. Accelerating, he'd climbed away towards the south before doubling back into the fray.

With just twelve hours in a Dagger, his inexperience in the cockpit of the supersonic fighter should have disqualified him from taking part, but, ignoring orders, he'd chalked his name up on the blackboard anyway. And he knew enough to know that if he could gain height he might be able to cover the tails of his two wingmen. But by the time he'd got eyes back on the fight one of them was already gone.

He saw the Sidewinder lance away from the leading Sea Harrier, the paler of the two British fighters. It seemed to snap from beneath the port wing like a firework from a bottle, 0 to 1,500mph in barely two seconds, its white exhaust trailing like the line of a harpoon.

'Watch out!' he shouted over the radio. 'Break!' Then he watched helplessly as the missile streaked inexorably towards his comrade and exploded.

Piuma tipped his Dagger into a dive towards the darker Sea Harrier, approaching from the British jet's seven o'clock. He flipped the safety catch on the control column and pulled the trigger. The Dagger shuddered as he loosed off a long burst of 30mm rounds. But without tracer it was impossible to adjust his aim. He released the trigger as his target flew into a valley and accelerated towards it in pursuit.

He was sure there was no escape for the British jet.

As he carved inside the Harrier's turn he caught sight of his RATON Flight comrade floating to the ground beneath a parachute. Momentarily distracted, he tore his eyes away from his friend and scanned the valley ahead in search of his target.

After witnessing his wingman's clinical despatch of two enemy jets, Ward had fire in his veins. Rolling out on to a westerly heading, he made a quick clearing check of the sky around him. From nowhere, a third Dagger slashed past below and to his right. And right into his Sidewinders' no escape zone. Ward turned in towards the bogey and called contact. He locked on and pickled the missile.

'Fox two.'

A deafening boom crashed through the airframe, a fierce explosion seeming to rip into the cockpit. 'My God, what's happening!' Piuma screamed as he lost control of his devastated aeroplane. At 450 knots and just 120 feet from the ground, he let go of the control column and pulled sharply on the yellow and black ejection seat handle between his legs.

Alerted by Ward's commentary, Thomas craned his neck back over his shoulder. A mile to his right he saw the Nine Lima strike the Argentine jet in the tail. It was blown to bits. Split seconds later the burning wreckage of the Dagger crumped into the hillside surrounded by a buckshot volley of fiery debris.

\*

Sharkey Ward and Steve Thomas now had five kills between them. And, just two days after her arrival aboard *Atlantic Conveyor*, ZA190 already had two of them.

Alberto Philippi led the flight of A-4Q Skyhawks at no more than 50 feet above the iron seas. He set his radar altimeter alarm to sound at 30 feet. The harsh electronic tone became a constant companion to all three as they skirted around the south coast of Gran Malvina to Cape Belgrano, the southernmost tip of West Falkland, before crossing the mouth of the Sound on a bearing of 069°. Salt spray bathed the three pale grey jets as they flew low over the waves. Only the constant rain stopped it from crusting on their windshields to obscure the view forward. And they were below the British search radars. You win, you lose.

Philippi advanced the throttle with his left hand. The Pratt & Whitney J65 turbojet behind him responded eagerly, pushing his speed up to 450 knots. He felt at home in the Skyhawk's snug-fitting cockpit.

*Like pulling on a backpack*, he thought.

As he approached the west coast of the Sound he turned on to a new heading of 025° towards San Carlos. Marquez and Arca followed him north, streaking low across the jagged spurs and inlets of the coastline beneath. The skies brightened a little as they traced their way northeast towards the British anchorage.

Thirty seconds out from the mouth of Brenton Loch, Philippi glimpsed the masts and radar antennae of a warship protruding from behind the rocky cover of the North West Islands. At the moment he saw it, the RT crackled into life.

It was Arca: 'A ship, sir.'

Philippi was tempted to keep on going, hopping over the Sussex Mountains and on towards the flotilla of British ships in San Carlos Water. But his orders were to go for the picket ship. It looked to him like a Type 21 frigate. Her stern buried low in a churning wake of white water, she was already manoeuvring to try to protect herself.

'We're going to attack,' Philippi replied.

At first glance, Sharkey Ward thought they were seagulls. After chasing down the Daggers to the west, the 801 boss was leading Trident

Flight back east towards the CAP station when, 10 miles away across the Sound, he spotted the three pale shapes describing a low turn over Grantham Sound towards the south.

*Were they seagulls?*

Ward got on the AAWC to *Brilliant.* 'Do you have any friendlies close to you?'

There was a brief pause.

'No, no friendlies close to us.'

'They're Skyhawks,' Sharkey told his wingman. He slammed the throttle forward again, accelerating at very low level across Port Howard to a speed of 560 knots. 'They're going for *Ardent*!'

# FORTY-FOUR

## Imminent peril

RED FLIGHT HAD a distinctly Phoenix Squadron flavour to it. The Flight Leader, Lieutenant Clive Morrell, had spent much of his career flying 809's Buccaneers from the deck of *Ark Royal*. He was universally known as 'Spag' after his surname had been misspelled 'Morreli' on the blackboard in the ready room. Spaghetti Morreli seemed to suit the long-limbed, olive-skinned ground attack specialist. His supremely sanguine approach to life only reinforced the Mediterranean impression.

Spag was only two months out of the Sea Harrier training course. After three tours on the Bucc, an exchange tour with the German Navy Marineflieger flying F-104 Starfighters low over the Baltic, and a posting to an RAF Germany GR.3 squadron, his instructors had done their best, as they put it, 'to make a fighter pilot out of him after years of bombing'.

Happily, Red Two had plenty of single-seat air defence experience. It's just that it was some years earlier, and none was in the cockpit of a Sea Harrier, a machine in which he had still only enjoyed around twenty hours' flying time, half of which was clocked up just deploying from Yeovilton to Ascension Island with Tim Gedge's new incarnation of 809 Squadron.

But John Leeming was champing at the bit. After a frustrating day kicking his heels aboard *Hermes* waiting for his slot to come up, he and Spag, a good friend from their time together on 3(F) Squadron at RAF Gütersloh, had been sitting on the deck strapped into their seats at Alert 5 for an hour when the tannoy barked, 'Scramble the Alert Harriers.'

As he followed Spag's SHAR off the ski-jump, he thought: *the ship must be in imminent peril.*

*Brilliant* cleared Trident Flight to cut across the AOA in pursuit of the three Skyhawks, but after coasting out over the Sound, Sharkey Ward realized that he and Thomas were never going to get there in time. He hit the transmit button.

'Red Section,' he called over the RT. 'Three Skyhawks, north to south towards *Ardent*. I'm out of range.'

A thousand yards off Ward's starboard wing, Steve Thomas barely had time to register the orange flashes streaking past his aeroplane before there was a loud thump in the cockpit. Immediately his radios went dead. A fuel pump failed. Thomas began to scan his instruments for any other signs of damage. He'd deliberately flown south of Port Howard settlement in an effort to avoid the flak. But the four 20mm armour-piercing rounds that had just sliced through his jet told him not far enough.

The frigate's sudden movement threw José Arca's aim. As Arca's Skyhawk slid out to the right of the formation, Alberto Philippi racked his own A-4Q round to port, away from the dark rock of the coastline. His wingtip nearly traced the water below before he levelled off on a heading of 250° and settled into his attack run, no longer able to manoeuvre to avoid the anti-aircraft fire from the ship. Ahead of him the British Type 21 steamed across his nose from left to right.

20mm shells from the ship's Oerlikon cannon kicked up the water ahead of him. He watched the frigate's 4.5-inch gun turret swing round towards him. Fifteen hundred yards out, approaching low from his target's port quarter, he pulled the trigger to return fire with the two 20mm Colt cannon mounted beneath the cockpit.

The guns rippled off only a handful of rounds before they both jammed.

Unable to provide himself with any kind of covering fire, the Flight Leader nudged back on the control column to climb to an altitude of 300 feet for the bomb run. He felt horribly exposed, but any lower and his bombs' fuzes wouldn't have time to arm. Philippi forced himself to put it out of his mind and focus on nothing but placing the reticle of his bombsight over the bow of his target. The ship filled his head-up display.

*It's dead on*, he thought, and pickled the bombs. With a satisfying thump, the ejector rack threw off the four 500lb Mk.82 Snake Eyes from beneath the A-4Q's fuselage.

Springloaded airbrakes on the tails of the bombs flicked open to retard their forward throw just long enough for Philippi to escape the blast. Careful not to let the sudden change in weight see him balloon into the sights of the frigate's Seacat missile system, he jammed the throttle forward to demand 102% rpm from the engine, jinked hard to the right and dived back towards the wavetops. As he urged the Skyhawk forward, the voice of his number two, following just eight or nine seconds behind, crackled over the RT.

'Very good, sir!' Arca told him as he watched the last of Philippi's bombs strike the ship.

Unable to set up a safe separation between himself and his Flight Leader, Arca had been half hoping that Philippi's bombs wouldn't hit. Instead, he thought, the view ahead of him looked Dantesque. He flinched as he flew through the pillar of fire and debris thrown up by Philippi's attack.

But his own bombs were on their way.

Philippi twisted round over his left shoulder to see a furious pall of smoke billowing from the stern of the British ship. He glimpsed water geysering heavily into the air 20 yards from the bow before he snapped back to flying.

'Let's get out the way we came in,' he ordered, before Marcelo Marquez, his number three, cut through the static.

'Another in the stern!' he reported, confirming that at least one of Arca's Snake Eyes had also hit home.

With Marquez joining the formation after his own attack, Philippi led his men low towards the southwest. Two miles separated the three jets.

*We'll use the same route to return*, he figured, *to avoid the enemy*.

Since coming on frequency, Spag and Leeming had listened in to the Trident Section show monopolizing the AAWC. On approaching

Falkland Sound in battle formation from the east, they initiated a steep descent from 30,000 feet in order to reach the CAP station at low level. Dropping fast through 10,000 feet over Darwin, Leems, 1,500 yards out on Spag's starboard beam, looked north and saw the ships of the Amphibious Task Group sheltered in San Carlos Water. To the west, though, he picked out an isolated ship, explosions ripping through her stern while giant flumes of sea water pistoned into the air around her. But if he was watching bombs going off right now, there was one obvious conclusion: *enemy close by*.

*Bugger it*, thought Spag angrily as he saw *Ardent* get hammered by the Argentine attack, thick oily smoke billowing from her stern. Neither they nor Trident Section had been close enough to stop it, but he realized that Red Section might now be in a position to make the attackers pay. He gave a moment's consideration to which way they were likely to try to make their escape. Assuming they'd try to egress to the southwest, he pulled the nose round on to what he reckoned was a likely intercept heading and poured on the coals, diving more steeply towards a gap in the broken cloud.

*They'll be out there*, he thought as the SHAR accelerated through 500 knots, its speed continuing to build.

Below him, the pale grey of an Armada Argentina A-4Q Skyhawk flashed past, conspicuous against the dark water beneath.

'There they are, Leems – follow me!'

Spag racked the SHAR into a tight descending turn, stooping down through the clouds like a peregrine towards his prey. Now out of sight behind him, Leems chased him down towards the fleeing Skyhawks. As they dived down, there was a radioed warning from Trident Section.

'Be careful,' Ward said, 'we're here. Don't shoot *us* up.'

'Would I do that, Sharkey?' Spag teased, before reassuring him, 'Don't worry, they're A-4s.' Morrell was much more concerned that, in dropping in behind the escaping fighter-bombers, he and Leems might expose themselves to any escorting Argentine fighters.

'Harrier! Sea Harrier on the left!' shouted Marquez over the RT as he watched Morrell's jet emerge through the cloud layer, nearly 2 miles ahead of him, and swoop into his Flight Leader's six o'clock. Perhaps mesmerized by the desperate sight ahead, the young pilot seemed oblivious to any possibility of an attack on his own machine.

Philippi had just started to believe they were in the clear when he heard his wingman's anguished radio call. He felt a chill run through him. He ordered his pilots to jettison their drop tanks and bomb racks in the hope they might just gain enough extra speed to reach the safety of low cloud ahead. Unsure of where any attack might come from he started throwing the jet into hard evasive turns in an effort to protect himself.

Spag levelled out below 100 feet with a high rate of overtake. The lead Skyhawk was barely half a mile ahead of him – close enough to allow him to pick out the Armada jet's distinctive blue and white painted rudder. He heard the Sidewinder acquisition tone growl in his headset, reached forward to the centre console to select the missile, and with the Skyhawk firmly in his sights, he fired.

The Nine Lima whooshed forward from beneath the starboard wing, spearing straight at the A-4's tailpipe. The missile was still accelerating when, barely a second or two after leaping off the rail, it struck its target. The solid-rocket motor was still burning at impact. There was a small explosion as the warhead detonated, followed immediately by the catastrophic destruction of the back end of the aircraft.

Philippi felt his jet buck as the explosion ripped through it. The nose pitched up and he grabbed the stick with both hands, pushing forward with all his strength in an effort to bring it under control. But the hydraulics were gone. Out of the cockpit he caught a glimpse of a Sea Harrier barely 150 yards away to starboard.

*Coming in for the kill*, he thought.

He was out of all options but one.

'They've got me,' he told his wingmen, 'I'm going to eject. I'm OK.' At least he was until he pulled the handle.

The Aircrew Manual recommended ejecting at 135 knots and at no more than 350 knots. Philippi was travelling at over 480 knots when the missile blew up his engine. He tried to throttle back, but there was no response. He tried to open the airbrakes, but there was nothing. Thoughts of expired ejection cartridges and a former comrade who, ejecting from an A-4Q in the seventies, had broken his neck flashed through his mind as he gripped the ejection seat handle between his legs. Holding on to the stick with his right hand to try to keep the wings level – *a naval pilot never lets go of the stick*, he told himself – he yanked hard, felt a stab of pain in his neck as the seat fired, and blacked out.

As he flew past the disintegrating remains of the first Skyhawk, Clive Morrell was already hunting for a second kill. The wingman seemed paralysed by the loss of the Flight Leader. As the seeker head of the second Sidewinder locked on to the A-4's jetpipe, he made no attempt to escape or evade. He was as good as gone. Spag pressed the fire button.

And nothing happened.

He stabbed at it again with his thumb, and again, but the result was the same. As the Skyhawk sat plumb in his sights, the much-vaunted 'death ray' clung stubbornly to its pylon beneath the port wing.

*Bloody hell*, thought Morrell in frustration, *what's the matter?*

Then, just as the SHAR pilot had given up on it, the missile streamed away towards the retreating A-4.

*Guiding nicely*, he thought as the Nine Lima darted towards its target before, a little over halfway through what looked like a good intercept, it seemed to just lose sight of the target and stopped guiding towards it. Morrell could only watch in helpless surprise as his Sidewinder went unexpectedly kaput and fell harmlessly towards the sea.

But in contrast to the supersonic Mirages and Daggers, the Skyhawk couldn't outrun the Sea Harrier. As the two jets roared across Falkland Sound just 50 feet above the water, Morrell was still glued to his enemy's six.

And, he thought to himself, *I've got two guns here.*

Spag selected the ADEN cannon and tried to bring the two guns to bear on his sea-skimming quarry. As he manoeuvred beneath the Skyhawk to compensate for the inclination of the barrels, the view through the HUD was only complicating his effort. The radar was locked on to the ground and feeding distracting nonsense into the gunsight. He berated himself for not switching the Blue Fox to standby on his descent towards the fight.

*It's useless*, he thought as he pulled the trigger, spraying high-explosive ammunition in more or less the right direction.

Still stunned by the sight of Philippi's jet exploding, José Arca was dragged rudely back to reality by the impact of 30mm shells thumping into his own. As the rounds punched into the Skyhawk's starboard wing he nearly cartwheeled into the sea. The little A-4 wobbled and dipped but he just managed to check its descent before disaster.

Unsure whether or not he'd hit the target, Morrell kept his finger on the trigger until he'd emptied his guns, despatching all 240 rounds in a lethal two-and-a-half-second blizzard.

A second burst of fire stitched across Arca's wing. Once again he managed to retain control of the aeroplane, but his problems were accumulating. Hydraulic failure and a loss of electrical power and oxygen saw him reaching for the ejection seat handle. But the rugged little attack jet was still flying. He decided to try to stay with his damaged machine and, instead of attempting to return to the mainland, coax her back to the runway at BAM Malvinas to the east. Without the hydraulics, he was without powered flight controls, though. Despite flying at over 200 knots, beyond the limit specified in the operating procedures, he switched to manual control. The stick was heavy in his hand as he tried to turn in towards the attacking Sea Harrier. With relief, he saw the British jet haul off in an ascending turn to port.

John Leeming dropped in from above the clouds on to the tail of the third Skyhawk. Pushing aside his anxiety over his own lack of cross cover he focused on the target ahead of him. The Sidewinder growled in his headset to signal it had locked on. He could still hear Trident Section talking over the AAWC. He tuned it out.

The pale grey and white A-4Q continued straight and level towards the southwest, the pilot apparently unaware of the danger lurking behind him. Against the frigid water below, the heat of the

Pratt & Whitney turbojet attracted the Nine Lima's seeker head like a beacon.

The picture was perfect, but for the fact that none of the missile's targeting symbology was projected in the HUD. The acquisition tone was there sure enough, though. Leems flipped the safety catch on the control column and thumbed the fire button.

Nothing.

As he continued his tailchase of the Skyhawk he tried pushing the button again with no more success. Seeing the prospect of a kill slipping away, Leeming's efforts to try to get the Sidewinders away became more frenetic. The cockpit was a blur of activity as he tried everything he could think of to get the recalcitrant Nine Lima to launch.

The acquisition growl continued to taunt him, but nothing worked.

He reached forward and selected 'GUNS'. As the graphics displayed in the HUD reconfigured in response, he couldn't help wishing he knew more about the SHAR's gunsight. The brevity of his introduction to the naval fighter was proving problematic as he overhauled the low-flying Skyhawk. Five hundred yards and closing fast.

Leeming squeezed the trigger.

The Sea Harrier juddered as he loosed off a couple of short volleys to find his range. Streams of ejected shell casings rattled against the bottom of the rear fuselage. A third burst peppered the water around the Armada jet.

That got his attention. Scalded by the realization that he'd been fired on, the A-4 pilot snap-rolled the little delta-winged fighter-bomber to starboard.

*Too late*, thought Leeming. Before the Skyhawk could pull into the turn, the RAF pilot placed the gunsight pipper right on the cockpit.

He pressed the fire control. And ahead of him, 30mm cannon shells blazed through the sky.

Leeming was little more than 150 yards away from his target and on a collision course when the first few rounds struck home with devastating effect. Hit along the fuselage behind the cockpit, the jet disintegrated spectacularly into an explosive maelstrom of fire and metal. Too late to dodge the fireball, Leems shrank into his ejection seat and closed his eyes as he flew through the debris cloud produced by his guns. The last thing he saw before emerging on the other side of the fireball was the sight of the Skyhawk's starboard wing breaking away from the fuselage.

*It's going to take me with it*, he thought as he shot through the gap between them.

His weaponry expended, Spag was out of the fight. As he climbed away from his attack on the second A-4Q, he looked back to see the burning remains of an aircraft falling vertically from the sky off his port beam.

*I hope that's not my number two*, he thought, realizing with a start that he'd not seen or heard from his wingman since first catching sight of the lead Skyhawk. He thumbed the RT.

'You OK, Leems?' he asked hopefully.

'Fine,' came the reply, 'how about you?'

Armed only with Leeming's two hung-up Sidewinders, Red Section regrouped and cruise-climbed back to altitude for the return flight to *Hermes*, leaving behind only debris strewn on the water and traces of smoke, soon dispersed by the crisp northwesterly breeze.

## FORTY-FIVE

### Flooding uncontrollably

ALBERTO PHILIPPI HAULED himself up on to the beach, so exhausted that he couldn't even get to his feet. His helmet and oxygen mask had been ripped off in the ejection. After parachuting into the freezing water about 100 yards from the coast, his dinghy had failed to inflate and he was forced to cut away his parachute lines when they got him tangled up in thick beds of kelp beneath the surface.

The knife had been a gift to his son Manfred. But when Philippi rejoined 3 Escuadrilla he'd figured his own need of a handmade 8-inch Puma White Hunter with a staghorn handle was likely to be greater than that of a two-year-old.

Once free of his lines, he'd wriggled out of his harness and swum backstroke to the shore where he triggered his emergency beacon and collapsed on to the sand to regain his strength.

He checked the time. It was not yet four o'clock local time, but sunset was fast approaching. He forced himself up and started scratching out a shallow foxhole with Manfred's knife. Without some kind of protection from the biting wind it was going to be a long and desperately uncomfortable night.

'I will not fall prisoner,' he told himself, 'I will not fall prisoner.' God, he was sure, was watching out for him.

The radar warning receiver picked up the familiar spokes of the radars clustered around Stanley, from the AN/TPS-43 search radar that remained such a thorn in the side of the British Task Force to the Skyguard fire control radars linked to the Oerlikon anti-aircraft cannon, and Roland SAM missiles. But transiting overhead at 30,000 feet, Red Section was out of range. And as the tide of adrenalin from the dogfight began to ebb, John Leeming tried to figure out what could have gone wrong with his Sidewinders. By the time he followed Spag down to low level for the last 50-mile leg back to Mother he had a horrible feeling he knew.

José Arca's effort to make it back to BAM Malvinas was proving even more stressful. He counted ten holes in the wings where Clive Morrell's rounds had doubled down on machine-gun fire aimed at him from *Ardent*: six in the port wing, four punched through the starboard one. Fighting with the heavy manual controls he crossed low over Lafonia, steering clear of Goose Green, then skirted up around the coast of Isla Soledad. Avoiding the undulating ground alone demanded his full attention, but his instrument panel was lit up like Times Square. Fuel bled from the tanks in his punctured wings. But his greater concern was the threat from his own side's defences around Puerto Argentino. Every fast jet pilot flying combat missions over the Malvinas knew about the tragic death of Gustavo Garcia Cuerva, the Fuerza Aérea Argentina Mirage pilot shot down by an Army flak battery as he'd approached the BAM Malvinas runway on the first day of the war.

Arca called the CIC, the Command and Control Centre attached to the AN/TPS-43 radar: 'TALA, this is TABANO 312 . . .'

There was no reply.

Unable to raise his wingman on the radio, Sharkey Ward had used every ounce of fuel retracing his steps to look for him. But with neither sight nor sound of him he feared Steve Thomas had been shot down. After the elation of their one-sided encounter with the Daggers, it was a bitter blow. He requested assistance in the search from *Brilliant* before climbing to altitude to conserve fuel, and with 80 miles to run he raised *Invincible* on the RT.

'Trident Leader,' he identified himself, 'be advised that I am very short of fuel. I believe my number two has been lost over West Falkland. Commencing cruise descent.'

'Roger, leader. Copy you are short of fuel. Your number two is about to land on. He's been hit but he's OK. Over.'

*

'TALA, this is TABANO 312 . . .'

Eventually, Arca made contact with an Army helicopter whose crew were able to act as a radio relay between him and controllers at BAM Malvinas. The air defences around the airfield were weapons tight as he joined the circuit.

He reached forward with his left hand and pulled the landing gear lever at the front of the side panel. He felt the reassuring clunk of the nose gear deploy beneath the cockpit floor. The indicator told him it was locked down. So too was the starboard main gear, but an ominous-looking red light told him all was not well beneath the port wing shredded by the Sea Harrier. He pulled the yellow T-bar emergency gear release lever, but the warning light stayed on. Looking out over the wing, the six entry holes were clean enough, but the exit wounds on the other side were likely to be a whole lot more ragged.

Arca called the tower to request a fly-by during which controllers could try to assess the damage.

Their verdict confirmed the worst.

'The left landing gear has gone,' they told him, 'there's just a hole where it should be. I can see the sky through the holes in your plane. Go and eject over the bay.'

He'd done his best to save the jet but he had no choice, there was no way of bringing her in safely. One last time, Arca pulled back on the heavy controls and climbed to 2,500 feet. Levelling off over the water, he cut the power and slowed to 170 knots. Making sure he was flying straight, level and pointing out to sea, he took off his oxygen mask and reached up to pull the ejection handle above his head.

After tumbling wildly through the air, the seat dropped away and his harness bit as the parachute opened above him. He inflated his lifejacket and watched as his jet, its balance upset by the ruined left wing, banked into a shallow turn to port and circled back towards him as he floated down into Port William Bay.

*It doesn't want to leave me*, he thought as the A-4 curled towards him. *I survived the attack and the fight with the Harrier and now my own plane is going to take me with it.*

The irony of it just seemed too cruel. Until, seeing the peril he was in, the anti-aircraft defences around BAM Malvinas intervened and shot it down.

While José Arca was fished out of the sea by an army UH-1 helicopter, the ship he'd attacked was dying. Twenty minutes after Arca's section shot through, *Ardent* was attacked by the second flight of Armada A-4Qs. The damage she absorbed became overwhelming. Already wounded from an earlier attack by a section of Air Force Daggers, at least three of 3 Escuadrilla's 500lb Snake Eye bombs exploded inside her to finish the devastation of the frigate's stern. Twenty-two officers and men were already dead. A grim assessment of the damage suggested that *Ardent*, on fire, flooding uncontrollably and unable to defend herself, could plunge at any moment. With the old Type 12 frigate HMS *Yarmouth* now alongside to assist, the only decision was to save the rest of them. Alan West gave the order to abandon ship.

As the light faded, he was the last man off, stepping off his ship's fo'c's'le on to *Yarmouth*'s flight deck at 1854Z. Tears streamed down his face. *Ardent*'s young captain had anticipated a tough day, but not for a moment had he imagined that it would end like this.

# FORTY-SIX

## A million flaming rivets

After losing both radios to ground fire over Port Howard, Steve Thomas could no longer communicate with the AAWC, the ship or his Flight Leader. But with both missiles gone, there had seemed little point in trying to follow Sharkey's tilt at the Skyhawks attacking *Ardent* across the Sound so he'd simply climbed away back towards the carrier.

'What was I supposed to think, then?' Ward asked in a half-hearted attempt to berate him for his thoughtlessness.

'You can look after yourself,' he told the boss with a smile. The junior pilot had been much more concerned about not being able to identify himself to British air defence ships. He had his IFF transponder switched on, but there was no way of being sure that it too hadn't been damaged. As well as the round through the cockpit radios, three others had hit the avionics bay behind the engine. Two had punched clean through from bottom to top, while a third had lodged itself in the box housing the TACAN navigation system.

Argentine troops dug in around the small settlement on West Falkland had clearly got their eye in, as the small 1(F) Squadron GR.3 contingent aboard *Hermes* had already learned to their cost.

The second Harrier pair had launched just before midday, ten minutes after Jerry Pook and Mark Hare's return from their attack on the helicopter dispersal west of Stanley. Unable to retract his undercarriage, Flight Leader Peter Squire was forced to return to the deck. His wingman, Jeff Glover, was authorized to continue alone to the AOA on what was his first operational mission. With no requirement for close air support around San Carlos, he was sent to Port Howard to find and attack Argentine positions.

When Clive Morrell and John Leeming recovered aboard the flagship at 1845Z there was still no word of what had happened to him. It was six hours since his last radio transmission to controllers aboard *Fearless*.

The remaining 1(F) pilots found a measure of sanctuary in the planning space they'd been able to secure in a cabin next to the 800 Squadron crewroom. While they closed ranks to consider the fate of their squadron mate and the cold reality of the danger inherent in their low-level mission, their gloom could do nothing to dampen the mood among the SHAR crews following Spag and Leems's triumphant return.

After satisfying the curiosity of deck handlers excited by the sight of one of their cabs returning with empty Sidewinder rails, Red Section climbed from their cockpits and signed the jets in. Both pilots reported the problems they'd had with the Nine Limas. The evidence of Leeming's inability to fire his missiles was there for everyone to see on XZ500. They were still hanging off the wings of the jet.

He walked into the crewroom with Morrell. Both wore big smiles. They unclipped their Mae Wests and began the inelegant job of sweatily extricating themselves from their thick, unyielding rubber immersion suits.

When he filled in his logbook after the mission, Morrell listed his attack on Arca as only a 'possible' kill. But after forcing the Argentinian's diversion to BAM Malvinas while at the same time taking out his landing gear, he'd sealed the 3 Escuadrilla Skyhawk's fate as surely as if he'd blown it out of the sky over Falkland Sound.

When the last CAP pair landed on in the dark at 2130Z, Dave Morgan was just about to take a shower when he got a call from the squadron's maintainers reporting back on their examination of Leeming's SHAR and its weapons. The constant rain and mist had been causing problems for both the electronics in the cockpit and the Nine Lima's seeker head. Neither was designed for the frequent soakings they received. But the solutions had been typically ingenious. To protect the instruments mounted horizontally in the side consoles, they were simply removed, wrapped in clingfilm and screwed back in. The Sidewinders' infrared seekers were dried out in the carrier's bread ovens.

On this occasion, though, they could find nothing wrong with either Leeming's aircraft or missiles. On his way back to the wardroom for a drink, Morgan popped in to see him. After listening to a detailed account of the engagement, Morgan asked him, almost apologetically, 'You did have the missiles selected, didn't you?'

'What do you mean?'

'The square button halfway down the panel behind the stick.'

'Oh, yes, the white one with "AAM" written on it.'

'Yup, that's the one. And it goes green and says "SELECT" when you press it.'

'Oh shit . . .'

Moggie had just confirmed what Leeming himself had feared as he reflected on what had gone wrong during his return to the carrier.

Later, over pints of CSB and cigarettes in the wardroom, Leeming continued to entertain his comrades with what was turning into a fine 'There I was' tale, complete with the necessary hand movements to illustrate the dogfight. 'The sky was full of a million flaming rivets . . .' he said. The sheer thrill of a danger-close guns kill more than made up for the ribbing he received for forgetting how to switch his missiles on. Affectionate taunts of 'Bloody crabs!' washed over him. It was worth it. Silhouettes of the three Skyhawks had already been stencilled on the wardroom bulkhead behind a row of optics.

Bill Covington, Hugh Slade and Steve Brown joined in the congratulations of their colleague. Covington, though, who had been 809's Air Warfare Instructor, couldn't help a nagging feeling that he'd somehow dropped the ball.

*It was my responsibility*, he thought as he enjoyed the bonhomie, *to make sure he knew how to do it!*

'No one told me,' Leems had suggested hopefully when Dave Morgan first got to the bottom of what had happened, 'that you had to push the bloody button in!' And for the purposes of bar-room banter it was a good line, but the truth was that in the heat of the moment the training had kicked in – the training for firing a Red Top missile from a Lightning F.6. 'In the Lightning,' he explained in his defence, 'if the missile growled it would fire, but the switchery's different in this shit heap.' But 809 Squadron's RAF recruit was irrepressible. It didn't matter. Leems could tell people: 'I gunned a Skyhawk!' And even Spag, unfazed by anything much, was prepared to concede that it had all been 'fairly exciting'.

News that one of their number had shot down a Skyhawk was similarly well received by the small Phoenix Squadron contingent aboard *Invincible*.

*Well done, 809*, thought Al Craig, who was particularly pleased that the new squadron scratched up by Tim Gedge had already made its mark. The boss himself, still doing his best to keep the 809 Squadron diary up to date, dutifully recorded it.

What Gedge didn't realize was that he'd seen it unfold with his own eyes. From his own position to the east, he'd caught sight of Spag and Leeming racing south over Falkland Sound in pursuit of the Skyhawks. And over his left shoulder he'd seen one of the Argentine jets explode in a fireball against the setting sun behind. It would remain one of his most vivid memories of the war.

Nor did the 809 CO know that his squadron might also claim a little satisfaction from the two Daggers splashed by Steve Thomas. The skill and aggression belonged to the young 801 pilot alone, but it was 809 that had furnished him with his aeroplane. Rather like one of James Bond's Aston Martins, ZA190 had been a gleamingly new machine when Thomas climbed into the cockpit. He'd then comprehensively beaten up the bad guys before handing her back to the engineers riddled with bullet holes. Unlike the usually terminal battle damage suffered by 007's vehicles, though, ZA190 was patched up and back on the frontline within twenty-four hours.

Being lashed down in the hangar deck away from the elements provided the perfect opportunity to paint over the 809 Squadron phoenix crest on her tail, an indignity suffered by all the Barley Grey jets within days of their arrival in theatre. But ZA190 would always be the jet that Tim Gedge himself had taken to war.

\*

Seconded from an RAF Germany Harrier squadron, John Leeming was really one of their own, but the RAF contingent from 1(F) Squadron were in no mood to raise a glass to his success. The small group of GR.3 pilots had been hit hard by Jeff Glover's loss. Before the night was done, though, their gloom was lifted when intelligence reached *Hermes* that suggested he might have survived.

A signals intercept referred to a Flight Lieutenant *William* Glover – Glover's middle name. A short time later, another signal confirmed that he was in Stanley suffering from a broken jaw and shoulder.

After he'd authorized his wingman to continue with the mission alone when his own jet had gone unserviceable, Peter Squire had carried an acute sense of responsibility for what had happened to him. Exhausted and relieved, but enjoying none of the adrenalin-flushed delight of the SHAR crews, he sat down to write a letter to his wife, Carolyn. Unable to share the source of his confidence, he simply told her that he was 'optimistic' about Glover's prospects.

Official confirmation that Glover was safe and had been flown back to Argentina as a prisoner of war didn't come until later.

On board *Invincible*, another snippet of information culled from Argentine radio traffic had raised the pilots' spirits. Word had reached the 801 crewroom that, in an obvious mark of respect, their opponents had taken to referring to the SHARs as 'La Muerte Negra' – the Black Death. Sharkey Ward urged the squadron to adopt it as a battle cry heralding their arrival over the Argentine guard frequency.

While Ward and his men enjoyed their success, good news at Río Grande was in shorter supply. The second section of A-4Q Skyhawks from 3 Escuadrilla had been on frequency during Red Section's mauling of their compatriots. It hadn't made for happy listening. They'd heard Marcelo Marquez's anguished cry of 'Harriers!' and Alberto Philippi's announcement that he was ejecting. All three of the second flight of Skyhawks had been able to make their attack on *Ardent* and escape Death Valley unscathed. One hundred and fifty miles out they had radioed ahead to ask about Philippi's flight. They were told none had returned. They checked their watches and they knew all three jets must have been lost.

In their first action, 3 Escuadrilla had lost 40% of their available airframes and a third of their pilots. News hadn't yet reached the mainland that any of them had survived.

The losses cut deep with the crews of 2 Escuadrilla with whom they were in such close proximity. The SuE pilots recalled the last words exchanged with their good friends – wishing them well as they walked out to the jets, still clutching the remains of a snatched lunch. And after an enforced lay-off following the sinking of the *Sheffield* and the retirement of the target-finding Neptunes, the Super Etendard pilots were eager to re-enter the fray. As it had been following the sinking of the *Belgrano*, a desire to avenge their fallen comrades was proving to be a great motivator.

They just needed reasonably accurate coordinates for the location of the British Carrier Battle Group.

On board *Atlantic Conveyor*, Mike Layard had been assiduous about keeping Ian North and his Merchant Marine crew up to date with the progress of the fight and what lay ahead.

'My instructions,' he said after gathering them together in the Officers' Lounge, 'are that we are to be ready to enter Falkland Sound in company with *Elk* on D-Day Plus Two.' The day after tomorrow. 'Any questions, gentlemen?'

'I've a question, sir,' replied Charles Drought, 'and I speak for all on board.' Since the Exocet attack on *Sheffield*, *Conveyor*'s Third Engineer had suffered from an unshakeable sense of foreboding. 'What sort of protection will we have from aerial attack when we go into the Sound? As you know, we've got sod all apart from a couple of peashooters on each side of the bridge.'

'Good question,' Layard replied. 'I can assure you that the *Conveyor* will be protected by frigates which will be stationed at each end of the Sound and also by Rapier batteries which have been set up ashore above where we'll be offloading our equipment.'

Layard wished he felt as confident as he sounded. At a meeting with Sandy Woodward aboard *Hermes* a few days earlier he'd not minced his words.

'I have no doubts,' Layard told the Task Force Commander, 'and you should have no doubts, about how vulnerable we are.'

'I'll make sure you're looked after,' the Admiral had reassured him. 'You'll have a permanent goalkeeper.'

That was once they got to the AOA. For now, as an extra precaution, while the *Conveyor*'s helicopters were put to work moving stores around the Battle Group, he ordered that her tall, brilliant-white superstructure be repainted in grey in a valiant effort to make it a little less conspicuous.

Back home in Somerset, Layard's wife Elspeth tried to get by on BBC reports and snippets of information from well-informed naval friends, but it was clear things in the South Atlantic were heating up. It was the wives of SHAR pilots that she really felt for. She was close to so many of them and knew they were going through agonies. Tomorrow would bring fresh sadness when she saw them all at EJ's memorial service.

'I trust,' she wrote in her diary at the end of the day, 'that Michael is well away from the action.'

# FORTY-SEVEN

## Deep water and clear horizons

THE SAFETY OF the *Atlantic Conveyor* was just one of a host of decisions over which Sandy Woodward had to balance risk against reward. It was long after midnight before the Admiral finally put an end to his appraisal of the day's events and tried to get some sleep. At the most basic level, D-Day had been a success. Over 3,000 troops and 1,000 tons of equipment had been put safely ashore. In securing the primary objective, though, a heavy price had been paid.

'*Brilliant* has one end only, and radar, and propulsion,' he wrote in his diary. 'By 2300 it seems that *Ardent* is sinking. *Argonaut* is stopped but has her weapons working. *Antrim* is floating and moving, but has no weapons and an unexploded bomb in her backside.'

Critically, he noted, all the amphibious ships had emerged unscathed. But while he was prepared to take losses, he couldn't sustain them at the rate he'd suffered this day, or in another two days his force of escorts, and with them the goalkeepers required to protect the carriers, would be no more.

The aerial equation looked a little better. Today alone, ten Argentine fast jets had been shot down. Alongside the six splashed by Ward, Thomas, Morrell and Leeming, 800 Squadron had despatched a further two Skyhawks and a Dagger. A Seacat missile launched from one of the Leander class frigates in the Sound took care of one more Dagger. If that loss rate continued over the days ahead, he thought, the enemy would be looking at attrition that might even give the Russians pause for thought.

According to his own estimates, though, that still left the enemy with around seventy serviceable aircraft. He remained dependent on just twenty-five Sea Harriers.

And so it came back to air superiority and the effectiveness of the SHARs and missiles. If they failed, if one of the carriers was lost before the ground war was won, the advantage would still shift decisively in favour of the Argentinians.

But in San Carlos Water, the landing of men and materiel needed to continue for days. After the weight of air attacks on D-Day it was decided to offload 42 Commando and sail P&O's 45,000-ton flagship *Canberra* to safer waters. The 'White Whale' was simply too conspicuous a target. But there were still plenty of ships Woodward had to shepherd in and out of the anchorage. Not least among them was *Atlantic Conveyor*.

She had already begun to prove her worth as a third deck, but it was the value of her cargo to the ground war where her contribution would really count. Aboard the requisitioned container ship were the means, through the 18 Squadron Chinooks and six 848 NAS Wessex HU.5s, to mount an effective air-mobile campaign. Each Wessex was designed to carry sixteen Royal Marines. Between them, the four Chinooks could chopper in another 200 – at a squeeze, perhaps as many as 300. The capability of moving battalion-strength numbers of troops to where they were needed could dramatically affect the course of the war. No less important was the aluminium matting with which a Forward Operating Base for the Harriers was to be built. Once the fast jets could operate ashore from a FOB, Woodward could relieve a little of the operational burden placed on the carriers. More importantly, he could spread his risk.

Until that point, though, the success of the campaign depended completely on the fleet's ability to provide defence against an Argentine air attack. And on the survival of the carriers. *At least,* he thought, *the Harriers are performing superbly, but the Args must soon come after* Hermes *and* Invincible *in a more determined way.*

Their only effective means of doing so lay with the Exocet-armed Super Etendards of 2 Escuadrilla.

\*

Woodward had no reason to believe that D-Day Plus One would see any let-up in the intensity of the Argentine air attacks. *And*, he felt certain, *they must surely wake up to the fact that proper escorts will cut down the losses inflicted on their bombers*. If the enemy started dropping jets armed with heatseeking missiles into each strike formation he was going to start losing SHARs, and yet, in order to protect the burgeoning British position ashore, he felt he had no option other than to be more front-footed in its defence.

Prior to D-Day, JJ Black and John Coward had urged him to push the air defences further out by establishing a missile trap west of the Falklands. A combination of Type 42 and Type 22, they argued, would not only act as an effective radar picket providing fighter direction for the SHARs, but would itself be capable of picking off incoming Argentine raiders with Sea Dart and Seawolf respectively. On the night of the landings, Bill Canning, the captain of *Brilliant*'s sister ship *Broadsword*, sent a signal to Woodward reiterating the suggestion. This time, the Admiral agreed. He moved the carriers as far to the west as he dared to try to give the SHARs a little more time on CAP.

*Coventry* and *Broadsword* were sent to patrol the waters north of Pebble Island. While David Hart-Dyke, the Type 42's captain, would have preferred the deep water and clear horizons 100 miles further west around the Jason Islands, early indications were that the 42/22 pairing would work well. The combination was quickly coined the 'Type 64'. And Woodward's fresh initiative to control the skies soon brought his ships into contact with their opponent's equally determined efforts to scan the seas in search of the Carrier Battle Group.

At dawn on 22 May, only damage to the launcher and salt encrustation caused by heavy seas saved a shadowing Fuerza Aérea Argentina 707 from a fiery demise at the hands of *Coventry*'s Sea Darts. By the time a sailor managed to fix the jammed flash doors with a lump hammer, the Burglar was out of range.

Later the same day, 1,800 miles to the northeast, another of Escuadrón II's 707s survived an even closer encounter with *Coventry*'s sister ship, HMS *Cardiff*, on her way south to reinforce the Task Force with the HMS *Bristol* group.

\*

The Boeing's Second Engineer was the first to see the Sea Dart missile streaking towards them, tracing a line of dark exhaust smoke behind it. In a desperate effort to save his aircraft, her captain, Vice-comodoro Otto Rittondale, stood the big airliner on its wing, throwing her into a maximum-rate turn to port to try to evade the missile. Extending the airbrakes, he rolled into a steep emergency descent. Warning alarms shrieked, while the airframe creaked and groaned in protest at its rough treatment.

Rittondale saw another Sea Dart flash past the cockpit windows before exploding. Worried that the shockwave had damaged his flight controls, the pilot kept a close eye on his hydraulic pressure as he held the Boeing in a steep dive.

To radar operators aboard *Cardiff*, their target's desperate evasive action looked almost suicidal.

It also saved the lives of everyone on board.

Fired at extreme range, neither missile had sufficient energy in the terminal phase of its flight to respond to the 707's manoeuvres. Levelling out low over the waves, Rittondale closed the airbrakes and pushed the four throttles forward to maximum power. Streaking close to the wavetops at over 375 knots, their escape left a scar of disturbed sea water in its wake.

The risk to the unarmed 707s was extreme, but the potential reward, in the shape of reliable coordinates for the carriers, was worth it. The outcome of the war depended on the Argentinians' ability to act on that intelligence. In essence, Woodward had concluded he was engaged in a straightforward *prizefight between the Royal Navy and General Galtieri's Air Forces*.

In response, the Sea Harrier squadrons mounted their most determined defence to date, launching sixty CAP missions in defence of the AOA between dawn and dusk. Every twenty minutes a fresh pair of fighters hurled themselves off one of the carriers and accelerated towards Falkland Sound at low level. At one point, ten of *Hermes'* fifteen SHARs were airborne at once, but hopes of adding to the previous day's tally were disappointed.

A low-pressure system hung over southern Argentina, blanketing in low cloud, rain and showers everything from the Andes to the west to the east coast north of Trelew. Fast jet operations from the mainland were all but scrubbed, leaving the SHAR pilots wondering what had happened to their opponents.

Argentina's day had not been without profit, however.

While, in San Carlos Water, reinforcement of the British beachhead had been able to continue without interruption, on the other side of East Falkland, the Air Force AN/TPS-43 radar operators of the Vigilancia y Control Aéreo had tracked and plotted the Sea Harrier flights as they transited in and out from their CAP stations. The sheer volume of British sorties ensured that the data given to their Armada colleagues in the Puerto Argentino Operations Centre for analysis were more comprehensive and revealing than ever before.

Their conclusions were transmitted to Comando de Aviación Naval commanders on the mainland, who in turn passed them on to Jorge Colombo's Super Etendard detachment at Río Grande. It was critical intelligence.

Unless and until 2 Escuadrilla intervened, the Sea Harriers were in the ascendant. While they might not be able wholly to contain the threat Argentina's fast jets posed to the success of the British operation, they could themselves fly over the TEZ with near impunity. As the new arrivals from 809 Squadron were finding out.

# FORTY-EIGHT

## Full chat

A THOUSAND YARDS to his left, John Leeming's Flight Leader flicked his jet on to its back and pulled into a steep dive. His voice crackled across the RT.

'Helicopter over the lake below me,' explained Dave Morgan. 'Going down.'

Leeming tipped in behind him, feeling a little more confident that, after the excitement of his last flight, he'd now got the better of the Sea Harrier's weapons system. They railed towards the target like a rollercoaster car coming down the hill.

Morgan had been lucky to catch a glimpse of it. It had been nothing more than a flash of spinning rotor blades over water in his peripheral vision that had exposed the helicopter. Flying low and slow over the dull tan and khaki ground it would have been near impossible to pick out from 8,000 feet above. And if he lost sight of it, there was no certainty of finding it again.

Descending in a hard left turn, Morgan fought the mounting Gs as he kept his eyes locked on the target. As he swooped to meet the bogey head on, Leeming carved round in a descending turn behind him to try to trap their quarry in a pincer.

Flying just 10 feet above the flat valley floor, Teniente Enrique Riis kept station at the rear of the formation, covering the tails of the three Aérospatiale Pumas ahead of him. Armed with 70mm rockets and podded 7.62mm machine guns, his sleek Agusta 109 could provide a measure of protection to the utility helicopters with their cargo of 120mm heavy mortars and ammunition. But when he saw the two fighters dropping out of the late morning sun, there was no time to do anything but shout an urgent warning: 'Planes! Planes! Get on the ground!'

'Hostile! Hostile!' There'd been no time to wait for the AAWC to report back on whether or not there were friendlies in the area, but as Morgan closed fast on his target from the north he recognized it as an Argentine Puma.

Leems was already looking beyond him. He thumbed the transmit button in reply.

'Visual,' he confirmed, 'I've got three more of them. Engaging the gunship.'

He streaked in from the south in pursuit of the armed escort, nudging the nose to starboard as the khaki-painted Agusta ducked towards one of the gulleys that sliced into the escarpment rolling down from the 2,000-foot-high ridge of the Hornby Mountains.

By the time he'd positively identified his target, Dave Morgan was too close and low to bring his guns to bear. Flying at 450 knots, he roared over the cockpit of the lead Puma, nearly close enough to make out the alarm on the faces of its Argentine Army crew. Barely 10 feet separated him from the helo's rotor as he pulled back hard on the stick, giving it a touch of left rudder as he hauled into a climbing turn to port to set himself up for a strafing run. He strained against the 5g load. As his field of vision faded to grey around the edges he grunted in resistance, wishing he'd chosen to wear his anti-g suit. Crisp white vortices streamed off the wings in the cold, damp air.

In the cockpit of the Puma the impact of the roiling air left in Morgan's wake felt as if they'd been hit by gunfire. The pilot, Teniente Enrique Magnaghi, thought he'd lost his tail rotor. The effect was much the same. The Puma, loaded with a 120mm heavy mortar and 2 tons of ammunition, began to spin around beneath the main rotor.

*We're going to die in the crash*, thought the pilot. Fighting to maintain control, he tried to slow down and control their descent until the Puma slewed into the ground and rolled on to its side in a whirlwind of violent disassembly. The cabin immediately began to fill with thick black smoke.

*Now the fire's going to kill us*, thought Magnaghi as he struggled with his harness and fought to clear his head. His co-pilot and crewman snapped his collarbone as they clambered over him to try to smash open the emergency exit. But they managed to drag him to safety before the ammunition started cooking off.

Morgan was astonished by the sight of the exploding Puma. He hadn't touched it. But whatever had brought it down it needed no further attention from him. He turned away and went looking for his wingman.

With the Agusta in his sights, Leems fired his guns. The reassuring judder that two days earlier had signalled the imminent destruction of Marcelo Marquez's Skyhawk thrummed through the SHAR's compact frame. He could only blink in surprise as his carefully aimed rounds chewed into the ground well short of his target. Perplexed by how he'd got it so wrong, he pulled back on the stick to recover from his dive as the escarpment began to loom large through his head-up display.

'Where is the target reference your fall of shot?' Morgan asked over the RT.

'One hundred yards to the east,' Leems was pained to admit.

*Christ*, thought Morgan, *how did he miss by that much?* He settled into his own strafing run. Holding the pipper over the target as he ran in, he dipped the nose, and pulled the trigger. He'd overcooked it, opening fire before he needed to. The first rounds hit ahead of the fleeing helicopter before walking back to within 30 yards of it. Angry with himself for squandering a perfectly good first pass, he held the SHAR in a steep turn as his wingman rolled in to attack again behind him.

Against another helicopter, ground fire or even a turboprop, Riis's weapons might have been of some help, but the only realistic defence against fast jets was to save yourself. Riis slowed the 109 with a smooth pull back on the cyclic, while hovering the collective to dump lift. A brisk correction cushioned them onto the ground. He and the engineer sitting next to him clambered out of the side doors, jumped down and ran across the soft ground, trying to put as much distance between them and their aircraft as they could as the Sea Harrier dived in.

'Off – no hit,' Leeming reported in frustration after his next strafing run, confirming 'in visual' as he pulled round for another go, slipping easily back into the radio calls and standard operating procedures of the seasoned ground attack pilot he'd been before he was press-ganged into a Fleet Air Arm air defence squadron. He *knew* he wasn't as bad a shot as his margin of error today was suggesting. Acceptably accurate shooting was supposed to be bread and butter to an RAF mud-mover. There must be another reason for it. And the fact that on both occasions his shells had torn up the turf the same distance short of his target suggested that.

'What the hell is the sight setting for these guns, Moggie?' he asked Morgan in exasperation.

His wingman filled him in, and Leeming reached for the WING-SPAN/DEPRESSION knob. He'd used the same sight settings as he would in the GR.3, but the SHAR was a heavier aircraft and the depression of the gunsight in air-to-ground mode took that into account. His truncated conversion to the FRS.1 had caught him out again.

The irony of it was that it was Leems himself who'd briefed the rest of 809 Squadron on the arcane art of close air support – of shooting at stuff on the ground.

Out of ammunition after a final pass he had to leave the Agusta to his wingman, who finished it off with a one-second burst from his ADEN cannon. Morgan's shells ripped through the grounded gunship in a series of small firecracker flashes before moments later the fuel tanks blew up. Just like in the movies.

But if Leems was still struggling to acclimatize to his new mount, there was nothing wrong with his eyesight. A couple of hundred yards from where Morgan's first victim lay crumpled and belching out thick black smoke he spotted another one of the three Pumas. He called it in.

'I'm out of ammunition,' he admitted through gritted teeth, but he thought he could at least act as a pathfinder for his wingman. 'I'll pull up right over the target.'

**Above left**: Scramble! An 801 Squadron Sea Harrier launches on another combat air patrol mission from *Invincible*'s 7° ski-jump. The location of the Sea Dart missile launcher on the carrier's fo'c's'le prevented the construction of a steeper 12° ramp like that fitted to *Hermes*.

**Above right**: An Argentine Air Force Dagger in among the British ships at San Carlos. Although undoubtedly courageous and skilful, these low-level attacks also meant fuzing the bombs correctly proved problematic.

**Left**: Type 22 Frigate HMS *Brilliant* in the crosshairs of an attacking Argentine Dagger. But they didn't have it all their own way. Three Daggers were shot down by Sharkey Ward and Steve Thomas in a single dogfight during the afternoon of 21 May.

**Below**: Starboard ventilation. Cannon shells from an Argentine Dagger tore through *Brilliant*'s Operations Room and caused a number of shrapnel injuries, including a wound that temporarily incapacitated Fighter Controller Laon Hulme.

**Above**: Shore-based at Rio Grande after the withdrawal of *25 de Mayo*, the pilots of 3 Escuadrilla pose in front of their aircraft before going into action for the first time on 21 May. From left to right: (back) Marquez, Lecour, Oliveira, Zubizaretta, Philippi, Castro Fox, Rotolo, Benitez; (front) Medici, Sylvester, Arca, Olmedo.

**Right**: A pair of 3 Escuadrilla Skyhawks carrying a heavy load of Snake Eyes. 3-A-312 would not survive its first operational mission.

**Below**: Hit by the 3 Escuadrilla Skyhawks, HMS *Ardent* burns while her crew abandon ship for the safety of HMS *Yarmouth*. By dawn the next morning only her foremast remained visible above the waves. Twenty-two of her crew lost their lives.

**Left**: Guns kill. Unable to fire his Sidewinder missiles, 809's John Leeming shot down one of the Skyhawks that had attacked *Ardent* with close-range 30mm cannon fire. He was lucky to fly through the wreckage of his disintegrating target without suffering damage to his own jet. His opponent, Marcelo Marquez, was killed.

**Below**: Job done. During the same sortie, Leeming's Flight Leader, Clive Morrell, accounted for two more of the 3 Escuadrilla Skyhawks. Morrell was new to flying air defence having previously flown with 809 Squadron from HMS *Ark Royal* in its previous incarnation flying Buccaneer strike jets.

**Above**: ZEUS Flight. A Grupo 5 A-4B Skyhawk of the Argentine Air Force sits ready for a mission at BAM Gallegos – one of six jets that launched on a mission from the base on 25 May. Note the ship kill markings below the cockpit.

**Left**: VULCANO Flight. In a carefully coordinated attack, two waves of Argentine Air Force A-4 Skyhawks attacked HMS *Coventry* and HMS *Broadsword* as they steamed north of Pebble Island. *Broadsword* survived this attack. *Coventry* would not be so lucky.

HMS *Coventry* was devastated by the explosion of two bombs dropped by ZEUS Flight, the second formation of A-4s from BAM Gallegos. Nineteen members of her crew lost their lives in the attack. By nightfall the destroyer had turned turtle and would soon sink to the bottom in 300 feet of water.

**Above**: 2 Escuadrilla Aeronaval de Caza y Ataque. From left to right: Rodriguez, Barraza, Colavino, Colombo, Bedacarratz, Curilovic, Francisco, unknown, Mayora. On 25 May they went hunting for the British carriers.

**Left**: In an effort to make *Atlantic Conveyor*'s bone-white superstructure less conspicuous, Senior Naval Officer Michael Layard had it painted grey. On 25 May, when the ship was ordered into San Carlos to unload her cargo, the job was still incomplete.

Just before sundown on 25 May, two Exocet missiles slammed into *Atlantic Conveyor*'s aft port quarter from the northwest. Unable to contain the fires, the ship's Master Ian North ordered the crew to abandon ship.

**Left**: After losing her bow, the burnt-out hulk of *Atlantic Conveyor* sank three days later, on 28 May. Twelve men lost their lives in the attack, including Ian North. He was last off his ship, but was unable to reach the safety of a life raft.

**Left**: The *Invincible* attack. With just one Exocet missile left in their arsenal, 2 Escuadrilla launched another attack. Supported by four Argentine Air Force Skyhawks armed with bombs, the plan was to take on fuel from a KC-130 tanker to give them the range to get in behind the British ships and attack from where they were at their most vulnerable.

**Right**: The six Argentine jets inbound to the Task Force during the 30 May attack. Equipped and trained to fly long distances over water, the Navy Super Etendard pilots led the way.

**Left**: After launching the Exocet, the Super Etendards turned for home, leaving the four Skyhawks to continue their attack against the British ships. This picture was taken from HMS *Exeter* as one of the A-4s streaked overhead. The raid ended in failure and only two of the Skyhawks survived the mission.

**Right**: Once the British forces were ashore in numbers, the Argentine garrison, unable to be meaningfully supported or resupplied from the mainland, were on borrowed time. After the Argentine surrender on 14 June, HMS *Hermes* sailed close to the islands for the first time.

**Above left**: Airborne early warning. Seen here in formation with its predecessor, the Fairey Gannet AEW.3, the Sea King AEW.2 helicopter was designed, built and put into service in just three months. These rapidly converted machines could detect low-flying targets at ranges of over 100 miles.

**Above right**: Journey's end. Before returning to Portsmouth, a rust-streaked HMS *Hermes* meets HMS *Illustrious*. The new carrier was hurriedly completed before sailing south to relieve her sister ship, HMS *Invincible*. As well as two of the new Sea King AEW.2s, she was also equipped with two radar-controlled Phalanx Gatling cannon to counter the Exocet threat.

**Left**: Michael Layard attended memorial services for his friend Ian North and, in Liverpool Cathedral, for all of those lost aboard *Atlantic Conveyor*.

**Below**: A hero's welcome. After being relieved by *Illustrious*, HMS *Invincible* returned to Portsmouth in mid-September to a rapturous reception. She'd been at sea for over five months.

IAN H. NORTH
Master of the 'Atlantic Conveyor'

DONCASTER PARISH CHURCH
(ST GEORGE'S)

SEA SUNDAY, 11th JULY, 1982

**Above left**: Fox Two. With the phoenix emblem restored to their tails, 809 Squadron returned to the Falklands to provide air defence after the war. Operating from HMS *Illustrious* and ashore from Stanley Airport, the enhanced SHARs were fitted with chaff and flare dispensers and could now carry two Sidewinders under each wing, as this post-war test firing illustrates.

**Above right**: With the completion of an extension to Stanley's runway, F-4 Phantoms from 29(F) Squadron RAF arrived to assume responsibility for defending the islands. Tim Gedge intercepted and escorted the first of them to arrive.

**Right**: Lessons learned. The Sea Harrier FRS.1 was replaced in the mid-nineties with the vastly more capable FA.2. Fitted with an advanced radar capable of tracking multiple targets and four medium-range AMRAAM missiles, the FA.2 served the fleet until 2006.

**Above**: Phoenix rising. In 2013 it was announced that 809 NAS would return to the frontline. Flying the F-35B Lightning, a supersonic fifth-generation stealth fighter capable of taking off and landing vertically, the squadron will fly from the Royal Navy's new 60,000-ton Queen Elizabeth class carriers.

Once again he dived towards the valley floor, skimming low over the rise and fall of the rough terrain towards the isolated Puma. Determined to hit his mark, he timed his ascent with care, before hauling back angrily on the stick, wringing out some of his frustration as he pulled the little fighter into the vertical, trading speed for height in an exhilarating zoom climb from ground level. Rolling out on top he watched Moggie dive in beneath him.

Mayor Roberto Yanzi had ordered his crew to jump out of the Puma's side doors and run before he'd even landed. A few yards on he put the wheels down and tumbled out behind them, throwing himself flat on the ground next to his men barely 10 yards from the helicopter. The main rotor was still spinning. He grabbed their hands and told them: 'It's an honour to die by your side.'

Then they heard the first rounds explode into the machine, followed a split second later by the report from the British jet's cannon.

Two rounds. That was all Morgan had left in his magazines. But his wingman's efforts to mark the target and his own good shooting had ensured they counted. Now short on fuel, Morgan and Leeming climbed away to the east for the return to *Hermes*.

The Argentine crew, pinching themselves that they'd survived the attack, checked the helicopter. One of the two 30mm rounds fired by Morgan's Sea Harrier had punched a hole into the tail pylon. It looked repairable, they thought, but she wasn't going anywhere for now. They salvaged what they could from the cargo hold and ran off to find better cover away from the helicopter. It proved to be a wise decision.

When Morgan heard Gold Section check in over the AAWC he called them up to report the position of his last victim. He reckoned he could hear the grin on Dave Braithwaite's face over the RT at the thought of getting some action.

Gold Leader, Tim Gedge, acknowledged and turned towards Shag Cove, pushing the throttle forward as he accelerated towards West

Falkland. Brave followed him. Since joining *Invincible*, more often than not the two most senior members of 809 had been operating as a pair. So far they'd been frustrated though.

'Make switches,' Gedge called as they coasted in over the straight bare-rock ridge that walled off the entire length of the eastern shore. Gedge was in the lead as they curled round in a hard left-hand turn towards the valley floor where Morgan had reported the Puma's last location. The pressure built in their inner ears as the altitude reading projected on to the HUD flickered like the numbers on a petrol pump to record their rapid descent.

Then once again, fifteen minutes after the departure of the first pair of SHARs, the snarl of Pegasus engines reverberated around the skies south of Port Howard.

Dark olive green against the dull peatbog, it wasn't at all easy to pick out the target from the background. A smoke signal would have helped, but the hulk of the nearby crashed Puma was all but burned out.

Gedge elected to make a dive attack. As boss of 800 Squadron, he'd consistently outpointed his pilots on the ranges, but it had been a while since his last trip to Lilstock. And the Puma was *very* difficult to see. He spotted it late on his first pass and elected to go round again. It seemed a reasonable expectation that a helicopter, put down and abandoned before reaching its destination, was not going to be a defended target.

Brave wasn't so sure. If there were men with guns, then get close enough to the ground, he reckoned, *and they'll always shoot over the top of you.* He glimpsed the shape of the Puma in the gully before dropping to low level.

*Eagle eyes*, he congratulated himself as he switched the HUD to air-to-ground mode, then took the SHAR down below the level of the surrounding high ground. Wide and shallow, there was room to manoeuvre between the arena sides of the valley. Gedge orbited above him.

*I'm not diving on it*, Brave decided, figuring that silhouetting the SHAR against the sky would just make him too conspicuous to any ground fire. Instead he kept on down towards the valley floor until the hills filled his peripheral vision. He reached forward to flip the gun selector switch to LIVE and double-checked the gunsight depression.

With his left hand he advanced the throttle all the way to the stops. Full chat. The speed climbed past 500 knots. At the same time the indicator of the bar display recording his altitude on the HUD dropped to the bottom. He was no more than 20 feet from the ground. When he cranked her into the turn, his port wingtip would be scoring through the air barely 6 feet over the grass and heather.

Time to go. With his right hand he moved the stick a fraction to the left, then pulled into the turn, the crisp response of the SHAR belying the fingertip touch of his control inputs. The inflatable bladders of the g-suit filled with air, compressing his legs and midriff as he was forced back into his ejection seat. He applied a little left rudder to prevent himself from swinging up and out of the turn like an out-of-grip Indy 500 driver. Keep it low. Just below the HUD the angle of attack indicator needle swung up towards the red as the little fighter's wings bit at the dense air. Clouds of condensation cooled by the suddenly reduced air pressure above the wing billowed and flared behind the cockpit. Two clean white vortices streamed behind him, tracing his arc.

The ground blurred past to his left almost touching distance away. He focused only on the view through the HUD of the nose hauling round to the west. He pulled the trigger to loose off a trial burst and the guns hurled 30mm shells ahead of him. He saw puffs explode in the ground to the right of him. That didn't look right. *How are my guns able to point over there?* he wondered for a moment before realizing it was defensive fire aimed at him. He pulled even harder into the turn.

*They'll always shoot over the top of you.*

But self-protection wasn't the only reason for coming in through the weeds. At this height he'd be able to frame the Puma against the background of the pale sky. It would stick out like a soldier standing on a ridgeline at sunset. Nor did he have to worry about the axis of the guns that had caused so many of his colleagues difficulty as they tried to get beneath their targets to bring the upward-angled barrels to bear on low-flying targets.

This way, spraying fire through a circular arc like some horizontal Catherine wheel, he'd scythe down anything that flashed across his sights.

He pulled the trigger again and the SHAR juddered from the percussive thrum of the two ADEN cannon.

As he dragged the jet's nose across the horizon, Brave saw the dark outline of the Puma traverse the length of the HUD from top to bottom before disappearing beneath him.

30mm high-explosive shells stitched across the tall fuselage. As he climbed away, Brave saw the main rotor come away as flames licked up around the engines and gearbox.

Now approaching bingo fuel after so long at full power, Brave told his Flight Leader he needed to return to Mother. Gold Formation climbed away from West Falkland, sufficiently satisfied with their day's work for Gedge to record it in the 809 Squadron diary on his return. They had good reason to be.

# FORTY-NINE

## Gutted, skinned and butchered

ONLY ONCE THEY were sure that the second Sea Harrier pair had left the scene did Roberto Yanzi and his crew return to assess the damage. Their Puma, after suffering minor damage from the first attack, had been written off by the second. All four helicopter crews were carried to safety by the one Puma that had escaped the attention of the British fighters along with whatever supplies they could salvage, but it was the last time the Army ever risked trying to resupply the Port Howard garrison by air.

More importantly, the destruction of the three helicopters at Shag Cove took another lump out of the occupiers' dwindling utility helicopter force.

Of the five Pumas the Comando de Aviación de Ejército, the Argentine Army's air wing, had deployed to the islands, only one now survived. Of their two heavy-lift Chinooks, one had been reduced to a pile of burned-out wreckage by cannon fire from an RAF Harrier GR.3 two days earlier; the other, suffering from incurable engine problems, hadn't flown since April. That left them with eight Bell UH-1H Iroquois. At first glance, they still had two-thirds of the fleet to work with, but because of the loss of the bigger Pumas and Chinooks they'd lost well over half of their capacity.

Since their arrival in theatre just days earlier, *Atlantic Conveyor*'s brood of 809 Squadron Sea Harriers and 1(F) Squadron GR.3s had been directly responsible for removing that third, and in doing so had determined that the Argentine forces defending the islands were effectively no longer air-mobile. Although there remained sizeable troop concentrations around East Falkland, Argentine commanders had lost their ability to rapidly reinforce them or to use air cavalry to outflank their British opponents. Degraded like this they would soon be able to offer little more than a static defence of their enclave around the capital.

Plans to airlift in another eight Hueys had had to be abandoned after the arrival of the Sea Harriers on 1 May. Only the wholesale removal of La Muerte Negra would restore the Argentine ability to reinforce the Malvinas garrison. And so, with the British now well established ashore on the west coast of East Falkland, Argentine commanders' hopes of a breakthrough rested, as ever, with the men of the Comando de Aviación Naval at Río Grande.

3 Escuadrilla received orders to mount a mission against the British anchorage in San Carlos just after midday on 23 May. The CO, Rodolfo Castro Fox, still unable to raise his arm to close his own canopy after his recent ejection, would lead in the surviving Omega-equipped jet. From his depleted pool of pilots he selected Capitán de Corbeta Carlos Zubizaretta as his number two. Tenientes Carlos Oliveira and Marco Benitez completed the flight of four A-4Qs.

The pilots planned their mission with the assistance of their comrades from the Super Etendard squadron. The SuE pilots, still waiting for their next opportunity to strike at the British, were eager to help. Many had come up through pilot training together. The grim conditions of their forward deployment to Río Grande only deepened the bond between the two COAN fast jet squadrons. They plotted a route across the hills, islands and inlets north of Gran Malvina that they hoped would protect them from the British radars until they were over the Sound and accelerating into their bomb runs.

Outside, beneath the usual smothering of thick cloud, the armourers had worked through the wind and rain to load each jet with four 500lb Snake Eye bombs.

With the mission planning and briefing complete, the Skyhawk pilots walked out to the apron and climbed into the waiting jets. As Carlos Zubizaretta settled into his ejection seat his friend, SuE pilot Alejandro Francisco, mounted the steps next to his cockpit and wished him well.

\*

A strong 30-knot crosswind blew in across Runway Two-Six from the north as Castro Fox led the four pale grey fighter-bombers into the air.

Oliveira was back on the ground an hour later after he'd been unable to transfer fuel from the KC-130H tanker to his drop tanks. The remaining Skyhawks continued without him, surviving Seacat missiles, heavy gunfire and further fuel transfer problems before returning to Río Grande unscathed.

Zubizaretta's mission had been a frustrating one, though, his flight home impeded by the 2 tons of bombs he'd had to haul back with him. While his two wingmen had launched attacks against the assault ship HMS *Intrepid* and HMS *Antelope*, the sister ship of their last victim, *Ardent*, Zubizaretta's Snake Eyes had hung up, stubbornly refusing to come off the pylons. And now, low on fuel, he had to put his heavy jet down in that crosswind gusting at over 40 knots at a right angle to the runway. Patches of ice on the strip only complicated his task.

Zubizaretta touched down gently enough, but the lateral force on the overweight jet from the wind caused his port mainwheel tyre to burst. The Skyhawk clunked hard on to the rim and slewed off the runway centreline, streaming angle-grinder sparks behind. As he veered uncontrollably off the paved surface riding 2,000kg of high explosive, the emergency procedure was clear: pull the ejection seat handle. But too low and too slow, he was already outside the seat's safe envelope, even if the time-expired cartridge fired properly. Sadly it did not.

The long leg of the nosewheel collapsed as it dug into the soft ground beyond the paved strip, and the nose pitched down as Zubizaretta's canopy was blown clear. The misfiring seat launched him forward out of the cockpit in a cloud of black smoke. The seat had barely released him when the drogue parachute deployed, throwing him face down on to the runway. The heavy seat smashed into his back on top of him, while in a pathetic coda his parachute partially deployed and flapped in the wind.

The Skyhawk had come to an undignified rest by the side of the runway. Other than its missing seat, the cockpit was undamaged. None of the bombs had gone off. As another 3 Escuadrilla pilot clambered into the cockpit to shut down the engine, an armourer placed fuze locks on the Snake Eyes. The jet was repaired. Tragically, Zubizaretta died from his injuries a short time later in Río Grande hospital.

Within an hour of Zubizaretta's terrible accident, a pair of 2 Escuadrilla Super Etendards, armed with Exocet missiles and an estimated position provided through analysis of the SHARs' movements, launched in search of the British carriers. They took on fuel and tracked in south of the islands at very low level under darkening skies. But when they popped up to scan the sea ahead with their Agave radars they could find nothing. At 2050Z they abandoned the mission to return to a sombre crewroom at Río Grande.

Their mission deemed complete by the rules set by Jorge Colombo, the baton was passed to the next pair of pilots, Capitán de Corbeta Roberto Curilovic and Teniente de Navío Julio Barraza. Alejandro Francisco's chance to avenge his friend would follow them.

That night, with full military honours and a rifle salute, Zubizaretta's coffin was loaded aboard a Navy Fokker F-28 cargo jet and flown north to Comandante Espora Naval Air Station at Bahía Blanca where his widow Ana was waiting with senior naval officers.

There was similarly grim news aboard *Hermes*. After taking Dave Morgan's place for a night strike against the runway at Stanley, Gordy Batt's bombed-up SHAR crashed into the sea about 5 miles ahead of the ship. Always a tidy flyer, the former helicopter pilot was keen to get everything squared away as soon as he could. But he was new to night flying off the ship. The suspicion was that instead of just trimming the jet after launch and settling into a nice comfortable climb away from ship, the popular West Countryman had been busy completing his post take-off checks. In the coal black of the South Atlantic night, he'd have had no visual cue of the nose-down pitch that needed to be trimmed out after leaving the ramp. But no one knew for sure, only that a much-loved member of the squadron was gone.

It only added to Dave Morgan's feeling of desolation. The adrenalin rush that followed his sortie with Leems hadn't lasted. After they'd recovered to the deck following their attack on the Argentine helicopters at Shag Cove, he'd climbed up to the bridge to brief the Captain. Middleton told him the ship had received intelligence suggesting that Jeff Glover, now a POW, was being moved from Port Howard to Stanley aboard a Puma that afternoon.

Unknown to Middleton, Glover had actually been flown out aboard a Huey the day before, but Moggie now thought he'd fired on the downed 1(F) pilot. And for once John Leeming had good reason to be thankful for his less than total mastery of the Sea Harrier's weapons system.

Ashore, near Darwin, while his squadron said goodbye to Carlos Zubizaretta, Alberto Philippi braced himself for another night out in the cold. He'd survived so far on chocolate, sweets and a couple of bottles of water from his survival kit. Hungry, he crept up on a small flock of lambs. He pulled out his .38 revolver, took aim, and was rewarded with a damp click. Instead he improvised a trap and snared six of them. Choosing one, he slit its throat with his son's hunting knife and carefully gutted, skinned and butchered it. He built a small fire from peat and after giving up on his wet matches, lit it with a flare. He roasted a leg and a shoulder before ravenously tucking into the warm meat.

*The Lord is my shepherd, I shall not want*, he thought again with a satisfied smile.

That evening, Lyn Middleton's second-in-command, Executive Officer Commander John Locke, spoke to *Hermes'* ship's company over the broadcast. 'There are four thousand men ashore,' he told them, but admitted that it had been 'a torrid time for the ships'.

It was about to become more so.

# PART FOUR

## STUFT

*The Royal Navy had deployed a large surface task force 8,000 miles from home without effective protection from air attack. Listening to false prophets, they had retired their large aircraft carriers as obsolete, depriving the fleet of airborne early warning and supersonic interceptors. To save money they had not funded the installation of existing cruise missile defenses nor made the investment in three-dimensional air defense radars for their ships. Now they began to pay a mounting price in blood and treasure.*

John F. Lehman Jr,
United States Secretary of the Navy, 1981–7

*Most of the pilots in the Argentine Navy were trained at Pensacola and at Kingsville, Texas. I had flown with several at Kingsville, and they were all of a very high quality.*

John F. Lehman Jr

# FIFTY

## Air raid warning RED

SANDY WOODWARD FACED a choice. He could keep *Atlantic Conveyor* out of harm's way until dark before she dashed in towards Falkland Sound to unload her precious cargo. This risked exposing her to daylight while still at anchor in San Carlos Water the next morning. Or, if he brought her into the Battle Group a couple of hours early, he'd put her at risk of a deep-water attack in the gloaming of the late afternoon as she approached from the northwest. It had been nearly three weeks since the Exocet attack on *Sheffield*. And, given the ferocity of the Argentine focus on San Carlos, the advantages of getting *Conveyor* unloaded and away before dawn seemed to outweigh the risk of bringing her within range of the Super Etendards before dusk.

There had barely been time to finish painting *Conveyor* when Mike Layard received the signal from the flagship.

'Be ready in all respects,' it ordered him, 'to proceed, under cover of darkness, to San Carlos Water to disembark all helos at first light.'

He looked up at the once gleaming white superstructure and funnel, now a muted battleship grey, rising high above the ship's navy blue hull. There were still three or four white containers to draw the eye, but the hastily applied camouflage to the most conspicuous part of the ship was a definite improvement. It wasn't much of a defence against air attack though. And Layard knew well what that looked like.

Four years earlier to the day, while serving as Commander (Air) aboard HMS *Ark Royal*, Layard had been launching 809 Squadron's Buccaneer S.2s to participate in Exercise SOLID SHIELD. For two days the Buccaneer crews had staged mock attacks against the 80,000-ton supercarrier USS *John F. Kennedy*. Standing in their way were the Grumman F-14A Tomcats of the *Kennedy*'s two fighter squadrons. The 809 Squadron Record Book noted that it was a convincing demonstration of the US Navy's capacity for self-defence, showcasing 'the abilities of this most advanced fighter'. In other exercises that same year *JFK*'s Tomcats had proved their ability to shoot down intruders from over 65 miles away.

Reliant on the Fighter Controllers aboard *Coventry* and *Broadsword*, and the 'Type 64' Seawolf and Sea Dart missile trap, the British air defence was a more white-knuckle affair. But after the SHARs despatched a Dagger on the 23rd, there was further encouragement the following day. Directed by *Coventry*, 800's CO, Andy Auld, and his wingman, Lieutenant David Smith, took just five seconds to splash another three Daggers as they approached low and fast from the direction of the Jason Islands to the northwest.

The next morning, eight oktas of cloud clung low over the Carrier Battle Group. Sandy Woodward had brought them in as close as 80 miles from Stanley to give his Sea Harriers more time on station before bingo fuel, but if they were clamped to the deck by fog it made no difference.

For now, *Coventry* and *Broadsword* were on their own.

Just before sunrise on 25 May, four Fuerza Aérea Argentina A-4B Skyhawks from Grupo 5 launched into clear skies from BAM Río Gallegos. Each carried a single 1,000lb Mk.17 bomb beneath the fuselage.

Any hope in Mayor Hugo Palaver's mind that his Skyhawk Flight might mark Argentina's National Day by springing a surprise attack on the British soon started to come unglued. Two of the A-4s turned for home before their rendezvous with the tanker. The remaining pair continued east towards Gran Malvina, but the low early morning light, lack of modern navigation equipment and uncertainty about their position saw them fired on by their own flak batteries at Goose Green.

Palaver's jet was hit, but he reported that he could still fly. Believing they'd encountered the anti-aircraft artillery defending the British beachhead at San Carlos, they broke north and south to complicate the gunners' task. While his wingman escaped to the southwest along Falkland Sound, Palaver emerged to the north and on to the radars of *Broadsword* and *Coventry*.

'VALID TARGET' confirmed the display of the Type 42's 909 fire control radar.

'Take it with birds,' ordered David Hart-Dyke, *Coventry*'s captain.

A single missile burst from the launcher ahead of the bridge, its solid rocket booster smothering the ship's bow cloaked in white smoke, before the ramjet engine drove it straight into Palaver's fleeing Skyhawk.

It was another success for the 'Type 64', but the aerial assault planned by the enemy had barely begun.

In Santiago, Sidney Edwards kept a tally of the number of Argentine aircraft that had fallen to the Sea Harriers and SAMs. Against this he kept count of the British warships reported as lost or badly damaged. The previous night had brought more bad news on that front. The 3 Escuadrilla raid for which Carlos Zubizaretta had paid with his life had added a second unexploded bomb to the one already lodged deep inside HMS *Antelope* following an earlier attack by Air Force A-4Cs from Grupo 4. At 2015Z one of the bombs had exploded, instantly killing one of the two Army bomb disposal engineers working to defuse it. Unable to control the resulting fires, her crew had abandoned ship.

At this rate, Edwards worried, *we might run out of warships before Argentina runs out of aircraft*. But, in total secrecy, beneath the top cover provided by his relationship with the Fuerza Aérea de Chile Intelligence Directorate, Operation SHUTTER continued. The network of Chilean surveillance radars, augmented by the RAF's S259 radar delivered through Operation FINGENT, supplied details of all Argentine air movements in and out of air bases along the Patagonian coast. At Edwards' urging, General Rodriguez had promised to push back routine servicing of the Chilean radar in order to keep it running day and night in support of the effort to protect the British fleet.

Radar was unable to determine the intent of the contacts that were detected, but at 1120Z on the 25th the team from 264 (SAS)

Signal Squadron reported via SATCOM, from FACh Intelligence HQ in Santiago, that four aircraft had launched from San Julián and were climbing out to the east.

This was TORO Flight.

Ten minutes later, under a lifting cloudbase, Tim Gedge and Dave Austin accelerated along *Invincible*'s flight deck kicking up rooster tails of spray behind them. They were the third CAP pair to launch from the ship after Action Stations had been piped at lunchtime.

At Yeovilton seven weeks earlier, the two of them had represented the sum total of 809 Squadron's complement of pilots. In ZA190, the squadron's single aircraft, Austin sharpened his dogfighting skills over three separate sorties against opposition provided by Fleet Air Arm Hawker Hunter GA.11s. Once he was done, Gedge took his first flight in a Sea Harrier since he'd handed over the reins of 800 Squadron to Andy Auld.

Today was the first time they'd been paired together since arriving in theatre. Silver Section streamed in at height before descending towards the northern CAP stations.

Gedge looked over at Austin flying in loose battle formation over half a mile off his starboard beam. Against the pale blanket of cloud beneath them there was no doubting the effectiveness of Philip Barley's camouflage. Barley wasn't to know that, since 809's arrival in theatre, there hadn't been a single engagement at the sort of altitude where it might have come into its own.

Silver Section checked in on frequency and settled into a low racetrack pattern above the Sound. They were sharing the honours with a pair from *Hermes*. Both eager for trade.

After nearly forty minutes on station, Dave Austin was just starting to get low on fuel. The constant jockeying required of a number two to stay on the wing of the Flight Leader tended to mean they went thirsty first. But until their replacement by the next pair they had responsibility for the CAP station.

They were under the direction of *Coventry*'s Fighter Controller.

TORO Flight came in low over East Falkland from the south. *Broadsword* and *Coventry*'s fire control computers were data-linked to ensure that the larger Type 42 could draw on radar information from the smaller frigate.

*Broadsword*'s Marconi 967 D-Band search radar was capable of picking up and tracking a sea-skimming missile from the moment it appeared over the horizon with 99.9% certainty. Pulse-Doppler technology allowed it to filter out clutter from the ground and rough seas. But it could not see through solid ground. And, obstructed by the ridge of hills that ran east across the top of West Falkland from Mount Adam and high ground south of San Carlos Water, TORO Flight's ingress was invisible to them.

A SHUTTER report might have alerted *Coventry* and *Broadsword* that TORO Flight was on its way, but until they were visible above the radar horizon, all they could do was wait at Action Stations, ready to pounce the moment the incoming raid showed itself.

When they crossed the ridge, San Carlos Water reached out ahead of them 700 feet below. Six or seven British ships presented themselves. Each of the Grupo 4 pilots chose his target and turned towards it, firing their cannon as they streaked in on their bomb runs. But the British anchorage was now a hornets' nest. The Skyhawks faced a barrage of fire from Bofors guns, 20mm Oerlikon cannon, shipborne Seacat missiles and the Rapier SAM battery ashore. It was one of the latter two that brought down Teniente Ricardo Lucero as he flew over HMS *Fearless*. Unable to control the A-4C, he ejected. The three remaining jets continued their attack against the frigates HMS *Plymouth* and *Arrow* but without success.

In making their attack, TORO Flight had exposed their position. They, not the British ships, were now the target. And one of them, suffering from hydraulic problems as a result of the fusillade it had flown through, was forced to climb.

'Air raid warning RED.'

The urgent bark of the AAWC whipped Silver Section from the monotony of their lazy to and fro over West Falkland with a stab of adrenalin. Gedge acknowledged, while he and Austin craned round in their seats towards San Carlos to try to catch sight of the enemy raid.

As the three surviving Skyhawks emerged from the northern

entrance of Falkland Sound and carved round towards the west they were picked up against the clutter by HMS *Broadsword*'s 967 radar. Aboard HMS *Coventry*, Fighter Controller Lieutenant Paul Bell called up the Sea Harriers and vectored them northwest on an intercept heading. Both waiting CAPs responded instantly.

Gedge and Austin slammed the throttles forward and rolled into a dive towards Pebble Island, accelerating down the hill towards the position where Bell had calculated they would roll out on to the tails of the retreating Skyhawks to be presented with a plum Sidewinder shot.

'Make switches,' Gedge told his wingman as he readied his own weapons system, selecting missiles in anticipation of a Sidewinder shot.

Bell asked Gedge to give him a countdown to when he would be in range.

In *Coventry*'s Ops Room, the ship's Captain, David Hart-Dyke, weighed up his options.

*Would the Harriers get there in time to intercept*, he asked himself, *or should we engage with missiles?* To his left, his Anti-Air Warfare Officer reported a lock-on with Sea Dart. Hart-Dyke knew that so far the SHARs' Sidewinder had proved to be the more dependable weapon, but encouraged by *Coventry*'s earlier Sea Dart kill, he made his decision.

'Take it with birds,' he ordered, and told Bell to haul off the SHARs and their Sidewinders.

The pilot and leader of TORO Flight, Capitán Jorge Garcia, survived the ejection after the Sea Dart hit his jet, but it might have been better for him if he had not. His body was found on a remote island beach in West Falkland over a year later where he'd washed ashore in his dinghy.

As Gedge cruised back to the carrier he felt pretty sure that, if *Coventry* had cleared him and Austin to continue their intercept, they'd have got missiles in among the escaping Skyhawks. But following the success of the Sea Dart strike it was difficult to argue with the decision made by the destroyer's Captain.

*Hundred per cent correct*, he accepted, despite being forced to return to Mother empty-handed.

*It's beginning to seem*, thought Sandy Woodward, *that the 42/22 missile trap is working.* Buoyed by the performance of *Coventry* and *Broadsword*, he'd brought the Carrier Battle Group to within 60 miles of Stanley, closer than at any time since the first few days of the war, as he covered *Atlantic Conveyor's* approach to San Carlos. The vulnerability of the ship still concerned him, but he'd done what he could to shield her. She was still upthreat of *Hermes* and *Invincible*, but he'd screened her behind three Royal Fleet Auxiliaries and the requisitioned tanker *Fort Toronto*. Steaming 25 miles ahead of them as a radar picket was HMS *Exeter*. And, as good as his word to Mike Layard, he'd given her *Glamorgan* and *Ambuscade* as goalkeepers. All these ships stood between *Atlantic Conveyor* and the Super Etendard base at Río Grande to the southwest.

# FIFTY-ONE

## Viva la Patria!

TENIENTE DE CORBETA Daniel Manzella had escaped his encounter with Sharkey Ward on day one of the shooting war with no more than a single cannon shell through the cockpit glass of his T-34C Turbo Mentor. But his aeroplane hadn't survived the SAS commando raid against Isla Borbón airfield that followed two weeks later. Since then, he and his fellow naval aviators had tried to contribute to the war effort in any way they could, from attempts to improvise artillery using the 70mm rocket pods once carried by the T-34s to firing small arms at attacking Harrier GR.3s.

But from the airfield that morning, he'd seen the British radar pickets steaming north of Borbón, the place the kelpers called Pebble Island. And he'd seen them take on his countrymen as they tried to make their escape from San Carlos Sound. After reporting the British ships' location to the mainland he was told, just after 1600Z, that the Air Force were going to stage an attack against them, and that the pilots needed his help. With an officer from the Comando de la Infantería de Marina he grabbed binoculars, radios, food and water. The two men climbed to separate vantage points to report back on both the position of the ships and the locations of the British combat air patrols.

Since its revival following the invasion, Escuadrón Fénix, the paramilitary Air Force unit joined by former RAF pilots Jimmy Harvey and Tito Withington, had been earning its keep flying decoy missions, providing navigational support and acting as airborne radio relays. It was in the last of these roles that a sky blue Learjet 35A, callsign 'RANQUEL', took off from BAN Comodoro Rivadavia at

1645Z and climbed to high altitude on a course towards the southwest.

From their perches high over the beaches, Manzella and the Marine could see the British ships 10 miles distant on the line of the horizon to the north. They reported the position to RANQUEL, who in turn shared it with two pairs of Grupo 5 A-4Bs that were inbound from BAM Gallegos: VULCANO Flight and, following in radio silence one minute behind them, ZEUS Flight.

Aboard *Coventry*, a Spanish-speaking officer listened in to the Argentine radio transmissions. The ship's own 965 long-range search radar picked up the approaching Skyhawks at a range of 180 miles. There was never any doubt about their intended target. But as the Argentine jets descended from altitude west of West Falkland and coasted in across King George Bay they dropped below the radar horizon. And with that, *Coventry* and *Broadsword* were blind.

'Careful,' warned RANQUEL, passing on a report from Daniel Manzella on the ground, 'there's a CAP approaching from the south over San Carlos strait.'

As he flashed over the north shore of Pebble Island, VULCANO Flight Leader, Capitán Pablo Carballo, hauled the Skyhawk into a tight starboard turn, staying below the cover of the rising ground to his right. VULCANO 2 was tucked in close, a little behind his starboard wing. He acknowledged the message from the Escuadrón Fénix Learjet with a click and pressed on. With the two British ships now visible to the northwest, he felt certain he could reach the target before the British interceptors caught him. With his left hand he advanced the throttle forward as far as it would go, juicing every drop of power out of the J65 turbojet. The little delta-winged attack jet's speed crept up towards 500 knots. Unable to contain the pride and adrenalin coursing through him, he thumbed the RT and cheered 'Viva la Patria!' as he rolled on to his bomb run.

*Broadsword*'s radar picked them up first against the ground near Mount Rosalie, and passed it to *Coventry* using the data-link. But until the raiders were clear of Pebble Island, they were as good as invisible to the destroyer's own radars. When, with barely a minute's warning, the Sea Dart's 909 fire control radar finally picked them up it was already too late to get off a missile shot. While the ship's Anti-Air Warfare Officer cursed the slow reaction time of the medium-range missile, Sub-Lieutenant Andy Moll, now Fighter Controller following a change of watch, directed the CAP in from the south.

Facing a hail of 20mm Oerlikon fire and the thump of radar-laid 4.5-inch shells fired from *Coventry*, VULCANO Leader told his wingman, 'Let's go for the one at the rear, it's less well defended.' Carballo and his wingman nudged their noses towards the trailing frigate. They fired their guns as they swept in.

Rounds rattled into the ship with the sound of ball bearings being thrown into a tin bucket. *Broadsword* returned fire with her own anti-aircraft cannon. The dark blue-grey water between them looked alive with gouges and spouts of white water.

Asked to choose between two targets in such close proximity, *Broadsword*'s Seawolf system glitched in exactly the same way as her sister ship *Brilliant*'s had when she'd been operating as part of an earlier 42/22 combination alongside HMS *Glasgow*. Unable to decide, the computer simply shut down like a rabbit in the headlights. On that occasion it had been *Glasgow* that took the hit. This time it was *Broadsword*'s turn.

Of four bombs dropped by the Grupo 5 A-4s, three missed. But a single 1,000lb bomb skipped off the sea like a Barnes Wallis Highball and speared up into the side of the ship's hull before punching out through the flight deck from below, taking off the nose of the Lynx helicopter that was lashed to it. Miraculously it didn't explode. *Broadsword* had been battered, but was unbowed.

'Are you through?' Carballo asked his wingman as VULCANO Flight streaked low across the target.

'Yes, sir. Behind you and visual.'

Then ZEUS Flight came on frequency: 'I have the visual on the target and I'm going in.'

\*

It wasn't just Gedge and Austin who'd been kept at arm's length. Half an hour earlier, an 800 Squadron CAP had been warned off *Broadsword*'s missile engagement zone and told to go hunting for Pucarás instead. This time it looked as if the SHARs' presence would be more welcome. Diving north at full throttle in pursuit of the Skyhawks, Neill Thomas and Dave Smith both saw the prospect of adding another kill to the one each of them already had to his name. The Nine Limas' infrared eyes scanned the skies ahead, ready to lock on to the attackers' jetpipes. Nudging 600 knots, the SHARs closed on the A-4s as the Argentine jets screamed low over the water tracing a wake across the surface in their slipstreams.

Within seconds they would be within range.

*Coventry*'s Sea Dart locked on to the second pair of Skyhawks. Now David Hart-Dyke was faced with the same dilemma as earlier in the day. The CAP had visual and was in hot pursuit but as they approached his missile engagement zone, either they must abandon the chase or he would have to holster his ship's defence and let them through. He wasn't sure the SHARs were quite going to overhaul the bombers in time.

Fighter Controller Andy Moll needed a decision. He leapt up from his screen and turned to the Captain.

'Do you want a Harrier to come in?' he shouted.

'Hold it off,' ordered Hart-Dyke as his ship turned to starboard to give his missiles a clearer shot. Once again the Captain opted for Sea Dart.

And for once, the Sea Harrier pilots' RT discipline let them down, their frustration clear to anyone tuned into the AAWC: 'You must be fucking joking. We've got them.'

Despite being hit in the attack from VULCANO Flight, *Broadsword*'s Missile Directors had been able to reconfigure the Seawolf system so that they could override the fully automatic mode and fire manually. Ready to take on the next pair of incoming Argentine fighter-bombers. The frigate's Captain, Bill Canning, was on the line to Sandy Woodward aboard *Hermes* as the two ZEUS Flight Skyhawks blazed in towards *Coventry*, their 20mm cannon firing ahead of them.

'Seawolf locked on.'

'Just a minute, Admiral,' Canning said, then, in a whisper, 'Oh my God . . .'

Seventeen men died instantly when two 1,000lb bombs ripped into *Coventry*'s port side. In attempting to bring her own missiles to bear, the Type 42 had sailed across *Broadsword* and the frigate's Seawolf missile arcs. Unable to fire, *Broadsword*'s Missile Directors could only look on helplessly as, with the radar lock on the Argentine jets broken, the Seawolf system reset itself.

Within half an hour of the devastating strike on *Coventry*, over 270 survivors had abandoned the ship. Half an hour after that she completely capsized. Only the black bottom of her hull and two five-bladed screws were visible above the surface, flanked by a couple of inflatable orange liferafts.

*Christ*, thought Sandy Woodward, *are we losing this?* Unable to risk exposing his true feelings of loss, doubt and sadness to the men around him, the Admiral retired to his day cabin to try to absorb and process *Coventry*'s destruction. He reached for his notebook and scribbled some immediate reflections on the day's tragic turn.

'The 42/22 combination does not work,' he began sourly, before berating the limitations of the ships' missile systems and bemoaning once again the crippling lack of airborne early warning.

'They really must come for the carriers now!' he concluded.

They were already on their way.

# FIFTY-TWO

## Both inventive and bold

It HAD STILL been dark when Capitán de Corbeta Roberto 'Toro' Curilovic first made his way through the cold and drizzle to the hangar. The engineers and armourers had worked through the night to prepare the jets, removing two AM.39 Exocets from their protective cases and bolting them beneath the wings of the two Super Etendards chosen for the mission. They were now crouched beneath the starboard wings with open black cases, running diagnostic tests on the big anti-ship missiles.

Like the squadron's rugged piston-engined Vought F-4U Corsair fighters before it, Curilovic's aircraft, 2-A-203, sported 2 Escuadrilla's distinctive club-wielding cockerel badge on its dark sea-grey flanks. He wore the same patch with pride on his leather flying jacket. As he walked around the jet, his thoughts turned to his fallen comrades from 3 Escuadrilla – Philippi, Marquez and Zubizaretta. He knew that his wingman for today's mission, Teniente de Navío Julio 'Mate' Barraza, mourned those lost friends the same way.

But once again the combined efforts of the Vigilancia y Control Aéreo Grupo 2 radar operators and the Armada flight controllers analysing the AN/TPS-43 plots from the Malvinas had come good. They were confident they had determined the position of the British Carrier Battle Group.

The atmosphere in the Operations Room had been expectant as Curilovic and Barraza planned their mission, reviewing the route, timings, emergency procedures and the latest intelligence. Above layers of warm clothing – thermal longjohns, thick socks and flightsuits – they'd pushed and pulled themselves into their thick rubber immersion suits. To a soundtrack of encouragement and good wishes from the rest of the squadron, they grabbed their helmets, walked out to the jets and climbed into the cockpits of the two waiting Super Etendards.

After carrying out pre-flight checks they started their Atar engines. For twenty minutes they then waited in the cockpits, their idling turbojets waffling the cold air behind into a pungent heat haze of burning aviation fuel, before they were told to shut down and return to the crewroom. The KC-130 tanker upon which their mission depended wasn't yet available. Back inside, squadron boss Jorge Colombo told his men to grab something to eat and be ready to go again as early as possible.

203 and 204 finally taxied out from the hardstanding a little before 1730Z. The SuEs' probing noses dipped on long undercarriages as the pilots checked their brakes before rolling forward again. From the side of the apron, the rest of the squadron stood watching and waving. Toro and Mate acknowledged their support with gloved hands through the cockpit glass.

When they at last opened the throttles, releasing their brakes and accelerating down the Río Grande runway, the morning's carefully considered mission plan remained the same.

It was both inventive and bold.

Hearts thumping, Curilovic and Barraza tucked up the undercarriage and climbed to 20,000 feet on a heading of 025° for their ocean rendezvous with the tanker.

Perhaps it was their track north-northwest towards Uruguay that caused those interpreting the radar plots produced by Operation SHUTTER in Chile to underestimate the threat posed to the British Task Force by the Argentine formation.

As *Coventry* and *Broadsword* came under attack, Curilovic and Barraza were plugging into the tanker around 200 miles off the Argentine coast east of Puerto Deseado. While fuel flowed, the two SuEs held position behind and below the KC-130, one attached to each wing via the hose and drogue. After topping off their tanks, they pulled back on the throttle to disengage, dropped back, retracted their refuelling probes and rolled away to the east, descending gently.

*Just sea and sky*, thought Barraza.

They flew on in radio silence, their radars turned off. Just two small aeroplanes cruising a few hundred yards apart enveloped by shades of blue and grey.

*It doesn't feel much like war*, he realized.

At the first tickle of a British search radar detected by the RWRs mounted in the jets' tails they dropped to just above sea level and accelerated. At a height of no more than 30 feet from the waves, salt quickly crusted the cockpit glass, obscuring the view ahead. This far from land birdstrikes were rarely a hazard, but at such low altitude the occasional leaping fish flicked past the pilots' canopies.

They had 150 miles to run.

A little over fifteen minutes.

As daylight began to fade, four of 801 Squadron's jets were still airborne, manning the CAP stations over Falkland Sound. Another pair, ordered to scramble following the Skyhawk raids against *Coventry* and *Broadsword*, was on the flight deck centreline poised to launch in support of the SHAR force defending the AOA.

Alongside Neill Thomas and Dave Smith, four more of 800 Squadron's Sea Harriers were flying combat air patrols over the islands, while two had been sent to bomb Stanley airfield in the company of one of the 1(F) Squadron GR.3s. Additionally, two more of the flagship's Sea Harriers had been despatched on a probe mission in search of ARA *25 de Mayo*. Lyn Middleton felt that the temptation to use her to stage a do-or-die spectacular on the National Day that gave the ship her name might be too much for Argentine commanders.

Tim Gedge and Sharkey Ward had just climbed into the cockpits of a pair of ghost-grey 809 jets, coded 000 and 002, ranged on *Invincible*'s flight deck, noses forward, alongside the island. As Gold Section, their launch was scheduled for 1940Z.

Fourteen SHARs in the air and another four preparing to launch.

And every single one of them was in the wrong place to deal with what was coming.

*

Mike Layard had ordered the prepositioning of stores in preparation for disembarking the helicopters. By 1900Z the job was done. All day, squadron personnel had worked to move equipment and spares to *Atlantic Conveyor*'s aft flight deck and below that to the C Deck Cathedral area near the ramp.

The initial plan to disembark the six 848 NAS Wessex HU.5s had been pushed back twenty-four hours. It would have been good to have got the helos off the ship sooner, but *Conveyor*'s Senior Naval Officer knew that no one was really sure how. There was no room on the carriers and the beachhead at San Carlos simply hadn't been ready to receive them. But today had been a decent day's work. There was a sense of urgency now.

An 845 Squadron Wessex, Whisky Delta, to which *Conveyor* had been a temporary home, was flown off to *Hermes* for an air test at 1910Z. And, after 18 Squadron engineers had reattached the six 300lb rotor blades to one of their Chinook HC.1s using a forklift truck, rope, brute force and bloody-mindedness, no time had been wasted putting her heavy-lift capacity to work resupplying the Battle Group. There'd been little sign of her since, save for the occasional sound of rotor slap carried south on a northerly wind.

While another Chinook underwent engine tests on the aft flight deck, some of Layard's officers and senior rates were enjoying a farewell drink at the invitation of the ship's Master, Ian North, and his officers. The men from Naval Party 1840 planned to make a serious dent in Cunard's profits before many of them left the ship at dawn with the helicopters.

Lieutenant Nick Foster, 848 Squadron's Senior Pilot, could see the convoy of ships running fore and aft to the horizon. As he stood on the bridge wing talking to the Master, North was, as ever, a genial, reassuring presence.

'Don't you worry about it, lad,' he told Foster. 'I was sunk twice in the last lot. You'll be OK.'

A little after 1930Z, Mike Layard left the comfort of Ian North's sea cabin, his accommodation since joining the ship, to make his way to the bridge.

*

A pale southern sun sat low in the sky behind them as the two SuE pilots pushed the throttles forward, accelerating to a speed of 500 knots. Just 200 yards separated them as they speared in towards their target from the northwest. From where, they hoped, the British would least expect them. Curilovic and Barraza flipped through books of ringbound flight reference cards, cycling through the checklists to prepare their weapons system. At a distance of 50 miles, Curilovic double-clicked the RT transmit button. Barraza acknowledged with a double-click in return.

They applied a little gentle back pressure to the control column. The jets responded, climbing to 300 feet before the pilots checked their ascent and switched their attention to the small radar display below the coaming of the instrument panel.

Two sweeps of the Agave radar was all they allowed themselves, but it was enough.

*I'm dreaming*, thought Barraza as he stared at three contacts, one large, two small. After their two-hour flight over featureless water, the intelligence from VYCA 2 at Puerto Argentino had been spot on. The target was where they had calculated it would be.

'Go for the biggest,' said Curilovic, breaking radio silence for the first time as they dived back down to the deck.

Barraza allowed himself the thought that the larger echo could belong to *Invincible*.

*Maybe*, he thought, *we could change the course of the war.*

A bead of sweat ran down his forehead and into his left eye.

'I'm tracking it,' said Curilovic.

'Ahead thirty-nine,' confirmed his wingman. 'I agree.'

*Exeter* and *Ambuscade* detected the transmissions from the Argentine jets' radars the moment they popped up above the radar horizon at 1936Z. Aboard *Ambuscade*, Leading Seaman Pierce, monitoring the ship's UAA-1 Abbey Hill ESM suite, called it in using the codeword 'Handbrake' that identified it as the racket from the Super Etendard's Agave radar. And that, in turn, meant the Battle Group knew that they were likely to be under attack from Exocet.

The Type 21's Ops Room erupted into a cacophony of noise that surprised even the ship's Captain. Two words above all others cut through: 'Handbrake' and 'Chaff'.

Steaming 4 miles southwest of *Atlantic Conveyor*, the 3,000-ton frigate fired chaff from her 4.5-inch gun a few degrees north of the 330° bearing of the threat. By sowing a chaff cloud 4 miles upthreat she hoped to confuse the enemy's targeting.

Thirty seconds later the *Ambuscade*'s 992 radar picked up two aircraft at a range of 28 miles.

Julio Barraza pressed the fire button to launch the missile. As he waited for the launch sequence to complete he saw his wingman's missile suddenly leap forward from beneath the jet and punch to transonic speed in an instant propelled by an explosion of fire and smoke. A split second later, his own aircraft bucked as the three-quarter-ton weapon dropped from beneath his starboard wing. He checked the SuE's roll to port. The Exocet fell for a moment, before the boom of its solid-rocket motor igniting thumped through the attack jet's airframe. It speared forward along the same path as the first missile, trailing dense white smoke behind it.

*Ambuscade* detected the missile release at 1939Z. Her radar operators saw the two attack jets turn immediately to port. Certain that she was the target, the Type 21 frigate sowed further chaff from her 3-inch rocket launcher.

'Air raid warning RED. Emergency stations, emergency stations!'

Mike Layard was running before the message ended. As he took the steps up to the bridge three at a time, the ship's siren screamed an urgent alarm in support of the warning over the ship's broadcast. Layard felt the ship move under him as *Conveyor* heeled to starboard. That was encouraging. The ship's crew was putting into practice the air raid drills as planned.

When he reached the bridge, he saw it was Ian North who'd swung *Conveyor* into a hard turn to port in an effort to present the thick steel of the ramp towards the southwest from where it was assumed any Exocet attack would come. Around him men were pulling on lifejackets. His efforts to drill the merchant crew on to a more martial footing had paid off.

The NP 1840 machine gun teams manned the 7.62mm weapons mounted on each bridge wing.

'What's the threat direction?' Layard asked, but he was told none had been passed on. He could see the dark grey hulk of *Hermes* on the horizon against a background of low cloud. A couple of miles ahead of her were the more compact, sleek lines of *Brilliant*. Both ships were firing chaff in patterns to screen themselves from the incoming attack. Without search radar or ESM of his own, though, Layard was blind. Without chaff delta, he was helpless. It was like standing in a darkened room waiting to be hit on the head.

As Layard watched the fireworks display around the warships, *Conveyor* continued her turn to port. And in doing so, instead of presenting her strong, narrow stern towards the incoming threat, she was now side-on, her bow facing due east.

Curilovic and Barraza held the jets low and flat in the turn. They kept their eyes on the horizon, controlling their sideslip with gentle pressure on the rudder pedals as the noses of the SuEs sliced through 180° back towards the direction from which they'd come. Rolling out to the northwest and into the low afternoon sun, their speed climbed back up to 500 knots.

Forty-one seconds after she'd detected the missiles' release, *Ambuscade* picked up the two incoming AM.39s with her radar. And causing palpable relief in the Ops Room, her radar operators reported that the missiles' flight path had veered away from the ship towards the first chaff pattern laid by her 4.5-inch gun.

Moments later, the brace of Exocets shot through the thick white cloud of aluminium and emerged, still skimming across the calm sea surface at just below the speed of sound in search of a new target.

About 5 miles on, a little to the left of their current heading, was the slab-sided steel hull of the *Atlantic Conveyor*, presenting an irresistibly large and isolated radar signature.

# FIFTY-THREE

## Exceeded in every conceivable way

THERE WAS A loud *whumph!* from behind and to the left of them. Standing on the bridge, Mike Layard felt it as much as he heard it. The ship shuddered as the first missile punched a hole in *Conveyor*'s port aft quarter about 10 to 12 feet above the waterline below the rear of the superstructure. The second Exocet javelined into the ship's hull through the hole ripped by the first, broke up after hitting a lift shaft and spread unspent rocket propellant in its wake as it hurtled along the 600-foot-long C Deck cargo hold. It was like spraying the inside of the ship with napalm.

On the starboard bridge wing manning one of the 7.62mm machine guns, 848 Squadron boss David Baston turned to the shocked-looking faces of those around him. The same question was on everyone's lips: 'What the fuck was that?'

With no knowledge of what might yet still be incoming, the order 'Hit the deck! Hit the deck!' was called over the ship's broadcast. But it hardly mattered. Within a minute of the initial strike, thick, acrid black chemical smoke was billowing from the ventilation flaps that lined the deck above the hold.

Warships were built to contain damage. At Action Stations, heavy hatches sealed the ship into separate airtight and watertight compartments, the theory being that flooding or fire in one could be isolated. It didn't make them invulnerable. Sufficient destruction, as *Coventry* had just discovered, could still sink a warship quickly, but *Ardent* had taken a monumental pounding before she had finally been overwhelmed.

By contrast, *Atlantic Conveyor* had C Deck, a cavernous open-plan space as long as two football pitches. And she was equipped with a $CO_2$ fire extinguishing system designed to protect the ship, in a worst-case scenario, from a deep-seated fire in a high-risk cargo like baled cotton. Success in dealing with something like that depended on the immediate and total sealing of the cargo hold and the rapid release of $CO_2$ to smother the fire in its infancy. The hold would then remain in lockdown while further gas was released at intervals until the ship reached harbour. Faced with the inferno caused by the double Exocet strike, it wasn't enough. Not nearly. Oily cotton had the potential to spontaneously combust at just 120°C. Solid rocket fuel burned at thousands of degrees.

Ventilation from the 8 by 10-foot hole torn by the first missile in the ship's side fanned the intense fire that took hold inside the Cathedral area. This was further fed by the large quantities of fuel, lubricant and paint moved aft in preparation for 848 Squadron's disembarkation. Nearby oxyacetylene welding equipment didn't help. The ship's ability to contain the conflagration was, as the Board of Inquiry report later put it, 'exceeded in every conceivable way'. What made matters worse was that, uncertain about whether or not survivors of the missile attack were trapped in the hold, North and Layard decided they couldn't risk triggering the release of $CO_2$ into A, B and C decks for fear of suffocating them.

*Conveyor*'s problems mounted rapidly. The ship's boilers went out immediately after the ship was hit, leaving her dead in the water. All remote control of machinery was gone and, when the diesel engine tripped, all electrical power was lost, and with that pressure in the ship's firemain. Fourteen minutes after the ship was hit the firehoses dried up. Ian North immediately ordered the $CO_2$ system to be activated.

In the engine room, the ship's small team of engineers started the emergency diesel generator only to find it feeding a dead supply system. One of the ship's two fire pumps had been damaged beyond repair. The other, though, housed away from the impact of the missiles in one of the stabilizer compartments, might work if they could provide it with power. After successfully connecting it to the diesel distribution board, the Chief Engineer spoke to his Third Engineer, Charles Drought.

'Charles,' he said, 'go and try to get to the fire pump remote control panel, and get that pump running at full speed.'

'On my way, Chief.'

Pulling on his gas mask, Drought fought his way back aft, through the thickening smoke.

'Thank God for that,' he said as he turned the starter switch and watched the needle swing round the gauge.

Just three minutes after they'd lost pressure, the firehoses bucked back into life. But, beaten back by heat and impenetrable chemical-tasting smoke, neither the forward nor the aft damage control parties could get near to the seat of the fire. Instead, they did what they could to boundary-cool the upper deck by hosing it with frigid sea water, adding steam to broiling smoke that had more or less divided the ship's company into those ahead of the fire on the forward flight deck, and those behind it.

As he turned back to the main control room, Drought heard cries from behind a steel hatch. As soon as he opened it, he was forced to his knees by a blast of heat and smoke.

'Help me,' said a weak voice from inside the annexe.

Drought crawled on all fours through the smoke until he found his colleague, Ernie Vickers, wedged in a doorframe. He tried to drag the man out, but unable to move him and beginning to feel himself burn from heat he realized he had to save himself.

As the rest of the engineers evacuated the control room, Drought went back down again with the Chief to see whether or not they could risk sending in properly equipped men to try to pull Vickers to safety.

At the first attempt the rescue party that followed their reconnaissance couldn't get to him. When they tried again, wearing fire gloves and breathing apparatus, they found only the mechanic's badly burned body.

*This isn't what I signed on for*, Drought thought sadly as the small band of merchant sailors was ordered by the Master to grab what warm clothing they could and make their way to the muster station.

As the sun set at 1958Z, explosions were reported from the C Deck Cathedral area. On the bridge, Mike Layard was trying to anticipate where further blasts might come from. Within three minutes of the Exocets first striking the ship, the liquid oxygen tank had been thrown overboard. The contents of the two huge bladders of AVCAT aviation fuel stored in containers port and starboard was pumped into the sea ten minutes after that. On the aft flight deck men were ditching small-arms ammunition and phosphor grenades, but the smoke was beginning to overwhelm them. It also prevented RFA *Sir Percivale*, one of the LSLs that had been leading *Conveyor* into San Carlos, from getting in close to help. But they were close enough to see the fire raging inside the ship through the petalled missile impact hole in the ship's port quarter.

An 848 Squadron Wessex was lashed to the deck just aft of the forward flight deck. Her folding main rotor blades had already been spread in preparation for flight. It looked like perhaps she still could fly. Layard had already discussed the possibility of getting her off the ship with David Baston, but the squadron boss wasn't sure it was possible to get through the smoke to reach her. Still, the idea of saving even just one of his ship's helicopters seemed too important to let go of lightly. When Baston's Senior Pilot, Lieutenant Nick Foster, arrived on the bridge to grab a survival suit, Layard tried again.

'What do you think about going down and flashing that up and getting airborne, Nick?'

Foster's reaction was no more enthusiastic than his CO's. He didn't need to think about it for long. Trying to get to the cab looked like asking for trouble.

'Sir,' he said to the Senior Naval Officer, 'if you're ordering me, I'll do it. If you're asking, then I'll decline.'

'I'm just asking.'

Foster made himself scarce. And, on reflection, Layard knew that, with the aft pad now untenable, he was going to need to keep the forward flight deck clear.

The pops, cracks and booms below decks now came with increasing frequency and volume. Faced with the inferno beneath them, Layard and North asked each other whether there was any more that could be done. Had they thought of everything? Tried everything? But within half an hour of the attack, the upper deck was already so hot it was beginning to melt the soles of people's shoes, night was drawing in, the sea state was rising, and the fire, despite the best efforts of the fire control teams, was clawing its way forward towards the thousands of gallons of kerosene and 220 BL755 cluster bombs on board. The two Captains reached the inescapable conclusion that their ship was lost.

*There's nothing more we can do to save her*, thought Layard. He knew that to give the order to abandon ship was a painful one for any Master to make, but he was impressed by his friend's composure and good sense. Less than twenty-five minutes after the double Exocet strike, Ian North picked up the handset and spoke over the ship's broadcast.

'The fire is out of control. We are going to abandon ship. Make your way to the starboard side where there are ladders and life rafts already deployed.'

# FIFTY-FOUR

## Shooting at shadows

FOLLOWING HER BRIEF check flight, Wessex Whisky Delta had returned to land on *Conveyor*'s forward flight deck at the moment the missiles struck. After fishing from the sea a near hypothermic RAF Sergeant who'd been thrown overboard by the impact, they flew him to *Hermes* before returning to the stricken ship to help pick up other members of the crew. Those forward of the fire had been cut off by it, unable either to communicate with those aft or to join them.

At first the Wessex crew lowered the winch, then thought better of it. Putting the cab down on the forward pad, they signalled for ten men to climb aboard. Then another three. As the pilot, Lieutenant Kim Lowe, pulled on the collective he realized he still had a little excess power. He let the helicopter's weight settle back on the undercarriage and told his aircrewman to wave two more on board.

His helicopter overloaded with survivors, Lowe radioed ahead to *Hermes* to warn them of Whisky Delta's impending arrival. The landing back aboard the carrier was going to be more than a little sporty. They'd need to clear the deck. He was coming in hot.

*Alacrity*'s slender hull crashed against the looming bulk of the container ship with the sickening grind and groan of scraping metal. The Type 21 frigate was standing by within fifteen minutes of the attack, providing reports of *Conveyor*'s material condition to Layard and North as she pumped gallons of freezing sea water over the freighter in a doomed effort to cool the hull. But thrown repeatedly against *Conveyor* by the swell, her Captain pulled her back from the burning ship's starboard side to a safer distance. After a month's pounding in the rough waters of the South Atlantic he wasn't sure his own ship was in any condition to survive collisions like that without sustaining lasting damage. With no hope of extinguishing the fires he needed to refocus his effort on saving *Conveyor*'s crew. In the fading cold grey-blue light, he ordered *Alacrity*'s duty diver into the water to help survivors.

Life rafts were thrown over the side of *Conveyor*'s starboard quarter, dangling from painters too short for them to settle in the water. And men were beginning to stream down the side of the ship's dark hull and drop into the sea.

Ian North insisted on being last off his ship. Mike Layard could hardly begrudge him that. They left the bridge together, forced to climb down on external ladders because of the smoke clogging the internal stairs.

On the upper deck, Layard looked out to starboard. *Alacrity* was there, still hosing the ship in a hopeless effort to provide boundary cooling. The frigate also fired Coston lines over the life rafts so that they could be hauled away from *Conveyor*'s heaving stern. Her divers were in the water, helping freezing survivors to rafts or up the scramble nets draped over her sides.

The choking smoke stung his nose and throat. Behind him, the auxiliary power unit used to start the Chinook turboshaft engines whined, apparently ignited by the heat convecting off the blistered steel flight deck beneath. It was over the heart of the furnace in the C Deck Cathedral area.

Ian North stood beside him in an orange one-time survival suit. He'd never looked more like Father Christmas. A vast column of black and grey smoke rose above them and blew south in the wind as Layard looked at his friend before grabbing the rope ladder and climbing over the gunwale.

As Layard scrambled down the ladder he could see the starboard side of the ship glowing red in places, her navy blue paint flaking and peeling from the searing heat. The rattle and clang of the ammunition cooking off on C Deck grew in volume, firing lethal shrapnel which punched through the ship's hull. Hot metal singed past his ears as he continued his progress, encumbered by the bulk of his survival suit.

*She's going to blow up any second*, he feared.

Above him, he saw the ship's Master struggling down the ladder. He was worried for his friend. North was neither in the first flush of youth nor fit. He'd wheeze going up and down a deck or two on *Conveyor*'s companionways, but somehow he was still hauling himself down.

Likely sheared off during *Alacrity*'s close manoeuvring, the ladder no longer extended all the way to the black sea below. With a sense of relief, on reaching its limit the Senior Naval Officer let go and fell the final 10 feet into the freezing South Atlantic. North soon dropped into the water next to him, disappearing beneath the waves before his lifejacket forced him back up to the surface. Layard quickly realized that any thought that they were through the worst of it might be premature. North looked like he was in trouble.

*Seems to be floating lower in the water than is good for him*, thought Layard as he kicked through the swell towards his friend. The hard clamber down the ship's side had exhausted the old mariner. Layard wrapped his arms around him and tried to hold him up out of the icy water.

To aid her fast passage through the sea, *Conveyor* had been designed with a hydrodynamically efficient cruiser stern. But the same elegant shape that reduced the drag of the water proved far less appealing from underneath. The smooth curve sucked at the water as the ship rolled in the swell, dragging rafts and swimmers in towards the hull with each upstroke. Then, inexorably, the massive stern would settle back down on top of those dragged beneath, forcing them underwater before the buoyancy of their survival gear pulled them back to the surface.

*What do you do*, wondered Layard after suffering one such dunking, *when you're pushed underwater like that?* The trick, he realized, was to kick away and carefully anticipate the moment you had to take a deep breath. But for the weaker swimmers it was impossible. And Ian North, already exhausted, was not a strong swimmer.

*Time's running out*, thought Layard. He had to try to get *Conveyor*'s Master into one of the rafts. After enduring two or three more dunkings together, he managed to push North towards a full life raft, surrounded by men clinging to the ropes around it. He hoped they'd help their Captain round to the entrance. Then, once again, Layard was dragged beneath the surface by that cruiser stern.

This time he wasn't sure he was going to make it. The plunge underwater seemed interminable, but when the dark sea finally released him to the surface, the view greeting him was very different. After gasping for air, he looked around but there was no sign of Ian North, nor the full raft he'd steered him towards; just an empty life raft and another body, not that of his friend, floating face down in the water.

Mike Layard possessed only what he was standing up in. *Conveyor*'s cold and bedraggled Senior Naval Officer was welcomed aboard *Alacrity* by the frigate's Captain, an old friend.

'Come on, sir,' he said gently, 'let's get you out of your wet clothes and into a shower.'

*Alacrity* took aboard seventy-four survivors and three bodies. In total, twelve of *Atlantic Conveyor*'s crew lost their lives. One of them was the ship's beloved Master, Ian North. On the verge of being rescued, it was thought that his heart had just packed up and that his body had drifted away in the late twilight.

He was never found.

Five miles away, Tim Gedge was still strapped into the cockpit of the Sea Harrier. He'd heard the air raid warning and watched in fascination as the carrier fired chaff rockets and scrambled the ECM-equipped Lynx decoy helicopter. Then, before *Invincible* turned to face the Handbrake threat, the two SHARs waiting on the centreline roared past him and off the ski-jump into the air. They were ordered to hold station to the north in order to avoid any possibility of suffering a blue-on-blue attack at the hands of the Battle Group. And there was no point in sending them after the SuEs.

With a head start of 30 miles on the SHARs at the point they'd launched their missiles and reversed their course, they were long gone. By now, even one of *Ark*'s much-missed F-4 Phantoms armed with medium-range AIM-7 Sparrow missiles would have struggled to overhaul them as they made their escape. With every passing minute the Argentine jets were 7 or 8 miles further away. In the slower Sea Harrier, with its short-range Sidewinders, there was no chance.

Instead, Gedge enjoyed a grandstand view of *Invincible*'s own Sea Dart system ripple-firing six missiles in quick succession, so fast away from the launcher that they appeared almost to score a solid straight white line of smoke away from the bow of the ship. It was an impressive display of firepower, but it was nothing more than that. *Invincible*'s radar operators believed they'd detected a low, fast contact at 20 miles. The *Hermes* Ops Room was under the impression that they'd locked on to her Lynx, or at least her chaff patterns. There was a detonation off the flagship's port quarter, another overhead and a third salvo that airburst nearby. All the Sea Darts detonated on contact with chaff.

*Invincible* had been shooting at shadows.

Gedge launched alongside Sharkey Ward at 2010Z. As they flew past the grim column of smoke rising from *Conveyor* towards their CAP station over Pebble Island, there were men jumping into the sea. In a night approach to the carrier an hour and fifteen minutes later, they saw only the glow of fires burning in the dark.

The following morning, Mike Layard gathered the survivors aboard *Alacrity* in the frigate's senior rates mess. He explained the sequence of events as he now understood it, describing the Argentine naval air arm's determined effort to strike at one of the aircraft carriers, and how the *Conveyor*'s 18,000-ton bulk must have looked, through the radar scope in the Super Etendard's cockpit, as if they'd had one of the British capital ships in their sights.

'This error has reduced the number of these deadly weapons held by the Argentine Navy to one, but that's not much of a consolation to us, is it?' Layard reached for a mug of tea and took a sip. 'It's dry work all this talking,' he said with a gentle smile. 'I wish it was something stronger.

'I am sad and angry,' he continued, 'that we were not able to complete our allotted task and land all our equipment. You are not gladiators, you are not trained for war, you are not trained to kill, but you all adapted to the rigours of wartime service with commendable ease. The shipmates who died bravely, doing their duty, upheld the best traditions of the Merchant Navy for which it is renowned. In times of war you have never been known to shirk your duty and let your country down and you all have been as loyal. I am full of admiration for you all and it has been a great privilege to serve with you.' He paused for a moment before continuing, 'That is all. May God be with you as you journey safely home to your loved ones.'

*Atlantic Conveyor*'s Senior Naval Officer saluted them and left the men in the mess to their own thoughts.

*The loss of the ship and her incomparable old skipper*, he reflected later, *left an ache in the hearts of all who'd been involved in her astonishing metamorphosis.*

At 1500Z that afternoon, the three dead who'd been brought aboard *Alacrity* were committed to the sea. Charles Drought, the Third Engineer, assisted in the ceremony.

'Victory,' wrote Winston Churchill, 'is the beautiful, bright-coloured flower. Transport is the stem without which it could never have blossomed.' He could have been referring to *Atlantic Conveyor*. She may have been, as Layard acknowledged, prevented from delivering *all* of her cargo, but in getting fourteen SHARs and GR.3s and their pilots to the TEZ the ship he described as the 'Thirty Day Wonder' – the total extent of her operational life – had substantially revised the odds in Britain's favour.

Before the end of the conflict, the single Chinook that had escaped the attack, Bravo November, had carried 1,500 troops, 95 casualties, 650 POWs and 550 tons of cargo. On one occasion eighty-one paratroopers were crammed into her hold and redeployed from Goose Green to Fitzroy, saving days of tabbing on foot. Kept flying without spares and specialist equipment for the duration of the war by a small 18 Squadron contingent of two crews and nine technicians, her nickname 'The Survivor' was stencilled on the side of the fuselage.

But on 25 May, *Atlantic Conveyor* delivered something more critical than desperately needed aircraft. The chaff fired upthreat from *Ambuscade*'s 4.5-inch gun had the unintended effect of nudging the Exocets in the direction of *Hermes*, steaming 9 miles behind her. *Conveyor* had been near equidistant between them. Had she not drawn the SuEs' fire, *Hermes'* own chaff patterns *might* have protected her. So too might *Brilliant's* Seawolf missiles have kept her safe, but as the *Coventry's* destruction had already demonstrated, they were not, despite shooting down Exocet missiles in trials, infallible.

No one had imagined that, in the end, it would be *Conveyor* herself and not just her cargo that would help absorb the Exocet threat to the carriers. Twelve men died in the COAN attack. Their sacrifice, and that of their ship, guaranteed the safety of the flagship and Britain's continued participation in the war.

As Mike Layard spoke to the crew aboard *Alacrity*, in Washington DC the CIA were distributing their latest assessment of this distant South Atlantic war. In it, they concluded, 'the British are in a strong position and should achieve victory in the next ten days'.

# FIFTY-FIVE

## An SIS officer of aristocratic bearing

JUST BECAUSE DAVE Braithwaite regarded the Blue Fox radar as about as effective as a lump of concrete didn't mean he wasn't going to try and put it to good use. As an air defence specialist he, like Sharkey Ward, kept a close eye on the cockpit display as he searched the skies for trade on CAP. Without effective low-level radar coverage from the ships he'd take any advantage he could, however inadequate it might be.

Despite being one of the most highly qualified of all the SHAR pilots in the South Atlantic, Brave had had a slightly frustrating time of it so far. Whether or not any CAP pair encountered the enemy was the luck of the draw. He'd listened in on the AAWC as others had seen action, and, flying alongside Tim Gedge, he'd destroyed a helicopter on the ground, but after fourteen missions over the islands he'd yet to be vectored towards an incoming raid.

Today had brought its own fresh excitement, though, when he'd been despatched with Mike Broadwater to a point 13 miles north of Pebble Island. They had orders to attack the *Coventry*.

On arrival at the coordinates loaded into the NAVHARS computer, they searched the surface for any sign of the ship. There was nothing. No trace of *Coventry*'s upturned hull on or beneath the surface, just a featureless patch of dark water.

*Orders are orders*, thought Brave, and he'd been told to strafe it. He settled into a dive attack on the position, flipped the safety catch down from the top of the control column and pulled the trigger. He kept the gunsight centred on the lat/long position as the jet stuttered. Ahead of him, the water flurried excitedly as if a school of piranhas was stripping a floating carcass. Fun, for sure, but it all seemed a little redundant.

'It worked a treat,' he told Sharkey Ward on his return to *Invincible*'s crewroom.

'What do you mean?' asked the puzzled 801 boss.

'I got a Delta Hotel on the piece of sea where the target should have been,' Brave replied with a smirk, and joking that there must have been enemy frogmen in the water.

An amused Tim Gedge listened in with the rest of the SHAR crews as his Senior Pilot regaled them with his tale of derring-do. Brave's direct hit and pioneering new attack tactic – NAVHARS strafing – probably deserved recording for posterity in the 809 diary. Another squadron first.

But after enjoying his moment in the sun earlier, now Brave was back stooging up and down the CAP station with Lieutenant Soapy Watson, one of 801's junior pilots. Then he spotted something on the radar screen: a contact down low over Falkland Sound at a range of 18 or 19 miles.

Brave locked on to it with the radar. As he told his wingman what he'd found he was already mashing the throttle lever forward and rolling into a diving turn towards the bogey. Watson hung on to Brave's wing, acclerating to combat speed as they carved down from altitude. As the CAP pair rolled into a shooting position the low-flying jet resolved into the shape of a Harrier GR.3.

*Give it up*, thought Brave as he hauled off and soared back up to medium altitude. No one had told him there were friendlies about. The Harrier was left alone to go about its business untroubled by Braithwaite's interest.

*Lucky boy.*

Braithwaite and Watson were hardly the only CAP pair to fly in circles for three-quarters of an hour wondering where the enemy was. Operating in clear weather 150 miles east of the Falklands, *Hermes* and *Invincible* had kept SHARs on patrol over the islands from dawn to dusk on 26 May. 801 Squadron had launched thirteen CAP pairs, their 800 Squadron counterparts on *Hermes* at least as many, and none had encountered either the Fuerza Aérea Argentina or Comando de Aviación Naval. In fact, not a single Argentine fast jet entered the AOA.

Bad weather over the Patagonian airfields had certainly hampered operations, but the challenges faced by the Argentine fighter-bomber squadrons were more deep-rooted. The weight of sorties launched against the British had collapsed, from claims of sixty-five on D-Day to a planned twenty-two on the 25th. The CIA estimated that Argentina had lost a third of its combat aircraft in a little over three weeks.

And yet they'd failed to prevent the British from either establishing or consolidating the beachhead at San Carlos. Over 5,500 British troops were now ashore, their positions defended by a ring of Rapier surface-to-air missile Fire Units that would make any attempt to attack from the air almost suicidally risky.

The Argentine Navy still chose to confine itself to coastal waters. Now the Air Force too had been forced to reconsider its position. They had been beaten in air combat on 1 May then depleted by the Sea Harrier CAPs and SAM missiles as they mounted brave but unescorted attacks against the ships in Falklands waters. Unable to displace British land forces nor, with the SHARs ascendant over the islands, able to support their own ground forces, they were out of targets.

No longer capable of meaningfully obstructing the British from the mainland, Argentine commanders' hopes of holding on to the Malvinas now rested on the 15,000 troops dug in around Stanley.

Unless 2 Escuadrilla were able to make their last Exocet missile count.

Aboard *Hermes*, that fear continued to preoccupy Sandy Woodward. It was a thought compounded by a further concern. *Argentina*, he realized, *might also find a way to replenish its supplies*.

Peru, Argentina's most prominent Latin American ally, had already supplied replacement drop tanks for Argentine Mirages and Daggers. She had promised to send surplus Mirages too. Libya was thought to be supplying Matra R.550 Magic air-to-air missiles and Soviet-built SA-7 Strela man-portable surface-to-air missiles. The greater concern was that either of these countries would get their hands on some Exocets.

In May, Peru, with four missiles on order to arm her Navy's small fleet of Sea King helicopters, was on the verge of having them delivered. Despite qualms about their contractual obligations, Aérospatiale cancelled plans to deliver the Exocets by air. While the possibility of their despatch by sea remained, Margaret Thatcher was urged by the Foreign Office to intervene directly to keep the missiles on French soil. 'There can be no doubt,' she wrote to President Mitterrand, 'that Peru will pass them on to Argentina.' She asked that they be delayed for at least another month. 'Naturally,' she added, 'we would prefer them not to be supplied at all.'

It would be July before Aérospatiale finally loaded them aboard the BAP *Independencia*, a Peruvian naval transport. But while the Peruvian missiles could be stopped at source by appealing to an ally, Colonel Gaddafi was altogether more biddable. The Libyan may not have had any Exocets at his disposal, but he knew a man who did: Saddam Hussein.

Wing Commander Jeremy Brown, the RAF's Air Attaché in Brazil, was tipped off that on 25 May a Fuerza Aérea Argentina Boeing 707, coded TC-93, had staged through Recife on its way to Tripoli. While the Ambassador covered for his absence in Brasilia by telling everyone he was having an affair, Brown left the capital to investigate.

When the big Boeing landed back at the east coast airfield at 2307Z two days later, Brown was waiting for it. And with the help of a local contact, during the hour that the Argentine 707 was on the ground, he got eyes on board. In the hold his agent discovered that, beneath a large number of other wooden boxes, six of the unmarked crates being freighted back from North Africa were approximately 5 metres long. Substantial enough to have contained Exocets. When TC-93 took off again just after midnight, Brown noted that it required a lot of runway – 'consistent', he said, 'with a heavy load of cargo'.

On returning to Brasilia, Brown briefed the Ambassador and the Embassy's resident SIS representative. In response, the spook recommended that Brown be trained in the use of plastic explosive so that he could sabotage the 707 on the ground at Recife by destroying its undercarriage when it next staged through.

'Should blow up,' said Our Man in Brasilia.

The Air Attaché wasn't so keen.

'What do *you* think we should do?' the Ambassador asked him.

Brown had noticed that the 707's track between Libya and Brazil took it within 150 miles of Ascension. 'A pair of Phantoms could be scrambled to intercept it and force it to land,' he suggested. On 24 May, three Phantoms from 29(F) Squadron RAF at Coningsby had deployed to Wideawake equipped with night vision goggles to maintain a round-the-clock QRA. This could see them gainfully employed. And, once the airliner's cargo was revealed to the world, Brown thought, Brazil's enthusiasm for supporting any further flights would falter.

Neither spy nor fighter pilot got his way. The Ambassador opted simply to have a quiet word with the Brazilian government to remind them of their professed neutrality. And while it was later learned that Colonel Gaddafi had been unable to supply Exocets, the episode was evidence of a worldwide effort, run from Whitehall, to stymie any possibility of Argentina replenishing her arsenal of AM.39s. It became an intricate jigsaw of information and initiative.

In Argentina, representatives of the South African helicopter company contracted to support their host's oil and gas industry wired details of NOTAMs issued by the Argentine aviation authorities to their head office in Cape Town. These were passed on to the Republic's National Intelligence Service who in turn shared them with their British counterparts at SIS.

In London, the Defence Intelligence Centre and Defence Procurement Department identified possible sources, both private and governmental, of further missiles. Plan A was always to apply diplomatic pressure either to persuade any government in possession of Exocets 'to retain the equipment in question or, alternatively, to make it available to the UK rather than to Argentina'.

Unable to exert the same kind of influence in the shadier corners of the international arms market, the Defence Sales Organization identified a couple of private companies, the state-owned IMS (International Military Services) Ltd and A. B. Jay Ltd, that could buy up any stray missiles that might otherwise find their way to Río Grande.

In the end they opted for a former Royal Marine called Tony Divall. The operation was run from Century House by an SIS officer of aristocratic bearing who, despite answering to the name, probably wasn't called Anthony Baynham.

Assuming responsibility for preventing Argentina from acquiring Exocets only added to Divall's exotic-looking CV, which already included Nazi hunter, racing driver, spy and arms dealer. While based in Hamburg he had been involved in clandestine work across the globe from Macao to the Congo.

Divall and Baynham first met at the Post House Hotel in Heathrow two days before the attack on the *Atlantic Conveyor*. The focus of their attention would be the Argentine Navy's effort, led by Carlos Corti and Julio Lavezzo in Paris, to buy Exocets on the black market.

Since April, after the SIS station in Paris acquired the number of Corti's private telephone line, GCHQ had been monitoring his calls. As a result, the British knew Corti had already been relieved of $6.3 million by a fraudulent American arms dealer. Divall decided to introduce the desperate Argentinian to someone who could help him navigate the treacherous waters of the international arms trade with more confidence. Based in Milan, former US Marine John Dutcher was barely less colourful than the man who'd employed him. A veteran of the wars in Korea and Vietnam, he'd also taught karate to Libyan commandos and assembled a mercenary force designed to dethrone Baby Doc Duvalier in Haiti. And he ran rings around Corti.

After the Argentinian accepted the charismatic American's offer to act as middleman, Dutcher, an agent run by SIS, then stood between Corti and any potential deal. All were kept at arm's length for the rest of the war. Ultimately, Corti knew he'd been played, but ordered by his superiors to buy Exocets at any price it had been impossible to refuse Dutcher's help.

While Divall and Baynham celebrated their successful infiltration of Corti's Parisian operation over a Michelin-starred lunch at the Roux brothers' Waterside Inn in Bray, aboard *Hermes* Sandy Woodward had allowed himself to feel a little more bullish. After the despondency that followed the double blow of losing *Coventry* and *Conveyor* in such quick succession, a few hours' sleep had restored some of his usual bite.

It seemed increasingly clear to him that the range of the Super Etendards had been extended through in-flight refuelling. The Admiral began to worry that if the Argentinians were able to refuel them twice, he might find himself under attack from behind with neither CAP nor picket ships upthreat to protect him.

But as he once again considered the risk to his ships, his thoughts inevitably turned to what felt like the hopelessly slow progress of the land forces he'd risked and sacrificed so much to put ashore. *What the hell are they doing?* he asked himself. *Digging bloody holes?* He took a clean sheet of paper and gave vent to his frustration.

'They've been here for five days,' he scrawled in block capital letters, 'and done fuck all!'

In fact, they were already on the move.

The plan to leapfrog Argentine positions between San Carlos and Port Stanley was just being finalized when reports arrived at Brigade HQ that *Atlantic Conveyor* had been lost. Without her cargo of Chinook and Wessex helicopters 45 Commando and 3 PARA were going to have to walk. But, with the Navy losing ships at sea and any prospect of swift action against the capital impossible without the helos, a hard yomp across East Falkland wasn't going to deliver results quickly enough for London's liking. Domestic political pressure and concern that international efforts to bring about a ceasefire would leave British troops isolated and exposed as autumn turned to winter forced Northwood's hand.

'Some action,' they told Brigadier Julian Thompson, the 3 Brigade Commander, 'is required.'

Despite subscribing to the view of his intelligence officer that Goose Green was little more than a 'self-administering prisoner of war camp' Thompson was ordered to send 2 PARA to attack the Argentine garrison there, 15 miles to the south of the British beachhead. *Unwelcome, but,* he conceded, *probably politically necessary.* He could live with that.

By nightfall on 26 May, the operation was underway.

# FIFTY-SIX

## Lit up like a Christmas tree

THE PARAS ARE *in serious trouble*. That was Bob Iveson's understanding as he was pressed into his Martin-Baker Mk.9 ejection seat by the Harrier's surging acceleration towards the ski-jump. It was the only conclusion to draw from the way 1(F) was being thrown back into the action again and again in support. After dropping cluster bombs on an enemy position at Goose Green, he and his wingman, Mark Hare, had landed back aboard *Hermes* only to be refuelled, rearmed and sent back into the fray. But while the urgency of the situation on the ground seemed obvious enough, it didn't mean that the GR.3 pilots had any clearer a picture of the progress of the battle.

'You're on standby to provide close air support for the raid on Goose Green,' they were told, 'but you will only be used if it's absolutely necessary.' There was good reason for that.

Unlike a carefully planned attack against a pre-briefed target, the Harriers would have little control over their approach to the target or the timing and track of their bomb run. Instead they'd be relying on the instructions of a Forward Air Controller, or FAC, on the ground. And that usually meant a straight line to the target from some easy-to-identify IP like a mountaintop. Considerations like using terrain masking or the position of the sun to offer a modicum of protection to the incoming jets rarely came into it.

It didn't help that the Air Liaison Officer (ALO) back at Brigade HQ kept losing contact with the FAC on the ground at Goose Green. Without eyes on the ground, the GR.3s were left holding at 8,000 feet above the battlefield waiting for targets. Any element of surprise had been lost before they even started.

The FAC eventually scared up six sets of coordinates, before deciding on a single 105mm gun emplacement at UC660626, but was unable to talk them on to the target. Without adequate direction the Harrier pilots found no sign of it. Instead, each pilot talked the other on to any target they were able to eyeball from the cockpit as they sped past through wall-to-wall tracer.

'Left of me now,' Iveson told his wingman. 'You follow me in, make the correction and you should see it in time.'

It was terrible terrain for identifying meaningful targets, but between them they managed to attack a small concentration of Argentine troops and, on his third pass, Iveson dropped his cluster bombs on a line of enemy foxholes. Both Harriers had been subjected to a barrage of small-arms and anti-aircraft fire for their trouble. Neither pilot saw either of the two Soviet-made SA-7 Strela surface-to-air missiles launched at them without success by the Argentine defences.

It wouldn't have made a difference. When Iveson and Hare arrived back over Goose Green a little over an hour later, the words of the duty Flight Commander, who'd come out on deck as they went through their pre-flight checks, were still ringing in their ears.

'The Paras,' he'd told them, 'are in urgent need of air support.'

Now alert following Iveson and Hare's first mission of the day, the anti-aircraft defences were waiting. As well as the SA-7 missiles the Fuerza Aérea Argentina had six radar-laid Rheinmetall 20mm gun emplacements surrounding the airfield. Not content with that, there were also the Army's two powerful 35mm twin-barrel Oerlikon cannon and their Skyguard fire control radar which had brought down Nick Taylor's Sea Harrier over Goose Green two weeks earlier.

As the returning GR.3s circled the IP at 8,000 feet, the FAC cut through the static over the RT with the coordinates of a 155mm field gun. Just fifteen minutes earlier, low fuel had forced another pair of GR.3s to return to *Hermes* without clearing their wings.

Left in no doubt about the situation on the ground, Iveson and Hare were determined to try to make their mission count.

Iveson went in first, but wasn't able to pick out the target. After directing Hare's bomb run towards an Argentine company position he sent his wingman back up to the IP to orbit out of reach of the flak. Iveson then set up his own re-attack. With no sign of the gun, the Flight Leader also dropped his cluster bombs on a concentration of Argentine troops, before making his escape back to altitude to join his wingman. Back up at 8,000 feet over the IP, the radio crackled into life.

'I've got another target for you,' said the ALO. 'Have you got any weapons left?'

'We've dropped all our bombs, but we've got guns,' Iveson told him. The Harrier pilot knew he was going to be pushing his luck if he returned to the hornets' nest below, but, he thought, *if the Paras are in trouble then I'm going to give this attack everything I have. It's a must.*

As he watched him descend once again towards the maelstrom of flak above the battlefield, Mark Hare could only conclude that his Flight Leader was crazy. Or suicidal.

Iveson virtually emptied his magazines during one long, fast strafing run low along Argentine trenches running east to west across Darwin Hill. He released the trigger. The buzzsaw judder of the two 30mm ADEN cannon came to an abrupt end as he pulled up then threw the jet into a hard evading turn back down below 100 feet and away from the track of his attack run.

Without warning, two or three violent thumps kicked the tail of his jet out of line, smashing Iveson's head against the canopy. So vicious was the Harrier's sudden yaw to starboard that the impact shattered the protective perspex visor of his helmet. Hit by a succession of high-explosive rounds from the lethally effective 35mm Oerlikon guns, Iveson's control column froze, then everything else went wrong at once.

*I must have been hit in both the hydraulic control systems.*

Ahead of him the arc of warning lights that rimmed the coaming of the instrument panel lit up like a fairground. A quick glance at them suggested he had the full set. Fire, hydraulics and the rest. His hydraulic pressure was crashing. He could smell burning. In peacetime he'd have tried to slow down, pull up and jump out, but he'd just been dropping cluster bombs on the people directly below him.

*They might not be best pleased to see me.*

He decided to try to stick with the stricken jet and try to put a little more distance between him and the Argentine positions. He reached forward with his right hand and punched the fire extinguisher button as he looked back over the GR.3's tail in the rear-view mirror. He could see flames whipping around the fuselage. They looked uncomfortably close to the jet's rear fuel tank, and the wayward factory of noises resonating through the airframe spoke of nothing good.

Smoke began to pour into the cockpit.

What little control authority he had from the stick was suddenly gone as the Harrier pitched down into a dive. Unable to pull the nose up with the stick, Iveson reached for the nozzle lever to his left. The Pegasus engine was still going strong. While he tried to keep the jet flying straight using the rudder pedals alone, he vectored the nozzles through 10 or 15°. The effect of VIFFing was immediate, arresting the Harrier's plunge towards the ground and bringing the nose back up. If he could just keep her going a little longer using the combination of nozzles and rudder he might make it back to the safety of British lines. With his left hand on the nozzle lever, he gripped the ejection seat handle with his right, steering with his feet.

Three or four miles on flames began to gust into the cockpit through the two ventilation louvres on the instrument panel in front of him.

He'd waited long enough. Iveson pulled the looped yellow and black handle without hesitation.

*I must have passed out*, he thought as he tried to process what was going on. For the next thing he knew, Iveson was flying feet first through the air at a couple of hundred knots looking through his legs at the fireball of his own burning aircraft. Just as the thought that he might actually hit it began to form in his mind, his parachute tugged at the air behind and quickly slowed his progress. But less than ten seconds after he felt its pull it had barely inflated when Iveson hit the ground, saved from serious injury by the downward slope of the hill away from him. That and the softness of the ground itself, so saturated with water that it was more sponge than solid earth.

*I don't feel hurt at all*, he realized as he got his breath back and took stock of his situation. But his eyes, unprotected by his broken visor from a near 500-knot blast of air, wouldn't focus. He'd been exceptionally lucky, but he knew that he was still on the wrong side of the lines. Through streaming eyes, he looked up the hill and picked out a group of blurry dots in the distance heading his way.

*Enemy troops*, he guessed. *Looking for me.*

He tried to focus, but couldn't sharpen the image. There was no time to lose. He grabbed the quick release fitting and gave it a sharp twist to release his harness, then got to his feet and ran as fast as he could in the opposite direction.

The Paras had yet to begin their assault on Goose Green and Darwin. On the ground, as the GR.3s had repeatedly run the gauntlet of the Argentine air defences, 2 PARA's O Group were 4 miles south at Camilla Creek House, going over their plans for the night's action. A pair of reconnaissance teams, sent forward to gather intelligence on enemy troop positions, had been spotted and fired on and there had been some inaccurate shelling from the Argentine 105mm guns, but it was desultory stuff. But now, because somehow the agreement to call in the Harriers only in extremis had been lost in translation between 2 PARA and *Hermes*, 1(F) were down to just four jets.

And Bob Iveson was on the run behind enemy lines.

# FIFTY-SEVEN

## The fundamental strength of the organization

At first it was just a suggestion on a brisk northwesterly wind, but the noise was soon unmistakeable. As much as Hendrix, the Stones and the Doors, it had been the soundtrack to the Vietnam War. Bob Iveson recognized the distinctive rotor slap of the Bell UH-1 Huey immediately. It had been a constant companion during his exchange tour with the US Marine Corps. This time, though, the familiar ra-tat-tat-tat clatter and thump beat out none of its usual reassurance.

Before daylight faded, Iveson had managed to put distance and high ground between him and where he'd come down. Now they were looking for him. Through the darkness he could see the beam of a spotlight streaming down from the sky. The Huey was hovering over a single spot.

*Must have found the remains of the aircraft*, he thought.

Then the high-power beam began walking across the ground towards him. Desperate for cover, Iveson tried to flatten himself into the low heather bushes.

The helicopter continued its slow hover-taxi towards him.

That was when the shooting started.

Across the water, 2 PARA launched their assault on Goose Green. The sharp crack of covering rifle fire was followed by the more expansive report of 84mm 'Charlie G' Carl-Gustaf recoilless rifles and grenades before being joined by the crump of artillery.

There was a change in tone from the blades of the Huey as the pilot poured on the power and pitched forward out of the hover, gathering speed before hauling the cab into a sharp turn back towards where it had come from.

*Better things to do*, thought Iveson with relief, imagining that the helicopter crew would want to be anywhere but airborne with all that ordnance flying about.

The rattle of the rotor receded into the night. Once he was sure of its departure, the Harrier pilot continued his trek away from the Argentine lines. He'd not been walking for long when he made out the dark silhouette of a remote shepherds' cottage. Despite the bitter chill, Iveson resisted the temptation to approach it immediately, instead maintaining his distance and watching for any sign of life. Only two hours later was he sufficiently confident it was deserted, and sufficiently cold, to let himself in.

He surveyed his surroundings. The cottage, called Paragon House, was a comfortable two up, two down, a shelter for the shepherds tending the local sheep farm. Upstairs there were mattresses and sleeping bags on the beds. Finally undercover, warming up and out of immediate danger, Iveson reflected on the circumstances that had brought about his shootdown.

'Single pass only' was the policy. It had been repeated at the briefing earlier in the day. 'If you miss, tough, come back to the ship.' But what choice had he had really? Without proper targeting or adequate forward air control the GR.3 pilots were forced to use a first pass just to find a target. There was no chance of actually hitting anything without going round again. And so, unaware that 2 PARA's assault on Goose Green had yet even to get underway, he and his wingman had ignored the risk to their own safety to provide the close air support they believed was so desperately needed on the ground. Iveson had nearly paid for it with his life.

He reached for the packet of cigarettes he'd tucked into the pocket of his flightsuit only to discover they'd been ripped away in the ejection. Happily, the hut was well stocked with tinned and dry food in anticipation of winter. He helped himself to a can of baked beans, climbed into one of the sleeping bags and watched the Battle of Darwin-Goose Green unfold across the water through a skylight in one of the upstairs bedrooms. While 3 Escuadrilla's Alberto Philippi had been forced to slaughter, butcher and barbecue a lamb, Iveson was able to tuck into one of Heinz's fifty-seven varieties and, if he could fire up the Rayburn, a full English breakfast. Already a

Falstaffian figure, 'Big' Bob knew there'd be no living that down when he got back to the squadron.

But the contrast between the experiences of the two downed airmen spoke volumes.

The war in the South Atlantic had undoubtedly exposed some cracks in the British war machine. There were, unsurprisingly, teething troubles as it was thrown at short notice into an unexpected war 8,000 miles from home. The machinery was not as well oiled as it might have been, nor were the three branches of the military, after nearly forty years of peacetime turf wars over funding following the end of the Second World War, as smoothly joined-up as they should have been. As guests of the Royal Navy, the small RAF contingent aboard *Hermes* were feeling that lack of cohesion more than most.

Even the SHAR pilots had noticed it. When Hugh Slade had gone to pick up his immersion suit he'd found Mark Hare on his knees trying to mark up target runs on a map spread out over the floor.

*This is really wrong*, Slade thought, as he saw pilots squeeze past Hare to grab their kit. It was symptomatic of the way 1(F) had been forced to try to go about their business. Still unable to properly align their navigation systems they were operating using dead reckoning and fixed gunsights. Their difficulties were compounded by the absence of a Carrier Borne Ground Liaison Officer.

'Seaballs', as the Navy referred to the position, had been a fixture aboard the Navy's strike carriers since 1943, when embarked Army officers first advised the Fleet Air Arm as they provided close air support for the Salerno landings in Italy. The arrangement grew to be so successful that by 1945 Admiral Chester Nimitz, the head of the US Navy, directed that, in anticipation of a long campaign against the Japanese, the US fleet should adopt the same system. But with *Ark Royal*'s retirement in 1978, the role had disappeared.

Now, operating from two carriers that were no longer expected or required to provide air support ashore, Peter Squire's men found themselves doing the best they could without adequate, timely intelligence about their targets or the defences they faced, in an aeroplane that, hobbled by its inability to make proper use of the avionics and weapons system, was barely offering them Second World War levels of technology.

But while it was easy to highlight British shortcomings, that the country was able to stage an operation as ambitious as CORPORATE *at all* was remarkable. Furthermore, mountains were being moved back in the UK to try to plug the gaps. As Argentina's resources grew increasingly depleted, her opponent, despite the extraordinary challenges she faced, was growing stronger.

In short order the RAF had revived or developed from scratch an in-flight refuelling capability for the Vulcan, Nimrod and Hercules, and fitted new navigation and electronic warfare kit to the Canberra, Harrier, Nimrod MR.2 and R.1, Victor and Vulcan. The Nimrod, Victor, Vulcan and Harrier had all been cleared to use a variety of new weapons. The RAF had also been the hub through which a valuable intelligence-gathering operation in Chile had operated. And while, with the loss of Bob Iveson's Harrier, there were just four GR.3s in theatre, 38 Group now had a proper pipeline in place to prepare pilots and jets that could practically provide replacements and reinforcements as required.

The fundamental strength of the organization was much in evidence, but what the Air Force really wanted was to have operational control of its own jets in theatre, free from the obstructions and vicissitudes they felt so keenly on *Hermes* where they remained at the mercy of the Captain's beck and call. From the moment the GR.3 deployment was first mooted by Ken Hayr, his thinking was to try to establish a FOB ashore as soon as was practically possible. But with the destruction of the *Atlantic Conveyor* much of the equipment with which they'd planned to do that was now sitting at the bottom of the Atlantic.

In the short term, they were stuck on *Hermes*, and forced to wrestle with Lyn Middleton over every requirement, from the need to fly attrition replacements direct from Ascension – a move the Captain had tried to veto as an RAF publicity stunt – to the angry exchange endured by Peter Squire following the receipt of a signal from the RAF's Central Tactics and Trials Organization containing guidance on how the Harriers should employ laser-guided bombs. It had run a little long. Squire was hauled into the Captain's day cabin where the South African tore strips off him.

'I will not,' he said, his voice all gravel and glue, 'have my communication channels blocked by these great books being written by the Air Force on how—'

'Now hang on,' Squire intervened. Instead of being cowed by Middleton, he stood his ground. 'This gives us the details of how to use what could be a battle-winning weapon that will enable us to take out targets with precision.'

To his credit, Middleton, instead of being provoked further by Squire's interruption, accepted the logic of his argument. It was typical Middleton: hard, but ultimately pragmatic. And yet the 1(F) Squadron boss couldn't shake the feeling that the Captain's resistance stemmed less from any concern about the signals traffic than it did from the possibility that, using laser-guided bombs, the RAF might actually distinguish themselves in what he considered to be a naval war.

Perhaps, thought Ken Hayr, if the Navy would prefer to reserve its ships for naval aircraft, the loss of the *Conveyor* might open the door to another possibility: a dedicated RAF aircraft carrier.

'In view of the long list of requests to the Americans,' began a memo from Hayr's Alert Measures Committee to Ben Bathurst at DNAW, 'why have we not included an aircraft carrier? If the Navy have any problems manning the ship, the RAF Marine Branch will be glad to help.'

Bathurst couldn't believe his eyes. But, jokes about the Marine Branch aside, Hayr was completely serious about an RAF bid for their own flat-top. As an additional asset to British forces in the South Atlantic, *it could have*, he felt, *a significant influence.*

The Americans, too, seemed willing to be accommodating. Defense Secretary Cap Weinberger's earlier intimation that a nuclear-powered supercarrier might lend weight to British efforts had been developed by Navy Secretary John Lehman into a more realistic and manageable plan. Under the direction of the Commander of the US Navy's Second Fleet, Admiral James 'Ace' Lyons, the 18,000-ton helicopter assault ship USS *Iwo Jima* was identified as the best potential replacement flat-top, should the Brits need it. And not only was the Pentagon prepared to provide the hardware, it had made provision to recruit a team of civilian contractors – former US Navy sailors with knowledge of the ship's systems – to act as advisers to any British crew who replaced *Iwo Jima*'s regular ship's company. After serving with distinction in Vietnam and recovering the crew of the ill-fated *Apollo 13* moon mission after their unscheduled splashdown in the Pacific, South Atlantic battle honours would have made an unlikely addition to the ship's storied history.

Ultimately, Hayr was forced to acknowledge that *the Navy didn't like the idea of an RAF flat-top.* And that was the end of it. The suggestion that the RAF Marine Branch had any meaningful role to play was also, as Hayr well knew when the idea was teased, a non-starter. It was an organization on its last legs, barely able to muster the handful of men required to operate the few rescue and target-towing launches still sailing under the RAF ensign, HMAFVs *Spitfire, Sunderland, Stirling, Halifax, Hampden, Hurricane, Lancaster* and *Wellington*. There would be no HMAFV *Iwo Jima*.

That the Marine Branch even existed, though, was a further illustration of the breadth and depth of the resources on which Britain could draw as the war rolled into its second month.

The UK still had its own sovereign capability across a broad spectrum of military endeavour even if, in some cases, it was suffering from a little ring rust and neglect. There also remained sufficient corporate memory to be able to revive some capabilities that had been allowed to wither. And in marshalling their own considerable resources, the RAF and the Royal Navy had drawn on the support of a huge range of government research and development organizations such as the A&AEE at Boscombe Down, the RAE at Farnborough and Bedford, the RSRE at Malvern, the Defence Operational Analysis Establishment and even, of course, the Aviation Bird Unit. Added to this was crucial support from Britain's allies.

The United States provided war-winning equipment like the AIM-9L Sidewinders and SATCOM radios as well as fuel, satellite intelligence, diplomatic support and staging for RAF aircraft en route to Chile. France had helped train British pilots and missile operators, denied Argentina and her allies further Exocet rounds and shared technical insight into the missile itself. At the same time her intelligence agencies aided the SIS effort to spike Argentina's Paris-based initiative to acquire AM.39s on the black market.

Despite a sharp decline in size over the preceding decade, the Merchant Navy contributed fifty-two ships to the campaign, including troopships, tankers, hospital ships and, in the form of the oilfield support ship MSV *Stena Seaspread*, a mobile battle damage repair facility for the warships. As well as *Atlantic Conveyor*, her sister ship, *Atlantic Causeway*, was also converted into a helicopter carrier in six days, while another container ship, MV *Contender Bezant*, was already on her way south carrying an additional four GR.3s.

Industry too had played a vital role. British Aerospace had accelerated Sea Harrier production, while developing both the SHAR's and the GR.3's weapons-carrying capability and self-defence suite. Ferranti and Marconi had tweaked, tuned and improved the fire control radars for the ships' Sea Dart and Seawolf missiles, even if the former's best efforts to get the GR.3's navigation and weapons system to align at sea had ultimately fallen short.

Meanwhile, under a veil of secrecy and on a strictly need-to-know basis, engineers at Westland and Thorn EMI were working themselves into the ground in pursuit of DNAW's urgent requirement for an AEW Sea King. After a frustrating ten days trying to source the necessary Searchwater radars, two prototypes were now under construction in a hangar at the manufacturer's Yeovil headquarters. 'Tell me,' Ben Bathurst told project manager Jim Schofield, 'if any of my staff ask for any equipment to be fitted which might delay its entry into service.' Nothing could be allowed to slow progress.

By the end of May, Bathurst would signal FONAC with a formal order to commission 824 Squadron D Flight to operate the newly modified Sea Kings. It was scheduled to happen on 14 June under the command of a former Gannet AEW.3 Observer.

But that was two weeks away. While the country had shown itself capable of sending high-altitude reconnaissance jets, sophisticated SIGINT spyplanes, long-range strategic bombers and even a make-shift aircraft carrier to the South Atlantic at short notice, Operation CORPORATE was still without airborne early warning.

It remained a critical hole in Woodward's defences.

# FIFTY-EIGHT

## A large single malt whisky

Dawn broke on Sunday, 30 May to clear skies and calm seas. The Met reported visibility of 20 kilometres. It was, noted JJ Black without enthusiasm, a lovely day for an Exocet attack.

*Invincible* was piped to Action Stations, and at 1115Z launched the morning's initial CAP pair. Two hours later, Dave Braithwaite and Al Craig launched on their first sortie of the day. In a welcome nod to the provenance of the 809 aircrew and aircraft absorbed into 801 Squadron, 'Phoenix' had been added to the list of callsigns used by the squadron. Today, Brave and Al were the first of the 809 alumni to use it. Apart from showing a little jet-fuelled moral support for HMS *Penelope* as she led another convoy towards the AOA on their return, the mission passed without incident. Phoenix Section landed back aboard at 1445Z. They had three hours for food, sleep, coffee and cigarettes before they were slated to return to their cockpits on Alert 5.

At 1645Z, an hour and a half before Craig and Braithwaite's next launch was programmed, *Invincible* received a SHUTTER report from Santiago warning that a Super Etendard attack was on its way. As ever, though, Sidney Edwards' operation to monitor the Argentine airfields could only give notice of aircraft movements, not of intent or tactics. And, once again, Jorge Colombo's squadron was mixing things up.

From Río Grande, the two SuEs tracked southeast. Only one, flown by Capitán de Corbeta Alejandro 'Pancho' Francisco, carried an Exocet – 2 Escuadrilla's last. Unusually, for this mission he and his wingman, Teniente de Navío Luis 'Cola' Collavino, were using a callsign: ALA. But, as they'd learned to their surprise a day earlier, on this mission, the SuEs were not hunting alone.

Forty miles out from the coast they were joined by the four Skyhawks of ZONDA Flight. The Fuerza Aérea Argentina A-4Cs each carried three 500lb bombs. Led to the target by the Super Etendards, it was hoped that the Air Force fighter-bombers would lend greater weight to the attack on the British carriers. The sinking of the *Coventry* had shown that, with luck, the A-4s could get through to inflict serious damage. The Armada pilots, given no choice in the matter, had hurriedly briefed the Skyhawk pilots on the route, tactics and operating procedures. They had stressed the importance of strict radio silence.

'Any indiscretion,' Pancho had warned them, 'could jeopardize the mission.'

After joining up, the mixed formation of six jets continued southeast towards a planned rendezvous with the two KC-130 tankers 400 miles out over the South Atlantic. After continuing east for another 180 miles as they took on fuel, by the time they unplugged they'd be almost as close to the tip of the Antarctic peninsula as they were to Tierra del Fuego.

*Far from everything*, thought Pancho, *over icy waters*. But it was worth it. The position of the British carriers given to them by the radar operators on Malvinas was 51°38S 53°38W, 186 miles east of the islands' capital. And he was going to lead the raid in from behind them to attack from the southeast, from where they least expected it.

Pancho rolled on to a north-northwest heading, leading the formation into a cruise descent over the next 80 miles down to low level to run in over the last 100 miles to the target below the radar.

Ian Mortimer, Sharkey Ward's AWI, had been scheduled to launch at 1715Z as leader of Phoenix Section alongside Charlie Cantan. But instead of enduring another long wait on *Invincible*'s deck at Alert 5, Morts was scrambled at 1635Z as a replacement for an unserviceable jet in the previous CAP pair. He was flying XZ458, one of the original 809 Squadron jets. It had been the first of Tim Gedge's SHARs to be stripped and repainted in Philip Barley's new air defence grey before John Leeming had flown it, with a faulty oxygen supply, to Ascension to embark on *Atlantic Conveyor*.

At 1719Z another pair of SHARs launched from HMS *Hermes*, steaming 7 miles northeast of *Invincible*. Aboard the smaller carrier, the Flight Direction Officer tracked their progress west on the ship's Type 992 search radar. They stayed low, out of sight of the Argentine AN/TPS-43 at Stanley.

On the flight deck, as Morts turned for home after a fruitless sortie to CAP station 33, Cantan, his former Phoenix Section wingman, remained poised on the carrier's centreline at Alert 5, ready to scramble at a moment's notice.

The SHUTTER report had warned of a Super Etendard strike three-quarters of an hour earlier, but it had failed to materialize. And, given estimates of time, speed and distance, it should have hit them by now. In the Ops Room aboard HMS *Invincible* JJ Black and his team could only conclude that it was another false alarm.

Then at 1730Z, on an old FH5 direction finder aboard HMS *Exeter*, urgent-sounding Spanish voices were heard. Moments later, two sweeps of a Super Etendard's Agave radar were detected approaching from the south. The crew of *Andromeda*'s Lynx helicopter flying as a picket 15 miles west of *Exeter* picked up the Argentine radar on their Orange Crop ESM equipment and reported it to *Hermes*. Then UAA1 radar warning receivers lit up aboard *Ambuscade*, *Cardiff* and *Glamorgan*.

They were under attack.

In *Exeter*'s Ops Room, Captain Hugh Balfour pulled his soft cotton anti-flash hood up over his head.

At the call of 'Handbrake!' ships throughout the Battle Group went immediately to Action Stations, employing now well-rehearsed responses to the Exocet threat, sealing hatches, firing patterns of chaff delta and turning either to bring their weapons to bear or to present the slimmest profile possible to the direction of the threat.

After the initial two sweeps the Agave radar transmissions were detected again in a sector scan lasting nearly thirty seconds. The SuEs were looking for targets. There was then a two-second pause. But it offered no respite, only a gnawing anticipation of what might come next.

When the Argentine radar transmissions returned they were no longer searching. A solid glowing dot on the RWR screen and a steady tone through the operator's headset indicated that the Agave had found its mark.

The missiles would soon follow.

*And I'm defenceless*, thought JJ Black as *Invincible*'s Ops Room erupted around him. After maintaining an unbroken 24/7 vigil since the day the ship had first entered the TEZ, *Invincible*'s Sea Dart missile system was down.

At 30 miles, on a bearing of 205°, the first of the inbound Super Etendards appeared over the horizon of *Invincible*'s 992 search radar. Black watched the orange glow of the contact trace north across the screen and a thought began to take shape in his mind. Twenty seconds later a second SuE appeared to the west of his wingman on a bearing of 204°. Just 28 miles away. But at the same time over 16 miles west of his ship and tracking north.

He could now see both jets quite clearly on the radar display and they were flying *away* from *Invincible*.

*Why*, he wondered, *can't they see us?*

Nor was his ship entirely defenceless. Her primary weapons were her aircraft. Within a minute of the SuEs' presence first being reported, she'd launched two. The ESM-equipped decoy Lynx from 815 Squadron got airborne, its pilot feeling enough adrenalin coursing through his system, he thought, to get the whole population of China buzzing for the next twenty years. Then moments later, after the command 'Scramble the alert Harrier' had sirened over the flight deck, Charlie Cantan slammed the throttle forward and accelerated down the centreline towards the ski-jump.

At a console near JJ Black in the carrier's Ops Room, the Direction Officer watched the SHAR's progress on the 992. Already 8 miles north of the ship by the time the SuEs appeared on radar to the southwest, the challenge was going to be trying to get Cantan past the screen of escorts positioned between him and the Argentine jets without getting him shot down by his own side.

Because the shooting had started.

\*

*Exeter* fired a Sea Dart missile within fifteen seconds of the first contact appearing over the horizon. And missed. Out at sea, over open water, Balfour was confident in a missile system he'd tuned to a fine pitch, but at a range of 25 miles they were operating at the edge of their capability against a low-level target. His effort had succeeded only in forcing a desperate evasive manoeuvre from *Andromeda*'s Lynx.

Less than a minute after they'd first popped up on to *Invincible*'s radar, the SuEs disappeared again as they dropped to sea level to make their escape. At the same time, Cantan was ordered to make chase on a bearing of 220° at an altitude of 1,500 feet. He picked up a momentary contact on the Blue Fox 12 miles to the southwest. He adjusted his heading and accelerated after it until his RWR sounded an urgent warning. Adrenalin surged through him. Illuminated by a 909 fire control radar from either *Cardiff* or *Exeter*, he threw the SHAR into immediate evasive action while at the same time broadcasting his identity on as many radio frequencies as possible. But breaking off from his pursuit would cost him dear. He'd never now get within range of his Sidewinders.

*Invincible*'s 'D' was relying on Morts, still around 80 miles distant to the west on his way back to Mother from CAP station 33. 'Fired out', as Sandy Woodward had recommended following the attack on *Conveyor*, along the raiders' escape route he might be able to cut them off as they were 'scampering out'.

801's AWI was descending to low level for the last leg of his transit back to the carrier when the call came. *Invincible* had trade for him: a contact detected 27 miles southwest of the carrier. Morts was vectored on to a bearing of 130°. He rolled into a hard descending turn to starboard and poured on the coals.

Barely fifteen seconds after they'd first appeared on *Invincible*'s search radar, the two Super Etendards turned sharply to port to reverse their course. Half a minute later they were gone. At exactly the moment the Armada jets dropped below the carrier's radar horizon, the UAA1 RWR aboard HMS *Exeter* had already picked up the 5000Hz pulse repetition frequency transmission of an AM.39 Exocet radar homing head. Bearing 166°.

'Exocet locked on to us,' reported Balfour over the ship's broadcast, 'hit the deck!'

The Captain paid no heed to his own directive.

Alongside his Anti-Air Warfare Officer and two electronic warfare operators he remained at his station, calmly providing his ship's company with a commentary on the fight. As the men prayed that the Sea Dart would do its job, the clock ticked down to impact. The missile had one minute to run.

But *Exeter* was not its target.

A little over 7 miles to the south, the Type 21 frigate HMS *Avenger* steamed slowly upthreat, the skies around her thick with blooming clouds of chaff delta. She'd detected six inbound bogeys at a range of 40 miles. After the two SuEs turned away, a close formation of aircraft continued to streak towards her at a speed of over 500 knots. The Skyhawks. *Avenger*'s gun controller was waiting until he could see the whites of their eyes before he opened up with the ship's 4.5-inch gun. He set the range for 9,000 yards.

*Exeter* shuddered as a second Sea Dart blasted away from the launcher.

Thirty-four seconds later a fireball 50 feet above the sea surface completely engulfed the Skyhawk on the port flank of the Fuerza Aérea Argentina formation.

When he fired his third missile, *Exeter*'s Sea Dart controller did so from underneath his desk, braced for the imminent arrival of the Exocet they knew was still spearing north at 600mph.

Between them, HMS *Avenger* was spitting 4.5-inch high-explosive shells at the three surviving A-4s, her semi-automatic GSA4 gun pumping out eight rounds in twenty seconds.

At 1734Z another explosion blew the tail off the Skyhawk to starboard sending what was left cartwheeling violently into the sea in a huge geyser of white water and spray just 50 yards to starboard of *Avenger*. The two remaining A-4s passed ultra low to port of the frigate, now wreathed in her own gunsmoke, where their bombs dropped harmlessly into the sea.

The Exocet had already swept through twenty seconds earlier, seduced by the patterns of chaff delta fired by the ship. Still armed and dangerous, the big missile lanced northeast on a bearing of 051°, low over the sea and unseen by British radars, searching for a new target.

This time, though, there was no *Conveyor* or any other ship in its path.

Unable to find a new target that lay within the narrow beam width of the radar homing head, it could do no more than fly on until its rocket fuel was expended. Nearly 30 miles north-northeast of *Avenger*, a missile with a high crossing rate was seen by her sister ship HMS *Ambuscade*. Still 7 miles distant, it splashed harmlessly into the sea.

Now *Exeter* had the two retreating Skyhawks in her sights. The Sea Dart's 909 fire control radars locked on to them both as they sped away towards the southwest. The Captain considered whether or not to take them down. It was sorely tempting, but his thoughts turned to the hours and days ahead. *Exeter* now had just seven Sea Dart missiles left in her magazine with no immediate prospect of replenishment. The two Skyhawks no longer posed any immediate threat to him or any other British ships. And the Direction Officer on *Invincible* had vectored the SHARs towards them. As the distance between the *Exeter* and the Argentine jets opened up, it made sense to leave them to the CAP to preserve what remained of his depleted arsenal for whatever action lay ahead. Balfour ordered his AAWO to stand down to leave them to the Sea Harriers.

It wasn't to be, though. Ian Mortimer got within 10 miles of the raiders but never caught sight of them. With no more hope of closing to within range of his Nine Limas than Charlie Cantan, Morts was hauled off the pursuit. There had been no more than thirty seconds in it. Had either of the two 801 pilots been just a little closer when the SuE's Agave radar was first detected they might have been in with a chance, but as Cantan continued to his CAP station, a frustrated Mortimer returned to *Invincible* empty-handed.

On board *Exeter* there was elation as crew members picked themselves up off the deck and emerged from wherever they'd taken cover. Their Captain had remained apparently unruffled throughout.

Balfour was a leader in the mould of JJ Black, projecting a calmness and composure from which his crew drew strength.

Six minutes after the first Spanish RT chatter had been detected, it was all over. Balfour ordered his steward to bring him a large single malt whisky to the Ops Room. As he sipped from the tumbler as if it were the most natural thing in the world, he spoke to his ship's company over the broadcast. 'Bravo Zulu,' he told them. Well done. And he suggested that they all treat themselves to a similarly well-earned drink too.

*It was a clever and ambitious plan*, conceded JJ Black of the Argentine attack as he reflected on the success of the Battle Group's response. And he knew that he'd been right to stand his ground over the SHARs' low-level, fuel-hungry ingress and egress from the carriers. The pilots hated it, but today, he thought, *that measure probably saved our lives*. During the attack on *Conveyor*, the position given to the SuEs, based on tracking the Sea Harriers in and out of the CAP stations, had been within 5 miles of *Hermes*. Today, the coordinates given to 2 Escuadrilla were 20 miles away from *Invincible* and nearly 30 from *Hermes*. When the raid turned north hoping to come in from behind the Battle Group's unprotected rear quarter to the east, it met only the defensive screen of escorts steaming west ahead of the carriers. Black was delighted at having forced an error from the enemy.

Aboard *Hermes*, Lyn Middleton was unimpressed. 'I'm getting bored with this fellow,' he announced later. 'It's not the nervous strain so much as the inconvenience. It's time we took him out.'

To all intents and purposes, they already had.

Subsequent analysis by Northwood examined the attack in detail. There remained some uncertainty about who had shot down what and how, but, they pointed out, 'One important overall conclusion must be remembered: ARGENTINA launched an attack against the high value units of the Task Force. IT FAILED. *The Task Force countered the attack SUCCESSFULLY.*'

And with its failure, Argentina's last realistic hope of winning the war was gone.

# FIFTY-NINE

## More appropriate to a James Bond movie

IN LONDON THE next morning, Attorney General Sir Michael Havers spoke briefly to the Prime Minister about a proposal to help contain the Exocet threat. The UK government's senior legal adviser followed this up in writing later the same day.

He was now having second thoughts about having troubled her with it, but, as a former Fleet Air Arm pilot himself, he believed the risk of Argentina acquiring further missiles justified consideration of every possible option to prevent it. And yet on re-reading his letter, he had to admit that the scheme dreamt up by his friend seemed pretty outlandish.

'More appropriate,' he told Mrs Thatcher, 'to a James Bond movie!'

But then, given that his friend was Charles Hughesdon, perhaps that was only to be expected.

Hughesdon had been an air racer, test pilot, decorated RAF flyer, champion ballroom dancer, equestrian and bon vivant whose marriage to film star Florence Desmond had proved no barrier to his enjoyment of long affairs with Shirley Bassey and Margot Fonteyn. But it was his long experience running a cargo airline, Tradewinds Airways, which prompted the idea he put to Havers. Because as well as Formula 1 racing cars and thoroughbred racehorses, Tradewinds also flew missiles for the MoD up to the NATO test ranges in the Arctic. Delivering missiles by air was one of the many and varied areas of his expertise.

If there was intelligence that Argentina had acquired further AM.39s on the black market, he would win the contract to airfreight them to Latin America using a Beirut-based airline like Middle East

Airways or Trans Mediterranean. But by installing his own inside man as Loadmaster on the flights he would then be in a position to hijack his own flights. Once the Loadmaster had taken control, the jet and its dangerous cargo could be safely diverted to a secure location like Bermuda for the missiles to be impounded.

Havers assured Mrs Thatcher that Hughesdon's loyalty and integrity were 'beyond question' and recommended that his friend's imaginative plan was 'an option we should keep open'.

But there was no need. The successful MI6 sting operation in Paris had already seen to that.

The Super Etendard detachment at Río Grande was ordered to return to Comandante Espora in the north. With their arsenal of five AM.39 Exocets now expended, 2 Escuadrilla's war was all but finished. Unable to acquire new missiles, there was some consideration given to arming the SuEs with bombs, but the Exocet threat to the British carriers was now over.

It had been something of a highwire act, but Sandy Woodward's fragile equation of distance, deception, picket ships, goalkeepers, CAPs, Sea Dart, Seawolf, chaff and sacrifice had succeeded in preserving *Hermes* and *Invincible*.

*The Args*, he thought, *started this game with five aces and they have now, incontrovertibly, played them all.*

The carriers, despite the odd warning that a Super Etendard raid might be brewing, were never again directly threatened. And while the Sea Harrier squadrons continued to fly a punishing programme of CAP missions, they rarely encountered the enemy. On one of the few occasions they did, five Grupo 5 Skyhawks attacking British landing forces in Choiseul Sound at dusk were routed by the SHARs, three of them shot down in quick succession by Dave Morgan and Dave Smith.

Despite a couple more high-altitude kills falling to Sea Dart missiles fired from HMS *Exeter*, the counter air war was largely over. While there continued to be debate about what exactly constituted air superiority and whether or not it had been established, among the Argentine pilots there were no such misgivings: the skies over the Falkland Islands belonged to the Sea Harriers.

\*

The CIA was in little doubt either. Argentina, they assessed, had lost a third of her combat aircraft. Langley's only curiosity was about why recent losses had been to missiles rather than the SHARs. Was there some issue affecting their ability to fight? There was none, other than the Fuerza Aérea Argentina's effort to avoid them wherever possible. Effective air defence could not simply be measured in terms of kills, for that failed to take into account the number of raids that had been deterred or turned back by the mere presence of the Sea Harriers patrolling between the attackers and their targets, warned off by the irritatingly durable, persistent and vigilant VYCA 2 crews at Puerto Argentino. Without precision-guided stand-off weapons, the British had been unable to stop them from warning incoming raids of the positions of the waiting CAPs using their powerful AN/TPS-43 radar.

The focus was now on the ground war, and that was beyond the ability of Argentina's mainland air power to affect. It was an impotence felt aboard the British carriers too.

'This war is getting dull,' announced Lyn Middleton.

'Let's hope it stays that way,' replied Sandy Woodward.

Privately, the Admiral was no longer in any doubt about the outcome though. It was a week now since he'd confided as much to his diary. 'The war will go on,' he wrote. 'Setbacks, yes. Defeat, no.'

He would be given no reason to revise that view.

# SIXTY

## Uniquely flexible

THE WAR WAS won on 14 June 1982. News of white flags over Stanley first reached *Hermes* after being reported from the cockpit of a GR.3 pilot. The day before, Peter Squire had made the first successful precision attack using laser-guided bombs when he scored a direct hit on an Argentine command post. 1(F) now had the ability to take out whatever target was required on demand, with certainty and impunity. The 'books' that Lyn Middleton had complained were clogging up his ship's communications had proved their worth. And, in the end, even Middleton, relieved of the pressure he'd endured throughout the fighting, was happy to concede of Squire's men that 'they did well'.

By the time 1(F) finally won the Captain's approval, Bob Iveson had already returned to the UK. Picked up from Paragon House by Royal Marines after the Battle of Goose Green and returned to *Hermes*, he flew a couple more sorties before back pain caused by his ejection grounded him. Capitán de Corbeta Alberto Philippi was similarly fortunate. After three days of escape and evasion, the 3 Escuadrilla pilot shot down by Spag Morrell was found and taken in by a Falkland Islander. Instead of turning him in, the farmer allowed his guest to be helicoptered out by his own side. A couple of days later Philippi was repatriated aboard a returning C-130 supply flight.

Over the two and a half months that followed the invasion, the Harrier and Sea Harrier had grown ever more capable. They may have had their shortcomings, but these were outweighed by their unique strengths. Had they been patrolling the same CAP stations, at the same time, in the same numbers, Phantoms would likely have shot down more Argentine jets, but the SHARs did account for nearly a quarter of the Argentine fast jet frontline without losing a single aircraft of their own to the enemy in air combat. Across over 1,700 sorties flown between 2 April and the surrender, the Sea Harrier also proved to be exceptionally reliable. Despite punishing climatic conditions and a thinly stretched logistics chain, 801's Air Engineering Officer reported over 99% availability for the missions tasked – a figure hailed by JJ Black as *quite extraordinary*. The complex and temperamental Phantom's serviceability had been anything but. The Harrier was uniquely flexible, too. Reinforcement and replacement of aircraft lost from the carriers would have been impossible with anything but the jump jet.

Those Harriers that *were* lost were lost to ground fire and accidents. There's no reason to suppose that the same number of Phantoms and Buccaneers would not have been lost to the same cause. That would have reduced *Ark Royal*'s air group to about fifteen aeroplanes. Add to that the jets that might have been lost because of the impossibility of trapping the three-wire at 130 knots in impenetrable fog or of diverting to the helicopter pad of an assault ship, and *Ark*'s air group begins to look somewhat threadbare.

A tanker could certainly have been launched to keep them flying, but for how long? On occasions the terrible South Atlantic weather curtailed flying for days on end. A tanker could, potentially, have given an aircraft stranded aloft the legs to divert to Chile, Uruguay or even Brazil. But on arrival it would have been impounded until a time of its host's choosing, as completely removed from the fight as an RAF Vulcan bomber that was forced to Rio de Janeiro after a failure.

Twenty Sea Harriers travelled to the South Atlantic with *Hermes* and *Invincible*. Over the course of the conflict six were lost to ground fire and accidents. Another four GR.3s were lost. Only the arrival of the fourteen aircraft aboard *Atlantic Conveyor* provided the combat mass necessary to sustain those kinds of losses and continue to fight the war. While the small five-strong squadrons normally deployed aboard the carriers put great store by the fact they'd been able to mount an unbroken CAP for days at a time during exercises, the reality is that ten SHARs would not have been enough to do all that was required of them. They'd simply have been unable to hold the line.

And it was only the Harrier's unique ability to stop then land rather than vice versa – to land *vertically* – that made it possible for any frontline RAF Harrier pilot to operate from the carrier without first becoming carrier-qualified. The very nature of the Harrier itself, not just the numbers possessed, meant that as fine as the thin dark grey line of *Sea* Harriers might be, through the land-based Harrier GR.3 the UK had useable reserves of both aircraft and pilots to throw into the fight as required.

Success in the Falklands War completely changed the way the jump jet was regarded. Having earned its spurs in difficult circumstances it had won the right to be taken seriously, no longer dismissed as an airshow novelty, but respected as a warplane. Reliability and flexibility were virtues that attracted fewer headlines than speed, endurance and weaponry, but victory in battle trumped them all, sealing a reputation that would endure.

At the 1981 Junior Olympics, a fifteen-year-old boxer from Catskill, New York knocked out his opponent after just eight seconds of round one to win the heavyweight gold medal. The following year, in the final of the same competition, his opponent's corner threw in the towel in round one to spare their fighter from further punishment. The young boxer's name was Mike Tyson. And he would go on to become the undisputed heavyweight champion of the world, cutting down all comers with clinical speed, power and accuracy. So fearsome would his reputation become that most of his opponents expected to lose before the first punch was thrown. The AIM-9L Sidewinder had a similar effect.

After photographs taken during the first interception of a Fuerza Aérea Argentina 707 in April showed that the Sea Harriers were armed with Nine Limas, the Argentine Mirage, Dagger and Skyhawk pilots believed they were at a disadvantage in any dogfight with the British jets.

In fact, during the fighting that followed, there wasn't a single Nine Lima kill that couldn't have been taken by the AIM-9G. And the Fleet Air Arm pilots were taking risks by dropping into the middle of formations of Argentine attack jets. Had the Fuerza Aérea

Argentina commanders included an R.550 Magic-, Shafrir- or Sidewinder-armed jet in every flight of bombers they might have picked off a few SHARs in reply. But for all their undoubted courage the Argentine pilots were intimidated by their perception of the enemy's superiority.

Of the twenty-three kills credited to the Sea Harriers, six fell to the pale grey aircraft brought south by 809 Squadron aboard *Atlantic Conveyor*. John Leeming shot down a Skyhawk during his dramatic encounter with the Armada Argentina A-4Qs alongside Spag Morrell. Tim Gedge and Dave Braithwaite strafed and destroyed a helicopter on the ground, while Leeming directed the gun attack from his wingman that had immobilized it in the first place. During his first mission over the islands Al Craig fired on the Pucará that was eventually despatched by Sharkey Ward.

The end of the war did not mean an end to 809's tour of duty. After being flown ashore in the last days of the war to try, at Sandy Woodward's behest, to sort out the air tasking in support of the battle on the ground, Gedge travelled back to the UK to prepare a new incarnation of his squadron to travel south aboard HMS *Illustrious*. Lusty would be replacing her sistership, *Invincible*, which had remained in the South Atlantic providing air defence since the war's end. There were a few new faces. Taylor Scott finally got to join the frontline again. War veterans Dave Morgan and Dave Smith, who between them had five kills to their credit, came over from 800 NAS. Spag Morrell returned to 809 for a third spell with the unit, but his first in a Sea Harrier rather than a Buccaneer. Simon Hargreaves, the young pilot who'd enjoyed the Fleet Air Arm's first encounter with the Fuerza Aérea Argentina when he intercepted the Boeing 707, was another. John Leeming also returned.

The squadron was flying a more battle-hardened and capable SHAR than the one which had first faced down the Argentine threat. Christened Ermintrude, Emanuelle, Ethel, Hot Lips, Cindy-Lou, Rosie, Phyllis, Esmeralda, Mrs Robinson and Myrtle, the squadron's ten jets all wore the pale Barley Grey camouflage they'd pioneered during the war. All now also carried AN/ALE-40 chaff and flare dispensers for self-defence. Larger 190-gallon combat tanks extended the jet's duration by nearly an hour. By September 1982, 809 was mounting long-range sorties against replacement ships sailing south from Ascension at a distance of 480 miles from the carrier, returning to Mother two hours and fifteen minutes after launching. Twin Sidewinder rails had also been added to the outer pylons. Each Sea Harrier now carried four Nine Limas rather than the two that had been available throughout the war.

But it was the arrival of the two Sea King AEW.2s from 824 'D' Flight that really transformed the capability of the new carrier's air defence capability.

Despite a shortage of spares, the new SKAEWs rapidly demonstrated their value. By the end of September, 824's radar operators were directing interceptions from 200 miles away with results that exceeded all expectations. Not only had they detected low-level raids mounted, unannounced, by *Invincible*'s Sea Harriers against *Illustrious* but they'd also picked up simulated Exocet attacks.

Instead of the two minutes the Battle Group had had to prepare for the arrival of the last Exocet on 30 May, D Flight could provide as much as eleven minutes' warning of an impending attack. That was enough time to vector the SHARs with some hope of making an interception. And, even if that failed, *Illustrious*, unlike her sister ship, had been fitted with two hastily acquired American Vulcan-Phalanx CIWS computer-controlled Gatling guns capable of acquiring, tracking and shredding any incoming missile in a hail of 20mm armour-piercing tungsten rounds. It hadn't just been the Sea Harriers that had benefited from a few important upgrades.

From the comfort of Stanley's Upland Goose hotel, Tim Gedge wrote a paper about the challenges of operating a naval fighter squadron ashore as 809, sharing responsibilities with Sidewinder-armed RAF GR.3s, provided the Falklands garrison with air defence. Between them they kept a jet on Alert 10 from dawn to dusk while SHARs embarked on *Illustrious* maintained the vigil throughout the night.

After work to extend the runway using steel matting was complete, the RAF arrived in force. On 17 October, the first of four 29(F) Squadron F-4 Phantom FGR.2s journeyed south from Ascension Island to pick up the baton from the SHARs. Gedge flew out to greet the new arrival, escorting the big interceptor all the way into Stanley where it landed using the newly installed arrestor wires. No sooner was the F-4 on the ground than it was being armed with four live medium-range Skyflash missiles, four AIM-9L Sidewinders and a single SUU-23 Gatling gun pod loaded with 1,200 rounds of 20mm high-explosive ammunition.

Once refuelled, XV468 took off again and flew beyond the western edge of the Falkland Islands Protection Zone where, watched by Argentine search radars, she accelerated to supersonic speed for the first of what were termed 'presence runs'.

Two days later, the Fuerza Aérea Argentina made an effort to reciprocate. Before getting anywhere near the 150-mile perimeter of the FIPZ, the Mirage turned away rather than challenge the waiting Phantom CAP.

For the six hours that followed the Argentine probe, 824 Squadron's Sea Kings maintained an AEW barrier, while heavily armed Phantoms and Sea Harriers, supported by a C-130K tanker, stood on Quick Reaction Alert. Another nibble later in the day triggered the scramble of another Phantom. Once again, though, the Mirage headed for home rather than press his luck, leaving Argentine commanders in no doubt about the efficiency of Britain's reinforced air defences.

With the arrival of the 29(F) Squadron Phantoms, 809's SHARs were relieved of their responsibility for the islands' air defence. Since the squadron's revival in April, its time on sentry in the South Atlantic had rivalled that of either 800 or 801.

*Illustrious* left for home on 21 October. Two months later, as the ship sailed within range of Yeovilton, the squadron disembarked from the new carrier for the last time. Filthy weather delayed their departure, then curtailed Gedge's plans to say goodbye to the ship with a memorable formation flypast. Instead, as the rest of his squadron climbed through the 25,000 feet of solid cloud blanketing the carrier, the CO tried to provide a solo farewell. Flying on instruments, he held the SHAR in an accelerating low-level orbit around the ship before levelling the wings and skimming past her along the length of the flight deck at over 500 knots just 50 feet above the waves.

As the roar of the Pegasus engine enveloped the carrier, Gedge pulled back on the stick and disappeared into the clouds.

For his extraordinary achievement in bringing 809 NAS back to the frontline, Tim Gedge was awarded the 1982 Boyd Trophy. The silver model of a Fairey Swordfish biplane was given annually to the individual, group or unit that, in the opinion of FONAC, had achieved the year's finest feat of aviation. In the year of the Falklands War it was deemed to be Tim Gedge, for 'Leadership on the ground and in the air, perseverance, skill, professional knowledge and control'.

On 17 December, 809 NAS was formally disbanded. The CO considered how they might mark the occasion with some kind of formal decommissioning ceremony, but the squadron was already scattered to the four winds. Many of his men were still aboard *Illustrious* alongside in Portsmouth, while others were on extended leave or had already left for new postings.

In the end, Gedge gathered those of his team still at Yeovilton around him and, standing on a soapbox, thanked them for all they had done to add another remarkable chapter to 809's storied history. There was little more to do after that but head home.

*It was all a little rushed*, thought Gedge. But that had been the defining characteristic of 809's return and what had made it so exceptional. It ended as it had begun. The squadron's revival had been an object lesson in the art of what was possible in the prevailing circumstances and the time available.

And while his squadron might once more have been placed into hibernation, some were already imagining 809 returning to save the day again. The squadron's last reporting signal read:

```
Alas too soon the day draws nigh
When the Phoenix Squadron must cease to fly.
Though fire and flames are forced to dwindle
The immortal spark awaits rekindle.
The snuffing out could hardly be faster,
But watch the Bird at the next disaster.
```

# EPILOGUE

## Phoenix Rising

*The F-35 fighter jet, which is, you know, almost like an invisible fighter. I was asking the Air Force guys, I said, 'How good is this plane?' They said, 'Well, sir, you can't see it.' I said, 'Yeah, but in a fight, you know, a fight like I watch in the movies – they fight, they're fighting – how good is this?' They say, 'Well, it wins every time because the enemy cannot see it. Even if it's right next to it, it can't see it.' I said, 'That helps. That's a good thing.'*

Donald Trump, President of
the United States of America, 2016–2021

With 809's return to the bench, Tim Gedge joined the Directorate of Naval Air Warfare in 1983. In his new post at MoD Main Building in London he was responsible for the Fixed Wing desk. Over the next two years he focused on two major priorities. The first was the selection of a new pulse-Doppler radar for the SHAR's mid-life update programme. The new set, developed on a shoestring in Edinburgh by Marconi, was christened Blue Vixen. And putting it inside the 1960s Hawker airframe of the Sea Harrier effected a dramatic transformation. It was as if someone had filled the elegant coach-built lines of a Jaguar E-Type with the state-of-the-art running gear of a Tesla.

The new radar would come to be regarded as one of the most capable sensors in the world. And armed with that, and four AMRAAM medium-range missiles hanging from the pylons, the Sea Harrier FA.2 became a hugely potent air defender, capable of tracking and destroying multiple different targets simultaneously at distances of 40 miles or more. In its combat debut over Bosnia in 1995 during Operation DENY FLIGHT, FA.2 pilots were denied the possibility of a few long-range kills. The NATO Air Commander had simply not believed Blue Vixen capable of picking up targets invisible to the patrolling AWACS jets. Once shown video of the SHARs tracking four bogeys flying low over land he was persuaded, though. The next day he briefed his staff that contacts detected by upgraded SHARs were to be believed because it was, he said, 'the little aircraft with the big dick radar'.

But as well as providing the SHAR with a world-beating radar, Gedge was looking further ahead still.

On day one at DNAW he was told he was responsible for drafting the document detailing the requirements for the Sea Harrier's eventual replacement. Naval Staff Target 6464 outlined an ambitious set of requirements. Supersonic speed, a powerful radar, medium-range air-to-air missiles and stealth were needed. And in a package that, like the Sea Harrier, could take off and land vertically and was compact enough to operate from an Invincible class carrier.

Gedge explored a number of radical technologies from voice activation trials at Farnborough to a proposal for a vertical landing version of the European Fighter Aircraft, the multinational project that would become the Typhoon. British Aerospace imagined the jet crabbing through the air with its nose pointing straight up, sitting on a pillar of thrust from the two jet engines in its tail, before hooking on to a hydraulically raised section of the flight deck by its nosewheel. The pilot would be entirely at the mercy of the computers, and Gedge was vehemently opposed to it.

Instead, in close cooperation with his USMC counterpart in Washington, he fleshed out the specifications required of a Harrier replacement aircraft in more detail. It would eventually grow into the biggest weapons programme the global defence industry had ever seen.

On 9 September 2013, during London Shipping Week, First Sea Lord Admiral Sir George Zambellas took to a podium in the ExCel Centre in Canning Town, east London.

In another era it might have happened south of the river, beyond the O2 arena that occupies the North Greenwich peninsula like a giant flying saucer, in the elegant Sir Christopher Wren-designed buildings of the Royal Naval College. But the Royal Navy had finally left the seventeenth-century campus in 1998, four years after Mike Layard had served as President of the College and a year before the dismantling and removal of the nuclear reactor JASON, housed inside the Grade 1 listed King William Building, was complete.

Zambellas was speaking at a maritime conference organized by the Royal United Services Institute as part of the Defence and Security Equipment International exhibition. Gathered in DSEI's naval theatre to hear Zambellas speak were manufacturers, journalists, consultants and commentators – anyone with an interest or stake in maritime defence.

British Harriers were long gone by this time. Under Bill Covington, the last of the Falklands SHAR pilots to retire from the Navy, the Fleet Air Arm's FA.2s had been rolled into Joint Force Harrier alongside the RAF's Harrier GR.7s. The hard-headed sense of realism that characterized the post-Falklands Sea Harrier community infused JFH. Neither bullshit nor ego was indulged in pursuit of excellence. For six years, from 2000 to 2006, JFH offered a powerful and effective combination of air defence and ground attack deploying successfully on operations in Sierra Leone and Iraq. But with the new command structure, the FA.2s were now answerable not to the Navy but to RAF Strike Command.

When budgetary constraints led to the premature retirement of the Sea Harrier in 2006, the Navy suggested using the money saved to throw in its lot with a modernized RAF Harrier force. As a result, Fleet Air Arm pilots converted to the re-engined Harrier GR.9 alongside their RAF counterparts, flying an aeroplane no longer owned or supported by the Navy. And, once again, they found themselves at war.

Despite the inevitable tensions, 800 Naval Air Squadron fought with distinction alongside 1(F) Squadron, just as they had in 1982 when they flew from the deck of HMS *Hermes*. This time, though, instead of fleet air defence, naval aviators flew demanding close air support missions from Kandahar airfield in Afghanistan as part of Operation HERRICK, until the Harrier detachment was replaced by Tornados in 2009.

Such demonstrable success was to count for nothing, though. In a shock decision that followed the 2010 Strategic Defence and Security Review, RAF GR.9s followed the FA.2 into retirement at the end of that year. Alongside them, HMS *Ark Royal*, the third of the Invincible class carriers to enter service, was also paid off.

Former Falklands Task Force Commander Sir Sandy Woodward viewed the Harriers' retirement with incredulity. 'Handling fixed-wing aircraft on the deck of an aircraft carrier is as complicated a business as it is to run the Bolshoi ballet, if not more so, and you do it for months on end as opposed to one evening at a time, and to get all that skill back will take you ten to fifteen years,' he thundered. 'That is a major problem, because if you want to do anything in terms of an expeditionary force in the world, you must have air cover, and we won't have it.'

As if to illustrate Woodward's point, just three months later

Prime Minister David Cameron asked whether it would be possible to return *Ark Royal* and the Harriers to service as part of Operation ELLAMY, Britain's intervention in Libya. It was already too late.

But the fixed-wing Fleet Air Arm – and with it an unbroken grip on the spirit that distinguished the SHAR force in the wake of the South Atlantic war – hung on by a thread, supported by a vigorous programme of fast jet exchange tours, primarily with the US Navy and Marine Corps. And by 2013, at the time of Zambellas's address, it was once more looking forward to a brighter future.

Two new 65,000-ton Queen Elizabeth class aircraft carriers were under construction for the Navy; they would be the largest vessels in the service's long history. And the origins of the state-of-the-art, stealthy, supersonic, vertical take-off and landing aircraft selected to fly from the new ships could be traced back to the work substantially begun by Tim Gedge in 1983.

Over time, other programmes on both sides of the Atlantic – USAF, USN and RAF – were folded into the development of what became known as the Joint Strike Fighter, but its origins lay in the Royal Navy and US Marine Corps requirement for a Harrier replacement as outlined in the NST6464 document drawn up by Gedge.

A decade and a half later, flying alongside their American counterparts at Edwards Air Force Base and Point Mugu in the United States, British pilots were putting the revolutionary new warplane born of those early draft studies through its paces. It was called the Lockheed Martin F-35B Lightning II. And the long and often controversial saga of its development was about to circle back to where it had started.

As a freshly minted young Fleet Air Arm pilot in 1982, George Zambellas had narrowly missed out on serving in the Falklands War, when *Invincible* and *Hermes* had proved so vital to Britain's cause. Now, after talking to the room at the ExCel about the broader challenges facing global maritime security, he focused on the 'quantum leap' forward in capability offered by the two new aircraft carriers, HMS *Queen Elizabeth* and HMS *Prince of Wales*.

'I am energized by the prospect of Air Force pilots operating alongside their Fleet Air Arm colleagues,' Zambellas said. 'That sense of joint endeavour is embodied in the fifth-generation Joint Strike Fighters.'

The Admiral said he approved of the RAF's choice of 617 Squadron, announced a couple of months earlier as the first light blue F-35 squadron, because, from the dams raid to the sinking of the *Tirpitz*, the legendary Dambusters had done much of their best work over water.

'And so they will do again,' he added.

But he was to finish with news that many in the audience had been briefed to expect: 'I am delighted to announce that the next Lightning II squadron, when it forms, will be 809. This squadron number is a golden thread which weaves its way through the proud history of carrier strike, from the Second World War through to the Buccaneers flying from the post-war HMS *Ark Royal* to the iconic Sea Harriers which served with such distinction in the Falklands in 1982. It could not be a more fitting squadron name for the new era of UK carrier strike.'

# GLOSSARY

| | |
|---|---|
| 1(Fighter) Squadron | RAF Harrier squadron |
| 2 PARA | 2nd Battalion, Parachute Regiment |
| 3 PARA | 3rd Battalion, Parachute Regiment |
| 39(PR) Squadron | RAF Canberra photoreconnaissance squadron |
| 40 Commando | part of 3 Commando Brigade, Royal Marines |
| 42 Commando | part of 3 Commando Brigade, Royal Marines |
| 45 Commando | part of 3 Commando Brigade, Royal Marines |
| 51 Squadron | RAF Nimrod R.1 Squadron |
| 700A NAS | Sea Harrier trials squadron. 'A' was reputed to stand for 'Arrier |
| 707 | American four-engined jet airliner built by Boeing; used by the Argentine Air Force for transport and reconnaissance |
| 800 NAS | British Naval Air Squadron – a frontline Sea Harrier unit |
| 801 NAS | British Naval Air Squadron – a frontline Sea Harrier unit |
| 809 NAS | British Naval Air Squadron, re-formed as a Sea Harrier unit in 1982 |
| 824 NAS ('D' Flight) | British Naval Air Squadron, equipped with Sea King AEW.2s |
| 845 NAS | British Naval Air Squadron, equipped with Wessex HU.5s |
| 846 NAS | British Naval Air Squadron, equipped with Sea King HC.4s |
| 848 NAS | British Naval Air Squadron, re-formed as a Wessex HU.5 squadron in 1982 |
| 849 NAS | British Naval Air Squadron, long associated with airborne early warning; re-formed in 1982 |

| | |
|---|---|
| 892 NAS | British Naval Air Squadron – first, last and only frontline Fleet Air Arm F-4 Phantom squadron |
| 899 NAS | British Naval Air Squadron – Sea Harrier headquarters squadron in 1982 |
| A-4 Skyhawk | US-made single-engine, single-seat naval attack aircraft |
| A-7 Corsair | US-made single-engine, single-seat naval attack aircraft |
| A&AEE | Aeroplane & Armament Experimental Establishment |
| AAM | air-to-air missile |
| AAR | air-to-air refuelling |
| AAWC | Anti-Air Warfare Coordination radio net |
| AAWO | Anti-Air Warfare Officer |
| ACAS (Ops) | Assistant Chief of the Air Staff (Operations) |
| ADEN | 30mm aircraft cannon, named after its development by the Armament Development Establishment in Enfield |
| ADF | automatic direction finder |
| AEO | Air Engineering Officer |
| Aéronavale | French naval air arm |
| AEW | airborne early warning |
| AFB | Air Force Base |
| Afterburner | US term for 'reheat' |
| Agave | French aircraft radar fitted to Super Etendard |
| Agusta 109 | Italian-made twin-engined utility helicopter |
| AIM-7 Sparrow | American-made medium-range radar-guided missile |
| AIM-9 Sidewinder | American-made short-range heatseeking air-to-air missile |
| ALO | Air Liaison Officer |
| AM.39 | air-launched Exocet anti-ship missile |
| AMC | Alert Measures Committee |
| AMRAAM | advanced medium-range air-to-air missile |
| AN/ALE-40 | airborne chaff and flare self-defence system |
| AN/TPS-43 | American-built long-range air surveillance radar |
| AOA | Amphibious Operations Area |
| AOC | Air Officer Commanding |
| ARA | Armada Argentina (the Argentina Navy) |

| | |
|---|---|
| ARA | Armada de la República Argentina (prefix to Argentine Navy ships' names) |
| ATC | air traffic control |
| ATREL | Air Transportable Reconnaissance Exploitation Laboratory |
| AV-8A | US military designation for the first-generation Harrier |
| AV-8B | US military designation for the second-generation Harrier |
| AVCAT | high-flashpoint JP5 aviation fuel used aboard aircraft carriers |
| AVTUR | kerosene-based aviation fuel used by land-based gas-turbine-powered aircraft |
| AWACS | airborne warning and control system |
| AWG-11 | American-made pulse-Doppler aircraft radar |
| AWI | Air Warfare Instructor |
| BAe | British Aerospace |
| BAM | Base Aérea Militar (BAM Malvinas was the Argentine name for Port Stanley airfield) |
| BAN | Base Aeronaval |
| Battle formation | loose defensive formation |
| Belfast | four-engined British turboprop transport aircraft |
| Bingo fuel | a pre-planned fuel level at which an aircraft has to turn for home |
| BL755 | cluster bomb |
| Blue Fox | British aircraft radar fitted to the Sea Harrier FRS.1 |
| Boeing 707 | see '707' |
| Bombhead | Fleet Air Arm slang for an aircraft armourer |
| Bootneck | slang for a Royal Marine |
| Bravo Zulu | Navy slang for 'well done' |
| Buccaneer | British twin-engined naval strike aircraft |
| C-5 | American four-engined jet transport aircraft |
| C-47 | military transport version of the Second World War-vintage piston-engined DC-3 airliner |
| C-130 Hercules | American four-engined turboprop transport aircraft |

| | |
|---|---|
| C-141 | American four-engined jet transport aircraft |
| Cab | slang for 'helicopter' |
| Canberra | British twin-jet bomber developed into a high-altitude reconnaissance aircraft |
| CAP | combat air patrol |
| CCTV | closed circuit television |
| Chaff | clouds of aluminium foil fired by cannon to decoy incoming missiles |
| Chinook | American tandem-rotor heavy-lift transport helicopter |
| Chipmunk | British piston-engined basic training aircraft |
| CIA | Central Intelligence Agency |
| CIC | Combat Information Centre |
| CINCFLEET | Commander in Chief, Fleet |
| CIWS | close in weapons system |
| CO | Commanding Officer |
| COAN | Comando de Aviación Naval (Argentine Navy aviation branch) |
| COIN | counterinsurgency |
| Coston line | rope/line-throwing cannon |
| Crab | Royal Navy slang for RAF personnel |
| CRT | cathode ray tube |
| CSB | Courage Sparkling Bitter |
| | |
| D | Navy slang for Fighter Direction Officer/ Fighter Controller |
| DACT | Dissimilar Air Combat Training |
| Dagger | Israeli-built version of the Mirage 5 single-engined supersonic jet fighter-bomber |
| Delta Force | US Army Special Forces unit |
| Delta Hotel | direct hit |
| DNAW | Department/Director of Naval Air Warfare |
| DOAE | Defence Operational Analysis Establishment |
| DoD | US Department of Defense |
| DoT | Department of Trade |
| Duff gen | RAF slang for 'bad information' |
| | |
| EAN | Estación Aeronaval |
| ECM | electronic counter-measures |
| Egg banjo | fried egg sandwich |
| Elk | Cargo ferry requisitioned from P&O |

| | |
|---|---|
| Escuadrón Fénix | Argentine paramilitary air force unit |
| ESM | electronic support measures |
| ETA | estimated time of arrival |
| EWOSE | Electronic Warfare Operational Support Establishment |
| Exocet | French-made anti-ship missile |
| | |
| F-4 Phantom | American twin-engined supersonic jet fighter-bomber |
| F-5 Tiger | American single-engined supersonic jet fighter |
| F-14 Tomcat | American twin-engined swing-wing supersonic naval interceptor |
| F-15 Eagle | American twin-engined supersonic air superiority fighter |
| F-16 Fighting Falcon | American single-engined supersonic fighter |
| F-35 Lightning | stealthy US/UK single-engined supersonic V/STOL strike fighter. Designated the Lightening II in US service |
| F-86 Sabre | American single-engined jet fighter |
| FAA | Fuerza Aérea Argentina (the Argentine Air Force) |
| FAC | Forward Air Controller |
| FACh | Fuerza Aérea de Chile (the Chilean Air Force) |
| FCO | Foreign & Commonwealth Office |
| FDO | Flight Deck Officer |
| FINRAE | Ferranti inertial rapid alignment equipment |
| FIPZ | Falkland Islands Protection Zone |
| FLIR | forward-looking infrared |
| Flyco | Flying Control |
| FOB | Forward Operating Base |
| FOF3 | Flag Officer Third Flotilla |
| FONAC | Flag Officer Naval Air Command |
| Fox Two | NATO brevity code used to indicate the launch of a heatseeking missile such as the AIM-9 Sidewinder |
| | |
| g | unit of acceleration |
| Gannet | British naval turboprop anti-submarine, transport and AEW aircraft |
| GCHQ | Government Communications Headquarters |

| | |
|---|---|
| Goalkeeper | missile-armed air defence ship riding shotgun for another ship, mainly the carriers |
| GPMG | general-purpose machine gun |
| Hack the Shad | Fleet Air Arm slang for intercepting an aircraft shadowing the fleet |
| Handbrake | codename for the detection of a Super Etendard radar |
| Harrier | British V/STOL single-engined ground attack aircraft |
| Heron | British four-engined light transport aircraft |
| HMAFV | Her Majesty's Air Force Vessel |
| HMAS | Her Majesty's Australian Ship |
| HMNLS | His/Her Majesty's Netherlands Ship |
| Horse's Neck | Usually whisky and ginger ale. Brandy and ginger ale in the Royal Navy |
| HP cock | high-pressure cock |
| HUD | head-up display |
| HUDWAC | head-up display weapon-aiming computer |
| Huey | nickname for the Bell UH-1, an American-made single-engined utility helicopter |
| Hunter | British-built single-engined jet fighter-bomber |
| IAF | Israeli Air Force |
| IFF | identification friend or foe |
| INS | Israeli Naval Ship |
| IP | initial point |
| ISTAR | Intelligence, Surveillance, Target Acquisition and Reconnaissance |
| Jetstream | British twin-engined regional airliner used by the Royal Air Force and Royal Navy |
| Joint Strike Fighter | original programme name for the F-35 |
| Junglie | a member of one of the Royal Navy's Commando helicopter squadrons (or the machine itself) |
| KC-130 | American-built four-engined turboprop tanker and transport aircraft |
| Kestrel | British single-engined vertical take-off and landing jet aircraft – a precursor to the Harrier |

| | |
|---|---|
| Lepus | Swedish-made air-launched parachute flare |
| Lightning | British twin-engined supersonic jet fighter |
| Long-slot | most distant extent of an air-to-air refuelling operation |
| LP cock | low-pressure cock |
| LSL | Landing Ship Logistic |
| Lynx | twin-engined British shipboard helicopter |
| | |
| Macchi MB-326 | Italian single-engined jet trainer and light attack aircraft |
| Mae West | aircrew slang for a lifejacket |
| MARTSU | Mobile Aircraft Repair, Transport and Salvage Unit (Royal Navy) |
| MASS | master armament selector switch |
| MCAS | Marine Corps Air Station (US) |
| Medevac | medical evacuation |
| Met | weather |
| MI6 | Military Intelligence, section six (British Secret Intelligence Service) |
| MiG-15 | Soviet single-engined jet fighter |
| MiG-17 | Soviet single-engined supersonic jet fighter |
| MiG-21 | Soviet single-engined supersonic jet fighter |
| Mirage | French single-engined supersonic jet fighter |
| MoD | Ministry of Defence |
| Mother | Fleet Air Arm slang for an aircraft carrier |
| Mud-mover | slang for a ground attack pilot |
| MV | Motor Vessel |
| | |
| NAAFI | Navy, Army and Air Force Institute (armed forces shop) |
| NAS | Naval Air Squadron (Royal Navy) |
| NASA | National Aeronautics and Space Administration |
| NATO | North Atlantic Treaty Organization |
| NATOPS | Naval Air Training and Operating Procedures Standardization (US) |
| NAVHARS | navigation, heading and attitude reference system |
| NBCD | nuclear, biological and chemical defence |
| NVG | night vision goggles (see 'PNG') |
| Nimrod MR.2 | British four-engined jet maritime patrol aircraft |

| | |
|---|---|
| Nimrod R.1 | British four-engined jet signals intelligence-gathering aircraft |
| Nine Lima | AIM-9L Sidewinder air-to-air missile |
| Northwood | British naval headquarters facility in north-west London |
| NOTAMS | Notices to Airmen |
| NP 1840 | Naval Party 1840, the military code assigned to personnel aboard *Atlantic Conveyor* |
| NP 8901 | Naval Party 8901, the military code assigned to the Royal Marine detachment at Stanley prior to the war |
| NRO | National Reconnaissance Office |
| NST6464 | Naval Staff Target 6464 (details the requirement for a Sea Harrier replacement) |
| | |
| O Group | Orders Group |
| Okta | unit of cloud coverage |
| Olympus | Rolls-Royce gas turbine engine |
| Operation ACME | codename given to RAF Nimrod R.1 operations during the Falklands War |
| Operation ALPHA | codename given to the Argentine military plan to occupy South Georgia |
| Operation BLACK BUCK | codename given to the RAF's long-range Vulcan missions during the Falklands War |
| Operation BLUE | codename given to the Argentine military plan to seize the Falkland Islands |
| Operation CORPORATE | codename given to the British operation to retake the Falkland Islands |
| Operation FINGENT | codename given to an RAF operation to set up a mobile air surveillance radar in Chile during the Falklands War |
| Operation FOLKLORE | codename given to RAF Canberra operations during the Falklands War |
| Operation GRAMMERIAN | codename given to the RAF Victor operation to provide refuelling support for a Sea Harrier launched from *Atlantic Conveyor* |
| Operation MIKADO | codename given to a planned SAS operation to attack a mainland Argentine air base during the Falklands War |
| Operation PARAQUET | codename given to the British operation to retake South Georgia |

| | |
|---|---|
| Operation PLUM DUFF | codename given to an SAS reconnaissance operation in Argentina mounted in preparation for Operation MIKADO |
| Operation ROSARIO | codename given to the Argentine operation to invade the Falkland Islands |
| Operation SHUTTER | codename for the British operation in Chile to provide the Task Force with early intelligence of Argentine air attack during the Falklands War |
| Operation SUTTON | codename for the British amphibious landings during the Falklands War |
| Ops | operations |
| | |
| P.1127 | British prototype vertical take-off and landing jet aircraft that led to the development of the Harrier |
| Picket ship | warship placed upthreat of the fleet to provide early warning of attack |
| Pickle | aircrew slang for firing/launching weapons |
| PNG | passive night goggles (see 'NVG') |
| POW | prisoner of war |
| PR | photoreconnaissance |
| Project LAST | crash programme to develop a helicopter-borne AEW system |
| Pucará | Argentine-built twin-engined turboprop attack aircraft |
| Puerto Argentino | Argentine name for Port Stanley |
| Puma | Anglo-French utility helicopter |
| | |
| QFI | Qualified Flying Instructor |
| QRA | Quick Reaction Alert |
| | |
| R.530 | French medium-range air-to-air missile |
| R.550 Magic | French short-range heatseeking air-to-air missile |
| R&D | research and development |
| RAAF | Royal Australian Air Force |
| RAE | Royal Aircraft Establishment |
| RAN | Royal Australian Navy |
| RAS | replenishment at sea |
| RCS | radar cross-section |

| | |
|---|---|
| RDX | royal demolition explosive |
| Red 90 | facing ninety degrees to port |
| Refam | refamiliarization |
| Reheat | fuel injected into an engine's jetpipe to boost thrust |
| RFA | Royal Fleet Auxiliary |
| RIC | Reconnaissance Intelligence Centre |
| RNAS | Royal Naval Air Station |
| RPC | request the pleasure of your company (party invitation) |
| RPF | radar proving flight |
| RPM | revolutions per minute |
| RT | radio telephony |
| RWR | radar warning receiver |
| S-2 Tracker | American twin-engined naval maritime patrol and anti-submarine aircraft |
| S259 | British-built portable air surveillance radar |
| SA-7 Strela | Soviet man-portable surface-to-air missile |
| SAM | surface-to-air missile |
| SAS | Special Air Service |
| SBS | Special Boat Squadron (renamed Special Boat Service in 1987) |
| SCADS | shipborne containerized air defence system |
| Seacat | British shipborne surface-to-air missile |
| Sea Dart | British shipborne surface-to-air missile |
| Sea Harrier | British single-engined V/STOL naval fighter-bomber |
| Sea Heron | British four-engined light transport and communication aircraft |
| Sea Jet | aircrew slang for the Sea Harrier |
| Sea Vixen | British twin-engined naval all-weather jet fighter |
| Seawolf | British shipborne surface-to-air missile |
| Shackleton | British piston-engined aircraft derived from the Avro Lancaster; originally designed for maritime patrol, by 1982 the RAF used it for AEW |
| Shafrir | Israeli-built short-range heatseeking air-to-air missile |
| SHAR | aircrew slang for the Sea Harrier |

| | |
|---|---|
| SIGINT | signals intelligence |
| SIS | British Secret Intelligence Service (also known as MI6) |
| Six/six o'clock | a firing position behind the tail of the target aircraft |
| SKAEW | Sea King AEW |
| Ski-jump | ramp built into the bow of British carriers to aid the launch of V/STOL aircraft |
| Skyflash | British-built medium-range air-to-air missile |
| SP-2 Neptune | American twin-engined maritime patrol aircraft |
| Spadeadam | British electronic warfare range in Cumbria |
| SPLOT | Senior Pilot |
| Stinger | American man-portable surface-to-air missile |
| STUFT | ships taken up from trade |
| SuE | aircrew slang for the Super Etendard |
| Super Etendard | French single-engined naval attack aircraft |
| T-34 Turbo Mentor | American turboprop training and light attack aircraft |
| TACAN | tactical air navigation system using radio beacons |
| TACSAT | tactical satellite radio |
| TEZ | Total Exclusion Zone |
| TFS | Tactical Fighter Squadron |
| TG 317.0 | British amphibious task group |
| TOPGUN | US Navy Fighter Weapons School |
| Tornado ADV | Air Defence Variant of the British/German/Italian-built twin-engined, two-seat multi-role combat aircraft |
| Triple A | AAA. Anti-Aircraft Artillary |
| Tu-95 Bear | Soviet four-engined turboprop bomber and maritime patrol aircraft |
| Tu-142 | Soviet four-engined turboprop maritime patrol aircraft |
| Type 21 | British frigate |
| Type 22 | British frigate |
| Type 42 | British destroyer |
| 'Type 64' | nickname given to a pairing of a Type 42 and Type 22 |

| | |
|---|---|
| Type 82 | British destroyer |
| Typhoon | European twin-engined supersonic fighter-bomber |
| | |
| U-2 | American single-engined high-altitude reconnaissance aircraft |
| UHF | ultra high frequency |
| USAAF | US Army Air Force |
| USAF | US Air Force, formed as an independent branch of the US armed forces from the USAAF in 1947 |
| USAFE | United States Air Forces in Europe |
| USMC | United States Marine Corps |
| | |
| VC10 | British four-engined jet airliner used by the RAF |
| VF | prefix to a US Navy or RAN fighter squadron |
| VHF | very high frequency |
| Victor | British four-engined jet bomber, developed into an air-to-air refuelling tanker for the RAF |
| VIFF | vectoring in forward flight |
| VLF Omega | radio navigation equipment |
| VMA | prefix to a USMC attack squadron |
| V/STOL | vertical/short take-off and landing |
| Vulcan | British four-engined jet bomber |
| VYCA | Vigilancia y Control Aéreo (Argentine air warning and control) |
| | |
| Wessex | British anti-submarine or utility helicopter |
| WRNS | Women's Royal Naval Service |
| WTI | Weapons Tactics Instructor (USMC) |
| | |
| XO | Executive Officer (a ship's second-in-command) |
| | |
| Z/Zulu | Zulu time – military term for Greenwich Mean Time (GMT) |

# BIBLIOGRAPHY

**Books**

Aldrich, Richard J., *GCHQ* (HarperPress, 2010)

Aloni, Shlomo, *Israeli Mirage and Nesher Aces* (Osprey, 2004)

Andrade, John, *Latin-American Military Aviation* (Midland Counties Publishing, 1982)

—— *Militair 1982* (Aviation Press, 1982)

Barker, Ralph, *The Hurricats* (Pelham Books, 1978)

Beardow, Keith, *Sailors in the RAF* (Patrick Stephens, 1993)

Beaver, Paul, *Fleet Air Arm Since 1945* (PSL, 1987)

—— *Invincible Class* (Ian Allan, 1984)

Beckett, Andy, *Pinochet in Chile* (Faber and Faber, 2002)

Beeny, Steven, *The Canberra Experience* (2017)

Benson, Harry, *Scram!* (Preface, 2012)

Bishop, Patrick and Witherow, John, *The Winter War* (Quartet, 1982)

Black, Admiral Sir Jeremy, *There and Back* (Elliott and Thompson, 2005)

Briasco, Jesus Romero and Huertas, Salvador Mafe, *Falklands Witness of Battles* (Editorial Federico Domenech, 1985)

Brown, David, *The Royal Navy and the Falklands War* (Leo Cooper, 1987)

Brown, Jeremy, *A South American War* (Book Guild, 2013)

Budiansky, Stephen, *Air Power* (Viking, 2003)

Burden, Rodney A., Draper, Michael I., Rough, Douglas A., Smith, Colin R. and Wilton, David L., *Falklands: The Air War* (Arms and Armour Press, 1986)

Buttler, Tony, *Hawker P.1127, Kestrel and Harrier* (The History Press, 2007)

Carballo, Pablo Marcos, *Dios Y Los Halcones* (Editora Abril, 1983)

Chartres, John, *BAe Nimrod* (Ian Allan, 1986)

—— *Westland Sea King* (Ian Allan, 1984)

Childs, Nick, *The Age of Invincible* (Pen and Sword, 2009)

Clapp, Michael and Southby-Tailyour, Ewen, *Amphibious Assault Falklands* (Leo Cooper, 1996)

Connor, Ken, *Ghost Force* (Weidenfeld and Nicolson, 1998)

Coram, Robert, *Boyd* (Little, Brown, 2002)

David, Saul, *Operation Thunderbolt* (Hodder and Stoughton, 2015)

de Saint-Exupéry, Antoine, *Wind, Sand and Stars* (Penguin Books, 1995)

Delve, Ken, Green, Peter and Clemons, John, *English Electric Canberra* (Midland Counties Publications, 1992)

Delves, Lieutenant General Cedric, *Across an Angry Sea* (C. Hurst and Co., 2018)

Dibbs, John, with Holmes, Tony, *Harrier* (Osprey, 1992)

Dildy, Douglas C. and Calcaterra, Pablo, *Sea Harrier FRS1 vs Mirage III/Dagger* (Osprey, 2017)

Dow, Andrew, *Pegasus* (Pen and Sword, 2009)

Drought, Charles, *N.P.1840: The Loss of the Atlantic Conveyor* (Countyvise, 2003)

Edwards, Sidney, *My Secret Falklands War* (Book Guild, 2014)

Ethell, Jeffrey and Price, Alfred, *Air War South Atlantic* (Sidgwick and Jackson, 1987)

Evans, Andy, *BAe/McDonnell Douglas Harrier* (Crowood Press, 1998)

Farley, John, *A View from the Hover* (Seager Publishing, 2008)

Forster, Dave and Gibson, Chris, *Listening In* (Hikoki Publications, 2014)

Freedman, Lawrence, *The Official History of the Falklands Campaign Volume 2* (Routledge, 2005)

Friedman, Norman, *British Carrier Aviation* (Naval Institute Press, 1988)

Gander, Terry, *Encyclopaedia of the Modern Royal Air Force* (PSL, 1984)

Garbett, Mike and Goulding, Brian, *Lincoln at War* (Ian Allan, 1979)

Gee, Jack, *Mirage* (Macdonald and Co., 1971)

Gibbings, David, *A Quiet Country Town* (The Military Press, 2015)

Gibson, Chris, *The Admiralty and AEW* (Blue Envoy Press, 2011)

Gledhill, David, *Fighters Over the Falklands* (Fonthill, 2013)

Godden, John (ed.), *Harrier: Ski-jump to Victory* (Brassey's, 1983)

Green, William and Swanborough, Gordon, *Commercial Aircraft* (Salamander Books, 1978)

Gunston, Bill, *Attack Aircraft of the West* (Ian Allan, 1982)

—— *Rockets and Missiles* (Salamander Books, 1979)

—— *Rolls-Royce Aero Engines* (PSL, 1989)

Hart-Dyke, David, *Four Weeks in May* (Atlantic, 2007)

Hastings, Max and Jenkins, Simon, *The Battle for the Falklands* (Michael Joseph, 1983)

Healey, Denis, *The Time of My Life* (Michael Joseph, 1989)

Henderson, Nicholas, *Mandarin* (Weidenfeld and Nicolson, 1994)

Hennessy, Peter and Jinks, James, *The Silent Deep* (Allen Lane, 2015)

Higgitt, Mark, *Through Fire and Water* (Mainstream, 2001)

Hobbs, David, *The British Carrier Strike Fleet After 1945* (Seaforth Publishing, 2015)

Hobson, Chris with Noble, Ian, *Falklands Air War* (Midlands Publishing, 2002)

Holland, James, *The Battle of Britain* (Ladybird Expert, Michael Joseph, 2017)

Hunter, Jamie, *Sea Harrier* (Midland Publishing, 2005)

Hutchings, Richard, *Special Forces Pilot* (Pen and Sword, 2008)

Inskip, Ian, *Ordeal by Exocet* (Chatham, 2002)

Jackson, Robert, *Sea Harrier and AV-8B* (Blandford Press, 1989)

Johnson-Allen, John, *They Couldn't Have Done It Without Us* (Seafarer Books, 2011)

Keijsper, Gerard, *Joint Strike Fighter* (Pen and Sword, 2007)

Kon, Daniel, *Los Chicos de la Guerra* (New English Library, 1982)

Leach, Henry, *Endure No Makeshifts* (Leo Cooper, 1993)

Lehman Jr, John F., *Command of the Seas* (Naval Institute Press, 2001)

Marston, Bob, *Harrier Boys Volume 1* (Grub Street, 2015)

Mason, Francis K., *Harrier* (PSL, 1986)

McCart, Neil, *Harrier Carriers Volume 1: HMS Invincible* (Fan Publications, 2004)

—— *HMS Hermes 1923 and 1959* (Fan Publications, 2001)

McCue, Paul M., *Dunsfold – Surrey's Most Secret Airfield* (Air Research Editions, 2002)

McManners, Hugh, *Forgotten Voices of the Falklands* (Ebury Press, 2007)

McQueen, Captain Bob, *Island Base* (Whittles Publishing, 2005)

Mercer, Neil, *Fleet Air Arm* (Airlife Publishing, 1994)

—— *The Sharp End* (Airlife Publishing, 1995)

Middlebrook, Martin, *The Fight for the Malvinas* (Viking, 1989)

—— *Task Force* (Penguin, 1987)

Moore, Charles, *Margaret Thatcher – The Authorized Biography: Volume One* (Allen Lane, 2013)

Morgan, David, *Hostile Skies* (Weidenfeld and Nicolson, 2006)

Nordeen, Lon O., *Harrier* (Naval Institute Press, 2006)

Núñez Padin, Jorge Félix, *McDonnell Douglas A-4Q and A-4E Skyhawk* (Serie Aeronaval #24, 2008)

Orchard, Ade, *Joint Force Harrier* (Michael Joseph, 2008)

Parry, Chris, *Down South* (Viking, 2012)

Peck, Gaillard R., *America's Secret MiG Squadron* (Osprey, 2012)

Polmar, Norman, *Aircraft Carriers Vol. 2* (Potomac Books, 2008)

Pook, Jerry, *RAF Harrier Ground Attack Falklands* (Pen and Sword, 2007)

Poolman, Kenneth, *Scourge of the Atlantic* (Book Club Associates, 1979)

Price, Alfred, *Harrier at War* (Ian Allan, 1984)

Pryce, Michael, *BAe P.1216* (Blue Envoy Press, 2011)

Ratcliffe, Peter, *Eye of the Storm* (Michael O'Mara Books, 2000)

Riley, P. J. 'Red', *Kisses from Nimbus* (Clink Street Publishing, 2017)

Rivas, Santiago, *British Combat Aircraft in Latin America* (Hikoki, 2019)

—— *Wings of the Malvinas* (Hikoki, 2012)

Royal Air Force Historical Society, *The Canberra in the RAF* (RAFHS, 2009)

Sciaroni, Mariano, *A Carrier at Risk* (Helion and Company, 2019)

Shaw, Mike, *From the Cockpit: Harrier GR3* (Ian Allan, 1988)

Shaw, Robert L., *Fighter Combat* (Naval Institute Press, 1985)

Southby-Tailyour, Ewen, *Exocet Falklands* (Pen and Sword, 2014)

Sturtivant, Ray, *The Squadrons of the Fleet Air Arm* (Air-Britain, 1984)

—— Burrow, Mick and Howard, Lee, *Fleet Air Arm Fixed-Wing Aircraft since 1946* (Air-Britain, 2004)

*Sunday Times* Insight Team, *The Falklands War* (Sphere Books, 1982)

Susans, Wg Cdr M. R., *The RAAF Mirage Story* (RAAF Museum, 1990)

Thomas, Andrew, *Royal Navy Aces of World War 2* (Osprey, 2007)

Verier, Mike, *Yeovilton* (Osprey, 1991)

Ward, Commander 'Sharkey', *Sea Harrier Over the Falklands* (Pen and Sword, 1992)

Weinberger, Caspar, *Fighting for Peace* (Michael Joseph, 1990)

West, Nigel, *The Secret War for the Falklands* (Little, Brown, 1997)

Westrum, Ron, *Sidewinder* (Naval Institute Press, 1999)

White, Rowland, *Phoenix Squadron* (Bantam Press, 2009)

—— *Vulcan 607* (Bantam Press, 2006)

Winton, John, *Signals from the Falklands* (Leo Cooper, 1995)

Woodward, Admiral Sandy, with Robinson, Patrick, *One Hundred Days* (HarperCollins, 1992)

## Newspapers, magazines and articles

Barraza, Julio, 'Un 25 de Mayo Cualquiera', *La Voz*, May 2014

Bencivenga, Jim, 'Rigging US Container Ships to Defend Themselves in Time of War', *Christian Science Monitor*, January 1981

'Brothers have come a long way from selling spare parts at Dublin Airport', *Irish Times*, August 1999

Campbell, Duncan, 'The Chile Connection', *New Statesman*, January 1985

Castro Fox, Rodolfo A., 'La tercera escuadrilla aeronaval de caza y ataque a 25 años del conflicto del Atlántico Sur', *Boletín Del Centro Naval*, Número 817, 2007

Colombo ARA, Cdr Jorge Luis, 'Super Etendard Operations During the Falklands War', *Naval War College Review*, Vol. 37, 1984

Copalman, Joe, 'Vertical Challengers', *Combat Aircraft*, November 2018

'Destino de aviador', *La Nueva*, May 2012

Dunnell, Ben, 'Falklands Confidential', *Aviation Historian*, 2013

'El aviador argentino que cayó dos veces en los mares del sur y sur-vivió', *La Capital*, March 2008

'The Falklands War', Centre for Contemporary British History, 2005

*Flight Deck*, Falklands Edition, 1982

'Fuego sobre el Atlántico Sur', *La Nación*, September 1997

Gaines, Mike, 'Sea Harrier School', *Flight International*, October 1985

Gainza, Maxi, 'Flying the Sea Harrier', *Pilot*, February 1990

—— 'Pucara', *Pilot*, November 1991

Griffin USN, Cdr Jim, 'Still Relevant After All These Years', *Proceedings*, 2012

Harper, Alan, 'Christ, Chief . . . It's Just Like a War Film', *Jets*, Summer 2000

Holloway, Don, 'Fox Two!', *Aviation History*, March 2012

Jackson, Paul, 'Harrier', *World Air Power Journal*, Summer 1991

'Jump Jets that Leap from Cargo Ships', *Popular Mechanics*, June 1983

LaGrone, Sam, 'Reagan Readied U.S. Warship for '82 Falklands War', *USNI News*, June 2012

Lake, Jon, 'BAE Systems Sea Harrier', *World Air Power Journal*, Summer 2000

—— 'Chilean Connection', *Air Pictorial*, December 1985

Laurance, Robin, 'Jumping into Place', *New Scientist*, June 1982

'Look Outs Afloat for T. Atkins', *Navy News*, 1/5/68

'Odisea de piloto correntino en cielo y mar malvinenses', *Norte de Corrientes*, May 2017

Otero, Pablo S., 'La primera gran tragedia británica', *La Prensa*, 2017

Peck, Michael, 'Project Cadillac: How the US Navy Invented the Flying Radar Station', *National Interest*, October 2016

Posey, Carl, 'Air War in the Falklands', *Air and Space Magazine*, September 2002

Professor John Fozard OBE (obituary), *Daily Telegraph*, 1996

Ramsden, J. M., 'America's Harriers', *Flight International*, 1976

The RAF in the Falklands Campaign, *Royal Air Force Historical Society Journal*, 30, 2003

Sciaroni, Mario (tr. Andy Smith), 'The May 30th 1982 Attack to the Task Force: A British View', *Minutes of the 3rd Argentine Air Force Congress*, September 2014

Smith RN, Lt David, 'Falklands Diary of a Harrier Pilot', *Popular Mechanics*, June 1983

Struminger, Brenda, 'la historia del primer piloto derribado en Malvinas', *La Nación*, April 2017

'Un aviador recordo como hundio un barco inglés en Malvinas', *La Capital*, 2/4/14

– 450 –

Vice-Admiral Sir Edward Anson (obituary), *Daily Telegraph*, November 2014

'Y Dios fue su copiloto', *La Nueva*, August 2004

## Archive documents

### Royal Navy, Army and RAF

700(A) Squadron Record Book

800 Squadron Record Book

801 Squadron Flight Authorization Sheets: April to October 1982

801 Squadron Record Book

809 NAS Fair Flying Log

809 NAS Squadron Diary

824 Squadron 'D' Flight Record Book

899 Squadron Record Book

Brown, Flt Lt Steve, 'Account of Attachment to the RN'

Flight Reference Cards: Sea Harrier FRS.1

HMS *Invincible*: The Falklands Deployment 1982

Leeming, Flt Lt John, 'A Falklands Diary'

Operation Corporate FONAC War Room Log

Royal Air Force Participation Op CORPORATE 1982, Air Historical Branch, 1988

Sea Harrier Standard Operating Procedures

Sea Harrier FRS Mk 1 Aircrew Manual

### British Library

C1379/27 – National Life Stories, An Oral History of British Science: Ralph Hooper

### National Archive

ADM 1/26496 – Sale of light fleet carrier to Argentina: memoranda by First Sea Lord

ADM 207/10 – 809 Squadron Diary

AIR 2/19850 – Operation Corporate (Falklands Conflict): No. 1 (Fighter) Squadron

AIR 2/19853 – Operation Corporate (Falklands Conflict): No. 1 (Fighter) Squadron

AIR 20/13030 – Operation Corporate (Falklands Conflict): Argentine combat reports

AIR 20/13033 – Falkland Islands: photographic survey by Canberra aircraft

AIR 20/13044 – Operation Corporate (Falklands Conflict): transcripts of interviews with personnel involved

AIR 20/13051 – Operation Corporate (Falklands Conflict): engineering reports; aircraft modifications and special fits

AIR 20/13102 – Operation Corporate (Falklands Conflict): Operation Fingent

AIR 20/13123 – Operation Corporate (Falklands Conflict): photographic reconnaissance

AIR 20/13126 – Operation Corporate (Falklands Conflict): reports and articles; Harrier aircraft operations

AIR 20/13127 – Operation Corporate (Falklands Conflict): Harrier aircraft matters

AIR 20/13128 – Operation Corporate (Falklands Conflict): Harrier aircraft policy

AIR 27/3535 – No. 10 Squadron

AIR 27/3536 – No. 11 Squadron

AIR 27/3565 – No. 29 (Fighter) Squadron (Falklands Conflict)

AIR 27/3572 – No. 39 (Photographic Reconnaissance) Squadron/No. 1 Photographic Reconnaissance Unit (1PRU) (Falklands Conflict)

AIR 27/3580 – No. 51 Squadron (Falklands Conflict)

AIR 28/2335 – RAF Belize

AIR 77/657 – Operation Corporate (Falklands Conflict): report on the involvement of the Defence Scientific Staff in air operations

AVIA 6/25983 – Defensive Weapons Department: research and development programme review, April 1982

AVIA 6/26122 – A further evaluation of paint schemes for camouflage of aircraft against ground to air detection

AVIA 18/3250 – Marcel Dassault Mirage 3A: evaluation by team from A&AEE at Istres, France

AVIA 18/3474 – Report on visit to USA to observe Harrier shipborne trials

CO 1024/161 – Sale of an aircraft carrier to Argentina

CO 1024/240 – Sale of an aircraft carrier to Argentina

DEFE 13/810 – Sale of Harriers to Argentina

DEFE 13/1121 – Harrier (including Sea Harrier): discussion of operational requirements and development

DEFE 24/2260 – Operation Corporate (Falklands Conflict): Anglo-French air combat training

DEFE 24/2709 – Airborne early warning (AEW) Sea King helicopter: development and cost

DEFE 24/2946 – Sea Harrier replacement

DEFE 31/233 – Operation Corporate (Falklands Conflict): Argentinian aircraft carrier Veinticinco de Mayo (25 of May)

DEFE 67/124 – Operation Corporate (Falklands Conflict): Harrier aircraft operations

DEFE 67/134 – Operation Corporate (Falklands Conflict): Exocet attack on CVBG 30 May 1982

DEFE 67/135 – Operation Corporate (Falklands Conflict): reconstruction of the anti-air warfare (AAW) conflict, volume 1, 1 May 1982

DEFE 69/622 – Sea Harrier: interception capability studies 1 and 2

DEFE 69/624 – Naval staff study: anti-air warfare

DEFE 69/660 – Maritime anti-air warfare equipment policy

DEFE 69/861 – Operation Corporate (Falklands Conflict): meteorological record

DEFE 69/898 – Operation Corporate (Falklands Conflict): reports, lessons learned; Vice-Chief of the Naval Staff (VCNS) commentary

DEFE 69/899 – Operation Corporate (Falklands Conflict): comments from the USA on lessons learned

DEFE 69/907 – Operation Corporate (Falklands Conflict): lessons learned; operations and logistics

DEFE 69/979 – Operation Corporate (Falklands Conflict): Equipment innovations

DEFE 69/1006 – Operation Corporate (Falklands Conflict): Special Projects Group

DEFE 69/1085 – Operation Corporate (Falklands Conflict): 801 Naval Air Squadron; operational diary

DEFE 69/1112 – Operation Corporate (Falklands Conflict): air matters

DEFE 69/1251 – Operation Corporate (Falklands Conflict): procurement from the USA; replacements for ships lost

DEFE 71/126 – Correspondence about Sea Harrier and advanced STOVL aircraft

DEFE 71/233 – Sea Harrier training

DEFE 71/810 – Operation Corporate (Falklands Conflict): Victor detachment report

DEFE 72/257 – Aircraft Specification No. 287 D&P: Sea Harrier, fighter, reconnaissance and strike aircraft

FCO 7/90 – Sale of HMS *Hermes* to Argentina

FCO 7/1490 – Sale of military aircraft to Argentina

FCO 7/3220 – Falkland Islands: contingency planning

FCO 7/3399 – Falkland Islands: contingency planning

FCO 7/3580 – Sale of aircraft to Argentina

FCO 7/3971 – Falkland Islands dispute between Argentina and the UK: contingency planning

FCO 7/5232 – Chile: Defence Attaché's Annual Report

FCO 33/5573 – French attitude to the Falkland Islands crisis

FCO 44/887 – Contingency plans for the Falkland Islands

## Miscellaneous

Canaday USN, LCDR John L., 'The Small Aircraft Carrier: A Re-evaluation of the Sea Control Ship', US Army Staff College

Farara, C. J., and Fozard, John William OBE, 'Biographical Memoirs of Fellows of the Royal Society', November 1998

Lokkings, Commander Craig J., 'The Falklands War: A Review of the Sea-based Airpower, Submarine and Anti-Submarine Warfare Operations', Air War College, May 1989

## Imperial War Museum Oral History

Neill Thomas
Ben Bathurst
Hugh Balfour
Sharkey Ward
Linley Middleton
Jeremy 'JJ' Black
Tim Gedge

David Braithwaite
Peter Squire

**Websites**

1982malvinas.com – Destrucción del *Atlantic Conveyor*
castrofox.blogspot.com – Malvinas
elchenque.com.ar – La Balada del Piloto Bahiense y el Estanciero
    Kelper
hmsalacrity.co.uk
hmsbrilliant.com – The Skipper
hmsexeter.co.uk
—— Balfour, Hugh, *Exeter: Antigua to the Falklands*
—— 30th May 1982 – The Last Air-launched Exocet Attack
infobae.com – Gaffoglio, Loreley, *El Letal Ataque al Atlantic Conveyor*
interesesestrategicoarg.com – 3-A-306: Un Avión, Dos Pilotos
    Argentinos
malvinasenlaradio.com – Board of Inquiry (Report) – Loss of *Atlantic
    Conveyor*
malvinasguerraarea.blogspot.com – El Hundimiento De La Fragata
    HMS *Ardent*
margaretthatcher.org
—— James Rentschler's Falklands Diary
—— The US and the Falklands War (1) and (2)
nottinghammalvinas.blogspot.com – Guerding, Eduardo C., *Skyhawk
    A4: Courage in the Air*
nuestromar.org – Argentina – El Último Exocet
radarmalvinas.com.ar – Diario de Guerra del Radar Malvinas
radionerds.com – Operators Manual AN/PSC-3
scribd.com – Borri, Lorenzo, *Halcones Con Alas Rotas*
thespacereview.com – Day, Dwayne, *The Lion and the Vortex*
ussduncan.org – Silas Duncan and the Falklands Incident
victorxm715.com – Beer, Mike, *A Close Run Thing*
wikipedia.com

# APPENDIX

Sea Harrier Cutaway

# British Aerospace Sea Harrier FRS.Mk 1

1 Pitot tube
2 Radome
3 Flat plate radar scanner
4 Scanner tracking mechanism
5 Ferranti Blue Fox radar equipment module
6 Radome hinge
7 Nose pitch reaction control valve
8 Pitch feel and trim mechanism
9 Starboard side oblique camera
10 Inertial platform
11 Pressurization spill valve
12 IFF aerial
13 Cockpit ram air intake
14 Yaw vane
15 Cockpit front pressure bulkhead
16 Rudder pedals
17 Cockpit floor level
18 Tacan aerial
19 Ventral Doppler navigation aerial
20 Canopy external latch
21 Control column
22 Windscreen de-misting air duct
23 Instrument panel
24 Instrument panel shroud
25 Birdproof windscreen panels
26 Windscreen wiper
27 Head-up display
28 Starboard side console panel
29 Nozzle angle control lever
30 Engine throttle lever
31 Underfloor control linkages
32 Lower UHF aerial
33 Radome, open position
34 Detachable in-flight refuelling probe

35 Pre-closing nosewheel doors
36 Ejection seat rocket pack
37 Radar hand controller
38 Fuel cock
39 Cockpit rear pressure bulkhead
40 Cabin air discharge valve
41 Canopy handle
42 Pilot's Martin-Baker Type 10H zero-zero ejection seat
43 Sliding canopy rail
44 Miniature detonating cord (MDC) canopy breaker
45 Starboard engine-air intake
46 Cockpit canopy cover
47 Ejection seat headrest
48 Drogue parachute container
49 Parachute release mechanism
50 Boundary layer spill duct
51 Cockpit air conditioning plant
52 Intake centre-body fairing
53 Ram air discharge to engine intake
54 Hydraulic accumulator
55 Nose undercarriage hydraulic jack
56 Boundary layer bleed air duct
57 Nose undercarriage wheel bay
58 Port engine air intake

59 Landing/taxiing lamp
60 Nosewheel forks
61 Pivoted axle beam
62 Nosewheel, forward retracting
63 Supplementary air intake doors (fully floating)
64 Intake duct framing
65 Air refuelling probe mounting and fuel connector
66 Engine intake compresso face
67 Air conditioning system ram air intakes
68 Boundary layer air spill duct canopy cut-out
69 UHF homing aerials
70 Engine bay access doors

71 Rolls-Royce Pegasus Mk 104 vectored thrust turbofan engine
72 Hydraulic filters
73 Engine oil tank
74 Forward fuselage integral fuel tank, port and starboard
75 Engine bay venting air scoop
76 Hydraulic system ground connections
77 Cushion augmentation strake, port and starboard, fitted in place of gun pack
78 Engine monitoring and recording equipment
79 Forward nozzle fairing
80 Fan air (cold stream) swivelling nozzle
81 Nozzle bearing
82 In-flight refuelling floodlight
83 Venting air intake
84 Alternator cooling air duct
85 Hydraulic pumps
86 Engine accessory equipment gearbox
87 Single alternator on starboard side
88 GTS/APU exhaust
89 Gas turbine starter/Auxiliary Power Unit (GTS/APU)

90 Aileron control rod
91 Wing front spar carry-through
92 Nozzle bearing cooling air duct
93 Engine turbine section
94 Wing panel centreline joint rib
95 Wing centre section fairing panels
96 GTS/APU air intake
97 Alternator cooling air exhaust
98 864-litre (190-lmp gal) jettisonable external fuel tank
99 Starboard inner stores pylon
100 Leading-edge dog-tooth
101 Reaction control air ducting
102 Aileron control rod
103 Starboard wing integral fuel tank; total internal fuel capacity 2864 litre (630 lmp gal)
104 Fuel system piping
105 Inboard pylon attachment hardpoint
106 Starboard twin Sidewinder installation
107 Starboard outer stores pylon
108 Wing fences
109 Vortex generators
110 Outer pylon hardpoint
111 Aileron hydraulic power control unit

*key continued overleaf*

112 Roll control reaction air valve
113 Starboard navigation light
114 Wing-tip fairing
115 Starboard outrigger fairing
116 Outrigger wheel, retracted position
117 Sea Harrier FA.Mk.2 ventral view
118 Blue Vixen radar
119 AIM-120 advanced medium range air-to-air missiles (AMRAAM), four
120 Fuel tank-mounted missile pylon
121 Rear fuselage stretched avionics equipment bay
122 Ventral gun packs
123 Starboard aileron
124 Fuel jettison pipe
125 Starboard plain flap
126 Trailing-edge root fairing
127 Water-methanol filler cap
128 Wing slinging point
129 Anti-collision light
130 Water-methanol injection system tank
131 Engine fire extinguisher bottle
132 Flap operating rod
133 Flap hydraulic jack
134 Fuel contents transmitters
135 Rear fuselage integral fuel tank
136 Ram air turbine housing
137 Turbine doors
138 Emergency ram air turbine (being removed)
139 Rear fuselage frames
140 Ram air turbine jack
141 Cooling system ram air intake
142 Air system heat exchanger
143 HF tuner
144 HF notch aerial
145 Rudder control linkage
146 Starboard all-moving tailplane
147 Temperature sensor
148 Tailfin construction
149 Forward radar warning receiver
150 VHF aerial
151 Fin tip aerial fairing
152 Rudder
153 Rudder top hinge
154 Honeycomb core construction

155 Rudder trim jack
156 Rudder tab
157 Tail reaction control air ducting
158 Yaw control port
159 Aft radar warning receiver
160 Rear position light
161 Pitch reaction control air valve
162 Tailplane honeycomb trailing-edge
163 Extended tailplane tip
164 Tailplane construction
165 Tail bumper
166 IFF notch aerial
167 Tailplane sealing plate
168 Fin spar attachment
169 Tailplane centre-section carry-through
170 All-moving tailplane control jack
171 Radar altimeter aerials
172 UHF stand-by aerial
173 Ram air exhaust
174 Equipment air conditioning plant
175 Ground power supply socket
176 Twin batteries
177 Chaff and flare dispensers
178 Dispenser electronic control units
179 Avionics equipment racks
180 Avionics bay access door
181 Ventral airbrake
182 Airbrake hydraulic jack
183 Liquid oxygen converter
184 Nitrogen pressurizing bottle for hydraulic system
185 Flap drive torque shaft
186 Rear spar/fuselage attachment point
187 Nozzle blast shield
188 Rear (hot stream) swivelling exhaust nozzle
189 Wing rear spar
190 Port flap honeycomb core construction
191 Fuel jettison valve
192 Fuel jettison pipe
193 Aileron honeycomb core construction
194 Outrigger wheel fairing
195 Wing tip fairing
196 Hydraulic retraction jack
197 Shock absorber leg strut
198 Port outrigger wheel
199 Torque scissor links

200 Outrigger wheel leg fairings
201 Port navigation light
202 Roll control reaction air valve
203 Wing rib construction
204 Outer pylon hardpoint
205 Machined wing skin/stringer panel
206 Aileron power control unit
207 Front spar
208 Leading-edge nose ribs
209 Reaction control air ducting
210 Port outer stores pylon
211 Twin missile adaptor
212 Missile launch rails
213 AIM-9L Sidewinder air-to-air missiles
214 Leading-edge fences
215 Inboard stores pylon
216 Inboard pylon hardpoint
217 Fuel and air connections to pylon
218 Port wing fuel tank end rib
219 Pressure refuelling connection
220 Wing bottom skin panel/fuselage attachment point
221 No. 1 hydraulic system reservoir (no. 2 system to starboard)
222 Centre fuselage integral fuel tank, port and starboard
223 Nozzle fairing construction
224 Leading-edge dog-tooth
225 Twin mainwheels, aft retracting
226 864-litre (190-lmp gal) external fuel tank
227 Fuselage centreline pylon
228 454-kg (1,000-lb) HE bomb
229 Ventral cannon pack
230 Frangible nose cap
231 Blast suppression ports
232 Cannon barrel
233 Aden 30-mm revolver type cannon
234 Link ejection chute
235 Ammunition feed chute
236 Ammunition tank, 100 rounds
237 BAe Dynamics Sea Eagle air-to-surface (anti-shipping) missile
238 RN 5.1-cm (2-in) rocket pack
239 Matra R.550 Magic air-to-air missile (Indian Navy aircraft only)

# PICTURE ACKNOWLEDGEMENTS

Although every effort has been made to trace copyright holders and clear permission for the photographs in the book, the provenance of some of them is uncertain. The author and the publisher would welcome the opportunity to correct any mistakes.

*First section*

Page 1: Hawker P.1127, first flight: Crown copyright; Sir Sydney Camm: Crown copyright; Harrier on HMS *Ark Royal*: © Lionel Smith; Harrier on ARA *25 de Mayo*: not known.

Page 2: John Farley and John Fozard: Crown copyright; Tim Gedge over HMS *Hermes*: © Tim Gedge; Tim Gedge with Linley Middleton on HMS *Hermes*: © Tim Gedge; SHAR over water, Pratt & Whitney factory: © Tim Gedge.

Page 3: SHARs with F-16s: © Tim Gedge; Tim Gedge on 1,000lb bomb: © Tim Gedge; SHAR flypast: © Tim Gedge; A-4 Skyhawk rounds the national flag at Base Aérea Malvinas: © Fuerza Aérea Argentina.

Page 4: *Hermes* stores for war: © Martin Cleaver, PA; Sandy Woodward: © Martin Cleaver, PA; JJ Black: © Martin Cleaver, PA; 809 NAS Commissioning Order: author's own/Fleet Air Arm Museum.

Page 5: SS *Atlantic Conveyor* approaching New York: © Michael Layard; *Atlantic Conveyor* conversion: © Tim Gedge; Ian North and Michael Layard: © Michael Layard.

Page 6: 1(F) Squadron crest: Crown copyright; Harrier with Sidewinders: Crown copyright; Argentine Air Force Boeing 707: Crown copyright; SHAR taken from Argentine 707: © Fuerza Aérea Argentina; Simon Hargreaves on deck of *Hermes*: © Martin Cleaver, PA.

Page 7: Farnborough camouflage tests: © National Archives; Bert Edwards building Airfix kits for camouflage research: © FAST Museum; SHAR in pre-war livery with newly painted SHAR in Barley Grey: © Phil Boyden; SHAR 330-gallon ferry tanks: © Phil Boyden.

Page 8: 4 x 809 Squadron pictures: © Phil Boyden; 809 crest: Crown copyright.

## Second section

Page 9: Canberra PR.9 at dusk: © Colin Adams; RAF on Easter Island: © Sqn Ldr Bill Ragg; Nimrod R.1: author's own; Operation ACME 4 route: © National Archives.

Page 10: 809 Squadron group photo: © Phil Boyden; Tim Gedge landing on *Atlantic Conveyor*: © Mike Layard; SHAR refuelling en route: © Tim Gedge.

Page 11: 3 Escuadrilla Aeronaval de Caza y Ataque logo: © Comando de Aviación Naval Argentina; A-4Q Skyhawk landing on *25 de Mayo*: © Comando de Aviación Naval Argentina; *25 de Mayo*: © Comando de Aviación Naval Argentina; Skyhawks being loaded with bomb for *Invincible*: © Comando de Aviación Naval Argentina.

Page 12: Nigel 'Sharkey' Ward: PA Images/Alamy Stock Photo; Argentine Navy Turbo Mentor: © Comando de Aviación Naval Argentina; Argentine Air Force Mirage III: © Fuerza Aérea Argentina; Argentine Navy Lockheed Neptune: © Comando de Aviación Naval Argentina.

Page 13: 2 Escuadrilla Aeronaval de Caza y Ataque logo: © Comando de Aviación de Naval Argentina; Exocet and Super Etendard: © Comando de Aviación de Naval Argentina; Exocet launch: © Comando de Aviación de Naval Argentina; HMS *Sheffield* after being hit: Crown copyright.

Page 14: 1(F) Squadron group photo: © Neil Corbett; Alert SHAR on *Atlantic Conveyor* pad: Crown copyright; *Atlantic Conveyor* underway: © Alastair Craig; Alastair Craig, Dave Braithwaite, Hugh Slade, John Leeming, Bill Covington and Steve Brown: © Alastair Craig.

Page 15: *Hermes* in South Atlantic: © Malcolm Smith, c/o David Oddy; Sea King HC.4 Victor Charlie: Crown copyright; *Hermes* deck with three Harrier varieties: Crown copyright; burning Argentine Chinook: courtesy of Santiago Rivas.

Page 16: SHAR taken from Al Craig's jet: © Alastair Craig; 809 SHAR launches from *Hermes*: Shutterstock; SHARs landing on *Hermes*: Crown copyright; Al Craig and Dave Braithwaite: © Alastair Craig.

*Third section*

Page 17: SHAR launching from *Invincible*: Crown copyright; Dagger at low level, San Carlos: Crown copyright; HMS *Brilliant* in the gunsights: © Fuerza Aerea Argentina; shot-up *Brilliant*: © David Oddy.

Page 18: 3 Escadrilla group photo: © Comando de Aviación Naval Argentina; Skyhawks carrying Snake Eyes: © Comando de Aviación Naval Argentina; burning HMS *Ardent*: Crown copyright.

Page 19: Keith Burns' John Leeming Skyhawk Kill: © Keith Burns; Clive Morrell in cockpit: © Martin Cleaver, PA.

Page 20: Grupo 5 A-4B Skyhawk: © Fuerza Aérea Argentina; FAA Skyhawk attack on HMS *Coventry*: not known; burning *Coventry*: Crown copyright.

Page 21: SuE pilots – Rodriguez, Barraza, Colavino, Colombo, Bedacarratz, Curilovic, Francisco, unknown, Mayora: © Comando de Aviación de Naval Argentina; *Atlantic Conveyor* painted grey: not known; burning *Atlantic Conveyor*: © Tim Gedge; burnt-out *Atlantic Conveyor*: © Tim Gedge.

Page 22: SuE refueling: © Comando de Aviación Naval Argentina; SuEs and Skyhawks: © Comando de Aviación Naval Argentina; Skyhawk overflying HMS *Exeter*: © Stephen Sloman, c/o Mick Murden; *Hermes* off the Falkland Islands after the war: Crown copyright.

Page 23: Sea King AEW.2 helicopters: Crown copyright; *Hermes/Illustrious* handover: Crown copyright; Ian North memorial: © Michael Layard; *Invincible* returns to Portsmouth: Crown copyright/Wikimedia Commons.

Page 24: SHAR firing Sidewinder: © Tim Gedge; Tim Gedge meeting F-4 Phantom: © Tim Gedge; SHAR FA.2: © Phil Boyden; F-35s landing on HMS *Queen Elizabeth*: © David Wa/Alamy.

*A Note for Model Makers:*

While I've done my best to ensure that *Harrier 809* was rigorously researched, it's a work of narrative history, not a reference book. So that extraneous detail doesn't hold up the story, I've been more casual in the way I've described the Sea Harrier's camouflage than some might like. For the record, the 800 and 801 NAS Sea Harriers that travelled south aboard *Hermes* and *Invincible* were painted all over in Extra Dark Sea Grey. I've often simply referred to this as dark sea grey. I've usually referred to the 809 NAS jets being painted in Barley Grey after the RAE scientist who devised their lighter camouflage scheme. This should properly be described as Medium Sea Grey, except for the undersides of the wings and horizontal stabilizers which really *were* painted in a shade formally known at the time as Barley Grey.

# THE POST-CREDITS STINGER

BOB IVESON WAS just relieved to be out of the Ministry of Defence. He'd hated it. The clue was in the name though. It was a ministry, not a military HQ, run by a combination of civil servants and treasury officials. And MPs. And he had a very low opinion of MPs. But flying a desk was what you got if the Air Force thought you were potential leadership material. And after he'd gone to war with 1(F) squadron in the South Atlantic the powers-that-be had decided Big Bob was their man. Iveson himself wasn't so sure. He reckoned they'd only sent him to Staff College because *they were desperate to hear the Falklands stories*.

Now, though, after getting out of Whitehall and being promoted to Wing Commander, Iveson was enjoying a job that was rather more to his liking. Posted to 1 Group headquarters at RAF Upavon in Wiltshire, he was travelling around the capitals of Europe helping set up military exercises with other NATO air forces. Until, during the summer holidays, a request from Personnel and Training Command landed on his desk. Was it necessary, they wanted to know, for the Air Commander in Belize to have had Harrier experience? The RAF maintained a small detachment of GR.3s and helicopters there to keep a lid on Guatemalan territorial ambitions and they were finding it tricky to fill the post.

With both colleagues who should have provided the answer away on vacation, Iveson drafted a reply that listed all the reasons why it was absolutely *essential* their man came from the Harrier world. On top of that, he explained that it would be hugely beneficial for the officer chosen to have 'the following experience' – and then listed his career to date.

Two months later he was asked whether he would take over in Belize.

'I'll go as long as it doesn't count as a flying tour,' he told them. The job at 1 Group counted as the second half of his Staff tour and he didn't want his willingness to help the Air Force out of a bind to delay his return to the frontline. For good measure, he added: 'Could you give me a squadron when I come back?'

'We can manage that,' they said.

After returning from Belize, Bob Iveson was sent to RAF Honington to learn to fly and fight the twin-seat, swing-wing Panavia Tornado GR.1, the Air Force's premier strike aircraft.

And, in May 1990, he took command of 617 Squadron.

The Dambusters.

Three months later, four Iraqi Republican Guard armoured divisions launched Saddam Hussein's invasion of Kuwait.

**THE STORY CONTINUES IN *DAMBUSTER 617***

# INDEX

Aberporth, RAE 56, 100
ACME, Operation 204, 205, 217, 227–8, 239, 248, 249, 250
Adams, Wing Commander Colin 88–90, 91, 95, 109, 120–21, 152, 154, 190–92, 200, 201
Aéronavale 69, 125, 127–8, 225, 237
  Hyères (air station) 225
  Marine Nationale air station (Landivisiau) 69, 85, 125, 237
Aeroplane & Armament Experimental Establishment (A&AEE), Boscombe Down 20, 22, 56, 82, 95, 159, 167, 405
Afghanistan 429
Air France Flight 139 266

**aircraft**
Aérospatiale 40, 84, 251, 391
  Puma 214, 341–3, 344, 346–8, 349
Airship Industries: Skyship 500 213
Avro
  Lancaster 30, 63, 212
  Lincoln 213
  Shackleton AEW.2 63, 212–13
  Vulcan 30, 64, 157, 165, 167, 185, 186, 189, 221, 224, 403
AWACS 427
Beechcraft Turbo Mentor (COAN) 169, 170, 171
Bell UH-1 'Huey' (helicopter) 291, 292–3, 350, 353, 400–1; (FACh) 269
Blackburn
  Buccaneer (Fleet Air Arm) 21, 27, 35, 36, 47, 56, 72, 147, 202, 219, 241, 297, 316, 357–8, 419, 421, 431; (RAF) 42, 64, 120, 241
  Skua 36
Boeing
  707 (FAA) 4–6, 111, 112, 114–15, 119, 223, 234, 236, 270–71, 338, 339, 391–2, 421, 737 151
  747-200 142, 217
  Chinook (helicopter) 52, 141, 143, 214, 372, 382, 386, 394; (Argentine Army Aviation) 291–3; see also Royal Air Force: 18 Squadron
  KC135 (tanker) 224
British Aerospace (BAe), Dunsfold 11, 44, 45, 76, 83, 100, 101, 103, 150, 183, 197, 224, 406, 428

Coastguarder 213
  Harrier GR.5 'Big Wing' 76
British Aircraft Corporation (BAC) Lightning 33, 121, 224; pilots 72, 95, 102, 122, 149, 158, 332
Dassault
  Mirage (FAA) 32, 59, 60, 61, 69, 82, 83, 87, 95, 115–16, 124–5, 126–8, 129–30, 133–4, 137, 165, 166, 167–9, 171–2, 173, 174–7, 178, 188, 191, 199, 248, 296, 326, 390, 420, 423; (RAAF) 82, 115; (Peruvian) 191, 390
  Mirage 50 248, 249
  Mystère/Super Mystère 59, 191
  Ouragan 59
  Super Etendard (SuE) (COAN) 33–4, 39, 64, 69, 83–6, 87–8, 106, 108, 129, 151, 188–9, 206–8, 237, 253, 254, 266, 334, 337, 340, 350, 357, 369–71, 373, 374, 375, 390, 394, 407–11, 413, 414; (Aéronavale) 69, 125, 127–8, 225, 237; see also Comando de Aviación Naval Argentina
De Havilland
  Chipmunk 62, 126, 144
  Comet 204
  Dash-8 commuter airliner 144
  Heron C.1 125–6
  Sea Heron xiv, 9
  Sea Venom 36
  Sea Vixen 11, 21, 48, 104
English Electric
  Canberra PR.7 90–91, 190
  Canberra PR.9 (RAF) 42, 88–91, 95, 96, 110, 120–21, 152, 153, 190–91, 192, 199, 200, 218, 246, 403; (FAA) 32, 119, 172, 178; see also Royal Air Force: 39(PR) Squadron
European Fighter Aircraft (Typhoon) 428
Fairey
  Fulmar 36, 223
  Gannet 62–3, 212, 213, 214, 241, 283 406
FMA IA58 Pucará (FAA) 32, 166, 244, 299–304, 367, 421
Focke-Wulf Fw 200 Condor 79, 222
Fokker F-28 352
General Dynamics F-16 Fighting Falcon 115, 136–7, 274
Gloster Sea Gladiator 36

(*aircraft, cont.*)
Grumman
  F-14A Tomcat 47, 48, 82, 358
  Martlet 78
  S-2E Tracker 85, 106, 150–51, 160, 309
Handley Page
  Herald 144
  Victor K.2 (tanker) 64, 119, 158–60, 185, 199, 224, 233–4, 235, 240, 403
Hawker Siddeley 35, 44
  Dominie T.1 74
  Harrier GR.1/GR.3 29–31, 33, 46–7, 56, 68, 72, 74–6, 81, 136; AV8A 19, 76, 81; GR.7/GR.9 429; 'Maritime' Harrier 34–5; *see also* Royal Air Force: 1(F) and 3(F) Squadrons
  HS125 (business jet) 74, 148
  Hunter 29–30, 42, 56, 65, 68, 92, 115, 122, 201, 360; (FACh) 94, 142; T.8M (camera ship) 146
  Hurricane 29, 30, 187, 222, 223
  Nimrod MR.2 98, 214, 403
  Nimrod R.1 204, 205, 217, 224, 227–9, 240, 248–50, 403; *see also* Royal Air Force: 51 Squadron
  P.1121 30
  P.1127 Kestrel 25–6, 31, 36, 75, 136
  Sea Fury 29
  Sea Harrier 4–5, 11, 13, 20, 29, 34, 35, 44–5, 60, 64, 67, 83–4, 86, 98, 102–3, 120, 427, 429; *see also* Fleet Air Arm; *Hermes* and *Invincible* under ships
  Sea Hawk 29
  Tempest 29
  Typhoon 29
Hunting Percival Pembroke C.1 102
IAI Dagger (FAA) 32, 61, 82, 87, 165, 167–8, 172, 177–8, 188, 281, 282, 294–5, 309, 310, 311–13, 328, 332, 336, 358, 390, 420
Learjet (FAA) 147–8, 364, 365
Lockheed
  C-130 (British: C.1) Hercules 9, 27, 41, 54, 111, 143, 153, 154, 186, 192, 201, 213, 218, 224, 250, 253, 403; (FAA) 108, 119, 271; *see also* Royal Air Force: 47 Squadron
  C-141 Starlifter 218
  C-5A Galaxy 218
  KC-130 Hercules tanker (FAA) 64, 85, 151, 188, 351, 370, 408
  SP-2H Neptune (COAN) 237–8, 253, 334
  U-2 (spyplane) 81
Lockheed Martin F-35B Lightning II 430, 431
Macchi MB-326 63
McDonnell Douglas
  A-4 Skyhawk (FAA) 32, 61, 87, 168, 160, 172, 282, 358, 361–2, 365–6, 367, 371, 408, 412, 413, 416; (COAN) 37, 38–9, 40, 106–7, 150–51, 160–61, 179, 182–3, 196, 252, 306–7, 322–4, 328, 330–32, 333, 334, 336, 343, 350, 351–2, 359, 369, 422–3; (RAN) 43, 63, 80–81; *see also* Comando de Aviación Naval Argentina; Fuerza Aérea Argentina
  AD-3W Skyraider 62

AV-8A/B 19, 46, 76, 81, 197, 261
AV-16 76
F-4 Phantom II 35, 43, 47, 48, 51, 67, 72, 103, 125, 136, 139, 199, 213, 224, 246, 302, 418, 419, 423; 29(F) Squadron 392, 422–3
F-15 Eagle 133, 136
F/A-18 Hornet 48
Messerschmitt Bf-109/110 36, 62, 222
Mikoyan
  MiG-15 136
  MiG-17 'Fresco' (Chinese) 50; (Ugandan) 266
  MiG-21 190; (Ugandan) 266
Nord Noratlas 2501 (freighter) 125
North American F-86 Sabre 136; (Taiwanese) 50
Northrop F-5 133; (FACh) 96, 153
Panavia
  Tornado ADV 214
  Tornado GR.1 429, 462
Supermarine Spitfire 30, 36, 213
Tupolev
  Tu-95 'Bear' 103
  Tu-142 'Bear F' 235
Vickers VC10 18, 54, 183, 201; *see also* Royal Air Force: 10 Squadron
Vought
  A-7 Corsair II 83
  F-4U Corsair 369
Westland (helicopters)
  Lynx 103, 251, 262, 264, 366, 384, 385, 409, 410
  Sea King 15, 52, 169, 213–14, 215, 241, 243, 244, 264, 265–6, 268, 271, 278, 391; AEW 250–51, 406, 422, 423
  Wessex 9, 25, 117–18, 141, 143, 151, 231, 284, 337, 372, 379, 381, 394

Airfix (model kits) 68
Airwork (company) 42
Allende, President Salvador 92
ALPHA, Operation 12
Amphibious Task Group (TG 317.0) 219, 220–21, 222, 224, 233–4, 235, 246, 254, 275, 280, 281, 286, 287, 288, 319
ARA, *see* Armada Argentina
Anaya, Admiral Jorge 12–13, 15
Anguita, Commander Pedro 204, 239
Anson, Rear Admiral Sir Edward 'Ted' 36–7, 41, 101, 126, 129–30, 139, 151
*Antrim, see* ships
ARAPAHO (programme) 79
Arca, Teniente de Navío José 306, 309, 314, 317, 318, 321, 322, 326, 327–8, 330
*Ardent, see* ships
Ardiles, Teniente José 178
Ardiles, Ossie 178
Area 51 (Nevada) 81
Argentina 15; invasion of Falkland Islands 20, 26–8; Air Force, *see* Fuerza Aérea Argentina; Army Aviation, *see* Argentine Army Aviation; Naval Aviation, *see* Comando de Aviación Naval Argentina (COAN); Navy, *see* Armada Argentina (ARA)

Argentine Army Aviation (Comando de Aviación de Ejército) 290; *see also* aircraft

*Ark Royal, see* ships

Armada Argentina (ARA) 32, 33, 69, 83, 86, 105; Task Force 79 150–51; *see also* ships

Ascension Island 9–10, 27, 41, 54, 111, 122, 131, 141, 149, 150, 159, 167, 183, 185, 192, 196, 198, 210–11, 215, 224, 403; Exiles Club 211; Wideawake airfield 52, 111, 150, 157, 183, 184–5, 210, 218, 224, 234, 392

*Atlantic Conveyor, see* ships

Auld, Lieutenant Commander Andy 15, 17–18, 21, 31, 69, 166, 241, 283, 358

Auld, Jacqui 216

Austin, Lieutenant Dave 42–3, 56, 219, 241, 264, 274, 307, 308, 360, 362

Aviation Bird Unit, Worplesdon 69, 405

BAe, *see* British Aerospace *under* aircraft

Balfour, Captain Hugh 409, 411, 412, 413–14

Banjul, *see* Gambia

Barkhorn, Lieutenant Colonel Gerhard 75

Barley, Philip J. 67, 68–9, 146, 360

Barraza, Teniente de Navío Julio 'Mate' 352, 369–71, 373, 374, 375

Barton, Flight Lieutenant Paul 18, 173–7, 178

Bassey, Shirley 415

Baston, Lieutenant Commander David 231, 376, 379

Bathurst, Captain Ben 34, 35, 71, 73, 211, 212, 213, 214, 217, 250–52, 253, 404, 406

Batt, Lieutenant Commander Gordon 198, 352

Battle of Britain 187, 188, 222, 275; Memorial Flight 213

Baynham, Anthony 393

BBC 12, 13, 15, 20, 167, 335; *Ark Royal* documentary 26; World Service 200, 208, 222, 283–4

Beckwith, Colonel Charlie 53

Bedacarratz, Capitán de Corbeta Augusto 207, 208

Beetham, Air Chief Marshal Sir Michael 65, 93

*Belgrano*, see *General Belgrano under* ships

Belize, RAF 90, 121, 152, 154, 190, 192, 200, 250, 461–2

Bell, Sub-Lieutenant Paul 362

Benitez, Teniente Marco 350

Bennett, Lieutenant Commander Alan 'Wiggy' 264, 265, 267–9, 271

Binbrook, RAF 121, 122, 158, 267

Black, Captain Jeremy 'JJ' 16–17, 28; and daughter's 18th birthday party 17, 22; and *Invincible*'s departure from Southsea 26; and gearbox failure 52; and Ward 87, 134, 162; and his pilots' sleeping arrangements 113, 131; addresses ship's company 131, 132–3, 162; has reservations about SHAR 134, 162; projects confidence 179, 221, 414; welcomes Gedge aboard 263; and Operation PLUM DUFF 271; and Operation SUTTON 281; and Woodward

338; and Argentine attack 407, 409, 410, 414; amazed by 801 Squadron 419

Black, Pam 16, 28

BLACK BUCK, Operation 157, 169, 185, 188, 189, 224

Blissett, Lieutenant Commander Mike 307

Bloch, General Paul 124

BLUE, Operation 12, 13

Boeing, *see* aircraft

Bond, Commander James (character) 204, 213, 415

Boscombe Down, *see* Aeroplane & Armament Experimental Establishment

Bosnia 427

Boyd, Colonel John 135, 136, 137

Boyd Trophy 424

Boyle, Flight Lieutenant Ted 121, 201

Braithwaite, Lieutenant Commander Dave 'Brave' 47–8, 49, 198; arrives at Yeovilton 58; his training programme for 809 Squadron 67, 102, 105, 210; knowledge of Argentine aircraft 80, 82, 126–7, 128, 130; against practising launching off ski-jump 123; produces report on Exercise TYPHOON 128, 133; and Ward 133; and Gedge 147, 149–50; flight to Banjul 158, 159, 160, 161–2, and on to Ascension 183–4, 185, 186; on 'a monster piss-up' 211; on deck alert 231; delivers air combat briefing 233; launches from *Atlantic Conveyor* aborted 234–5, 240, 241; moved to *Invincible* 241, 264, 286; sorties 274, 308, 345, 346–8, 388–9, 407, 421

Brawdy, RAF 122

Brice, Squadron Leader Derek 217, 239

*Brilliant, see* ships

Bristol Engine Company: BE53 Pegasus engine 3, 30, 31, 75, 81, 112, 225, 258; Olympus engine 30

British Aerospace, *see* aircraft

British Army 28, 46, 282

  2 PARA (2nd Battalion, Parachute Regiment) 219, 220, 278, 285, 395, 399, 400, 401

  3 PARA (3rd Battalion, Parachute Regiment) 220, 280, 394, 395, 399

  264 (SAS) Signal Squadron (Royal Corps of Signals) 250, 359–60

British Carrier Battle Group, *see* Royal Navy

Brize Norton, RAF 18, 54, 109, 142, 155, 217, 238

*Broadsword, see* ships

Broadwater, Lieutenant Commander Mike 18, 215, 274, 388

Brown, Wing Commander Jeremy 391–2

Brown, Flight Lieutenant Steve 101, 102, 149, 150, 219, 241, 243, 257–8, 260–61, 274, 283, 308, 331

Brüggen, RAF 246

Burton, Petty Officer Colin 'Ollie' 218–19, 226

CADILLAC, Project 62

Calderón, EAN 244

Cameron, David 430

Camm, Sir Sydney 29, 30, 31

Canning, Captain Bill 338, 367, 368
Cantan, Lieutenant Charlie 408, 409, 410, 411, 413
Carballo, Capitán Pablo 365, 366
Casey, William J. 254
Castro Fox, Capitán de Corbeta Rodolfo 37, 38–9, 40, 180, 181, 306, 307, 350, 351
cavity magnetrons 62
Central Intelligence Agency (CIA) 157, 237, 254, 387, 390, 417
chaff and flare 100, 121, 201, 252, 374, 375, 384, 385, 386–7, 412–13, 421
Child, Lee 164
Chile/Chileans 32, 65–6, 83, 90, 91, 92–3, 96, 142–3, 152, 153, 191, 192, 199, 269, 403; Air Force, see Fuerza Aérea de Chile (FACh); Navy 204; radar 359–60; see also Concepción; Punta Arenas; Santiago
Chinook, see Boeing under aircraft
Choiseul Sound 229, 416
Churchill, Winston 167, 222, 386
Clapp, Commodore Mike 221–22, 244, 280, 283
COAN, see Comando de Aviación Naval Argentina
Cole, Squadron Leader Brian 91, 120–21, 191, 201
Collavino, Teniente de Navío Luis 'Cola' 407–8
Colombo, Capitán de Fragata Jorge 39–40, 85–6, 188, 206, 239, 254, 266, 340, 370, 407
Comando de Aviación Naval Argentina (COAN) 32, 33, 39, 61, 272, 350
 1 Escuadrilla Aeronaval de Exploración 237
 2 Escuadrilla (Super Etendards) 33–4, 39, 64, 69, 83–6, 87–8, 106, 108, 129, 151, 188–9, 206–8, 237, 253, 254, 266, 334, 337, 340, 350, 357, 369–71, 373, 374, 375, 390, 394, 407–11, 413, 414
 3 Escuadrilla (Skyhawks) 37, 38–9, 40, 106–7, 150–51, 160–61, 179, 182–3, 196, 252, 306–7, 322–4, 328, 330–32, 333, 334, 336, 343, 350, 351–2, 359, 369, 422–3; see also Philippi, Capitán de Corbeta Alberto
 Escuadrilla Aeronaval Antisubmarina 150–51, 160
 Escuela de Aviación Naval (flight school) 169
Concepción, Chile 205, 227
Condor, BAM 299
Coningsby, RAF 124, 125, 126, 128, 133, 392
COPE THUNDER, Exercise 115
Corino, Comodoro Carlos 115, 177, 188
CORPORATE, Operation 28–9, 43, 65, 70, 71, 90, 190, 216, 245, 403, 406
Corti, Capitán de Navío Carlos 86, 393
Coventry, see ships
Covington, Lieutenant Bill 46–7, 48–9, 198, 308; arrives at Yeovilton 58; as Air Warfare Instructor 67, 210; organizes painting of Harriers 67–9; on mission to find out about Argentine planes and missiles 126, 127, 128, 129; misses his wife and daughter 130; and report on Exercise TYPHOON 128, 133; and unfamiliarity of Sea Harrier 149; flight to Banjul 158, 159, 160; on Ascension 210;

and Al Curtis's death 216; and Pook 233; on Atlantic Conveyor 240, 241; moves to Hermes 259–60; leads Tartan Flight 260–61; leads Trident Section sortie 274; with old friends 283; and Leeming 331; heads Joint Force Harrier 428–9
Covington, Penny 130, 216
Coward, Commander John 289, 296, 310, 338
Craig, Lieutenant Commander Alastair 'Al' 56–7, 198; new to flight controls 149; arrives at Wideawake 184–5; in hospital 211; and deaths of Curtis and Eyton-Jones 215–16; on Atlantic Conveyor 254; cross-decks to Invincible 241, 264, 273, 274, 286; first sortie 297, 298, 300–1, 302, 303, 304–5, 307, 421; pleased with 809 Squadron success 332; further sorties 407
Crete, Battle of (1941) 288
Culdrose, RNAS 9, 52, 78
Cunard 78, 79, 209, 232, 372
Cunningham, Admiral Andrew 282
Curilovic, Capitán de Corbeta Roberto 'Toro' 272, 352, 369–71, 373, 375
Curtis, Lieutenant Al 18, 214–15, 216, 236
Curtis, Pam 216
Curtiss, Air Marshal Sir John 90, 91, 190, 245, 246, 247

Daily Star 199
Daily Telegraph 137
Darwin 284, 297, 319, 353, 399, 401
Dassault, Marcel 124
Davidoff, Constantino 12
de la Billière, Brigadier Peter 65–6
Defence Operational Analysis Establishment, West Byfleet (DOAE) 70, 130, 405
Delves, Major Cedric (SAS) 118, 243–4, 245
DENY FLIGHT, Operation 427
Department/Directorate of Naval Air Warfare (DNAW) 9, 34, 36, 51, 67, 69–70, 73, 80, 103, 151, 212, 213, 250, 251, 404, 406, 427; Naval Staff Target 6464 (Sea Harrier replacement) 427
Desmond, Florence 415
DETHRONE (programme) 251
Devonport Naval Dockyard 9, 99, 139, 141, 143
Divall, Tony 393
DNAW, see Department/Directorate of Naval Air Warfare
DOAE, see Defence Operational Analysis Establishment
Doolittle, Lieutenant Colonel Jimmy 123
Drought, Third Engineer Charles 210, 334, 377–8, 386
Duncan, Captain Silas 8, 14
Dunsfold, see British Aerospace under aircraft
Dupeyron, Capitán Luis 4–5
Dutcher, John (agent) 393
Duvalier, Baby Doc 393

Easter Island 91, 109, 110, 201
Edwards, Wing Commander Sidney 65; on covert mission to Chile 65–6, 92, 93–4, 96–7, 110, 153; attempts inspection of radar site 154–5; and the press 199; orders

Robbie to clear Chilean territory 201;
inspects San Félix 204–5; sets up radar
surveillance 218, 250, 270, 407; told of end
to SIGINT missions 249–50; concerned
about loss of British warships 359

El Palomar, BAM 114

ELLAMY, Operation 430

Espora, Comandante 85

Everett, Lieutenant Bob 223

*Exeter, see* ships

Exocet missiles
AM.39s 33, 39, 40, 84, 85, 151, 188, 206,
207, 253, 269, 271, 369, 374, 376, 377,
386, 390, 391, 392, 393, 405–6, 407,
411–13, 415–16
MM.38 34, 251
defences against 87, 88, 129, 130, 210, 264,
266, 373, 375

Eyton-Jones, Lieutenant Commander John
'EJ' 18, 19, 214–15, 236, 335

Eyton-Jones, Sally 216

FAA, *see* Fuerza Aérea Argentina

FACh, *see* Fuerza Aérea de Chile

Falkland Sound 229, 275, 277, 280, 281, 284,
285, 288, 294, 295, 297, 319, 321, 332,
334, 339, 357, 361–2, 371, 389

Farley, Chief Test Pilot John 33, 35, 44, 120, 197

Faslane Dockyard 9

*Fearless, see* ships

Federal Bureau of Investigation (FBI) 53

Ferranti (company) 122, 149, 275, 406; *see
also* FINRAE; NAVHARS
AWG-11 pulse-Doppler 103
Blue Fox 20, 102, 103–4, 114, 149, 168, 208,
228, 252, 270, 276, 281, 187, 297, 307,
308, 322, 388, 411
Blue Vixen 427

Fieldhouse, Admiral Sir John 13

FINGENT, Operation 155, 205, 218, 250, 359

FINRAE (avionics kit) 122, 261, 270, 275

Flag Officer Naval Air Command (FONAC) 9,
10, 15, 36, 41, 60, 213, 406, 424

Flag Officer Third Flotilla (FOF3) 10, 11, 13,
21, 23, 24, 29

Fleet Air Arm 6, 34, 35, 36, 59, 212, 213, 215,
224, 226, 429
700A NAS (Sea Harriers) 22–3, 48, 63, 103
764 NAS 11, 24, 99
800 NAS (Sea Harriers) xi, 3–4, 15, 18,
19–20, 21–2, 29, 35, 49, 113, 146, 166–7,
195, 225, 258, 259, 275, 293, 294–5, 309,
336, 367, 371, 389–90, 429; *see also* Auld,
Lieutenant Commander Andy; Morgan,
Flight Lieutenant David; Ramsay,
Lieutenant Commander David
801 NAS (Sea Harriers) xi, 15, 19–20,
26, 35, 60–61, 63, 87, 178–9, 214–16,
236–7, 252, 273, 389–90, 419; *see also*
Ward, Lieutenant Commander Nigel
'Sharkey'
802 NAS 79
804 NAS 223
809 NAS (Sea Harriers) 36–7, 41, 68–9, 71,
82, 100, 103–4, 120, 137–9, 140–41, 146,
156, 197, 209, 218, 219, 222, 226, 236,

243, 258–9, 273, 407, 421–2, 423, 424,
431; *see also* Austin, Lieutenant Dave;
Braithwaite, Lieutenant Commander
Dave; Brown, Flight Lieutenant Steve;
Covington, Lieutenant Bill; Craig,
Lieutenant Commander Alastair; Gedge,
Lieutenant Commander Tim; Leeming,
Flight Lieutenant John; Slade, Lieutenant
Commander Hugh
815 NAS 410
824 NAS 406, 422, 423
845 NAS 372
846 NAS 243, 264–6, 267–9, 271
848 NAS 141, 231, 337, 372, 376, 377, 379, 381
849 NAS (Fairey Gannet AEW.3s) 47, 62–3
892 NAS, *see Ark Royal under* ships
899 NAS 18–19, 20, 22, 35, 42, 43, 133,
259, 273; *see also* Thomas, Lieutenant
Commander Neill
Headquarters, *see* Yeovilton, RNAS

'Junglies' 15, 151, 264–5

Flying Tiger Line 142, 155, 217

FOLKLORE, Operation 91, 109, 110, 121, 143,
152, 153–4, 190, 192, 200, 203, 204, 250

FONAC, *see* Flag Officer Naval Air Command

Fonteyn, Margot 415

Fort Bragg (Delta Force) 53–4, 110

Fort Southwick 13, 15, 20, 28, 31, 37, 71

Foster, Lieutenant Nick 372, 379

Fozard, John 30, 81, 102–3

France/French pilots 34, 40, 83, 124–8, 225,
237, 405–6

Francisco, Capitán de Corbeta Alejandro
'Pancho' 350, 352, 407–8

Frederiksen, Lieutenant Commander Rod
'Fred' 283, 293, 294–5

Freetown, Sierra Leone 208–9

Fuerza Aérea Argentina (FAA) 32, 33, 60, 61,
64, 82, 87, 95, 112, 125, 137, 147, 148,
165, 188, 213, 221, 390, 396, 417, 421;
*and see* aircraft
Grupo 1: reconnaissance missions 6
Grupo 2 172, 178
Grupo 3 299
Grupo 4 (A-4C Skyhawks) 249, 369, 360–61,
362
Grupo 5 (A-4B Skyhawks) 358, 365, 366, 416
Grupo 6 168, 294, 309
Grupo 8 de Caza 115, 172, 177
DARDO Flight 172–7
LEON Flight 293
PERRO Flight 294, 295
RATON Flight 312, 313
TANDU Flight 294
TORO Flight 168, 360–61, 362
VULCANO Flight 365, 366, 367
ZEUS Flight 365, 366, 367
ZONDA Flight 408
Escuadrón Fénix 147–8, 364–5
Grupo 2 Vigilancia y Control Aéreo (VYCA 2)
108–9, 168, 188–9, 253, 340, 369, 373, 417

Fuerza Aérea de Chile (FACh) 66, 93, 94,
96–7, 110–11, 121, 152, 153–4, 192,
248, 250, 359
Grupo 7 96
Intelligence 97, 111, 218, 249, 360

al-Gaddafi, Colonel Muammar 391, 392

Gallagher, Lieutenant Commander Leo 67, 103–4, 137, 138, 149, 151

Galland, Adolf 87

Galtieri, General Leopoldo 12–13, 15

Gambia, The 150, 160, 161; Banjul (capital) 149, 161, 183, 184

Gambia Airways 238

Garcia, Capitán Jorge 362

Garcia Cuerva, Capitán Gustavo 'Paco' 168–9, 172, 173, 175, 176, 326

Gedge, Monika 37, 146

Gedge, Lieutenant Commander Tim 10–12; reports to Northwood 10, 12, 13; contacts Auld and Ward 15, 17; audits status of Sea Harrier force 20; produces four more planes 21; approves construction of flight decks on *Canberra* 24–5; and departure of *Hermes* and *Invincible* 28–9, 31; forms new 809 Squadron 37, 41, 42–3, 45, 49, 57, 58, 67; obtains Sidewinder missiles 49, 51–2, 56, 57, 59, 70–71; flies Sea Harriers (ZA190) 56, 58, 307–8, 360; and French planes 69, 83, 115, 124, 129, 225; clashes with DOAE scientist 70; and conversion of *Atlantic Conveyor* 99–100, 104–5; and a shortage of pilots 100, 101–2, 103–4; surprised at Woodward's appointment 112; and in-flight refuelling 119–20; meets 1(F) pilots Iveson and Squires 122–3; proves SHARS' superiority to F-16s 136–7; not allowed to take test pilot south 139; lands SHAR on *Atlantic Conveyor* 143–4; tops up the tanks at Plymouth City Airport 144–5; proud of his new squadron 147; checks flight plan with Braithwaite 149–50; takes delivery of last SHAR 150; at send-off for 809 pilots 156; stops off in Gambia 161–2; on Ascension Island 183–4, 185, 196–7, 210, 211; and Nick Taylor's death 198; keen to shoot down Argentine Boeings 223; calculates radius of action 225–6; keeps Sea Harrier on deck alert 231; and North 231–2; his launch aborted 233–4; a superb CO 241; witnesses Brown's narrow escape 257–8; moves to *Invincible* 262–3; and Ward 273–4; keeps 809 diary up to date 274, 332; as Flight Leader in XZ491 308, 345–6; downs enemy Puma 346, 348, 388; paired with Austin 360; forced to abort intercept 361–3; prepares to launch with Ward 371, 384, 385; and sinking of *Atlantic Conveyor* 385; and Braithwaite 389; prepares new squadron for HMS *Illustrious* 421; writes paper on operating naval fighter squadron ashore 422; escorts F-4 Phantom into Stanley 422–3; provides a solo farewell to *Illustrious* 423; awarded 1982 Boyd Trophy 424; joins Directorate of Naval Air Warfare 427; provides SHAR with world-beating radar 427; drafts NST6464 detailing requirements for Sea Harrier replacement 427–8, 430

Gellett, Petty Officer Bob 140–41, 209

*General Belgrano*, *see* ships

George, Sub-Lieutenant Andy 101

Germany 14, 34, 75, 78, 79, 87, 131, 148, 220, 246, 316, 333; *see also* Brüggen *and* Gütersloh

Gibraltar 24, 112

Glover, Carolyn 333

Glover, Flight Lieutenant Jeff 260, 270, 329–30, 333, 353

Goering, Hermann 187

Goose Green 245, 304, 358, 386; British air attacks 166, 198, 221, 229, 236, 244, 299, 395–6, 399, 400; Paratroopers' assault 394, 396, 300, 400, 401

Gorshkov, Admiral Sergey 2

GRAMMERIAN, Operation 224, 233

Grytviken (South Georgia) 117, 118

Gunning, Lieutenant Commander Jock 43–4, 101, 146

Gütersloh, RAF 101, 102, 261, 283, 316

Haig, Al 55, 157

Hale, Lieutenant Martin 293, 294, 295

Halifax, Admiral David 17

HAMPTON (programme) 251

Hanrahan, Brian 167

Hare, Flight Lieutenant Mark 290, 291–3, 329, 395, 396, 397, 402

Hargreaves, Lieutenant Simon 3–4, 5–6, 111–12, 421

Harrier, *see* Hawker Siddeley *under* aircraft

Harris, Squadron Leader Pete 260

Hart-Dyke, Captain David 338, 359, 362, 367

Harvey, Jimmy 147, 148, 364

Havers, Sir Michael 415, 416

Hawaii 201

HAWK TRAIL deployment 192

Hayr, Air Vice-Marshal Ken 64–5, 72–3, 74, 77, 92, 97, 98, 110, 204, 205, 249–50, 403, 404, 405

Healey, Denis vii, 25

Heath, John 278–9

Henderson, Nico 202

Hercules, *see* Lockheed *under* aircraft

*Hermes*, *see* ships

HERRICK, Operation 429

Hitler, Adolf 148, 187

Honduras 190–91

Honington, RAF 42, 121, 462

Hooker, Joseph 211

Hooker, Sir Stanley 30, 31, 75

Hooper, Ralph 30–31, 75, 136

HUDWAC (head-up display weapon-aiming computer) 149, 301, 302

Hughes Aircraft Company 50

Hughes, Lieutenant Commander Des 259

Hughesdon, Charles 415–16

Hulme, Lieutenant Commander Laon 289–90, 296–7, 298–9, 309–10

Hunt, Rex 41

Hussein, Saddam 391, 462

Hutchings, Major Richard 264, 265–6, 267–9, 271

*Illustrious, see* ships

Imrie, Leading Aircrewman Pete 264–5, 267–9, 271

Indian Navy 104

Inman, Admiral Bobby Ray 157

International Military Services (IMS) Ltd 392

*Invincible, see* ships

Irish, Aircraft Engineering Artificer Noel 140–41

Israeli Air Force 59, 82; Commandos raid on Entebbe 266; Six-Day War (1967) 59

Iveson, Squadron Leader Bob 73, 76–7; inspects *Atlantic Conveyor* 74, 77; enjoys his first take-off from her ramp 98–9; brings Gedge up to speed 122–3; in mock combats with French jets 126; opinion of Mirages 128; on *Atlantic Conveyor* 219; and North 232; ferried across to *Hermes* 260; ordered into the air by Middleton 261; and failure of FINRAE 275; on bombing raid with 1(F) Squadron 276–8; back in action 395, 396–8; bails out behind enemy lines 398–9, 400–2; returned to *Hermes* 418; grounded by back pain 418; post-Falklands career 461–2

Iveson, Hank 74

Jay (A. B.) Ltd 392

Joint Force Harrier 429

JOURNEYMAN, Operation 14, 26

'Junglies', *see* Fleet Air Arm

Kendall, Squadron Leader E. P. 218

Kent, Lieutenant Commander Robin 18

Kinloss, RAF 267

Knight, Air Vice-Marshal Sir Michael 121, 154

Lambert, Squadron Leader Gordon 217, 227–8, 229–30

LAST, Project 213, 250, 251

Lavezzo, Capitán de Navío Julio 84, 86, 393

Layard, Elspeth 78, 141, 145, 216, 335

Layard, Captain Michael 78, 357–8; appointed Senior Naval Officer aboard *Atlantic Conveyor* 78, 79, 80; and Captain North 79–80, 209, 231, 334, 372, 374; and Gedge 99, 122, 262; and conversion of *Atlantic Conveyor* 99–100, 140; meets Iveson and Squire 122; and First of Class trials 141, 143, 144; and sinking of *Sheffield* 210; and 809 Squadron 222, 225, 240, 241; orders ship to Action Stations 254; and Brown's narrow escape 258; on *Atlantic Conveyor's* vulnerability 334–5; ordered to proceed to San Carlos Water 357, 363, 372, 374–5; and Exocet attack 376, 377, 378–80, 381, 382–3; tries to save North 383–4; speaks to survivors on *Alacrity* 385–6; as President of Royal Naval College 428

Leach, First Sea Lord Sir Henry 10, 28, 196, 202, 253

Leeming, Flight Lieutenant John 'Leems': ordered to RAF Yeovilton 101, 102; given brief training 102, 149, 150; suffers oxygen failure 158, 159, 160, 408;

seconded to 809 aboard *Hermes* 241, 243, 260, 261, 274, 283; first sortie 316–17, 318–19, 322–4, 326, 333, 336, 421; and failure of Sidewinder 330–32; a further sortie 341, 342, 343, 344–5, 352, 353, 421

Legg, Captain Andy (SAS) 265–6, 268, 269, 271

Lehman, John F. Jr 55–6, 356, 404

Leston, Capitán de Corbeta Proni 207

Libya 390, 392, 393, 430

Locke, Commander John 262, 353

Lockheed C-130 Hercules, *see* aircraft

López, General Mario 93

Lord, Flight Lieutenant David 121, 201

Lossiemouth, RAF 63, 136

Lossiemouth, RNAS 11, 99, 297

Lowe, Lieutenant Kim 381

Lucero, Teniente Ricardo 361

Luqa, RAF 89

Lyneham, RAF 143

Lynx, *see* Westland *under* aircraft

Lyons, Admiral James 'Ace' 404

McAtee, Major Willard T. 18–19, 43, 101, 150, 201–2

McDonald, Ian xi, 284

McEvaddy, Intelligence Officer Ulick 238

McLean, Dr William B. 50

McLeod, Flight Lieutenant Murdo 102

McQueen, Captain Bob 183, 184, 196, 214

Magnaghi, Teniente Enrique 342–3

Malvinas, BAM, *see* Stanley

Manzella, Teniente de Corbeta Daniel 169, 170, 171, 364, 365

MAPLE FLAG 9, Exercise 73, 102

Marconi

radar 406, *and see* radar

Marham, RAF 158, 224, 267

Marquez, Teniente de Fragata Marcelo 306, 309, 314, 318, 319–20, 333, 343

Matkey, Terry (USMC) 74

Matthei, General Fernando 66, 93, 94, 97, 153, 154

Mayne, Paddy (SAS) 244

Mayora, Teniente de Fragata Armando 85, 207, 208

Medici, Teniente de Navío Félix 272

Merchant Navy 144, 209–10, 232, 406

MI6, *see* Secret Intelligence Service

Micheloud, Primer Teniente Juan Luis 299, 300

Middle East Airways 415–16

Middleton, Captain Lyn 21, 36, 212; requests AIM-9L Sidewinders 50; has *Hermes* on war footing 113; on Sea Harriers 189; dislikes colour of 809 SHARs 258–9; orders GR.3 pilots into the air 260, 261–2; his abrasive manner 262; agrees to recognize 899 Squadron as separate entity 273; and Pook 293; and Glover 352–3; and ARA *25 de Mayo* 371; clashes with Squire 403–4; unimpressed by Argentine attack 414; finds the war dull 417; concedes that Squire's men have done well 418

Middleton, Ray 262

MIKADO, Operation 266, 269

Mirage, *see* Dassault *under* aircraft
missiles
   AIM-7 Sparrow 295, 384
   AIM-9, *see* Sidewinder missiles
   AMRAAM 427
   AS12 141
   Blowpipe 94
   Exocet, *see* Exocet missiles
   Fritz X 34
   Matra R.530 128, 137, 168
   Matra R.550 Magic 115–16, 128, 137, 165,
     168, 173, 390, 421
   Rapier 280
   Roland SAM 325
   Seacat 181, 288, 318, 336
   Sea Dart 61, 85, 138, 181, 252, 281, 338,
     339, 358, 362, 366, 367, 385, 406, 411,
     416
   Sea Eagle 197–8
   Seawolf 181, 252, 280, 289, 296, 310, 338,
     358, 359, 366, 367–8, 406
   Shafrir 421
   Skyflash 423
   Soviet missiles 34, 390, 396
   SS11 141
   Stinger 53, 54
Mitterrand, President François 84, 391
Mitterrand, Jacques 84
Moll, Sub-Lieutenant Andy 366, 367
Moore, Major-General Jeremy 90
Morgan, Flight Lieutenant David 'Moggie'
   22, 101; scrambled in pursuit of
   unidentified contact 113–14; aircraft
   damaged in sortie 166–7; and news
   of *Belgrano*'s destruction 195–6; on
   *Hermes* with 800 NAS 283, 284; and
   Leeming's 'failed' Sidewinder 330–31;
   successful sorties 341–5, 346, 416, 421;
   fears he's fired on Glover 352–3; *Hostile*
   *Skies* xi
Morrell, Lieutenant Clive 'Spag' 316; on
   *Hermes* 283; successful sortie with
   Leeming 316–17, 318–22, 324, 326, 330,
   332, 336, 418; returns to 809 Squadron
   postwar 421
Morris, Flight Lieutenant A. 143
Mortimer, Flight Lieutenant Ian 'Morts' 61,
   181, 182, 408–9, 411, 413
MUSKETEER, Operation 264–5
Mutual Weapons Development Program 75

National Aeronautics and Space
   Administration (NASA) 75
National Reconnaissance Office (NRO) 203
NAVHARS (avionics kit) 149, 160, 182, 229,
   261, 263, 388, 389
Nelson, Admiral Lord Horatio 256
Nicaragua 190, 200
Nimitz, Admiral Chester 402
Nimrod, *see* Hawker Siddeley *under* aircraft
Nine Lima, *see* Sidewinder missiles
Nord Aviation, France 34
North, Captain Ian 79–80, 144, 209, 231, 232,
   242, 258, 262, 372, 374, 377, 379–80,
   381, 382–4
North Luffenham, RAF 119–20

Northwood Headquarters 10, 13, 15, 17, 60,
   64, 65, 90, 95, 140, 152, 195, 225, 230,
   245, 249, 269, 271, 297, 414
Nott, John 10, 28, 55, 193, 222

OCEAN VENTURE, Exercise 38
Ogilvy, Lieutenant Commander Tony 283
Okinawa, Battle of (1945) 63
Oliviera, Teniente Carlos 350, 351
Olympus engine, *see* Bristol Engine Company
Omega Air 238
O'Reilly, Primer Teniente Enrique 249

P&O (company) 24–5
Paez, Captain Jorge Luis 147
Palaver, Mayor Hugo 358–9
PARAQUET, Operation 117–19
Paratroop regiments, *see* British Army
Pearl Harbor (1941) 195
Pebble Island 169, 176, 243–5, 266, 277, 287,
   338, 362, 364, 365–6, 385
Pegasus engine, *see* Bristol Engine Company
penguins, gentoo 70
Perona, Primer Teniente Carlos 'Daga' 168–9,
   172, 173, 174, 175, 176
Peru 153, 191, 390–91
Phantom, *see* McDonnell Douglas *under*
   aircraft
Philippi, Capitán de Corbeta Alberto 105–6,
   160–61; leads 3 Escuadrilla Skyhawks
   180–81, 196, 271–2; photographs his
   men 278; and mission planning 306–7;
   leads attack 308–9, 314, 317–18; shot
   down by Morrell 320–21, 322; survives
   325, 333, 353, 401, 418
Philippi, Manfred 325
photographic reconnaissance 88–91, 95, 96,
   110, 120–21, 152, 153, 189–91, 192, 199,
   200, 218, 246, 403
Pierce, Leading Seaman 373
Pinochet, General Augusto 92, 97
Pita, Capitán de Navío Miguel 267
Piuma, Mayor Gustavo 312–13
PLUM DUFF, Operation 265–6, 271
Plymouth City Airport 144–5
Point Mugu, *see* United States Navy
Pook, Flight Commander Jerry 232–3, 234,
   260, 261, 263, 275–8, 290–93, 329
Poole, Lieutenant Commander Dave
   'Hooligan' 139–40
Port Egmont, West Falkland 14
Port Stanley, *see* Stanley
Portsmouth 9, 13, 17, 20–21, 28, 61, 113, 424
Pucará, *see* FMA *under* aircraft
Puerto Argentino, *see* Stanley
Puerto Soledad, East Falkland 14
Puma, *see* Aérospatiale *under* aircraft
Punta Arenas, Chile 90, 96, 153, 154, 156,
   192, 249, 269
PURPLE DRAGON exercises 266–7

RAAF, *see* Royal Australian Air Force
radar 62–3, 88, 188–9
   Agave 129, 208, 248, 352, 373, 409–10, 413
   Airpass 121
   AN/APS-20 62, 63, 213, 214

AN/APS-38 151, 181–2
AN/TPS-43 108–9, 165, 188–9, 190, 245, 253, 267, 325, 326, 340, 369, 409, 417
Cyrano 165
Ferranti
  AWG-11 pulse-Doppler 103
  Blue Fox 20, 102, 103–4, 114, 149, 168, 208, 228, 252, 270, 276, 281, 287, 297, 307, 308, 322, 388, 411
  Blue Vixen 427
Marconi AN/AR118228/6 Sky Guardian 95
Marconi Foxhunter 214
Marconi S259 42, 97, 155, 205, 218, 248, 251, 359, 361
Sea Searcher 215
Searchwater 214, 250, 406
Seaspray 103
Superfledermaus 292
Type 909 85, 182, 252
Type 965 222
Type 967 218, 289, 299, 310, 361
Type 992 295, 374, 409, 410
Type 1022 215
RAE, see Royal Aircraft Establishment
RAF, see Royal Air Force
Ramsay, Lieutenant Commander David 43, 56, 70–71, 80, 82, 101, 115
Ray, Admiral Bobby 157
Raytheon (company) 50
Reagan, Nancy 156
Reagan, President Ronald 15, 156–7
Reeve, Squadron Leader John 157
Reffell, Rear Admiral Derek 10, 12, 28–9, 71
Rentschler, James 55, 157
Riis, Teniente Enrique 341–2, 343–4
Río Gallegos, BAM 61, 96, 165, 169, 172, 358, 365
Río Grande, BAM 61, 96, 97, 108, 165, 188, 206, 208, 238, 254, 266–7, 268, 269, 270, 271–2, 278, 294, 306, 333, 340, 350, 351–2, 363, 370, 392, 407, 416
Rittondale, Vice-comodoro Otto A. 339
Robbie, Squadron Leader Peter 109, 110, 152–4, 190, 192, 201
Rochfort, Flight Lieutenant John 260
Rodriguez, General Vicente 93, 94, 96–7, 110, 204, 205, 249–50, 359
Rojas Galdames, René 278–9
ROSARIO, Operation 15
Royal Air Force (RAF) 11, 22, 30, 35, 36, 41, 51, 64, 88, 98, 247, 403; see also aircraft
  1(F) Squadron (Harrier GR.1s and GR.3s) 57, 72–3, 77, 98, 129–30, 192–3, 211, 219, 224, 241, 243, 247, 260, 261, 275, 283, 288, 329, 330, 371, 395, 396, 399, 402, 418, 419, 429, 461; see also Iveson, Flight Lieutenant Bob; Pook, Flight Commander Jerry; Squire, Wing Commander Peter
  3(F) Squadron (Harrier GR.3s) 101, 102
  10 Squadron (Vickers VC10s) 41, 54, 109–10, 201, 218
  18 Squadron (Chinook HC.1s) 141, 219, 337, 372
  29(F) Squadron 392, 422–3
  30 Squadron 143
  39(PR) Squadron (Canberras) 88–91, 95, 96, 110, 120–21, 143, 152, 153, 190–91, 192, 199, 200, 218, 246, 403
  47 Squadron (Hercules) 266–7, 269
  51 Squadron (Nimrods) 203–4, 214, 217, 218, 227–8, 229, 238–9, 247–50
  70 Squadron 111
  360 Squadron 251
  617 Squadron 431, 462
Alert Measures Committee 41, 42, 64–5, 404
ISTAR (Intelligence, Surveillance, Target Acquisition and Reconnaissance) 88–9
Marine Branch 404–5
Royal Aircraft Establishment: Bedford 405; Farnborough 67–8, 247, 405, 428
Royal Australian Air Force (RAAF) 80, 82, 115
Royal Australian Navy (RAN) 10, 26, 43, 63, 80
  VF-805 Squadron 43, 80
Royal Fleet Auxiliary support ships 14, 49, 132, 140, 363
Royal Marines 1, 25
  3 Commando Brigade 25, 220
  40 Commando 280, 285
  42 Commando 117, 280, 284, 337
  45 Commando 280, 284, 394
  Naval Party 8901 10, 41, 285
Royal Naval College, Greenwich 428
Royal Navy 4, 6, 55–6, 63, 282, 430; see also ships; aircraft; Fleet Air Arm; Royal Marines
  Britannia Flight 144
  British Carrier Battle Group 26, 31, 132, 220, 222, 287, 334, 338, 358, 363, 369; and ARA 25 de Mayo 60, 160, 180, 181, 195, 196
  Mobile Aircraft Repair, Transport and Salvage Unit (MARTSU) 209
  Submarine Service 112, 113
Royal Signals and Radar Establishment, Malvern 214, 405
Russia, see Soviet Union

St Athan, RAF 20, 43, 307
St Mawgan, RAF 192, 267
Salt, Captain Sam 208
Sampson, Squadron Leader Ian 248
San Carlos/San Carlos Water 244, 245, 250, 271, 285, 287, 296, 309, 319, 337, 340, 350, 357, 358, 361, 363, 364, 372, 390, 394
San Félix Island 204–5, 217, 227, 228, 230, 238, 239
Sandys, Duncan 30
Santiago, Chile 92, 142, 152, 155, 199, 238, 269, 278; Sidney Edwards in 66, 92, 97, 110, 204, 249, 250, 359, 407
SARDIUS, Operation 12
SAS, see Special Air Service
satellites 88, 152, 203, 405; see also SIGINT
  Soviet spy satellite 110
  VORTEX (US) 203
Sayeret Matkal 266
SCADS (shipborne containerized air defence system programme) 79, 80

Schofield, Jim 251, 406
Scott, Taylor 44–5, 56, 101, 120, 421
Sea Harrier, see Hawker Siddeley under aircraft
Sea King, see Westland under aircraft
Secret Intelligence Service (SIS: MI6) 391, 392, 393, 406, 416
Shackleton, Ernest 117
Shag Cove 345, 349, 352
Sheffield, see ships

**ships**
25 de Mayo, ARA 32–3, 37, 38, 60, 83, 107, 160, 179, 180, 182, 195, 196, 203, 371; Skyhawk squadron 105, 106, 150, 151, 179, 180, 181, 182, 196
Alacrity, HMS 14, 177, 179, 381–2, 383, 384, 386, 387
Albion, HMS 59
Alferez Sobral, ARA 108
Ambuscade, HMS 363, 373–4, 375, 386, 409, 413
Andromeda, 409, 411
Antelope, HMS 220, 351, 359
Antrim, HMS 117, 118, 119, 280, 284, 287, 293, 294, 295, 296, 336
Ardent, HMS 220, 284, 288, 315, 317, 326, 328, 329, 333, 336, 351, 376
Argonaut, HMS 220, 222, 234, 294, 336
Ark Royal, HMS 27, 198; and BBC documentary series 26; Buccaneer S.2s (809 Squadron) 27, 36, 47, 57, 72, 219, 316, 357–8, 419, 431; F-4 Phantoms (892 NAS) 11, 22, 27, 44, 47, 48, 72, 102, 103, 295, 384, 419; retirement 34, 35, 402, 429, 430
Arrow, HMS 177, 179, 361
Atlantic Causeway, MV 406
Atlantic Conveyor, MV 78, 79–80; formation of landing pad 99, 100, 104–5; loading of jets and pilots 101, 122, 126, 139, 140–41, 184; transformation of 140; Naval Party 1840 (crew members) 140, 144, 209, 225, 231, 372, 375; trials 143, 144; departs for Ascension Island 144, 145, 150, 197, 208–10; embarkation of 809 Squadron 214, 216, 218–19, 308, 419, 421; journeys south as part of TG 317.0 formation 219, 222, 224–5, 231–2; and enemy planes 234, 235, 236; and bad weather 240–43, 247; jets made ready 254, 260; a near disaster 257–8, 260–61; camaraderie 273; Gedge leaves 262–3; pilots cross-deck to Invincible 264; 1(F) Squadron GR.3s leave 270, 288; her vulnerability 334–5, 336, 363; her valuable cargo 337, 357; approaches San Carlos 363, 372; sinking of 374–5, 376–80, 381–7, 394, 403, 404, 408, 414; see also Layard, Captain Mike
Audacity, HMS 78–9
Avenger, HMS 412
Belfast, HMS 16
Brilliant, HMS 132, 252, 276, 280, 285, 288–9, 296, 298, 299, 309–10, 315, 317, 326, 336, 338, 366, 375, 387
Bristol, HMS 237, 338
Broadsword, HMS 132, 262, 280, 285, 288–9, 284, 338, 358, 359, 360–61, 362, 363, 365, 366, 367, 368, 370, 371

Bulwark, HMS 59
Canberra, SS 24–5, 220, 280, 337
Cardiff, HMS 338, 339, 409, 411
Clio, HMS 14
Conqueror, HMS 182, 194, 195, 196
Contender Bezant, MV 406
Coventry, HMS 132, 281, 338, 358, 359, 360–61, 362, 363, 365–6, 367, 368, 370, 371, 387, 388–9
Dedalo, SNS 120
Dreadnought, HMS 14, 26
Dwight D. Eisenhower, USS 202, 203
Eagle, HMS 59
Eilat, INS 34
Elephant, HMS 21
Elk, MV (cargo ferry) 334
Endurance, HMS 10, 12, 14
Europic Ferry, MV 280
Exeter, HMS 363, 373, 409, 411, 412, 413–14, 416
Fearless, HMS 10, 220, 221, 233, 241, 244, 245, 280, 290, 296, 330, 361
Fiskerton, HMS 15
Formidable, HMS 63
Fort Austin, RFA 251, 280
Fort Toronto (tanker) 363
General Belgrano, ARA 182, 194–6, 206, 221, 238, 334
Glamorgan, HMS 167, 170, 171, 173, 174, 177, 179, 244, 284, 363, 409
Glasgow, HMS 132, 208, 252–3, 281, 289, 366
Halifax, HMAFV 405
Hampden, HMAFV 405
Hercules, ARA 61, 85, 106
Hermes, HMS 21, 25, 26, 48, 257, 375, 385; Sea Harriers 13, 15, 20, 21–2, 32, 60, 146, 197, 419; Westland helicopters 15, 251, 271; bombs on board 20; departs for Ascension Island 28–9, 31, 52; pilots on board 21–2, 43, 241, 257, 258, 283–4, 294–5; planned missions by SHAR squadrons 60–61; SATCOM sets 111; as Woodward's flagship 112, 114–15, 262, 280–81; Sea Harrier kept on alert 113; Sea Harriers launched from 3–6, 135, 166–7, 178, 246–7, 270, 275, 285, 287, 290, 307, 316–17, 318–24, 339, 344–5, 352, 389–90, 395, 396–9; crew hears of Belgrano's destruction 195; protection given to 220–22, 251, 416; Sea Harriers grounded 237; and night-flying 261–2, 263; 1(F) Squadron GR.3s 288, 329, 333, 396, 402, 403, 418; Locke addresses the crew 353; Wessex Whisky Delta given air test 372, 381; given protection by Atlantic Conveyor 386–7; and end of war 418; see also Middleton, Captain Lyn
Hipolito Bouchard, ARA 194, 267
Hornet, USS 123
Hurricane, HMAFV 405
Illustrious, HMS 251, 421, 422, 423
Indefatigable, HMS 63
Independence, USS 75
Independencia, ARA 105
Independencia, BAP (Peru) 391

*Intrepid*, HMS 10, 220, 271, 280, 296, 351

*Invincible*, HMS 10, 15, 25–6, 131–2, 162, 168, 181–2, 304, 409, 414; Sea Harriers 13, 15, 20, 32, 60, 197–8, 216, 419; Westland helicopters 15, 251–2, 264, 271; pilots 18, 87, 214–16, 241, 263, 264, 273–4, 304–5, 345; bombs on board 20; sets sail 15, 28–9, 31; gearing coupling breaks 52; picks SAS man 111; Sea Harriers launched 114, 135, 170–72, 198, 215, 228–9, 246, 259–60, 287, 297, 307, 371, 384–5, 389, 407, 411, 413, 414, 419, 422; protection given to 220–21, 251, 363, 416; grounded by weather 27; 809 Squadron subsumed within 801 273, 274, 332; shoots at shadows 385; *see also* Black, Captain Jeremy

*Iwo Jima*, USS 404–5

*John F. Kennedy*, USS 358

*Jupiter*, HMS 11

*Karel Doorman*, HMNLS 32

*La Salle*, USS 75

*Lancaster*, HMAFV 405

*Lexington*, USS 8, 14

*Mary Rose* (flagship) 22

*Melbourne*, HMAS 43

*Norland*, MV 219, 232, 243, 280

*Penelope*, HMS 407

*Phoebe*, HMS 14

*Phoenix*, USS 195

*Piedra Buena*, ARA 194

*Plymouth*, HMS 361

*Prince of Wales*, HMS 430–31

*Puerto Rosales* (tanker) 194

*Queen Elizabeth*, HMS 430–31

*Raleigh*, USS 75

*Resource*, RFA (stores ship) 49

*Roma* (Italian flagship) 34

*San Luis*, ARA 289

*Santísima Trinidad*, ARA 61, 85, 106

*Seahawk*, HMS 78

*Sheffield*, HMS 132, 207–8, 210, 211, 212, 215, 221, 237, 238, 250, 263, 334

*Sir Galahad*, RFA 220, 280

*Sir Geraint*, RFA 220, 280

*Sir Lancelot*, RFA 220, 280

*Sir Percivale*, RFA 220, 280, 379

*Sir Tristram*, RFA 220, 280

*Spartan*, HMS 12

*Spitfire*, HMAFV 405

*Splendid*, HMS 9

*Stalker*, HMS 36

*Stena Seaspread*, MSV 406

*Stirling*, HMAFV 405

*Stromness*, RFA 280

*Sunderland*, HMAFV 405

*Superb*, HMS 12

*Tyne*, HMS 14

*Valiant*, HMS 270

*Vanguard*, HMS 16

*Venerable*, HMS 32

*Victorious*, HMS 11, 36, 63, 98

*Warspite*, HMS 34

*Wellington*, HMAFV 405

*Yarmouth*, HMS 328

*Zealous*, HMS 34

Short Brothers, Belfast 89

SHUTTER, Operation 111, 205, 250, 359, 361, 370, 407, 409

Sidewinder missiles 81, 82, 122
AIM-9 50–51
AIM-9G 20, 49, 51, 52, 116, 420
AIM-9L (Nine Lima) 4, 49–50, 51–2, 55, 56, 57, 59, 111, 115, 135, 137, 172, 174, 175–6, 178, 197, 218–19, 224, 225, 226, 233, 234, 241, 281, 294, 298, 311–12, 313, 320, 321, 323, 330–31, 362, 405, 420–21, 422, 423

SIGINT (signals intelligence) 203, 227, 229, 239, 249, 406; *see also* satellites

Skyhawk, *see* McDonnell Douglas *under* aircraft

Slade, Hannah 63, 130

Slade, Lieutenant Commander Hugh 61–2, 63; contacted by DNAW 80; joins 809 Squadron 82, 123, 308; and French flyers 126, 127, 128; and DOAE report 130; misses his family 130; co-produces report on Exercise TYPHOON 133; arrives at Ascension Island 184–5; lands on *Atlantic Conveyor* 219; cross-decks to *Hermes* 241, 259, 260, 274, 283, 402; on first CAP sortie 307; and Leeming's success 331

Slade, Josephine 63, 130

Smith, Lieutenant David 358, 367, 371, 416, 421

Smiths Industries 149, 301, 302

Sobey, Senior Engineering Officer Bruce 77

SOLID SHIELD, Exercise 357–8

South Georgia 12, 70, 117–19, 285, 289

Soviet Union
MiG fighters, *see* Mikoyan *under* aircraft
missiles 34, 390, 396
reconnaissance aircraft 35, 103, 235
spy satellite 110
Victor II submarines 9, 12

Spadeadam, RAF 121

Special Air Service (SAS) 53, 265, 266, 299, 364
B Squadron 53–4, 265, 266–9
D Squadron 22 111, 117, 118, 243–4, 245, 266, 271
G Squadron 271, 290

Speed, Wing Commander Brian 217, 227, 230, 248, 249

SPRINGTRAIN, Exercise 112

Squire, Wing Commander Peter 56, 73; orders Iveson to inspect *Atlantic Conveyor* 73–4; brings Gedge up to speed 122–3; flies mock combats with the French 126; reports on Harrier tactics 128; lands on *Hermes* 260; ordered into the air by Middleton 261–2; training mission 270; first operational mission 275–8; forced to return from sortie 329; and Glover's disappearance 329, 333; and failure of technological support 402–3; clashes with Middleton 403–4; scores direct hit on Argentine command post 418

Stanley/Port Stanley, Falkland Islands (BAM Malvinas; Puerto Argentino)
airfield 27, 40, 60, 61, 108, 151, 157, 165, 169, 173, 177, 185, 186, 252, 253, 280, 299, 322, 326, 327, 328, 330, 371, 418
local radio station 37
Moody Brook Barracks 10
radar 245, 254, 292, 325, 326
Stanley, Lieutenant Commander Ian 118
Stenzel, Third Officer Martin 209
Stirling, David (SAS) 244
Stokes, Air Electronics Operator Tony 247–8
STUFT ('ships taken up from trade' programme) 24, 78
Suez Crisis (1956) 25, 36, 55, 59
Super Etendard, see Dassault under aircraft
SUTTON, Operation 221, 250, 253, 271, 279, 288
Swaby, Major Don (USMC) 48
Swan Island 287

TACSAT (satellite radio) 54, 110
Tahiti 91, 201
TANSOR, Operation 224
Taylor, Lieutenant Commander Doug 98
Taylor, Lieutenant Nick 198, 210, 216, 221, 246, 247, 396
Testard, Major Jean-Yves 124–5, 126–7, 129
Thatcher, Margaret 12, 84, 117, 118, 196, 391, 415, 416
Thatcher, Mark 89
Thomas, Lieutenant Commander Neill 18, 19–20, 21, 22, 42, 43, 189, 241, 273, 276, 283, 307, 367, 371
Thomas, Lieutenant Steve 173–7, 178, 297, 298, 299, 300, 302, 304, 310–14, 317, 326, 329, 332, 336
Thompson, Brigadier Julian 244, 394
Thorn EMI (company) 214, 250, 406
THUNDERBOLT, Operation 266
Tierra del Fuego 27, 61, 96–7, 153, 154, 266, 269, 270, 282, 408; see also Río Grande
Tomba, Mayor Juan 299, 300, 303–4
TOPGUN, see United States Navy
Tracy Island (Thunderbirds) 204
Tradewinds Airways 415
Trans Mediterranean Airways 416
Trump, President Donald 426
TYPHOON, Exercise 125, 128, 133
Tyson, Mike 420

United States 14, 54–5, 62, 75–6, 88, 156–7, 201–2, 404, 405; National Reconnaissance Office 203; see also Central Intelligence Agency, Federal Bureau of Investigation, and below
United States Air Force 29, 53–4, 75, 133, 135, 430; and see aircraft
Andrews Air Force Base 53
Edwards Air Force Base 430
March Air Force Base 109
Military Airlift Command 218
Pope Air Force Base 53
4th Tactical Fighter Squadron 136
United States Air Forces in Europe (USAFE) 201

United States Army: Delta Force Special Operations unit 53–4
United States Marine Corps 47, 75–6, 136, 233, 430
VMA-513 Squadron 46–7, 81
VMA-542 Squadron 74, 77
United States Navy 38, 50, 62, 63, 76, 119, 121, 402, 404–5; and see aircraft
China Lake (Naval Ordnance Test Station) 50–51
Kindley Field (naval air station) 121
Marine Air Warfare Training School 49
Miramar (naval air station) 48
Point Mugu (naval air station) 47, 80, 82, 126, 430
Test and Evaluation Center, Patuxent River 76
TOPGUN school 47, 48, 80, 233
VF-121 Squadron 48
VX-4 Squadron 47, 48
Upavon, RAF 461
Upper Heyford, RAF 201
USAF, see United States Air Force
Ushuaia naval base 96, 155

Varela, Admiral Benigno 33
Veinticinco de Mayo, see 25 de Mayo under ships
Vickers, Ernie 378
View to a Kill, A (film) 213
VIFFing (vectoring in forward flight) 81, 136, 233, 398

Ward, Alison 216
Ward, Lieutenant Commander Nigel 'Sharkey' 87; with 700A NAS 22–3, 63, 103; leave cancelled by Gedge 15; chooses pilots 18, 19, 20, 22, 43; lands SHAR on Invincible 22–3; requests AIM-9L Sidewinder 50; as leader of 801 Squadron 52, 60; conducts threat reduction exercise 87–8; makes extravagant claims for Blue Fox radar 104; rubbishes SHAR pilots' report on TYPHOON 133–4; worries Black 134, 162; has a frustrating time 167, 168; sorties 170–72, 228–9, 244; forced to stand down due to weather 236–7; and Gedge 241, 273–4; briefs 801 Squadron 286–7; in favour of using radar 297; further sorties and successes 298, 299–303, 304, 305, 308, 310–11, 312, 313–15, 336, 364, 421; and attack on Ardent 317, 319, 329; fears for Thomas 326; urges squadron to adopt 'La Muerte Negra' as battle cry 333; and destruction of Atlantic Conveyor 371, 385; Sea Harrier Over the Falklands xi
Watson, Lieutenant Ian 'Soapy' 170, 171–2, 244, 389
Wattisham, RAF 42, 97, 155, 205
WD-40, use of 138–9, 223, 253
weaponry; see also missiles; Exocet missiles; Sidewinder missiles
2-inch rocket 60, 122, 141
3-inch rocket 223, 374
7.62mm GPMG 100, 169, 341, 375, 376
70mm rocket 169, 299, 341, 364

ADEN cannon 4, 135, 175, 219, 225, 275, 291, 300, 321, 348
Browning Hi-Power semi-automatic (pistol) 210
'Charlie G' Carl-Gustaf rifle 400
cluster bombs 141, 166, 275, 277, 290, 291, 380, 395, 396, 397
DEFA cannon 310
Durandal (bomb) 59, 60
Gatling guns 422, 423
laser-guided bombs 403, 404, 418
M16 assault rifle 244
M-72 LAW (anti-tank) 244
Mk.8 torpedoes 194
Oerlikon cannon 166, 177, 198, 288, 292, 317, 325, 361, 366, 396, 397
Snake Eye bombs 160, 180, 181, 272, 308, 318, 328, 350, 351, 352
Sura rocket 92
thousand-pounder (1,000lb bomb) 20, 31, 60, 166, 167, 189, 221, 246, 294, 358, 366, 368
Zuni rocket pod 47
Weinberger, Caspar 'Cap' 55, 201, 202, 404
Wessex, *see* Westland *under* aircraft
West, Commander Alan 288, 328
West Drayton, RAF 218
Westland Helicopters, *see* Westland *under* aircraft
whales 289
Wibault, Michel 30, 75
Williams, Captain Peter 70, 156
Withers, Flight Lieutenant Martin 185, 186, 189
Withington, Tito 148, 364
Wittering, RAF 11, 29, 43, 57, 72, 98, 122, 126, 130, 283
Woodward, Admiral John 'Sandy' 112–13, 282; makes *Hermes* his flagship 112, 280–81; requests permission to shoot Argentinians down 114–15; and retaking of South Georgia 117, 119; relieved at news of *General Belgrano*'s destruction 195; and loss of SHARs 216–17; tries to protect carriers 221–2, 416; and failure to destroy Argentine radars 244–5, 247, 277; and Operation ACME 249–50; and Middleton 262; plans air defence 282–3; and defence of Amphibious Task Group 284–5, 287, 338, 339, 358; fails to protect *Atlantic Conveyor* 334–5, 336, 337, 357, 363, 393, 411; and sinking of *Coventry* 367, 368, 393; concerned that Argentina may replenish supplies of weaponry 390; angry with land forces 394; and lack of early warning system 406; sure of victory 417; and Gedge 421; incredulous at proposal to retire Harriers 429–30
Wyton, RAF 88, 91, 95, 121, 200, 203, 217
Electronic Warfare Operational Support Establishment 95

Yacimientos Petrolíferos Fiscales (oil company) 148
Yanzi, Mayor Roberto 345, 349
Yeovilton, RNAS 9, 15, 18, 19, 35, 36, 41, 42, 43, 46, 49, 56, 57–8, 70, 71, 80, 98, 99, 100, 102, 115, 119, 122, 123, 128, 129–30, 138–9, 149, 150, 156, 158, 202, 261, 271, 360, 423, 424
Sea Harrier Operational Conversion Course 102
Sea Harrier Simulator 42

Zambellas, First Sea Lord Admiral Sir George 428, 430–31
Zubizaretta, Ana 352
Zubizaretta, Capitán de Corbeta Carlos 350, 351–2, 353, 359

# ABOUT THE AUTHOR

**Rowland White** is the author of four critically acclaimed works of aviation history: *Vulcan 607*, *Phoenix Squadron*, *Storm Front* and *Into the Black*, as well as a compendium of aviation, *The Big Book of Flight*. Born and brought up in Cambridge, he studied Modern History at Liverpool University. In 2014 he launched Project Cancelled to produce apparel inspired by the best in aviation, space and other cool stuff. Find it at projectcancelled.com

For more information on Rowland White and his books visit his website at rowlandwhite.com or find him on Twitter @rowlandwhite

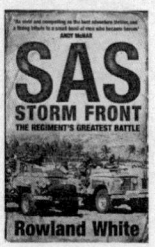

# SAS
# STORM FRONT

### Rowland White

Dawn. 19 July 1972. A force of nearly three hundred heavily armed, well-trained guerrillas launches a surprise attack on the small fishing village of Mirbat. All that stands in their way is a troop of just nine SAS, aided only by an elite band of fighter pilots overhead.

Two years earlier a Communist rebellion had threatened the Arabian Peninsula, in the strategically critical Sultanate of Oman. Following a covert intelligence mission, 22 SAS deployed their largest ever assault force against the rebels.

But this was to be a bitter and hard-fought campaign culminating in the Battle of Mirbat which would become a defining moment for the Regiment. Their heroism that day would remain part of the SAS legend for ever.

'As vivid and compelling as the best adventure thriller, and a fitting tribute to a small band of men who became heroes'
ANDY MCNAB

'Gripping, revealing and extraordinarily well-researched, this is a riveting new account of a little known but crucial war'
SIR RANULPH FIENNES

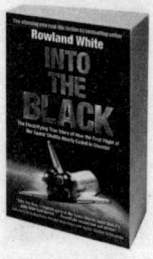

# Into The Black

*The electrifying true story of how the first flight of the Space Shuttle nearly ended in disaster*

## Rowland White

'Tells the true, complete story of the Space Shuttle better than it's ever been told before . . . Beautifully researched and written'
COLONEL CHRIS HADFIELD, FORMER ASTRONAUT AND SPACE STATION COMMANDER

On 12 April 1981, the world's first real spaceship, NASA's Space Shuttle *Columbia*, blasted off on her maiden flight.

On board were men with the Right Stuff. Never before had a crew been so well prepared for their mission, yet less than an hour after their spectacular departure they found a problem. Tiles designed to protect *Columbia* from the blowtorch burn of re-entry were missing from the heat shield. There was no way of knowing whether she could make a safe return to earth. To save *Columbia* and her crew, NASA turned to a spy agency hidden deep within the Pentagon. Together, they would attempt something that had never been done before. Success would require skill, pinpoint timing and a massive dose of luck . . .

*Into the Black* draws on brand new interviews and newly declassified documents to tell this dramatic story for the first time. It is an extraordinary race-against-time thriller, a gripping high-stakes Cold War story and a celebration of our love affair with the stars . . .

'*The Right Stuff* of our times'
DAILY MAIL

'*Into the Black* told me stuff I never knew before – and I worked at NASA for 30 years . . . a deep and enthralling read'
MIKE FOALE, FORMER ASTRONAUT AND INTERNATIONAL SPACE STATION COMMANDER

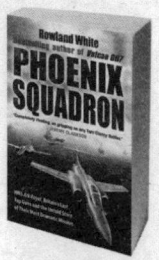

# Phoenix Squadron

*HMS Ark Royal, Britain's last Topguns and the
untold story of their most dramatic mission*

### Rowland White

---

'A true story as gripping as any Tom Clancy
thriller. It's completely riveting'
JEREMY CLARKSON

January 1972: the tiny outpost of British Honduras is threatened
with imminent invasion by battle-hardened, US-trained Guatemalan
paratroops. Britain's response must be immediate and decisive. But
there is only one deterrent the government can offer: HMS *Ark
Royal*, once the Navy's most powerful warship, now a white
elephant on the verge of being scrapped.

To save the small colony, she must launch a pair of Buccaneer fighter
bombers on an unprecedented long-range mission. But first the old
carrier must make a high-speed, 1,500 mile dash across the Atlantic
towards the Gulf of Mexico. The odds of arriving in time are very
slim indeed . . .

Drawing on extensive first-hand accounts and previously unseen,
classified documents, Rowland White has pieced together one of the
most audacious and thrilling missions of post-war British military
history.

'Combines pulse-pounding tension with riveting detail.
If only all military history was written like this'
ANDY McNAB

'[A] page-turning thriller of a book . . . White's obvious passion
infuses every page . . . This gripping, hugely entertaining book is a
powerful reminder that we sacrifice strike power at our peril'
JAMES HOLLAND, *TELEGRAPH*

# Vulcan 607

*The Epic Story of the Most Remarkable
British Air Attack since WWII*

### Rowland White

---

'I more than enjoyed it, it could have been written specially for me'
JEREMY CLARKSON

It was to be one of the most ambitious operations since 617 Squadron bounced their revolutionary bombs into the dams of the Ruhr Valley in 1943 . . .

April 1982. Argentine forces had invaded the Falkland Islands. Britain needed an answer. And fast.

The idea was simple: to destroy the vital landing strip at Port Stanley. The reality was more complicated. The only aircraft that could possibly do the job was three months from being scrapped, and the distance it had to travel was four thousand miles beyond its maximum range. It would take fifteen Victor tankers and seventeen separate in-flight refuellings to get one Avro Vulcan B2 over the target, and give its crew any chance of coming back alive.

Yet less than a month later, a formation of elderly British jets launched from a remote island airbase to carry out the longest-range air attack in history. At its head was a single aircraft, six men, and twenty-one thousand-pound bombs, facing the hornet's nest of modern weaponry defending the Argentine forces on the Falkland Islands. There would be no second chances . . .

'Exciting and breathtakingly pacy . . . This is exactly
how modern history should be written'
ANDY MCNAB

'Gripping, endlessly fascinating detail. I read the book in one
sitting: it is an utterly compelling war story, brilliantly written'
SIMON WINCHESTER

'A masterwork of narrative history'
CLIVE CUSSLER